# 100 Vicious Little

# Vampire

## Stories

# 100 Vicious Little

# Vampire

## Stories

*Edited by*

ROBERT WEINBERG,
STEFAN DZIEMIANOWICZ,
& MARTIN H. GREENBERG

BARNES
&NOBLE
BOOKS
NEW YORK

The acknowledgments appearing on page 583 constitute an
extension of this copyright page.

Copyright © 1995 by Robert Weinberg, Stefan Dziemianowicz,
and Martin H. Greenberg

This edition published by Barnes & Noble, Inc.,
by arrangement with Martin H. Greenberg.

1995 Barnes & Noble Books

ISBN 1-56619-558-6 *casebound*
ISBN 0-76070-206-3 *paperback*

Book design by Mario A. Moreno

Printed and bound in the United States of America

MC  9  8  7  6  5  4  3  2  1
MP  9  8  7  6  5  4  3  2  1

BVG

# Contents

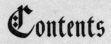

# Introduction

**W**hat is a vampire?

Nearly a century ago, this question wasn't difficult to answer. If you subscribed to the image of the vampire immortalized in Bram Stoker's 1897 novel, *Dracula*, the vampire was evil incarnate, a creature whose supernatural existence and gruesome means of sustenance contradicted the norms by which civilized human beings measured what was natural and morally proper. With his nocturnal habits, the vampire served as a potent symbol for humanity's unenlightened superstitions; in his evocation of primal darkness, he became a counter-symbol of the divinity who turned the darkness of the void into light.

In time, Stoker's well-defined boundaries for the vampire eroded. Critics interpreted his vampire as a metaphor for everything from repressed sexuality to foreign immigration. Other writers, inspired by Stoker's example, wove scenarios around their undead that were deliberately different from their model, dressing the vampire up in a variety of different guises and subjecting him to experiences that Count Dracula never knew. As their stories became progressively more modern, so did the vampire, shedding his medieval garb and aristocratic demeanor to better adapt to the contemporary lifestyle and fashions of his time and place.

The end result of the vampire's evolution is *100 Vicious Little Vampire Stories*, a collection of 100 vampire tales from nearly as many hands in which no two vampires are exactly alike. Here, the vampire runs rampant through the worlds of fantasy, horror, and science fiction, and even mundane worlds in which any suggestion of the supernatural is conspicuously lacking. In the variety of their approaches to the vampire theme and the diversity of their treatments, these stories unconsciously show that there is no simple answer to the question "What is a vampire?"

More important, they indirectly ask a more problematic question: *What is not a vampire?*

The enduring popularity of the vampire is attributable to a number of factors, but surely the most important is that the vampire's relationship to those around him suggests an entire gamut of recognizable human relationships. Typically, the vampire-victim relationship is thought of in terms of predator and prey. Among some of the *atypical* predator-prey relationships to be found herein are the Internal Revenue Service stalking tax delinquents, viruses attacking the bloodstream, and radio "shock-jocks" baiting their audiences. The classic bloodsucking vampire lives off the life force of his victims; but some of *these* vampires feed on the sympathy rendered them by unsuspecting caregivers, the affection of incautious lovers, or the tithes donated by the religious faithful. The undead life the vampire gives back to those infected by his bite is a scourge in most vampire fiction; but, ask some of the authors represented here, might not the immortality imparted be a boon to some: the writer, the written word, the terminaly ill?

In putting together this anthology, we did not intentionally seek modern reinventions of familiar vampire lore. Indeed, there are quite a few traditional vampires lurking between these covers. But some of these creatures are conjured deliberately to undermine all the expectations that traditional vampire fiction has inculcated. In their efforts to wreak original variations on the vampire theme, the writers have imagined ingenious new means of vampire disposal, envisioned vampires interfacing with computers and piloting time machines, and even proposed more than a few reasons why people might want to be vampires—or at least have one as a close friend. There are vampires here to suit every taste—an intentional pun meant to warn that several of the selections are intended as comic relief.

Although all of these stories are short, their cumulative impact is tremendous, for they reveal the vampire to be one of the most malleable myths of the modern age, a creature whose characteristics have an eerie resonance for many fundamental human situations and experiences. Their brevity notwithstanding, these stories show a wealth of imagination: in them you will find the writers' hearts and souls—and some of their blood.

—*Stefan Dziemianowicz*
*New York, 1995*

# And to See Him Smile

## Donald R. Burleson

All the old-timers knew the legend and the song. That much Lloyd Bailey came to know, but not until he had lived in the building for a while. Most of the people in the other apartments, he found, were pretty much inclined to keep to themselves. It wasn't just that they didn't talk much to him, the new tenant; they really didn't talk to one another much either, so far as he could tell. People drifted down the dreary hallways, nodded to you perhaps, went behind doors, and were gone. It was a lonely place, all in all, if you were used to a more outgoing life; but in his current economic doldrums he guessed he was lucky to have anywhere to live at all.

He had been in the building the last stale and sultry weeks of summer and the first few slate-gray days of autumn when he first heard the song, heard it from the lizard-visaged lips of an old woman out on the crumbling front steps. Squatting there like a gargoyle, she was crooning to a pack of ragamuffin children gathered on the dirty sidewalk:

"He comes in the night in the pale moonlight, he comes when the cold winds sigh; he comes from the gloom of his terrible tomb, and to see him smile is to die."

Surely a fine thing to be singing to impressionable children, Lloyd thought, annoyed. The kids merely jeered at the old woman and scattered, but he thought he detected, on their grimy faces, a certain furtive apprehension mingled with their defiance. As they dispersed, there might have been a ghost of a smile on the woman's ancient face, or there might not; it was

1

hard to tell. But if there was, it was a smile that carried with it not the faintest trace of humor.

Lloyd spent the rest of that day, as he had so many others, in fruitless job hunting, returning to the bleak old building on the corner of Ipswich Avenue and Twelfth Street only late in the day and with only minimal enthusiasm for coming home. It was hard to feel at home in a place to which you had come down in life, a place in which you had no roots and no real friends. And as the mid-October sun had set by the time he climbed the stairs to his third-floor apartment, he thought anew about something that had crossed his mind a number of times before.

With rare exception, no one ever seemed to be out and about in the hallways or on the stairs after dark. Even outside, on the infrequent occasions when he went for a stroll and a smoke, the sidewalks were generally deserted, at least near the building. If you walked far enough down Ipswich Avenue or far enough up Twelfth, away from this corner, you would eventually meet up with the usual scowling little knots of sullen teenagers or the quiet older couples walking dogs; but around the building where he lived, the sidewalks were peopled only by rows of wanly lit windows where unseen hands drew dingy blinds down to shut out the night. On these occasions, Lloyd found his loneliness giving way to another, less comprehensible feeling, a vague nervousness that made him wish to be off the streets as well. Increasingly, he found himself spending whole evenings indoors.

Among the other tenants there seemed to be only one who, in time, proved to be a little given to conversation. This was a retirement-age chap who had introduced himself simply as Jack, and Lloyd ran into him in Phillips Park over on Thirteenth Street one crisp Saturday morning; they sat on a bench drawing their collars tight to their throats, talking quietly and smoking. Lloyd brought up that troubling memory of the old woman and the song, and Jack arched an eyebrow.

"So you heard the song? Well, you'd have to, sooner or later. I'm not surprised you heard it from her. Old Mrs. Day. She's been in the building longer than most anybody can even remember, I guess, and her family before her. Some of those families have lived there for generations. Place was built in the 1830s, you know. Mrs. Day's father and my grandfather was

2

playmates in the building when they was kids if you can believe that. Mrs. Day has seen everything that ever happened around the place. She could tell some stories, I imagine, but she don't talk much."

"Huh," Lloyd said. "Just sings her creepy songs to the kids."

Jack shook his head. "Not songs. One song. And it ain't hers. My grandfather taught me that song when I was a kid, and he knowed it when *he* was a kid."

"I don't understand," Lloyd said. "Why—"

"Nobody's told you about—him."

"Who?"

"Him. The one the song's about. There's a whole legend about him."

"Go on," Lloyd said, intrigued.

"Well, he's supposed to be around the place sometimes. Outside, or in the halls or in the stairwells. At night. His kind can only be out after dark."

Lloyd laughed. "Oh, come *on*. Gimme a break. A vampire?"

Jack shrugged, and did not look amused. "Call him what you want, don't make no difference what you call him. There's them has seen him. My grandfather seen him. My mother seen him. I seen him once myself, from a ways off. Half the folks in the building has probably seen him, if you could get them to talk about it. And other folks has disappeared, from time to time. Like the little Jameson girl last summer. They say he probably got her. And maybe he did."

Amazing, Lloyd thought, the bizarre folklore that could grow up around a place. "Well, what's he supposed to look like?"

"Just an old man," Jack said, lighting another cigarette and looking thoughtful. "An old man in ragged clothes and a big heavy overcoat throwed around his shoulders like a cape, you know, kind of the way a wino might look. And always has a scarf or something covering up the lower part of his face.

Lloyd thought out loud about the song. " 'And to see him smile is to die.' "

"You got it," Jack said. "That's the story they tell. If you ever run across him and he drops that scarf or whatever it is and

3

you see his mouth—well." The man fished something up from beneath his jacket; it turned out to be a little silver cross on a chain around his neck. "I ain't never been all that religious, but I wear this. All the time. You'll say it's silly, I suppose."

"No, no," Lloyd protested, "not if you're really afraid. It's just that—well, I mean, after all those old stories and movies about—and here you tell me there's really a—is that cross really supposed to protect you?"

"That's the worst part of it," Jack said. "The old folks all say don't ever be without one, not if you want to have a chance. But they say something else too: They say if it ever comes down to running right smack into him, and he smiles at you, why, then that cross ain't going to be enough."

It was ridiculous, of course, but the man's face was dead serious. Lloyd, that afternoon, feeling a little foolish, walked up Twelfth Street to a shop he knew and bought himself a silver cross and a chain. He hadn't worn one since he was a kid, and he wasn't wearing one now because of Jack's wild story; he just felt like wearing it, and he didn't have to have a reason. Not as a free person living in a rational age.

Or so he preferred to think.

It was near the middle of November, with the sky turning blustery and the nights bitter cold, that he first saw something himself.

Even though his unemployment benefits and his savings were running dangerously low, he had walked uptown and treated himself to a movie, which had let out rather late. He was coming along Ipswich Avenue and nearly home when, walking past the entrance to an alleyway between his building and the adjacent one, he glanced down the dark crevice between buildings and thought he glimpsed a suggestion of movement somewhere in there.

He quickened his pace, but not before someone leaned close to him out of the shadows. It was all over in a moment, but in that moment he had the crazy impression that he was looking into a veiled face, though the face itself, or what was visible of it, was apparently a man's. The eyes, bulging from beneath great shaggy brows, were bright and transfixing, almost feverishly so, and Lloyd had to will himself to snap his own gaze away from the strange half-face, noting, nevertheless, that the mouth was covered by what looked not so much like a scarf as like the tattered fringe of some larger filthy garment that lay below. Dashing up the steps into his building, Lloyd didn't realize until he was halfway up the stairwell that his hand, back there, had unconsciously gone to his pendant cross, which he was still clutching when he locked himself in his rooms.

He didn't sleep much that night, but it was just as well, because he didn't think that he would have liked his dreams.

The day after that encounter, he had tried to tell Jack about it, but Jack seemed either not to want to hear it or to know already what Lloyd was going to say, or both. Lloyd found this disappointing, because he *needed* to talk about it. Also about this time it began to happen that when he passed other tenants on the stairs or in the hallways, their curt nods seemed to contain something more, about the eyes, than they had contained before, a subtle little expression that might have said: You know now, don't you. You've *seen*. Old Mrs. Day in particular fixed him with a look that he found somehow intolerable. Had gossip gone around—or could they tell just from looking at him? If they could, his nerves must really have begun to suffer more than he knew.

He resolved to keep his mind on healthy subjects, and indeed largely succeeded in doing this, mostly by stepping up his job search, which was, for a while longer, still unfruitful, but which served to direct his mind away from unpleasant thoughts. In the end he did find a job washing dishes in a diner over on Fifteenth Street, replacing a boy who had suddenly stopped reporting for work. It wasn't a spectacular job, but Lloyd was glad to have it.

The only thing was, it was always dark by the time he got off work.

But despite the disturbing memory of the encounter at the entrance to the alleyway, he made up his mind to brook no more nonsense—this wasn't the Middle Ages, or the mountain passes of Transylvania, and he was *not* going to be afraid, like some wide-eyed and superstitious schoolchild, to walk home in the dark. Now that he had at least a small income again, he realized, upon reflection, that a person unemployed and depressed and insecure could all too readily become credulous, foolishly imaginative, even downright gullible. He felt like telling that character Jack what he thought of his idiotic folktales, except that he hadn't seen Jack around for a while. Anyway, just because the old-timers were uptight about some loony derelict haunting the building, there was no reason to imagine crazy things. In short, it was good to get his composure back.

He kept it for nearly a week.

The first few walks home, past the alley opening, were uneventful. Fleeting impressions of movement within the maw of darkness between the buildings were surely nothing more than the late-autumn wind twirling bits of paper rubbish; with the nearest street lamp half a block away the light here was uncertain, but at least no febrile-eyed wraith leaned to him out of the shadows.

On the night after the first light snowfall, in fact, the walk home along Ipswich Avenue was quite pleasant, with the clouds clearing away to unveil a gibbous moon that made the snow sparkle on the sidewalks and in the doorways where the rising wind silted it in gossamer drifts. And strolling past the alley he felt emboldened even to go back and explore a bit. There was about an inch of snow on the ground, and even the fact that there were vague footprints in the snow around the alley entrance didn't particularly bother him. He followed them back some distance into the alley, where the moon rode just high enough over the brick walls to show him that the prints angled rightward to approach the shattered remains of a basement window dimly outlined in the shadows. He was sure that this was the sheltering place of some poor homeless wretch who might well have been living in the building's basement for years.

Or he would have been sure of it, had the two yellow eyes that smoldered there looked more nearly human.

Lloyd was back out at the alley entrance, down the sidewalk, and halfway up the steps to his building before he realized that he was running. *He comes in the night in the pale moonlight,* some corner of his mind intoned as he flung open the door and bolted inside and up the stairs. He was on the second-floor landing before he looked back down the dusky throat of the stairwell. Was something moving down there? *He comes when the cold winds sigh.* Lloyd was bounding up the next flight of stairs, sprinting down the dimly lit hallway, and fumbling with his key in his door. *He comes from the gloom of his terrible tomb.* The key turned in the lock, thank God, and he was inside, slamming the door shut and locking it. His heart pounding, he leaned on the inside of the door and tried to get his wind back. When his breathing calmed he listened with an ear against the door; outside in the hall everything was quiet.

And then the singing began.

As if in uncanny response to his own troubled thoughts, a chorus of lilting, mocking voices seemed to be crooning from somewhere down the hall, possibly from down in the stairwell. "He comes," they sang; "comes in the; comes in the night; night in the; in the pale moonlight; moonlight." The voices were de-ranged-sounding, out of agreement with each other. "Comes when; when the; comes when the cold; when the cold winds sigh." It was whiningly high-pitched and ragged, like a gaggle of children trying unsuccessfully to sing together. But whatever was going on, at least this was something one could confront, Lloyd reflected, somewhat relieved; it was a group of *people,* even if they were drunk or crazy. He unlocked his door and stepped out into the hall.

"Winds sigh. He comes from; comes from the; from the gloom." The voices were emanating from somewhere down the stairs. "Gloom of his; of his terrible tomb; tomb." Lloyd snorted; he'd see about this. Stepping smartly back down the hall, he felt his annoyance grow; hadn't he been through enough? He started down the stairs.

And stopped halfway down, between floors.

The voices were here, all right. But only one figure stood on the shadowy stairs below him.

Lloyd's hand went to his throat, fished under his collar, found the chain, the cross.

For the figure standing below him was familiar. It had a heavy overcoat draped over its shoulders, and a swatch of cloth covered its face below the fiery eyes. "Terrible tomb," the voices sang. How could there be so many of them? "And to see; to see him; and to see him smile," they sang. The eyes appeared to wince slightly at the sight of the cross, but held their gaze upon him. And the gnarled hands went up and grasped the cloth and pulled it down and off.

Lloyd's earlier impression had been right. The "scarf" was only the broad fringe of a kind of mantle or shroud that had covered most of the creature's front like some grotesque bib.

The thing was face all the way down. And all the mouths were singing.

"Him smile; see him smile."

One puny silver cross certainly wasn't enough—maybe it would have taken dozens of crosses, one for each needle-fanged mouth. "And to see him smile is to die." Lloyd tried to back away, but it would have taken running up the stairs backwards. The nightmare face lurched upward, and some of the mouths were still singing when they reached him.

# The Witness

MIKE ASHLEY

Once again sleep eluded him. Leigh stretched and forced himself out of bed, looking blearily out of the window across the acres of fields. It was a dark, overcast day, threatening rain, just as it had all week. He cursed. Would the sun never appear to allow him to finish his painting? He had only hired the cottage for the week, and at this rate he was never going to finish his assignment.

Frustrated, Leigh dressed and made himself some coffee. He busied himself more from the need of something to do than for any purpose. He knew he could complete the paintings within the cottage, but he needed the open space and fresh air to invigorate and inspire and to give the full flavor of atmosphere. His publisher's commission had been to capture the spirit of the battlefields of Europe for a forthcoming book and to do that he needed to be there, not cooped up in this one-bedroom cottage. He was going to have to venture forth again with his sketchpad and do his best.

But he was tired. Why had he not slept? No sooner had he

started to slumber than something, he wasn't sure what, disturbed him and he was awake. All he could remember was that sudden jolt when you dream you are falling. Only he wasn't falling. Not really. It was more as if he were sinking, or being sucked, downward.

He shook himself from his thoughts. The gathering wind was blowing the branches of a tree just outside the cottage and they were scratching at the window. It brought back memories of sounds in the night. He hadn't remembered the wind, but the rustlings had come and gone.

*Oh, pull yourself together Leigh.* He downed a second cup of coffee and finished a slice of toast, and went again to the window. The fields of the Somme stretched out to the horizon, a patchwork of colors. Small hedgerows partitioned the fields into ancient shapes. He could have been almost anywhere in western Europe, but for the knowledge of the many tens of thousands of men who had died in battle in these fields, not only in the First World War, but throughout history. Leigh shuddered, not for the first time, at the thought of the carnage. The fields must have been almost perpetually soaked in blood.

A vision flashed in his mind for his painting and he snatched his sketchpad and pencil to capture the image before it was lost. As he did so his eye was suddenly drawn to a shape in a distant field. Something dark and huddled, like a man stooping. It seemed to shift slightly in the wind, as if it was hobbling. It was difficult to see at this distance, and a part of his mind assumed it was someone walking through the fields, stopping to study something on the ground. The rest of his mind was intent on capturing the image of the rivers of blood flowing down through time.

Having caught something on paper he felt better. Slipping into his waxed jacket and boots he decided to go for a walk. Since he had arrived nearly a week ago he had only considered the area to the east and he felt he needed to have a fresh angle on the land. He had been to the visitors' center and local museum to study the history and detail, but he was more in need of the atmosphere and the real essence of the land. He wanted to get away from the modern-day memorabilia and find the natural world.

Once outside the cottage he immediately felt better. Despite the lowering sky it was light, the air was fresh and the wind was not too cold. Leigh had his sketchpad and a hat tucked in his poacher's pocket, with his usual array of drawing implements, so he felt suitably prepared. Maybe the rain would keep off and give him a chance to complete some additional rough sketches.

The narrow road outside his cottage ran up a slight incline before falling away toward a shallow valley. As Leigh crested the rise he stopped to look out across the fields. He remembered the photographs he had seen at the visitors' center of the anguished and haunted faces of the men, caught in a second of time awaiting their fate. Looking out across the fields he could almost hear the cries of dying amidst the thunder of battle. He knew little about the detail of the battles, and felt it was not necessary. The author of the book was taking care of that. Leigh's assignment was to bring the real essence of those moments back into focus.

Suddenly a flock of crows rose from the field and Leigh was taken aback by the impression of the souls of the dead parting from the battle. Before he knew it, pad and pencil were in hand and he was lost in his art.

It must have been five or ten minutes before he became aware of a further movement in the field. He squinted. He could see again that huddled shape, but now in a nearer field. Thinking of the time since he had first seen it he was surprised it was still in view but perhaps the person, like himself, was in no hurry and intent on taking in the atmosphere of the land. But then a change in the clouds lightened the scene and he became aware that it was not a person but a scarecrow, with the wind whipping its rags. Strange he hadn't noticed it before, but perhaps his thoughts had been elsewhere.

He put his pad and pencil back in his pocket and continued along the road, down into the shallow defile, where a small stream guttered under the road, and on toward the next bend. An embankment and hedgerows temporarily obscured the field, but as Leigh turned the corner a new scene opened to him, looking down toward a large wood. He knew from the map that a footpath led across from these trees to a ridge overlooking one of the main defences of the war, where tens of thousands of soldiers had fallen in a futile offensive.

The flock of crows that had been his vision of souls had

settled in the trees but now on his approach they launched themselves again, their cawing sounding hoarse against the softness of the land. As Leigh neared the trees the hedgerows fell away and he was again exposed to the wind, which was now blowing stronger and had a slight chill to it. You wouldn't think it was May, he mused, as he climbed over a stile into the field opposite the copse.

As his feet touched the field he felt almost a shock. It was as if the very soil had gripped him and pulled him toward it. It reminded him all too suddenly of his dream, or whatever it had been, during the night. It lasted only a second, but in that moment Leigh felt a weariness spread through him, a lethargy that took longer than the moment to pass. It was with a heavy heart and a slow tread that he followed the path up a steep hill toward the ridge, which he knew would overlook the river Somme.

It was the river he now felt he needed to capture in his painting. Blood, the river of life, amidst the Somme, a river of death for so many thousands over the centuries. The picture was becoming clearer in his mind, and he hastened to the crest of the hill.

There was a sudden flapping sound and he became aware of the scarecrow he had seen earlier. It was on the other side of a small hedge he was approaching. He couldn't help noticing how bloated it looked. The farmer, for whatever reason, had fashioned a full face out of an old plastic container, the kind Leigh had seen containing a litre or two of creosote or stainer. The streaked dark brown of the plastic, together with the eyes, nose, and mouth, which were just cut into the container, gave it an earthy, hollow countenance. Leigh paused to look at the scarecrow, wondering why the farmer had gone to that extreme. Rather than the type he was used to—a couple of poles, an old coat, a straw head, and a hat—this one was like a manikin. It was complete with arms and legs. Its shirt and trousers were made from black plastic garbage-bin liners and were stuffed heavily with something. It had a smoother, more liquid effect than straw and was enough to make the clothing bulge, giving the appearance of a fat old man. Over the shirt and trousers was a long coat with a high collar. It was this coat, which reached to the ground, that was flapping so noisily in the wind. There was no doubt that it was an effective bird scarer, as the crows circled all around, but none came near.

The most disturbing aspect though, apart from the sinister face, was the way the scarecrow was fixed to the ground. It was not a single pole, but a cross, in an X shape. Two poles were forced into the ground, these same two poles being both the legs and arms of the scarecrow. It gave the overriding impression of a man crucified, and as that thought entered Leigh's mind, so did another vision of the battlefields, and death. The scarecrow became a symbol of death as it witnessed the carnage and destruction of the war.

Leigh's pencil soon captured the image on paper. As he sketched, he looked again at the scarecrow and noticed how the poles darkened as they entered the ground. He presumed the farmer had treated the poles with some preservative, but he couldn't help thinking that the wood was staining upward, as if it was drawing something out of the ground, something dark and brown.

Leigh shivered at the imagery and finally forced his eyes away from the scarecrow. It was only a few more yards to the top of the hill and the view of the Somme, but he was feeling tired and sluggish and it was all he could do to move his feet. They felt almost rooted to the spot. But he finally reached the top and there before him was the view he wanted. Stretching out down below the escarpment was the flat marshy plain of the river. The fields were alive with poppies, the final image that he required. Linked to the rivers of blood and death, the crows as souls of the dead and now the crucified witness, Leigh felt he was able to capture both the stark horror and the hope of rebirth.

He unrolled a plastic groundsheet from one of his pockets and lay it under a tree against which he could rest his back. He sat down on the incline and was soon lost in his sketching.

Some while passed, and he began to realise how tired he was. The last few restless nights had taken their toll, but the invigorating air and the imagery had also had their effect. Before he knew it he was dozing. And as he dozed there came a sinking sensation as if the earth was opening below him. With a jolt he was awake. He leaned back against the tree but before long his head began to droop again. This time the sinking sensation was not so sudden. Instead he felt he was drifting, buoyed on the crest of a mighty wave. It was almost restful, welcoming.

And then the wave passed and he began to slide down toward the trough, and the sky and land darkened and water turned to . . .

He suddenly woke and shook his head. The sensations faded fast, but Leigh felt unnerved. He stretched and looked up at the tree above him, his eyes following the intricate tracery of branches as they waved and crossed in the wind. They soon became a blur of pattern and he found himself becoming almost hypnotised by their incessant movement against the violent clouds. The branches and new growth rustled and whispered, shifting suddenly as if to hide a secret. And then, within the branches, just for a moment, something looked back at him. As his eyes refocused the image vanished, but Leigh was left with the impression of two dark, slit eyes and a slit mouth.

He forced himself to his feet. This lack of sleep was making him delirious, he felt, and he needed to pull himself together. He looked back at the scene of the former battlefield, and envisaged the futile attempt by the thousands of infantrymen to storm this escarpment. All those lives wasted, for what? A few yards of mud and filth.

As he surveyed the scene something touched his neck, and his hand reached up instinctively to flick it away. His fingers felt something cold caught in the collar of his jacket. He pulled it out and looked at it. It was a small piece of black plastic. He flicked it away and watched the wind catch it and whip it up and over the fields below.

He settled down again on his groundsheet and continued with his sketching, but before he knew it his head began to droop and his eyes closed. Into his mind came the sight of the dead and the dying and the blood-drenched fields. The men were looking at him imploringly, with hollow eyes, seeking a saviour, someone who would take them back to the golden fields of home and the arms of their loved ones.

The men were calling to him in voiceless whispers. He began to feel himself slipping, soaking into the soil. But it was pleasing, welcoming. The land recognised him as a friend, a sympathetic soul that could release the pain. The soil was rippling, like small waves, rising about him, caressing his body. . . .

He shivered and woke again, looking about him for reassurance. The sky had darkened and rain looked imminent. He really ought to get back to the cottage. A warm soup and bread and he'd soon be replenished and able to get on with his painting. But it was such an effort to move. Just a few moments more, and then perhaps he could take a short-cut back across the field. He couldn't be much more than thirty minutes from the cottage.

But sleep beckoned. Again his head drooped, his eyes closed. Again he was drawn into the earth, the warm, welcoming earth, where thousands of souls had rested before their flight. He could feel something tightening around his wrists and ankles and neck, and a rustling sound was in his head. He tried to move but was rooted to the spot. Something cold and wet smothered his face and he began to struggle for breath. He gasped, and the reaction woke him. At that moment the sky flashed with lightning and there was a distant rumble of thunder.

He rubbed his eyes and face, forcing himself to move. Invisible bonds seemed to lash him to the earth, but with a determined effort Leigh at last was able to rise. As he did so the groundsheet was caught in a strong gust of wind and flapped up, wrapping itself around his legs and body, pushing him toward the poppy-strewn fields. It required every last breath to force himself against it. When the wind suddenly dropped he stumbled forward, but another gust caught the groundsheet and carried it away. It rose, black against the sky, and Leigh couldn't help thinking about the crows and feeling he was witnessing his own soul rising. The effort to regain it was just too much. Leigh suddenly felt very lonely and very tired.

With leaden legs he forced himself back toward the hedgerow and some shelter from the wind. He looked around for his bearings. Out of the side of his eye he was aware of a movement behind the tree. As he turned his head to look it was gone, though he was left with the impression of something black. Probably more of that black plastic caught in the wind, he thought.

It started to drizzle and that brought his mind back to the

cottage. He knew the way he had come, but was hoping to spot a quicker route back, perhaps through the field with the scarecrow. But the rain was now starting to fall heavily and it wasn't easy to see clearly. He reached inside his coat for the hat in his poacher's pocket and touched something cold and wet. His hand jerked back in a natural reaction and then he felt again. He unzipped his coat and looked inside the pocket. It was soaked by some dark liquid. In horror he whipped out his pad, checking his sketches. They were okay, though the pad was stained brown around the edges. He started to put the pad away into one of his outer pockets only to find this was soaked as well.

He pulled out his hat, which was stained with the dark brown liquid. The puzzlement overrode any repulsion, as Leigh first wondered whether he'd left his coat somewhere wet, or just what he had done. Then he began to think more about the liquid and what it was. It looked like the brown stain he had seen on the scarecrow's legs; in fact, it almost looked like blood after it had soaked into cloth.

As the rain beat down Leigh felt compelled to put his hat on, though he felt a little queasy about it. He rationalised the liquid had come from the outhouses at the cottage where he had rummaged on the first day, and though this didn't convince him, he tried not to think any further. His prime concern was to get back to the cottage.

He looked up, right into the face of the scarecrow, and the shock made his heart thump. The evil slit eyes looked straight into Leigh's and the mouth grinned. The scarecrow's coat flapped noisily in the wind. Leigh couldn't understand how he came to be standing by the scarecrow as he had no recollection of crossing into the field.

He stepped back . . . and the scarecrow stepped with him.

A trick of the light? A sudden gust of wind? Leigh had no idea, but it unnerved him. He stepped to one side and almost felt the eyes follow him. He looked away from the scarecrow for a moment to work out where to go, but the rain and wind were beating against his face and he couldn't be sure. The scarecrow's coat was flapping in the wind. Then it moved again.

This time Leigh was sure. No matter how much his rational mind told him it had not, his eyes told him it had. Leigh turned and ran, but his feet sank into the earth, which the rain was rapidly turning to mud. His mind briefly captured a vision of the mud-strewn battlefields of the Somme, the soldiers up to their ankles in water in the trenches. Then the flapping of the scarecrow's coat reminded Leigh how close it was and he struggled again to move his feet. But with each step he was getting deeper and deeper in the mud. He was drained of all energy and could not move.

It was then, in a dreadful vision, that Leigh saw his groundsheet again, rising on the wind and flapping toward him. A flock of crows, frightened by the sight, took cawing to the air, their wings turning the sky to black. Like a twisting wraith the sheet curled in the air, alive with the storm. Rooted to the ground, hypnotised by the sight, Leigh heard a squelch in the mud behind him. Before he could turn his head the flapping coat of the scarecrow closed over him. He was aware of a damp, oily smell and a wetness around his neck.

Then he was struck by the full force of his groundsheet as it wrapped around him, bonding him to the scarecrow. Its arms became his arms, its legs his legs, and with that came a sudden surge of strength from the soil. The blood of centuries bubbled from the ground and Leigh heard the screams of armies in his head. The whole agony of war paralysed his brain, and the sense of anguish and futility permeated his veins. His body relived a thousand dying moments.

And then all went quiet. The wind dropped. The rain ceased. The clouds began to part allowing a watery sun to cast a wan light across the mud-streaked fields. A lone scarecrow, fatter now than ever, bowed its head from the light and waited.

# Conversion

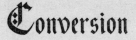

RAMSEY CAMPBELL

You're in sight of home when you know something's wrong. Moonlight shivers gently on the stream beyond the cottage, and trees stand around you like intricate spikes of the darkness mounting within the forest. The cottage is dark, but it isn't that. You emerge into the glade, trying to sense what's troubling you.

You know you shouldn't have stayed out so late, talking to your friend. Your wife must have been worried, perhaps frightened by the night as well. You've never left her alone at night before. But his talk was so engrossing: you feel that in less than a night you've changed from being wary of him to understanding him completely. And his wine was so good, and his open-throated brightly streaming fire so warming, that you can now remember little except a timeless sense of comfortable companionship, of communion that no longer needed words. But you shouldn't have left your wife alone in the forest at night, even behind a barred door. The woodcutter's cottage is nearby; at least you could have had his wife stay with yours. You feel disloyal.

Perhaps that's what has been disturbing you. Always before when you've returned home, light has been pouring from the windows, mellowing the surrounding trunks and including them like a wall around your cottage. Now the cottage reminds you of winter nights long ago in your childhood, when you lay listening to a wolf's cry like the slow plummeting of ice into a gorge, and felt the mountains and forests huge around you, raked by the wind. The cottage feels like that: cold and hollow and unwelcoming. For a moment you wonder if you're simply anticipating your wife's blame, but you're sure it's more than that.

In any case you'll have to knock and awaken her. First you go to the window and look in. She's lying in bed, her face open as if to the sky. Moonlight eases darkness from her face, but leaves her throat and the rest of her in shadow. Tears have gathered in her eyes, sparkling. No doubt she has been crying in memory of her sister, a sketch of whom gazes across the bed from beside a glass of water. As you look in you're reminded of your childhood fancy that angels watched over you at night, not at the end of the bed but outside the window; for a second you feel like your wife's angel. But as you gaze in, discomfort grows in your throat and stomach. You remember how your fancy somehow turned into a terror of glimpsing a white face peering in. You draw back quickly in case you should frighten her.

But you have to knock. You don't understand why you've been delaying. You stride to the door and your fist halts in mid-air, as if impaled by lightning. Suddenly the vague threats and unease you've been feeling seem to rush together and gather on the other side of the door. You know that beyond the door something is waiting for you, ready to pounce.

You feel as if terror has pinned you through your stomach, helpless. You're almost ready to flee into the woods, to free yourself from the skewer of your panic. Sweat pricks you like red-hot ash scattered on your skin. But you can't leave your wife in there with it, whatever nightmare it is, rising out of the tales you've heard told of the forest. You force yourself to be still if not calm, and listen for some hint of what it might be.

All you can hear is the slow sleepy breathing of the wind in the trees. Your panic rises, for you can feel it beyond the door, perfectly poised and waiting easily for you to betray yourself. You hurry back to the window, but it's impossible for you to squeeze yourself in far enough to make out anything within the door. This time a stench rises from the room to meet you, trick-ling into your nostrils. It's so thickly unpleasant that you refuse to think what it might resemble. You edge back, terrified now of awakening your wife, for it can only be her immobility that's protecting her from whatever's in the room.

But you can't coax yourself back to the door. You've al-lowed your panic to spread out from it, warding you farther from the cottage. Your mind fills with your wife, lying unaware of her plight. Furious with yourself, you compel your body forward against the gale of your panic. You reach the door and struggle to touch it. If you can't do that, you tell yourself, you're a coward, a soft scrabbling thing afraid of the light. Your hand presses against the door as if proving itself against a live coal, and the door swings inward.

You should have realized that your foe might have entered the cottage through the doorway. You flinch back instinctively, but as the swift fear fades the panic seeps back. You can feel it hanging like a spider just inside the doorway, waiting for you to pass beneath: a huge heavy black spider, ready to plump on your face. You try to shake your panic out of you with the knowledge that it's probably nothing like that, that you're giving in to fancy. But whatever it is, it's oozing a stench that claws its way into your throat and begins to squeeze out your stomach. You fall back, weakened and baffled.

Then you see the rake. It's resting against the corner of the cottage, where you left it after trying to clear a space for a garden. You carry it to the door, thinking. It could be more than a weapon, even though you don't know what you're fighting. If your wife doesn't awaken and draw its attention to her, if your foe isn't intelligent enough to see what you're planning, if your absolute conviction of where it's lurking above the door isn't false— You almost throw away the rake, but you can't bear the sense of your wife's peril any longer. You inch the door open. You're sure you have only one chance.

You reach stealthily into the space above the door with the teeth of the rake, then you grind them into your prey and drag it out into the open. It's a dark tangled mass, but you hurl it away into the forest without looking closer, for some of it has fallen into the doorway and lies dimly there, its stench welling up. You pin it with the teeth and fling it into the trees.

Then you realize there's more, hanging and skulking around the side of the door frame. You grab it with the rake and hurl it against a trunk. Then you let your breath roar out. You're weak and dizzy, but you stagger through the doorway. There are smears of the thing around the frame and you sway back, retching. You close your mouth and nostrils and you're past, safe.

You lean on the rake and gaze down at your wife. There's a faint stench clinging to the rake, and you push it away from you, against the wall. She's still asleep, no doubt because you were mourning her sister all last night. Your memory's blurring; you must be exhausted too, because you can remember hardly anything before the battle you've just fought. You're simply grateful that no harm has befallen her. If she'd come with you to visit your friend none of this would have happened. You hope you can recapture the sense of communion you had with him, to pass on to your wife. Through your blurring consciousness you feel an enormous yearning for her.

Then you jerk alert, for there's still something in the room. You glance about wildly and see beneath the window more of what you destroyed, lying like a tattered snake. You manage to scoop it up in one piece this time, and you throw the rake out with it. Then you turn back to your wife. You've disturbed her; she has moved in her sleep. And fear advances on you from the bed like a spreading stain pumped out by a heart, because now you can see what's nestling at her throat.

You don't know what it is; your terror blurs it and crowds out your memories until it looks like nothing you've ever seen. It rests in the hollow of her throat like a dormant bat, and indeed it seems to have stubby protruding wings. Its shape expands within your head until it is a slow explosion of pure hostility, growing and erasing you. You turn away, blinded.

It's far worse than what you threw into the forest. Even then, if you hadn't been fighting for your wife you would have been paralyzed by superstition. Now you can hardly turn your head back to look. The stain of the thing is crawling over your wife, blotting out her face and all your sense of her. But you open your eyes an agonized slit and see it couched in her throat as if it lives there. Your rage floods up, and you start forward.

But even with your eyes closed you can't gain on it, because a great cold inhuman power closes about you, crushing you like a moth in a fist. You mustn't cry out, because if your wife awakens it may turn on her. But the struggle crushes a wordless roar from you, and you hear her awake.

Your seared eyes make out her face, dimmed by the force of the thing at her neck. Perhaps her gathered tears are dislodged, or perhaps these are new, wrung out by the terror in her eyes. Your head is a shell full of fire, your eyes feel as though turning to ash, but you battle forward. Then you realize she's shrinking back. She isn't terrified of the thing at her throat at all, she's terrified of you. She's completely in its power.

You're still straining against the force, wondering whether it must divert some of its power from you in order to control her, when she grabs the glass from beside the bed. For a moment you can't imagine what she wants with a glass of water. But it isn't water. It's vitriol, and she throws it in your face.

Your face bursts into pain. Howling, you rush to the mirror.

You're still searching for yourself in the mirror when the woodcutter appears in the doorway, grim-faced. At once, like an eye in the whirlwind of your confusion and pain, you remember that you asked his wife to stay with yours, yesterday afternoon when he wasn't home to dissuade you from what you had to do. And you know why you can't see yourself, only the room and the doorway through which you threw the garlic, your sobbing wife clutching the cross at her throat, the glass empty now of the holy water you brought home before setting out to avenge her sister's death at Castle Dracula.

# Apotropaics

NORMAN PARTRIDGE

I was heading for the creek, whistling "Heartbreak Hotel" and minding my own business, when Ross caught up to me and told me about the vampire at Todd Palmer's house.

"Jason," he gasped, doubling over as he caught up to me. "Man, we thought you'd never get home from vacation. Todd and Dave and me, we didn't know what to do. But now that you're back . . ."

He left the sentence unfinished. Suddenly, he wore the relieved look of a tired pitcher who'd just been pulled from a tough game. He straightened, still a head shorter than me even though we were both eleven, and he shot the look my way one more time, just to be sure that I hadn't missed it.

I flicked his Brooklyn Dodgers cap off his head. "Pull the other one, Ross. You guys have probably been planning this for two weeks." I sighed. "C'mon—Bela Lugosi in corn country? Is that the best you can do? Isn't it bad enough that my folks dragged me through twenty-two states in fourteen days? And, man, all I've got to show for it is this chintzy knife from Yosemite."

I pulled the knife fast enough to make Ross jump (he's a hopeless coward). It wasn't really chintzy, but it wasn't the one I had wanted, either. That one cost ten bucks and had an authentic ivory handle. My old man wouldn't go for it though, so I had to settle for the two-buck special that had a genuine plastic handle with a hand-painted view of Half Dome.

Hand-painted in Taiwan, that is.

Ross stared at the knife. No, he did more than stare—his gaze was riveted on the shiny blade. "Oh, man," he said. "This is scary. I mean, you buying a knife. It's like you're psychic or something. I swear to God it is!"

"What're you talking about?"

"C'mon and I'll show you."

Ross scooped up his cap and we walked the short distance to Palmer's cornfield. We hopped the fence and blazed a trail between two rows of dead cornstalks. I was surprised that Mr. Palmer hadn't plowed the field and planted another crop. Todd's dad was usually real quick about that kind of stuff. My dad always said that Mr. Palmer was a hard man, a man who didn't brook nonsense. That was the way Todd's dad managed his farm, pushing its crop potential to the limit, and my dad seemed to think that was the way Mr. Palmer handled his kids, too.

But something had slowed Mr. Palmer's clockwork pace. Maybe for once he hadn't had time, or maybe he'd wanted a vacation of his own, or maybe . . .

Maybe anything. Who knows why things happen? I mean, really? People say things. They do things. But who ever knows why? Really?

Ross pushed between two tall stalks that crackled like ancient parchment. I followed. We cut through a couple more rows and came to the center of the field.

And there it was. A naked mound of dirt, dark clods dried gray and hard in the hot sun.

*A grave,* I thought, shivering. It wasn't an ordinary grave, either, and not just because it was in the middle of a cornfield. Imbedded in this grave, punched into it like it was some weird pincushion, were dozens of stakes and knives. Tent stakes, sur-

22

vey stakes, Boy Scout knives, ordinary silverware, putty knives, and fancy stuff that must have been pure silver.

Ross was talking again. "We had to steal some of 'em. Christ, my mom'll kill me if she finds out I took Aunt Alma's silver. But we had to, 'cause we can't let him come back. Oh, man, he'll be pissed if he comes back, and I don't want to think about what he'd do to Todd, and to me and Dave because we helped Todd." He bent low, making sure that the stakes and knives were firmly planted in the hard ground. "So we stuck this stuff into the grave, and he can't get out without killing himself again. That makes sense, don't it, Jase? I mean, you know how this stuff works. . . ."

Ross kept talking, the way he always does, but I wasn't listening.

It was my turn to stare.

My turn for riveted gazes.

The churned, dry dirt of the grave. The stakes, brown and hard and smooth, like weird roots. The knives, hilts glistening in the morning sunlight. The clumps of earth, like dead fists.

Not dead. Undead.

Because this was a vampire's grave.


Standing there surrounded by oak trees that were a good hundred years old, Todd's big house looked small. The Palmers had lived on the outskirts of Fiddler for three generations, and the house had stood the test of time. A couple coats of white paint every two years helped, and so did old man Palmer's skill as a carpenter, but I always thought that there was something about the way the house rested under those big trees that helped protect it.

Today it didn't look protected. It looked trapped, ensnared by a hundred gnarled arms, all twisting toward it and holding it down.

Todd answered our knock. He didn't look right. There was a deep green bruise on his jaw, and his eyes were red, and it didn't take a rocket scientist to figure out that he'd been crying.

Ross opened his trap and started to whisper too loudly, and Todd held a finger to his lips. "My folks are gone," Todd said. "They headed down to see Grandma in Earlimart. They don't think she's gonna make it this time, and she won't go back to the hospital. Sis is upstairs, sleeping again. That's all she does lately." He opened the screen door. "Come in, but be quiet."

We followed Todd through the living room. It was stark, like a room where no one lived at all. No TV, no hi-fi, no coffee table, certainly no magazines or flowers. Just a worn rocker, a few chairs so stiff that even the doilies on their arms seemed out of place, and a big wrought-iron cross hanging over the fireplace.

*A cross that a hard man would appreciate,* I thought, and then I felt kind of weird, because it was a thought my dad would have.

Anyway, Todd moved down the hallway, his right shoulder rubbing the flowery wallpaper. He came to a little table by the staircase and picked up the telephone.

He didn't have to dial. It was a party line, and Dave's mom was in the middle of a call. "I hate to interrupt, Mrs. Sanchez," Todd said, his voice quiet but firm. "Can I talk to Dave? It's kind of important."

Mrs. Sanchez must have agreed, because Todd didn't say anything else. In a town like Fiddler, where everybody thinks they know everybody else's business, a kid with a dying grandma can get away with anything.

We stood in the quiet hallway, waiting for Dave to come to the phone. I stepped to the foot of the staircase. A doorway stood open on the landing above. I saw a bed, and someone's arm dangling over the side. The person in the bed rolled over just as I started up the stairs, and I saw long blond hair and a white nightgown dipping low over a white shoulder.

Janet Palmer, Todd's sister. Her eyes caught mine, but it was like they weren't quite focused. "Dave?" she whispered. "Is that you? I'm sorry, Dave. I'm so sorry."

I backed down the staircase, embarrassed, and didn't say a word. Todd said a couple words to Dave, because that was all it took. Then he grabbed my shirttail, and I turned and saw those red eyes of his.

I couldn't read them at all.

Upstairs, Janet was crying.

"C'mon," Todd said. "Meeting time."

We sat under Todd's front porch. The air was still and cool. There was enough room for kids to sit comfortably, but not enough room for adults, so it was the perfect place to go when we didn't want to be bothered.

"Tell us what to do, Jase," Ross said. "Tell us if we done right. I mean, you know about this stuff. You read all those monster magazines and see all those movies."

"Yeah." I nodded. "You've said that about a jillion times today."

Dave laughed, twirled his drumsticks, and did a little drum roll on the rubber pad the band teacher had given him so he could practice over the summer. His folks weren't too well off and he couldn't afford a snare drum, let alone the fancy set he wanted.

Dave carried the practice pad with him everywhere. He put up with concert band, but he really wanted to rock 'n' roll. He said he was going to get out of Fiddler and tour with Ritchie Valens or somebody like that. Dave was the coolest kid I knew, the leader of our group, and I felt like he was about five years ahead of us in almost everything. Girls liked him, and he didn't put on a show with them or pretend that he minded their attention.

"So who's going to tell me what's going on?" I asked.

Ross started blabbing again, and I cut him off with a hard glance. Todd didn't look like he was up to talking. Dave shrugged and started in, setting his drumsticks aside.

"I guess I was the first one to figure out what was going on." He sighed. "But I don't really want to talk about it. It was hard enough to tell Todd the first time, and to do it again . . ."

"You gotta tell," Ross put in, and then he buttoned up before anyone could punch him.

"Yeah, I gotta tell." Dave sighed again. "You know that we've got a party line with Todd's family. Well, I got so I would listen in every now and then. At first it was just for fun. One time, I heard Mr. Palmer cussing out some tractor salesman. And I heard Mrs. Palmer gossiping with Ross's mom almost every day." He paused, his eyes locked on his drumsticks as if he didn't dare look up at me and speak at the same time. "But, to tell you the truth, Janet was the one I really wanted to hear when I picked up the phone."

I glanced at Todd. His eyes were glazed over, and he was rubbing the welt on his jaw. I knew then, even before Dave said what he was going to say, that Todd would rather get punched out than listen to Dave's story again.

Suddenly, I knew what kind of story it was going to be.

People say things. They do things.

And sometimes they even tell the truth.

Dave went on, still looking down at his drumsticks. "I know that she's six years older than me. I *know* that. But when I'd hear Janet talking to her girlfriends, I didn't miss a word. And when she wouldn't tell them the name of the guy she had a crush on, I'd imagine that she was talking about me. And when she told Ross's sister that she was in love with a guy who was in love with her, too, I imagined that she knew how I felt about her without me even saying, and that she felt exactly the same way about me."

"Without even saying," Todd whispered, still rubbing his jaw.

Dave nodded, still looking down.

"Tell him what happened next," Ross blurted. "Tell him about the vam—"

"Shut up, Ross," I said.

"Yeah, shut up," Dave said, but his voice didn't have any strength. He looked at me, and I knew that it took everything he had just to hold my gaze. He didn't look like a leader anymore. He didn't look like a guy who had everything figured out. He looked like an eleven-year-old boy who'd been scared by an expert.

He kept talking. "It was two weeks ago, just about the time you left on vacation. I got up around midnight to get a drink of water. I don't know why, but I picked up the phone, even though it was late.

"I heard him then. I had to strain to understand him, because his voice was so quiet and smooth. Her voice sounded the same way. But I'd never heard Janet talk like that before. It made me feel sick, some of the things she said, and the hard way he laughed when she said them." Dave swallowed. "And I felt sick, too, because suddenly I knew she hadn't been talking about me when she talked to her girlfriends.

"I wanted to hang up, but I couldn't. And then came the worst part. He said, '*You think your little friend is listening? You*

26

*think he's gettin' a thrill!'* and she just laughed. I hung up then. I didn't even try to be sneaky. I'm sure they heard me.

"I tried to go to sleep, but all I could do was toss and turn. I knew that I'd never be able to look Janet in the eye again. And then, in the middle of the night, I heard a motorcycle out on the road, full open and racing fast. I got out of bed and ran to the window just in time to see Janet riding with him, her arms wrapped around his chest, her fingers digging into his leather jacket, her blond hair blowing in the wind. They headed up the road, toward wherever he was from, I guess, and they came back about an hour before dawn.

"That should have been the end of it. Even then, I thought it was spooky that they knew I was listening to them that night. I mean, I knew it was weird. Too weird." Dave's voice quavered with shame. "But I couldn't stop listening. I heard them every night. The things they said . . . some of them they said to me, because they knew I was listening. And I heard the motorcycle. Roaring out on the road, coming and going night after night. And then one day I heard Todd's mom talking to Ross's mom—"

"I heard it too," Ross said. "I mean, Mom told Dad about it. She said that an evil boy was sucking Janet Palmer dry, sucking the blood of Jesus right out of her and dragging her straight down to hell."

"Your mom is pretty wild with the fire and brimstone bit," I said. "She's said worse stuff about me, I'll bet."

"No way," Ross said. "She was serious. She knew that this guy was a vampire! She knew it! But she was afraid to say the word!"

Dave shook his head. "I don't know, Jase. Maybe you're right. But if you'd heard this guy. If you'd heard the things that he said—"

"Or if you'd seen what he did," Ross put in. "I didn't see it. Not myself. But Todd was there when it happened. Todd saw the whole thing."

Todd stopped rubbing his jaw. He started talking, but his voice was distant, like it wasn't a voice at all but a little machine that had clicked on inside of him. "We went to see Grandma. Mom and Dad and me. You guys know how sick she is. Janet didn't go. She said she wasn't feeling well. She whispered something to Mom about the way she felt, and Mom blushed and said it was okay for her to stay home.

"Grandma talked for a long time. It was fun to listen to her. She talked about her courting days, and how wonderful Grandpa was back then. It was like she wasn't sick at all. She fell asleep with a smile on her face.

"We got home late. Dad saw the motorcycle parked by the barn. He stopped the car at the end of the driveway, got out, and started for the house. He was walking fast, but he didn't run. Mom just sat there in the front seat, not moving at all. I sat in the back, staring at her hair. It was all neat in a bun and it didn't move, either. It was like she was a dummy or something. I remember thinking that."

Todd lay back and closed his eyes—maybe it helped him remember, or maybe he wanted to hide from us. He said, "I heard Janet scream, and I scrambled out of the car. Mom was yelling at me, but I didn't stop running. I banged through the screen door and the screaming was really loud, like it was bottled up in the house.

"I almost stopped running when I got to the foot of the stairs, but it was too late. I took them three at a time and then I was in Janet's room. She was in the corner, all twisted up like she wanted to hide. She didn't have any clothes on and I saw the bruises on her neck where he'd . . . and there were bruises on her boobs, too." He sobbed. "And then I saw the blood. I saw where she was . . . bleeding. It was on her legs and . . . and . . ."

Todd was crying now, and there was no stopping his tears. "And there was blood on the sheets. Dad pinned the vampire to the floor with his knees, straddling him. The guy—the thing—it was real white. Its arms and legs were long and skinny, like it was a big spider. Dad had the wrought-iron cross in his hands, and he bashed . . . and he hit the thing again and again, and the guy—the vampire—was twitching and Janet was crying and . . . its arms and legs were twitching . . . and the cross . . . it worked and . . ."

Dave's hand dropped onto Todd's shoulder. Todd stopped talking, but he couldn't stop sobbing.

"That was what happened," Dave said. "Todd's dad sent him to bed, hit him hard when Todd tried to go back to Janet's room. He told Todd that the guy was okay, that he'd only beat him up so he wouldn't come back and hurt Janet again. But Todd knew that wasn't true. He could see the cornfield from his bedroom window, and he saw his father go out there that night and dig a grave."

"But Mr. Palmer didn't put a stake in the vampire's heart," Ross said. "At least we don't think so. That's why we put the knives and stakes in the grave. 'Cause Todd saw Janet. He saw that blood. He knew what really happened."

"It really happened," I said. "Everything you told me. It really happened."

They nodded. No one said anything for a long time. Then Ross started in again. "It's just like they said. It's true, every word. I mean, the vampire only came at night. On the phone, he knew that Dave was listening. They can read minds, right? And the things it said to Janet, and the things it made her say. They can hypnotize people, y'know, make them say or do anything. And the blood. Todd saw the blood." Ross hugged himself, rocking back and forth. "It's scary. I mean, I found where Todd's dad hid the vampire's motorcycle. It's down by the creek. It's black. It's all busted up now, but it doesn't have any mirrors, and I bet it never did. Understand? It doesn't have any mirrors!" He was rocking like crazy now. "I don't think the vampire can come back. We did the right thing, didn't we Jase? It can't come back, can it?"

I shook my head.

Dave's drumsticks thrummed gently on the practice pad, but he couldn't find a beat. "It's hard," he said, and he almost sounded like Ross. "It's hard to know what we should do next."

I looked at them, and I was with them, and I wanted to help them.

I looked at Todd. He couldn't do it. He was the son of a hard man, and he'd been broken.

Dave couldn't do it. He was still in love. If he heard Janet say how sorry she was, he'd never forget it.

Ross couldn't do it. Not on his best day. Not ever.

"She won't get up," Todd said. "She won't eat . . ."

Dave started to cry.

Gently, I slid the drumsticks out of his hands.

I opened my new knife.

Sometimes people say things. Sometimes they do things. But nobody said a word, and nobody moved, while I sharpened the stakes.

# Camera Shy

## T.E.D. Klein

*EDITOR'S NOTE: This story was originally written to accompany a series of photographs.*

hy would anyone take a picture of an empty chair?"

The front door slammed; he was back early today. In silence Mrs. Melnick worked her pudgy fingers through the dough, a cookbook propped open before her. Jennifer and Laszlo would be coming home later this evening, and she wanted to have the cake ready in time for their arrival. Only yesterday, it seemed, she had waved goodbye to them as they'd marched up the steps of the airplane; later she had watched the plane's winking yellow taillights disappear into the eastern sky. Yet soon—in a matter of hours—the two would be returning to the States, their honeymoon behind them. *Imagine,* she thought, *married one whole month. . . .*

"I swear to God," called Mr. Melnick from the living room, "it's nothing but a goddamned empty chair!" The closet door banged open as he hung up his coat. "I *told* you not to hire that photographer!"

Mrs. Melnick stopped what she was doing. "Photographer? What photographer?"

"The one who took the wedding pictures."

"You mean they're here?" She hurried from the kitchen, wiping her hands on her apron. "So don't keep me in suspense. How did they come out?"

"Terrific—if you like pictures of furniture!" He was sitting *penseur*-like upon the edge of the couch, gloomily examining the photo in his hand. Others lay before him on the coffee table, piled atop a large manila envelope. He looked up as she came in.

"I found them in the mail just now. God knows what to make of this one." He held up the photo for her inspection. "See? If you ask me, it's a waste of perfectly good film."

Mrs. Melnick glanced at it and shrugged. "Just practice, I guess. Come on, let's see the others." Seating herself heavily beside him, she reached for the pile, then drew back her hand. "Go ahead. I don't want to get them sticky."

The photo on top showed the same empty chair from a slightly different angle, but the one beneath it was an ordinary snapshot in which wedding guests stood stiffly round a punch bowl. Behind them a trio of musicians were setting up their instruments, perspiration gleaming from their faces. The reception had been held at a local country club, early on a warm September evening. The sky, she recalled, had been brilliantly flooded with moonlight, yet in the photograph—due, no doubt, to some trick of the flashbulb—a row of windows in the background appeared to look out on a world of impenetrable darkness.

Her husband turned over the next photo, and the next; smiling pink faces passed glossily in review. "A nice shot of Aunt Ida," he said, apparently surprised, "and this one of you and Jennifer is decent enough."

The sight made her wince. "God," she moaned, "I look so *fat!* And so does Jennifer. I only hope she's had the sense to keep her weight down over there, with all that continental cooking." She thought briefly, guiltily, of the cake she'd been preparing for Jennifer's return, and of the letters they'd received from her this past month: ecstatic reports of the Alhambra by moonlight, Paris after dark, the best night-spots in Rome, dining by candlelight in Vienna—and then that odd, half-scrawled postcard from Laszlo's native village outside Budapest. . . .

"Jennifer's not fat," Mr. Melnick was saying. "She's just a little on the *zoftig* side. And better *zoftig* than *this.*" He pointed grimly to the next photo in the stack.

Turning to it, Mrs. Melnick sighed and shook her head. "Poor Pamela," she said. "Such a tragedy. Jennifer will be so upset when she finds out."

Pamela Lebow had been the bridesmaid. She had been ill at the time of the wedding, but she nonetheless managed to attend, rising from her sickbed to join, albeit lethargically, in the nuptial rites. Afterward, however, as if exhausted from the strain, she had taken once more to her bed. While the bride and groom were winging majestically toward Europe, she had sunk into the all-embracing darkness of a coma. Less than a week later she was dead. The doctors had blamed an obscure form of anemia, and checked to see that their malpractice insurance was paid up.

"She looks so *happy,* somehow," observed Mrs. Melnick. "As if she knew she hadn't long to live and didn't really care."

Mr. Melnick nodded. "Sad, very sad." He avoided mentioning to his wife that, with her deathlike face and shadow-haunted eyes, the young lady had in fact given him the creeps. In the photograph the two Melnick women, mother and daughter, were beaming at the camera like a pair of Brueghel peasants, shoulders broad and foreheads shining rosily, while Pamela stood beside them looking pale and oddly distracted. She was smiling a wan Mona Lisa smile and seemed to be staring at someone just beyond the edge of the picture.

Perhaps she was looking at Laszlo. The two of them had dated for a while, shortly before he'd met Jennifer, and they'd remained close even during Laszlo's engagement. Pamela had proved a good friend to them both; she had never shown an ounce of jealousy.

"The poor thing," said Mrs. Melnick. "It meant so much to her to come to the wedding." She handed the photo back to her husband. "We'll have to send a copy to her parents. You really must admit, dear, the photographer did a very fine job."

He grunted noncommittally, already peering at the next one in the pile. "Well, this shot of the three of us is okay, I guess, except my goddamned tie is crooked."

"Of course it is, silly! That's what I kept *telling* you."

"And look, here's one of that woman Seymour brought, who drank so much—"

"Ugh! Don't remind me!"

"—and who made that awful scene outside the ladies' room." He flipped through several more. "This one of Cousin Oliver's not bad"—Oliver had doubled as Laszlo's best man, since Laszlo's friends and family were, all of them, in Hungary—"but I still say I've taken better pictures myself, and for a hell of a lot less money." He reached for another. "The trouble with these so-called 'professionals' is that they don't know the first thing about— Hmm. Now *this* is strange."

Mr. Melnick squinted at the photo in his hand. His own plump face grinned back at him above a crooked tie. He was standing by the doorway of the reception room, one arm thrust awkwardly in the air. There was something terribly unnatural about the pose, something in the placement of the arm. He felt a tiny chill.

His wife leaned forward to study the photo more closely. A smile crossed her face. "He's certainly caught you at an odd moment," she said. "You look just like a lamppost!"

*Or a gallows,* he thought. He searched his memory, then gave up. "I can't understand it," he said, "I'm sure I never posed this way for anyone. Believe me, I'd remember if I did. The closest thing was . . . Well, you remember, don't you? That photographer asked me and Laszlo to get together for a close-up, and Laszlo didn't seem to want to, and I made a joke about how maybe he was afraid to have his picture taken alongside a handsome guy like me. In the end, of course, he agreed, and we posed together by the doorway—me and Laszlo, standing arm in arm. . . ."

He fell silent.

"Well," his wife said at last, "Laszlo certainly isn't in *this* one."

Mr. Melnick frowned. "The odd thing is . . ." He cleared his throat. "The odd thing is, he doesn't seem to be in *any* of them."

Indeed, he was not. What's more, the photographs looked terribly strange without him. Cousin Oliver turned up in another close-up, but from his position at the left half of the picture it was clear that a second figure was supposed to have been standing by his side. Jennifer, in a later photo, was shown feeding a slice of wedding cake to thin air, while a ring of smiling faces looked on. In still another, the young woman appeared to be dancing with herself, while poor Pamela gazed longingly at the place where Laszlo should have been.

"Why, it's the silliest thing I've ever heard of," sniffed Mrs. Melnick. "Laszlo's been completely left out! Do you suppose they misplaced his pictures?"

"Maybe," said Mr. Melnick. "Or someone's playing a rather elaborate joke on us." He reached for the phone book. "What was the name of that agency?"

"Celebrity Associates," said his wife. "Aunt Ida recommended them, remember? She said that since Laszlo had aristocratic blood and all, he was practically a celebrity, and so I thought—" But Mr. Melnick was already dialing the phone.

The man on the other end was soft-spoken and cordial, but the cordiality receded as the nature of Mr. Melnick's call became clear. "No groom?" he cried. "Impossible! Our guys follow a routine, it's the same at every wedding: bride with bridesmaid, bride with groom, bride with father and mother, father of bride with groom—"

"There *is* no groom!" It was hard to keep from screaming. "And I'll be damned if I pay good money for someone who's not there. Your man was hired to take wedding pictures—that means pictures of a *couple*, a *pair*. If I'd wanted just my daughter I'd have taken them myself."

"Okay, mister, okay. Maybe there was some kind of screwup. Do you happen to remember the photographer's name?"

"Jerry something, I think. I'd like to ask him if—"

But the voice had disappeared, to be replaced by silence.

No, not silence. Echoes—echoes just beyond the edge of comprehension. Mr. Melnick pressed the phone to his ear and strained to make sense of them. He half fancied he heard wails, a hissing, laughter, the chattering of a hundred demons skipping rope amid the phone wires; brigades of ghosts were whispering the names of the condemned, his own doomed name among them. . . .

"Mr. Melnick?"

He jerked back, startled. The voice had returned.

"Listen, I just spoke to Jerry. He says—"

"I'd like to speak to him myself."

"Uh-uh, we've got him down in the darkroom today. He can't come to the phone. But he told me he remembers the wedding, and that he had a lot of trouble with the groom. He says it was very hard to get the guy to sit still and have his picture taken. You know how it is, some people are just camera shy. Jerry says he got him, though, in all the standard shots. Bride with bridesmaid, bride with groom—"

"He isn't *there*, I tell you!"

The man gave an exasperated sigh. "Okay," he said wearily, "here's what you do. Send us back the negatives so we can look them over, and I'll see to it you don't get charged. Of course—" His voice was all business again. "—if you order extra prints, you're gonna have to pay for them just like everyone else."

Mr. Melnick was grumbling as he got off the phone, and continued to do so all evening—especially when, shortly after midnight, with still no sign of Jennifer and Laszlo, he telephoned the airline and learned that their flight was three hours late. "That's it for me" said his wife. "You can wait up if you want to, but I'm going to bed." Yawning, she moved toward the stairs. "And for heaven's sake, stop worrying about Laszlo. If you absolutely *have* to have his picture, you can take it yourself in just a few hours, when he and Jennifer come home." She paused at the landing. "And be sure to wake me when they do."

The house, once she'd gone up, seemed unnaturally empty, a stage set with the props all in place but with the performers yet to appear. Entering the kitchen, Mr. Melnick nearly failed to recognize the face that scowled and peered at him through the windows near the sink; it was his own face reflected in the glossy blackness of the panes, yet subtly altered, imbued now with an almost spectral pallor caused, no doubt, by the glare from the fluorescent bulb. Upstairs he heard the sounds of washing, the snapping off of lights, the creaking of floorboards and bedsprings as his wife made ready for sleep. Pouring himself a cup of coffee in the kitchen (fortified with a shot of Jack Daniels), he returned to the living room and settled back on the couch with a half-completed crossword puzzle from that morning's *Times*, which, as usual, his wife had tried and then abandoned. He stared at the puzzle for a moment, thinking of what she'd said earlier. Perhaps, some time tomorrow, he *would* ask Laszlo to pose for a picture or two. Just for the record, of course; just to have something to include among the wedding photos. He could really use a few of Laszlo. . . .

The air outside was growing colder. Around him, like a sleeper, the old house shifted and groaned, drawing itself closer for the night.

Odd, come to think of it—he didn't have a single picture of Laszlo. Not a one. Even though he'd always been something of a camera buff, he had never managed to include Laszlo in a shot;

the fellow always had some excuse for staying out of range. "Camera shy," the man at the agency had said.

Not that Laszlo had anything to be ashamed of. He was a decent-looking young man with what Jennifer liked to call "dark, European good looks," albeit a bit sallow of complexion. But then, what could you expect from someone who kept such ridiculous hours? "I guess I am just—how you say?—a 'night person,' " he'd explained, with an apologetic smile.

Well, habits like that were easy to break; Jennifer would soon set him right. She was a trifle on the heavy side, perhaps (she took after her mother), but she'd always been a strong, healthy girl of formidable enthusiasm and energy. Some of this was bound to rub off on Laszlo. No doubt their honeymoon together had put a little color in his cheeks.

Yet what if, in fact, the opposite had occurred? What if Laszlo and his ways had proved the stronger? The Old World, he knew, had a certain allure, especially to an impressionable young woman seeing it for the first time. He remembered that last, hurried postcard of Jennifer's, written just after meeting Laszlo's family. *"Dear Mom and Dad,"* it had said. *"Laszlo has shown me a whole new way of life. Can't wait to let you both in on it."*

Somewhere deep in his stomach he felt a tiny, hard knot of unease. The feeling seemed distinctly inappropriate so near to his daughter's return. He got up to make himself another drink, this time omitting the coffee.

Outside, there was movement. A chill October wind had risen from the east, scattering the dead leaves in the yard and stripping the branches of the trees. The old house stirred. In the kitchen, with a terrible suddenness, the refrigerator fell silent. Its noisy little motor had been churning steadily all evening, but until this moment he hadn't really been aware of it. Now the sound was, as in the old expression, conspicuous by its absence. . . .

*Just like Laszlo.* The thought had come unbidden to his mind. Setting down his drink, he opened the manila envelope and looked once again at the photos.

They still made no sense. Here young Laszlo should have been beside him, son-in-law and father-in-law standing arm in arm. Here his daughter, in the dance, appeared to have her arms around a phantom, yet one that she apparently could see. Even Pamela—poor Pamela!—was staring, it seemed, in Laszlo's direction.

Holding the photos to the light, studying the faces of the wedding guests, Mr. Melnick frowned. Laszlo, for all his nonappearance, seemed curiously *present* in scene after scene, visible to all but the camera—as if the very chemicals in the film had balked at recording his visual image.

The notion, of course, was absurd. It contradicted all the laws of physics; though on a fairy-tale level it seemed reasonable enough—like that legend, half-remembered from his childhood, about vampires casting no reflections. Dimly he recalled a scene from a long-ago Sunday matinee: Lugosi lunging for someone's pocket mirror and smashing it to the floor, preserving till another hour his dreadful secret.

Perhaps the same process was operating here. If vampires passed unseen before the silver in a looking glass, wouldn't they have the same problem with—what was it again?—the silver nitrate in a roll of film?

He forced himself to stop. One didn't apply logic to patently illogical concerns. Laying aside the photographs, he turned back to the puzzle. *Seventeen across, Rhode Island river; twenty-two down, author of "Casting the Runes"* . . .

But illogical concerns kept crowding at his mind. His wandering gaze, in search of other puzzles, settled on the topmost picture in the stack: the photo of his wife and daughter standing beside Pamela Lebow. *Poor Pamela!* he thought automatically. *To die so young!* He remembered her funeral and, before that, her illness, and—

And before that, her brief romance with Laszlo. . . .

Feeling inexplicably more nervous, he scrutinized the image of her face. She looked drawn, pallid—drained of life. Was she pining away for Laszlo? Or merely ill?

Or was she, in fact—

Outside, the night-breeze moaned softly. Dead leaves sprang into the air as if on tiny wings and hurled themselves against the windows. His thoughts, like driven things, rushed on ahead. What if—just for the sake of argument, of course—what if Laszlo *were* some sort of vampire? And Pamela, in fact, his first victim?

This late at night, with the house creaking and shuddering around him, the idea didn't seem so outlandish. Maybe it was just the Jack Daniels, but it seemed to make a queer, uneasy kind of sense.

Still absorbed in Pamela's picture, his gaze dropped to her neck. He half imagined he could make out, concealed behind the collar, two telltale reddish marks. . . .

If Pamela were the first victim, it suddenly occurred to him, then his daughter would be next.

His wife's suggestion came back to him again. "If you absolutely *have* to have his picture, you can take it yourself." Well, yes, perhaps he would. Just to put his mind at ease.

Rising, with an effort, to his feet, he moved unsteadily to the closet and hauled down the small black Polaroid she'd bought him last winter. Carefully he loaded the film pack and attached the flash, then returned to the couch and settled back to wait, the camera in his lap. Jennifer and Laszlo would be along soon. Right now they'd be nearing the airport, perhaps, their jet circling somewhere overhead. He could almost see it in the sky, a great predatory birdlike thing, pale against the night. It was spiraling inexorably toward him, ravenous for life, and the darkness echoed with its roaring. . . .

He awoke with the camera still cradled in his lap. The roaring was the sound of a taxi pulling up before the house.

Hurriedly he jumped to his feet and switched off the table lamp beside him. Clutching the camera like a weapon, he retreated into the shadows behind the stairs. From outside he could hear the sound of voices, the slamming of a car door and a trunk. With a rumble of its engine the taxi pulled away, disappearing somewhere up the block, and in the returning silence he heard footsteps advance across the porch, the jingle of a key-ring, the click of a key in the lock. *Why am I doing this!* he wondered, but it was too late to change his mind; the front door was already opening, and a hand was groping for the hall light.

He burst into the hall, camera raised, just as the light snapped on. Two figures were standing in the doorway, their baggage at their side. Behind them, past the little square of porch, yawned the night. His thumb found the button; the flash went off in their startled faces. "Surprise!" he said. He brought the camera down, the photograph already emerging from its base.

The two regarded him in silence.

"Welcome home," he added nervously. He forced a smile. "Forgive my little experiment, I just—"

"You shouldn't have done that, Mr. Melnick," said Laszlo. He stared down at the camera, shaking his head. "You shouldn't have wasted good film on *us*."

"I think he deserves a kiss," said Jennifer. She stepped into the light. He saw, as she came toward him, that she had lost weight. Her face looked very pale. "Come on, Daddy. Let me give you a kiss."

Laszlo was still staring at the camera. There was a kind of sadness in his eyes. Glancing down, Mr. Melnick saw the photograph and drew it forth. Somehow it hadn't yet developed; the hallway was an empty pool of light, with a black sky stretching endlessly behind it.

Jennifer was by his side now; he bent down for her kiss, but his gaze remained fixed on the photograph. As he felt his daughter's lips brush his cheek and move gently to his throat, he watched the pool of light, waiting in vain for the figures to appear.

# Snip My Suckers

LOIS H. GRESH

Chuck's heat steams my leaves. "So sweet," he says, "you're always so sweet in the first flush of spring."

My petals strain to his cheek. His whiskers are raw; a thousand blades shredding the hot velvet of my bud.

His nose dips. His eyes close.

A quick prick, and I'll have him. I crawl up the side of his house, sharpen my thorns on the stucco.

Chuck sprays me with the bone meal and the heavy phosphate.

Up my naked canes and out my tender sprouts, I pump the perfume that drives him wild: the honey cloves and the morning dew.

Chuck's nostrils widen. He sprays me again.

I quiver by the nectar that pounds through his neck. My thorns graze his skin, probe for the pulse; and now—

I plunge.

He screams and slaps his neck, and my branch whips back against the stucco. "Dratted mosquitos," he says, and his blood dribbles and my sepals curl and tighten and lap the hot juice.

His fist tightens around silver shears. "Think I'll snip off some suckers. It'll give you more strength, Glory, more roses. You look a bit peaked."

Go ahead, Chuck, snip my suckers. Prune me, baby, like a madman.

His shears are sharp. They sever me down at the root trunk where I'm most sensitive. Buds bust from my stems. Perfumes pump from my anthers.

"You look like you're gonna die, Glory. Wish I knew what kind of rose you are." He leers at me, then wipes his paws on his pants and gathers his tools.

I'm an unnamed seedling, Chuck, born from the roots of wild stock and fed on the mush of bony phosphate. The mice and the kittens know, and even the neighborhood dogs stay away from me.

But Chuck shrugs—we just don't communicate on anything but a physical level—and then he fondles a leaf and saunters away with two withered blooms.

The fence gate creaks. My little bud eyes swivel. Chuck is behind the house, stooping by his wife's grave. Even from a distance, his steam scorches my sap.

His paw rests upon the stone cross. The paw that stroked me. And now my two flowers are on the cross. They wilt. They die. Their corpses fall to the dirt.

What does Chuck see in dead bones? Why does he love *her* more than *me?*

The screen door slams. He's entered the safety of the stucco house. If only I could come with you; oh Chuck, you succulent hunk of bloody raw steak. I curl my tendrils over his roof gutters and sweat.

The afternoon sun streams down, plasters me like melted dough against Chuck's house. I'm all alone. My branches ache. My leaves are soggy mash. And the sky frowns and dumps its rain.

At the far end of the yard, Chuck's garden sucks up the water and laughs. Beans bulge and split their seams. Tomatoes throb like hearts; they mock me. Garlic surfs the breeze, and when I lash at the fumes, they curl from my grasp and snicker.

I break out with cankers and crown gall, with mildew and blackspot.

I need nightfall. I need it badly.

I cling to the house. I shrivel.

I bake for an eternity. Finally, the sun buries itself behind the cemetery. Night comes down and gives me a black kiss. And now my stems surge and my buds explode into crimson roses.

Something sniffs my bottom buds and nibbles. I turn twenty branches toward the ground. Dozens of my bud eyes peer through the gloom.

And there it is: a mouse scurrying along the base of the house, trying to slurp water from my leaves.

Twenty branches descend.

A thousand thorns thrust, retract, and thrust again.

The corpse is warm. My leaves smother it, and my stomata open wide and drink. Blood runs thick through my stems.

I leave the skin and bones. Eventually, they'll rot into the soil and nourish my roots.

A cat approaches, cautiously. I pop a root from the ground and poke its belly. It howls and runs into the night.

By morning, I've sucked dry three stray dogs and a host of rodents.

Chuck is yawning. He drinks steam from a clay cup. Gracing the side of the cup is a picture of a *Rosa roxburghii:* pink and anemic, a water drinker.

The sun's rays tear into me. My flowers close into tight balls and hide.

Chuck sets aside his cup and packs manure around my lower extremities, down by the sensitive spots where he snatched my suckers. The manure is cold and smells of rot. Chuck must love me.

"Jesus! What the hell is this?" He leaps back, and the blood drains from his face. He pulls on gloves and grabs a shovel. He heaps the remains of the mouse and the dogs and the other beasts into a green bag. I know that I'm a sloppy eater, but why is he so angry?

He drags the plastic bag somewhere behind the house, then returns with a hose and several cans and a spray gun.

He spritzes me with the bone meals and the phosphates, and to thank him, I scratch his arms and drink his nectar. He squirts insecticides from bright yellow cans with crossbones on them. He cuts my cankers and tumors; sprays me with lime sulfur, with folpet and zineb and ferbam. And with streptomycin to cure my crown gall.

I'm so lucky to be loved by Chuck.

The cross in the cemetery casts a shadow across us. It's the dead wife. She won't leave us alone. Even dead, she tries to win him back. I break out with mildew. Chuck does not notice. He stares at his wife's grave.

Now he turns to me with a big grin. "You know what you need, Glory? To be transplanted next to Rosemary. The soil's good there, and besides, you'll be good company for her. Rosemary always loved you when she was alive."

*Rosemary:* the witch who planted white Madonna lilies and wore a gold cross around her neck. *Rosemary:* the witch who planted the garlic. I said to her once, "Go on, honey, snip my suckers—ha, if you dare," and fool that she was, Rosemary dared.

Her blood was thin and bitter.

Now Chuck is packing all his cans and spray guns into a wheelbarrow. He thrusts a shovel into the ground by my roots. He cackles. "Don't really know much about gardening, but one thing I do know: you need *something* to make you healthy. You're always breaking out with diseases. And your flowers look sick."

But I'm always so sweet in the first flush of spring. . . .

Ack, the shovel splinters my stems. Chuck's weight heaves against the handle, thrusting into me, snapping me, killing me, draining my sap. He hacks and he hacks, and soon I'm screaming inside and everywhere, the rodents titter at me; and if all that were not enough, Chuck rips me from the ground.

42

And now, I am naked to the world. My shame burns. I want to die I want to die I want

to die.

Chuck plops me atop the folpets and the zinebs, and he carts me across the yard.

His gloved paws pack me into a small hole by *her* grave. My bud eyes turn from the cross. I will not look I will not

look, but I do look and half a dozen branches splinter and fall from me, and instantly they turn to dust.

Chuck does not notice. "Oh, Rosemary, how I miss you. Perhaps the fragrance of Glory's roses will cheer you."

My tender sprouts are splayed across her grave. I'm so weak I can barely move.

Chuck drags the hose across the yard. He fills the hole with water—

with *WATER*—

and now I'm sopped in oxydemetonmethyls and nicotine sulfates

and dimethoates and carbaryls and manebs and folpets and ferbams

and I'm dying from it all, and yet

I need Chuck.

I need *his blood.*

But he leaves me, as all lovers do, and again the screen door slams. My roots slip deep into the earth and slither to Rosemary's coffin. The wood is rotting, and easily I pick through the debris and slide within and find the cold bones.

*This is what Chuck loves. This is what Chuck prefers to me.*

I cross my roots over her ribs. My thorns drill into the bone. I try to suck the marrow, but it's dust.

All night, I wait; all night, I plan. And when morning comes, I know that Chuck will be mine.

He slurps from the *Rosa roxburghii* cup. His greasy whiskers shine in the sun. "I have a gift for you," he says.

Ooh, possibly a fat blood-glutted dog?

"This will help you grow huge flowers, Glory."

Must be a special treat . . . a neighbor; or better yet, a priest or rabbi.

I want to thank him, so I scratch his ankle and lap the blood.

"Dratted mosquitos, driving me nuts." He pulls his leg from me, then drags something large across the lawn and through the creaking cemetery gate. "Your gift," he says.

Ooh, it's a . . .

. . . a cross-hatched trellis?

I wilt against the gravestone.

He pulls a hammer from his workbelt. He drives the stakes into my roots.

I scream and I lunge, and my thorns are deep within his throat, stabbing and stabbing—

and he's slapping at me and howling, and thick worms of blood stream down his neck,

and he runs into the house and the screen door slams.

His blood has made me strong. My roots snake under the lawn and drill into his basement. They wait until nightfall.

Inside the coffin, roots tangle and twist around Rosemary's bones. One root rips the cross from her chest and crushes it. Others slither up the trellis, knot into fists, and pull the cross-hatched monstrosity to the ground.

And now I'm ready. Across Chuck's lawn, my roots poke through the grass and spring into the night air. I will be everywhere, always, for Chuck.

The thrum of his heart calls to me. I'm hungry, and dogs and cats won't do. I've loved Chuck for so long. I want to make him happy. I will give him back to Rosemary.

My roots curl up his walls, slither like snakes up the basement stairs. I find him snoring in the bed.

The bed he shared with *Rosemary.*

This time, he will share it with *me.*

# Blood and Silence

## David Langford

'mm. I did think we'd manage a better turnout for *this* meeting. It's not just another boring weekly update on a crank project—you ought to know that. So much has happened since last Monday! With any luck we're headed for a Nobel Prize, and my little presentation today is going to be famous . . . not just through a lot of pop-science best-sellers but in *history* books, for goodness' sake. Of course you and the team will all receive full credit.

So. Hello John, hello Carol, hello Patrick, and I have three faxed apologies for not coming in to the lab today, plus four more by e-mail.

As you know, last Tuesday we had our lucky break and the V-syndrome hypothesis can now be taken as strongly confirmed. I also have an extra surprise for you, just in this morning! But first, let's have a look at Patrick's splendid scanning electron micrograph of V itself. When I finish my paper I shall certainly give him special credit. Will you do the honours, Patrick? What? Throat? Laryngitis? Doesn't stop you working an overhead projector, does it? Ladies—lady—and gentlemen, the star of the show . . .

*Awash with false colour, the image of the giant virus resembles nothing familiar . . . perhaps a half-melted triumphal arch painted in the hues of delirium by Salvador Dali. It cannot possibly look sinister. It is too abstract. Nevertheless, to those armed with foreknowledge, it radiates a certain cool menace.*

I'm thinking we should call it the Alucard retrovirus, ha ha. According to Carol's initial report, which she'd read to us right now if it weren't for a nasty case of toothache (sorry to hear it, Carol, and I hope that swelling goes down soon), the job it seems to have done on the DNA in our sample is *radical*. We have some interesting confirmation in that area . . . that's the surprise I was talking about, and it came from New Scotland Yard.

As you may know, this whole project started over there with one of their backroom geniuses, a chap called March who specializes in weird crime patterns. He runs what they call (not for public consumption) the Department of Queer Complaints, with a devil of a lot of computer power processing the kind of reports any sane person would throw in the bin—or send to the *Fortean Times*. And when they correlated a bundle of stuff about burglaries with nothing missing, puncture wounds, blood loss, unbelievable speed and strength, and so on and so on . . . he suggested the V hypothesis. We don't use the V-word itself because we're reasonable scientists, but the way March put it was that if there were something that *behaved like* such a creature, he or she or it, bloody well ought to be investigated.

His database seeming to be hinting at a centre of activity in southwest London: Richmond or Kingston. Since they outsource so much forensic work to us, we were the natural choice to help design the equipment for that empty flat in Latchmere Road. Two years waiting. Never in the history of civilization has one room been so massively monitored and booby-trapped for so long. And even then . . .

This isn't the video you saw last week. It's been image-enhanced and generally cleaned up. Much clearer now. Here we go.

*There is something at the window, streetlights throwing a hunched, malformed shadow on the curtains. The shadow's deformity is a lie: the figure that enters wears an impossible perfection of poise, moving to the bedside with silent, fluid grace. Even in the room, though, it remains featureless, a grainy silhouette against the white dazzle that is what image amplifiers make of the window's dim glow. Those who watch the video picture know that lying beneath the sheets is a dummy, artificially warm, its breath and heartbeat an endless tape loop: the policewoman chosen for her close fit to the victim pattern has retired to another fortified room after conspicuously drawing the curtains here. This bedroom is not a safe place to sleep. . . .*

*. . . as becomes evident when the man (man?) in close-*

*fitting black bends too closely over the false sleeper. An instant's total whiteout as unleashed energies jolt the power lines. There is a violent metallic clatter, followed by a steady hiss. Pale clouds are billowing from the innocuous-looking wardrobe, and a device like an oversized handcuff is seen to have clamped itself around the visitor's left ankle. The body flicks through a dozen positions as though in strobe lighting, but that leg is shackled, immovably, to heavy machinery underneath the bed. There can be no escape.*

*It is the lack of pause for thought that chills. As though trained in this gesture through years of some murderous ballet school, the captive whips out a glinting blade and within four seconds of blurred movement is messily free. All in a silence that screams. The narcotic gas never has time to act. There is still a certain appalling grace in the one-legged, headlong leap through the window.*

*On the floor, the severed foot is a dark blot lying in a dark pool.*

Serendipity, that's the word. The way he got away tells us so much! There's absolutely no tourniquet work in that video, yet the artery has closed off before he's moved a step. You couldn't have a stronger hint that the . . . V-word . . . legend about regeneration might have a basis in reality, a genuine foothold in the real world, ha ha.

When Rosie in Pathology dissected the specimen, she found the muscle density was medically impossible. (In my draft paper she does of course receive due credit.) But that's not as bad as the real eye-opener on Friday, when our radioisotope analysis of the bone cores came through with the news that—unless the software has gone completely haywire—this fellow had been alive and kicking since *approximately* 1820. Give or take a decade. And yet the skin was fresh, unscarred, like a kid in the early teens. Quite a few of us have this strong hunch that our friend is walking on a brand-new foot by now. Er, yes Carol, don't look like that: I know you were first with that little idea, and believe me you will get the credit for it.

Well. All of a sudden the V virus starts to look highly desirable! We'll have to keep our samples under lock and key! Luckily it can't be particularly contagious, or these retooled people would be everywhere. An injection, though, of enough infected blood or culture medium . . .

Well may you nod, John, well may you nod. You're right to look worried.

But before we get too fussed about half the country fighting over the chance to be biologically reengineered by the V agent, I have a new video to show you. This puts matters in a slightly different light, and may also clear up the tooth question. We expected, didn't we, to find the traditional overdeveloped canines? That side of it must be an unfounded part of the V myth. We've been over all the trap records, and both the flash X-ray and ultrasound scan seem to agree that the guy's teeth were no pointier than yours or mine.

About the garlic thing and the sunlight thing, we just don't know until we have an experimental subject of our very own. They're hard to hire. Ha ha.

It was March who passed on this new video, another spot of serendipity. I really will have to acknowledge the New Scotland Yard assistance in my coming major paper. They were trying an experimental surveillance system in a certain public toilet near Richmond Park, where naughty things are supposed to happen by night. And what they saw . . . lights! action! camera!

*The image of one dark figure against a background of white-tiled glare seems momentarily to be a still picture; but then it flicks to a new position, and another, like poor stop-motion animation. In this spy camera, moving-picture quality has been traded off against better resolution. The man busies himself at the public urinal . . . and blink, blink, blink, another figure is at his side. Both figures begin to grow, in a flickering zoom-in: the moron software behind the camera takes note of supposed anomalies like two men standing side by side at adjacent urinal stalls, when English reserve indicates the keeping of a discreet distance unless forced into proximity by a crowd. Perhaps there will be a brief encounter in a lavatory cubicle, thinks the prurient program, zooming in to get mugshots that might one day be credible in court. . . .*

*Blink, blink, blink.*
*It is an encounter. One man has his arms round the other.*

*There is no recourse to a cubicle. It is an anomalous encounter. The man in black leather with the beautiful, feral face (but oddly plump and full cheeks) has accosted the older, greying, respectable-looking gent. Things tend to be the other way around. Blink, blink, blink. With movement chopped into this salami of freeze-frames, it is hard to be certain that the older man is struggling to escape. But the emotion on his jowled face is not lust.*

*Blink, blink, blink. It emerges frame by frame from the young man's wide-open mouth. It ought to be a tongue but is huge and alien, glistening black: the bloated thing must fill the entire mouth when retracted, but now it extends, stretching and thinning like a questing leech. Blink, blink. White fear in the old eyes behind their bifocal spectacles. Blink. Needle-tipped, the leech-organ stabs for the jugular vein. For many frames thereafter the picture is unchanged, except that the victim slowly, very slowly, wilts. . . .*

God, that gives me the creeps even the second time around. I gather they nodded it through as death by exposure. March said there are some stories for which a British coroner's court is not yet ready, and I suppose he's right.

Well, this is what we call strong confirmation, isn't it! Affected persons must find it hard to hide: open their lips and they're condemned out of their own mouths, ha ha. So the V agent does indeed remodel the body. Incredible. And yes, Carol, I know that insight was originally yours. You needn't sulk. In my paper . . .

Look. I think we ought to have this out. I really expected you to be bubbling over with ideas and analysis after the first public showing of that little video nasty from the Yard. Not just sitting there looking glum. I know there are some bitter feelings in this lab, simply because protocol absolutely demands that as Director I should write the official paper on all this. I happen to be aware—because I've seen e-mail that wasn't meant for me—that some of the team, naming no names, think I burnt out as a scientist twenty years ago. They reckon I'm too slow on the uptake to deserve any glory. No doubt *you* all saw the possibilities of the V virus last week while you were working hands-on with it and I was busy with the hard slog of coordinating the reports and arranging our press conference. Nevertheless I promise that everyone will receive proper credit. And indeed you can all have a voice in the preparation of the paper.

Aren't you going to *say* anything?

Have I been sent to Coventry?

Cat got your tongues?

. . . oh, *dear* . . .

# And by a Word, Immortal

MARK KREIGHBAUM

I think Ellie is a vampire, but not the usual kind.

For one thing, she doesn't seem to have any trouble making it to her classes, though she usually comes up with some excuse to avoid gym class when it's outside. She loves garlic. I saw her eat two helpings of the spaghetti surprise in the cafeteria the other day and there was garlic in that sauce, for sure. Well, as much as you can be sure of anything when you're talking food in a high school cafeteria.

But the main way she can't be a traditional vampire is that her whole family is real religious and I've seen them all wearing big silver crosses. Ellie even wears one as an earring. I don't know. Is there such a thing as a vampire whose mom teaches Sunday School?

On the other hand, I've seen her in the library doing her vampire thing. She sneaks back into the corner shelves and comes out a while later with a big grin. Once, I saw her fangs when she was smiling extra wide. There was *stuff* on the fangs, I'm sure of it. Plus, she wears these tinted glasses to hide the red in her eyes. But you can see it, if you look close. Not that I'm following her around staring into her eyes, or anything, but we have homeroom together and you can't help but notice that sort of thing. Mrs. Bell, the homeroom teacher, is a nicotine fiend, so she always sends us down to the library during homeroom so she can go to the faculty lounge and ruin her lungs for an hour.

So, I decided to tell my best friend, Rick, about all this. We were playing chess in Mr. Krupa's room after school. Rick laughed so hard, I thought he was going to break his throat, or something. Finally, he calmed down enough to talk.

"C'mon, Davie," he said, in that voice like he's talking to his cocker spaniel, Hammie, who is the stupidest dog on Earth, I swear. "Let's be logical—"

"Oh no," I said. I hate it when he does the "let's be logical" thing, like he's Mr. Spock.

"No, really. Think about it." Rick adjusted his glasses and started counting off points on his fingers. Fourteen years old and he's already studying to be William F. Buckley. "She's not afraid of crosses. She walks around in the daytime. And why would a vampire bother to take Algebra I? What do the undead care about factoring polynomials?"

"I *said* she wasn't a normal vampire. Maybe kid vampires are different. She's probably just pretending to be a kid anyway so she can suck the blood of other kids. Who'd ever suspect?"

"Okay," said Rick, but impatient and smug. He's got a killer argument, I can tell from his tone of voice. "But here's the most important thing: If Ellie Rusman is fanging people in the library, how come you never see anybody else come out of that corner in the stacks?"

"Huh." Actually, he's got a point there. "Well . . ."

"So?"

"I don't know. But she's doing something there. Maybe she knows I'm watching her and uses her hypnotic powers on me to keep me from seeing her victims."

"Why wouldn't she just make you forget she was a vampire completely? Or just fang you?"

"I don't know." Rick is making sense, but I know what I know. "Why don't you come and watch tomorrow? She usually bites 'em during homeroom. Just meet me in the library."

"Right."

"No, really."

He argues with me some more, but I can tell he'll do it, just so he can give me the business about it for the rest of my life.

So, the next day, during homeroom, we're sitting at one of the round tables reading magazines in those stupid wood dowel things with the plastic covers. I always feel like I'm reading a flagpole. Most of the other people in my homeroom are either out in the parking lot listening to music, or skipping out early. One or two of the brains are in the study carrels doing homework. Usually, I'm reading a book. I've read pretty much all the adventure and science fiction. Right now, I'm working my way through the biography section, which is really interesting. My parents can't afford to buy me books, so I use the library a lot.

The librarian, Mrs. Gertroschen, otherwise known as Gert the Lert, is in her office typing up index cards for the card catalog at about a million words a minute. But she still has time to keep an eye on everybody with her peripheral vision. Somebody asked her once how come they didn't replace the card catalog with a computer database, or a CD-ROM, or something from the twentieth century and she looked down her nose (which is skinny and sharp enough to cut paper) and said in the sincerest voice you ever heard that it was far more important to purchase a spare set of down markers for the football field so that children could be instructed in the true meaning of education without the anxiety of wondering how many yards were left. Gert the Lert is kind of weird.

Anyway, Rick and me waited at the table, keeping an eye out for Ellie Rusman. Rick kept giving me these looks, opening his eyes really wide, curling his hands into claws and pushing his upper teeth out over his lower lip. Really funny.

Then Ellie shows up. She's always late for homeroom because she has to help Mr. Riski, the social studies teacher and football coach, put away the audiovisual equipment after class.

Ellie is short, with red hair and she wears really strange clothes, ripped black leotards, army jackets, weird berets. She looks like the lead singer of a punk band. She's always smiling, like she knows a joke that you don't. Well, sure, she's an immortal bloodsucker and I guess that must be pretty funny.

Anyway, she stopped at the round table and looked at me. She always does this.

"Greetings, Monsieur Davie," said Ellie, doing this goofy little curtsy thing.

"Uh, yeah. Hi, Ellie," I mumble. I blushed, like I always do. Which is not because she's a vampire, but because I can't talk to girls at all without blushing. It's so stupid.

"Bonjour, Ricardo," she said.

Rick grins at her and answers back. "Bonjour, ma chère." Of course, they have French together. I forgot that. Suddenly, I wondered if maybe this is all a setup. Maybe Rick and Ellie are pulling a joke on me. But no, why would Ellie bother?

Ellie waved and strolled to the back of the library, heading for the corner stacks. Sure enough, she vanished from sight.

"Well?" I asked.

Rick just looked at me. "Well, what? So she's looking for a book."

"She's fanging somebody."

"Pfff." But he's interested.

"Let's go back there. Catch her in the act." I'm amazed to hear myself make this suggestion.

"And what? Did you bring a wooden stake?"

"Huh." It's a good point. I mean, if Ellie Rusman *is* a vampire, what do we do? I mean, she's in my homeroom and is kind of a friend, sort of. But suddenly that doesn't matter. I just had to know. "I don't know. Are you coming?"

Rick shook his head, but at least he wasn't laughing at me. "I'll back you up, distract the Lert."

Right. Gert the Lert didn't like girls and boys making out in the back, or even hanging out there plotting mischief. Come to think of it, she would never have let Ellie go back there with anybody, so how could she be fanging anyone? Rick's major point was a good one. Nevertheless.

I slipped past the nonfiction stacks. Ellie was in the corner with the fiction shelves, my favorite part of the library. I glanced back to see Rick hovering at the Lert's office, asking her to explain something in the magazine he was reading. I hoped it was something that would keep the librarian from coming out of her cubicle to do research. The Lert loved to march you around her domain showing you how to use all the materials to answer some question that she could have answered for you in two seconds.

Finally, I got to the side of the shelf behind which Ellie was hiding. I could hear a little low slurping sound. It was chilling. My heart beat a thousand times faster than normal. I hadn't really, truly believed. What would she do if I surprised her in the middle of her unholy afternoon snack? But I couldn't stop myself. I had to know.

I turned the corner. Ellie's back was to me. She was hunched a bit and I could hear the squelchy sucking sounds clearly. But there was no one else back there with her.

I must have made some kind of noise because she spun around. In her hands was a library book. She'd taken off the dustcover and had sunk her teeth into the binding. When she saw me, she yanked the book out of her mouth and hid it behind her back. There was a little trickle of black liquid at the corner of her mouth. She licked it up with the tip of her tongue and just smiled at me guiltily.

"What are you doing?" I asked.

Still keeping the book behind her back with one hand, she took off her glasses with the other and I saw that her eyes really were red, bright red and glittery like a Fourth of July sparkler. I started to feel weak at the knees, but then I closed my eyes and the feeling vanished.

"You *are* a vampire!" I said.

"Keep your voice down."

"Are you going to . . . fang me?"

"Ewww. You mean, like, drink human blood? Ewwww."

I opened my eyes. Ellie had put her tinted glasses back on. And she was grinning.

"Sorry about that. You surprised me and I didn't want you to start yelling until I had a chance to explain."

"Explain what? That you're undead? A vampire?"

"Well, jeez," she said, putting her hands on her hips. Apparently, she'd returned the book she'd been sucking back on the shelf while I was dizzy from her gaze. "You make it sound like I'm evil, or something."

"Aren't you?"

"Of course not." Her voice quivered a bit and I felt rotten.

"I'm sorry." I couldn't believe I was apologizing to a vampire for hurting her feelings.

"I wouldn't ever hurt anybody. I'm not a bad vampire. In fact, most of us are really nice. You get one guy in your family who goes around impaling people over five hundred years ago and everybody thinks all vampires are bad. It's not fair."

"I'm sorry, Ellie." I felt awful. She wasn't quite crying, but close. "I didn't know."

"That's all right. I guess it's not your fault." But she still sounded sad.

"Well, um, I thought vampires all drank blood."

She made a disgusted face. "Who would want to? Yech."

"What *are* you doing, then?"

Ellie scrunched up her face and squinted at me and I felt like she was looking right into my head. Maybe she could do that. After a second, she turned away and took a book off the shelf. It was a book by H. G. Wells: *The Time Machine.* She lifted off the dustcover and I could see two little toothmarks in the spine, but they were rapidly disappearing. As I watched, they vanished completely.

"You suck paper?"

Ellie giggled. We were standing close to each other, closer than I'd ever stood next to a girl before, but I didn't feel that nervous. She grinned up at me, her usual grin.

"It's more a psychic thing. Books are like houses, you know, they keep a bit of everyone who has touched them, a little of their aura."

"And you suck up the . . . the aura?"

"Yeah. Every book tastes different, depending on what it is, and who has read it. Science fiction and adventures are my favorites."

"Really? Me, too!"

"And it's good for the book, too," she said. "A book that's been bitten by a vampire never dies, you know."

I grinned. Ellie was keeping my favorite books alive forever, for me and for every kid whose parents couldn't afford to buy them books. She was a hero.

Just then, Gert the Lert loomed around the corner with Rick in tow. Rick stood behind her. He shrugged in apology when I looked at him. Then he nodded toward Ellie and made the fang thing over his lower lip again. Ellie burst out into giggles. I blushed.

"Discussing the ramifications of Proust, I suppose?" said the Lert.

"No, I'm on a diet," said Ellie.

I laughed. The Lert gave all three of us detention. But it was worth it.

55

# The Kwik-Mart Vampire

## ROBERT WEINBERG

The sound of a car pulling into the parking lot wrenched Rick's gaze from the shivery delights of Anne Rice's latest vampire novel. Quickly folding over the corner of the page, Rick closed the paperback and hid it beneath the counter. Reading on the job, even with the store empty, was strictly forbidden at Kwik-Mart. All of the advertising for the twenty-four-hour convenience store chain stressed that, no matter what the time, the clerks paid close attention to their customers' needs. More than one unfortunate had been fired at 3:00 A.M. when caught napping at their post by a territorial manager secretly making his monthly rounds.

Rick sighed in relief when he saw the familiar black and white of a Wayne County squad car. Instinctively, he checked the clock over the entrance to the store. It read a little after 2:00 in the morning. His visitor had to be Sgt. Stan Gilmore on a snack cake and coffee break. Shrugging his shoulders, Rick turned on the burner beneath the coffee pot. Seconds later, the big, burly policeman pushed his way through the Kwik-Mart's glass doors.

"Hey, boy," said Gilmore, his voice gravely and deep, "get that mud you call coffee brewing. And dig me up some Twinkies. I need me some sugar."

"Coming right up," said Rick with a false cheerfulness, as he swung over the counter and headed for the dessert cake rack in the rear of the store. A heavyset man with a huge pot belly and bright red cheeks, Gilmore was the laziest individual Rick had ever met. The officer never took a step more than necessary. He knew exactly where the snack cakes were located, but he invariably had Rick get them for him.

"Get me the fresh ones from the back of the shelf," called the policeman. "None of them out-of-date ones you push to the front."

"Be polite, be cordial, and remember the customer is always correct," Rick muttered under his breath as he grabbed several packages of Twinkies. He needed to remind himself of the Kwik-Mart service motto every time Gilmore stopped in his store. *Several* times during the course of the patrolman's visit.

Located at the crossroads of two major county roads, Rick's store was a regular layover for most of the highway police in the area. In most cases, Rick welcomed their visits. Isolated convenience stores were a prime target for robbers. Nothing discouraged would-be criminals more than the sight of a police car parked in the Kwik-Mart lot. Thus, Rick normally was pleased when the officers arrived at the store for a break. Except when that caller was Sgt. Gilmore.

Rick didn't like the big policeman. Something about the officer didn't ring true. He wasn't like the rest of the patrolmen who made the rounds of the all-night convenience marts. Maybe it was the big man's habit of discussing the most grisly crimes imaginable while he gulped down his snacks. Or his sarcastic comments and obvious dislike of teenagers. Or his tendency to forget to pay for the goods he devoured until reminded. Whatever the reason, Rick never felt at ease when Gilmore was around.

"Man, I've been dreaming about these babies for the past half-hour," said the cop, nearly ripping the Twinkies out of Rick's hands. Tearing the wrapper off the snack cakes, Gilmore messily shoved the yellow cylinders into his mouth. "Gimme some coffee. Can't eat a Twinkie without hot java."

Rick poured the policeman a steaming cup of black coffee. Sloppily, the big man took a deep gulp of the scalding liquid. "That's more like it," he declared after a few seconds. Leaning on the counter in front of the cash register, he grinned at Rick. "Hear the latest about the Kwik-Mart vampire?"

Mentally, Rick groaned. For the past month, Gilmore had insisted on sharing with him every detail of the gruesome killings. Rick didn't want to hear a word more. He had his own theory about the murders. One he definitely didn't want to share with the obnoxious policeman.

"That monster got another clerk the other night," said the big cop, tearing open another package of Twinkies and dropping the wrapper on the floor. "Same as all the others. No sign of a struggle. No alarms. No clues. Just a dead teenager found behind the counter, blood drained right out of him. Dry as a bone!"

"I'm really not interested," said Rick, fiddling with the stock invoices clustered by the cash register. Maybe if he appeared busy, Gilmore would take the hint and leave. Usually Rick welcomed company late at night. Working the night shift at a convenience store was lonely business. But, given the choice between the loud-mouthed policeman and his Anne Rice book, the paperback won easily.

"That's five late-night clerks killed in the past two months," declared Gilmore, showing no signs of departing. He leaned forward on the front counter, his bulk causing the wood cabinet to groan in protest. "Five murders and not a hint as to the motive or the killer's identity. Even the state cops are starting to believe there's something spooky about the crimes."

Rick snickered. "That's crazy. Ain't no such things as vampires."

Gilmore stuffed another Twinkie into his mouth. "Whadda you know?" he said smugly. "You ain't nothing but a dumb clerk in an all-night Kwik-Mart."

"I am not dumb," retorted Rick, his annoyance getting the better of his good sense. "Just 'cause I work at night doesn't mean I'm a total idiot. Jobs aren't easy to get these days. It took me a month before I found this one. Besides, I like working here. The pay is good and there's not much traffic after midnight."

"Sure you do," said Gilmore sarcastically, wiping his sticky fingers on his pants. "Get me a container of milk, kid. None of that two percent or skim stuff. The real thing. Chocolate if you got it. The richer the better."

Chewing his lower lip, Rick hurried to the refrigerator units in the rear of the store. He should know better than to blow his cool. He hadn't been exaggerating about how hard it was to find a job. If Rick lost this position at Kwik-Mart he would be in big trouble. He grimaced as he grabbed a carton of chocolate milk from the refrigerator. Clerking in a convenience store was no thrill, but it sure beat the hell out of the alternative.

Gilmore was grinning broadly when Rick returned to the front of the store. For a second, Rick wondered if the big cop had rifled the cash register while he was gone. Everything appeared in order. And opening the electronic register quietly would take more brains than Gilmore possessed. Rick dismissed the smile as more evidence of the officer's mental instability. Recounting the so-called "vampire murders" to Rick gave the cop a tremendous charge.

Instinctively, Rick glanced down at the silent alarm located on the floor at the base of the counter. The concealed buzzer was hooked by a direct line to the local police station. A brush from Rick's foot would have the local law enforcement officers here in less than a minute. Faster, most likely, with the convenience store murders so prominent in the news. It was a comforting thought.

"You like vampires, huh?" asked Gilmore, his grin growing wider than ever. From behind his back he drew out a copy of *The Vampire Lestat*. Rick's copy. "Been studying up about them, I see."

Rick stifled a curse. He should have guessed the big cop would look beneath the counter when he was in the rear of the store. He ought to have hidden the book better. Too late to worry about that now. The damage was done. "There's no law against reading vampire novels," said Rick, defensively. "It's all make-believe stuff."

"Yeah," said the big cop, thumbing his way through the paperback. "Tell that to those five dead kids. Bet they don't think vampires only appear in these here best-sellers."

"There's no proof that a vampire killed those clerks," blurted out Rick angrily. Gilmore's sticky hands were making a mess of the book's pages. By the time the policeman finished mangling it, the paperback would be too gross to touch. Frustrated and upset, he snatched the novel from the officer's huge fingers. The cop chuckled nastily but made no attempt to retrieve the book.

"Someone smart and tricky," Rick continued without thinking, as he tried to flatten the bent pages, "is using the monster story to hide the real solution to the murders. It's all part of a slick cover-up but the newspapers and state police are too stupid to realize the truth."

"But you're smarter than all of them," said Gilmore, grinning again. There was a nasty look in the policeman's eye that made Rick wish he had kept his mouth shut. "Typical wiseass teenager," continued the cop. "Think you know more than everybody else."

The big man folded his arms across his chest, his dark eyes fixed on Rick's face. Menace hung heavily in the air of the convenience store. "Let's hear your idea, kid. If it wasn't a vampire, who killed those teenagers? And how?"

Nervously, Rick shuffled his feet and drew in a deep breath. His vague suspicions about Gilmore suddenly seemed terribly real. Rick started to sweat. One foot toyed with the silent alarm. Unless the big cop actually did make a threatening move, Rick knew he dared not stomp the buzzer. He couldn't accuse the patrolman without evidence. The local police weren't going to arrest a fellow officer without hard facts. And nobody would believe a teenager's wild accusations.

Carefully resting his foot on the alarm, Rick explained his theory. "I've read lots of novels about vampires. They're my favorite horror stories. After a while, you can't help noticing a few similarities in all the books."

"Sure," said Gilmore, smirking. "The main character drinks human blood, sleeps in a coffin, and can be killed by a stake through the heart. I don't read nothing and I know that."

"The Undead shun two things" said Rick, ignoring the cop's remarks. "They can't stand bright sunlight . . . or publicity."

Gilmore's face twisted into an odd expression evidently indicating concentrated thought. "What'd you mean?" he finally asked, sounding puzzled.

"Vampires aren't real," said Rick, repeating his earlier statement. "But, if they were, the last thing they would want to do is broadcast their existence to the world. Think how vulnerable the monsters are during the daytime. They can't move around in the sunlight, they would be easy pickings to anyone hunting them." Rick shook his head. "The vampires in these novels always try to blend in with their surroundings. They would never blow their cover like that."

"So who killed those teenagers?" asked Gilmore, sounding unconvinced. "A werewolf?"

Rick edged his foot closer to the alarm. He was about to step out onto thin ice. With the emergency buzzer his single lifeline.

"At first, I asked myself the same thing. And, like everyone investigating the murders, went nowhere. That's when I realized I was approaching the mystery from the wrong direction. Assuming the killer wasn't supernatural in origin gave the whole case a different meaning. Who would want to make it appear as if the crimes had been committed by a vampire? The answer was obvious."

"What are you saying?" asked Gilmore, his voice soft and very, very cold.

"The vampire story successfully diverted attention from the real riddle involving the killings. How come there was never any sign of a struggle at the scene of any of the crimes? And why didn't the clerks set off an alarm when confronted by their killer?"

"The monster hypnotized them," whispered Sgt. Gilmore, his eyes shining strangely. "Like in that *Dracula* movie."

"Or," said Rick slowly, resting his foot on the top of the buzzer, "the clerks knew their killer and trusted him completely. Thus he was able to lure them away from their alarms and kill them when their backs were turned. Afterwards, he carried them back to their stations and used some sort of makeshift pump to suck out their blood, establishing his vampire alibi."

"Fascinating," murmured Gilmore, a ghoulish smile plastered across his face. "You explained everything except why this criminal mastermind killed the clerks. And how he got them to leave their cash registers."

"He's a homicidal maniac," said Rick, his muscles tensing. "A serial killer, this lunatic murders because he likes it. As to how he got the guys to abandon their posts, I'll bet he asked them to get him a bottle of chocolate milk."

Gilmore bellowed with anger and lunged at Rick with astonishing speed. Darting to one side, Rick punched the emergency alarm with his foot. Then hit it a second time for certainty. Before he could stomp on it yet again, the big patrolman had him by the shoulders.

"Pretty damned smart for a punk kid," said the officer, his eyes burning with maniacal fury. From his rear pocket, Gilmore pulled out a long silk scarf and wrapped it tightly around Rick's wrists. Another scarf effectively bound his ankles.

"The soft material don't leave no marks," declared the policeman, letting Rick drop painfully to the floor. "I learned that from watching that sexy bondage murder mystery in the movies. You wait here, okay? I got to go out and pull my equipment from the trunk of the squad car."

Gilmore stomped off, leaving Rick alone on the floor. Rick didn't bother trying to untie his bonds. The local police should be arriving any minute. Finding him trussed up like this would be further proof of Gilmore's insane scheme. Raising his head, Rick listened for the telltale wail of the police siren. Seconds passed and turned into minutes. Not a sound broke the silence of the night.

The insane policeman returned a few minutes later, lugging behind him what looked like an industrial strength vacuum cleaner. Horrified, Rick noted the two huge hypodermic needles connected to the nozzle of the machine's suction tube. Gilmore chuckled and nodded. "This baby will drain your body clean of blood in five minutes. And the incisions made by the needles look enough like tooth marks to fool the coroner."

"You're crazy," said Rick, desperately straining to hear the scream of approaching sirens. "Absolutely nuts."

"Yeah," said Gilmore checking the mechanism of his vacuum. "I guess I am. Been killing people for years. For a long time, I went after hitchhikers and runaways. Picked them off the street, pretended to arrest them." The officer grinned. "By the time they realized I wasn't taking them to the station it was too late for them to do anything. I disposed of their bodies in the swamp."

"How many?" gasped Rick, anxious to keep Gilmore talking. Anything to waste time until the local police responded to the silent alarm.

"Thirty-one," announced the officer proudly. "I kept track of each and every murder in my diary. That shelter they started in town cut into my fun. That's when I came up with the idea of the vampire murders."

Gilmore chuckled ghoulishly. "Some day, I plan to sell my story to the movies. That's why I'm keeping accurate records of each killing in my diary. I'll be famous."

"Like Jack the Ripper," retorted Rick. "Sooner or later, you'll be caught. And pay the price for your actions."

"Maybe," said Gilmore, wiping the needles with his handkerchief. "But not tonight, wise guy."

The patrolman drew a small pair of wirecutters from his coat pocket. "I know how the alarm systems in these buildings work, stupid. When you were in the back, I clipped the connections. You can stop listening. Nobody at the police station suspects a thing is wrong."

Rick grimaced. He was in deep trouble. Then he was struck by sudden inspiration. There still might be a way out of his dilemma.

"You mentioned a diary?" he asked.

"That's right," said Gilmore. "It's hidden under my bed at home." The madman raised the tube with the two needles. "Juicy reading if the wrong people found it."

Gilmore's gaze met Rick's . . . and froze. His motion suddenly ceased. The cop stood immobile, as if petrified in place. Blood rushed to his face as the muscles in his arms and chest tightened with effort. But he remained rooted to the spot.

Nodding pleasantly to himself, Rick jerked his hands apart. The silk scarf binding his wrists exploded into fragments of cloth. Reaching down, he ripped off the ties binding his ankles. Smoothly, sinuously, he rose to his feet.

"I think discovering you in your squad car dead of an apparent heart attack will push the investigation in the right direction," said Rick, thoughtfully. "Especially if this bizarre contraption of yours is resting on the back seat. The honest cops in town are pretty dumb but they shouldn't have much trouble piecing together the whole story once they discover that wonderful diary you mentioned. It will lay to rest the whole notion of a vampire killer while providing a full confession to your crimes. Perfect."

"I—I can't move," whimpered Gilmore.

Rick nodded. "You shouldn't have looked directly into my eyes. I can overwhelm the will of an ordinary person with a single glance. Inducing a heart attack, especially with your diet and weight problem, won't be difficult either."

"Who are you?" whispered Gilmore hoarsely. *"What are you?"*

"I suspected for weeks that you were the serial killer," said Rick, not bothering to answer the patrolman's question. "But I never said a word to anyone because I didn't want to create a stir. Remember what I said earlier about avoiding publicity? Besides, I couldn't risk jeopardizing my position here at Kwik-Mart. Not all of us were born rich noblemen. I need money to pay for my lodging, clothing, and entertainment. And the hours are perfect."

"You—you can't be real," stuttered Gilmore. "You're just a teenager."

"My kind never age," said Rick smiling. "I've been a teenager for three hundred years." He laughed. "You only pretended to be a vampire, Gilmore. *But I'm the real thing!*"

# Forever Young

## MARTIN R. SODERSTROM

The group of kids pushed through the bush and immediately ran up the hill once they were free of the thistled branches. There were five of them, not counting Josh's little sister, who was still battling the bush and screaming for Josh to wait. The rest of the kids tore up the hill and disappeared from sight, as if they were ignorant of Maggie's calls. Josh looked back a few times, unsure, but even he continued over the top of the hill without waiting. Only Max waited. But Max was different.

Max reached in and pulled some branches aside so Maggie could wiggle out of the foliage without being snapped across the face by the sharp vines. Once free she pushed her shoulder-length blonde hair out of her face.

"Where dey go? Where dey go?" she demanded as Max let the branches snap back into place. But before he could answer she heard the shouts coming from over the hill and she was off without a word. Max ran along behind her, half to catch her if she slipped, half to get to the top so he wouldn't miss anything.

"Jeez, Max, whose side are you on, man? Why do you gotta always help her?" Scotty said when Max and Maggie had reached the top of the hill. Scotty was seven years old, like the rest, but his red hair made him stand out in a crowd. And of all the gang, he was the one most full of the devil.

Max ignored Scotty, as he'd found it was the only way to deal with him, and stared into the distance. The tracks seemed to stretch on forever. He tried to listen over the commotion (Scotty was pushing Guy around again—Guy being the smallest kid, not counting Maggie) but could only be half sure that no trains were approaching.

"Let's take the bike path, guys," Max tried, though he pretty much knew what the answer was going to be. If not for Maggie, Max would have been in front leading the charge.

"I'm the engine!" Scotty shouted as he began running down the center of the tracks.

"I'm a load of race cars!" Josh shouted, falling into line behind Scotty.

"I'm rocket engines!" Guy shouted, following suit.

Todd was a carload of super secret spies and Maggie was a shipment of ice cream. Max, thanks to Maggie, was stuck with the dishonorable position of caboose. He trotted along behind Maggie, who continually tripped on the ties, arguing with himself about how she was Josh's sister and why did he care?

Scotty woo-wooed every now and then as they meandered their way through the brush toward their eventual goal of the Dairy Queen. *I'll probably get stuck buying Maggie a cone,* Max thought as he grew less and less enamored of his job as surrogate big brother. When they made the final turn, he'd had enough.

"And the caboose breaks free! Look out, the caboose is passing the engine!" Max shouted as he turned on the speed and rocketed past all the other kids, giving Scotty a shoulder for good measure as he passed him.

"No fair! No fair!" The other kids shouted as they too turned on the speed. Soon all the cars had broken rank and the train became a horse race. Max easily outdistanced the others and was the first to reach the path that lead down from the tracks to the bike path behind the Dairy Queen. He leaped the last few feet and slammed his sneakers onto the path before turning around to see by how much he'd won. To his surprise, no one was on the path behind him.

He looked up at the top of the path and saw the backs of all the other kids. They were jumping up and down and shouting something. Max couldn't hear them. The train's air horn was just too loud.

"Maggie," Max said as he vaulted forward and raced back up the hill. Once at the top, he pushed through the other kids and saw her—and the train. She was sitting on the tracks crying. The blood on her chin told Max what had happened. *She doesn't even hear it!*

Even if she stopped crying, got up and ran for all she was worth she'd never make it now. The train was too close—and getting closer. All the kids, even Scotty, were screaming for her to look behind her. But she just continued crying at the top of her lungs. Max knew what he had to do.

Summoning a power that had lain dormant for almost sixty years, Max concentrated, not sure if even he could save Maggie. All at once the kids stopped yelling, their jaws dropping open as they backed away from Max. His legs were the first to shrivel up, but before he fell into the dirt, the rest of his body diminished until he'd taken on his other form. After a few swoops to get his bearings, Max's bat form rocketed down the tracks. It was only a few seconds before he reached Maggie but it was plenty enough time to realize what he'd just sacrificed. He'd have to move again. Find another neighborhood with kids who didn't know his hideous secret. They'd all think he drank blood and cringed at crosses, now. It wasn't true, but that didn't matter. In fact, nothing mattered right now. Nothing, but Maggie.

Max circled when he was a few feet away from Maggie and concentrated. His panic must have supercharged his power, for he shifted shapes while still in the air. Fully a boy again, he fell hard onto the tracks. Fighting to gain his wind back he looked up and saw that Maggie was still crying, with her eyes closed. She hadn't seen it. *Thank God for little favors,* Max thought as the train's air horn ripped into the air again, the sound of screeching brakes just slightly less loud. Maggie turned and saw the train barreling down on her and screamed. Max grabbed her and vaulted down the side of the hill that supported the tracks. They rolled and bounced down until they landed in a thicket of ivy at the bottom. Safe.

Max pushed Maggie's blonde hair out of her face as the train roared by up above. Her eyes were red and swollen from crying and she had a scrape on her cheek besides the cut on her chin from tripping on the tracks, but she seemed intact.

"You okay?" Max asked.

"A lot you care," Maggie said before she pushed Max aside, stood and stomped out of the bushes toward the bike path. "Josh!"

Max stood, brushed himself off, and trotted out behind her. When he emerged from the bushes he was met by a line of shocked faces, some jaws still open in amazement. *Here it comes*, he thought. *The ridicule, the cries of "freak," the unfounded stark terror*. He braced himself as he looked into their faces and waited. After what seemed like an eternity, Scotty was the first to speak.

"M-Max?"

"Yeah?" Max said, trying to hide the waver in his voice.

"That was cooo-ool!"

"Totally awesome, man," Josh said next.

"Do it again! Do it again!" Guy shouted.

Now Max was the one with the shocked look on his face.

"I want a cone, Josh," Maggie said, pulling Josh's sleeve toward the Dairy Queen.

# Moving Day

## Scott A. Cupp

When Jerry and I pulled up in front of the house, I was all in favor of calling up the turkeys at Allied Vans and giving them the job. The house was that bad.

Not that I was afraid or anything like that. I've moved people out of houses that I wouldn't have leased to a family of cockroaches if they had brought me an ironclad ten-year lease at $500 a month. This place wasn't like most of them. It was just sort of creepy.

And the whole deal smelled creepy, anyway. The boss didn't even get a call from the guy. One day a letter showed up and said to send two strong people to this address and to move out everything that wasn't tied down. The guy wasn't even going to be home. We were to put everything into storage until we heard from him.

Jerry and I were to be the muscle. We'd worked with the moving company for Jerry's Uncle Nick since we'd been in high school. It was hard, backbreaking work, but Nick paid well and it went a long way toward our school expenses.

Still, this move was weird, but I could go for it. The check had been more than enough to cover the expenses of the move and several months worth of storage. And I, for one, could do without the nosy homeowner standing over my shoulder, telling me how much he had paid for this awful painting or to be careful with the dinosaur of a hide-a-bed that must have been thrown out by Attila the Hun. This was going to be a nice, quiet move.

That was what I thought before I saw the house. The rats must have been wearing hard hats to crawl through it. I saw why the guy didn't want to be there for the move. *I* didn't want to be there.

I told Jerry to turn the truck around and head back. He glared at me. My best friend in the world, and he glares at me for being concerned about his health.

"Sammy, we do the job. Uncle Nick needs the money and we said that we'd do it. So, we do it. End of conversation."

Jerry's pigheaded that way, but he made some sense. Nick did need the money. So I crawled out of the truck and began to direct Jerry as he backed that monster into the drive. We directed our energies into a work mode.

The place looked like a furnished mausoleum. There were pieces of furniture strewn about, covered with stained white sheets. I thought the place must have been abandoned for years.

We began by casing out the big items first. They needed to go toward the front of the truck. There were a couple of big rectangular tables and several bureaus. I moved one of the bureaus to assess its weight and determine how hard it would be to move. I called Jerry over to look at it.

"Make a note of this one, Jer. No glass in the mirror here. Don't let this guy stick us for anything. I don't want Nick to pay for anything we didn't bust."

Jerry brought out the clipboard with the exception report on it and made the notation. As he walked away, he stopped suddenly and called to me. "Look, Sammy! All of the mirrors are broken."

"Write 'em all down," I said. "Don't miss a one."

I pulled off my shirt and we got down to work. Occasionally, I looked down at the muscles on my chest and arms. I wasn't any Mr. Universe or even Mr. Local Football Jock, but I could hold my own in turning girls' heads or in a fair fight. Good, honest labor would put muscles on you and there was nothing like moving for that. It wasn't great for the mind, but Jerry and I played mind games as we worked. It drove some clients nuts when we played Botticelli, but, hell, sometimes it drove us nuts. It always seemed so easy once you learned who the mystery celebrity was. I had Jerry on the ropes with Dante Gabriel Rossetti. He'd been going at it for twenty minutes and hadn't established much. Pre-Raphaelite poets were not his strong suit, though he knew I was really fond of the period. One of these days, I was going to graduate school and work in that particular area. Jerry's strength was accounting. He was going to work for Nick in the general offices when he got out next.

Time passed quickly and without much trouble. One odd thing did happen. Jerry was moving one of the bureaus when his hand caught a sharp corner and he scratched his hand and arm pretty badly. It looked worse than it was and he just sort of grimaced and said, "Get me a purple heart!"

I started to laugh, when the room was filled with this howling sound. It was like there was a pack of wolves, trying to beat down the walls.

There wasn't much blood, though, and the noises soon went away. It was hard to ignore and present a brave facade. But we still had a job to finish, so we went on.

The guy had acquired a lot of really nice stuff. I particularly admired an old trunk in the corner. The workmanship on it was impeccable, obviously Victorian and used for more than decoration. This trunk had traveled and seen ports of call that I would never see. I pointed it out to Jerry. He was impressed and examined it closely. He found the nameplate that I had missed. "J. HARKER, ESQ. SOLICITOR. LONDON, ENGLAND."

"Our client must have picked it up at an estate sale or

something," said Jerry. "The client's not named Harker. The check was signed A. R. Claud. I wonder how much he had to pay for this beauty?"

An hour later, we found out that our client was a dentist. I had emptied out a closet and found several cases of dental floss and toothbrushes. Probably sold them to his patients and made a healthy profit.

By the late afternoon we had the main floor and upstairs loaded onto the truck. The letter had specified that the contents of the basement were to be loaded last. Some clients think that they know everything that there is about moving. But, for the money he was paying, we were willing to humor him. At least until we unloaded the stuff into storage.

There wasn't a great deal in the basement, just a few crates and boxes, lots of cobwebs, a rat or two, millions of shadows. I almost overlooked the coffin.

The coffin was covered by a couple of old canvases, hidden way back in the shadows. It was made of wood, not fiberglass like the ones my cousin Sidney tries to sell me every Thanksgiving when we get together. It was old, too.

The coffin was plain with rope handles and a small brass nameplate at the head. I dusted off the nameplate and tried to make out the minute, ornate script. "V. TEPESCH" it said. This guy Claud sure had some weird stuff in his house. I figured he must have been sniffing the laughing gas at the office a few too many times. Me, I wouldn't have one of these in the house for a million bucks.

I ran my hand down the side of the coffin. This sucker had been in the ground! You could feel where the weather and Nature had worked it over for a long time.

I wondered what Claud was doing with a coffin in his basement. I was sure there were laws against it. Maybe he was moving his great-uncle Victor or Victoria from the Old Country over to America. Or maybe he liked dead people. Some people are weird that way.

Whatever the reason, the coffin still had to be moved. It would certainly add some spice to my "What I Did on My Summer Vacation" essay that I would have to do in my creative writing course that was scheduled for the fall. I could hear it now. "Yes, Dr. Kalbach. I moved a coffin out of this crazy dentist's house during July. Yes, sir. It was a real coffin, one that had been in the ground, and *it had someone else's name on it!"* The class would howl, but I would be the center of attention for a few days. Might even get a date or two out of it. Never can tell.

I tackled one end of the coffin and tried to lift it. It was as heavy as it looked. Wood is not light. Ask anyone who has ever carried an old fashioned hide-a-bed up two circular flights of stairs. Things like that can make you curse Yankee ingenuity.

I called up to Jerry and told him to get his strong, but dumb, body down into the basement on the double. I heard him drop something and cuss at me the entire time he was coming, telling me, half-heartedly, that I wasn't pulling my own weight on this job.

You should have seen his face when he saw the coffin. His eyes got really wide and his face paled. "Is that what I think it is?"

I said that it was and that the sucker was heavy and was he going to stand over there all day like a nerd or did he plan on helping me out with it. Reluctantly he came over and tried to get a handhold at the foot of the coffin. We lifted it up. Damn thing must have weighed three hundred pounds. We both shifted our hands to get a better hold on it and to stabilize it.

We look a tentative step. Rats began running out of the shadows, must have been fifty or sixty of them, nipping at our jeans and getting underfoot.

We jostled the coffin a bit, something shifted inside. I wasn't about to look and see what had shifted. The rats, however, stopped suddenly, as if stunned. They filed silently back under the stairs and didn't come back out. Weirdest thing I ever saw. But I was glad to see them go. I hadn't been bitten yet, but they had shredded the edge of my jeans. Nick was going to have to spring for new ones. I asked Jerry if he was okay. He said that he hadn't been bitten, so we continued on.

It took forever to negotiate the stairs. They were steep and we had to stop and rest every few steps. I felt sorry for Jerry, since he was at the foot and supporting most of the weight. But not sorry enough to change places.

From the stairs to the front door was a short trip. We had to tilt the coffin some to get it through the door. I heard the body inside shifting some more. Outside in the heat of the day and the direct sunlight, sweat just seemed to pour out of my body. As we approached the truck, I could feel the coffin slipping at Jerry's end. I began to yell at him to set it down for a better grip when it fell out of his hands.

The coffin smashed into the concrete and rolled on its side away from us. The lid latch must have broken, because the lid flipped up and open. From where we were we couldn't see inside. We were looking at the base and side.

"Now look at what you've done!" I started to say more, when suddenly there was this loud shriek and something that sounded like a wolf screaming in pain. Things like that just don't happen around here. Jerry looked at me and I looked at him. I didn't want to see or smell what had to be inside that box. But it needed to be done and no one was going to do it for us. I took a deep breath. "Ready when you are, C.B.," I said. He nodded. I took one more deep breath and held it in.

We grabbed the coffin side and righted the coffin on the drive. The damage wasn't too bad. We had chipped the corner slightly and the lid was open. I didn't see anything inside that looked like a body. There was a lot of dust and dirt inside the coffin. I let my breath out. The smell of decaying flesh that I had expected was not there.

I made Jerry dump the dirt out. I didn't want it to get in the truck and soil the other items inside. Not that it would be likely, considering the condition of most of the merchandise that we had just moved.

We picked the coffin up and began to load it into the truck. For some reason, the coffin felt a whole lot lighter as we loaded it in. As we sat there mopping our brows, I told Jerry to get the exception report. "Make sure that you note this on the report. The lid hinge was broken and the side was slightly chipped. I don't want us or Nick to have to replace or repair that thing."

Jerry just looked at me. "Mr. Claud isn't going to like what we did to it."

"Look," I said, "it's against the law to have these things in a private dwelling, anyway. So, he's not going to press the issue. Besides, he probably won't even notice it."

# Aqua Sancta

## Edward Bryant

Father Callahan stood miserably alone in the absolute darkness of the cathedral basement, wondering when the vampire would return to drain his blood. "You might well try praying for a miracle, Father," the vampire had said, smirking, as it frogmarched the priest to the thick, plank door. "But I caution you. Notre Dame's in the middle of another losing season. Don't expect a whole lot." With unnatural strength, it had shoved Callahan down the stone steps. The priest had tumbled, but managed to protect his head as his glasses skittered away and smashed on the cement floor. Then the door had slammed shut.

The priest waited in his solitude. He listened for the quick, arrogant steps outside the door. Outrage at this unnatural abomination infuriated him. There was something worse than death, something more insidious than worldly evil. And he was helpless.

He feared for his parishioners. The dial of his watch was not illuminated, though he could hear its old-fashioned ticking when he brought his wrist close to his ear. He guessed that the appointed moment for midnight mass was now far less than an hour distant. Who would save those unsuspecting souls? Certainly not a weak clergyman locked impotently within brick walls three feet thick.

He stood, fighting vertigo, and thought furiously. Everything hurt. Joints aching, head throbbing, his bladder nigh unto bursting, the priest suddenly found inspiration. It was a brilliant white light bursting behind his eyes. "A miracle," he whispered. Maybe. But he would try. There was one thing he could attempt. "In the name of the Father, the Son, and Holy Ghost—" He fumbled.

The door crashed open, rebounding from the wall. The vampire stood at the top of the steps, outlined by the blinding, electric glare. "Keep praying, Father." The unholy creature laughed, somehow embodying a keen hunger in the sound. "I always appreciate the saying of grace before dinner." The vampire stepped nimbly down the flight. "You're the hors d'oeuvre," it said. Then the creature paused a moment, apparently startled. "Been thinking of reneging on your vow of celibacy, Father?"

"In the Name of Our Lord, no!" Father Callahan turned fully toward the vampire and did his best to aim.

The vampire screamed. Burst into flame. The creature's cry keened up the scale for only a few hideous seconds. Then the fire abruptly subsided, guttering like the peaceful votive candles Father Callahan knew were set out above. The vampire whimpered and . . . was gone. Ash remained.

When the priest had stopped shaking, he adjusted his button fly before the immolated vampire. Father Callahan prayed again, first silently, then aloud. He thanked God. Miracles—and holy water—came from unexpected sources.

# Something Had to Be Done

### DAVID DRAKE

He was out in the hall just a minute ago, sir," the pinched-faced WAC said, looking up from her typewriter in irritation. "You can't mistake his face."

Capt. Richmond shrugged and walked out of the busy office. Blinking in the dim marble hallway were a dozen confused civilians, bussed in for their preinduction physicals. No one else was in the hallway. The thick-waisted officer frowned, then thought to open the door of the men's room. "Sergeant Morzek?" he called.

Glass clinked within one of the closed stalls, and a deep voice with a catch in it grumbled, "Yeah, be right with you." Richmond thought he smelled gin.

"You the other ghoul?" the voice questioned as the stall

swung open. Any retort Richmond might have made withered when his eyes took in the cadaverous figure in ill-tailored greens. Platoon sergeant's chevrons on the sleeves and below them a longer row of service stripes than the captain remembered having seen before. God, this walking corpse might have served in World War II! Most of the ribbons ranked above the sergeant's breast pockets were unfamiliar, but Richmond caught the little V for valor winking in the center of a silver star. Even in these medal-happy days in Southeast Asia they didn't toss many of those around.

The sergeant's cheeks were hollow, his fingers grotesquely thin where they rested on top of the door or clutched the handles of his zippered AWOL bag. Where no moles squatted, his skin was as white as a convict's; but the moles were almost everywhere, hands, face, dozens and scores of them, crowding together in welted obscenity.

The sergeant laughed starkly. "Pretty, aren't I? The docs tell me I got too much sun over there and it gave me runaway warts. Hell, four years is enough time for it to."

"Umm," Richmond grunted in embarrassment, edging back into the hall to have something to do. "Well, the car's in back . . . if you're ready, we can see the Lunkowskis."

"Yeah, Christ," the sergeant swore, "that's what I came for, to see the Lunkowskis." He shifted his bag as he followed the captain, and it clinked again. Always before, the other man on the notification team had been a stateside officer like Richmond himself. He had heard that a few low-casualty outfits made a habit of letting whoever knew the dead man best accompany the body home, but this was his first actual experience with the practice. He hoped it would be his last.

Threading the green Ford through the heavy traffic of the city center, Richmond said, "I take it Pfc. Lunkowski was one of your men?"

"Yeah, Stevie-boy was in my platoon for about three weeks," Morzek agreed with a chuckle. "Lost six men in that time and he was the last. Six out of twenty-nine, not very damn good, was it?"

"You were under heavy attack?"

"Hell, no, mostly the dinks were letting us alone for a change. We were out in the middle of War Zone C, you know,

75

most Christ-bitten stretch of country you ever saw. No dinks, no trees—they'd all been defoliated. Not a damn thing but dust and each other's company."

"Well, what did happen?" Richmond prompted. Traffic had thinned somewhat among the blocks of old buildings, and he began to look for house numbers.

"Oh, mostly they just died," Morzek said. He yawned alcoholically. "Stevie, now, he got blown to hell by a grenade."

Richmond had learned when he was first assigned to notification duty not to dwell on the ways his . . . missions had died. The possibilities varied from unpleasant to ghastly. He studiously avoided saying anything more to the sergeant beside him until he found the number he wanted. "One sixteen. This must be the Lunkowskis'."

Morzek got out on the curb side, looking more skeletal than before in the dappled sunlight. He held his AWOL bag.

"You can leave that in the car," Richmond suggested. "I'll lock up."

"Naw, I'll take it in," the sergeant said as he waited for Richmond to walk around the car. "You know, this is every damn thing I brought from Nam? They didn't bother to open it at Travis, just asked me what I had in it. 'A quart of gin,' I told 'em, 'but I won't have it long,' and they waved me through to make my connections. One advantage to this kind of trip."

A bell chimed far within the house when Richmond pressed the button. It was cooler than he had expected on the pine-shaded porch. Miserable as these high, dark old houses were to heat, the design made a world of sense in the summer.

A light came on inside. The stained-glass window left of the door darkened, and a latch snicked open. "Please do come in," invited a soft-voiced figure hidden by the dark oak panel. Morzek grinned inappropriately and led the way into the hall, brightly lighted by an electric chandelier.

"Mr. Lunkowski?" Richmond began to the wispy little man who had admitted them. "We are—"

"But, yes, you are here to tell us when Stefan shall come back, are you not?" Lunkowski broke in. "Come into the sitting room, please. Anna and my daughter Rose are there."

"Ah, Mr. Lunkowski," Richmond tried to explain as he followed, all too conscious of the sardonic grin on Morzek's face, "you have been informed by telegram that Pfc. Lunkowski was—"

"Was killed, yes," said the younger of the two red-haired women as she got up from the sofa. "But his body will come back to us soon, will he not? The man on the telephone said?"

She was gorgeous, Richmond thought, cool and assured, half smiling as her hair cascaded over her left shoulder like a thick copper conduit. Disconcerted as he was by the whole situation, it was a moment before he realized that Sgt. Morzek was saying, "Oh, the coffin's probably at the airport now, but there's nothing in it but a hundred and fifty pounds of gravel. Did the telegram tell you what happened to Stevie?"

"Sergeant!" Richmond shouted. "You drunken—"

"Oh, calm down, Captain," Morzek interrupted bleakly. "The Lunkowskis, they understand. They want to hear the whole story, don't they?"

"Yes." There was a touch too much sibilance in the word as it crawled from the older woman, Stefan Lunkowski's mother. Her hair was too grizzled now to have more than a tinge of red in it, enough to rust the tight ringlets clinging to her skull like a helmet of mail. Without quite appreciating its importance, Richmond noticed that Mr. Lunkowski was standing in front of the room's only door.

With perfect nonchalance, Sgt. Morzek sat down on an overstuffed chair, laying his bag across his knees. "Well," he said, "there was quite a report on that one. We told them how Stevie was trying to booby-trap a white phosphorous grenade—fix it to go off as soon as some dink pulled the pin instead of four seconds later. And he goofed."

Mrs. Lunkowski's breath whistled out very softly. She said nothing. Morzek waited for further reaction before he smiled horribly and added: "He burned. A couple pounds of willie pete going blooie, well . . . it keeps burning all the way through you. Like I said, the coffin's full of gravel."

"My God, Morzek," the captain whispered. It was not the sergeant's savage grin that froze him but the icy-eyed silence of the three Lunkowskis.

"The grenade, that was real," Morzek concluded. "The rest of the report was a lie."

Rose Lunkowski reseated herself gracefully on a chair in

front of the heavily draped windows. "Why don't you start at the beginning, Sergeant?" she said with a thin smile that did not show her teeth. "There is much we would like to know before you are gone."

"Sure," Morzek agreed, tracing a mottled forefinger across the pigmented callosities on his face. "Not much to tell. The night after Stevie got assigned to my platoon, the dinks hit us. No big thing. Had one fellow dusted off with brass in his ankle from his machine gun blowing up, that was all. But a burst of AK fire knocked Stevie off his tank right at the start."

"What's all this about?" Richmond complained. "If he was killed by rifle fire, why say a grenade—"

"Silence!" The command crackled like heel plates on concrete.

Sgt. Morzek nodded. "Why, thank you, Mr. Lunkowski. You see, the captain there doesn't know the bullets didn't hurt Stevie. He told us his flak jacket had stopped them. It couldn't have and it didn't. I saw it that night, before he burned it—five holes to stick your fingers through, right over the breast pocket. But Stevie was fine, not a mark on him. Well, Christ, maybe he'd had a bandolier of ammo under the jacket. I had other things to think about."

Morzek paused to glance around. "All this talk, I could sure use a drink. I killed my bottle back at the Federal Building."

"You won't be long," the girl hissed.

Morzek grinned. "They broke up the squadron, then," he rasped on, "gave each platoon a sector of War Zone C to cover to stir up the dinks. There's more life on the moon than there was on the stretch we patrolled. Third night out, one of the gunners died. They flew him back to Saigon for an autopsy, but damned if I know what they found. Galloping malaria, we figured.

"Three nights later, another guy died. Dawson on three-six . . . Christ, the names don't matter. Sometime after midnight, his track commander woke up, heard him moaning. We got him back to Quan Loi to a hospital, but he never came out of it. The lieutenant thought he got wasp stung on the neck—here, you know?" Morzek touched two fingers to his jugular. "Like he was allergic. Well, it happens."

"But what about Stefan?" Mrs. Lunkowski asked. "The others do not matter."

"Yes, finish it quickly, Sergeant," the younger woman said, and this time Richmond did catch the flash of her teeth.

"We had a third death," Morzek said agreeably, stroking the zipper of his AWOL bag back and forth. "We were all jumpy by then. I doubled the guard, two men awake on every track. Three nights later, and nobody in the platoon remembered anything from twenty-four hundred hours till Riggs' partner blinked at ten of one and found him dead.

"In the morning, one of the boys came to me. He'd seen Stevie slip over to Riggs, he said, but he was zonked out on grass and didn't think it really had happened until he woke up in the morning and saw Riggs under a poncho. By then, he was scared enough to tell the whole story. Well, we were all jumpy."

"You killed Stefan." It was not a question but a flat statement.

"Oh, hell, Lunkowski," Morzek said absently, "what does it matter who rolled the grenade into his bunk? The story got around and . . . something had to be done."

"Knowing what you know, you came here?" Mrs. Lunkowski murmured liquidly. "You must be mad."

"Naw, I'm not crazy, I'm just sick." The sergeant brushed his left hand over his forehead. "Malignant melanoma, the docs told me. Twenty-six years in the goddamn army, and in another week or two I'd be *warted* to death.

"Captain," he added, turning his cancerous face toward Richmond, "you better leave through the window."

"Neither of you will leave!" snarled Rose Lunkowski as she stepped toward the men.

Morzek lifted a fat gray cylinder from his bag. "Know what this is, honey?" he asked conversationally.

Richmond screamed and leaped for the window. Rose ignored him, slashing her hand out for the phosphorous grenade. Drapery wrapping the captain's body shielded him from glass and splintered window frame as he pitched out into the yard.

He was still screaming there when the blast of white fire bulged the walls of the house.

# Chains

## MICHAEL SKEET

oo much blood. The full bucket was too much for her to deal with; even chilled as it was, the blood-smell assaulted Susan, constricting her throat and making her dizzy. She would have known it was cow's blood by the smell, even if Katherine hadn't just told her: There was something slow and bovine in the scent of it that repulsed her. She turned away, trying to avoid Katherine's eyes.

It was no good. "What the hell is the matter with you?" Katherine whispered, setting down her own bucket and gripping Susan's shoulder. Susan felt the warmth and strength of Katherine's fingers searing through her, and wished that some of that strength would transfer itself to her. Now the others were looking at her, too. They were nine in all, sifting through the shadows around a Pape Avenue fast-food chicken franchise. "Losing your nerve, Susan?" She heard mockery in Katherine's voice, now, and that hurt the most.

"It's the smell of the blood," Susan said, choking out the words. "It's making me sick."

"It makes all of us sick," Katherine said, stepping back from her. "But there's always a price to be paid when you believe strongly in something. Tonight, having to smell and maybe touch the suffering of other animals is the price we pay. Now, pick up your bucket."

It's not my bucket, Susan thought. I'm doing this for you. She turned back, willing herself not to let the sweet-acrid scent touch her palate. It was no good, though: The bitter decay seeped in with the hot and humid air and she gagged, choking up bile and frustration. She fled out of the shadows to the street corner, bending over a newspaper vending box and trying to stifle her coughing before she alerted the whole neighbourhood.

"Oh, for Christ's sake," Katherine hissed. "Can't you behave older than you look, Susan? Larry, pick up that bucket. Let's do this before somebody calls the cops. Okay," she said to the group as she picked up her own bucket of blood, "put up the posters."

Katherine had developed a special flour-water paste that made posters almost impossible to remove once it had dried. Now, Lynn, one of the new members of the group, slapped blood-red posters on the door and walls of the Chik'n Shak. The older guy who was the other new member boosted Angela onto his shoulders so that she could clamber up and glue a large sheet to each side of the illuminated plastic sign. The Chik'n Shak now screamed out a new allegiance: "STOP TORTURING ANIMALS," it said, paste dripping down plastic, glass, and painted brick.

"Larry," Katherine said, and Larry took Susan's bucket and began to splash blood on the door and along the sidewalk out front of the restaurant. When his bucket was empty, he nodded to Katherine. "Okay, everybody, head out. We'll meet at Withrow Park in twenty minutes for debriefing."

As the others scattered and Susan walked miserably into a nearby alley, Katherine hurled her bucket of blood through the large plate-glass window at the front of the Chik'n Shak. Susan bicycled away to the jangling of a blood-spattered burglar alarm.

"We ought to do well from this one," Katherine said to them from the moonshadow cast by a large maple. Her voice, pitched low, was nearly muffled by the quiet of the park. "The police won't have a clue who's done this until we issue our communiqué. And the blood was a wonderful idea. We'll get terrific TV coverage this time. Who knows"—Susan couldn't see in the darkness, but she knew that Katherine was smiling—"I may even be asked to do an interview about this latest 'outrage.' "

Katherine stepped out from under the tree. "Time to go our own ways," she said. "As usual, no one has any contact with the others for at least two weeks. Except, of course, for those of you in my philosophy class; I'll expect to see you tomorrow evening at six-thirty. Good night, all. You've done good work tonight."

As the group began to drift apart, Katherine began her ritual, stopping people with a touch, a smile, or a soft question, pitched so only the recipient could hear. A smaller echo of the group began to form; these would go home with her, some to talk until dismissed, one or two others to stay for the remainder of the night. Susan desperately wanted to be one of the chosen, had wanted to since the moment she first saw Katherine at the university. She had not been thus far blessed, though, and her luck did not change tonight. Gripping the handlebars of her bike ever tighter, she watched Katherine gather three others around her and vanish into the trees, her deep, honeyed laughter trailing behind her.

Susan settled herself onto the seat and began pedaling slowly, automatically toward home. She lifted a hand to wipe a tear from her cheek, and smelled the sour dead coldness of the rubber handlebar grip on her fingers. The night, which only an hour ago had been alive with excitement and promise, was now as lifeless as the scent that filled her nostrils. She didn't want to go to class tomorrow night. Katherine hadn't once so much as looked at her after Susan had backed away from the bucket of blood.

At home, she could not rest. Her mind would not let go of the night's events—the anticipation, the humiliation that had followed. Her third-floor apartment had jealously held onto the day's heat and humidity, and dampness clung to her like shame. Giving up, she had a quick, cold shower, dressed, and went outside for a walk.

It had cooled somewhat, especially this close to the lake, and the air moved a little thanks to the nightly offshore breeze. There wasn't enough movement in the air to clear her head, though. Why was she making such a fool of herself over Katherine? Why hadn't she been able to analyze, to understand the attraction and then deal with it rationally, instead of trailing after the woman like a baby crying after a negligent mother? All of her reason seemed to have deserted her lately, and the realization made her furious—when she could bring herself to try to think about it. Most of the time, it just made her utterly miserable.

When she stopped chastizing herself long enough to pay attention to her surroundings, she realized that she had crossed the Don Valley and was back in lower Riverdale. A few blocks more and she'd be in Withrow Park—practically in Katherine's backyard. She was furious with herself. She turned toward the park anyway.

A police car slowed as it passed her, both occupants scrutinizing her carefully. She hoped the car would not stop, and it didn't; she left the street for the purple trees and grass of the moonlit park. As she made her way up the gentle slope she met a pack of dogs making its way south, one of those loose, spontaneous affiliations of middle-class hearth-dogs unexpectedly set free for the night by carelessness with gate latches. The pack orbited her for a moment, tawny-coloured moons tasting her scent, until some other more interesting smell drifted north on the feeble breeze and one by one the dogs forgot her and drifted south again.

Perhaps the dogs had distracted her; she was at any rate unaware of the man's presence until he spoke to her. "Another one of us can't sleep," he said, and she started even though she knew the voice. B, he called himself, and always with a small laugh to show he was aware of the absurdity of this flirtation with pseudonymity. The newest member of Katherine's group, he'd had been with them only a couple of months.

He had also, she remembered with a flare of anger, been one of the ones Katherine had taken home with her.

"You seem upset," B said, now walking beside her. "Surely it's not because of your reaction to the blood tonight. That could have happened to anyone."

"It didn't; it happened to me." She clipped the words, hoping he would understand the code and leave her alone.

He didn't. "It seems to me," he said with sudden solicitousness, "that what is upsetting you is not what you did or didn't do tonight; it's our noble leader's reaction to you that bothers you. How old are you?"

Susan stopped so abruptly that B continued walking a half-dozen paces before realizing she was no longer with him. She was furious that he had pointed it out—and shamed that someone who scarcely knew her had noticed. She was not accustomed to being so transparent, and she resented it. She found herself well-supplied with resentment; there was even some for Katherine. "Eighteen," she finally said.

"You seem older than that to me, even if not to her."

"I feel as though I've been eighteen for a long, long time," she said.

"I apologize if I've been too blunt," B said. He had a slight accent, Susan realized. It went well with his mild self-mocking and his old-fashioned courtesies. "I simply wondered if I'd found in you a kindred spirit. There's something about you."

"Kindred?" Susan suddenly found him interesting.

"I have for some weeks now despaired at Katherine's failure to understand the limits against which she is singularly failing to push," B said. "Her espousal of animal rights is all well and good. But she is being either hypocritical or naive in not realizing that the animals for whose rights she campaigns are not a closed system unto themselves." B had started walking again, and now Susan found herself moving her shorter legs faster in order to keep up with him. Moonlight stuttered through the trees and danced on the grass, then on pavement as they left the park.

"A closed system?" she said after thinking a minute. "I'm pretty sure she knows that animals can't be compartmentalized. Sometimes, though, you have to simplify issues in order for the public to understand them."

"Yes. That's what Greenpeace has done. And what is Greenpeace? It's a media circus, not an environmental movement. Most members of Greenpeace and the organizations that subscribe to its philosophy are intellectual couch potatoes, Susan. They watch the commercials and the news reports of stunts on TV, and they live their commitment vicariously through the tube. They convince themselves that by sending in their twenty-five or fifty dollars they are somehow 'supporting the environment.'

"That's what Katherine is doing, isn't it, Susan? She's more interested in getting her simplistic philosophy on television than she is in any practical attempt to understand how humans bear a responsibility to the ecosystem and food chain of which they're a part."

"I hadn't really thought about that," Susan said. More honest to herself, she decided that the whole question of animal rights didn't much concern her. Animals were simply part of the landscape. Her interest had been in Katherine, and if Katherine espoused a radical approach to animal rights, then Susan was interested in that, too.

What B was saying made some sense, though. She might not have thought much about animals, but Susan was definitely interested in her place in the world. It was a question, she now realized, around which she had been circling for nearly a year, much as the dogs had circled her a few minutes ago. Perhaps B could offer the insight that had so far been denied her by Katherine.

"How do you think we fit into the environment?" she asked. "You said something about responsibility."

"We're at the top of the food chain," B said. "Plus, we are so far as I am aware the only reasoning animals on the planet. As such, we bear a much greater responsibility to those below us on the chain. It's all a question of power and suffering."

Suffering she understood. Susan had hopes of being able to understand power. B, she now saw, was much older than she had assumed, even older than Katherine. He was what her father might have called a portly man, but he carried himself with a physical grace that seemed to cloud her perception of his bulk. Thin gray and black hair was slicked back from a high forehead, presumably to cover a bald spot somewhere.

"Where are we going?" she asked. They had, without her really being aware of it, walked for some time, into a neighbourhood her nighttime walks had not thus far taken her to. She assumed without thinking too much about it that B was directing their steps.

"I thought we might continue our discussion at my house," he said, gesturing to an old semidetached. The brick walls had been painted a long time ago, and the house was now in the process of shedding its acrylic skin, which was hanging in strips in places. He led her down the driveway to a side door. "Have you eaten tonight?"

She had not. The smell of the cold cow's blood had drowned her appetite, but a twisting in her vitals let her know that hunger was finally returning to her. "That brings up an interesting question," she said as she followed him down an old, but carefully maintained set of steps into the house's basement. "You say you respect not just animals, but everything below you in the food chain. Does that mean that you don't eat meat—and you don't eat vegetables, either?" B shook his head, unlocking a door at the foot of the stairs. "Then what on earth do you eat?"

"There is only one thing we can eat if we truly believe that we have a responsibility to all other living things on the planet,"

B said. He opened the door and smiled, his eyes shining even in the dim basement light.

"We eat each other."

The smell of blood, fresh and stale, warm and cold, rushed through the door and into Susan's nostrils. This was not cow blood, however, mocking her hunger with its refusal to be metabolized by her kind. This was human blood, and the harsh, sweet steel of it set off rockets of pleasure and longing in her. "I've watched the way you look at the others," B said, "and I have a feeling you're a kindred spirit. Would you like to join me for dinner?" He giggled, a light, nervous sound, and stepped through the doorway. Susan followed. After month upon month of loneliness, she was prepared to do without Katherine's strength of personality if B turned out to be another, like herself, who had been touched by the night.

But he hadn't. The room was semifinished, dominated by two old chest freezers, their chipped white enamel spattered with blood; a long, roughly finished workbench ran between them. There were body parts on the bench, and hanging from hooks above it. The skin had been stripped from most of them, and from the ones best illuminated by the single bulb swaying from the ceiling Susan could see that sections of muscle had been neatly cut away. She looked up at B, who smiled at her. His teeth were relatively straight and even. He was not like her, except that his tastes were a distant mockery of her needs.

"I've prepared a special dish for you," he said, and gestured to the far corner.

In the gloom a woman was chained to the wall, her nakedness dusty grey in the poor light. Susan widened her eyes and looked again. Katherine stared back at Susan, eyes pleading, a piece of duct tape over her mouth. "And now, a practical lesson in philosphy," B said, moving toward Katherine. He held an old-fashioned straight razor in his hand, the blade reflecting paper-thin slivers of light as he trembled with anticipation.

Anger burst out of Susan, anger at this pathetic, perverted imitation of what she was, and anger at having willed herself into being misled by him. With a wordless howl of rage she seized his left wrist and swung him through a circle. She felt as much as heard his arm leave its socket. Then she released him, and he slammed headfirst into one of the freezers.

For a moment Susan stood there, the adrenalin and hunger surging through her. Then a sour, earthly smell began to fill the room as B's dying bowels emptied themselves. There would be no feeding from that one. She turned and walked to the corner.

Katherine was whimpering hysterically, her shaking causing the chains to rattle. Susan stood over her, looking into Katherine's eyes. Katherine stopped shaking. Susan tried to look at Katherine's body, but the nakedness she had often imagined was not here. What she saw was nothing more than unclothed flesh, an awkward bag of skin sprawled in the dust.

"I didn't want it to be this way," Susan said quietly. "I've been alone so long. I admired your strength, wanted you to share it with me. I need someone like that, Katherine. At least I thought I did. But you never understood. You never listened. I wonder if you ever even noticed me." Katherine's eyes were half-closed, her whimpering almost inaudible now. Susan brushed her fingers along the trembling throat.

Katherine was overfond of the sun, and the skin on her neck was dry and leathery. Susan's fingers nevertheless found a place, below the ear and behind the jawline, where the skin was still soft and supple. "I would have spared you this," she breathed into Katherine's ear. "If you had asked me to be with you even once, I would have been slow and careful and tender with you.

"You would have liked it."

# Blood Gothic

NANCY HOLDER

She wanted to have a vampire lover. She wanted it so badly that she kept waiting for it to happen. One night, soon, she would awaken to wings flapping against the window and then take to wearing velvet ribbons and cameo lockets around her delicate, pale neck. She knew it.

She immersed herself in the world of her vampire lover: she devoured Gothic romances, consumed late-night horror movies. Visions of satin capes and eyes of fire shielded her from the harshness of the daylight, from mortality and the vain and meaningless struggles of the world of the sun. Days as a kindergarten teacher and evenings with some overly eager, casual acquaintance could not pull her from her secret existence: always a ticking portion of her brain planned, proceeded, waited.

She spent her meager earnings on dark antiques and intricate clothes. Her wardrobe was crammed with white negligees and ruffled underthings. No crosses and no mirrors, particularly not in her bedroom. White tapered candles stood in pewter sconces, and she would read late into the night by their smoky flickerings, she scented and ruffled, hair combed loosely about her shoulders. She glanced at the window often.

She resented lovers—though she took them, thrilling to the fullness of life in them, the blood and the life—who insisted upon staying all night, burning their breakfast toast and making bitter coffee. Her kitchen, of course, held nothing but fresh ingredients and copper and ironware; to her chagrin, she could not do without ovens or stoves or refrigerators. Alone, she carried candles and bathed in cool water.

She waited, prepared. And at long last, her vampire lover began to come to her in dreams. They floated across the moors, glided through the fields of heather. He carried her to his crumbling castle, undressing her, pulling off her diaphanous gown, caressing her lovely body until, in the height of passion, he bit into her arched neck, drawing the life out of her and replacing it with eternal damnation and eternal love.

She awoke from these dreams drenched in sweat and feeling exhausted. The kindergarten children would find her unusually quiet and self-absorbed, and it frightened them when she rubbed her spotless neck and smiled wistfully. *Soon and soon and soon,* her veins chanted, in prayer and anticipation. *Soon.*

The children were her only regret. She would not miss her inquisitive relatives and friends, the ones who frowned and studied her as if she were a portrait of someone they knew they were supposed to recognize. Those, who urged her to drop by for an hour, to come with them to films, to accompany them to the seashore. Those, who were connected to her—or thought they were—by the mere gesturing of the long and milky hands of Fate. Who sought to distract her from her one true passion; who sought to discover the secret of that passion. For, true to the sacredness of her vigil for her vampire lover, she had never spoken of him to a single earthly, earthbound soul. It would be beyond them, she knew. They would not comprehend a bond of such intentioned sacrifice.

But she would regret the children. Never would a child of their love coo and murmur in the darkness; never would his proud and noble features soften at the sight of the mother and her child of his loins. It was her single sorrow.

Her vacation was coming. June hovered like the mist and the children squirmed in anticipation. Their own true lives would begin in June. She empathized with the shining eyes and smiling faces, knowing their wait was as agonizing as her own. Silently, as the days closed in, she bade each of them a tender farewell, holding them as they threw their little arms around her neck and pressed fervent summertime kisses on her cheeks.

She booked her passage to London on a ship. Then to Romania, Bulgaria, Transylvania. The hereditary seat of her beloved; the fierce, violent backdrop of her dreams. Her suitcases opened themselves to her long, full skirts and her brooches and lockets. She peered into her hand mirror as she packed it. "I am getting pale," she thought, and the idea both terrified and delighted her.

She became paler, thinner, more exhausted as her trip wore on. After recovering from the disappointment of the raucous, modern cruise ship, she raced across the Continent to find refuge in the creaky trains and taverns she had so yearned for. Her heart thrilled as she meandered past the black silhouettes of ruined fortresses and ancient manor houses. She sat for hours in the mists, praying for the howling wolf to find her, for the bat to come and join her.

She took to drinking wine in bed, deep, rich, blood-red burgundy that glowed in the candlelight. She melted into the landscape within days, and cringed as if from the crucifix itself when flickers of her past life, her American, false existence, invaded her serenity. She did not keep a diary; she did not count the days as her summer slipped away from her. She only rejoiced that she grew weaker.

It was when she was counting out the coins for a Gypsy shawl that she realized she had no time left. Tomorrow she must make for Frankfurt and from there fly back to New York. The shopkeeper nudged her, inquiring if she were ill, and she left with her treasure, trembling.

She flung herself on her own rented bed. "This will not do. This will not do." She pleaded with the darkness. "You must come for me tonight. I have done everything for you, my beloved, loved you above all else. You must save me." She sobbed until she ached.

She skipped her last meal of veal and paprika and sat quietly in her room. The innkeeper brought her yet another bottle of burgundy and after she assured him that she was quite all right, just a little tired, he wished his guest a pleasant trip home.

The night wore on; though her book was open before her, her eyes were riveted to the windows, her hands clenched around the wineglass as she sipped steadily, like a creature feeding. Oh, to feel him against her veins, emptying her and filling her!

*Soon and soon and soon . . .*

Then, all at once, it happened. The windows rattled, flapped inward. A great shadow, a curtain of ebony, fell across the bed, and the room began to whirl, faster, faster still; and she was consumed with a bitter, deathly chill. She heard, rather than saw, the wineglass crash to the floor, and struggled to keep her eyes open as she was overwhelmed, engulfed, taken.

"Is it you?" she managed to whisper through teeth that rattled with delight and cold and terror. "Is it finally to be?"

Freezing hands touched her everywhere: her face, her breasts, the desperate offering of her arched neck. Frozen and strong and never-dying. Sinking, she smiled in a rictus of mortal dread and exultation. Eternal damnation, eternal love. Her vampire lover had come for her at last.

When her eyes opened again, she let out a howl and shrank against the searing brilliance of the sun. Hastily, they closed the curtains and quickly told her where she was: home again, where everything was warm and pleasant and she was safe from the disease that had nearly killed her.

She had been ill before she had left the States. By the time she had reached Transylvania, her anemia had been acute. Had she never noticed her own pallor, her lassitude?

Anemia. Her smile was a secret on her white lips. So they

thought, but he *had* come for her, again and again. In her dreams. And on that night, he had meant to take her finally to his castle forever, to crown her the best-beloved one, his love of the moors and the mists.

She had but to wait, and he would finish the deed.

*Soon and soon and soon.*

She let them fret over her, wrapping her in blankets in the last days of summer. She endured the forced cheer of her relatives, allowed them to feed her rich food and drink in hopes of restoring her.

But her stomach could no longer hold the nourishment of their kind; they wrung their hands and talked of stronger measures when it became clear that she was wasting away.

At the urging of the doctor, she took walks. Small ones at first, on painfully thin feet. Swathed in wool, cowering behind sunglasses, she took tiny steps like an old woman. As she moved through the summer hours, her neck burned with an ungovernable pain that would not cease until she rested in the shadows. Her stomach lurched at the sight of grocery-store windows. But at the butcher's, she paused, and licked her lips at the sight of the raw, bloody meat.

But she did not go to him. She grew neither worse nor better.

"I am trapped," she whispered to the night as she stared into the flames of a candle by her bed. "I am disappearing between your world and mine, my beloved. Help me. Come for me." She rubbed her neck, which ached and throbbed but showed no outward signs of his devotion. Her throat was parched, bone-dry, but water did not quench her thirst.

At long last, she dreamed again. Her vampire lover came for her as before, joyous in their reunion. They soared above the crooked trees at the foothills, streamed like black banners above the mountain crags to his castle. He could not touch her enough, worship her enough, and they were wild in their abandon as he carried her in her diaphanous gown to the gates of his fortress.

But at the entrance, he shook his head with sorrow and could not let her pass into the black realm with him. His fiery tears seared her neck, and she thrilled to the touch of the mark even as she cried out for him as he left her, fading into the vapors with a look of entreaty in his dark, flashing eyes.

Something was missing; he required a boon of her before he could bind her against his heart. A thing that she must give to him . . .

She walked in the sunlight, enfeebled, cowering. She thirsted, hungered, yearned. Still she dreamed of him, and still he could not take the last of her unto himself.

Days and nights and days. Her steps took her finally to the schoolyard, where once, only months before, she had embraced and kissed the children, thinking never to see them again. They were all there, who had kissed her cheeks so eagerly. Their silvery laughter was like the tinkling of bells as dust motes from their games and antics whirled around their feet. How free they seemed to her who was so troubled, how content and at peace.

The children.

She shambled forward, eyes widening behind the shields of smoky glass.

He required something of her first.

Her one regret. Her only sorrow.

She thirsted. The burns on her neck pulsated with pain.

Tears of gratitude welled in her eyes for the revelation that had not come too late. Weeping, she pushed open the gate of the schoolyard and reached out a skeleton-limb to a child standing apart from the rest, engrossed in a solitary game of cat's cradle. Tawny-headed, ruddy-cheeked, filled with the blood and the life.

For him, as a token of their love.

"My little one, do you remember me?" she said softly.

The boy turned. And smiled back uncertainly in innocence and trust.

Then she came for him, swooped down on him like a great, winged thing, with eyes that burned through the glasses, teeth that flashed, once, twice. . . .

*soon and soon and soon.*

# Child of the Night

## BRIAN McNAUGHTON

ranz was no more than six years old when some impulse that he later took as proof of precocious genius prompted him to open a nursery window to better gaze upon the glory of the full moon, to better feel the touch of the far-wandering night breeze, to better hear the liquid fluting and trilling of the nightingale.

The night! It held beauty and mystery and a promise of adventure. The day was crude and plain, it made no promises at all, only threats of study and drudgery and duty. Why were all those stupid grownups *sleeping?* Why weren't they wandering in the silvered fields, which surely no longer rippled with humdrum barley, but with angelic grain that would impart all knowledge and eternal pleasure? Why weren't they out gazing in stunned wonder at the moon? Why weren't they running barefoot through the woods, pursuing fireflies whose flashing message, if decoded, might make one God?

With thoughts like these (as he later reconstructed them in adolescent verse) tumbling through his brain, he fell asleep over the windowsill. There his nurse discovered him the next morning, more out of the window than in it, his nightshirt soaked with dew and his flesh pimpled by mosquito bites.

Gretchen beat him, an almost unprecedented event, and she did it in a tearful hysteria that terrified him far more than the pain inflicted by her big, red palm. When his mother dashed from bed to investigate the commotion, she raised his terror to a new level of shrieks, convulsions, and shameful incontinence.

Instead of protesting the nurse's brutality, she grabbed a handful of his long, yellow curls and jerked his head from side to side as she screamed in his face that he was either an idiot or a demon, who had been switched for the real Franz in infancy to wreak destruction upon their ancient house.

His father, the count, came roaring like a bear from its den to sort things out with words that Franz had never heard before.

The nearly demolished boy was left alone for some hours to—as his mother put it—think upon his sin. In fact he thought upon the exasperating wilfulness and stupidity of adults, and vowed that he would never become one. He believed he at last understood why his Aunt Magda had celebrated her thirteenth birthday by drinking lye.

Consoling him later with kisses and chocolates and promises of a trip to the zoological gardens in Vienna, his mother told him that no proper Christian slept with his windows open.

"Did Jesus' house have windows?" asked Franz, who was often distracted by lines of inquiry that others found irrelevant, if not downright queer.

"Of course it did!" His mother seemed bemused by an equal irrelevancy, the painful mosquito bites he had suffered, but only by those on his throat. "The question flirts with blasphemy, young man. Our Blessed Lord was a carpenter, Franz, and his house must have had the sturdiest windows with the strongest fastenings that could be fashioned by professional skill combined with divine powers. You don't suppose Our Savior would have run the risk of being bitten by a vampire!"

"What's a vampire?" he asked, and his flustered mother told him that she had spoken no such word, that in fact no such word existed, and that, unless he immediately recanted his error, his hearing would be corrected with a triple dose of Dr. Hapfstengel's Universal Purgative.

"What's a vampire?" he later asked his father, who was far more reasonable, but whose statements could be irksomely oracular.

"Vampires, like virgins or priests, are things that women believe in. We must never fail to humor them in such matters."

Later, by ingratiating himself with crones and lackeys and woodcutters; by paying closer heed than most did to the muttering of Grudin, the village idiot; and by devouring sensational novels that he had to conceal from his mother, Franz learned all there was to know about vampires, except the most important fact of all: Where to find one?

Of course he understood that the undead haunted graveyards and wastelands and ruins, but in a countryside that had been disputed for millennia by nearly anyone who could read a map and raise an army, such likely locations left scant room for the fields and villages of honest folk. He took to haunting the accursed spots himself until, his surprise not unmingled with a certain satisfaction, he noticed that the peasants had taken to crossing themselves or making less orthodox signs at the sight of his gaunt, pale figure.

It was true that he slept by day and prowled by night, and that he scorned the daylight world of commerce and industry, of sport and fellowship. He secretly longed to become a vampire, to indulge fully his passion for night and solitude, to command strange powers and live forever. Could it be that one of those bites he had suffered in childhood had not been made by a mosquito at all? Could it be—but except in certain of his darker verses, he was forced to reject this speculation. He had no thirst whatever for blood. To the extreme displeasure of his father, who counted no day complete without killing some bird or animal, the sight of blood, sometimes even the mere mention of it, made Franz vomit.

At the university, he discovered that vampirism was held to be a quaint fantasy of untutored rustics. Having mentioned his obsessive interest to the wrong people, he was ever after pictured by his peers as a forelock-tugging bumpkin who wore lederhosen and practiced clog-dancing in his room.

In the depths of the library, however, he came upon forgotten books in ancient tongues that advanced a far different view. In the popular press, too, vampires were not taken lightly, and he collected enough clippings in his student days to overflow five massive scrapbooks. Straining his allowance, he would often take trains to Prague, Munich, or Bucharest, pursuing further complications of trains and coaches and footpaths to investigate personally the more horrific hints. With infuriating similarity, the supposed eyewitnesses told him that the events he tried to verify, although indisputably true, had happened to someone else, somewhere else, at some other time.

The only good that came of this was that his father assumed he was squandering his time and substance on gentlemanly vices. He increased Franz's allowance and grew more benign.

Although no one else did, Franz considered himself a poet. Meanwhile, almost by accident, he established himself as an expert (by academic standards, a hopelessly unsound one) on folk-lore, and as a journalist whose articles earned favor on the most sensational frontiers of the press. This proved a godsend when the renewal of an obscure quarrel among the factions that claimed his homeland made it impossible for him to make a living, as his now-deceased father had done, merely by being a count.

Franz was astounded when the dusty little priest who happened to share his table at the inn proved to hold provocative opinions on the subject of his own obsession.

"They are not fools, you know," Father Teodor said. "How could any fool survive for a thousand years, two thousand?"

"But they must eat." Franz remembered and addressed the pork and cabbage on his plate, which only a long and tiresome journey could have made palatable.

"Of course they must." The priest lived in this remote outpost on just the other side of the known universe, and perhaps since he had suffered no such journey, his plate remained untouched. "But it is absurd to imagine that they flap brazenly through the world like Mr. Stoker's creature, seizing, as the whim strikes them, virgins or real-estate salesman."

"How, then?"

"Protective coloration would be essential. The vampire can no longer be a wicked nobleman in a shunned castle, for who would shun it in this day and age? Journalists like yourself would descend upon it like a flight of . . . ah . . . vampires, if you will, and take it apart stone by stone in search of the hidden crypt."

"Drinking blood would surely attract some notice," Franz said, "no matter what his disguise."

"Would it draw notice on a battlefield, where one might be free to wander among the wounded, to kneel beside them, lean close to them? Who bothers to measure all the spilled blood of our fallen heroes? Imagine the modern vampire as a military physician, a stretcher-bearer, a looter."

"Or a priest," Franz said, for he was annoyed to hear his romantic fantasy translated into pedestrian terms.

"Exactly, my son!" cried Father Teodor, not at all put out. "The normal course of my duties requires me to drink blood several times a day in full public view, and no one has ever once suggested driving a stake through my heart."

Although not at all devout, Franz was scandalized to hear a man of the cloth flirt with blasphemy. The priest laughed as if to prove he was joking; and, as if to advance further proof, touched the oddly patterned crucifix at his breast.

"However, your local vampire has ignored all this good advice," Franz said, gesturing at the low-ceilinged room around them. Except for the innkeeper drowsing in a corner, it was empty. The windows were tightly shuttered and hung with garlic blossoms. Arriving late at night on a lame horse, he had pounded on the door of the inn for nearly an hour before gaining admittance, and only then after demonstrating his ability to recite the Lord's Prayer without error or hesitation, a feat that had taken three tries. "He has not, obviously, escaped notice."

"What has been noticed is the absence of several young persons, who no doubt grew bored with village life and ran off to sample the cosmopolitan dazzlements of beggary and prostitution. Since we cannot blame the stupefying dullness of their parents for driving them away, we must search for miracles, wonders, vampires."

"But the bodies?"

"A girl who died from refusing to eat, a boy bleached white when he was recovered from the stream where the paper mill dumps its bleach. And you mustn't forget the drunkard who glimpsed a wolf in the graveyard, or the spinster who heard a man whispering obscenities at her window." For the first time the priest fixed him directly with his eyes. They were surprisingly deep and knowing, and they belied his rather frivolous manner and his dusty, inconsequential appearance. "No, Franz, you've come to the wrong place entirely to fulfill your lifelong ambition."

"My—?" He found himself blushing as he had not done since he was a young man, and that was a long time ago.

"I've read some of your verses. Not entirely unlike Baudelaire, I thought. But consider, my son: If the well-disguised vampire I have described lurks in the modern world, why would he endanger his long career by taking on an apprentice whose notions have been fuddled by Gothic fiction?"

Franz's only answer seemed as lame to him as the Ontological Proof of God's existence: If I want it to be so, it must be so. He refrained from speaking this aloud.

"Some would find your preoccupation unhealthy, or even sinful, but I submit that it reflects a deep longing for spiritual transcendence. If you want mystery and awe and eternal life, you really should give the Church a try."

Franz smiled sourly. For a priest in such an obscure parish, he was remarkably skillful at fitting his sales talk to the potential customer. He had been stringing Franz along with his prattle about vampires.

Ignoring the suggestion, Franz said, "What about the local suspect, this Valdemar Trusis?"

"Just a poor lunatic who murdered his wife and children many years ago. As madmen often do, he made curious remarks. They are now given more weight than they deserve. But he surrendered to Christ before he was hanged, and his body was interred in the family vault. Which vault has remained, I assure you, undisturbed for the past fifty years."

"You've checked?"

"Of course." The priest smiled. "Mr. Conan Doyle's detective advises us to eliminate the impossible from our inquiries, but he doesn't tell us to ignore it completely."

Lying in his bed later, after opening both windows of his room on the night, tossing the garlic blossoms into the street, turning the mirror to the wall, and hiding the innkeeper's crucifix in the chamber pot, Franz savored the priest's praise of his poetry. Only after a while did it strike him that saying his verses were not entirely unlike Baudelaire was no praise at all.

He decided before drifting off that Father Teodor's exile to this backwater was no mystery. Advancement in the clergy had never been the reward for mordant wit.

Given over to mangy dogs and knots of suspicious old men by daylight, the town itself seemed undead. Houses and factories gutted in the late war, or perhaps in some previous war, had never been repaired. The paper mill whose defluxions had bleached the dead boy lay in ruins, but Franz was willing to grant that its poison might still linger in the dead, still stream.

The graveyard was more populous than the town, but no better kept. Climbing steeply through a tangle of broken slabs and brambles, Franz at last reached the precinct of nobler tombs. That of the Trusis clan was square and squat and ugly, and securely locked. Footprints were evident in the dried mud on the portico, but they had been left by those who had defaced the walls with a disturbing mixture of religious and lubricious symbols and wreathed the door with garlic. Unbroken by any motion of the door, the wreaths had withered long ago.

Franz felt very old on his way down the hill, and even older when he made a second climb through the ruins after dark. Slipping on a rain-slicked headstone, he cut his hand, and this lifted his spirits. The incidents in this town had been too numerous, their explanations too glib. As never before in his long and frustrating career, he sensed the near-presence of the uncanny. Valdemar might not be the vampire; but the real one might be drawn by a trail of fresh blood leading to his tomb.

And what then? "Wait!" he would cry, given half a chance. "Unlike your other victims, I welcome you! We are the same, you and I, born into the service of darkness and the worship of night. Drink the blood I have saved for you and show me the way."

The rain fell harder. He shrank tighter into his cloak and huddled for shelter against the door of the suspect tomb, which opened.

A thin cry escaped his lips as he struggled for balance. His first, shameful impulse was to dash headlong down the hill and regain the safety of the inn, but he found the strength to resist. It took strength, too, to hold and operate his electric torch in hands that didn't merely tremble, but shook violently.

The dancing light revealed a bare chamber where coffins lay in niches about the walls. The oldest were of bronze, fancifully ornamented and undisturbed; the newest was a plain pine box whose lid had been removed and placed standing against the wall, as if awaiting the return of the occupant.

As he had known it would be, it was empty. He sagged against it, pressing his forehead hard against the edge, unable to determine whether the ragged sounds that tore from his throat were sobs or giggles. Either way, his eyes stung with tears. As he came to himself, he noted that the coffin held a stronger odor than one might expect from an occupant who had resisted the importunities of the worm.

He stood and consulted his watch, which had stopped. The rain pattered on the roof, a chill crept into his wet feet from the stone floor. His best estimate suggested a long wait.

With a shrug to placate the Powers of Darkness, he hoisted himself into the niche and lay down in the vacant coffin, which was a tolerably good fit. He planned to get out as soon as he had relieved the strain on his feet and rested his eyes.

It was so deliciously comfortable, though, to lean halfway out the window and try to discern patterns in the multitudinous glimmer of the fireflies as they rose to the glorious moon. . . .

The rain must have stopped, Franz thought when his eyes opened to a burst of sunlight, and he just had time to reflect that this was a shoddy last thought for a poet. And last thought it must surely be, to judge by the unbearable, tearing pain that had exploded in his heart.

"Fa . . . ?"

"Rest, my son," said Father Teodor, pounding the stake a final time.

With a strength that seemed nearly preternatural to those huddled behind him, the priest severed the vampire's head with one stroke of a butcher knife. Before anyone could get a good look at the ineffable Valdemar, he reversed the head as tradition dictated and pressed the still twitching and drooling face against the pine planks.

"So much blood!" Granny Karen quavered. "And after so many years! I was just a little girl when Val tried to corner me in the woodshed and lift my dress, but—"

"Go!" the priest commanded. "Our long ordeal is over at last. Leave me now. I must pray."

"Shouldn't we burn it?" asked Gregor, the butcher, who was troubled about the future use of the good knife he had lent the priest. "I once read that—"

"Get out!" Father Teodor shrieked, his eyes seeming to start from his head for a moment, then added in a milder tone, "My children. This is yet a place of great evil and spiritual peril, and only a consecrated servant of Our Lord is truly safe. Please go. Now. At once! And close the door."

"Considering what Val used to do to cats, I can't say he didn't deserve it, but what a way—"

"Believe me, Granny, no one ever pursued his fate with so much willful persistence as this man," he said, giving her a shove that would have seemed extremely rude if he hadn't been in such obvious physical distress. Everyone remarked that Father Teodor looked pale and shaken, that he averted his eyes from the sunlight as if in pain.

Young Peter's ears were soundly boxed when he asked why, before the door clanged shut, he had glimpsed the priest greedily licking his fingers.

# Coffin Nail

RICHARD PARKS

RECEIVED BY LSUAC·EDU «MAILER-DAEMON» 6 '94
TO: MVH@LSUAC·EDU
SUBJECT: VAMPYRES·INFO

Mike thought the electronic mail message looked promising, but there was something wrong with the heading. Computers were nothing new to him but the university's Internet connection was; the global network was a big place and it was easy to get lost without a guide. He looked around the Lowry Hall basement computing center for anyone who looked vaguely like a Sherpa, or even a grad student.

"Elizabeth?"

A black-haired young woman with pale makeup and impossibly red lips looked up from a game of computer Solitaire. She recognized him and smiled brightly. "Doctor Mike! What brings you to the catacombs this time of night?"

"Trying to track down some research sources. Do you know anything about this e-mail program?"

She walked over, still smiling. Elizabeth Simmons was a very attractive young lady, but the thing Mike always remembered about her was her smile. There was a definite strain of somber romanticism that infected most of his students' actions and dress, but, unlike most Gothic Studies majors, Elizabeth smiled a lot. She leaned close over the console and Mike caught a faint hint of cinnamon.

"Looks like an anonymous remailer," she said. It must have been obvious from his expression that Mike didn't have a clue, so she went on. "It's a special e-mail relay site. People can send mail to that computer's address, and it in turn sends the message on to its final destination without revealing the source. Good for privacy." She looked at him. "Got something special here, Doctor Mike?"

"I don't know yet. I've been making inquiries over the net for a few weeks and this just showed up."

*No sense going farther than that. Most of my students think I'm crazy enough as is.*

Elizabeth reached down and tapped a few keys, too fast for Mike to follow most of it, then shook her head. "There's no way to track the source. Do you know what it is?"

"I guess I'll find out. Thanks."

Elizabeth went back to her game. Mike called up the mail message to his screen and read:

```
COFFIN.NAIL 453,543 bytes
/pub/gothic/binary
KNACKER.COM
```

The name and size of a computer file, its location in a distant computer's file system, and the Internet address of the computer. That was all. The address was unknown to him, but that meant nothing. He knew just a very few of the thousands of computers on the network. Mike rubbed his eyes and checked his watch. It was after midnight, and he was in no shape to pursue the lead now. The kind of answers he sought demanded full attention and care, neither of which he had at the moment.

*It's not enough to know your enemy's weakness. You have to know your own.*

The saying was an old one in his family; he didn't know where it came from and neither did anyone else, but Mike had his suspicions. He printed the message out, tore the single sheet off the printer and tucked it into his pocket before logging off.

\* \* \*

He heard about Elizabeth the next morning. She was found at her computer, right where Mike had left her. The official verdict was heart failure. Mike would have liked to believe that, but when he finally recovered from his first shock he remembered the one word he'd been able to make out from Elizabeth's frantic typing, and finally realized what it meant.

*Oh, God . . .*

Mike went down into the computer center and found an available computer. Getting into Elizabeth's account was no problem; as faculty advisor he had set up most of his students' accounts and passwords in the first place. It didn't take long to find what he was looking for. Her curiosity apparently aroused, Elizabeth had copied Mike's strange letter into her own account the night before. The chain of events following that were pretty easy to construct, with what Mike already suspected about the nature of the message.

*I'm sorry, Elizabeth. I didn't know. I should have known. . . .*

Mike cursed himself for a very long time.

Mike stopped off at the Computing Services manager's office before class.

"Tom, I need a favor." He handed him a sheet of paper covered with diagrams and instructions. "Can you do this?"

Tom Matthews looked at him with that distracted air that Mike associated most with computer people. They were friends and had been for years, but Mike didn't pretend to understand him. Tom shrugged. "Sure. We have an old AT-class machine we're about to retire anyway, and the program seems simple enough. What's it for?"

"To test a theory. I need an isolated machine in case something goes wrong."

Tom frowned. "You're not playing with a computer virus, are you?"

"Something like that." Mike sighed. "How soon?"

Tom shrugged again. "I hope you know what you're doing. . . . Okay, I just finished a big database project, so I'm free until Wednesday. I can have it by tomorrow afternoon."

Mike nodded, started to leave, and then hesitated. "There's just one more thing—it has to work the first time. None of this 'fine-tuning' you're so fond of. Sometimes I think you break programs just so you can fix them."

"You wound me, sir," Tom replied, smiling, "but all right. Count on it."

Mike nodded. "I have to."

Class let out early the next day for Elizabeth's memorial service, but there were still a few questions from students. None about Elizabeth; those closest to her had cut class completely and the rest seemed intent on pretending nothing had happened. Mike didn't blame them; he wished he could do the same, and the predictability of the questions itself was comfort of a sort. In fact, one particular question seemed almost new again.

"You've touched on the heart of the matter," Mike said. "If the vampire is limited to night travel, then even with its special powers of transformation its range is limited. If you'll recall your reading assignments, it's clear from Dr. Van Helsing's account in the original *Dracula* that this was part of the reason the vampire relocated to London. Its source of supply was dwindling, and worse, its prey knew how to defend themselves more and more. The vampire needed a greater hunting range to survive, and more complacent victims."

The student, a too-serious looking young woman who still reminded him of Elizabeth, persisted. "But wouldn't that be less of a problem now? Transportation is much better."

"But not foolproof. Suppose our modern vampire took a plane? People get bumped. Schedules can be disrupted. Planes have mechanical problems. The same for driving; in either case a delay of a few hours could be fatal. Not to mention that all of this makes the creature more visible and traceable—exactly what it does not want. A modern-day vampire would still have Dracula's problem."

"So what's the solution?"

"Good question. I think we should all think about that one for next time."

"You're all set."

Tom had set up the spare machine in Mike's office. The network cabling had already been installed for the new machine that hadn't arrived yet, but Tom had installed a fast modem at

Mike's request. "Just don't let anyone see this, or they'll assume you've already got a machine and they'll give your new computer to someone else."

"Not to worry. And . . . thanks, Tom."

"Just let me know how it works out, whatever it is."

Mike managed a weak smile. "You'll be the second to know."

When Tom was gone Mike flipped the power on and brought up the system. It ran an older version of the campus system software, but it worked. Mike connected his machine to the remote computer with a few memorized commands and then started the file transfer. After a few minutes the screen flashed a message.

«TRANSFER COMPLETE»

Mike reached for the cable connection, then hesitated. He had the file, but files were copied, not transferred physically. There had to be more to it than simply possessing the file, and odds are he would have only one chance to get it right.

*I have to be sure.*

He did a search of the directory and finally identified the file:

rwx-rx-rx bin June 1994 coffin.nail

A binary file, then. A program. Mike took a deep breath and activated the file. For a few long moments nothing happened, then the modem lights began to flash again on their own, bringing something else across the wires. Mike smiled.

*So that's how it works. Ingenious . . .*

Mike waited as long as he dared, then put his fingers to the keyboard and felt a shock, numbing his fingers to the wrist. The numbness grew higher, creeping up his arms like a glacier. His hands would not lift from the keyboard, though he could still move his fingers. Mike prayed that would be enough. A message came up on his screen and the computer's small speaker repeated it in hissing tones.

THANK YOU FOR THE INVITATION.

"So kind of you to come," Mike said, though his teeth were chattering with fear and cold. "Thank you."

FOOL! YOU'RE MINE. IT'S ALREADY BEGUN.

"I thought 'the blood is the life.' Has that changed, too?"

LIFE IS THE LIFE. THAT NEVER CHANGES,
AND THERE'S MORE THAN ONE WAY TO TAKE WHAT I
    NEED. . . .

*And more than one way to stop it.* Mike typed out the code. He had no sensation at all in his hands; it was like trying to type with a handful of icicles but he managed to get the command in:

CROSSES.BIN

Mike punched down on the «ENTER» key and the computer's small speaker shrieked like a soul in torment. The sound was almost painful but Mike wasn't listening now—every free memory location in the computer suddenly filled with a new pattern. Mike felt a great rush of relief as he saw the result; even the machine's video memory locations were affected, echoing the pattern over and over across the entire display:

```
00011000
00011000
11111111
00011000
00011000
00011000
00011000
```

The compulsion to remain at the keyboard was weakened, but it still took every ounce of Mike's will to jerk his hands away from the keyboard and free himself from contact with the creature. He breathed a silent thanks to Tom's programming skills. The crosses would probably be enough to contain the creature but there were no guarantees. Mike's fingers were still a little numb, but with a little fumbling, he managed to pull the phone plug out of the modem, breaking the connection completely. "Gotcha."

The cross pattern obliterated the words a second after they appeared, the echo from the speaker was gibberish.

### I WIO11LL OO DESTROY 11 YOU!

"I don't think so," Mike said as he rubbed some feeling back into his hands. He opened a drawer in his desk and pulled out a small stoppered bottle. "I couldn't quite figure out what a virtual stake would be, but I'm betting this stuff still works well enough. This is for Elizabeth Simmons, by the way." He opened the bottle and held it over the computer. "In case you wondered. It is, unfortunately, the most I can do now. Damn you and me both."

The screen was still garbled, crosses flashing across the screen in near-random patterns, but another message managed to get through.

### WHOOO11AREOO YOU???

"Dr. Michael Van Helsing. And the answer is 'yes.' My great-grandfather."

There was nothing showing now on the screen except the flashing crosses. The first searing drops of holy water rained down and soon the sparks and flames of the dying beast rose up to meet them.

# Setup

## Rick Hautala

I don't spoze there's anyone that thought Ed Marlboro didn't have to die.

Wait a second, that sounds kinda confusing, don't it?

Must be a double negative in there or something. People are always telling me I use them "double negatives," but I ain't too sure what they mean by that.

What I mean is, just about everyone I know pretty much wanted Ed Marlboro to die.

Well, maybe not *die*, actually, but I figured, sooner or later, something was gonna have to happen to such a royal pain in the butt.

It's just one of them inevitable things in life, you know? . . . like taxes and the Mets sucking.

I guess I'm a little upset that *I* had to do it, but—as far as I could see—no one else was quite up to the task.

So once I decided to do it, the only other question, really, was *how* to do it.

One thing I sure as heck didn't want was for me to get caught at it. It didn't make no sense for me to rot away in jail for the rest of my life when I'd only gone and done what everyone else at the newspaper wanted done anyway.

A'course, at the time, I didn't talk this over with anyone.

Tell no secrets, and leave no witnesses, my mama always used to tell me.

I had to figure out the best way to do it with the least chance of me getting caught . . . but still, I wanted to make sure Ed got what he deserved, okay?

And I didn't want no half-assed attempt that was gonna backfire on me, neither.

Lemme back pedal here just a touch.

My name's Tom Martin, and I work at the *Portland Sentinel*, one of the local newspapers here in town.

No, I ain't no reporter.

What, you thought I was? . . . The way I talk?

You make me laugh.

No, I been working at the newspaper for a lot of years, doing general clean up . . . janitorial-type stuff.

I never could write no good. Probably never will be able to, neither. I never got beyond third grade, and I didn't even do all that hot in there.

But take Ed, now.

He's a real reporter, a real smart guy. He can read 'n write *real* good. 'Least, that's what people 'round the office are always saying. I think he even got some awards for what he wrote.

The thing of it is, though, if you ask me, Ed thinks he's some kinda big shot. Heck, even if you *don't* ask me, I'll tell you that.

Working 'round the office, a'course I hear plenty of stuff. All sorts of rumors and gossip and such. I probably know more about some people's lives than they know about themselves.

Anyways, this guy Ed's been a real pain in the butt to just everyone there, but 'specially to Nancy Garvey.

She's one of the secretaries there. Real pretty lady.

Yeah, I *do* kinda like her.

How'd you guess?

I guess you have to be pretty smart to be a detective, too, huh?

Oh, yeah . . . sure—Ed was mean to me. More often than not, though, he pretty much just ignored me. Every now and again he'd get it into his head to get on my case about something or other. 'Specially once he figured out I was kinda sweet on Nancy.

Lots of times, whenever there was something missing from his desk or something, he'd accuse me of swiping it or—you know, of throwing it away when I was emptying wastebaskets or something. He called me "dumb" a lot of times, too, but I learned to ignore that from just about everybody.

A'course I wouldn't never do nothing like steal from him. My mama taught me that stealing ain't right.

Oh, yeah, sure—she taught me 'bout how it ain't no good to kill no one, either, but—well, with Ed, I figured even the God my mama was always praying to would see that there's always gotta be exceptions.

Is that the right word?

*Exceptions?*

Yeah, I guess so.

But I didn't do this, trying to impress Nancy, like you suggested earlier.

Heck no!

I don't think she even knows I like her.

But anyways, like I said, I was casting about, trying to think of some way I could get rid of Ed.

Right off the bat, I decided not to use any of them usual ways you see all the time on TV and in movies—you know, guns, knives . . . stuff like that. And I didn't want to run him over with a car, neither. A'course, I don't even know how to drive, so that wouldn't've been no good, anyway.

When I heard a couple of the secretaries in the office talking about that place just out of town, that haunted house, I figured that might be the way to go.

I'm sure you've heard of this place, ain't you?

It's that big old house out in Gorham, on Route 25. It's right by some old cemetery or something, and it's spozed to be haunted.

Hell, no. I don't believe it's *really* haunted.

Matter of fact, I know it ain't 'cause I went out there one night not too long ago and talked with the lady who lives there.

I had to set the whole thing up with her first, you see.

I introduced myself and told her that I had this friend—a newspaper reporter—who was investigating . . .

That's the right word, ain't it? *Investigate?*

Yeah—okay.

Well, you must remember how, a couple of years ago, there was all them kids who disappeared out that way. Wasn't it something like ten kids in just a couple of months? The whole state was in an uproar about it.

Anyways, I told this lady that I had a friend who was investigating what might've happened to them kids, and that I wanted to play a practical joke on him. I figured it all out with her that we could set something up to scare Ed . . . maybe even scare him to death.

That's what I was hoping, anyway.

At first she didn't cotton to the idea. She said she lived alone way out there 'cause she didn't want any other people around. I couldn't quite figure out why 'cause she was—well, you know, she was kinda pretty.

Yeah, *sexy* is a word that might describe her, but *you* said it first.

She offered me something to drink, and after that, she finally agreed to help me out. Actually, we got to be pretty good friends that night, 'cause when I was leaving, she even gave me a little kiss.

No, not on the mouth. On the neck.

I ain't never been kissed like that by no lady before . . . 'cept my mama, of course, but that don't rightly count.

I figured I could cook up some wacky-doodle story about that house to get Ed to go out there with me. I could tell him that the place was haunted or something, and that he should do a story about it. Might even win another one of them awards.

Sure, it was gonna take some convincing, but I figured I'd make up something real good that would bring him out there.

'Course, as it turned out, things got a little more serious than I intended.

I got Ed out there a couple of nights later, all right. He and I drove together 'cause, like I said, I ain't got no driver's license.

I could tell by the way Ed was treating me that he didn't really believe none of what I was telling him, but I told him I'd been out there and seen some really *weird* things. I couldn't think exactly what to tell him, so I just said I wanted him to see for himself.

He went along with it 'cause—you know, Halloween's coming up, and he must've figured he'd at least get an interesting article in the paper or something.

When we got there, I was scared that the lady wasn't going to go along with what we planned. She was supposed to be hiding upstairs and jump out at us as soon as we went up the stairs, but she answered the door right away when we first knocked.

I thought maybe we were too early, or that I'd gotten the wrong day . . . or that she had forgot all about it.

Right away, though, I could tell that *something* was wrong. For one thing, she didn't look quite right.

She'd been real pretty the first time I seen her, but now—I don't know, she didn't look so good.

Kinda sickly.

Her skin was real pale—almost white, and her teeth . . . her teeth looked kinda funny whenever she looked at me and smiled.

I didn't even get to say nothing to her, though, before she attacked Ed.

*Attacked.*

Yeah, *attacked* is the right word.

She was just standing there in the doorway, looking at the both of us and smiling at us, and all of a sudden she just went for Ed's throat.

It all happened so fast, I didn't know what was happening. I barely had time to react.

At first I thought she had come up with something better than what we'd planned, but after a moment or two, I knew something was seriously wrong.

You're a cop, right? So you must've seen some of them pictures they took of Ed.

She just grabbed onto him and hugged him real tight with both arms.

At first I just stood there, thinking I wished she'd a held me like that, but after a minute or so, I saw that Ed or she was bleeding.

One of 'em was, anyway.

I couldn't move, I was so scared.

I just stood there, watching what she was doing. Ed tried to fight back, but it was like she was too strong for him.

She had her face pressed real hard against his neck and was making all these strange sucking and moaning sounds, like she was really enjoying herself.

After a couple more seconds . . . I don't know, it might've been longer, but once Ed's face was—God! It was bone white. Then he just sort of folded up and fell down on the front steps. His feet were hanging out over the edge of the stairs, still twitching like he was being 'lectrocuted.

When she looked at me, her face was all smeared with blood, and she was smiling something wicked. Her teeth looked really funny—glistening like sharp little pieces of bone sticking up out of a bloody wound.

It scared the bejezus out of me, I don't mind saying.

I don't remember what I said to her . . . if anything.

I looked at Ed, thinking she was gonna do the same thing to me; but after a second or two, she wiped her mouth with the back of her hand and smacked her lips.

"Satisfied?" she said.

It still gives me terrible shivers to remember what her voice sounded like, all gurgley like her throat was full of water.

But I knew it wasn't water.

I know I didn't say anything to her after that.

God, I couldn't hardly breathe.

I just stood there, looking down at Ed's body, lying there in the doorway.

I knew he was dead, and I remember thinking that maybe Nancy would be real happy about it when she found out. At least he wouldn't be bothering her at work no more.

I started backing up away from her real slow, but she just stood there in the doorway, watching me. I didn't like the way her eyes looked all silvery and shiny.

Just before she closed the door, she said something else to me, something about how she was angry that she was going to have to move again. But the last thing I heard her say was that she was sure we'd see each other again.

Real soon.

I didn't know how to drive the car, so I had to hitchhike all the way back to my place in Portland.

Right after I got home, I called you guys to go out there and find Ed.

I didn't mean for it to happen quite the way it did, so I don't see why you're keeping me here in jail.

It's gonna be daylight soon, and I'm feeling kinda . . . I don't know, kinda tired and . . . and really thirsty.

Oh, yeah—I know I shouldn't have set Ed up like that, but you have to believe me that I didn't mean to kill him.

Besides, I didn't do it.

She did.

Is it my fault that you can't find her?

Sure, I shouldn't have set Ed up like that, but I didn't have no idea she was gonna do something like that.

You have to believe me when I say how much I regret it. Heck, there's *lots* of things I shouldn't have done.

I probably shouldn't have let her kiss me that first night when I met her, either.

And I know darned well that I shouldn't've had that drink with her!

Could you step a little closer to the bars here?

I'm *really* thirsty!

# Single White Vampire

### GARY JONAS

**K**evin Bradford couldn't believe his luck. He'd answered a personal ad and wound up getting a date with a gorgeous blonde named Virginia. She'd called him at work to set up a meeting time. The date was fantastic. Virginia was intelligent, witty, and fun. He didn't want the evening to end, but it was late, so he took her home.

"I had a great time tonight," he said. They were sitting in his car in front of her apartment building. "I'd love to see you again. If you're willing, that is."

Virginia hesitated, then nodded. "You can call me, if you like."

Kevin smiled. He couldn't believe his luck. A beautiful woman wanted him to call her. All he could think was: Wow! But he kept his wits enough not to vocalize that thought; he'd eaten his shoe enough already tonight.

"I guess I should give you my number," she said. "But I just got the phone and the number is upstairs. I can't remember it."

Great, Kevin thought. He just knew she was scrambling for an excuse not to give it to him. He'd bored her to tears. She thought he was a moron. A fool.

"So," she continued, "maybe you'd like to come upstairs for a few. We can have a drink and I'll find the number."

"I understand," he began, then realized what she'd said. Quick save time. "Uh, I've had my phone for years and I still can't remember the number."

"Really? I was going to ask for it."

"555-2341."

Virginia smiled. "Coming?"

Her apartment was small—cozy. She didn't have much furniture and no pictures adorned the walls. It lacked the feel of being lived in. Kevin reminded himself that she was new in town. Maybe her stuff hadn't arrived from New York.

"Grab yourself a beer if you like," she said.

Kevin walked into the kitchen and tugged open the refrigerator door. The metal bar on the inside of the door fell off and the contents crashed to the floor. Kevin jumped back. "Oops!"

"What happened?" Virginia asked, running into the room.

Kevin looked up sheepishly. "I'm sorry, the bar came off and—"

"Oh no." Virginia closed her eyes and sighed.

The bottles of ketchup, mustard, and mayonnaise survived the crash, but the bottle of cherry Gatorade broke. So did two other bottles labeled AB.

"Back up," Virginia said. "You don't want to cut yourself. There are some towels in that bottom drawer. Hand them to me."

Kevin found the towels and passed them to her. He knelt and began picking up shards of glass. "This looks like blood," he said.

She shot him a look. "What?"

"Uh, nothing. I just said it looks kinda like blood."

"It isn't."

"I know, but it looks like it. What is it?"

"Gatorade."

"Sure, some of it, but not all. It's too thick."

He dipped a finger into the redness and touched his tongue. "Jesus!" he said. "This *is* blood! What the hell?"

"I can explain," Virginia said, rising.

Kevin backed away from her. "Okay," he said. "What are you doing with blood in your refrigerator?"

"I'm type AB. It's very rare and last year I had an accident. I almost died because they couldn't find a donor. Now I keep some on hand, just in case."

It didn't ring true, but Kevin wanted to believe her. She was so gorgeous! "I'm type O," he said for no reason.

"I know."

"You do?"

"Not that you were O," she said, though he could tell she was lying. "Just that you weren't AB."

Kevin nodded. "Okay." The way she looked at him, he felt certain he'd have nightmares. He had to lighten the mood, so he cracked a little joke. "You act like you're a vampire or something."

She stared at him. "What did you say?"

He backed up a step, then shook his head and smiled. "You had me going for a second."

She smiled, too, and looked almost relieved. "You're pretty gullible, Kevin. Vampire indeed."

"You don't have fangs," he said and laughed. "Plus, I talked to you this morning on the phone and if you were a vampire, you'd have been tucked away in your coffin."

"No coffins here," she said with a sweeping gesture that took in the entire apartment.

"Yeah. Uh . . . I'd better go."

Amazingly enough, Virginia accepted a second date with him the next night. Maybe no one was calling her about her ad. Maybe she just liked him. Kevin wasn't sure. On the drive over, the radio announcer recapped the big news story of the day: Five gang members had been slain—one of them drained of blood. The crime took place only a few blocks from Virginia's apartment. He made a mental note to tell her to be careful.

She wasn't ready when he knocked on her door. "Come on in," she said. "I'll finish getting dressed."

He waited in the living room. There were no magazines to look at except a copy of the *Singles Preview* where he'd seen Virginia's personal. It still bugged him to stoop to a singles mag to get a date.

Someone knocked on Virginia's door.

"Could you answer that?" Virginia called.

116

"Sure," Kevin said, hoping she hadn't accepted a date with someone else. That could prove awkward.

He opened the door and his jaw dropped.

Elvis Presley stood in the doorway, a smirk on his face.

Kevin stared at him a moment—took in the wide girth, the sequined jumpsuit, the trademark sideburns. "Elvis?"

"Uh-huh-huh," Elvis said.

Kevin blinked, stepped back. What should he say?

A man wearing a snakeskin jacket, Tony Llama boots, faded blue jeans, and a big white Stetson squeezed in front of Elvis. "Howdy," he said. "Ginny around?"

"Who are you?" Kevin asked.

"Name's Jake. The big guy's name is Bob." Jake leaned forward. "He wants to be an Elvis impersonator, but we don't hold it against him none."

Kevin turned. "Virginia, could you come out here, please?"

Virginia stepped out of the bathroom. "Oh my God," she said. "Jake and Bob!"

"Howdy, ma'am. Ol' Nate wants you to come on back to the big city."

"Kevin, get rid of them!"

"Me?" Kevin backed toward her. "What's going on here?" he asked.

"Ginny, this skinny little runt ain't gonna be able to protect you. Come peaceable like and no one gets hurt."

"Uh-huh-huh," Bob said and smiled revealing fangs. He looked at Virginia and sang to the tune of "Hound Dog":

> I ain't nothin' but a vampire
> And you could be my wife
> I ain't nothin' but a vampire
> And you could be my wife
> But if you try and run
> I'll put an end to your life.

Virginia grabbed Kevin. "Meet me at your car," she whispered. Then she shoved him toward the two vampires and slammed the bathroom door.

Jake and Bob didn't waste time on Kevin. Jake pushed him out of the way and launched himself at the bathroom door.

Kevin screamed and ran out of the apartment and down the three flights of stairs to the ground level. When he reached his car, Virginia was already there waiting.

"How did you . . . ?"

"I'll explain later, let's get out of here!"

"Vampires?" Kevin said.

He sat on his futon couch, safe in his suburban home. Virginia sat in a chair across from him. "That's right. You saw them."

"I don't know what I saw. Could have been fake teeth. You expect me to believe in vampires?"

She nodded. "We exist."

Kevin shook his head. "You aren't a vampire."

She opened her mouth and extended her fangs.

"Whoa!" Kevin said. "But I talked to you in the daytime. You'd have burned to ashes or something!"

Virginia rolled her eyes. "That's so Hollywood."

"What?"

"In the daytime we're like regular people. At night, we have supernatural powers."

"But you ate regular food."

"For appearances. We can eat and digest food, even though we don't have to."

"So you, like, drink blood?"

"Preferably type AB. Other types upset my stomach, but they'll do in a pinch."

"That's gross!" Kevin said. "So what's the deal here. Why do they want you?"

"The man who turned me into a vampire doesn't want me to be free. He sent Jake and Bob to capture me and take me back. At the start, I guess I thought Nathaniel and I were going to be husband and wife, but what he wanted was a mistress. A sex slave who would never lose her beauty."

"Jesus."

"Sucks, doesn't it?"

Kevin didn't want to admit how cool it would be to have a sex slave who would never grow old, so he nodded. "Yeah."

"Well, Nate grew tired of me, so I took what cash I could find, packed my supply of AB, and took off. I knew they'd look for me, but I thought I could keep a supply of blood on hand—avoid killing anyone."

"And I broke your only two bottles."

"That's right. I had to kill last night to survive."

"You killed someone who answered your personal?"

She laughed. "Actually, I killed some gang members who attacked me."

"Oh. That's okay then."

"How do you figure?"

"Self-defense." Kevin rubbed his chin. "So what happens now?"

"Now we have to be ready for Nate. Jake and Bob will call him in now that I've been located."

"They can't find us here."

"Hate to tell you this, but once they found out what city I was in, it was easy to trace me. Vampires can always find their own. They'll be here in no time."

Kevin was ready for action when the doorbell rang. Bob stood waiting with Jake. "Where's this Nathaniel guy?" Kevin asked.

"In the car," Bob said. "Virginia needs to come outside now."

"No," Kevin said. "Nathaniel has to come in here to get her. But before you go get him, I gotta ask you. Why Elvis?"

"He's the King," Bob said. "He and I have a lot in common. I even have type O blood. Just like Elvis."

"I'm type O too, pal. It just so happens to be the most common blood type."

"I'm not liking you much," Bob said.

"Get Ginny out here," Jake said.

Kevin smiled. Feeling smug, he said, "You're vampires. You can't come into my house without an invitation."

Jake frowned. "What, you think we're polite or something?" He shoved Kevin back, stepping into the house. "Ginny!" Jake called. "Come on out! Nate's waitin' in the car and he's mad enough to eat the Devil, horns and all."

But Nathaniel didn't wait in the car. He entered the house behind Jake and Bob. Kevin stared in awe at the master vampire.

Nathaniel was slender, but seemed to radiate power. He

looked distinguished with a touch of gray at the temples. His eyes gleamed with dark wisdom. "Where is she?" he said.

Kevin found that he could not deny this man anything. "Upstairs, sir."

"Get your butt outta the way," Jake said and shoved Kevin again.

Nathaniel glided up the stairs with grace and a motion born of fluidity. "Virginia, you have kept me waiting. You know I don't appreciate such behavior."

Jake and Bob followed Nathaniel up the stairs. At the same instant Jake reached into his snakeskin jacket and Bob reached into his sequined jumpsuit and they pulled out short wooden stakes.

Kevin put a hand to his face. They weren't planning to capture her; they intended to kill her! And there was nothing he could do to stop them.

Virginia appeared at the top of the stairs, her hands behind her as she gazed at Nathaniel. "I'm sorry if I upset you," she said.

"You should be sorry," Nathaniel said. "I've decided to end your existence. I've found another woman to take your place. One who won't defy me." Nathaniel looked back at Jake and Bob. He smiled when he saw the stakes already in their hands.

"You ready?" Jake said.

Nathaniel nodded. "I am."

Virginia grinned. "Now!" she yelled and pulled a stake of her own from behind her back. She, Jake, and Bob all lunged at Nathaniel and slammed their stakes into his body. He screamed in agony as one punctured his heart. He clawed at them, but his strength faded quickly and he crumpled to his knees. He looked at Jake and Bob in wonderment, then toppled backward and slid down the stairs, coming to rest at Kevin's feet.

Kevin looked up at the three vampires. "You had this planned all along?"

They all nodded. "We were sick of being ordered around," Bob said. "I wanted to go to Vegas and fulfill my desire to be the King." He smiled. "I'm free at last. Uh-huh-huh!"

Jake grinned and removed his Stetson. "I took a liking to a cowgirl, but Nate wouldn't let me have her. Now he ain't got no say in the matter."

Virginia came down the stairs and embraced Kevin. "You were perfect," she said.

"Huh?"

"Nathaniel was powerful enough to read mortal minds. Centuries of practice. You believed the whole gig so he did, too. We had to lure him out of his mansion where he had too many loyal servants."

"You used me," Kevin said.

"To a degree, yes. However, you remember the LTR part of my ad?"

Kevin nodded. "Long term relationship?"

"That's right," Virginia said. "With emphasis on the long. How would you like to become one of us?"

"Say what?" Kevin gazed into her beautiful blue eyes. He felt as if he were falling in love with her, but he wasn't sure if it was natural or some sort of hypnosis on her part. Couldn't vampires seduce with a glance? Hmm. Maybe he could do that, too.

Virginia smiled. "Do you want to live forever?"

# Worthy of His Hire

LAWRENCE WATT-EVANS

Mike thought he heard something; he looked up from the kitchen table and saw the water leaking out under the cabinet door, but for a moment it didn't register. Water on the floor? Had something spilled?

Then he realized that the water was coming pretty fast, and there was a lot of it, and he decided that he'd better check, right *now*. He dashed to the sink, knelt down, and opened the cabinet.

Once the door was open he could hear the hissing clearly; he pushed aside a soggy roll of paper towels and saw the water spraying from the cracked copper pipe.

"Damn," he said. It must have burst when he got that drink of water a few minutes ago.

He'd have to turn it off at the main valve; that would hold it until morning. He could call a plumber—some of them advertised twenty-four-hour emergency service, but he knew that usually meant they'd take a message now and send someone in the morning.

He stood and hurried for the main shut-off valve in the basement.

As he stumbled down the cellar stairs he cursed quietly to himself. This is what he got for buying this house. The ad had called it a "handyman special"; he should have known it was trouble.

He wasn't much of a handyman, really—they just hadn't been able to afford anything better and hadn't wanted to rent any more. Maggie had *so* wanted a house of their own!

Well, she had it now—and she was up in bed, probably asleep by now, as any sensible person would be at this godforsaken hour of 1:30 in the morning. She didn't know that something else had gone wrong with her suburban dream.

He pushed aside a box of Christmas lights and found the valve; he grabbed the rusty knob and turned it, hard.

Metal groaned, and the knob snapped off in his hand.

He stared at it in horror.

"Oh, my *God!*" he said.

He dropped the broken valve and ran for the stairs.

His first stop was the broom closet, where he snatched up the big mop bucket. Then came the cabinet under the kitchen sink, where he shoved the bucket under the leak, and almost broke his neck sliding on the wet floor—the puddle now covered everything from the refrigerator to the end of the counter, and it was creeping toward the breakfast table at an alarming rate. Then he splashed his way over to the phone, hauled the yellow pages out of the drawer, and opened it to "Plumbing."

Half a dozen ads in the first few pages listed "24-Hour Emergency Service," as he had expected. George Miller & Sons, heretofore his regular plumber, was not one of them—he knew that he'd just get an answering machine there. He'd settled on Miller because he was reliable and didn't charge an arm and a leg, not because he was convenient.

He looked over the ads, trying to clear enough of the panic out of his thoughts to decide who to call, and his gaze fell on a neat little box in the bottom corner of one page.

"Midnight Plumbers," it said. "Open 8 P.M. to 5 A.M. Why

pay extra for nighttime service? Late-night emergencies are our specialty. Over fifty years experience." And the address was only a dozen blocks away.

It sounded too good to be true. Mike punched the number into the phone.

He expected it to ring half a dozen times, or to connect him to an answering machine, but instead it was picked up on the first buzz, and a voice that did not sound at all like a machine said, "Hello?"

He didn't mention the company name—a bad sign. "Is this Midnight Plumbing?" he asked.

"Yes, sir, Midnight Plumbing, Al speaking."

"Listen, I've got a burst pipe here, and the main shut-off is broken—how soon can you get someone here?"

"Where are you, sir?"

Mike gave his address.

"I'll be there in ten minutes, sir."

"Fine, I . . . wait. Is this going to cost me an arm and a leg?"

He heard a chuckle from the other end of the line. "Not exactly. I think you'll find our rates quite reasonable. And our work is guaranteed one hundred percent."

"All right."

"Ten minutes, then." With a click, Al hung up.

"Honey? Who were you talking to?" Maggie called from upstairs.

Mike hesitated, then shrugged and called back, "The plumber, dear. We've got a broken pipe."

Then he slogged across the kitchen and looked under the sink. The bucket was more than half full already; he dumped it quickly and slid it back into position.

Maggie appeared in the kitchen doorway. "A leak?" Then she saw the puddle. "Oh, damn. How bad is it?"

"*Very* bad," Mike told her, "but the plumber says he'll be here in ten minutes."

"Well, let's mop up some of the water, then." She headed for the broom closet.

No more than eight minutes after Mike had hung up the phone, the doorbell rang. He looked out the window.

The van at the curb didn't have a company name on it, but

it otherwise looked like a plumber's truck; a rack on the roof held a ladder and several lengths of PVC pipe.

The man at the door was tall and thin and pale, not the usual hale, hearty, and hairy sort of plumber, but he wore gray overalls and black boots and a tool belt, and carried a steel box.

"Hi," he said. "I'm Al, from Midnight Plumbing—you the guy that called?"

A minute or so after that Al looked at the broken shut-off valve, shook his head, and said, "You wouldn't happen to know where the water company's shut-off is, would you? The outside one, like a little tiny manhole cover?"

"Not exactly," Mike admitted. "Somewhere in the sidewalk, maybe."

"I'll find it."

"Need a flashlight?"

"No, thanks."

Mike assumed that Al had his own flashlight, but if so, he didn't use it; he found the outside shut-off in the dark and did something to it with a huge black T-shaped thing.

The hissing from under the sink began to fade.

That done, Al came back up to the door.

"Now," he said, "before we go any further, it's time to talk about price."

Mike cringed. "You *do* charge an arm and a leg," he said.

"Nope," Al said. "Just blood. Plus parts."

Mike blinked. He supposed that was meant as a joke, but it wasn't funny. "Ah . . . how much?" he asked.

"I figure for this job, about two pints would be fair—I saw your wife in there, that'd be one from you, one from her. Plus five bucks for parts."

For a moment the two men stood in utter silence as Mike gaped at Al. At last he said, "What?"

Patiently, Al explained, "I'll fix your leak, replace the supply line to the sink and the main shut-off valve, for two pints of fresh human blood and five dollars for the parts."

"*Blood?*"

Al sighed. "I'm a vampire," he said. He bared his fangs. "See?"

Mike backed away, trying to remember where he'd put his grandmother's rosary.

"Look, it's like this," Al explained. "Most vampires, they figure hey, I'm a dread creature of the night, I've got hypnotic powers, I can turn into a bat or a mist, I have a supernatural appeal to the opposite sex, I can take whatever I want, as long as I want! So they go around preying on people, and sooner or later people get mad, and next thing you know the vampire's got a stake through his heart and his head cut off. That's not for me, thanks. If you want to get by you can't just take what you want, you've gotta give something back. So fifty or sixty years ago I sat down and thought it over and tried to figure out what I, as a vampire, could do that people would want enough that they'd pay blood for it."

"Plumbing?" Mike gasped. "You decided on plumbing?"

"Sure. I saw that one thing I had was that I was up all night, when most folks weren't, and I tried to figure out how I could use that. I didn't see much use for turning to a bat or a mist, and hypnotizing guys or seducing women just gets other people ticked off—I can't hypnotize *everyone*, and sooner or later there's some smartass with a sharpened stake who gets angry because his secretary's mooning about with a pair of holes in her neck."

"Plumbing," Mike said.

"Plumbing," Al agreed. "And locksmithing, too. And I'm on call to chauffeur sick pets to the animal hospital—regular ambulances won't do that."

"And you take payment in blood."

"Sure. Not enough to do any real harm—I mean, you've probably donated a pint or two to Red Cross, right?"

"You're really a vampire? You sleep in a coffin and everything?"

"In a spare tool locker, actually. So, is it a deal? Two pints and the cost of the parts and I fix your little problem here?"

Mike glanced toward the kitchen and remembered the spreading puddle.

"It's a deal," he said.

An hour later the pipe and valve were replaced and the water back on, and Mike watched woozily as Al bent over an all-too-willing Margaret's throat and sucked thirstily.

Looking at Margaret's expression, Mike could see how people would be jealous of vampires. He began thinking vaguely in terms of wooden stakes himself.

It was as if Al had heard his thoughts. The vampire looked up, Margaret's blood dribbling down his chin.

"Just remember," Al said, "how hard it is to get a *human* plumber at this hour!" Then he turned, wiped his mouth with a rag from his back pocket, checked to be sure he had the five-dollar bill Mike had given him, packed up his tools, and left.

Mike thought about that, and remembered all the years of waiting until morning, of staying home from work to let trades-men in, of paying outrageous prices. As the door closed behind the vampire Mike called after him, "Don't worry!"

And a moment later, as he helped Margaret up to bed, Mike laughed. "He charged us for parts," he said. "At least he didn't want an arm and a leg!"

# Night Flight

## MIKE BAKER

I hate flying," the polyester-clad man said as he settled into seat 11A and fastened his safety belt. "It really sucks the big one, if you know what I mean." Flashing a wide grin, exposing a set of the finest, brightest, whitest teeth that money can buy, he turned to face the well-dressed, overweight man squeezed into the too-tight confines of seat 11B. "It's a necessary evil, though, right pal. If you want to stay on top of things, you've got to hit the air."

The overweight man's head turned, his attention shifting away from the service tray inset in the back of the seat in front of him.

"Coleman's the name," the polyester-clad man said. "Lee Coleman." Raising a bright pink, fleshy, diamond-studded 14k-gold pinky-ring-bedecked hand from his lap, he extended it toward his seatmate.

The overweight man's beady eyes, which were nearly as dark as the night outside the plane's window, glanced down at

Coleman's hand, then up at his puffy, bestubbled face. "It is a pleasure to meet you," he said, his slightly accented voice devoid of all emotion. Ignoring the proffered hand, he nodded his head ever so slightly, smiled a cold, tight-lipped smile, then returned his attention to the seatback in front of him.

Guy's got all the warmth of a snake, Coleman thought as he lowered his hand and scratched his leg with it, as if that had been the true reason for it being extended in the first place.

Coleman's rumpled off-the-rack Sears suit itched. He squirmed in his seat, trying vainly to find a comfortable position as the plane taxied down the runway and took off. Normally Coleman didn't mind business trips, especially ones that took him to Europe, but this one had been a real bust, bad news all the way. The foreign investors he'd spent years courting hadn't merely said no to his proposal for installing easy-listening music systems in world-class museums—first up, the Louvre—they'd shown outright contempt toward both the project and him. A couple even seemed so put out by the idea that if a pistol had been handy, Coleman figured they probably would have shot him right then and there.

Deciding that it was best if he just cut and ran, he'd checked out of his hotel earlier than planned and booked a flight on the next available plane home.

Yawning, Coleman cast a sideways glance at his seatmate; he was still staring intently at the seatback, as if the serving tray were inscribed with writing only he could read.

Might as well get some sleep, Coleman thought. Closing his eyes, he reached for the button that would recline his seat.

"I do not care for airplanes," the overweight man suddenly said, catching Coleman by surprise. Eyes snapping open, he sat up straight, smiling at his seatmate as he did.

"I do not care for them one bit," the overweight man continued. "They are never punctual." As if to drive home his point, the overweight man glanced at his watch, a plain-faced platinum Bulova, then shook his head, uttering a disgusted snort as he did. Reaching inside his perfectly tailored suit, he withdrew a silk handkerchief he used to blot the beads of sweat that had formed on his brow.

"You hit the nail on the head there, buddy," Coleman replied, relieved that a conversation had finally begun. If there was one thing he hated to do on airplanes, it was sleep; every time he did he woke up cramped, cranky, and, more often than not, more tired then when he first closed his eyes. "That two-hour delay before takeoff was inexcusable. Happens all the time, though. Once, when I was flying out of O'Hare—"

The overweight man spoke again, his deep, smooth voice cutting into Coleman's ramblings like a knife. "I should not have taken this flight," he said, speaking more to himself than to Coleman.

"Why's that?"

Ignoring Coleman's question, the overweight man looked at his watch yet again. "I do not care for airplanes," he said, bringing the conversation back to where it had begun. That done, he returned his attention to the seatback.

Deciding that he'd rather risk cramped muscles and a sore back then try to pry anything else out of his stuck-up, eccentric flying companion, Coleman leaned back, lowered his seat, and closed his eyes.

Four hours later Coleman was jostled back to reality when the plane bounced through some turbulence. He glanced down at his watch, a full-service digital wonder with thirty-six functions (or so the salesman had said; so far Lee had only been able to get it to display the time, date, and relative barometric pressure), which he had reset to New York time before takeoff. It said five-thirty, which meant that they were about a half-hour away from landing.

Raising his seatback, Coleman cast a quick glance at his neighbor. The overweight man appeared to be in a highly agitated state, as if he were extremely nervous about something. His beady-eyed gaze darted about the plane, then shot back to his watch every few seconds. Rivulets of sweat rolled down the overweight man's pale face, passing tightly clenched bloodless lips to settle in the folds of his triple chins.

Fear of flying, Coleman thought. Wimp.

The overweight man's head turned toward Coleman. "It is as I feared," he gravely announced. "Our flight is behind schedule."

"So what's new about that," Coleman replied. "No flight is ever on time; it's one of life's unwritten laws."

"You fail to understand," the overweight man cried. "I can't be late."

"Hey, I understand," Coleman said, nodding his head sagely. "There's a guy I work with just like you; if he's so much as a second late to anything, he gets all paranoid. It's just a minor phobia, nothing to be afraid of. Besides, we aren't going to be *that* late; the way I figure it, we'll be landing just after dawn."

Cringing at Coleman's words, the overweight man ran his sodden silk handkerchief across his brow, his fear-filled beady black eyes darting to his watch as he did.

"Good morning ladies and gentlemen," a tinny-sounding voice announced over the cabin's speakers. "This is your captain speaking. I'm afraid I've got a bit of bad news for you. The fog's a bit heavy over Kennedy Airport right now, and it's caused a bit of a backup. There shouldn't be too much of a delay, though; the sun will be up soon, and that ought to clear—"

The overweight man's terror-filled scream drowned out the rest of the captain's speech. Fingers as thick as sausages clawed at the seatbelt embedded in his prodigious stomach in a desperate attempt to unfasten it.

A stewardess suddenly appeared. She leaned over the overweight man, giving Coleman a much-appreciated glimpse inside her blouse, reciting reassuring clichés as she did in an effort to calm the overweight man before his panic spread to the other passengers.

"Help me," the overweight man wailed as his sweat slick fingertips slid across the smooth metal of the seatbelt clasp, failing to gain purchase. "I beg of you, set me free before it is too late."

Isn't this just the perfect ending to the worst day of my life, Coleman mused. Disgusted and embarrassed by the scene the overweight man was causing, he tore his eyes away from the stewardess's cleavage and glared at him. "What is your problem?" he snapped, earning an angry glance from the stewardess in the process. "For God's sake, calm down."

"If you're seated on the right side of the aircraft," the captain announced over the speakers, "look out your window and you'll catch the start of a beautiful sunrise."

Shaking his head at the pathetic scene taking place beside him, Coleman reached for his lowered window shade.

Eyes growing wide with fear, the overweight man suddenly froze. "No!" he yelled. Shoving the stewardess back into the aisle with the sweeping wave of one arm, he reached for Coleman with the other just as the salesman raised the window shade.

Sunlight streamed in through the window, striking the overweight man's hand. Wherever the sun's rays touched, pale flesh burned.

Screaming, the overweight man yanked the charred remains of his hand out of the sunlight.

The stewardess fainted.

Gagging at the stench arising from the blackened flesh, Coleman shrank back into his seat in an effort to get as far away from his seatmate as was humanly possible.

Ignited by the overweight man's scream, the flames of panic spread through the airplane.

Outside, the sun continued to rise. As it did, its rays crept across Coleman's seat, inching closer and closer to the overweight man.

Equal measures of pain and fear lining his sweat-soaked face, the overweight man thrashed about in a frantic effort to escape from seat 11B.

Sunlight touched the armrest separating seats 11A and 11B.

Disengaged by a flailing hand, the overweight man's seatbelt clicked open.

Sunlight caressed the edge of the overweight man's slacks.

With a mighty burst of energy, the overweight man pulled himself free of the constricting confines of seat 11B, escaping from his flesh-searing foe. Gasping for breath, he stumbled into the aisle.

Its right wing dipping, the plane banked into a turn.

The sunlight leapt at the overweight man.

Wisps of smoke rose lazily from the collar and cuffs of the overweight man's suit as he fell to his knees in the aisle. Throwing his head back, baring his fangs, he screamed, "NOT LIKE THIS!!!" at the top of his lungs. An instant later his head caught fire, igniting as swiftly as dry tinder.

With a sickening crackle, what little remained of the overweight man's body collapsed in upon itself, falling to the floor to form a foul-smelling, smoldering pile of charred bone and ash.

Airborne ashes danced in the sunlight as Lee Coleman closed out his bad day in a fitting manner by throwing up all over his new suit.

# The Flame

FRED CHAPPELL

Many women are wonderfully attractive to men. Beautiful or unbeautiful, witty or dull, rich or penurious, they draw males to them and keep them about them the way the greater planets in our system capture and keep at arm's length rings of disappointed asteroids. But some women are attractive only to certain kinds of men. The leggy freckled blonde probably has an athlete or two awaiting her leisure, while the tweedy and precise brunette has gathered scholars to her like homely footnotes cuddling a dissertation. A cheerful mother once described her daughter as "working on her fourth banker." But for Andrea Greenleaf the situation was not so happy. Andrea attracted vampires—a half dozen or so at a time.

At first she had no idea that they were vampires, only that wherever she went at night—to films, to concerts, to the productions of the Gatesboro Opera Company, to restaurants—she always spotted two or three or even four pallid and slender men in dark suits who stared at her with fever-cold eyes. And then at midnight she would hear on the steep slate roof of the old house she had inherited from her Aunt Embry the muffled beat of pads and click of claws, and slitherings and shiftings unidentifiable but certainly unpleasant. As her house was situated on the outskirts of Gatesboro with no close neighbors, Andrea suffered a ragged nocturnal restlessness.

It was her friend Moon Crescent who enlightened her. "That man?" she asked, looking across the clattering restaurant to the gloomy thin man who sat at the bar, devoting all his disconcerting attention to Andrea. "He's a vampire, my dear. He calls himself Count Estragu, though of course that's not what

131

his mother named him, any more than mine named me Moon Crescent. He's quite well known in Gatesboro—in some circles, I mean." She patted Andrea's hand in a rather patronizing manner and added: "Not in yours."

Though she couldn't help feeling a small seethe of impatience, Andrea would have to admit that her friend was correct. She didn't run with the same crowd as Crescent, having no interest in reincarnation, pyramids, Atlantis, crystals, or apocalypse. She pronounced the name of Edgar Cayce as if it rhymed with "second base." She couldn't decide whether she believed in ghosts or not. But she was not pleased at having drawn the notice of a vampire, especially of one with such an intense gaze. It would not be inaccurate, she thought, to describe that gaze as *hungry*. "What does he want?" she asked her friend. "Is he going to hurt me? He could have injured me long ago if that was his plan. Why is he following me?"

"Well," Crescent said, "why don't we go ask him?" She completed her nibble of spinach salad and began to push her chair from the table.

"Oh no." Andrea blushed to the roots of her amber-colored hair.

"Why not?"

"I'm scared. And I feel silly. What if you're wrong? What if he's not a vampire?"

"That part I'll guarantee," Crescent replied. She rose and laid her crumpled napkin in her chair. "I'll go find out what else is happening."

This sort of embarrassment was more than Andrea was accustomed to endure. In fact, she rarely had occasion to be embarrassed. But now she tried to avert her eyes from the colloquy taking place at the bar. Crescent was expostulating, making jerky elbow movements in her black leotard top. What if people guessed that this animated conversation concerned her? She realized afresh that one of the reasons she liked Crescent was because she admired her brash courage. Who else would have the nerve to walk up to a vampire and confront him face to face?

When her friend returned to the table Andrea asked, "Is he really a vampire?"

Crescent looked at her as if taking her in for the first time. Andrea was not a gorgeous woman, nor even a pretty one, in the ordinary way of magazine photographs. She was by no means obese, but her body was too ample entirely. Her hair spilled over her plumpish shoulders in a tangle of dark fire, her mouth was large and as luscious-looking as an overripe peach, her brown eyes were both active and melting at once. She was simply too much. Her words flew from her like little startled flocks of goldfinches. Crescent became aware of a desire to press her face between Andrea's opulent breasts in the forest-green sweater and giggle like a schoolgirl with a naughty secret.

But she only answered half carelessly: "He's a vampire, all right. That was never in question, Flame."

"Flame? Why do you call me that?"

"That's what he calls you. What *they* call you. The Flame." She leaned across and took Andrea's plump, strong hands in her slender, cool fingers. "They're dead, you know. Where vampires are it is black and cold and lonely. I can't express how lonely it must be in the place where they are. And they're always there. Even when we see them now, right here in the Open Gate Cafe, they are also in the other place."

Andrea's sympathies were easy. "Oh, that sounds dreadful." She sneaked a glance at the Count but he had turned away to stare into the unresponsive bar mirror.

"Don't look at him," Crescent told her. "He's shy. He doesn't want you to look at him while I explain. He's a little ashamed."

"Will he hurt me? What are they going to do?"

"They call you Flame, he says, because you are so full of life. You are very rare that way. Everybody sees that, even if you don't. And vampires see it more quickly because they need it more."

"I don't understand what *it* is."

"Oh, you know—life force. There are some people who make the rest of us seem like shadows. They are like natural springs while we are like tap water. We are like smoldering matchstems while they are like—well, flame. Just as the vampires say. Hearth fires."

"I don't believe I'm that way." Andrea's judgment was firm.

"If you could believe it, you wouldn't be," Crescent answered. "Your lack of egoism is one of the reasons you're the way you are."

"It is very confusing," Andrea said. She had always thought of vampires as inimical creatures who did harm to God's other creatures out of sheer malicious perversity. She had not thought about them as abandoned animals condemned to fare lonesome through the dark and freezing nights and forbidden the light of the warming sun. They were dangerous, she knew that, but abandoned animals are likely to become feral, if they don't die beforehand. Vampires, it seemed, died first and then became feral. She had imagined a vampire sinking venomous fangs into her, tearing away painful gobbets of flesh, beating his coarse-haired chest and howling at the blood-red moon. But now she thought the situation would be different, more like finding another stray cat beneath her viburnum, the dull-eyed animal frightened and shivering with sickness and too anxious to defend itself. "I really don't understand," she concluded.

"That's why I've invited the Count to visit you," Crescent said. "He will explain everything better than I ever could. And he's promised to show you how to fix up your house so you'll feel safe. They're not going to harm you, but they know you don't *feel* safe."

"You invited him to my house? When?"

"Thursday evening," Crescent replied. "You and I were going to the movies then anyhow. So now we'll do this instead."

"I don't know. It's pretty scary."

"I'll be there with you. And, believe me, he's not—*they*'re not—going to hurt you. If you treat him as an envoy, as a sort of ambassador from the Vampire Nation, everything will work out fine."

"Really?"

"Oh, come on, Andrea," Crescent said. "You've never turned down a request in your life. From anyone. About anything."

It was true. Andrea's body was generous, her mind was generous, her heart was as generous as a Kansas wheat harvest.

Thursday evening chez Andrea was not a great success. Things started badly when Crescent teased the nervous guest about his chosen name. "He's Romanian, all right, but he

134

doesn't belong to the nobility. He was actually just a trouble-some peasant two centuries ago. He gave himself a title when he came to America. Isn't that so, *Count* Estragu?''

He admitted the fact readily enough, but his demeanor changed. Unused to social company, he was extravagantly shy. Of course, Andrea gave her all to make him feel at home, but just when he had begun to unbend Crescent had made her remarks about his title. After that he became sullen as well as withdrawn. It was easy to see that he did not blame his hostess for this gaucherie, easy to see that he adored and even worshipped her and would like to remain in her company. But Crescent put him off with her impertinence, she violated his sense of propriety. Andrea had observed that her friend affected many others in the same way, and the situation was worse with this vampire because of his painful diffidence.

After the faux pas he became all business and toured Andrea around her own house—with which he showed an unsettling familiarity. He had the air of a contractor planning to replumb as he took her from room to room, showing where she might place ropes of garlic, basins of holy water, silver crucifixes, and so forth. When Crescent observed that it was like installing burglar alarms, he ignored her. When he had entered the house, he had spoken in an almost normal tone of voice, but after Crescent's first sally he muttered his sentences in a quick but broken fashion. Now that she made her lame joke about burglar alarms, his voice subsided to a whisper when he said to Andrea, "I'm telling you these things because you ask. These precautions you do not need. Neither I nor any of my . . . confreres would ever do you any harm. You must believe me."

She reassured him warmly. "Oh I do, I do believe you," she said. "It's only that—well, I expect to get married someday and have children. Messy hordes of children. Dozens. And I want them to be safe and not frightened. That's when I'll take advantage of this information you've been so kind about imparting. I'm sure you won't mind when that happens."

The Count was slow to reply, and before he did he exchanged a long and darkly knowing look with Crescent. A recognition passed between them that Andrea could not guess at. Then he whispered, putting his words together with exquisite care: "If you have children, we shall never harm or frighten them. We shall go away from this house and not return. In fact, we will do so now if you request us to."

His earnest and wistful tone quite overcame her. "Oh no," she said. "You mustn't leave. . . . But if you might keep just a little more distance. All those noises on the roof at night." She essayed a cheerful little confession. "I enjoy my sleep just terribly much. I really do."

He looked for the first time into her eyes and his yearning was so boundless that her heart quaked and her knees trembled. "I know you do," he said. And then, as if he'd given himself too much away, turned to his demonstrations again. But now he was cursory and in haste and though the women tried to insist he took leave of them in so brusque a manner he was almost rude.

After his departure Crescent asked her hostess for a glass of scotch and Andrea was surprised. Her mystic friend usually eschewed hard liquor because it disordered her aura or astral body or karma or something.

"I have some white wine in the fridge," Andrea said.

"It will have to do," Crescent replied and strode purposefully to the kitchen where she helped herself.

Andrea followed. "I wish he hadn't left so soon," she said. "I had lots of questions I wanted to ask."

"About what?" Crescent drained her glass of chardonnay too quickly and poured another.

"About being a vampire. What it's like and—"

"—And how you can help?"

"Well, no. Not exactly."

"Yes. Exactly. That's you. You want to help. But I know that bunch better than you do. You don't want to get too involved, let me tell you."

"Why not?"

"You just don't."

"All right. But what was that about between you two?"

"What was what about?"

"I saw the look you gave each other. When I said I wanted lots of children."

"Nothing. It was nothing."

"*Crescent.*"

"Well—" Her body slumped, then straightened as she made

up her mind. She looked directly into Andrea's eyes. "They're right, you know, to call you The Flame. That's what you are. The flame of life. You're just too much, Andrea. You are too much."

And now she had the sorrowful experience of watching as Andrea began to understand, as her blooming complexion drained white and her warm brown eyes welled hot with tears. The flame she was could warm the dead and cheer them for an hour or two of their black eternity. But a living man could not withstand it; he would be consumed utterly.

# First Love

## Hugh B. Cave

At midnight the leader of the group, the big fellow named Vladim, decided they should draw lots to determine who was to guard her through the night. "There is no need for all of us to go without sleep until the professor gets here," he said.

So Lasloc, whose house it was, left the bedroom for a few minutes and returned with seven straws from a broom. He broke the straws into different lengths, and Vladim held them in a huge fist, and each of the others stepped forward to draw one.

When the straws were compared it was Vladim himself who held the longest one. The other six men departed, leaving her lying spread-eagled on the bed with her wrists and ankles roped to its posts. Roped so tightly, so cruelly, she could scarcely move enough to draw air into her lungs.

She would gladly have gone without breathing in that stinking room if it were possible to stay alive while doing so. When, dear God, had the window been opened last? When had anyone assaulted the shroud of dust that blanketed everything? Even the naked light bulb dangling from the ceiling was so encrusted with grime that it gave out no more light than a candle.

"You just stay quiet now until the professor arrives,"

Vladim snarled at her. "I'm warnin' you, don't try any of your filthy vampire tricks on *me* or you'll regret it."

The man they called "the professor" was someone's cousin, it seemed, but what else he was and where he was coming from, Marya did not know. Judging by their conversation, he had only recently arrived in the United States from eastern Europe, which was the homeland of so many in this Appalachian mountain village. Apparently he had told them on the telephone that he could not be expected to get here until about daybreak.

At least it was quiet now, she thought. The bedlam had all but deafened her when all seven were arguing about what they should do with her.

"The only way to kill one is to cut the head off."

"No, you are wrong. We must drive a wooden stake through the heart."

"No, no, no! You have to burn them!"

"Well, to be certain she will never prey upon us again, why don't we do all three?"

Where was Bela? Dear God, what if he didn't know this terrible thing had happened to her? What if *no* one came to save her, and the professor believed what they said about her?

Looking at the huge, bearded man on the chair against the wall only added to her terror, so she turned her head. But then the events of an hour ago rushed back into her mind, and there they were, as though the grimy ceiling at which she stared had become a motion-picture screen.

There they were and there *she* was, sixteen-year-old Marya Cochenko, and she saw herself arriving home in the dark after a late-night tryst with the boy she loved. Saw herself kissing him goodnight at the top of the lane—kissing him as though she had known him forever, not just for a few weeks—because, as usual, he declined to come the last hundred yards to the house. "Your parents might be angry," he said sadly. "Remember, they forbade you to see me again."

"I should be angry with *them*, for being so unreasonable!"

"Perhaps. But if we wish to continue seeing each other, we must be discreet."

She had every right to be angry with her parents, she told herself. Purely by accident one night while walking home from her job at the grocery store she had met this wonderful young man from the old country, newly arrived in America. He introduced himself politely before walking home with her, yet they did not like him, would not even talk to him, simply because he was from some place in the old country they did not approve of.

How silly! How totally silly! But they would not listen to reason.

So after that first night she had to meet him in secret, and always at night because she worked days at the store. Always in different parts of the village, too, so they would not be seen together by some well-meaning busybody who might inform her parents.

And never, of course, could they be together very long. It was hard enough to find excuses for going out at all, without having to invent some for staying out really late.

Which brought her to tonight. They had met at the old mine and stayed there maybe an hour. Just long enough for her to know for sure that she loved him. Then, considerate of her problem as always, he had walked her home. Or at least to the top of the lane.

Going alone to the house after their last goodnight kiss, she had looked back and seen him standing there, and waved to him. Looked back a second time and waved again. A third time and . . .

And then—then—Vladim and his cronies stepped out of the dark trees bordering the lane, three on one side, four on the other, and seized her. Vladim himself was the one who clapped a hand over her mouth to smother her cries for help.

They hurled her to the ground and bound her hands and feet with rope. Tied a stinking rag over her mouth and another over her eyes. Then picked her up and took turns carrying her to this old house in which she was now a prisoner.

A prisoner waiting for the professor. Whoever he was.

She knew who *they* were, of course. In a village as small as this, everyone knew everyone. Unless a person happened to be a newcomer like her beloved Bela.

She turned her head to look again at the man guarding her. "What's got into you, Vladim?" she found the courage to ask. "How can you say I'm a vampire? You've known me my whole life!"

He had been dozing, it seemed. Lifting his head, he returned her gaze. His thin lips, so red they were like a knife-slash across his ugly face, curled downward at the corners in a kind of snarl that made him look like a wildcat ready to pounce. "Things've been happenin' 'round here," he snarled.

"Well, I know that. Everyone knows that. But what in the world have *I* got to do with it? Tell me that, if you will!"

"You been seen out at night, most nights they happened."

"I had a reason for being out at night!" she heard herself wailing.

"What reason?"

"I've been—" No, she couldn't tell him. He knew her parents. If she confessed that she'd been slipping out to see Bela, he would go straight to them and tell them.

"You been what?" he said, leaning forward on his chair to accuse her with his beady eyes.

"Never mind. I didn't have anything to do with those things you're talking about."

"Those things I'm talkin' about are dead people," he growled. "Dead *kids*, for God's sake. Three of 'em now, with marks on their necks and some of the blood sucked out of 'em. And two of the three nights it happened, you were seen near where they was found."

"No," she sobbed. "It wasn't me who did it!"

"You done it all right, Marya Cochenko. We held a meetin' and took a vote. You done it, and when the professor gets here you'll pay for it." He leaned back on his chair and turned his head away to let her know he was done talking.

Biting her lip in frustration and fear, Marya looked up at the ceiling again and silently addressed her next question to someone she hoped would be more understanding.

"Dear God, why are you letting this terrible thing happen to me? You know I didn't do what they're saying I did. All I've ever done is sneak out of the house nights to be with Bela, because we love each other. Please, God, help me! If you don't, they're going to cut my head off or drive a stake through my heart!"

Would Bela come? He *must* have seen the men seize her; he was right there at the end of the lane. But he was only a boy and they were men—seven of them, big and determined. Would he dare challenge them?

Vladim seemed to have dozed off again. At least, his head was on his chest and as best she could see in the dim light, his eyes were closed. If only she could get loose, she might have a chance!

In movies, tied-up people sometimes got loose by twisting their wrists. She tried it, but it didn't work. Still, she continued to struggle. Something might give in the end.

What gave in the end was her strength. As though she had lost her footing while wading across Cutler's Creek when it was in flood, and grabbed an overhanging branch with both hands, but the rushing water was pulling at her and at last, in spite of herself, she had to let go.

When she woke up, her arms and legs were free and Bela was standing beside the bed, reaching out to her. "Come, Marya," he whispered.

Beyond him, the man supposed to be guarding her was still asleep on his chair, but with a difference. His head drooped sideways now and his arms hung limp. Had Bela caught him dozing and knocked him out with something? Brave Bela!

"Come, beloved," he said again, and she realized—God be praised!—that she was free.

Squirming off the bed she would have fallen, but he held her steady until the room stopped spinning. Then he took her by the hand and led her to the door, which was closed. Funny, she thought. If he had sneaked in and caught Vladim by surprise, why had he shut the door? But it was only a fleeting thought. In only a minute or two they were outside the house, hurrying through tall, scratchy weeds. Overhead, a pale half moon hung low in the sky.

What time was it? With the moon so low, it must be close to daylight. But who cared? She was safe again with the boy she loved!

"Where are you taking me, Bela?" she asked when they had reached the road and were hurrying along it.

"To my house. We can't go to yours. Yours is the first place those men will look for you." He gave her hand a little squeeze. "You've been asking me where I live. Now you'll see."

Yes, she had asked him where he lived. He had not taken her there because someone might see them and tell her parents. All she knew was that it was on the bog road somewhere, and he lived alone. He would get a job soon, he had said, but there was no hurry because his folks in the old country had left him plenty of money to live on. They had died of some sickness that nearly wiped out their village. It was why he had come to America.

Her heart sang as they hurried along. Think of it! This boy she adored had saved her life! In defeating Vladim he had overcome one of the meanest, strongest men in the village! And he so young and handsome!

She tugged him to a halt to tell him how much she loved him. "And I you," he said, his smile a beautiful thing to see in the pale moonlight.

When they stopped again he said, "Here, Marya Cochenko. This is my house."

She was surprised, a little. It was a very old house, even older than the one he had rescued her from. Almost falling down, in fact, with weeds and grass standing tall all around it. Even the key that he unlocked the front door with was old-fashioned. Perhaps he had not yet found the kind of house he wanted and was just making do here temporarily. That must be it, of course. In darkness she followed him down a musty hall, past a sitting room almost empty of furniture.

He unlocked another door, pushed it open, and stood aside to let her walk past him. Just over the threshold she stopped in bewilderment.

This room, too, was almost empty. It was meant to be a bedroom, she guessed, but there was no bed in it. The pale shaft of moonlight from its single window disclosed only an oblong box made of some strange wood in the middle of the floor.

A box shaped like a coffin.

Frowning, she turned to face him.

He smiled. "I said to myself, if Count Dracula could take his grave-earth to England, why should I not carry mine to America?" His voice was like a crooning as he reached out and gently drew her into his arms. "Yes, dear Marya, I am one of those. And when I make you one, we will be lovers forever!"

She would have screamed then, but the warmth of his lips on her neck cut off the sound as it rose in her throat. Then as the pressure continued, her unborn scream became a sigh of ecstacy and she put her arms around him, holding him close.

Crash! The sound came from the hall as the front door

shuddered open. A thunder of racing footsteps and a snarling of voices followed. Releasing her, Bela threw his arms wide and whirled to face the bedroom doorway.

Into the room rushed the men she had escaped from, with a tall, bearded stranger in the lead. Hurling himself at Bela, the stranger thrust out a hand that held a cross.

A silver cross a foot high, with a silver figure of the Christ on it.

Bela spun like a top as though frantically seeking some way to escape, but there was no time. In only a moment he was on the floor, on his back, with two men holding his arms down and the bearded stranger kneeling astride him.

The stranger held the crucifix over Bela's contorted face.

Another man stood by with what looked to Marya like the sharpened leg of a kitchen chair.

A third stepped forward with a sledgehammer.

Two others seized Marya then and turned her away so she could not see what they were doing. But when the screaming stopped, all of them turned their attention to her.

"Do you still believe this one is innocent, Professor?" someone asked.

"Unless we have arrived too late." Holding a flashlight now, the professor stepped toward Marya and tipped her head back to examine her throat. "Yes, thank heaven, we got here in time," he said. "Someone should take this poor child home."

The youngest of the group, a sturdy youth with whom Marya Cochenko had gone to school, stepped forward. Taking her hand, he led her down the hall to the front door, which hung open now on only one hinge. As he walked her out to the road, she looked at his face in the first light of a new day and saw that it was full of concern for her.

In fact, the first thing he said was, "I am sorry for what happened to you tonight, Marya. I hope you understand and will forgive us."

Marya Cochenko nodded. But being only sixteen and heartbroken, she knew for certain she would never love anyone again.

# The Need

## Jay R. Bonansinga

*For Janey*

Jewel found another victim around nine o'clock Monday night.

"There—lower right—dark hair." Jewel pointed a slender fingertip with chipped black polish at the glowing cameo at the bottom of the monitor. The Macintosh had been dissolving from one earnest young mug shot to another for over an hour now, with no results. Jewel had been close to giving up. But now, all at once, she found herself staring at the cathode likeness of another ladykiller.

"I think we have a spark," the saleswoman said, eyes twinkling, sugary smile creasing her dimples. She turned to her computer fan fold and thumbed through the data for a moment. A plump woman in her early thirties with big hair and big makeup, the saleswoman had agreed to keep Video Matchmakers open well past closing time for Jewel to make her selection. "Here we are," the saleswoman said, finally locating the entry. "Name's Alex Nunnaly, Box Number Twenty-three."

Jewel watched the saleswoman climb out of her swivel and go over to the wall.

There were columns of videos racked along the stucco panels. Neon hearts and K-Mart glamour shots festooned the adjacent walls. Gauzy beefcake, smiling singles, dating game schmaltz; it made Jewel want to puke. Jewel watched Miss Big Hair select the appropriate cassette, turn back to the conference table, and present the video like it was some kind of an award. "Here's Mister Alex Nunnaly; you can get acquainted in booth number three." The saleswomen pointed through an archway at a row of cubicles. "Happy hunting," she winked.

"Yeah, thanks," Jewel muttered.

She got up, went into booth number three, put the cassette

144

in the machine, pressed PLAY, and waited for the snow to go away. Barely out of her teens, whip smart, and sullen as a monk, Jewel was wearing her standard garb. Spandex flayed open by razors, camo pants, and Doc Martens. Her head was shaved to the nubs on one side, the other side a brilliant purple. Delicate little black filaments of human bones twined down each arm, the tattoos terminating in matching skulls and crossbones on each wrist. Only her face, pale as porcelain and innocent as a Raphael cherub, belied her grim getup.

Jewel had been using various video dating services as a method for choosing victims ever since she'd become a vampire. It was a highly effective way to pinpoint the right type of victim. The red-blooded misogynist. The kind of man Jewel hated most. Drop-dead gorgeous hunks, often attorneys, usually alumni of major college fraternities, often the possessors of too much money, horsepower, testosterone, and time on their hands. Their blood was always rich and blue, and tasted of expensive dope. They deserved to be slain and drained and pissed away; and Jewel was just the woman to do it.

The picture flickered to life.

*"Yeah, uh, hello, hi,"* the man on the TV was murmuring, looking morosely into the lens as if facing a shooting squad. He wore a tattered black shirt buttoned up to the collar. His face was subtly different on video. Darker. Maybe even a little tormented. *"Name's Alex. I'm a photographer, live alone. I like music, I guess, I dunno. Goth rock, Nine Inch Nails, Ministry, stuff like that. Favorite photographers are Diane Arbus, Mapplethorpe. Favorite color's black—"*

Jewel poked the PAUSE button.

Her throat had gone dry, and her heart was beating all of a sudden. She had never been wrong about a man before. Never. But now it looked as though her record was coming to a shattering end. This guy wasn't even remotely like her other victims; this guy was almost okay. And that bothered Jewel more than anything else. Like chopper gunners in 'Nam who dehumanized their earthbound targets in order to sleep at night, Jewel had dehumanized her victims. Called them bleeders, or wigglers, or shriekers. But this guy, this guy was actually interesting.

She couldn't resist letting it play some more.

*"—I'm a little embarrassed, you know, about this whole*

*video dating thing. I'm sorry, I'm kind of screwing this thing up. Okay, anyway, I'm a night owl. I like the solitude, I guess. I dunno. I had a pretty crappy childhood, but, I get lonely sometimes. Late at night—"*

Jewel slammed the PAUSE button again.

This was no good, this was no good at all. This guy wasn't good for killing. This guy was positively cool. Jewel fished in her pocket for a Merit, pulled one out, and noticed her hand was shaking. Was it the craving? Was it The Need? Or was it because this Alex guy was almost attractive to her? She felt like smashing her boot through the TV, like ripping the circuitry out with her teeth, like torching this whole fucking neon-hearts and Barbie-and-Ken-building to the ground.

Instead, she pressed PLAY again and watched the somber young man twisting on his stool.

*"—is this sounding pathetic? I always sound pathetic when I talk about myself. I'm sure you've probably turned this tape off by now, but anyway, if there's anybody who wants to just hang out, I dunno, you could call me, or whatever."*

Jewel punched EJECT. The tape rattled for a moment, then spat out of the slot. Jewel ripped it out of the machine and carried it back out into the main room.

"Well?" Miss Big Hair was over by the tape cases, standing behind a push sweeper, batting her eyelashes with saleswoman-of-the-month anticipation.

"This was a mistake," Jewel handed the cassette back to Big Hair.

"Oh—" Big Hair was crushed. "You're not interested, huh?"

"He's not really, he's not my—"

Jewel paused for a moment. She felt the hot wire in her spine, seething, the acid gathering in her mouth. Across the room, beyond the hearts and photographs, through a narrow window, a thin crescent moon rose like a silver suture in the sky. It made Jewel's stomach tighten. The Need was upon her. Jewel turned back to the saleswoman and looked at the cassette, licking her lips and deliberating as if standing at the threshold of a banquet table. "You know," Jewel finally said, "maybe a phone call wouldn't hurt."

Miss Big Hair smiled.

*  *  *

Baneberry Street was a carnival midway. Arc lights slashed the cool air along the neon facades of bars and after-hours clubs. Street musicians shrilled. And the nameless nightcrawlers huddled in doorways, queuing in sheaths of monoxide and smoke. A dirty mist had fallen earlier in the evening, and now the streets and sidewalks were streaked with dirty rainbows.

Jewel navigated the promenade like a shark in black leather, always moving and scanning and hating.

She met Alex Nunnaly in the deserted rear section of a place called No Exit. Sitting at a booth. Haloed by the blue fog of a Sherman. Half empty cognac in front of him. Head cocked at a weird angle, eyes closed, he seemed to be receiving subsonic signals from the beat-box thunder in the other room. When Jewel appeared next to the booth, he looked up and got all wide-eyed. "Oh, hi, you're the one, I mean, you're the woman who called," he stammered, motioning at the opposite bench. "Sit down, please, have a seat."

Jewel sat. "I usually don't do this," she lied. "The dating service thing, I mean."

"You and me both." He pointed at his drink. "Get you anything?"

"Burgundy."

They ordered the drinks and did the routine. Talked the small talk. Went through the motions. What Jewel did for a living, where Alex was born, where Jewel went to school, how many brothers or sisters, favorite bands, isn't it a shame about Kurt Cobain, isn't the price of good weed outrageous, did you see Porno for Pyros on their last tour, whatever happened to blah, blah, blah, blah, blah, blah.

Then Jewel saw the man smile.

"I know what you mean about that dating place," Alex said, and for the first time that night, he grinned his crooked, lazy grin. And all of a sudden everything changed for Jewel. The way the man's eyes narrowed and shimmered, the way his head bowed slightly. The painful shyness melting away momentarily. It was a beautiful thing to behold. "I felt like a rube on some sleazy game show," he continued. "Like I was doomed to live the rest of eternity in some kind of television purgatory."

Jewel laughed in spite of her hunger. "Tell me about it—I

felt like at any moment the ghost of Burt Convy was going to jump out and stick a microphone up my ass."

Alex laughed, but it was a flinty, weary laugh, and Jewel could smell the pain behind it. The pain and the loneliness and the black despair. She wondered if his blood would taste of antidepressants.

"Tell me, Alex," she finally said after the laughter shrivelled away, "you come to places like this very often."

Alex glanced across the blue haze of the club. There were cliques hunkered in various corners, giggling, drinking, and trading intimacies. A few of the more intoxicated souls were stumbling around the strobe-lashed dance floor, diving off the stage onto one another as the industrial grind went on, endlessly churning and hissing. After a moment, Alex turned back to Jewel and said, "I despise these places."

"I know what you mean," Jewel told him.

Killing this poor soul was going to be difficult. Very difficult. For once in her life, Jewel was actually feeling vaguely attracted to a man. *A man.* The same gender that had abused her as a little girl, forcing her down into the cellar of her foster home, making her do unspeakable things in the dark, turning her psyche into a brittle fun house of shattered mirrors. The same gender that had picked her up along a deserted stretch of the Tyrolian Highway during a European visit three endless summers ago, taking her high into the Carinthian Alps, sucking her dry as a ruin, infecting her. The same gender she had dedicated her eternal un-life to devouring.

A goddamned *man.*

"My place," Jewel enunciated so that Alex could hear her over the din, "is over by the canal, not far from here."

He looked up at her for a moment like a man trying to read a subtitle. "You want me to—you and me—?"

"C'mon."

They left the bar and headed east on foot.

The night was a dark cold wave cresting over the tops of the tenements. The air smelled of cordite, and the hot metallic melange drifting up from the steelworks south of the city. Jewel and Alex walked briskly, faces downturned, hands in their pockets. Their boot steps echoed like horses' hooves.

"It's just up ahead," Jewel informed him. "Right around the corner."

She was trembling now, but it was more than The Need worming in her belly. It was a realization. Radiating outward from her stony heart, warming her bitter blood, the notion swelled encephalitically in her brain. And she caught herself thinking the unthinkable. A companion. Perhaps this was the way to put a salve on her lonely existence. It would be so easy to transform him, just as she had been transformed. A simple nip, a break in the skin. A trading of the cursed bodily fluids. And he would bring the one thing she could never in all her immortal rage and unearthly power find in this world.

He would bring her love.

"Home sweet home," she muttered, fumbling through her keys outside a decaying Victorian flat. Her hands were palsied with tension.

She got the outer door open, and she took him up a flight of stairs to her meager little studio. Inside the apartment, the air was fetid and clammy, like the inside of a refrigerator that had been turned off for a few days. Jewel rarely kept blood in her place, as other vampires often did, but she occasionally brought up a small animal, a cat or a possum, from which she could harvest blood for weeks. She liked to keep the thermostat at about sixty to prevent rotting.

"Make yourself comfortable," she said and turned on the overheads. Cool, fluorescent light spilled across a narrow room cluttered with broken-down antiques, audio equipment, and stacks upon stacks of rare books; one of the few advantages to being undead was that you had plenty of time to read. "I'll put on some music," Jewel said, going over to the stereo.

Alex huddled in the foyer, his eyes on the floor, looking exceedingly sheepish.

Jewel opened the CD cabinet and selected a disc by Throbbing Gristle. Plucking the silver wafer from its box, she knelt down by the player and shoved the disc home. Her gums were starting to sting, her stomach tightening. The Need was blooming inside her, a black flower opening, and she didn't want Alex to see her eyes changing. Sudden music leapt from the speakers, a tidal wave of feedback.

Jewel went over to Alex.

"Care to dance?" she said and wrapped her painted arms around him. This was going to be much more than some messy evisceration in some anonymous sewer tunnel. This was going to be unprecedented: *Jewel's first keeper.*

They swam across the floor to the surge of the music, the squeal of electric guitars. Jewel could feel the stirring of his heart beneath hers, the faint shiver of his hands on her back. She closed her eyes and let the change rise in her. It came like a jackal in her chest, bifurcating her vision, splitting her soft palate down the middle and extruding two large white thorns from the roof of her mouth.

She was about to pierce the pale flesh above Alex's carotid when two needle sharp incisors struck the cool skin of her own neck.

Pain howled inside her, the shock swirling through her neck and her chest. She instinctively pulled away. Strands of blood and saliva threaded off her mouth, off his mouth, a cat's cradle of sticky spoor between them. She stared at him. His soulless, pupilless eyes stared back. His fangs were already fully protracted. Two obscene tusks. But his expression was pure shock, his face coloring with humiliation.

"I'm sorry," he said, "I didn't know—you were—"

"Bastard!"

She lunged at him.

Their bodies collided and went sprawling to the floor, knocking over an Edwardian bookcase. Glass shattered and volumes rained down on them as they rolled and struggled across the hardwood. Jewel dug her nails into his neck, hissing feral bursts, spraying bloody saliva. Alex countered with inhuman strength. Wriggling out of her grasp, he lifted her and tossed her across the room as a petulant child might toss a rag doll.

She landed on a Hepplewhite. The hutch collapsed on impact, sending shards of wood and glass across the room. Jewel tumbled to the floor. The engine inside her was revving madly, threatening to burn out.

"It isn't my fault!" Alex hollered at her, struggling to his feet.

*"Fault?!"* Jewel shook off the pain and stood up on wobbly knees. Her fangs were aching, The Need twisting inside her like

razors. "You don't get it, do you?!" she said. She was speckled with blood now, her own blood, Alex's blood. She took a step toward him, tears burning her eyes, her first tears ever. "You just don't fucking get it!"

"Wait—" Alex started to say something else.

Jewel swung at him.

The blow struck Alex in the jaw, whiplashing him backward. He hit the wall hard. Framed lithographs toppled, and dust puffed from the cracked plaster. Alex howled, the sound of his voice a hellish, ululating roar. Jewel lunged at him again. Their bodies tangled and slammed against the wall.

Jewel's growl was not of this earth. *"I was going to turn you—!"*

Their eyes locked.

All at once, an ancient process, a process that had mesmerized so many victims, began to take hold of the mesmerizers. Jewel gasped. She felt a tingling at the base of her spine, a light-headedness wash over her, and a syrupy, sensual feeling slithering through her midbrain. The sensations poured out of Alex's eyes. Jewel sent them right back. But just as the twin hypnotic glares seemed to coalesce between them like a glass cocoon, Jewel absorbed one final truth.

An unexpected truth.

It came on a wave of voices, strangled voices, a child's anguished pleas, and the angry reproachments of drunken stepparents. A metal rod across a boy's bare ass, nylon cord drawn tight around his wrists, cigarette burns, and fumbling fingers pulling down his little trousers. A wave of memories, ugly, horrible memories buried deep in Alex's fractured consciousness. And soon Jewel knew the real common bond between the two creatures, a bond that would tie them for eternity.

Their faces came together then.

And they did what came unnaturally.

Jewel was the first to tap an artery, Alex following close on her heels. Razor canines plunged home; yellowed, elongated fingernails digging in; inhumanly strong arms locking and embracing, clinging, holding desperately tight. But there was something distinctly new about this clinch, something neither Jewel nor Alex had ever experienced, consummating itself in their mutual syphoning, the wonderful, endless transfusing, for better or for worse, in the name of all dark gods.

Forever and ever.


Some time later.

They sat at their breakfast table.

As the last light of day swirled down the drain outside the apartment, they sat together, eating their breakfast, quite content. Alex was reading the *Village Voice* and nursing a goblet of Cabernet. Jewel was smoking a lime-green Sherman and gazing out across the balcony at the serpentine lights below. She was smiling wistfully.

For the first time in either of their miserable un-lives, they were full of cold, empty peace.

And behind them, in the nursery at the end of the hallway, the children of a new order slept in shadows.


# The Rose Cavalier

### BEN P. INDICK


**T**he clerks at the Food Emporium snickered and raised their eyes when Margy came in. They always did, and Margy always smiled innocently back at them, raising her own eyes. Her humor only made it worse. Her brightly lipsticked mouth revealed her discolored teeth. "I never see her smoking, but what teeth!" Annie whispered to Jack as he ostentatiously swept the floor near her register. "The better to bite you with, my dear!" he whispered back, and they giggled. "Why doesn't she just act like a nice little old lady, instead of all that crazy makeup, and all those *clothes!*" Annie was forced to whisper because Mr. Lowzicki, the manager, had instructed the staff not to ridicule the customers, "no matter what!"

Margy pretended she was receiving compliments. She was a fat little woman who could have been in her eighties. She complemented the flaming makeup with an even more florid wig. As though in fear of imminent snowfall, although it was nearly June, she wore a hodgepodge of thrift shop clothing or worse, one sweater on another, a coat over all, and shoes that appeared several sizes too large for her. Still, she was always cold. She shuffled along, pushing a cart and nodding at the overstuffed shelves.

Margy delicately dropped a box of chocolate chip cookies into the cart, knocking a few others down to the floor. She stared thoughtfully at them for a moment, then reached down and picked one up. As she straightened up, she noticed Mr. Lowzicki standing next to her, a frown on his face. She dropped the cookies into the cart. "I like to have enough," she explained to him. He shook his head in resignation, picked up the others and replaced them.

"Sure you do, Margy," he said. "Just try to handle them with care, dear," he urged. "They get broken when they fall."

Margy apologized profusely and her cart knocked a few cartons of ginger snaps off their perch. She looked back sheepishly at the manager. "Oh, there I go again." She appeared as though she were about to cry, but the manager just shook his head and picked them up after her. "Thank you, Mr. Lowzicki," she cooed, "what would us old folks do without nice people like you to help." He nodded and walked off sharply as though he had just remembered an urgent task he had forgotten.

Margy watched him vanish and reached with extra caution for a ketchup bottle. She nodded approvingly. "Plastic!" she noted, giving the bottle a squeeze. She was startled as another cart collided jarringly with hers. She looked up at its driver and the ketchup plopped from her hands into her cart. The woman was staring at Margy, who knew the collision was no accident. She looked familiar. Memory came. "Is it," she asked hesitantly, "Ilsa?"

The other woman was tapping her manicured nails against the handle and nodding disapprovingly at Margy's outfit. "Yes, Margy." She allowed the last word to slide out disparagingly. Her eyes stared out through huge sunglasses as dark as Margy's, but she wore a suit in rich violet with a scarlet scarf across her throat. Her black hair was drawn back tightly across the temples into a bun. She was a foot taller than Margy. She held a tentative hand toward the little woman. "Just what is *all this?* Are you a bag woman now?"

153

Margy gathered up her clothing. "It's mine. I've always had these things. I need them. I'm not so well. This cold weather."

The woman's voice was sinuous as she leaned across the carts and stared closely at her. "Margaretta, under all that paint and garbage, you look terrible! Are you also living in cardboard packing cartons on a sidewalk grating, huddling in the occasional exhaust of warm air and surviving on rats and refuse?"

Margy pushed her cart into Ilsa's, jarring her for a moment. "I have a room, a nice room," she answered defensively, "and I eat as I please. I did not ask you to come bothering me, and I wish you would leave me alone." Her abrupt belligerence faded into sudden weakness as she looked down helplessly. "Go away, Ilsa," she concluded in a subdued voice. "I have managed without you and your kind for a long time."

Ilsa seemed affected. Her demeanor became almost supplicating. "I have looked for you because you were special to me and you always will be. *This*," she pointed at Margy's bunched clothing, "is not you. You cannot survive like this." Margy only looked away. "I don't worry about surviving," she mumbled. "Not much more anyway."

A young Hispanic woman pushing a cart with a baby on it stopped near them as she studied the packages of crackers. Margy suddenly tried to disengage her cart and push away but Ilsa prevented her. "Wait," she whispered. "Margaretta, come with me." Her eyes appeared to glow, violet as her suit, even through her glasses as she stared intently at Margy. The young mother, happening to glance their way, was startled at her urgency. "Go away!" Margy said desperately. The woman, mistaking Margy, quickly pushed her cart off. Ilsa continued. "I have been looking for you. You must leave. It is not safe here." She leaned forward to whisper. "Too many of them are diseased. It is dangerous. It is in the Life, in the blood. You cannot live if you get that disease."

Margy shoved the cart again and Ilsa fell back, slipping a bit. Margy was alarmed until she saw the woman was not injured. "It does not matter to me. I don't have anything to do with anyone. I am not interested. I don't know what you are talking about anyway and I live alone. I don't—visit—anyone any more. You should know that. No more. Never. Go away, Ilsa! I told you that last time, I don't care!"

Ilsa pulled her cart out of her way. "This is the last time," she snapped. "I'll not look for you again. I . . . Oh, Margaretta, look at you! How could you allow this to happen? Please listen; it's not too late!"

Margy, about to go, looked back. She saw tears beneath the glasses but the woman turned away. "Ilsa," she said at last, "I'm old. I don't remember things like I once did. I don't think the same. I don't talk the same. I don't act the same. I cannot forget there was a little girl, a child, somewhere. . . . After that I did not want to live anymore. Certainly not like *that*. No, I don't want to remember."

Ilsa whispered to the shelves. "It wasn't your fault, Margaretta. It happened, but it's over, and I want you back. You can still return, be Margaretta, live forever!" She heard the squeak of the shopping cart's wheels and looked up. Margy was already at the end of the aisle, and she was wiping her eyes. Margy slowly turned around to face her friend, but there was only an empty cart.

Margy carried her shopping bag into the old brownstone. She was cheerful again. It was all forgotten, and she was humming her favorite music, a snatch of Strauss's *Der Rosenkavalier*. The hall light never worked and it was comfortably dark in here. She removed her sunglasses and carefully put them into her purse. She started up the first of the three staircases but she heard the sound of a radio or a phonograph from the apartment on the left. The music was her Strauss! She hummed with it softly, and smiled with recognition as she recalled some of the lines in their German. She sang one lightly, pleased to realize there was still some lilt to her voice, even if it was rusty and reedy. She suddenly sang aloud with pleasure. " 'Spur nur dich.' Oh, the career I might have had! 'Spur nur dich allein!' "

The apartment door opened and a young man with a towel in his hand looked out. He saw Margy. "I'll be damned, it's Margy from upstairs! Ezra says he could have sworn he heard a Rose Cavalier out here," he said with a grin. "Did you see anyone, Margy?"

Margy drew herself up. "Don't you 'Margy' me! I know what goes on in there!" She started up again. The young man approached her and reached to her arm. His grin had vanished. "Margy—" he began but she recoiled from the towel. He noticed and withdrew but still looked at her with an earnest, pleading expression. "You were singing. Ezra heard you. I heard you. It's his favorite. Strauss. I see you all the time, Margy, you know me. Margy, could you just, I know I'm asking a lot, I mean, could you just come in for a minute, and—sing? Just a little. Just for fun." Suddenly he took her arm. "Just for Ezra, Margy. He would love it so much. He needs company. Please?"

From behind the door Margy heard a young man's voice, weakly calling. "Richard, don't, please don't."

Richard released Margy's arm, and she looked blankly at it. He looked at her a last time, but he was downcast now. He shrugged his shoulders and started back.

Margy tried to sound forceful. "I know you two. Namby pamby boys. You can't fool me." But the words just tailed off. As Richard closed the door she could hear the boy's voice over the music. "Thank you anyway, Richard. You're kind." Margy trudged up to the first landing, no longer singing, just mumbling to herself. "Namby pamby boys, that's what." Her mind was clouded. "Rosencavalier, Reinhardt, Strauss. Boys. Namby pamby boys. Sick. He's sick, that one in there, sick. And Ilsa? My Ilsa?" She turned to listen. The music swelled and after a moment she swayed her head in time to the waltz melody. She looked down at their doorway. Slowly, she began walking down the steps, quietly, to the door and carefully, soundlessly, reached into her shopping bag. She took out one of the two packages of cookies and laid it at the doorway. She turned and went upstairs to her room.

For a few days after this Margy would glance at the door where the two young men lived whenever she entered or left the house. She heard no music, and indeed, no sound of any sort. Had they, perhaps, left? Had she made them feel bad? It wasn't her fault they were what they were! She had her own problem. She had given it up forever, whatever it was, she added to herself, and tried to sneer, but she couldn't. Once there was a night, once, such a long time ago, in Paris, she thought, she could remember that, although it were best to forget it, yet it had been such a very special night, eyes, lips, that chin with a little dimple in it, the white swan's neck, the music, the violet eyes! She forced away the ghost of the memory, as she had done for many years now. She sighed and opened the outside door. Nothing she could do, she told herself, and clutching her coat and sweaters, she would look into the ancient mirror in the vestibule, to see that her lipstick was on properly, perhaps add another dab of rouge, not to look more pale than she was. It was night and she did not need her glasses, but she was terribly cold. Maybe she could find another sweater.

It was just one week later that Margy came home with her meager groceries and Richard was pacing in front of the stoop. He tried to appear casual but she could see he was quite disturbed. He tried to joke. "Margy," he said, "do you think you are ready to give us an aria yet?" She merely stared at him. He was blocking the steps anyway. He wanted to say something, she knew. "Margy," he finally said, blurting it out, "I know you don't know me, or Ezra either, and you aren't responsible for us, but you do live here, and I need some help. There is no one else."

Margy stood back suspiciously. "I don't have any money." He laughed nervously. "No, no, not money. Not that I couldn't use it. Margy, I need a big favor. Ezra won't go to a hospital, and I can't make him. It's too much, I mean," and he began stuttering with emotion, unable to speak. "And just when I have to be away a few days. Only a few days," he emphasized. She noticed a dufflebag beside the stoop. She looked from it to him, in suspicion and doubt. She interrupted his flow. "What are you trying to say?"

"Margy, he has no one. While I'm gone, can you look in on him? He can take care of himself, but just be sure he has his food. Look, here," and he reached into his pocket and came up with a handful of bills. "Use these and buy whatever he needs. Only till the end of the week, then I'll be back." He held his head in his hands. "I can't watch. I have to go. I'll be back. The end of the week." Without waiting, he felt his way around the stoop, grabbed the bag, and stumbled off. He stopped for a moment, and looked back at her. She stood in astonishment and she could see he was biting his lip in restraint, and then he staggered off.

Margy looked at the money and snorted at his vanishing figure. "Does he think I'm a babysitter, or a nurse? He thinks I don't know what's going on? His boyfriend is sick, and I'll bet it's that AIDS. Thats what's going on! AIDS! I can't go near it. Ilsa said it. 'Stay away,' she said. Saturday. Three days! *If* he is coming back! It's not for me! I'm telling him so!" She took a deep breath and climbed the steps. She went to the door and after a moment knocked firmly. A weak voice responded, "Come in. It's open."

Margy opened the door. She smelled the bad air before she saw anything inside. There was a passage and she felt her way down. A room opened to her right and she looked in to perceive a bed with a young man lying in it, staring at her in surprise. He was in white pajamas and raised himself with some difficulty up on an elbow. He coughed several times. "Where is Richard?" he asked.

"I don't know. He said he had to go away for a few days." Margy held out the money. "He said I should bring you food. I can't." His face and arms seemed to be very shrunken and the eyepits were dark and hollow. She could not take her eyes off him but she could see tables with towels, medicine bottles, pans, and a vaporizer steaming.

"You're Margy?" he asked. She nodded. "I'm Ezra." He slowly swung his legs out of bed. They were thin, like the rest of him, and she could see blotches on his white skin. "He will be back soon, I'm certain," he said, with a rueful smile. "Don't blame him, Margy, he is a good person. Too good for me. But I don't want to trouble you. You look like a good person too, but I can take care of myself. It isn't your problem." He raised himself, but had difficulty standing. He shuffled to a radio-CD player and returned to his bed with a remote control. "It's too much work to change the record, but it doesn't matter. I play only one now. I think you know which." He smiled at Margy and she nodded. "Please, Margy, if I may call you that, since I don't even know you, you don't have to trouble yourself. I'll manage. I was going to call some of my relatives anyway to come over. I think I need a little help. In fact, I think I'll go to the hospital." He began coughing again, hard, racking coughs. When the paroxysm had ceased he fell back into bed. "Please Margy, go. I'll manage. I'm not your problem. I'll be all right." When she still did not move, he looked up at her, his eyes dark caverns on the white sea of his face. "Please. I want to rest. I have my music."

Margy left, and as she closed the door she could hear Strauss again. She knocked at the door. She heard the surprise in his voice as he told her to come in. "I'll be back," she said simply, and left.

She was back that very night, with some soup she made for him. He smiled with pleasure, although he could eat very little, and nothing else. She asked about a hospital, but he smiled wistfully, and said it was not time for that. He would get better by himself. She knew this was not true. He was helpless. "How could your friend, Richard, leave you?" she asked. "He loved you, didn't he?"

"He still does, Margy. I think that's why he could not stay. I know he will be back, but maybe not till . . ." He waved a hand and left the words dangling. "I don't mind. I love him too, and it's better this way. I'll call the hospital. Soon." He smiled sadly. She wiped his perspiring forehead and for an instant he took her hand. "Oh, I'm sorry, Margy," he said, releasing it. She replaced it, silently.

In the next few days he obviously was weakening, and the coughing was worse. There could not be much more. She begged him to call the hospital, but he would not hear of it. "Richard will not know where I am, unless I wait here for him." He smiled wanly at her. "Dear Margy! You are not taking care of yourself, worrying over me!"

That night when Margy came to Ezra, his eyes were closed and he seemed very still. She listened for his breathing; it was very slow. She bent over him, over his white face, over his thin white neck. She touched it.

Something long forgotten stirred in her, and she sat up with a shock. Her body tingled and she felt that familiar craving she thought she had forgotten. She welcomed it now, and the years along with the clothing fell away from her. She was young again, a cloud of golden hair over her forehead, clad in a satin pink jacket and knee britches. She bent over him again. She called him. "Ezra. Come to me. Come." Her lips touched his neck gently; the newly grown incisors pricked the skin lightly. He stirred and his eyes opened wide. She stood up before him, smiling radiantly. "It isn't Margy?" he asked in disbelief. "Margaretta," she replied. "Listen!" She touched the remote, and the familiar music filled the room. "Before I met Ilsa I sang for Strauss himself. I was Octavian, his Rose Cavalier!"

"I don't understand," he said.

"There is no understanding. You must simply believe. After I met Ilsa, I became an Undead." She touched his mouth. "Accept. I committed a sin, however, and after that I left, to live and at last to die." Her teeth bit gently into his neck. He did not wince, but held her head to his. "And now, I too shall die."

"No!" he protested, but again she touched his lips.

"I choose to. Even the Undead must one day die. Only love or even the memory of love is forever. The love you have known and that I choose to give."

He had not thought he had tears left. "You are the most beautiful thing I have ever seen, Margaretta." She bent over him again and he held her to him until at last she looked up into his sad eyes.

"Please sing for me, Margaretta. As Octavian!"

She waited for the music, and then leaned over him and sang. *"Spur nur dich, spur nur dich allein, und dass wir beieinander sein!* I only know you, only you alone, and we are together, loving, each other. *Geht all's sonst wie ein Traum dahin, vor meinem Sinn.* Everything else passes like a dream, a vision of you."

He was silent as she bent over him again, and then she was silent too.

The next day Richard returned, remorseful and pained. When he came in, he found them, Ezra, smiling even in death, and Margy, the old woman, peaceful and dead in his arms. The red on her smiling lips was not lipstick.

# The Lady of the Fountain

DARRELL SCHWEITZER

It was in an old land that the battle had taken place; a country of empty halls and deserted castles where ruined walls stood protecting nothing from nothing, and roadways faded into the earth and led nowhere. For three days in this place the swords of the two armies sang their terrible song on shields and armour, and when the fighting was done and all was still, a deep fog covered the sodden ground.

I rode away from the field of slaughter, at the edge of a wood where the land sloped upward into the mountains, and I heard still the whimperings and curses of the dying behind me. I shuddered with cold and revulsion, and wrapped my cloak more tightly around me. I pressed on.

I reminded myself that I was on a quest. Thus far I had journeyed over lands unknown to geographers, braved marauders and wolves, seen wonders and met hardships, and still I sought my perilous goal. I knew that mine was indeed a goodly and forthright mission, and that once it was ended I would become a hero and perhaps a saint, and all Christendom would sing my praises. At the moment, though, this was all very far off and it meant little, for I was exceedingly weary. Yet I would not lie down and rest among the dead, so I forced my horse on a little further.

At length the land began to rise about me, the path twisted between hills and grew steep, and I knew then that I could not stop, lest in my weakness I lie down and freeze, or fall prey to whatever wild beasts might be roaming about. It was in the fall of the year, and winter already lurked in the highlands.

The way grew harder and harder, and I felt my horse struggling beneath me. The creature's every breath was laboured; foam poured from its mouth, and I could see that the animal was as near to exhaustion as I was. So it seemed like a miracle, a boon from God in answer to my unspoken prayers, when in the midst of all those cliffs and steep ways I found a low and sheltered valley, where fair blossoms bloomed and tall trees stood all about. The sun was almost down, but as I entered the valley the chill of the mountain night seemed to leave me.

It was not long before I came to the fountain. It stood in the very centre of the valley, nestled among shrubs, its splashing waters breaking the silence of the velvet evening. Above me the clouds broke, and the hunter Orion peered down out of a darkened sky.

I dismounted and drank, and washed the grime from my face. My horse drank also. After I was refreshed I sat and strove to forget all the things I had done that day, how many I had slain, how many I had crippled. My sword was a wreck in my scabbard and it troubled me not. I cared little that Count Mordantas of Grey Mountain lay slain in the mud with all his thanes, or that his hireling host was scattered. I too had fled the battle when all was clearly lost, for I had no wish to perish. I chose life over chivalry even though the Count had been good to me and given me bread and shelter during the Holy Days. Somehow my breach of honour seemed like the only sensible thing and it meant nothing that the army of the red banners now held all the land from Thandaroum to the sea, or that the army of the blue banners would charge no more. And it did not strike me as wrong that I failed to mourn for my squire Jon, my faithful companion in all my wanderings who was now lost to me, and was now doubtless the object of ravens' feasting. These things passed through my mind like a masque, something distant and strange, and I had no strength left for sorrow.

After a time I came to notice the engravings on the marble base of the fountain and ran my fingers over them. Old and worn they were, only half legible, in a script like some rare and ancient Latin carved by the noble Romans of centuries past, or perhaps something even more ancient, something unspeakably timeless and without age.

I could not think more on it. I rose, stumbled a few paces until I found a comfortable spot, dropped to the ground and slept.

That night I dreamed I saw all the kings of the past before me, all the empires rising and falling before my gaze, crumbling as the years fell aside. Rome I saw, Carthage, Nineveh, and Thebes. I saw the handwriting on the wall of Babylon, the last days of Ur of the Chaldees, and then I was carried back more quickly through the ages to the years when strange gods trod upon the earth and there were lands where there are now seas, and seas where now stand mountains. I saw towns other than those of history, and in my dream I knew their names, strange to my ear: Belhimra, Gldathrion, Sithuil, and Kosh-Ni-Hye. All these did I glimpse before they faded. Great men and small walked the world, and in their ships they rowed to the very edge where all oceans plunge downward into the abyss. To the farthest North they went, to the lands of endless snow and ice where the Ell Kingdoms still stand, and to the West where jungles creep into ancient holdings where in legend King Aznaroth quested forever after the golden sunset city.

Still onward I was swept on the river of dreams, until at last I came to a timeless span before the coming of years; when gods unknown to Christ had freshly hewed the world out of primal Chaos, and Garil the Builder raised up in the morning of the Earth the blest Throramna, the Father of Cities. It was here that I came to rest, and I found myself before the golden gate of that city. I climbed a low hillock and read the inscription above me. It was written in an ancient tongue, but the voice of my dreams whispered to me its meaning: HERE STANDS THRORAMNA, MEMORIAL TO THE FORTY-NINE GODS THAT WERE.

I pondered on this a minute before entering. I found the gate unlocked and unguarded, and I was drawn by the sound of laughter from within.

Five maidens met me in the courtyard, which I was told was called The Place of Coming Sun, and they danced about me and caressed me, saying: "Put away your weapons, you who are tired and weary of battle. Lay down your sword and your shield and your helm, for the gods are good and there is no war in this land. Come, for we have wine and soft music, and there is feasting."

In a daze I was, and half bewitched, and I left my armaments in a heap on the cobblestones, and went with the five. We passed down streets wide and narrow, lined with houses of coloured marble, each exquisitely and uniquely carved. At last we came to a great hall made of wood and bright stones, and inside there were men and women gathered around a vast table. Much laughing and joking and singing filled the room as wine flowed freely and a great feast was laid out before them. He who sat at the head of the host rose and bade me come and sit by his right hand, that I might join in the merrymaking. This I did and we drank a toast to his gods, whose names I did not know. Now always had I been taught that there is but one God, namely the Christ, but the world I knew was far from me then, and in the joy of the moment my sin passed by me unnoticed. I accepted the good drink offered me and toasted with the rest, and after the toasting was finished the meal began. Fine meats and rare fruits were served, while birds sang the songs of the Beginning, poets recited lines from the Epic of The Lost Gods, and maidens danced before the assembled company. Soon all was warm and hazy, and a drowsiness overtook me.

I vaguely remembered being carried away by many hands and laid on a soft bed, and all the while I heard somewhere not far from me a light and beautiful voice which said, "Be gentle with the stranger, for his world knows not the peace of ours, and he has suffered much."

It was a bright and peaceful morn when I awoke after what seemed many days, and I sat up in bed and stretched myself, glad to find my strength renewed and my muscles no longer sore. Soon I saw that my wounds were healed, and I felt restless and eager, like a youth who has been kept inside all winter. I rose, and without thinking sought my armour. Then I heard the voice again.

"There is no need for your things of metal. What would you do with them here?"

"Aye, there is truth in that," I said, and in turning I beheld for the first time Llania the Fair, Princess of this city, whose name means Flower of The Morning Sun. At the sight of her my eyes were bedazzled, my heart sounded to the very core. I knew then the sweet wound of love, and I was hopelessly ensnared in a silver web. More wondrous of form and face was she than any other maiden; like a goddess she was with her long golden hair, yet at the same time earthly and warm. I knew at once that whatever gods ruled this place were good, and that it had been fated for the two of us to meet like this and to remain together always.

We wandered through the city that day, and she spoke of things great and little, and whenever I worried that these things might not be true, she rendered them so with a kiss. Soon I forgot all about my Christian God and my quest and my world. Indeed, I forgot even the name by which I had been known during my former existence. She gave me a new one, Arandil Re' Neth, meaning in her own tongue, He Who Is Reborn. No longer was I the knight Julian, born of a mad duke and baptised by a bishop. Now I was Arandil Re' Neth, the lover of Llania, and nothing else mattered. I had started my life anew.

Summer came and went, and autumn was mild. Not once did we toil or know sorrow in all those months. Often we rode the hunt with the lords and ladies of Throramna and stormed through bushes after the hart. Aye, that was goodly sport. And again there were times when the two of us would go off into the forest alone without fear, and speak with the friendly sprites that dwelt there. We heard them tell things clever and marvellous, and we both laughed merrily when a water nymph told the story of Why The Centaur Comes Not Into The Daylight.

Always I was with my Flower of The Morning Sun, and like the orb of her name, her radiance shone upon me always, soothing me, driving away my little fears. I knew a peace not granted to ordinary men. Time did not seem to pass, and I did not age. I dwelt in a golden pocket of the universe, where pain and strife were always excluded. I loved my Llania deeply, so much that my heart would flutter like that of an unbearded boy when I was with her, but again her kisses would remove all anxieties. Kings, wars, monsters, and other matters seemed trivial and meaningless, like a bad dream nearly forgotten.

One night we climbed a tall mountain beyond the city, so that we might gaze at the stars and speak to the spirits of the upper airs. And as we sat there breathing the deep freshness of the heights, I drew Llania close to me and whispered into her ear: "On the morrow we shall be wed, and dwell always within the city. We shall raise ten tall sons and many daughters. Never shall we leave this place."

And she replied. "It is good!"

We kissed then, but as we did there was a rushing of winds, and a darkness fell over the stars. The moon in its brightness was blotted out, and I felt the ground crumble away beneath me. Suddenly, I was falling through space, and far away from me I could hear the fading voice of my Llania, screaming and calling out my name.

"I shall never leave you!" I cried.

She screamed all the louder, and there was agony in her voice.

Then all was still.

I awoke on a wet lawn, cold and still, dressed in my damp and battered armour. For a moment I knew not where I was, but then I saw Jon my loyal squire standing over me, he whom I had thought dead.

"Oh Jon! I have had a wondrous dream! I wish I had never awakened!"

"It was not a dream, Lord," he said, "but a terrible reality."

"Terrible? Nay! It was beautiful! I loved a damsel. Her name Llania."

"Not Llania, Sir, but Lamia, the Vampire. I thank God that I could save you from her in time. Hear now my tale: When I was separated from you in the battle I lost all heart, thinking you slain. I hid in a glen until the fighting was over and the victors had departed. I searched among the corpses for you and had a reborn hope when I did not find you. After that I followed this road, knowing that you had to come this way, for all other roads are held by the enemy. This night I came into the valley and found you here in the arms of the vampire, which through the grace of Our Lord Jesus I destroyed."

I was too dazed to say anything to this. I tried to stand, but was suddenly overwhelmed by nausea. My legs collapsed beneath me, and Jon caught me before I fell. My head throbbed as if it were a gong and a giant was beating on it, and the landscape, which seemed far more barren than it had been before, danced about me. When it grew steady Jon took me by the arm and led me, speaking as we went.

"She was lying on the ground beside you, her lips red with your life's blood. Already she had stolen much, and you had begun to grey, as you have now. With my cross I drove her back to her tomb behind yonder fountain, and with my sword I cut her head off."

"This is madness," I was able to mutter.

We passed by the fountain which was filled with rainwater and scum, not flowing, and came to the wreck of a house, or perhaps a palace. Great chunks of broken stone lay about, and fallen columns sank into the mossy ground. Indeed there was a tomb there, half covered with weeds and stained green with age, so old that its very marble was beginning to crumble. There was an inscription at the base, long since worn to illegibility.

The lid of the tomb had been pushed aside, and in the blood-splattered tomb lay the body of a maiden, her head cut off and lying with her. I knew her face in an instant. It was my Llania.

"Murderer!" I screamed. I pulled away from Jon, then turned to face him, my strength renewed by grief and rage. "She loved me! She loved me as no other woman has! For once I was not a pauper knight, but one who was to wed the fairest lady in all creation. Now you have murdered her!"

I drew my sword. It was battered but it could still slay.

Jon drew back from me in horror. "No, my Lord! She is a fiend out of Hell! Look at the fangs in her mouth! Behold the tomb she resides in!"

My blade rose and fell, and there was silence in the valley. All around me even as I watched, the trees faded like smoke and were gone. The blossoms were no more; the land was bare of grass as the last illusions passed from it. I turned once more to the sepulchre and beheld not my beloved, but only dust.

I looked down at my hands, and at my beard, and saw the hands and beard of one older than myself. Truly years had passed —or been stolen—and after a single night I was young no longer. Only the body of Jon remained as it was. His red blood poured forth onto the ground, and I knew by it that I was thrice damned. I had loved a vampire out of the darkest Pit, and a great sin this was. I had toasted her pagan gods, which is something the Lord forbade in his first commandment to Moses—this too was a great offence. And I had slain my pious servant, who had done no wrong. For this there could be no forgiveness.

I mounted my horse and rode away from the tomb and the fountain as the new day dawned. I descended the far side of the mountain range and continued on my journey, heading away from all the lands I knew. By noon the last wisps of fog were gone and the day was bright and clear.

Occasionally, I would come across a fallen warrior with flies on his face, and bucklers and spears discarded in hasty flight. The battle had reached even this far. I spurred my horse to a rapid trot, and all this time I thought of nothing but the beautiful Llania, of my sins, and the paradise that could never be. I paid no attention to where I was going, and it was only for the intelligence of my mount that I did not stray from the path and become lost.

That afternoon I passed through a squalid village, and filthy little peasant brats ran after me and tried to seize my horse's tail, but ceased when the beast kicked one of them. I glared at the bent and ugly hags that laboured over churns, ran their petty errands, or gossipped on street corners. Here and there a man with a low brow and a face like a monkey crossed my path, and with a wave of my sword and an angry shout I would send him scurrying. A maid in the window sang a happy song and I spat on the doorstep of that house, and she was silent. I departed that place and was glad to be again on the road, alone with my thoughts and my sorrow.

And so I continued on my quest of a goal whose worth escaped me.

# The Shape of Turmoil

### H. ANDREW LYNCH

Bisa's cup of coffee grew cold. She poured in more sugar, captured by the senselessness of the gesture. The granules failed to blend, as she failed to blend, as all vampires failed to blend, within their vacuum of undying.

She studied the occupants of the toadstool tables in the bookstore coffee shop, then sighed, disgusted with herself for wasting so much time contemplating humdrum candidates. She watched a raft of bubbles circumnavigate the coffee's oily surface as the ache in her jaws returned for the third time that evening. After 143 years, the ache, always unpredictable in its duration or intensity, still annoyed her.

A waiter with large amber eyes and thick fingers helped an

old woman to her feet and led her to the Biography aisle. Gisa had seen the waiter once or twice near Dupont Circle, around noon. That was when she liked to run errands, around noon. Even if she had nowhere to go or nothing in mind to accomplish, she made sure she was out, at noon, enjoying a time of day during which normal vampires lay torpid in states of jealous waiting.

She threw down a wad of ones, unable to recall the victim from whom she'd lifted them. She made customary stops in the Biography and Special Interest aisles, but she'd read it all. Turning past Cookbooks, she paused in the Psychology aisle. A new title caught her attention: *Identity: A Closer Study of the Human Shield . . . And the Void It Often Masks.*

Her hand trembled as she lifted the book from the shelf and opened it to the table of contents.

She'd long ago accepted the futility of human psychology. Therapy could not cure her of the twenty-four-hour stretches following a feast. Whenever she drank from human veins, she took, for a day, the strongest and weakest facets of the victim's persona, struggling, often in agony, to regain her sense of self. The hunger forced her to take enormous chances. To how many neurotics had her mind and body played host? To how many borderline psychopaths?

She supposed it was the price she paid for embracing sunlight, for profiting by its warmth. The others—the so-called brethren—were fragile creatures, in many ways weaker than the humans who fed them. Those she'd encountered railed against their nocturnal prisons, but none of them escaped. She was not completely divorced from the culture: running water, fire, and wood splinters were as baneful to her as they were to the brethren. Yet the poison-crazed vampire who'd killed her had made her almost a species of one.

Gisa returned the book to its shelf and left the bookstore. A limousine with tinted windows sat on the street out front, motor thrumming. A man in the back seat studied her, clearly confident the windows obscured him. Moving closer to the limo's side, Gisa pretended to scan the street for a taxi.

The rear door opened and he stepped out. Beneath the street lamp, his wide, handsome face was a riddle of sharp plateaus. "You may have some trouble finding a taxi this late at night." He stepped closer; while far from a threatening move, it made her nervous enough about being accidentally touched to back away. She softened her retreat with a smile. "I sometimes spend half my nights," she said, "waiting for cabs."

"Tell you what," the stranger ran a hand over his wide jaw. "If you let me take you home, you won't have to use your cab-waving hand at all."

"Awfully kind," she said. "But I'm not in the habit of getting into strange vehicles with men I don't know." She cocked her head toward the limousine, but stared straight into his eyes. "I mean . . . I'd have to be crazy, right?"

She knew she could do better, but she was hungry and tired, and the idea of riding to her next meal in a limousine was irresistible.

Within half an hour, they were in Gisa's ninth-floor apartment. She poured her guest a glass of Evian, careful not to splash. "So, Winston, you 'buy and sell things.' What does that mean?"

"Jaded socialite jargon. Thanks to my parents, my fortunes were made before I was born. I guess you could say I'm a career shopper."

"Sounds . . . rigorous," she said, crossing her legs. "Tell me more."

As he talked, she lowered her defenses and probed, smiling all the while, for signs of psychological disturbance. Now and then, she'd say something to spur him on, but beneath their chat's icy surface, she fished for evidence that he was unsuitable. Finding none, she decided that adopting the playboy for a day would be relatively unremarkable.

She set the glass she'd pretended to drink from on a table and moved behind his chair. "I suppose I should seduce you," she whispered, placing her hands on the collar of his shirt.

She braced herself for his predictable response: He slid his hands over hers, guiding them as she loosened muscles in his taut shoulders. Her hands burned where their flesh met. Reflexively, she tightened her grip.

"Hey, hey, hey," he squirmed. "Be gentle. I break easy."

Hot sulfur raced through the veins in her hands and forearms; each moment of contact increased the pain. She pinched his ear, crushing cartilage as she jerked his head to the left. White and corded, his neck stretched.

Winston's protests became yells. Gisa shoved her fist into his mouth, sank blunt incisors into his jugular. His eyes unfocused, his legs whipped empty air, and thank God his bowels were empty, because they surrendered without a fight.

She drank her fill and fell to the floor behind his chair. His body lay lifeless, his golden head a mop of tarnish and sweat. She remained still for an hour, waiting for the feeding hangover to pass. She avoided looking at Winston's face as she broke his neck and smashed his nose into his brain. There could be no doubt the man was dead: The last thing she needed was an undead victim bearing a grudge.

She took a canvas sack from the closet, slid his body into it, checked the corridor through the peephole, cracked the door, checked again. She then lifted the bag over her shoulder, took the maintenance elevator to the basement, and exited through a service door. Gliding over cherry-blossom droppings, she reached into the limo's front window and snapped the chauffeur's neck. With both bodies in the trunk, she drove the limo into a bridge abutment below Arlington Cemetery, and then ran toward home.

Dawn approached, and for that she was feverishly grateful. Across the street from her building, Meridian Hill Park yawned as the first sun beams scrambled through elms, dappling the worn stonework beneath them with miniature blobs of light. Fountains spat loudly, agitating both the living and dead goldfish that inhabited their coinless basins.

Gisa sat at the fountain's edge. Her neck ached where she'd been bitten fourteen decades ago. She rubbed the spot, then studied her fingertips. A splash of color streaked her field of vision. How was he going to explain the limousine? Better yet, how was he going to explain that he was dead, smoldering in the trunk of an abandoned vehicle next to the chauffeur's crackling corpse? Father would scream. And Mother . . .

Gisa twisted around, squinting through colorblind eyes at a single spot on a vine-covered wall. No! She folded her arms tightly across her chest. No! It wasn't safe to be out, in broad daylight, at times like this. She needed to get back to the apartment, lock all the doors, turn the TV up loud, and rock on her haunches until the intruder went away. She laughed. Of course, being dead, he was going to be late for his appointment with the Tunisian Ambassador and her grisly husband. How the hell was he going to explain that? He smacked a palm against his forehead and turned back to the fountain. Excuses, excuses, he spent his adult life making excuses. He didn't want to piss off his father, for fear of losing the largesse. And Mother . . .

Quite by accident, Gisa bit her tongue. Color returned to the park around her, but when she saw a rat scurry from one bush to another, the park exploded and a dozen breeds of green rocketed away from her on the backs of fireworks sparks. She blinked. And Mother . . .

And Mother . . .

"Christ!" Gisa pressed her face into her palms.

A giant goldfish somersaulted and splashed. She recoiled from the lethal spray. Cautiously, she leaned over the ripples and saw his face: the broad jaws, the thickness of her fingers as he stroked them. The ripples spread until calm water threw a woman's face back at her. Her reflection was an anchor in sanity, a constant reminder that she was, and would always be, more human than her lifeless brethren. A sudden adrenaline rush forced her to her feet. She could run. For miles and miles, she could run. Sometimes, extreme physical exertion exhausted her uninvited guests. She ran. Through neighborhoods he didn't recognize, past black-owned corner stores he'd never think of entering. He knocked over a young boy on a skateboard; when he turned to apologize, the boy called her a bitch.

At Logan Circle, she dashed into the bushes and threw up. A taxi stopped, the driver rolled down his window. "You all right, lady?" "I'm fine." He was fine. He staggered into the cab and gave the driver Gisa's address. Mother would be so disappointed.

Gisa slept for two and a half days, the first R.E.M. rest she'd enjoyed in nearly a month. While she slept, Winston had vacated her, leaving nothing behind but the impression of his uncertainty.

In the bathroom, she toyed with the shower handles, then sat naked on the toilet while water ran. It was an old habit; she wasn't sure when or where she'd picked it up. Watching, listening to water shoot from the shower head soothed her, allowed her to wander through regions of mortality the brethren would never willingly trespass. Water was power, to those who sustained themselves on it and to those, like Gisa, who would kill to protect themselves from its venom. Careful to avoid stray drops, she turned off the shower. She was restless for something to do. She wandered into the closet, chose a pair of jeans, olive leather boots that bunched at the ankles, a matching silk blouse.

Downstairs, the lobby attendant hailed her a taxi, smiling widely as she slipped into the back seat. "Hirshhorn," she said, and within ten minutes was at the art museum's Twelfth Street entrance. She whisked past the permanent exhibits on the ground floor and walked up a broken escalator to a second-floor exhibit called *The Shape of Turmoil.*

The dimly lit exhibit occupied a huge, pie-wedge room. Four sculptures of deformed humans, hewn seemingly from onyx, towered in the room's center. They rotated slowly on a platform threaded with optical cable: yellow, pink, green, and orange pinpoints of light traveled the figures' bodies, softening their pronounced disfigurements. Gisa moved closer to the humming platform. Although she was the only person in the hall, she felt as if she were being studied. Glancing up at the figures' heads, she noted with growing uneasiness that they were not made of something hard, like onyx, but of something soft—rubber, perhaps, cast with a technique that evoked an oily, black sheen.

The four figures shared six eyes. One was apparently blind, devoid even of eye sockets. Another had two eyes, while a third had only one, which focused on the forehead of the blind figure. The final three-eyed figure was the source of Gisa's discomfort. Two eyes occupied anatomically correct positions and seemed, from every angle, to stare at her. The third eye stared at her also, but through an abscess in the figure's elbow.

Gisa stepped back, suddenly breathless. A rash of discarded personalities stormed through consciousness. Dizziness swept her and she pitched forward into the base of the rotating platform. A low growl erupted from her throat; she felt the human veneer slipping away, the animal, the vampire beneath, surfacing.

Then she smelled it, a human. Felt it, a hand on her shoulder. She turned in slow motion and saw an older woman with enamel gray eyes and the faintest glow of cinders in her hair. She couldn't respond to or recoil from that unwanted touch.

"Who—" she croaked.

The older woman blinked, said something, blinked again. When she placed her other hand against Gisa's cheek, Gisa stiffened. The animal retreated, the room stopped spinning, and a current of familiarity with a feeling Gisa couldn't identify flowed into her through the older woman's pale, cool hand.

Gisa heard herself say something. Before she blacked out, the older woman smiled.

Fuzzy light. A loft overhead. Potted Wandering Jews swaying in a breeze. The creak of leather. A running faucet. An armless human made of glistening black rubber.

Jerking upright, Gisa gasped. The unfinished rubber sculpture sat on a dais of the same material. It had no eyes, no mouth, but it faced her directly as though it had guarded her while she slept.

Painfully, she pried herself from a black leather couch and surveyed her surroundings. The room was long, uncarpeted; narrow panes striped the cathedral ceiling. Blank painting canvases crowded an entire wall. On the coffee table in front of her, magazines and old books lay in disarray.

"Hello?"

She crossed to where the armless sculpture sat and leaned over it. Even this close to it, she felt none of the discomfort she'd felt in the museum. . . .

The museum. The woman!

"Hello?" she said, louder this time.

Someone in a nearby room turned off the running faucet. Gisa stepped away from the sculpture as the older woman she'd seen in the museum entered the room, carrying two glasses of ice water.

"I'm so happy you've come around," the woman said. "I was afraid I'd have to take you to the hospital, despite your wishes."

"Despite my wishes?"

174

The woman set the two glasses on the coffee table, wiped her hand on a pant leg and extended it to Gisa. "I'm Barbara Yerle."

"You're the sculptor," Gisa said. She did not take Yerle's hand.

The sculptor gracefully withdrew her hand, smiling stiffly as she offered Gisa a glass of water. Her back was slightly stooped and her eyes, Gisa noted, while perhaps once bright and blue, were now alarmingly gray. The woman seemed sad, distracted, but beneath her worn surface something boiled. Gisa had felt it in the museum.

"Thank you," Gisa said, taking the glass. "And thank you for not taking me to the hospital."

Yerle nodded. "Oh, you made it quite clear I should avoid that course of action at all costs. I had to do some fast talking to explain to the staff that I knew you and would take you home with me. I was—both suspicious and intrigued."

Gisa's preblackout directive must have been a century of survival habits at work: an emergency room scene, with all the probing hands and pricking needles, would have turned into something ugly.

"What happened at the Hirshhorn?" Yerle said, sitting lightly on the couch's edge.

Gisa set her glass carefully on the coffee table.

"I don't know what happened," she said. She didn't, but she'd have to feign complete naïveté to learn more about the enigmatic artist sitting before her. "Something about your sculptures—bothered me."

"So I gathered." Yerle crossed her legs. "Why are you here? Who are you?"

"I don't know why I'm here," she said, choosing honesty over evasion. "The sculptures stirred something in me I thought—" She shook her head. "—Something I thought I'd lost. I need to understand what that is."

"What about the work tied you in such knots?"

*Be honest with the woman.* "Pain." *Be honest with yourself.* "Desperation."

Softly, her eyes sparkling white in the afternoon sun, Yerle said, "I don't see a desperate woman standing in front of me. I don't see the shape of turmoil."

Gisa began to understand that the spell she thought Yerle had cast over her was her own need to regain mortality. Yerle, more by chance than by design, had captured roaming, ceaseless suffering in her sculptures.

Gisa was potentially immortal. It had taken Yerle's art for her to recognize how horrible that could be. How inconclusive.

Yerle was saying something about taking Gisa home. Again, Gisa's human shields crumbled as hunger and supernatural sensitivity blossomed. This time, she welcomed the wave as it cleaved Yerle's voice, exposing imperceptible threads of emotion and heredity.

From a distance of light-years, she watched her fingers clamp around Yerle's wrist. Her other hand whistled through air, slapping the woman's shocked face so harshly blood splattered the blank canvases yards away. Within seconds, she was on her knees, her knees were on Yerle's chest. The woman shrieked, but a second blow to the head knocked her unconscious.

Gisa cupped the woman's head in her hands. Even before the bite, the surge within her of Yerle's personality began. Gisa drank slowly, lovingly, as a motley memories, perceptions, opinions, and fears exploded behind her closed eyelids.

Finally, she broke Yerle's neck.

After collecting herself, she staggered out of the house; within two blocks, she found a cab to take her home. At the apartment, she stripped, carefully reducing her outfit to strips of confetti and arranging them in a large circle in the middle of the living room floor. She sat in the middle of the circle and weighed new postures for pain, new studies in suffering.

An itch in her palms drove her into a mad cat's pace. She was in the bedroom, looking fruitlessly for the sketch pad, the charcoal tin, the black clay bricks she was certain she'd picked up from Piotr's place the day before the Hirschorn opening. She tried the kitchen, but her search there was equally fruitless. Goddamned Piotr! Didn't he know? Didn't he know how much she hated not having enough of what she needed? Didn't he know what it did to her, how it left her incapable of thinking straight and impossible to deal with? For studies, she needed clay bricks! Black clay bricks!

She opened the refrigerator, but it was empty and unlit. Why? In the living room, exhausted, despondent, she sank into a chair and counted backward from ten. Where had she gone wrong? Why had the sculptures failed? *None* of them understood that the figures were displays of dread. They saw only the guise of innovation, never the heart of her loneliness. Was she Gisa, was she Barbara, was she Gisa?

A couple of laughing youths passed her apartment door in the hall outside. She wondered where they were going and what they'd be doing once she was dead.

Dead.

The word brought the artist and Gisa clashing together. No longer were they oil and water struggling to separate. They shared an unspoken wish for the permanence neither, on her own, was capable of defining. Yerle had buried the seed of self-destruction, too weak to give it life. Gisa had absorbed the seed, given it a full complement of boughs and roots.

She fell out of the chair, tears racing down her cheeks. She plucked the recliner off the floor and threw it through the window. Trembling, she watched it straddle a branch, hesitate, and tumble to the ground.

She felt as if someone had poured acid on her face. Horrified, she ran to the bathroom and stared at herself in the mirror. Since her murder and rebirth, Gisa had never cried. Now, the body punished itself for the release, baring tracks of blistered flesh where salt water had run. The sculptor, empowered by liberation, screamed for more. Gisa, weak from the communion, exploded with fresh tears.

The world warped as her features grew distorted beneath the torrent. The sculptor's eyes saw Gisa's deformity as Gisa's mouth spat horrible insults at the cruel specter of undying.

Her fingers clenched and the marble sink top crumbled. She'd been fooling herself for years, convinced she could survive comfortably in a world of ignorant, insensitive critics. No, not critics. Food. Not food. Humans.

The pain in her face was greater than any she'd experienced, but the movement of tears was also marvelous agony. She pried her fingers from the sink top and sat on the toilet. Slowly, she popped the shower curtain off its rings, shuddering violently as the sculptor wrapped Gisa in a suicidal envelope.

Hands twisted the shower handles, releasing spumes of hot water. Steam tickled her nostrils. She inhaled it. She inhaled Yerle's fatal reassurances.

Before her second leg had entered the stream, her body began to smoke.

# Crucifixion

ADAM-TROY CASTRO

He first tried to kill it during the Napoleonic era, early in his damnation, when the lover he tried to Turn instead merely died, her body repelling the blood he attempted to mingle with hers. He had imagined that if he could make another creature like himself he wouldn't be so lonely anymore. But Madeleine merely writhed in agony for a day and a night and a day and a night, aging decades even as he watched, her beautiful milk-white skin turning to dessicated parchment, her devotion to him turning to hate. She cursed his name with her last dusty breath. He needed to die, then—not the false death that he'd lived for only a few short years at the time, but the true death that he imagined would free him from the guilt of his betrayal. And so he'd placed a pistol to his head and pulled the trigger. The blood so violently driven from his body became a scarlet flower on the wall, like a last bouquet for the lover now turning to dust by his side.

He'd fallen to the floor, dead. His wound was an open mouth, facing the ground—a perfect invitation for his blood to return to him. And the blood obliged, pouring down the wall in a hundred hungry rivulets, each one moving much faster than gravity alone could have pulled it, each one so much in control of its own destiny that the wall it abandoned was left dry and unstained in its wake.

The puddle it formed on the floor flowed quickly back into his wound, which just as quickly closed, leaving him to sit up, cursing the fire that burned inside him.

But the blood didn't care what he wanted.

It didn't care if he strode naked across battlefields, letting the cannonfire rip his flesh to ragged shreds. It didn't care if he was blown into a hundred pieces and mingled with the corpses of a thousand martyred soldiers. It didn't care if he was decapitated, or buried, or burned, or gassed, or eaten. It was just blood. Every drop was just like every other drop, all infinitely divisible; and as long as so much as one drop survived, even if only as a stain on a scrap of cloth, it gathered his pieces together, and made him whole, and sent him forth to feed.

Once, he leaped from the deck of an ocean liner in the dead of night, and sank gratefully into the cold and black, certain that this, at last, would be enough. It wasn't. His lungs filled with water. He drowned. Small fish came to feed on him. Blood mingled with the currents. He found himself reborn, long enough to drown a second time; then lived and died twenty years of hell, living and dying again and again before he made his way to the nearest land. By then, the blood was ravenous within him. Nobody in the small fishing community that found him survived that night. The blood drove his limbs, forcing him to take them all—the good, the evil, the young, the old, even the babies in their cribs—before the sun rose the next morning. He faced its unwelcome light across streets filled with pale, dessicated corpses, cursing it for not taking him, the way he had once heard it was supposed to. But it was just daylight, the giver of life, the force that gave strength to the blood of all men; and which could never hurt the beast that pounded in his veins.

That was decades ago, now. Decades of growing despair and self-loathing. Decades of obsessing on the day he'd become what he was; a lazy summer day so beautiful that he'd gone off by himself and taken a nap in a field, only to waken and (imagining it a dream) see a single glistening red spot leap from the grass beside him, flow up his cheek like a reverse tear, and enter him through the corner of his left eye. Decades of remembering what it had been like to feel the blood boil inside him, as it all changed in a moment of flaming pain. Decades of suspecting that whoever played host to the blood before him must have somehow succeeded in driving it away; leaving him with the colossal bad luck to lie down on this spot, and be chosen. Decades of wondering how many centuries his predecessor must have had to live with it—centuries? Millennia? And decades of killing himself again and again, only to be repeatedly brought back to life by the damned slavemaster blood.

Until now.

He has spent years gathering the knowledge and resources he needed to build this place; a year more in putting it together, and making the hundreds of little adjustments necessary to make his little solution as thorough as it needs to be.

It has to be thorough. It is not enough for his flesh to die—not enough for his spirit to wither inside him. His flesh is just ambulatory meat; his spirit just the cool wind that drives it. It's the blood that is tainted, the blood that makes him what he is, the blood that makes his existence a sick compromise between life and death. It is the blood itself that must die. He can't permit a drop to remain.

And so he hangs from a hundred hooks, bleeding from a hundred wounds, onto the hot grill that boils his blood one steaming drop at a time. Every drop that hits the broiling-hot metal below screams audibly as it turns to steam. Whenever he looks like he's going to stop bleeding, the steel clamps that grip him from either side squeeze him tighter, inexorably wringing him dry. When there is no more blood to have from him, he will be dropped onto the stove like a piece of meat, and cooked for an hour or two . . . at which point the chamber will fill with acid.

It is agony. He doesn't care.

He is only afraid it won't be enough.

And as the blood screams, and the clamps wring him tighter, he thinks the last sane thought of his long existence:

MADELEINE.

# Bingin'

## Greg Cox

Roxane posed in front of the full-length mirror stuck onto her closet door. The glass showed most of her small, cluttered bedroom, but not Roxane. Fine, she thought. She didn't need a reflection to know how she looked.

She knew she was fat.

Heavy metal posters decorated the walls. A crescent moon shone through the lacy white curtains over the window, casting a spotlight onto the rumpled sheets of Roxane's small single bed. Rox had not actually slept in the bed for months; these days she preferred the shade and privacy of the basement. Her parents didn't object, at least not since she had buried them alive in the same basement. She had the house all to herself now, and could bring boys home whenever she wanted.

Like tonight.

Rox stepped away from the mirror, almost tripping over the body stretched out on the carpet, the body of a good-looking teenager with shoulder-length blond hair. His torn leather jacket, with imitation silver studs, was spread out like a miniature cape beneath him, revealing a black Nirvana T-shirt. Jeans and briefs gathered in a clump around his ankles. An ugly red gash stretched across his throat, just below his Adam's apple, but only a few stray drops of drying blood dappled the carpet beneath his head. His flesh was ashen, cold, and lifeless.

His cheap leather wallet, emptied as well, rested on Rox's dresser next to a crumpled heap of coins and bills. Only $46.72, she thought bleakly. Shit, that was barely enough to cover utilities. Good thing she didn't have to pay rent.

He called himself "Dutch," Rox recalled. She didn't need to turn on the lights to see him clearly. She knelt and closed his eyes for him: ugly eyes, full of fear and disgust, just like they were right from the start. Proof for sure that she still wasn't thin enough. When she'd first found Dutch, outside the Bloodsnares concert at City Center, the grossed-out look in his eyes told her right away that he wouldn't come freely, that she'd have to use the old Bela Lugosi stare to bring him back here.

Major mass depressing. If I was pretty enough, Rox knew, I wouldn't have to use the magic. Madonna never needed to use her eyes to catch guys. But Madonna isn't fat like I am. She never felt as full, as bloated as I do now.

Suddenly she couldn't stand it anymore. She ran out of her room and down the stairs to the kitchen. She yanked opened the the refrigerator door and let one tiny bulb struggle to light up the entire house. Frosty racks and shelves, empty except for a few plastic bags and foil-wrapped souvenirs of past dates, smelled of baking soda and raw meat. Frantically, Rox snatched out a Zip-loc bag full of garlic and threw it on the chipped formica counter. Her hands could not move fast enough, but somehow she managed to get the bag open. The fumes immediately attacked her eyes and throat.

Good, she thought. It's still fresh.

An inch-long fingernail sliced a sliver off the bulb of garlic, then cut the sliver in half. Rox nodded grimly; that should be enough. Holding her nose with one hand, she lifted the garlic fragment and dropped it down her throat.

Oh fuck! Rox clenched her fangs together to hold down the scream. Like always, the stuff hit her right away. It burned its way down, then exploded in her gut like a ball of flame. Scarlet droplets broke out like sweat over her forehead and back. An icy chill rushed through her trembling body, followed by a sudden wave of sweltering heat. Her skin was too tight. Stolen blood pounded in her temples. Her stomach churned, and she felt the burning coming back up. Rox leaned over the kitchen sink and watched as a flood of crimson fluid rocketed out from between her jaws.

*Scarf 'n barf,* she thought. Same as always.

Afterwards, as she spat out the last few gulps of Dutch's life, Rox felt shaky but content. Puking up blood was never fun, but, hey, what was the point in living forever if you couldn't stay thin and hot-looking.

Another chill came over her and she leaned on the counter for support. She waited for the sink to drain, but the tub stayed filled to overflowing with cooling gore. Damn, she thought.

Clotted again! How am I going to explain a sinkful of blood to my next boyfriend? Probably have to call in a plumber and kill him after the sink's fixed.

The clock on the stove read 2:30 A.M. It was nowhere near dawn, yet Rox felt like calling it a night. Totally wasted, she stumbled towards the basement stairs. She ought to hide Dutch's body, she knew, just in case some snoop drops by, but she didn't have the energy. Anyway, why bother. Now that Dutch had croaked, he'd be changing. His throat would have started healing already. By tomorrow night, he'd be able to walk out of here on his own two legs.

Rox sighed wistfully. It would be nice if he stayed, of course, but she couldn't count on that, could she? If only she could see what she looked like! . . .

Dutch, a.k.a. Andrew William Voris, was trapped in a nightmare that just went on and on. Neon-red demons, like the monsters on a Meat Loaf album, swooped down from a thunderous sky, snapping at his head. He tried to fend them off with his hands, but his arms turned into batwings before his eyes. He ran through an empty parking lot glittering with broken glass, the demons hissing and shrieking overhead, until he stopped abruptly, frozen by the sight of a blood-red tidal wave rushing toward him. Frothing with pink foam, the wave crashed over him, washing him away. He found himself drowning at the bottom of a warm, sticky, salty ocean. He flapped his wings wildly against the thick, murky redness, swimming against pulsating currents, and fought and battered his way to the surface. . . .

He opened his eyes. The sea of blood was gone. Instead, he found himself lying on his back in a room he didn't recognize. It was dark, but he could still see. A life-size poster of Axl Rose stared down at him from the ceiling. Where in the hell am I, he wondered. Last thing he remembered, he was strutting home from the concert when . . .

He shuddered suddenly from something he couldn't bring himself to recall. Dutch sat up with difficulty. His arms and legs were cold and numb; they seemed to belong to someone else. His mouth felt strange, too, like it was shaped different maybe. For a second he feared his jaw was broken, but, no, there was no pain. His mouth was dry, though, and hungry for something he couldn't quite place.

Another flash of memory hit him: After the concert and parking lot. Running down empty suburban streets. Legs aching, gasping for breath, but unable to stop. Compelled. *Controlled.* Then a house, some stairs, a bed with pink sheets . . .

"NO!" Dutch yelled, his eyes pinched shut, his face contorted. "Stop, please, stop." He pounded his head with his fists. He ground his teeth together, slicing his tongue to ribbons, anything to keep from remembering.

Then something stirred behind him. "Welcome back," said a dry, scratchy voice. "Remember me?"

Dutch turned his head and knew he was insane.

A half-naked mummy stood posing in the doorway, silhouetted against the darkened hall beyond like a photographic negative. She was a skeleton in a bra and torn cut-offs, barely covered by a thin layer of flaking, brown skin. One bony hand rested on her hipbone. She stretched her other thin, emaciated arm towards him and a spiked wristband slid all the way down to her shoulderbone. The eyes in her skull were roiling globs of luminescent jelly, and she smiled without lips, gnashing rows of chipped, yellow tusks. A clump of dyed blue hair dropped off her skull, but she appeared not to notice.

"C'mon, lover," she croaked hoarsely. "The night is young." She sauntered towards him in a hideous parody of seductiveness. "You want to go for a bite, or dance, or . . ." Her glowing eyesockets turned towards the bed. ". . . Well, you know." Sharp black nails on a skeletal hand reached out for Dutch's face.

Sheer, blind panic overcame Dutch. With a wild, wordless shriek that emerged as a howl, he rolled away from the decaying horror and scrambled to his feet. He did not think or try to understand what was happening; he just had to get away! His desperate gaze searched the room, then seized upon the moonlit window. He staggered towards the window. Through the curtains he saw a fenced-in backyard that looked as though it had not seen a lawnmower for many months. He glanced down. It was a two-story drop to the grass. Dutch didn't care.

"Wait," said the monster, coming nearer. "Don't go." She

took another step closer, her clawlike hands outstretched, her shriveled breasts caked with blood.

Retching on pieces of his own tongue, Dutch threw himself at the window. Glass shattered. The lacy curtains clutched at him like cobwebs, but he was free and away from that place! He expected to fall, but instead he felt the warm summer wind lift him up. Strange new instincts kicked in, and dark leather membranes blossomed from his arms even as his body shifted and grew smaller. Fleeing the ghastly terror in the bedroom, Dutch soared towards the moon on wings of night.

Roxane considered flying after him, but gave it up. She didn't have the strength or the confidence. Blood was better than Prozac, but at times like this she missed the pills. Talk about your mega-rejections! He hadn't even said good-bye.

She slumped onto the blood-speckled carpet and glanced, mournfully, at her empty mirror. If ever she'd had any doubts about her figure before, Dutch's frantic retreat had killed them forever.

And yet the hunger still boiled inside her. Her mouth watered and her fangs ached for the taste of fresh human meat. It would be so easy, she knew, to find another snack, just like Dutch. Or better.

No way, Rox thought. Not tonight. She had all of eternity to go hunting in. First, though, she had to lose weight.

# Slice of Life

## Dan Perez

Your day begins at 9:32 P.M. in the humid darkness of a southern city called Houston, Texas, and it begins with a whimper, not a bang. The whimper comes from a homeless man underneath one of the city's sprawling freeway interchanges. He's wearing Desert Storm camo pants and a T-shirt and he just got a good look at you in the actinic glare of the lights from a nearby supermarket parking lot. He backs away, that low sound gurgling in his throat and that hollow trapped look in his brown eyes. He was sweating before but now it's beading up fresh on his face, heavy with the mingled scents of grime and terror. He stumbles and falls back onto the corrugated incline of an on-ramp support. Scrabbling up the incline like a crab, he tries for words, to somehow convince you to stop advancing, but the only sound is a gasping "Don'—"

Then, faster than his dilated pupils can follow, you're upon him, slashing his throat with sharp yellow fingernails until your hand is slick and wet, and his wild flailing has ceased. You take a mouthful of his blood; it's as hot as the air here, and it tastes of nicotine and Mad Dog 20-20.

After drinking a bit more, you leave him on the incline and turn toward the supermarket, listening to the *thok-thak* sound of cars driving across the expansion joints in the loops of freeway high overhead. A wail behind you. "Oh, Pixie, man! Oh what they done to you, Pixie?"

You cross against the traffic to reach the parking lot, and the cars swerve to miss you. There are honking horns and the screech of tires, and, muffled inside the cars, cries of fear and disgust.

Then you're crossing the parking lot of the ethnic supermarket, with Latinos and blacks and a few whites scrambling to hide behind the parked cars as you pass. The elderly security guard near the entrance fumbles his revolver from its holster and shouts, "Stop! *No entre!*" You continue to advance and he fires, four of the shots missing entirely and two connecting with your right shoulder and chest. There is pain, but it's only a fleeting spasm as the bullets pass through and the wounds close up.

Moaning, the guard claws at his belt for more bullets, but you slash out and he tumbles back, clutching his mangled throat. Now there are nearly constant screams, which, to you, have become the night's anthem. Glass doors slide open and you enter the store.

People rush to the head of the aisles to see what's happening, get a glimpse of you and then run away again. You stop in front of the magazine rack. There it is on the cover of *Newsweek* and *Time* and the front page of the *Houston Post:* stories about your recent appearances in Chicago, Tulsa, and Little Rock. *Newsweek* has a grainy picture of you stalking past a burning warehouse in Tulsa. Your pale skin is stained red with blood and your dark long hair snarled and matted. Your face, as it always is in photographs, is blurred, indistinct. The lurid headline above the photo says UNSTOPPABLE? You laugh at that. To those who have long forgotten the old rituals and defenses (or the few deluded souls who have guessed what you really are, but cling to all that movie nonsense about crosses and hardwood stakes) you most likely *are* unstoppable. That's one reason you've taken up your current cross-country spree. To see how unstoppable you really are.

Soft sobbing comes from behind a counter with watches and cheap silver rings for sale. You vault over and a wide-eyed teenager with nut-brown skin cowers before you. She tries to scream, but it comes out a pathetic squealing sound. You toyed with the concept of mercy for your prey decades ago, but now you're too jaded: You can't help but see them for what they are. This girl is to you what the lamb, the kid, and the veal-calf are to her kin. You reach out for her.

By midnight, you're moving along Main Street toward the glittering glass skyscrapers of downtown Houston. There is blood and fire and anguish in your wake. Two helicopters shine their spotlights on you and the air is shattered by the sound of pistol and riot shotgun fire: The local police have converged upon you now. They fire from the doorways and from the cover of police cruisers, and amid all the noise, you can hear cursing, confused flurries of orders, and frustrated shouts. "Why doesn't he go down?" someone yells over and over again. The air reeks of cordite.

A sound bearing down on you, from behind. You spin to see a police car speeding at you, a wild-eyed officer gripping the wheel. Shouts of "Hold your fire!" go up as the car accelerates, now just a few feet away. You time it, and vault up onto the hood just as the car gets to you. The cop hits the brake about the same time you smash through the windshield with your fist. Momentum hurls you through the air. *Whee!* Laughing, you crash through a chainlink fence and tumble to a stop on a neatly manicured St. Augustine lawn. The crunching impact of the police car skidding to a halt reaches your ears. At that moment, an air raid siren blares to life from the vicinity of downtown Houston. What a wonderfully surreal touch.

By 2:30 A.M. you're doing battle with the SWAT team in the shadow of the downtown skyline. They fire high-powered rifles at you, but the slugs, even those designed to expand and tumble in human flesh, just zip right through you. They're lobbing those stun grenades at you, though, and it's annoying to keep getting knocked down again and again. So you jog over to the grenadiers' positions before they can scramble away and you snap some necks. There. That's better. Just for fun, you take some grenades with you to toss at the gauntlet of regular police surrounding you. The flash and bang of the grenades and the popping gunfire are exhilarating, but it's missing something. A pulse-thumping musical soundtrack, perhaps.

You glance up at the sky. Houston has come alive. The skies are full of helicopters, many of them news choppers, and the streets are clogged with police and news vehicles. One idiot photographer rushes up to snap your photo and is cut down by the hail of bullets that swarm around you like angry Texas mosquitoes. You step over his torn body and keep going.

The National Guard shows up around 4 A.M., as you climb up the limestone facade of the One Shell Plaza building. Bullets constantly plink around you, shattering the glass windows and spitting out little puffs of limestone dust. There's a loud, screeching impact behind you, and you turn to see a CNN copter and a Houston police copter going down after shearing off each other's rotors. They explode in flame as they strike the parking lot near an armored personnel carrier twelve stories below.

The stakes are higher now. A lot of automatic weapons fire from the ground strafing your position and a big National Guard chopper circling the building. In a lighthearted moment, you pause to wave as the olive drab bird sweeps past.

The gunfire stutters to a halt as you lever yourself over the edge of the building's roof. You're completely coated with limestone dust, white as a ghost. You notice that nearly all the copters, except a few police units shining their spotlights on you, have pulled back. That big green chopper is still close by, too—

hovering patiently, its side door still closed. Something big is coming up, that's for sure.

Which is fine by you because that's why you're doing all this. The epiphany of the century hit you a few weeks ago, before Chicago. You realized that the ultimate curse of immortality boils down to one rather simple thing.

Boredom.

The side door of the Guard copter slides open. Main event time, you figure. You stride out toward the edge of the building, and a few of those crazed cops fifty stories below still squeeze off potshots at you. You lean out over Houston and shake your fists, shouting, "Top o' the world, Ma!" It strikes you as ironic— your mother died six centuries before movies were even invented. Still, it sounds so *appropriate* up here. "Top o' the world!"

The guardsman in the chopper doorway shoulders a tube-like rocket-propelled grenade launcher. Today is definitely going to end with a bang.

"RPG!" you shout. "Dig it!"

The conical grenade whiffs out of the tube and sizzles toward you and there is a *very big concussion,* like all the stun grenades in the world going off at once. All light and pain and noise and *dissipation.*

Wisps of night fog coalesce over a southern city that buzzes like a disturbed hornet's nest. Carried on a light breeze, the strands of fog twist together and drift down, heavier than the night air, collecting into a vague oblong in an alley behind a convenience store. The oblong continues to solidify and then it —*you* open your eyes to see the first light of dawn creeping into the skies overhead.

Houston's been pretty fun, you think, searching for a place to sleep during the daylight hours. Tomorrow night you'll continue on west, perhaps to Albuquerque or Phoenix or maybe north to Denver. It doesn't matter, really. Now things are *rockin'.*

# Charity

## ADAM NISWANDER

The sign read CAROLVILLE, ARIZONA. POP. 509.

Giuseppe slunk into town after dark, hugging the shadows, large dark eyes scanning the street for watchers. He saw no one. The town simmered, reflecting the accumulated heat of the day. He ran a shaky hand over his bald head, scratching at the short fringe that began just above his ears. Turning, he looked into a blank storefront window. The lone street lamp lit the walk where he stood, causing the glass to reflect like a mirror. He wished again he had a reflection.

He remembered being human, just barely—but his memory had to reach back many decades. He knew what he looked like, though. With his nearly bald pate and his pear-shaped form, he most resembled the stereotype of an Italian barber. The cruel comments of men who were long dust did not seem so far away. They had called him names. He had no trouble remembering that. Chromedome. Skinhead. Baldy. After the change, he had hunted them down and fed, the blood tasting even sweeter when it slaked his hunger for vengeance. An ironic smile haunted his lips as he thought about how all things come full circle.

Now he was the hunted.

The newspapers called him the last vampire . . . and press coverage of the hunt for him had been rife. Man had finally decided to rid himself of his parasite. Over the past three months relentless pursuers had chased, harried, and driven his kind to extinction—save for himself. Only he survived of all the arrogant, supposedly immortal, undead. He had been tracked as far as New Orleans. There, it seemed, they had lost his trail. But how much longer would he remain free? When would one of the finders come at him with a stake or an ax or fire?

He knew he had been lucky to escape detection even this long. His normally dark skin lightened perceptibly when he hungered, but the resulting tone—though pale—appeared almost normal. In a new town, after sunset, he looked . . . human.

They shouldn't be looking for him this far west, but suspicion and paranoia are hard for the hunted to overcome.

Despite the seeming emptiness of the streets, he stayed in the shadows. This might be a trap. He had a new identity—papers, license, social security card, even a blood donor's card, all taken from the most recent victim. But careful observation might prove embarrassing to this counterfeit "Wilbur Crane."

No traffic moved on the street. No one stirred. The town looked eerie and desolate. *Where the hell is everyone?*

Cautiously turning a corner, he saw the sudden brightness ahead and heard the low murmuring of human voices. A hospital—with a small crowd gathered in front. Ambulances sat parked in long rows. Some kind of accident?

He could not avoid them at this point. His choices had disappeared.

He moved up to the rear of the crowd. Though outcast and hunted, his kinship with humans remained the one fragile thread connecting him to this world. He looked hungrily, longingly, at a woman standing a little to the side.

She met his gaze with mournful eyes.

"Pardon me," he said in a low tone. "What happened? What's going on?"

She stared at him for a moment, then looked back at the well-lit building before them. "You been lost in a cave or somethin'?" She ran a weary hand over her face and rubbed tear-laden eyes. "The school bus turned over. Every kid in town's in there. They were pretty badly cut up. We may not have enough blood for all the transfusions."

"What?" He didn't have to pretend surprise. "No, I just got into town, not five minutes ago. I didn't know."

"They're lookin' for O+ blood, mister." Hope momentarily lit her face. "What kind ya got?"

Giuseppe looked stricken for a second, then remembered. "Uh, just a moment." He fished out the wallet and fumbled the donor's card from the pocket. "I'll be damned," he muttered.

The card said TYPE: O+

"We'll all be damned if'n we don't save them kids," she said.

He looked at her and nodded. "You're right," he said quietly.

"Ya got that right, mister. Now what type blood ya got?"

"The right stuff," he said making up his mind. "O Positive."

"Praise the Lord," said the woman, relief lighting her face. She stepped onto the long front porch and called out. "Barton! Barton Russell! We got another O Plus out here."

The harried white-coated doctor came outside, his face pale, etched with deep worry lines. "Who is it, Ellie?"

She pointed at the stranger. "This fella here."

Dr. Russell came forward, took the proffered card from the man's outstretched hand, and read it eagerly. "We sure are glad to see ya, Mr. Crane. We need your help."

Giuseppe felt a sudden, uncontrollable urge to laugh aloud, but covered his mouth with his hand, faking a cough.

When he recovered, he said, "Miss Ellie explained it to me, Doctor. Are you asking me to let you take my blood? Do you think I should?"

"This card says you gave blood four days ago, Mr. Crane, so you must be okay. We haven't got time for the usual tests. I have a half a dozen children in there who's lives are in your hands."

The vampire straightened up, his sense of justice lending him an aura of dignity. "I appreciate being invited, Doctor. That has always been important. Let's get to it, then," he said quietly. "I'm glad I came here tonight. You have no idea how happy I'll be to donate my blood to the cause."

"You're a hero, Mr. Crane, though you won't get a medal or anything. Why, if you stayed in this town long enough, future generations would thank you. Come on in here, my friend, and we'll get you hooked up."

Giuseppe took a deep breath and nodded. Without further words, he stepped through the door and into Vampire history— as the savior of his race.

# 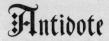Antidote

### BILLIE SUE MOSIMAN

Carmine made it through the long tunnel and halted across from the park in the darkest part of the street to pry a quarter inch of hard bio-metal scab from the knuckle of his right hand. It would grow back, of course. All the small patches growing over the surface of his skin like a creeping cancer would eventually merge until the only opening was a vent for his nose and eyes. Thus encased in his new skin, immobile, he would die of starvation.

Vampire punishment, cruel and unusual, heartless. A strain of insecticide had been developed in the late twentieth century to control moth and butterfly larvae. It effectively encased them in their skins so they starved. This technology had been further enhanced to be used on the undead man. By the age of twenty-one Carmine had been caught in his native Italy and strapped to a gurney and injected. Nothing else killed his kind, not the traditional stake through the heart, that only pissed them off; not burning, for they could walk out of any fire; and not beheading, for they could carry their heads under their arms and have them stitched on again.

The Hosts had won the war in the nick of time and it was through geneticists who had been working to save crops. Or rather, they thought they had won the war. For a half century Vampires and Hosts coexisted, killing and being killed in turn. Now a majority of the vampires had been captured and inoculated with the deadly vaccine. There were few left who were disease-free. When an innoculated beast bit a Host, making him a vampire, that beast too carried the tainted blood that would finally bring him down.

It was rumored, however, that Fondren, the King of the Vampires, had commissioned his brightest people to seek an antidote to the vaccine. It was further rumored that one of their kind working in research in the far reaches of the East Texas wastelands had done just that.

A cure!

But only if Carmine was able to stay alive long enough to arrive at the enclave and be inoculated with the antidote. Only if Fate allowed him time to reach Texas before his nights ran out and his skin turned to a solid case of shiny metal armor with him lying slobbering behind the cold hard mask, his eyes wild and rolling from the suffocation. It was worse than being buried alive. He'd be able to see his enemy, smell his fresh blood, hunger for him with every molecule, and yet not be capable of the pounce, of the rendering and tearing of the carotid, of drinking his fill, of satiation.

A girl's voice broke through Carmine's reverie to ask, "Do you have somewhere to go tonight? Would you like some company?"

He sneered at this approach before he turned and showed his face, his fangs. Even today the Hosts had their women on the streets offering their bodies, never knowing if they would be used for pleasure or for food. It was walking suicide, and he hadn't any remorse in his heart when he took down one of these idiot whores.

He swiveled slowly, his upper lip rising as he did so to show her true terror. When she came into view, his lip froze in place and he blinked and his heart stuttered in his chest.

She was a great old one who had been taken in her youth; she was a queen. From the fiery furnace of her gaze he trembled and shrank back. She hissed, showing him her own fangs. She was far stronger than he, her physical power rippling the muscles beneath the fair skin of her biceps as if they were full of snakes. "I'm not your supper," she said. "You mistake me for another sort of female, one weaker than I."

"How did you know I was a vampire?"

"I saw you tear off the bio-metal and fling it from you."

"Are you infected too?"

"Not me! I'm too clever to be caught. And so was my Master who made me. I doubt even now these years later that they've gotten their hands on him. So will we walk together or are you intent on your solitude?"

"Come along," he said, turning and moving on through the shadows, staying close to the buildings' walls. "I'm on my way out of this morbid city. You can come with me to the outskirts if you want."

"Leave Mobile? Why would you want to do that? From your accent I can tell you're foreign. Italian, perhaps? We've had an influx of Italians lately. Mobile takes in the foreigner quite nicely. Besides, you're doomed and there's no better place than here beneath the century oaks to die. Then again, perhaps one place is as good as another. We do have the stench of death here, our kind falling so rapidly sometimes you must step over them on the sidewalks and in the gutters come early morning." She shuddered involuntarily.

"I won't die." Carmine straightened his shoulders and walked with more purpose.

"Certainly you will. You've got the metal growing on you even as we speak."

Carmine nodded his head. He picked at an imaginary fleck of the metal he thought might be growing on his left wrist. "Yes, but Fondren made finding an antidote his highest priority and I've heard one of our scientists in Texas has found it. I'll be saved. I've come halfway around the world to reach him."

She laughed, the sound so sudden and unappealing in its derision that Carmine stopped again and glared at her. His lips rose in automatic response and his fingers spread, yearning to find themselves wrapped around her young, tender throat. Strength of fury would cause him to challenge her if it came to that even though he knew she would not be overcome.

"It's a lie!" She laughed no more, seeing his face. She spoke again, more quietly, knowing his dignity ruffled, his hope shattered. "We've all heard the same, but it's not true. It's just moonbeams on a summer's night. It's wispy fog along a swampy bank. It's a child's tale told to ward off the nightmare."

"How would you know that?" He knew he was speaking out of turn, that if she chose she might take him prisoner, bind him, and keep him still until the bio-metal did its harsh work, but he must know why she called it a lie.

She lowered her head and black glossy hair hung past her cheeks like a curtain. "I had a friend who believed the rumor and made the trip. He came back just days before his final encasement within the bio-metal. He had searched out the entire southeast portion of the state of Texas looking for this miracle worker and found no one remotely familiar with the legend. It's a scurrilous lie. More horrible because it sends so many like you on a fruitless last march cross country for no reason."

"Your friend might have been wrong. He might not have . . ."

She hissed. Silence settled between them like a heavy dew fall. Finally she said, "There is no cure. There is no antidote. You've wasted your time coming this far if you thought otherwise. Where are you from?"

"Italy," he said. "You guessed correctly." He resumed his walking again though now his steps were no longer purposeful, and hope had fled from his face the way a butterfly races across the sky to flee the sticky petals of a poison blossom.

"A beautiful country, I've heard."

"Disseminated," he said, thinking of his homeland and the terrible journey he had made on the strength of what his companion now called a deceit. His ship, with him in the hold, had landed in Miami and he'd traveled by night for a week to get as far as Mobile, Alabama.

"As is this country," she said sadly. "Not even many of the Hosts are left to rule. It's all collapsed."

"The world," he said, "will soon be a wilderness, overgrown with weeds, and ruled by the rodent."

She shrugged. "So why waste what precious time you have left to go to Texas? They say the Hosts have cleared out from Houston to the panhandle. The ones left alive are in a fort near Abilene. You could starve to death looking for game or man."

"And here? I've had no luck all across the state of Florida either."

"There's many Hosts left yet in this place."

"But no hope," he said, walking faster as if to leave her behind.

She must have halted for she spoke from his back. "How much do you want saving? I see you would travel on to a desolate empty place even when you're told there is nothing there to help you, but would you kill off the Hosts with a disease worse than the bio-metal, if you could? Even if you knew it meant the end of your human source of blood and you'd be forever dependent on the lower animals?"

He hesitated, his steps slowing. He turned to her again. She was mesmerizing, a Merlin with riddles at her command. "What does this mean? That you can save me, that you have some magic to stop *this*?" He pushed up the sleeve on his left arm and with long fingernails plucked a metal scab the size of a silver dollar from just above his elbow. The exposed raw skin glowed red a moment and then freely oozed his blood. He pitched the metal bit and heard it jangle as it hit the pavement of the street.

"What if I told you that I am the antidote? That I am this city's liaison to gather vampires who have heard of the cure in Texas and decide which ones I'd like to save and which ones to let wander on toward death? That there are others like us scattered across the states, seeking out the wanderers? That, yes, Fondren ordered an antidote and it was created, and I was injected, and I am it?"

"I'd say that was farfetched."

"More impossible than a phantom in Texas waiting with vials to save you?"

He cocked his head and studied her. "Why do you tease me with all these stories? Just to confuse me so that I don't know truth from lie? I have *no time* for games! Even now there are bio-metal spots I can't reach formed on my back, and if I were to pull down my trousers, I'd find patches on my thighs. If I took off my shoes, they'd be there glittering between my toes, and here . . ." He grabbed one of his ears and pulled the lobe forward from hiding behind shoulder length hair. "Here is one trying to take over my skull!" With a wrenching movement and a groan he tore skin and metal and threw it at her feet. Long damp strands of his hair clung to it and blood now poured fresh down his throat.

"Come to me," she said in the seductive voice of the hunter. "Let me drink from you and save you all at once. I promise it is not a lie, nothing I have said is an untruth. If you wish for life immortal as was promised in the beginning, come to me now."

Her hushed voice filled and thrilled him. It blinded his eyes, dampened the taste buds on his tongue, stilled the rapid beat of his heart, stole memory and fear and desire from his thoughts. He lumbered clumsily into her embrace, no more in control of his actions or emotions than he had been when he was made by his Master half a decade earlier. She was very powerful. A queen with skill enough to put him on his knees or to bay like a wolf at the stars. She could not be denied; no matter if it meant his admittance to final darkness or redemption into the everlasting life of the undead with no worry of bio-metal encasement. He had lost all choice and did not even miss it or know the moment it actually deserted him.

She leaned her head near the wet, soggy hair that lay across his throat. With her long tongue she licked it aside. His heart slowed and he wrapped his arms around her body, pulling her in close to him, loving her, wishing to be one with her forever. It had been years, a lifetime, since he had felt such peace and serenity. Perhaps she did have the antidote in her bite, coursing through her rich blood, the miracle that would return his immortality.

Just before she bared her teeth she said softly, "Now I will tell you the real truth."

He sighed against her, his strength draining from him as it would if he had been hypnotized and told his limbs were turned to tubes of rubber.

"There is no antidote in Texas. There is no antidote in me. There are no Hosts left on this entire continent, my dear friend. The few of us who are left must prey either on one another or on foreigners who come to this land. We spread the rumors that brought you. Many of us sailed to other shores, some who had the skills flew planes, but the rest, like me, who cannot leave, simply lie in wait for you."

"Noooo," he said, drawing out the word in a whisper of breath. He felt her heat and it reminded him of the emptiness of Miami and of all the state of Florida, how he had not had a human meal since he landed. Other vampires he encountered had looked haunted and frail, but none had the power of this one to capture him.

"Yesssss," she cooed, sinking her fangs into the carotid and drinking deep while Carmine silently cried in his mind for it to be over quickly.

The fangs fastened, his head lay back, and he submitted to the last death. As he slipped from the bounds of his body he knew she had been right all along. She was the authentic antidote, the surcease from despair. He sighed with the breath of stale air left in his lungs and took the echo of that sigh with him into the blind darkness, stepping away almost happily from a world ravaged and beyond any hope of repair.

# All Through the Night

JEDEDIAH ELYSDIR HARTMAN

The pale predawn light in the eastern sky blinked out and was replaced with a handful of stars like sparks tossed from a fire into darkness. Cherna stepped through the door as it hissed open, then turned to wait, cocking her head to better hear the faint strains of music that drifted across the lawn. The door slid gently closed; and a momentary, almost indiscernible brightening of the light beyond it heralded Ilya's arrival.

The door opened once again and Ilya stepped out. Strips of black silk rustled and swirled about her legs, allowing an occasional glimpse of pale thigh and ankle as she walked.

"Shall we?" Cherna murmured. Arm in arm, they strolled across the lawn toward an archway.

"Where are we this time?" Ilya asked.

"Who knows?" Cherna said. "Mika didn't say. Istanbul, perhaps?"

Ilya glanced around. "Where is Mika?"

"He must have gone on ahead."

They continued through the archway into the courtyard beyond, into the hubbub of laughter and music, into the party.

The synthesist's break after his second set was nearly over when Ilya finally cornered him near a table of punch bowls and glasses on the third floor of the mansion under a crystal chandelier. She lifted one black eyebrow and the corner of her mouth to catch his attention, then moved closer to him before he could turn away.

"Aren't you Terry Winters?" she asked innocently.

He laughed, surprised and pleased. "You've heard my music?"

"I've heard a lot about you. You're earning quite a name for yourself."

He laughed again, with a touch of self-deprecation. "In some circles, maybe."

She smiled, a brief flash of white teeth. "Would you like to accompany me outside?" she asked. "It's very nice out tonight."

"I'd love to."

Ilya led the way to the ornate French doors at the end of the room. Winters followed her out onto the stone balcony beyond. The quarter moon had moved nearly halfway up the sky, lending a silver glow to the courtyard below them. Guests wove back and forth in intricate patterns, laughing, dancing, singing.

"You know," Winters mused, looking down at them, "I sometimes think if I watched people moving around for long enough, I could translate the motion into music. A theme or a melody for each of them, weaving through each other until—"

Ilya's soft touch on his arm interrupted him. She put a pale index finger, half-sheathed in black silk, to her too-red lips. "Shhh," she breathed.

Surprised, he forgot to blink for a long moment, lost in her eyes. Then: "You're very—" he began, but she stopped him again.

"Don't talk." She lifted her face toward his—hardly lifted at all, really; she was almost his height—and he bent toward her. Their lips met, opened. Winters brought his left arm up behind her back and pulled her toward him. He reached backward with his right hand to set down his wine glass, but it slipped from his fingers, shattering with a crystalline susurration on the stone floor. His vision blurred.

He felt his knees buckle, but something held him upright. From a great distance, he heard her soft voice: "Beautiful. Such a prize." Then came a stabbing pain at his throat, and blackness.

Ilya shut the French doors gently behind her as she returned to the room. Mika, obviously bored, watching the well-dressed partygoers surrounding the punch bowl, leaned against the wall by the door, one black boot at the end of a bent leg resting at the top of the wainscoting. His bright red lips turned up at the corners when he saw Ilya, one black eyebrow lifting above his dark glasses. He pushed himself away from the wall as she approached, leaving a dusty footprint on the mahogany.

"What of the night, dear sister?"

She smiled back, a flash of white teeth. "A true prize, dear brother. Have you noticed our hosts' appalling lapse of taste? The musicians have been playing without a synthesist for nearly an hour."

The eyebrow again, and a gesture with the red wine in his left hand toward the balcony doors. "Terry Winters?"

Ilya nodded.

"That *is* quite a catch, my dear. My congratulations."

They kissed. Drawing back, Mika licked his lips and said, "Sweet."

Ilya touched the corner of his mouth, brushing away a tiny spot of red. "Yes. Music in the blood, or so it's said."

Mika nodded. "I've been only a trifle less successful. Jacqueline Pierce."

"The senator? Well done," Ilya said. "And Cherna?"

"Little luck thus far tonight, I'm afraid," Mika said. "Only a dancer, and an unknown one at that."

Ilya licked her lips. "Well, there should be time for one more round before we move on."

Cherna's pale face and hands were barely visible in the dimness, despite subdued lamplight seeping in from the hallway and starlight through a high window. Mika stepped all the way into the darkened room, shut the door behind him, removed his sunglasses.

"What brings you here, dear brother?" Cherna asked. She leaned back in her chair, her short, fashionable black leather jacket falling open to reveal a thin blouse.

"Looking for you, my sweet," Mika said.

She stood, and they kissed, hungrily. After a minute, Cherna stepped back, breaking the embrace. She laughed: A high, wild sound that stopped abruptly. "You haven't had your second turn yet."

"No," Mika said. "But I'm about to rendezvous with a certain important personage. . . ."

Cherna asked, "And who might that be?"

Mika smiled, slowly, starlight glinting in his pale eyes. "Chris Washington," he said.

"Very nice," Cherna said.

"Ready to concede?"

Cherna glanced at the door. "Not quite yet, dear brother. I've a prospect arriving shortly who should put me solidly in the lead. Would you be so kind . . . ?"

"Best of luck," Mika said. He replaced his glasses, opened the door a crack, and slipped out. Back in the room, Cherna sipped her wine, moistening her red, red lips, and settled back in her chair to wait.

The moon was gone from the sky, and pale talcum light powdered over the easternmost stars. Cherna and Ilya toasted each other with champagne across the remnants of a tableful of hors d'oeuvres, then kissed. Recorded violins whispered from speakers hidden in the foliage. Of the other remaining guests scattered across the courtyard, a few still chatted quietly, but most had drifted off to sleep in chairs or lounges.

Mika stepped from the shadows of an ornately carved doorway to join Ilya and Cherna. To Cherna he said, "Ah, there you are, dear sister. Ilya told me of your success; I congratulate you." He drew her close, and they kissed.

At length, Mika stepped back and turned to Ilya. "Shall we depart?"

"Cherna's turn, I think," said Ilya. "Winner's choice. Though how you managed Sarah Fiona Cheng, dear sister, is quite beyond me."

"It was merely luck, dear sister," said Mika.

"Skill, rather," replied Cherna. "*You* wouldn't have managed it, dear brother. Remember Hans Frieling?"

A black eyebrow twitched with annoyance, above dark glasses. "Very well. Point conceded. Your choice."

Cherna smiled, white teeth behind red lips against pale skin, a curve of dark wine on chalk, blood spilled on snow. "I know just the place," she said.

The three strolled back through the arch, back toward the booth. Ahead of them another group of guests, laughing, blinked out one by one, going home. When they were gone Cherna stepped in, adjusted the settings, vanished.

"Good night, dear sister," Mika whispered to Ilya as he followed Cherna.

As she waited for the door to cycle open again, Ilya whispered to herself, "Yes. Yes, it is." A good night: The fading night now part of the long night past, and the renewed night to come, to be followed by night after night after unending night, free of interfering daylight, uninterrupted darkness stretching forward into eternity. . . .

The door opened, and she stepped through.

# The Dark Nightingale Returns

### THOMAS MARCINKO

Here's how I got started as a superhero:
I slipped past security and made my way to the elevator. Nobody saw me unless I wanted them to. Berkwell, the worst slumlord in Philadelphia, lived in a luxury suite on the twentieth floor. He wouldn't live much longer.

It felt good to be back on the prowl. Especially now that I had a new purpose.

I found Berkwell's suite. Locked, of course. But over my three centuries I'd picked up some useful skills. If you had all that time on your hands and were as nosy as I, you too would excel at breaking and entering.

I opened the door quietly and padded in on soft-soled shoes. On a skyscraper roof just across the park, I saw the flare of paranormal combat. It looked like a couple of dynamicals going at it. Colonel Quantum versus the Electric Eye, as far as I could tell by their registration colors. I wondered what they were fighting about.

I didn't care. After three hundred years of loneliness, I didn't feel so alone any more. My days of hiding were over.

I wanted to shout: Brothers and sisters in paranormality, I come to join you on your Crusade for Justice. You have shown me the way. Like you I will use my powers in the Service of Good. You got your superpowers in radioactive and chemical accidents, or through drugs and implants and suits licensed by the Paranormal Control Commission. I got my superpowers from a bite in the neck and an obscure metabiological process. What's the difference? Power is power. What's important is how you use it.

Berkwell shambled out of the bedroom. He was a fortyish slab of suet, in the middle of dressing for dinner.

"Who the hell are you?" he asked, startled.

"One of your tenants."

"Yeah, buddy? You from the tenant's co-op? The rent's due on Friday. Now beat it."

"I'm not just any tenant."

"Yeah? I suppose you're the goddamn King of England?"

"I am your death."

I sunk my teeth into the fat bastard's neck and drank him dry.

He tasted delicious. Much better than my last long-ago feeding, because this time I'd done it in a good cause. My methods might be somewhat unconventional even by current standards of paranormality. And I chose to attack white-collar rather than street criminals out of long-held political conviction. But nobody could deny that I was as effective as Colonel Quantum, Madame Morphosis, the Dark Oracle, or any other licensed paranormal.

I expected the Paranormal Control Commission would offer me a license. Sooner or later.

I found my assistant—my Renfield, if you will—working up a sweat on the stationary bike, the dermal patch on his shoulder drip-dripping life extenders into his bloodstream. He had a handsome face, a sinewy body, and he'd kept his skin a healthy, sensible, and rather attractive pale white.

"So you got him," he said between puffs.

"Climb off the bike and kiss me."

"A few more minutes." Puff. Puff. Poor bastard. Some people will do anything to live forever. Try telling them it's not worth it. They never believe you.

But he came to me like he always did. He'd left a few drops of blood from a shaving cut. I shoved him away.

"Don't tempt me."

"You know I want it."

"Can't we just go to bed?"

He wouldn't let it go. He was using me in the hopes that I would give him the Big Bite and grant him eternal life.

Me, I was just using him for sex. At least one of us was getting what he wanted.

Afterward we watched the news while I lay cradled in Renfield's arms. I had to laugh when Epsilon's holo manifested and he began to denounce me. Tall, bronzed, muscular—he looked pretty good in that long underwear. Nice buns. The mask was of course purely decorative. Everybody knew that Epsilon was George Epstein, though the media always referred to him as "reputed" paranormal. His energy-nimbus crackled and sparked. He pointed challengingly at the imager.

"Know this, bloodsucking fiend!" Epsilon bellowed. "Your obscene crimes will not go unavenged! We of the Paranormal Control Commission will find you; we will track you down; we will turn you over to the proper authorities; there is nowhere that you can run—!"

"Off," I told the deck. To Renfield: "I'm disappointed."

"I told you so. Why bother with those jerks? If you want to do something worthwhile for a mortal, why don't you transform *me?*"

That argument again. I'd say I was sparing him decades of untold boredom. He'd accuse me of harboring a death wish and warn me that I was the last of my kind. I'd say maybe that was for the best, and he'd say, then why didn't I just end it if a potentially eternal life was so unbearable? I'd say that wasn't the point. He'd say I was on a power trip.

Maybe I was. But what did that make Epsilon, or the rest of the licensed paranormals?

The city stank of corruption. Politicians on the take. Mob bosses. Corporations were the worst.

Making a dent was hard. One or two per night was my

limit. With binging and purging I could sometimes take out five or six.

By now I'd collected a nice bunch of headlines from the newsnets.

PARANORMALS TO VAMP VIGILANTE: DROP DEAD!

NOSFERATU NEMESIS HITS MAYORAL HOPEFUL.

BLOODSUCKING BEAST OFFS EURO AMBASSADOR.

GOVERNOR CALLS FOR PARANORMAL CRACKDOWN.

MADAME MORPHOSIS DENIES CORPUSCLE KILLER LINK—"I AM NOT A BAT."

EMPOWERED MOMS: "SAY IT AIN'T ONE OF US!!"

I had a costume of sorts. I hadn't even had to commission it from the usual suppliers to paranormals. It was a large black T-shirt with red bloodstains dripping down the front. I'd bought it from a street vendor. I was a tourist attraction. If the organized paranormals didn't want my help, I still had my fans.

I liked being famous. Or infamous. If I couldn't be a superhero, I was glad to be a supervillain.

"This crimefighting thing," Renfield said as he cooled down from an intense session of weightlifting. "Wouldn't it go easier if you had an ally?" He raised his chin invitingly. He did look delicious, his throat pulsing from heavy breathing.

"It's not for you," I said.

"I could get myself a power," Renfield said. "I know where to get Anodyne. Or Enlightenment. Or any of the drugs linked to paranormal syndrome. Or implants. Or just a powersuit."

"What are you saying?" I challenged him. "If I don't sip your blood and make you one of the living undead, you'll go get another superpower?"

He flexed his biceps. "Wouldn't I look great in tights?"

Target: Kevin Tarmak, a local politico who'd diverted billions of dollars in drugs from FedHealth, condemning thousands of poverty-level viral-carcinoma victims to an early and painful death. He was getting away with it. The court called it a mistrial. I called it a crime.

A crime that must be avenged.

"I am your death," I muttered to myself, practicing on the way to his place. "Kevin Tarmak, I am your death."

I broke into his place in the usual way. Tarmak saw me. He screamed and dropped his beer.

"I am your death."

Epsilon crashed through the skylight. He crackled with stray sparks of energy as he dropped to the two-inch-thick imported carpet and knocked over a shelf full of rare coin displays.

I was startled. I stopped in mid-bite. A mistake. A forest of long, thick tendrils poked through the skylight, wrapped themselves around bug-eyed, silk-pajama'd Tarmak, and reeled him up through the light to safety. The tendril-bearing figure lowered himself from the skylight and touched the carpet with tiptoes. His vinelike appendages whipped around me with rodeo grace, pinning my arms to my sides.

Another figure fell through the skylight. (I had to pick a penthouse with a skylight.) She did a passable gymnast's roll, untangled herself from her black mock-judicial robes, and tossed back her mane of curly red hair. She faced me, green eyes glaring through an elegant ballroom-style masque. She pointed a slender finger at me and said:

"I am Judge Miranda—and you have the right . . . *to tell me everything!*"

It worked. Over the centuries I'd dealt with mesmerists, charismatics, and hypnotists of many kinds, and they'd never been able to get a thing out of me. Clearly, I was dealing with something very different here.

Under her patient questioning, while she sifted and rummaged through my most private thoughts, I told her all. When she released me from her psionic grip, I knew how my early victims had felt. I've looked at vampirism from both sides now.

We'd been joined by a few other paranormals. I recognized the Spinner, and the Strange Attractor, and True Gamester. One costumed figure I did not at first recognize was documenting the scene with a holo-camera.

"Renfield," I said. His costume was purple and black, the color of a registered sidekick. He did look good in tights. All that work on the stationary bike had paid off. "How the hell did you get a license?"

"I'm sorry," he said apologetically. "They promised me a superpower if I led them to you."

I couldn't believe he'd done it, particularly since his betrayal led me to be psionically raped.

"Can they offer you what I can?" I asked.

"You were never about to give it to me. If I have to live a mortal lifespan, at least I can live it as *something* special." He turned to Epsilon. "I'd like to be able to walk up walls, if that ability is available for licensing."

Epsilon's electric-bright eyes were full of contempt as he looked at Renfield. "Take him away."

The Tendril caught him. He lifted Renfield up through the skylight, to the police copter whose whir grew closer.

That's what I got for picking beauty over brains. I might have told him the paranormals would never accept him. Too much guilt by association.

Epsilon turned to me. "We want you to stop. God knows I sympathize with what you're trying to do. The world's better off without the scum you've erased."

"Then why interfere?"

"The feds have been reaming our butts since you went to work. They think one of us is responsible for the Nosferatu Murders."

"Not murders," I said. "Executions."

He shook his head. "That is *not* the way we do things. I don't know what country you're from, but this is America. We turn evildoers over to the police and the courts. We have a thing called due process. Maybe you've heard of it."

I bristled. The nerve of this pompous, bureaucratic, holier-than-thou. "Don't you dare lecture me about due process. Was it due process when they burned my village? Killed my family, my sponsor, my mentors? Dragged them into the light and watched them go up in smoke? I was young then. Naïve, like you. But don't talk to me about due process. Nobody gave *me* due process."

"You've put this city through a reign of terror."

"You don't know what terror is."

Epsilon was silent for a moment. I thought it might be a thoughtful silence.

"This is America," he said. "We don't do stuff like that here."

"You can't stop me."

"I don't want any of my buddies mistaken for you. Or caught in the crossfire. We'll do what we have to. Three of the tabloid nets have already posted a reward for the apprehension of the Fearful Vampire Killer.

"We'll try anything," he continued. "Stakes, garlic, crosses."

I laughed.

"Miranda has your psi-print," he reminded me.

I stopped laughing.

"We can track you down," he continued. "You've already shown one vulnerability. You must have others. Sunlight, maybe. Chemicals. Radiation. At the very least we'll make your half-life a living hell."

I knew he was right, for the time being at least. But I wouldn't go quietly.

"It's my method, isn't it?" I shouted. "You don't even mind that I go after the white-collars you usually lay off of. I want justice as badly as any of you, and God knows I'm at least as smart as most of you. You just can't stand the association with somebody who has the paranormal ability that I do. It's the blood thing that bothers you, doesn't it?"

He had no answer.

"I'm not that different from you," I said. "Am I? Tell me I'm different."

I got no reply. I made my escape. Nobody saw me unless I wanted them to.

I claimed one more victim before I temporarily retired. You should never let a Renfield get away with betrayal.

He'd wanted me to feed on him and turn him into one of me.

He got the first half of his wish.

I've gone back into hiding. The licensed paranormals continue to operate under official sanction. But evidently some paranormals are more equal than others. I hate them, the fascist bastards.

I wonder if they taste any good. I have a feeling I'm going to find out. But I'm still outnumbered.

I may have to make more of my own kind after all.

# Up in the Air, Junior V-Men

### GREGORY NICOLL

The vessel was warm against his gloved fingers, but the gun was cold.

Duke smiled and raised the little white styro cup to his lips. His coffee was still too hot to drink, but inhaling the dark, earthy aroma of the smoky joe was one of the few pleasures available out here. Squinting, he looked down the blue steel barrel of his rifle at the heavily barricaded farmhouse.

All around him, grim men wearing bulletproof vests were huddled behind Treasury Department vehicles, watching the embattled Branch Jeffersonian compound through binoculars and riflescopes. They smoked cigarettes as they waited, occasionally glancing up at the setting sun. The evening chill nipped hungrily at their flesh. Conversation was low, tension high.

Duke noticed that the cold didn't seem to bother Steve Boggs, the jovial blond-haired agent who shared the car with him. He didn't know quite what to make of Boggs. The kid was excited about something but he wouldn't let on what it was, although every few minutes he rechecked the mechanism of the smoke grenade launcher he'd laid across the Chevy's trunk. Weighted down by their vests, Duke and Boggs leaned uneasily against the ice-blue sedan, cradling their assault rifles and their coffee cups.

And waiting.

From time to time one of them would whisper the name of their fallen comrade, Koch.

"Koch. . . ."

"Yeah, Koch. . . ."

The name was passed slowly up the line of men, repeated in whispers as each agent spoke it with reverence, nostalgia, disgust, contempt, or awe. Or, as in the case of Boggs, a curious sense of anticipation. Duke wondered if any group of fighting men on the American continent had been as inspired by a simple phrase since *"Remember the Alamo!"* rang from the lips of Texan avengers two centuries earlier.

Not that Special Agent Koch had been a hero on the order of Davy Crockett or Jim Bowie. In fact, Koch had been a vile little creep, always cheating on his weekly timesheet and bitching about being passed over for promotions that everyone knew he didn't deserve. But Koch's brutal, merciless slaying by the tax protestors holed up in the Branch Jeffersonian farmhouse had made quite an impression. Every agent on the case had seen it happen. None of them would ever forget it.

"Koch," someone said again. "Damn shame what happened to Koch. . . ."

A diesel engine rattled as a small blue van rolled up behind the line of cars. Its tailpipe coughed smoke and condensation as its motor was switched off. Two bulletproof doors creaked open at the rear. The H13, commonly called "the Drainer," had arrived. Five and a half gleaming feet of stainless steel, the Drainer was rumored to be able to draw every usable ounce of blood from an average human corpse in less time than Mr. Coffee could brew twelve cups of joe. A petite young technician—Duke thought he remembered her from Waco as Marybeth something —hopped out. She began to assemble and adjust the Drainer's many tubes and suction valves.

Another vehicle, a long black Cadillac hearse, rolled up and drifted silently to a stop alongside. Two sullen agents opened the rear doors and removed a massive oak coffin, which they placed on the ground near the Drainer. The casket's lid eased open with a late-night horror movie sound effect, and Special Agent Gibbs, "V-Man," climbed out.

Duke felt his stomach turning. Gibbs was playing the part to the max, complete with a high-collared black satin Lugosi cape. Duke took a jolt of very mortal pleasure at the sight of an ugly brown stain on the edge of the cape, no doubt a trace of Gibbs's native Carolina soil.

He watched as young Boggs stepped forward to the V-Man with that smoke-grenade launcher and, following a plan they'd apparently discussed the previous night over a cellular phone, Gibbs quickly shapeshifted into a fine mist. The vampire then slowly condensed his mist-self and, with a hiss like the sound of escaping steam, inserted himself into the steel green grenade canister.

Boggs gestured to a group of men manning the huge Air Force spotlights. They fired up the carbon-arc lamps, turning the hot white beams on the little farmhouse. This lit the scene up so brightly that it seemed strangely artificial, like a movie special effect sequence just before the effect was about to happen. Duke shook his head at the irony; in a way, that's exactly what this was.

Then Boggs turned, grinning, to Duke. "Okay, Mouth Marine," he said. "Get on that bullhorn and tell 'em that Avon's calling."

Duke flicked the toggle, switched on his loudspeaker. There was a brief shriek of feedback as he adjusted the volume. He raised it to his lips.

*"Branch Jeffersonians,"* he said calmly but forcefully. *"Throw out your weapons, and come out now with your hands in the air. This is your last warning."*

Their answer was a volley of gunfire. A window shattered on one of the blue Chevys and two bullets thumped harmlessly into the side panel of the Drainer van. It took only a moment for Marybeth to recover the slugs. She immediately verified that the projectiles were neither silver nor hardwood, just plain ol' gray lead.

"Rock and roll," said Boggs. He raised the grenade launcher and wrenched back the trigger, sending the small green canister spiraling straight toward the broken main window of the farmhouse.

It stopped dead in mid-flight at the windowframe, and fell harmlessly to the ground.

V-Man Gibbs, still in the form of a mist, plumed out of the canister and shapeshifted into corporal form. He looked around in startled amazement. Blinded by the spotlights, he was obviously baffled as to why he now found himself standing outside the house instead of inside. As he turned and faced the window, a resounding *twang* of high-tension string came from the darkness within. A wooden crossbow bolt poked through the back of Gibbs's cape, and the undead special agent fell to the ground dead for the second—and last—time. His body began to decay rapidly, collapsing like a sandcastle in the surf.

Boggs was speechless. A chorus of *what-the-hell*'s and *those bastards* echoed up the line as the agents marveled at what they had just witnessed. Duke just shook his head and sipped his coffee.

Then, with a mothlike fluttering, a small gray bat descended from the evening sky and shapeshifted into corporal form behind them. The agents had been surprised before on this job, but nothing had prepared them for this—the second vampire was Koch.

Laughing, Koch said, "You fellahs look like you're seeing a ghost. Dont'cha know the difference between a ghost and a vampire?"

"B-but *how?*" somebody asked.

Koch chuckled again. "I had Gibbs 'tap' me a coupla nights ago, at my own request. Didn't hurt much, really. Then yesterday I just took a chance on rushing the farmhouse door. When the protestors nailed me, it was no big deal. I knew that when it happened I'd be right back—as one of the undead."

The men shuddered and began to whisper among themselves.

"*Hey,*" said Koch, a touch of annoyance now coloring his tone, "this way I'm now a fully vested V-Man, with a three-grade promotion. And I get to keep all my benefits too, even though I'm dead. Plus, the Treasury Employees' union and the Equal Opportunity Office negotiated a whole new set of fringe benefits for us V-Men."

Duke shrugged. "Well, all that sure didn't do Gibbs much good."

"I was watching that farce," said Koch, "from up in the trees there. You guys forgot something important, one of the basic rules of vampirism. Ya see, I read the V-Man manual cover-to-cover last week, and I know exactly what went wrong: Gibbs wasn't *invited* in. Now, let's try that tactic again, shall we?"

\* \* \*

It took a while, but Duke worked the bullhorn like the solid professional he was. At last a series of deliberately provoking threats got the Jeffersonians stirred up enough to issue the challenge that the agents had all been waiting for: "Come on in and *try* to take us!"

V-Man Koch now had the invitation he needed.

This time Boggs's smoke grenade breached the window-frame and planted a full-blown hungry vampire directly behind them. The protestors dropped their crossbow and fled the farmhouse, firing automatic weapons to clear their path. Koch bounded after them in wolf form. Four surgical gunshots from the Treasury Department snipers dropped all the fugitives dead in their tracks.

Marybeth rolled the Drainer up and attached it to the Jeffersonians' bodies, tapping off the blood with a low, surging sound. Koch shapeshifted to human form and watched hungrily, his fangs bared and saliva drooling over his lips.

"The union and the EEO Office got us new fringe benefits," Koch reminded everyone.

Duke shook his head as he watched the Drainer at work. He leaned over to whisper in Boggs's ear. "Can you believe it?" he said. "In this new age of V-Men revenue agents, all those old taxpayer jokes about us are now true . . . the I.R.S. *really does* want their blood."

The Drainer, its task complete, made a loud sucking sound and switched itself off.

Duke and Boggs picked up their coffee cups from the hood of the Chevy. The styro mugs left twin imprints of moisture in the painted logo, like the punctures of two enormous fangs.

*Internal RevenOO Service*

# Cross Examination

## BRAD STRICKLAND

**C**ount Wolfort Rokosh was good on the stand—good enough to make me sweat blood. From the moment my opponent, "Sleazy" Sydney Hisch, asked his client, "Now, are you a naturalized citizen of the United States?" the Count's suave assurance, air of melancholy, and brooding authority shone. A handsome man he was, impeccably dressed and groomed. I wondered how he managed that without a mirror.

"I have been a citizen since February of 1862." More than a century in the U.S.A. had blunted the Count's Transylvanian accent. "I could have remained an alien until the Civil War ended, but I wished to fight for the Union. I am a patriot."

Natch. He even said it with the right air of diffidence, the good citizen being humble. A glance at the jury told me that the women on it were feeling sympathetic toward him already. Syd let the witness tell of his long career, then got to business. "You know the plaintiff, Miss Myra Quattlebaum?"

Rokosh assumed a sweet, sad expression. "I used to call her 'my bountiful winepress.' "

My client tugged my sleeve. "That's not true! The creep just flew in, satisfied his thirst, and never had the decency to call later—"

"I know the type," I whispered back. "Just 'Fang, bang, and tell the gang.' Let's hear what he has to say." Night court was new to me, and sleepiness kept trying to pry my mouth open in a yawn, but I had to pay attention. The Count was miles ahead on points, and I wasn't sure I could sway anybody on the jury, but my meager bank account said I had to try. Since Rokosh had accumulated a fortune over the years, and since my thirty percent contingency fee rode on the jury's decision, I had quite a stake.

When at last Syd said, "Your witness," I stood. A glance told me the jury (one half of them women, the other half-asleep) had bought Rokosh's act. I licked my lips, trying to come up with an angle, as I approached the witness. I had to get him on cross—that was my only hope, my only chance. "Let me see if I have this straight. You claim you met Miss Quattlebaum at a party and tried to start a conversation. She wasn't interested. Later you followed her home, correct?"

"I felt attracted to her. She was—my type." A juror giggled.

My face stayed straight. "I see. Would you say you were stalking her?"

Syd objected; the judge considered; finally he let me have the question. Rokosh showed his pointed teeth. "I would not use that term."

"And at about two-thirty that morning you entered Miss Quattlebaum's apartment. You didn't tell us how. What was your route of entry? Did you come through the front door?"

Rokosh squirmed—not much, but he squirmed. "No."

"Tell the jury how you entered."

With an uncomfortable glint in his eye, Rokosh said, "I changed myself into a bat—"

Juror Three made a face of disgust. "A bat?" I interrupted. "The flying mammal, so often infested with vermin or infected with rabies—"

Syd objected on behalf of bats. Sustained. "I apologize," I told the witness. "What I said was no reflection on you." It was only a small victory, not enough to win me the case, but I had made my point.

Rokosh continued. He had fluttered up to the bedroom window, had watched my client undress for bed (he didn't mention whether his voyeurism was in human or chiropteran form), and then tapped on the glass. Surprised to see him on the ledge outside her sixth-floor apartment, my client expressed concern for his safety and asked him in. "So I was invited," Rokosh concluded with a smirk. "Everything by the rules."

The rules. Of course. I paced, remembering all the ground rules of vampirism that years of midnight movies had made clear to me, to everyone on the jury. If only he hadn't obeyed the rules, if only—

Dawn broke. Maybe. Or maybe it was just the false dawn of a forlorn hope. But there were other rules. My mouth was dry. I cleared my throat and asked, "By the rules?"

"Exactly."

I shouted, "You expect this jury to believe that lie?" The sleepy ones jolted awake.

Rokosh looked flustered. "What lie? I tell the truth!"

"I put it to you that you are lying," I shot back. "Answer this: Did you at any time ask my client's permission to bite her neck?"

"Ask her per—" Rokosh furrowed his brow. "I don't understand."

"It's a simple question. Did you obtain Miss Quattlebaum's informed consent before indulging in vampiric activity with her?"

"She—she wanted me to bite her neck," stammered the count. "I could tell—"

"Your honor," I said, "please direct Mr. Rokosh to respond."

"The attorney for the plaintiff is calling for a straight answer, Mr. Rokosh," the judge said. "Give it to him."

Attaboy, Judge. He was a Republican appointee, a by-the-book guy, and also democratic enough to follow my lead in dropping the "count" hogwash. Best of both worlds.

Rokosh muttered, "I don't remember quite what you asked—"

The court reporter read back my question.

"Well," said Rokosh, oozing a cold-looking moisture that probably passed for sweat, "I did not exactly ask her verbally—"

"You didn't?" All six women jurors were leaning forward, the fire in their eyes warming my heart. Just to hammer home my point, I said, "You mean that in contemporary America you entered a woman's bedroom well past midnight, remained there in her presence, placed your mouth on her throat, pierced her jugular with your teeth, sated yourself on her blood, and never once asked her permission orally or in writing?"

"I—she *wanted* it, and, uh, she didn't say I couldn't, and, uh—"

The judge gave him a stern frown. "Answer the question."

His Honor's implacable tone pounded the last nail into the coffin. Looking hunted, haunted, pinned down at last, Rokosh muttered, "Well—not as such, no."

\* \* \*

217

On another evening some weeks later, my client signed a check and handed it over. "It isn't the money that's important. I'm just happy we fixed Rokosh so he can't pull the same thing on another woman."

"It isn't the money at all," I agreed, trying not to salivate on the check. My cut came to a million and a half. "And don't worry about Rokosh. We've taken care of him. He probably can't even afford the payments on his mausoleum." No joke. We had bled the sucker dry. "So what are you going to do with your award?"

"First thing, take a vacation. I hear Carlsbad Caverns are nice this time of year." Her sharp-toothed smile was radiant. "I may buy them."

I saw her out. A pale woman was waiting for me in the anteroom. She asked, "Are you the bloke wot took Rokosh for five million?"

Blame the TV tabloids. This kind of thing happens all the time. "Right," I said. "But no more vampire cases. I can't stand the hours."

She shook her head. "It ain't vampires. I want to bring a sexual harassment suit against me employer. He acts proper towards me one time, acts as'f I'm dirt the next. I'm sure the doctor'd never treat a man that way."

"Doctor? You work for a *medical* doctor?"

"That's right."

I took her arm and opened the office door. "Tell me all about the terrible way you've suffered working for this nasty, rich Dr.—"

She smiled at me. "Jekyll," she murmured.

# It All Comes Out in Analysis

HOBEY WIDMOUTH

D r. Glassman popped an antacid into his mouth and rubbed his stomach. It had been a very long day.

Squinting through the office window at the darkness and the rain, he muttered a short German curse he'd learned as a boy.

Wouldn't you just know it, the one day of the week he worked late. . . . It never failed. Another rainy night in Manhattan, with street lights reflected in the gutter and taxis splashing pedestrians who stood too close to the curbs.

He pushed the miniature orange tree aside and stared at the sidewalk thirteen floors below. From this height, the shifting umbrellas down there looked like moving targets.

Thursday was always a long day. As usual, Dr. Glassman had arrived at 8:15 this morning to find Mr. Shapiro already here, perched stiffly upon the edge of the bench in the waiting room, holding the *Wall Street Journal* before him like a commuter on a train. Damn it, the man knew very well his appointment wasn't till 8:30! He knew Dr. Glassman needed those extra fifteen minutes to go over his notes, schedule appointments, and do all the things a psychiatrist has to do to prepare himself for twelve hours of human misery. . . .

Still, there he'd sit, hoping Dr. Glassman would make an exception just this once and would fit him in just a few minutes early so that, God help him, he could be down at the Stock Exchange by 9:30. Or hoping, at least, that the doctor would feel guilty about keeping a patient waiting for fifteen minutes. (He'd have to talk to Mr. Shapiro about that next week; perhaps that was part of the man's problem, always forcing guilt upon those around him. Dr. Glassman reached for a pad and jotted down a little reminder to himself.)

As usual, Mr. Shapiro had spent the whole session glancing

at his watch, as if the state of the market were more important to him than the state of his own psyche. (Come to think of it, maybe it was.) As usual, too, he'd yielded up his dreams grudgingly, like some secret investment portfolio, and had made it clear that he had better things to do with his day than spend it spinning fantasies and recollecting nightmares for some stout, ugly headshrinker who was probably a fraud anyway, and whose whole profession was just one big racket. . . .

Ah, yes, Mr. Shapiro was a suspicious one. A healthy dose of paranoia and a dab of anality—the perfect businessman, from 8:30 to 9:20 every Thursday morning.

And then came Mrs. Osterman, of course, with the hot flashes and menopausal angst, followed by Joanie Weems, with her adolescent drug hobby. ("Not a habit," she would say. "It's just a hobby.")

And after her Jill Kirkbride, convinced that men only liked her for her looks; then poor Miss Ritter, who was so homely she couldn't look men in the eye. And then Anita Gates (now beginning to "transfer" onto Dr. Glassman), who loved her father a little too passionately; and jolly Mr. Doldus, who dreamed of slitting his father's throat. . . . Then there was Mrs. Barnett— sorry, *Ms.* Barnett—whose marriage was on the rocks. And Mr. Crane, whose marriage to another man was working out splendidly. And then, of course, there was Miss O'Brian, and Mr. Phelps, and Mrs. Reinhardt with the weight problem. . . .

With just enough time, amid that welter of names, to gulp down a mouthful of lunch. And on late nights such as this, several mouthfuls of dinner.

Which helped account for the doctor's sour stomach. Although there was another reason, too. . . .

Swallowing the remains of the antacid mint, he drew the curtains, blotting out the glossy blackness of the night.

Yes, the warm sunshine of Aruba was going to be very pleasant indeed, after a schedule as hectic as this. Only three more weeks of it. . . .

And only one more patient left for tonight.

Stoat.

The man responsible for Dr. Glassman's stomachache.

The doctor sighed and knelt before the file cabinet in the corner, his plump knees cracking from the strain. (Must get back to those isometrics, he decided, especially with vacation coming up. Or maybe he could schedule himself a few more tennis lessons. He'd jot that down just as soon as he got to his feet.)

Stoat—yes, it was time for him at last. His most unpleasant patient. Disagreeable. Infuriating, even. Each session with him was, for Dr. Glassman, a test of nerves: Keep your professional cool with this man and you can analyze anyone. . . .

And the worst thing about him was that he tried so hard to be *nice.* To avoid giving offense at all costs.

That was what was so offensive.

Dr. Glassman yanked open the drawer marked

Q - R - S

and rifled through the folders. There it was, still relatively thin and new, not dog-eared like (God help her) poor Miss Ritter's.

He removed the folder and, with a groan, stood up and moved back to his chair. "Uuuh, Mrs. Dundee," he said, pressing the button of the intercom, "send in Mr. Stoat, please."

While waiting, Dr. Glassman ran his eye down the first sheet in the folder.

STOAT, SIDNEY W.

was typed neatly across the top, the "E" showing only faint signs of erasure where Mrs. Dundee had misspelled the name. (*"Sidny"*—how typical! Decent secretaries were impossible to find these days.) Below it, in the doctor's own handwriting, appeared the inscription,

"Infantile oral aggression manifested in
obsessions of 'vampirism.'"

Outside his office door, someone cleared his throat.

Yes, it was starting again. . . . Dr. Glassman clenched his fists, then reached into his pocket and feverishly began peeling another antacid mint from the roll.

The sound was repeated, followed by a nervous little cough.

221

Glassman waited tensely in his chair, his teeth clamped on the mint like a wounded man biting a bullet.

Again the throat was cleared. The man was nothing if not patient, he'd wait an hour if need be. . . .

Sighing with exasperation, Dr. Glassman got · up and opened his office door. Outside stood a pale, sheepish-looking little man, nervously shuffling from foot to foot. But for a certain air of insecurity that clung to him like too much aftershave, there was nothing particularly distinctive about his appearance: gray suit narrow at the shoulders, shoes a little *too* shiny, tie a bit too tight, hair cropped just a drop too close for fashion. . . . He was the sort of man who invariably got dandruff on the couch, and invariably apologized for it.

Dr. Glassman stood holding the door for him. The man stood where he was, staring at his shoes in embarrassment.

Finally the doctor capitulated. "Well for God's sake, come in, come in. You know you don't have to wait for me to open the door."

The man shuffled into the room and threw himself down on the couch. He lay there trembling slightly, lines of exhaustion in his face.

"The point is," he said, "I *do* have to wait. I'm not allowed in till you *invite* me." His voice was high, edged with desperation, as if at any moment he might break into a scream.

Dr. Glassman closed the door and returned to his chair. He wasn't particularly anxious to pursue this subject; it had defeated him too many times before.

"Yes, well . . ." His words trailed off into a sigh. "We're going to have to talk about that. Perhaps later in the session—"

"Oh, I do *hope* so," the other interrupted. He sounded eager.

"But for now, Mr. Stoat, I think we ought to pursue the direction we were taking last week. Let me see. . . ." He studied the folder in his lap. "When the previous session ended you were saying something about 'too many commitments.' " Dr. Glassman read from his notes. " 'I just can't meet them all,' you said. 'The pressure . . . it's too much.' " The doctor paused, staring pointedly at his patient. "What sort of pressures did you have in mind? Family pressures? Your business? Or perhaps—"

222

He leaned forward and smiled ingratiatingly. "—sexual pressures that sometimes appear . . . overwhelming?"

"No, no, it's nothing like that." Stoat shook his head. "I wish it was! It's the pressure I feel about—being, *you* know. . . ." He concluded in a small, slightly embarrassed voice. "A vampire."

"All right." Dr. Glassman hoped his professional tone would disguise his distaste. "I suppose it is time to deal with this problem. Now why don't you take a minute to calm down" —it was he himself who needed time to calm down—"and then tell me exactly what sort of pressures you feel about . . . this, um, activity."

"It's not an activity, doctor. It's an *identity*."

"Yes, all right, you're quite right, an identity. Why don't you tell me about it." He settled back in his chair, stomach churning, molars pulverizing the mint.

"Well, the problem is . . . you see . . . I can't *exist* any more as a practicing vampire. This horrible city has got me going in circles." Shutting his eyes, Stoat shook his head, the very picture of misery. "It's impossible to secure victims these days. There are just too many *rules* you have to keep if you're going to do it right."

"'Rules'?" Dr. Glassman paused in his chewing. "What sort of 'rules' are you referring to?"

"Rules of what vampires can and cannot do," Stoat explained. "Like coming into your office."

"Oh?"

"Believe me, doctor, I feel like a damned fool waiting outside in the hall each session, but I'm just not allowed to walk in here without being invited. It's a matter of—Well, call it self-respect."

"Self-respect?"

"Professional ethics."

"I see," said the doctor, somewhat doubtfully.

"Look, have you ever read *Carmilla*? Or Montague Summers's books on vampirism in Europe? How about the studies by Ludwig Prinn, or that monograph of Byron's?"

"No, I must confess I've never delved into that area," said Dr. Glassman, loathe to admit an ignorance of any subject. "Frankly, it's always left me a little cold. . . . But I'm well acquainted with the more clinical aspects of the phenomenon. The psychology behind the folklore, you might say. And I assure you, Mr. Stoat, that your condition is by no means unfamiliar to me. Why, I've no doubt I could teach you a few things you've never even suspected."

"Wonderful!" said Stoat. "In that case, I'm sure you already know that a vampire cannot enter a home—and I guess that extends to a psychiatrist's office—unless he's asked in by the owner. You'll see it mentioned in *Dracula*."

"Ah, I understand."

"And the frustrating thing is, in this day and age it's extremely hard to get yourself invited anywhere! In the eighteenth century, say, I used to be able to walk right in, claiming I was a traveler who'd lost his way. But now . . ." He shook his head and smiled. "Have you ever tried to talk your way into a New York City apartment? Not a chance! I've covered whole buildings, a hundred doorbells, without a single word of welcome. People today are so—so paranoid!"

"Hmm . . . Why not leave such terms to me?" said the doctor mechanically. He paused, scribbling something into Stoat's folder. "I notice you said, 'In the eighteenth century *I* used to . . .' I assume you meant '*one* used to,' yes?"

Stoat opened his mouth, then hesitated a moment, as if confused about what to say. A small sigh escaped him.

"Yes," he said finally, "I suppose you're right. It was just a slip of the tongue."

"Ah, but it's little slips like these that can reveal so much about the inner workings of the mind. Believe me, Mr. Stoat, in analysis there's no end of things the tongue can tell us!"

Seeing the other roll his eyes upward in obvious exasperation, Dr. Glassman realized that he'd been waving his finger like a professor. Perhaps, he decided, he'd sounded a little too gloating. He cleared his throat and continued:

"We'll come back to that question later. We were talking about *rules*. Now it's obvious to me, though perhaps not to you, that this supposed 'rule' about being invited inside is nothing more than a rather vivid way of warning people about what happens when they trust too readily in strangers. Picture, for example, a village elder talking by a fire, some time during the Dark Ages. These are perilous times, and he knows there are dangerous men about—desperate men, robbers, thieves, and what-not. But he can't speak of these things directly. No one would take him seriously. So he couches his warnings in the form of a rather picturesque legend. That way, it sticks more firmly in the memory. It's the sort of trick Moses used. He went up onto Mount Sinai and carved his ten commandments—or 'rules,' if you like—and then he came down the mountain and told everyone that *God* had given him the tablets. He realized, you see, that making a little story out of the affair was the only way to bring the lesson home."

Stoat's eyes widened. *"Really!"* he exclaimed. "Gosh, *I* didn't know that about Moses. I'd always thought those commandments came from"—he pointed toward the ceiling—"you know who."

"From God."

"Yes, but I can't say that. That's another rule. If I utter His name He'll blast me to cinders. I'm not even supposed to *think* about Him too much. It makes me nauseous."

Dr. Glassman leaned forward. "I'm a little surprised, if you'll pardon me, that till now you've taken these teachings so literally. As a thinking man you should have developed a few *doubts* and *questions* by this time. I'm not asking you to give up your . . . religion, of course, but to examine these beliefs intellectually, in light of modern scholarship."

"Wow!" exclaimed Stoat. "This is really opening me up, all this talk. I can feel it! It's good to get the lowdown on you know who! Maybe I *have* been taking these things a bit too literally. . . . But sometimes I've got to—there's just no other way to take some of them. Like the rule about water. Did you know that vampires can't cross over running water?"

"And yet you commute to the city every day from Brooklyn."

"Yes," said Stoat, "but I take the subway. *Under* the river. That's allowed. Bridges are forbidden."

"How quaint!" The doctor permitted himself an indulgent smile. "But it's all really quite transparent. You see, ever since the first baboon used urine as a territorial marker, magical properties have been attributed to all the fluids of the body: the mother's milk, the semen, the blood." He noticed that Stoat was blushing. "Yes indeed! To the primitive mind, fluids represent the archetypal life-force, with holy water—and, by extension, all water—its special cleansing agent. Hence the dead and the un-dead cannot cross. It is too clean, too 'pure,' too full of life for them." He chuckled. "But that can hardly apply to the filthy, polluted river *you'd* have to cross! Take my word for it, it's a lot deader than your great-grandfather."

"You mean, the East River would be just as safe as"—Stoat's eyes widened—*"Blood?"*

The doctor nodded, a trifle hesitantly.

"And you say Holy Water's just a—"

The doctor beamed. "A rather sweet symbol."

Stoat lay back on the couch, mulling over this new wisdom. For the first time tonight he seemed relaxed.

Staring idly toward the window, his eye fell on a small wall plaque hanging nearby. It was an icon of Saint Octavius display-ing a formidable gold cross—souvenir of the doctor's Mediterra-nean cruise several years ago. Immediately Stoat's expression grew grave.

"But you can't say that about the cross," he muttered darkly. *"That's* no symbol. It really works. I can feel it."

He pointed to the cross, wincing.

Dr. Glassman eyed him skeptically. "You mean the legend about vampires and the cross? Really, Mr. Stoat, that should have died out years ago! True, the cross was once invested with certain spiritual qualities. People were devoutly religious then. But I ask you, how many still read the Bible today? We live in such a secular world that I, for one, should think of the cross as . . . well, as a symbol robbed of its power." He pointed to the wall. "That little Greek icon—*that* worries you?"

"Yes," said Stoat. "I feel weak whenever I come in here."

"Because you think you *ought* to feel weak. It's psychoso-matic, a result of your early conditioning. Look, I hang that on my wall because it's pretty, nothing more. Most of my patients say they like it. It makes them feel comfortable here, reminds them of their childhood. As for me, it reminds me of a rather pleasant vacation, that's all. It has no religious significance. I'll be perfectly happy to take it down if it upsets you."

"No, really. . . ." Stoat waved his hand, unwilling to give offense. "Please don't do that for my sake. I'm sure you're right. Better I learn to deal with it, and—and overcome it. . . ."

"That's the spirit! But say, rather, overcome your own unpleasant *associations* to it. As a thing in itself, that little wall plaque has no meaning. It's you who gives it one.

"Mind you, I'm not ridiculing superstition," he added. "It's a very human thing. Why, just look at the number on my office door—14-B—and all because the builders had a bad association with 'thirteen.' "

Stoat nodded pensively, still staring at the icon. His gaze fell to the window—and again his face registered alarm.

"But the night!" he cried.

"Pardon me?"

"Night. I have to come up here at night. I can't go outside during the day."

"Oh, yes, I remember." Dr. Glassman nodded. "All the trouble you've had finding suitable employment—"

"And getting you to agree to *see* me at night!"

Both men laughed.

"Ah, well," shrugged the doctor, settling back into the chair. "I'm a busy man."

"But you're telling me that my—my pain and sickness when I'm exposed to sunlight are just . . . psychosomatic? Good God, I even—"

"There, you see?" Dr. Glassman almost leaped from his chair. "You *said* it! And nothing happened!"

"Said what?"

" 'Good God.' And you haven't been burned to a cinder."

Stoat's jaw dropped in amazement. "Why, you're right! Gee . . . God! Lordy me! I feel so . . . *liberated!*"

Dr. Glassman nodded sagely, with just a touch of smugness. "You see? It's like I always say: It all comes out in analysis."

"I'm awfully grateful to you, doctor." Almost visibly the man was beginning to loosen up, to shed some of his ever-present tension.

Encouraged, the doctor began to relax, too. "Now tell me about this problem with sunlight." His voice was almost chummy.

"Well, as I was saying, if even a beam of sunlight happens to fall on my skin, it causes a horrible burn. You're not going to tell me *that's* only in my mind!"

"Have you tried a good skin specialist?"

"Please, doctor! That's not funny."

Dr. Glassman sighed. "My friend, I'll have to recommend a few good books on allergies to you. Many of them—hay fever, for instance, or reactions to cats, or textiles, or certain foods—are just psychosomatic responses. There are cases on record of patients who don't begin to sniffle till they read in the newspaper that the hay fever season's begun."

"But the garlic people hang up to keep vampires away . . ."

The doctor smiled. "Garlic keeps *anyone* away! It's an old joke that somehow got taken seriously. Every culture is filled with stories of demons being driven off by foul smells—demons, werewolves, even the devil himself. Merely an attempt to reassure the listeners that these rather frightening myth figures have their share of human qualities. If you don't like the smell of garlic—and few people do—why not simply hold your nose?" He stifled a belch. "You've no doubt noticed that I myself may reek a little of garlic. That's simply the price I pay for eating at that abominable Italian restaurant around the corner. Frankly, I don't like the smell any better than you do." He peeled himself another mint.

"And the soil I have to sleep on?" persisted his patient. "Soil from my native Transylvania?"

The doctor smiled. "Sounds uncomfortable."

"You have no idea!" Stoat rolled his eyes comically.

"Simply a mutation of the Antaeus legend, if you ask me. They say a dog fights best in his master's yard. Outside of it he'll turn and run. A man, too, is strongest when he's standing on his own territory—it's a human need you can trace back through the primates and down to the reptiles. Keep a bit of territory with you at all times—symbolized by the proverbial 'coffin filled with earth'—and you'll thereby maintain your strength. Makes a childish kind of sense, doesn't it?"

"How about the rule about vampires only drinking the blood of young girls?"

Dr. Glassman really had to laugh; it was so hard not to feel superior. "My dear Mr. Stoat, I can't begin to tell you all the psychosexual origins of *that* belief! Suffice to say that a male—such as yourself—might confine his fantasies to young, sexually desirable females out of a need to reaffirm his own masculinity. Each one of us, of course, feels tenderness toward members of both sexes; tenderness, and its natural opposite, *hostility*, both of which are often repressed. I should think the truly liberated man might feel free to indulge in his aggressive fantasies—uh, 'vampiric,' in your case!—toward *either* sex."

This revelation seemed too much for poor Stoat. Shaking his head as if to clear it of these warring ideas, he got to his feet and staggered toward the wall plaque, panting slightly from excess of emotion. Tentatively, timidly, he reached out and touched Saint Octavius's cross; then, with growing assertion and confidence, he placed his whole hand over it.

He gasped. Nothing had happened! He hadn't been burned!

"Doctor!" he cried, smiling dizzily. "I feel so . . . so *liberated!*"

Dr. Glassman smiled benignly from his chair. His stomachache was gone.

It was marvelous, really—and he'd accomplished it all in one session. He beamed at the young man like a proud parent watching his son graduate from college; and he reserved a special congratulation for himself. This was the sort of thing that made being a psychiatrist—the training, the tension, the aggravation—all worthwhile.

He leaned forward to catch what his patient was saying. Standing near the window with his hand on the icon, the man looked close to ecstasy, and his words were becoming hard to follow.

"I think . . ." Stoat was panting more heavily now, his eyes bulging. "I think . . ." He swayed forward.

"What's the matter, Stoat?" Damn it, the man looked as if he were choking! Perhaps the treatment had been a bit too sudden, too traumatic.

Stoat bent double, grunting and snorting. Alarmed, the doctor rose and hurried over to him.

"What's the matter with you, Stoat?" He grabbed him by the shoulders and jerked him erect. The man's mouth was trying to form words, but his body was now quivering as if from pain or orgasm. "Stoat! Listen to me! What's the matter? What are you trying to say?"

229

Stoat stiffened, eyes rolling upward to show the whites. "I
. . . I . . ." His chest heaved, his breath coming in gasps.

Dr. Glassman shook him by the shoulders. "Stoat! Damn
it, man, what *is* it!"

"I think—" Suddenly Stoat made a low, wet choking
sound; something bubbled deep in his throat. His face seemed to
grow, turning purple, then darker, then . . .

The doctor backed away, hands upraised to ward off the
sight of those glaring red eyeballs. He screamed at what came
slithering from between the thing's lips—a thin, pink, tubular
tongue, as long as an anteater's and glistening with saliva.

The lips curled into a smile, and the thing spoke.

*"I'm cured!"*

Just before it sprang, it croaked another word. Dr. Glassman couldn't hear it very well, for by now the thing's tongue
was fully extended and he himself was busy screaming, but he
thought it sounded quite a lot like *Thanks.*

# The Early Decision

## STEVE ANABLE

T he man at the wheel of the blue Rolls Royce was beginning to lose confidence in himself—a new experience for him. He was almost ready to admit to his wife
and son that he might be lost. He was unfamiliar with
this part of northern New England—and the low stone walls, the
abandoned farms, and the ancient family graveyards run riot
with briars all looked the same.

Archibald Armstrong was thirty-eight, overweight, and,
some said, overbearing. But no one denied that he was a genius.
He had been a scholarship student at M.I.T., and was the son of
schoolteachers from Ripley, Massachusetts, a mill town of peeling clapboard houses with yards full of dust, children, and angry
mongrel dogs.

Archibald had vowed to use his brains to move up and out
of Ripley—and he had, founding his own software firm and be-

coming a millionaire at a time when most of his contemporaries were applying for their first credit card. Archibald was an odd combination of his past and present, of poverty and success. His shirts were custom-made, but he kept their monogrammed pockets crammed with cheap, leaky pens. He wore elegant wool suits—and thick eyeglasses with the same marbleized plastic frames he'd bought in high school. He was an expert on wines who compulsively chewed gum. But he wanted all traces of his family's hardscrabble origins eradicated from his only child, his son, Andy.

"You're lost," his wife, Janet, suddenly snapped. "Let's just go home. Andy can go to Country Day. This place gives me the creeps."

But all of New England gave Janet the creeps. She was a diehard Californian, the daughter of a poor Baptist oil worker from Bakersfield. Archibald had met her when she was crowned "Miss Software World" at the Computer Universe Expo in Las Vegas, and Andy was the result of a romp in the jacuzzi in the Presidential Suite at the Desert Bud Hotel.

"What was that?!" Andy asked.

"That was just a raccoon!" Archibald lied. In fact, the animal in the road had been bigger than a dog.

"Why can't we have a house in California?" Janet began complaining. There was a wonderful school in Bel Air that Andy would just love. The lead singer of the Viruses sent his twins there. Janet pulled off her gold shrimp earrings and dropped them into her alligator purse. For all the flash of her showgirl past, she still adamantly refused to pierce her ears. Pierced ears and loose morals go hand in hand, her mother swore.

"Dad, it's getting dark! Our appointment was for three-thirty! We're late and we're lost!" Andy whined.

At least he was assertive enough to say so, Archibald thought.

"Let's just skip it," Janet said. "Let's get back on the highway and head home."

Archibald slammed on the breaks and cut the engine. He squinted at the map the Burroughs School had mailed them. "This damn thing makes no sense at all!" he said. "Left on Burnt Church Road, then onto Wenn Lane. Now I'm looking for some moccasin outlet. . . ."

231

"Dad, there!" Andy said.

Around the bend, through some blighted balsams, Archibald discerned a plaster totem pole and a low building made of varnished logs. A neon sign burnt feebly out front, no brighter than swamp gas. "Moccasin City," it said.

The moccasin outlet smelled like leather, not the rich fragrance of new shoes, but stale and wet, like boots that have grown mildew in a cellar. There were bins and bins of factory-reject moccasins inside; no two seemed alike. Andy began yanking moccasins from the bins while Janet clutched her alligator purse as if angry panhandlers were present. A blond youth, all sneer and Adam's apple—the palest human being Archibald had ever *seen*—announced "We're closing!" as soon as Archibald moved in his direction.

"It's only quarter-to-four!" Archibald said, offended by the youth's tone and this affront to the work ethic, closing so early.

"We're closing; we're going out of business. I forgot to turn off the sign."

"Listen, I don't want any of your crummy moccasins! Both of *my* feet happen to be the same size! I just want directions to the Burroughs School!"

The clerk was only slightly Andy's senior. He wore a plaid flannel shirt and jeans that were raggy along the seams, but a signet ring gleamed on his finger, an oddly patrician touch on this raw rural specimen, Archibald decided.

"The Burroughs School? Never heard of it," the clerk snapped.

"Let me use—"

"The phone's outside."

A chill wind from the wilds of Canada cut through Archibald's camel-hair coat. It had come from the Arctic wastes, over the igloos of Eskimo shamans, over dense forests where trappers froze, muttering prayers to French saints. It chilled Archibald Armstrong so much that he actually lost his confidence—something that had not happened since his freshman year at M.I.T., on his test essay about Lady Macbeth in "Shakespeare for Scientists," his humanities course requirement.

Thank God, the school number was actually ringing! "Good afternoon!" the receptionist said, as if this were a May

232

morning all tulips and bluebirds instead of an autumn dusk with the odor of roadkill on the wind.

The receptionist disarmed Archibald with her cooing apologies about the school's map. "This happens *all the time*," she said. "I'll bet you're at that awful Moccasin City!"

The school would send a car to guide them. They were the last appointment of the day and Dr. Stark, the headmaster, was eager to meet them but behind on some paperwork, so their late arrival would cause no inconvenience. "Oh good!" Archibald said. Then, to his chagrin, he became the polite boy waiting on the mill owner's son back in Ripley, handing him his tenderloin steak at the butcher's where he worked on Saturdays. "Thank you," he said, like a servant.

Janet and Andy were now shivering beside him. The neon sign blinked off, as did the lights of the outlet. "He just threw us out; he couldn't have been more rude!" Janet said. "These New Englanders!"

"Dad, I'm starving!" Andy whined.

Archibald lived in fear that Andy would follow in his footsteps (to the refrigerator) and eat himself fat. Andy was so lethargic, spending hours playing video games, slaying monsters, and dodging death-rays and asteroids.

Then, from out of nowhere, a big Dusenberg came gliding through the murk. It was hemmhorage-red with blackened windows. "What a cool car!" Andy said. The window of the driver's side rolled down a crack and young but pompous voice told them, "Follow me, Mr. Armstrong. We'll be at the school shortly. So sorry you're lost. . . ."

The Dusenberg impressed Archibald; he admired a machine that survived. In the computer industry, products became outdated before they were first shipped.

So Archibald surrendered; he allowed himself to be led. He would remember this drive the rest of his life: the roads that twisted like spirochetes, the sputum-white fog that came toward the car like breath. It seemed a journey not through miles, but through time. . . .

Then the Burroughs School seemed to rise up out of the mists, like the ruins of some ancient, mythical city appearing slowly on the bottom of a draining, enchanted lake. It was dark, but the school was bustling. Boys ran between the mock-colonial quadrangles, shouting, laughing, lugging lacrosse sticks. The cross-country team came panting by. . . . But they all looked so *pale*, Archibald observed. And some, in blazers, looked very old-fashioned; Archibald swore they wore brilliantine; their hair looked solidified, parted straight down the middle of their scalps.

The driver of the Dusenberg did not emerge, but the Armstrongs caught a glimpse of his blond hair and of his ear, which was as pale as a shell that has been bleaching on the sand for centuries.

"Go straight under that portico—Dr. Stark's study is on the right."

Janet blew her nose into some scented Kleenex. "Honey," she whispered, "this place gives me the creeps!"

It was chilly inside Memorial Hall, in its long corridor with its oak-panelled walls hung with sepia-toned photographs of graduates killed in wars.

"Memorial Hall, that's a cheery first impression," Janet remarked.

Andy was suddenly alert. "There's photographs of guys killed during the Civil War, the Spanish-American War, and World War I," he was saying, surveying this gallery of the young dead. "How come there's no one killed in World War II? Or in Korea or Vietnam? Isn't that weird?"

"That's *influence*," Archibald whispered to his son. "That's knowing the right people, that's telling the local draft board who's boss." Privately, he thought it *was* puzzling. He didn't know much about history, but somewhere he'd read that World War I was "the last gentleman's war." He'd read about those English officers from Eton who'd brought hampers of food from Fortnum & Mason to the front—smoked salmon, brandied peaches. And hadn't they brought their own valets?

At last Dr. Stark appeared. He shook the Armstrongs' hands with the kind of exaggerated *bonhomie* a fraternity president would use during rush week. Archibald was ready to become peeved at his blatant insincerity when the headmaster disarmed him by exclaiming, "You look even *younger* than your picture on the cover of *Software News!*"

Dr. Stark, by contrast, looked positively unhealthy: he was pale as a maggot. He smelled of pipe tobacco and wore a rumply suit of heather-green tweed. His tie was stitched with a pattern of small wolves' heads—odd, Archibald thought, he'd have expected golf clubs or squash racquets or silhouettes of Martha's Vineyard, the kind of ties favored by the few preps his company hired.

To Archibald's embarrassment, Janet began a tirade about the school's map. "When was that map made? Fourteen ninety-two? And that clerk at that sleazy Moccasin City—"

"Yes, Harold is *so* rude," Dr. Stark stated.

That clerk had *never heard* of the Burroughs School, Archibald remembered. Or so he'd said. So how did the headmaster know *his* name? Archibald was about to ask when Dr. Stark said, "I hope you didn't mind *us* being so bold as to contact *you*?"

Archibald was baffled.

"Oh, honey," Janet said, "I forgot to tell you. Dr. Stark wrote to us just after you got all that publicity—about all your millions—just after the *Software News* story. That's when I added the Burroughs School to our list of possibilities for Andy." Janet popped a cough drop into her mouth. "So you can blame me for this disaster," she muttered.

Dr. Stark just smiled. He opened a manila folder on his desk. "Andy's transcripts," he said.

Andy's grades were nothing to smile about. "He's . . . a classic underachiever," Archibald said. Andy tested badly. He was brilliant, brilliant, but he was so busy with his own . . . inventions that he'd let his schoolwork sort of slide. "He's just written a computer program that helps him clean up his room, helps him organize his things." While Archibald lied, Janet yawned and Andy was blank as the screen of a short-circuited computer.

Dr. Stark pressed a buzzer, summoning a thin, waxen boy with a pointed face and a silver tray burdened with a Paul Revere tea service, china cups, and a plate of pastries. "This is Jeremy," Dr. Stark said.

Solemnly, Jeremy shook the Armstrongs' hands. His fingers were cold as a cod fillet just off the ice, Janet Armstrong later would recall.

The pastries made Archibald's stomach turn somersaults— they were oozing congealed raspberry jam and shaped vaguely like aborted fetuses. But the headmaster's study—the Oriental rugs, the Tudor tables, the prints of horses jumping hedges—all spelled "class" to Archibald, almost out loud. At last, gentility was within his reach! He remembered his own boyhood home: the worn linoleum in the living room, the mousetraps hidden behind the kitchen stove, his father's wet T-shirts flapping on the clothesline. . . . So he ate the pastries and praised the tea, and, for once in his life, he tried to be charming. He had to compensate for his roots, Janet's boredom, and his son's plump inertia. He told anecdotes about the software industry. ". . . Then, just as our chief engineer—"

"It's time for your tour," Dr. Stark gently interrupted. "Jeremy here will be your guide."

Jeremy's demeanor changed radically outside the headmaster's presence. He went from being the shy lackey to the Big Man on Campus in a matter of minutes. He began reciting the prizes he'd collected last June, including the Wainwright Cup, awarded to "the best winter athlete who's under sixteen." Just looking at the Armstrongs seemed to animate Jeremy, as if he drew some sort of nourishment from their presence.

"Where are you from?" Archibald asked.

"Grosse Pointe, Michigan, sir," Jeremy said crisply. "But the school is home now."

"Do you like it here?" Archibald wondered.

"I could stay here forever," Jeremy said.

Wherever they went at the school, knots of boys stopped what they were doing to turn and stare. They stopped talking, stopped gazing at bulletin boards, stopped swigging their ginger-beer at the Snack Shop. And their eyes became bright in their pallid faces and some bit their lips, as if suppressing a laugh. So Archibald checked his fly to make sure that it was zipped and worried that his chalk-stripe suit was too ostentatious.

They toured the science building, the library, and now the gym. Someone had tipped off Archibald that you could judge a prep school's wealth by its gym. Victories in sports gladdened alumni hearts and opened alumni wallets. So the richest schools had the biggest, best gyms. Lawrenceville supposedly boasted an indoor polo field. (What was that quote about the polo fields of Eton?)

But Archibald was disappointed by the gym, by its murky

pool and basketball court with buckling floors, by the weight room that dated back to the Coolidge administration. And the whole building reeked of disinfectant.

The Armstrongs were pausing in the trophy room, where ancient footballs lay withering like shrunken heads in the display cases.

"This gym is pretty old-fashioned," Archibald said.

"It's an old-fashioned school," Jeremy said proudly.

(Jeremy's skin, Andy would later remember, was white as the belly of the frog he'd dissected last spring in biology lab.)

"This whole setup—"

"Dr. Stark feels tradition is very important," Jeremy interrupted, now every bit as rude as that clerk at Moccasin City.

"And you gave up the tradition of hanging photographs of the war dead right after World War I? In Memorial Hall?" Archibald asked. "There's something fishy—"

"The school underwent a change then," Jeremy said. "The Stark family came here, you know, new blood."

"I think we've seen enough," Janet said curtly.

Something howled. Was it a happy boy—or some sort of animal?

Andy acted uneasy.

Archibald was beginning to agree with Janet that this part of New England was somehow sinister. He moved to comfort his son, to squeeze his shoulder or pat his back, but he had no energy; he could barely lift his own arm.

The chapel bell began tolling as the Armstrongs descended the gym steps. That frigid wind from the Arctic wastes cut through their clothing once again. What was in that tea Dr. Stark had served them? It had a musty, ancient taste and now it was affecting Archibald's vision. He was following Jeremy toward the chapel, a great Gothic structure made of scab-brown sandstone.

"I'm dizzy," Janet said.

Now the chapel seemed to be *alive*; its buttresses seemed to rise and fall, rise and fall, as if the building somehow were *breathing*. The stained-glass windows seemed to undulate like great webs and the stone saints in their niches trembled like spiders sensing prey.

Something deep in Archibald told him to run, to run all the

way back to Ripley, Massachusetts, to his room under the eaves with his chemistry set and mineral collection. But a stronger force made Archibald keep trailing Jeremy.

As Jeremy ushered the Armstrongs through the entrance to the Burroughs School chapel, their ears were overwhelmed by baroque organ music that seemed to reach down the aisle to pull the dazed family toward the altar.

Hundreds of pale boys in blazers stared. So did the faculty wives, all pale as their identical strands of pearls. And the teachers and coaches stared too—and spoke. "Good to see you, Archibald!" "Hello, Janet, and welcome." "Congratulations on your early acceptance, Andy!"

How did they know their names, the Armstrongs wondered? It was uncanny, unsettling—yet at last we are being *accepted*, Archibald thought.

Dr. Stark was waiting in the distance, at the altar. When he smiled, his mouth was bright as a cut.

Suddenly, Janet shrieked. "There's no cross!" she cried, her voice thin with fright. "There's no cross in this whole church! *Archibald, let's get out of here!*"

A tall, blond youth, an acolyte, was lighting long *black* candles on the altar. He turned—his blood-red robe whirling—to smile a haughty familiar smile the Armstrongs had seen before. He was pale as a shell that has been bleaching on the sand for centuries.

"Dad!" Andy shouted. "That's that guy from that moc—"

At Armstrong Software, the company founder and legend disappeared. Rumors circulated about a nervous breakdown or a blood disorder, that he had fled to the wilds to meditate or join some cult.

The Burroughs School took no new applications for decades—despite the construction of the new Armstrong Memorial Gymnasium, with its Olympic-sized pool, its basketball courts, its high-tech weight rooms, and indoor track.

But when applications were again being accepted, a plump, pale boy began clerking at Moccasin City, while his parents stacked boxes in the back room.

# Blood Brothers

## PETER CANNON

t was Vampire Appreciation Week at James Buchanan High, and as the bell rang for his initial Monday morning class Jake Valter, rookie English teacher, nerved himself for another bout with the multicultist curriculum. Only yesterday, it seemed, his ninth graders were honoring Werewolf Americans, and next week they might be celebrating Zombie Americans or even Invisible Americans, but for now the powers-that-be had deemed Vampire Americans the cult du jour. Needless to say, teaching such a subject was like strolling through a graveyard at midnight—you never knew what might jump out and surprise you. Being young and idealistic, however, Jake welcomed the challenge, or so he often had to remind himself.

Selecting a text on which to build his lesson had been problematic. There used to be available, of course, a good variety of modern vampire literature, from the classic *Dracula* to the Lestat saga of Anne Rice. But then certain education watchdog groups had pointed out that the best-known books about vampires were not written by vampires. Indeed, these strident advocates claimed that nonvampires, even a novelist as empathetic as Anne Rice, couldn't really begin to understand the vampire experience and hence had no business in the multicultist classroom. In the end Jake had settled on Dan Leslie's angrily eloquent autobiography, *Blood Brother*, which would be sure to stimulate plenty of lively discussion despite its deficiencies as a work of art.

The truth was, instructional materials were meager. Vampires didn't start arriving in America in large numbers until the turn of the century, after that bungler Van Helsing failed to stop the Transylvanian Count from infecting a significant percentage of the English population. A colleague of Jake's in the history department had once complained to him about having to teach from a textbook that made a run-in, probably legendary, between a vampire and some Hessian soldiers near Princeton around the time Washington was crossing the Delaware sound like the pivotal event of the Revolution.

The dozen or so students who regularly showed up for Jake's first section were no more rambunctious and obstreperous than most youngsters suffering through the throes of early adolescence. Some of the boys were still undersized with high-pitched voices, while more than a few of the girls sported makeup and jewelry to enhance their shapely figures.

With the ringing of the late bell, Jake closed the classroom door, which automatically locked—standard procedure at a school like James Buchanan. On the blackboard he had already chalked the "aim" or leading question for the day's lesson, "What is a vampire?"

Quentin, a troublemaker who liked to bait him, provided Jake with his opening. "Are you a bloodsucker lover, Mr. Valter?" the boy asked, his tone as cocky as the angle of his baseball cap.

"Please, Quentin, you're old enough to know it's very bad to use a name like 'bloodsucker.' The people in the cult we're studying this week are called vampires or Vampire Americans." He wrote both terms on the board. "Note for the word 'vampire' it's okay to use lowercase, but 'Vampire Americans' you should always capitalize."

"How come if you're not supposed to use that word, Mr. Valter, there's a group that calls itself the Bloodsucker Brotherhood?" continued Quentin.

"Some of the more militant vampires, in their efforts to promote the rights of the undead, have tried to defang the epithet, as it were, by taking it from the vampire haters and making it their own. But be careful, class. Coming from a nonvampire it's still an offensive cultic slur."

"My mother says sucking blood is nasty!"

"Yes, Fiona, vampires are hemo-dependent—which brings us to today's aim. Everyone knows vampires need blood to survive, but how else can we describe their life- or rather, death-style?"

To Jake's satisfaction his pupils were eager to volunteer their opinions, and soon he had a long list on the board. Among other traits, vampires slept in coffins, could turn into bats, didn't show up in mirrors, and avoided sunlight like the plague. Jake had his own personal feelings about the undead, but as a teacher it wasn't his role to sway his young charges to his views. On the other hand, it would be derelict of him not to try to disabuse them of any wrong-headed or ignorant notions. At their impressionable age they tended to accept too much nonsense uncritically.

"First of all, a lot of what is commonly believed about vampires is false. These ideas come from folklore or have been spread in the popular media until they've been accepted as real. For example, vampires do reflect in mirrors, and thanks to modern science they can take medication that allows them to go about during the day like ordinary human beings, just as hemophiliacs can now take medicine to stop them from bleeding to death."

"I saw this movie once where the vampires were afraid to cross water."

"Well, Graham, you don't believe everything you see in the movies, do you?"

"I've heard that it's the ghouls and the poltergeists who control Hollywood and the media who are responsible for making vampires look so evil."

"An interesting point, Victoria. It's a fact that many of the early motion pictures showed vampires in stereotypical ways. In recent years, however, filmmakers have become more sensitive. Later in the week, if we get our reading done, I'll bring in a video of one of these more sympathetic vampire movies. Maybe *The Hunger* with David Bowie."

The cheers that erupted at the prospect of watching a video helped relieve the heaviness Jake feared was creeping into the discussion. He was feeling pretty relaxed when Algernon raised one of the more delicate issues regarding vampires.

"Don't they want to convert nonvampires, Mr. Valter?" said the boy. "Don't they try to turn people into night creatures like themselves?"

"Yuck!" piped one or two of the more immature voices.

"Again, that's a myth, Algernon. Yes, a few selfish and inconsiderate individuals might do that, but the vast majority of vampires feed at blood banks set up specifically for the purpose. Or they prey on each other."

"You can always tell when somebody's a bloodsucker, can't you, Mr. Valter. The way they stare at your neck and start to drool."

"No, Quentin, you can't tell by appearances." Jake decided to ignore the lad's use of inappropriate language. "Because their fangs are retractable, vampires look just like other people. I will say, though, I don't think it's utterly impossible for one vampire to instinctively recognize another vampire."

Jake immediately regretted expressing this sentiment. As many as two or three members of the class might be vampires, he suspected, and such a remark could lead to an embarrassing situation where one student would accuse another of being "in the coffin," followed by painful denials or even tears. Fortunately, apart from an isolated guffaw, no one took advantage of this slip, which he later attributed to his inexperience. He was able to move on smoothly enough to the next part of the lesson.

"All right, class. Let's open our copies of *Blood Brother*," he announced. "Daphne, will you please start reading at the top of page 9?"

Two of the more appealing features of *Blood Brother* were its brevity and its readability. All five of Jake's sections easily covered the text in three periods, and certainly the author sparked a range of responses, from "fresh" to "whack." In all honesty, Jake wasn't sure just how much his classes had absorbed the book's message of respect and tolerance, but at least they'd learned a great deal about the morbid career of one rather idiosyncratic and, he had to admit, self-pitying vampire. Happily, *The Hunger*, the showing of which exactly filled the final two periods of the week, met with almost universal approval. In theory one had to obtain the principal's permission to bring in a film from the outside, especially a film as sexy and violent as *The Hunger*. In practice, however, the enterprising teacher often had to proceed without official sanction, given the principal's fear of putting her signature on any activity request that could conceivably provoke controversy or complaint. Part of a good learning facilitator's job, as Jake well knew, was knowing when to bend the rules and take risks.

Students, of course, were always pushing the limits of higher authority. Throughout the week it troubled Jake that young Quentin was especially disruptive. Talking about vampires and their habits clearly brought out the silly side of the boy, as it did others his age, but that didn't excuse flagrantly antisocial behavior. Throwing his copy of *Blood Brother* out the window in feigned disgust was one thing, but laughing or otherwise making rude noises during the most solemn scenes of *The Hunger* was quite another. On Friday Jake felt he had no recourse but to arrange a conference with Quentin after ninth period to discuss his negative attitude.

Jake had his doubts that the youngster would actually show up for the appointment, but he was gratified when a few minutes after the final bell the boy slumped into his classroom, looking so small and vulnerable in the long-billed baseball cap and low-riding baggy trousers that were *de rigueur* among the male fashionable at Buchanan High.

"Have a seat, Quentin. And please shut the door behind you." Jake gestured to a desk in the front row. Expressionless, the lad did as he was told. So as not to appear any more intimidating than necessary, Jake took the adjacent front-row desk and turned it to face Quentin. This way they could communicate at the same level.

"Quentin, do you have any idea why I asked you to see me alone?"

The student, his face hidden by his cap, nodded.

"What was that, Quentin?"

"Yes, Mr. Valter," the boy squeaked.

"Yes what, Quentin?"

"Yes, Mr. Valter, I think I know why you asked me to see you alone."

How different a student could be when he didn't have an audience to play to! So tough and smart-alecky on the surface, but really just a scared little kid beneath the skin.

"Now, Quentin, I understand the subject of vampires makes some of us feel uncomfortable. Especially young adults like yourself." In fact, he was being generous. Quentin looked no older than a child of ten.

Jake heard a catch in the boy's throat.

"What is it, Quentin? Look at me."

The youth slowly raised his head. His eyes were moist. Obviously he was very upset. It was so hard sometimes to figure what bothered kids at this difficult, transitional stage. It could be anything, from problems at home to an unrequited crush.

"What's wrong, Quentin? How can I help?"

At this Quentin started to cry. Jake was afraid he might try to run out of the classroom, but he just sat where he was, his face behind his lowered hat, which quivered with his sobs. Like many attention-getters, Quentin probably had low self-esteem or possibly was confused about his identity. In the circumstances only a heartless monster could refrain from offering a comforting hand.

One of the cardinal rules drilled into you at normal college was to avoid any and all physical contact with your students. His first year at Buchanan, however, Jake had been puzzled to discover a double-standard at work. His female colleagues could blithely display their fondness, through friendly pats or hugs, but woe be to the male teacher who so much as brushed the eight-ball-jacket sleeve of one of his pupils. The slightest, most innocent touch could lead to a charge of sexual harrassment before the faculty disciplinary committee.

"Quentin, we must try to act like grown-ups."

"I'm sorry, Mr. Valter, I know once in a while I act up. I'm sorry."

Jake reached across the gap between their desks to place a fatherly finger— In the next moment the lad had thrown both arms around him and was weeping on his shoulder.

Then Jake started to feel the urge—the urge he had tried for so long to suppress. Dry-mouthed, he was helpless to prevent his fangs from springing into the boy's jugular, excited perhaps by the two tiny pricks in his own neck.

# Hunting the Vampire

## C. Bruce Hunter

**G**eoffrey led the way into the cellar of the ruined abbey, while Marcus followed close behind. The first man held a hastily sharpened stake in his left hand, a heavy mallet in his right. His companion carried a large brass carriage lamp to guide them through the lower chambers, and in his free hand he clutched a crucifix.

"Be careful," Geoffrey whispered, "Dracul could be anywhere in this labyrinth."

"At least he's not there," Marcus said, nervously pointing to an empty room. Its open door was laced with cobwebs, and the dust of decades lay undisturbed on its floor.

"Don't be so sure," Geoffrey said. "These creatures can change themselves into anything, even a cloud of mist. He could pass right through those webs without touching them."

They moved slowly down a flight of steps and into a long corridor whose thickly plastered walls were broken in a dozen places by doors. Most stood open, revealing storage and utility rooms. What lay behind the others, they could only guess. Dust and cobwebs were everywhere, yet there was nothing out of the ordinary to mark the passing of the beast they hunted.

At the far end, the corridor opened into a massive room that stretched sixty feet into the bedrock on which the abbey was built. It was nearly as wide as it was long and piled high with barrels and crates. But there were still no traces of the vampire.

"I'm damned if his coffin isn't here somewhere," Geoffrey sighed, as he stepped into the room.

Marcus held the lamp higher, and its yellow light showed the extent of their plight. The room was ringed with doors that no doubt led to still more rooms and corridors.

Suddenly, the hunt seemed hopeless. Their quarry could be almost anywhere, and he was probably rising at this moment from his coffin.

Geoffrey turned to warn his companion of the danger they faced. But he was too late.

With a shrill shriek, a dark shape swooped down from the ceiling. It grasped Marcus, tore out his throat and lapped frantically at the blood that flowed from the wound.

For precious moments, Geoffrey stood frozen by fear, but something inside him retched at the sight of Marcus's death and forced him to action. With the stake held high, he lunged at the vampire.

Dracul saw the motion and pulled away from his lifeless prey. He jerked quickly to one side then lunged forward.

The attack threw Geoffrey off balance. Its force slammed him against the wall. The stake flew from his hand, bounced on the floor, and rolled under a wine barrel that rested slightly off the floor on wooden blocks.

Geoffrey half fell, half scrambled to his knees, desperately trying to recover the stake.

Just then he felt a sear of pain in his shoulder as the vampire's fangs ripped through his clothes and pierced his flesh. The pain was unbearable. Geoffrey screamed. He trembled uncontrollably as spasms of white hot pain surged through his arm.

Then the pain spread to his back. He lurched violently. Forgetting the stake, he tried to pull away, twisting and squirming to free himself of the vampire's terrible grip.

The pain seemed to ease. Dracul had released his hold, not much but enough for Geoffrey to regain his feet.

Seizing his last chance to survive, he spun around and desperately swung the mallet as hard as he could. It hit the vampire squarely in the face.

Both men staggered backward. Dracul shook his head fiercely, while Geoffrey braced himself to keep from falling again.

They stood in the semidarkness for a long time, too stunned to act, staring downward. There, scattered on the floor between them, lay Dracul's teeth.

Geoffrey and Dracul shrugged and exchanged knowing glances. Then Geoffrey turned and limped painfully back through the corridor, while the vampire sadly dissolved into a cloud of mist.

# The Heart of Count Dracula, Descendent of Attila, Scourge of God

THOMAS LIGOTTI

Count Dracula recalls how he was irresistibly drawn to Mina Harker (née Murray), the wife of a London real estate agent. Her husband had sold him a place called Carfax. This was a dilapidated structure next door to a noisy institution for the insane. Their incessant racket was not undisturbing to one who was, among many other things, seeking peace. An inmate name Renfield was the worst offender.

One time the Harkers had Count Dracula over for the evening, and Jonathan (his agency's top man) asked him how he liked Carfax with regard to location, condition of the house and property, and just all around. Ah, such architecture, said Count Dracula while gazing uncontrollably at Mina, is truly frozen music, a pretty figure of speech incarnate.

Count Dracula is descended from the noble race of the Szekelys, a people of many bloodlines, all of them fierce and warlike. He fought for his country against the invading Turks. He survived wars, plagues, the hardships of an isolated dwelling in the Carpathian Mountains. And for centuries, at least five and maybe more, he has managed to perpetuate, with the aid of supernatural powers, his existence as a vampire.

*This existence came to an end in the late 1800s.*
*Why her? Count Dracula often asked himself.*

*Why the entire ritual? when one really thinks*
*about it. What does a being who can transform*
*himself into a bat, a wolf, a wisp of smoke,*
*anything at all, and who knows the secrets of*
*the dead (perhaps of death itself) want with*
*this oily and overheated nourishment? Who would*
*make such a stipulation for immortality?*

*And, in the end, where did it get him? Lucy*
*Westenra's soul was saved, Renfield's soul was*
*never even in any real danger . . . but Count Dracula,*
*a true vampire, one of the true children of the*
*night from which all things are born, has no soul.*
*Now he has only this same insatiable thirst, though*
*he is no longer free to alleviate it. (Why her?*
*There were no others such as her.) Now he has only*
*this painful, perpetual awareness that he is doomed*
*to wriggle beneath this infernal stake which those*
*fools—Harker, Seward, Van Helsing, and the*
*others—have stuck in his trembling heart.*
*(Her fault, her fault.) And now he hears*
*voices, common voices, peasants from the*
*countryside.*

*Over here, one of them shouts, in this broken*
*down convent or whatever it is. I think I've*
*found something we can give those damn dogs.*
*Good thing, too. Christ, I'm sick of their*
*endless whining.*

# Misapprehensions

## DON D'AMMASSA

Inspector Bartleby frowned as the cadaverous foreigner stood over the exsanguinated body of Lord Northby and resisted the urge to rearrange the nobleman's limbs into a more dignified position. He was skeptical of this entire line of investigation, but he had his orders.

"The body has not been disturbed, I take it." The accent was almost undetectable.

"That is my understanding, Dr. Van Helsing. Lord Northby's personal physician was quite indignant when the constable barred him from the house." Bartleby's voice betrayed his own dissatisfaction with the situation.

"An admittedly distasteful arrangement, but necessary to the pursuit of truth." Van Helsing crouched by the bed, his eyes only inches from the bloodless wounds in the dead man's throat. "It is just as I feared," he said quietly, then stood abruptly and walked to the window.

"If you're through here, sir, the undertaker is waiting downstairs."

"What? Oh, yes, the undertaker. There's a family vault, I assume?"

"Naturally."

"And the interment is to be . . . when?"

"This very day, sir. The heat, you know." As if suddenly remembering the stubbornly oppressive summer weather, Bartleby started to raise a hand to loosen his stiff collar, but let it fall back rather than demonstrate weakness in front of Van Helsing.

"Very good. We will need to make certain preparations before the ceremony."

"Preparations, sir?"

Van Helsing described them, apparently oblivious to the growing rage on the Englishman's face. "Surely you can't mean to do such a thing! It's . . . it's inhuman, sir!"

"Indeed. That's what I've been trying to tell your government ever since they requested my assistance. Believe me, Inspector, I don't suggest such drastic acts lightly."

"I can't authorize such a thing. The family will have to be consulted, and Lord Northby's brother is in Brussels presently."

"There's no time for such niceties. Our difficulties will only be compounded if we hesitate. It was my understanding from Sir Humphrey that I would have your complete cooperation."

Bartleby colored at the implied criticism, but fought down his anger. "You are correct, sir."

Van Helsing sighed. "We gain nothing fighting with one another, Inspector. Your reservations are understandable but surely my sponsor's endorsement was persuasive."

"Mr. Holmes was most insistent about your qualifications, sir," Bartleby admitted. His shoulders slumped resignedly. "All right, what must I do?"

"Arrange for a pair of your bravest constables to accompany us to the vault immediately after dusk. And I will require certain items, a willow shaft twice the thickness of a man's thumb and shaved to a point, a carpenter's mallet, some fresh-cut wild roses, and a physician's bonesaw."

Bartleby was still shaken the following morning when he arrived at Van Helsing's temporary lodgings, and a largely sleepless night had left its signature on his face. Their mission had been ghastly enough in its conception, but the sight of Lord Northby's animated corpse struggling to pull free the stake driven through its chest even after Van Helsing had sawed off the dead man's head had shattered the Inspector's self-confidence.

Van Helsing greeted him cheerfully, gestured toward a basket of fresh breakfast rolls.

"No, thank you, Doctor. I really couldn't." He did, however, accept the offer of a seat.

"You'll regret it, Inspector. The engine of the body cannot function long without fuel."

"Perhaps later. Dr. Van Helsing, I feel I should apologize for my previous skepticism."

The older man shook his head. "Not necessary, Inspector.

A man in your profession is perfectly justified in demanding tangible evidence. I only regret that time works not in our favor in this matter."

"Then how should we proceed?'

"You have a list of the previous victims?"

"Yes, of course." Bartleby withdrew a notebook from his pocket, unnecessarily since he recalled the names as readily as those of his children. "A fortnight past, Sir Martin Choate was found dead in his stable by the liveryman. Prior to that, and at intervals of three to fifteen days, the victims were Le Comte de Beauvais—a Frenchman, the Earl of Cholmondesley, Lord Godalming, and a foreigner who styled himself a Prince, Vlad Dracul, from some outlandishly named region on the continent."

"And each man died in the same fashion?"

"That's my understanding, sir. The deaths were initially attributed to the attack of some nocturnal animal, as you might expect."

"From the unimaginative, yes, indeed I would. An animal that confines its attacks to distinguished male members of the nobility. A prince among predators." He sighed. "I would like to speak to the examining physician in each of these cases, Inspector, and as quickly as possible."

Bartleby hesitated. "The previous victims. Would their remains be similarly . . . affected?"

"I fear so. We must intrude upon the resting place of each before nightfall, and deal with them in the same fashion."

"Yes, sir. I will make arrangements immediately." He rose and started for the door. "There is one slight difficulty, Doctor. Lord Godalming's physician was killed several days ago."

"How killed?"

"An animal attack of some kind." Bartleby saw the change in Van Helsing's expression, hastened to explain. "Not like the others, Doctor, not even in London. Dr. Seward was on a hunting holiday with an American chap out in the country. He was separated from the rest of the party and apparently stumbled into a bad situation. Torn up quite badly. There wasn't even a viewing of the body, if you know what I mean. Unfortunate, but it has no bearing on this case."

"Perhaps not." But Van Helsing's voice was laden with doubt.

The interviews did not go to Van Helsing's satisfaction. None of the four physicians considered the lacerations significant, and three were adamant that the deaths were the result of a "failure of the heart." The fourth, who had attended the body of the foreign Prince, seemed particularly inept, though voluble.

"Some foreign disease, most likely. No offense intended, Dr. Van Helsing."

"None taken, Dr. Marsh. And you saw nothing unusual about the throat wound, then?"

The portly doctor appeared mildly discomfited. "Well, as to that, I didn't actually see it, don't you know? I mean, it had already been covered by that time, and I saw no reason to question Dr. Seward's observations."

Van Helsing and Bartleby exchanged startled looks. "Would that be Dr. Jack Seward?" the Inspector asked mildly.

"Yes it would. Did you know him then? Wasted his career working among madmen, if you ask me, but a sound mind. Terrible waste, his death."

"How is it that you were both called in, Dr. Marsh? Surely one physician would have been adequate to sign the death certificate."

"Certainly. Dr. Seward's arrival was coincidental with my own, but his visit was for purely social reasons. He was a recent acquaintance of the Prince, who had represented himself as knowledgeable of diseases of the blood, if I recall. They were to have dined together that evening."

"It might be no more than happenstance, Doctor." The two men sat facing each other in the hansom carriage as it jolted its way back from Dr. Marsh's offices.

"Inspector, we have six victims, two of whom were examined by the same physician, who is himself killed under unusual circumstances, all in the space of two months."

"It does look strange; there's no denying that."

"I wish to learn how Dr. Seward made Prince Vlad's acquaintance."

"I will make inquiries straightaway."

"There's a more pressing issue just now, Inspector."

"Yes, the other . . . victims."

"We must act quickly, you realize. Indeed, it may already be too late. The newly wakened linger near the grave, but with the passage of time they grow more adventurous."

"Unfortunately, the two foreign gentlemen are beyond our reach. Their bodies were shipped to their respective homelands."

"I feared as much. But we must deal with the others, and promptly."

But someone had anticipated them. Sir Martin Choate, the Earl of Cholmondesley, and Lord Godalming all lay in their coffins, each with his head separated from his body and a shaft of wood protruding from his breast.

"Seward?"

Van Helsing nodded. "So I believe. Unhappily, his identity was obvious to another as well."


Bartleby's face betrayed his eagerness to speak when he arrived at Van Helsing's rooms the following day. "Dr. Seward was present at a dinner party given by the Westenra family approximately two weeks before the Prince's death. Prince Vlad attended as well and it is there presumably that they first met."

"Excellent, Inspector. I wish to speak to their host at the earliest possible opportunity."

"I assumed such and have an appointment for early this evening. But there's more, Doctor."

Van Helsing waited for a few heartbeats. "Well, what is it, man? Don't stand there looking smug or your face may freeze into that expression permanently."

Bartleby huffed good humoredly. "It seems that Dr. Seward did not ordinarily attend Lord Godalming, and his presence there was somewhat a mystery. He'd begged audience with his Lordship on an unspecified matter of some urgency, but arrived only a few moments before the discovery of his Lordship's body."

"I see. Dr. Seward seems to be the key to this entire puzzle. You say he was accompanied by an American at the time of his death?"

"Yes, one Quincey Morris. A rather flamboyant fellow by all accounts."

"Is he still about somewhere?"

"He has a flat in London. I just learned the address this morning and I have a carriage waiting."

"You anticipate me, Inspector."

"I am not without some resources of my own, Doctor."

Unfortunately, their expedition was less than satisfactory. Quincey Morris lay cold in bed, his throat torn out along with most of his internal organs. The walls of the room were dark with dried blood.

"I don't understand," admitted Bartleby. "Why wasn't he drained like the others?"

Van Helsing sniffed. "Our quarry is an epicure, Inspector, with a taste for noble blood. This was an enemy, not prey."

"I appreciate your seeing us on such short notice, Miss Westenra, and at such a late hour." Van Helsing bent to kiss her proffered hand, noting with interest the delicate jeweled pendant that lay across her breast.

"It's a welcome diversion, gentlemen. I've been abandoned by my family these past few days while they chase an inoffensive fox around the countryside and most of my proper companions have accompanied them, I regret to say. If it weren't for Mina, I'd go quite mad, I think."

The two visitors waited until Lucy was seated before doing the same, the Inspector with a noticeable air of uneasiness. He always felt awkward dealing with the aristocracy, a discomfiture apparently not shared by his companion.

Van Helsing waited until a servant had finished lighting candles against the encroaching darkness before speaking to the issue. "We wish to ask you about Dr. Seward, Miss Westenra."

"Yes, poor Jack. He was a true and dear friend. I will miss him."

"When did you last speak to him, may I ask?"

"Why, I believe it was in this very room. We were arguing about the merits of the hunt, as I recall, rather than listen to a rather tedious conversation in the dining room."

"That would have been the night of the party your parents arranged for Prince Vlad?"

"Yes." Her eyes narrowed. "You have the advantage of me, it seems. May I ask the purpose of this interrogation?"

"It's hardly an interrogation, Miss Westenra. . . ." Bartleby tried to smooth things over, but Van Helsing overrode him.

"I apologize for any indelicacy, but the matter is of some urgency. We are investigating the circumstances of the death of Vlad Dracul, who was also, I believe, a guest of yours that evening."

Lucy nodded thoughtfully. "A rather stuffy sort, actually, though Mina found him frightfully interesting. A touch of the exotic, I suppose. He entertained some grandiose plan to refurbish Carfax Abbey as I recall."

"Mina?"

"My dearest friend and companion. Am I to understand that there is some question concerning the Prince's death?"

"We're attempting to address that possibility, yes. Would you be able to recall who else was in attendance that evening?"

"Well, my parents of course, and Mina. Dr. Seward and the Prince you know of already. Mr. Stoker was there, but not, I believe, his wife, and . . ." With occasional pauses, Lucy went on to list a virtual who's who of London society, during which recital two names stood out—Lord Godalming and Quincey Morris.

They took their leave a few moments later, after solemnly promising to apprise Lucy of any discoveries they might make.

Their efforts the following day to interview the other guests at that fateful party were universally frustrated. The Stokers were in France visiting friends, the Marrowbys had accompanied Lord Cheltenham to Gibraltar, and everyone else on Lucy Westenra's list had gone to the countryside for the hunting season.

"All those still alive, at least," Bartleby added pensively. "You're quite certain young Morris died by the same hand?"

Van Helsing remained stonily silent.

"Foolish question, I suppose." The Inspector sighed. "Someone Miss Westenra forgot, perhaps?"

"Not necessarily."

"I don't understand."

"I think it's time we made our report to Miss Westenra."

Bartleby frowned. "Even if we had anything to reveal, it would hardly be appropriate to convey such information to the young lady, Doctor."

"Inappropriate, perhaps, but possibly revelatory as well."

Bartleby glanced out the window. "I suppose there's time before nightfall if we hurry, but I still don't understand what purpose this will serve."

"There's no hurry at all, Inspector. In fact, I think we should dine first; I fancy Miss Westenra would far rather receive us after nightfall. It would be best if we sent a message ahead, something to the effect that we have discovered the truth surrounding Dr. Seward's death and wish to keep our promise."

"But we haven't . . ."

"Don't be so certain, Inspector. Sometimes we don't realize what knowledge we possess."

This time they were ushered into a slightly larger room, where they were presently joined by Lucy Westenra and a dark-haired young woman.

"Inspector Bartleby, Dr. Van Helsing, this is my friend Mina Murray."

Mina acknowledged them shyly, never raising her eyes to meet their's. A silver cross pressed against the flesh at the base of her throat, and her bodice was cut with unfashionable modesty. In contrast, Lucy's gown was so daring that Bartleby felt considerable embarrassment and studiously averted his eyes, hastily evicting what he considered impertinent thoughts.

"I understand you have something to tell me, gentlemen."

"We've made rather a startling discovery, Miss Westenra." Dr. Van Helsing rose casually and began walking around the room. "You may be surprised to learn that several of your recent guests have succumbed to an evil creature whose very existence modern man has contrived to forget. Or perhaps it comes as no surprise."

Lucy turned her head to follow Van Helsing's progress. "I don't understand, Doctor."

"Do you not?" He moved casually behind Lucy's chair, his hands clutching the lapels of his jacket. "That's a beautiful necklace you're wearing, Miss Westenra."

"Yes, isn't it? It's been in my family positively forever."

"Yes, so I would imagine. Not really the style though, is it?"

"I beg your pardon?"

"The Christian Church has adopted many of the pagan traditions and made them their own, but I hardly think the sign of Pan is one of them."

"Is that what this is?" She dropped her chin to regard the pendant.

Van Helsing quickly removed something from his inside pocket and thrust it rudely toward Lucy's face. "Wouldn't this be a more appropriate ornament?"

Lucy rose and stepped away from the chair so suddenly that it would have toppled had it been of less solid construction. Her eyes flashed angrily and she held both hands clasped at her bosom. Van Helsing advanced toward her, holding an ornate, jeweled crucifix at arm's length.

"What in the world are you about, Dr. Van Helsing? I find your behavior most peculiar, even insulting."

"Do you now?" Van Helsing moved to interpose himself between Lucy and her friend, who sat motionless, her eyes wide in apparent shock. "Well, then, let me present you with this gift, as reparation for my breach of manners."

Lucy's eyes flickered to the crucifix, then back to meet Van Helsing's gaze. "Sir, I fail to grasp the purpose of this game."

"Then perhaps you'd just humor me and grasp this instead." He advanced a half step, the crucifix still extended.

"Sir, you presume upon my hospitality."

"Not without reason. Will you accept my gift or will you not?"

She hesitated, glanced toward the room's single doorway, then seemed to resign herself to the inevitable. With a sudden, spasmodic gesture, she reached forward and snatched the crucifix out of Van Helsing's hand.

"Are your bizarre motives now satisfied, sir?"

Van Helsing's expression would have been comical in another context, but to Bartleby it appeared the man had aged a decade in a heartbeat.

"I thought . . . I was certain . . ." Van Helsing shook his head. "It appears, Miss Westenra, that I have made a complete fool of myself."

257

"Not a complete fool, Dr. Van Helsing."

The voice was so unexpected, so unfamiliar, that no one reacted at first. Then three heads turned as one to stare at Mina Murray, who had risen from her chair and advanced toward her companions.

The candles flickered and several went out, but enough remained to illuminate a transformed Mina, still slight of build but with eyes now deepset and glowing. Her slender fingers were tipped with razor sharp nails and bright red lips barely concealed emergent fangs.

"But you wear the cross!" Van Helsing protested, just before Mina reached out and tore away his throat.

"Foolish man," she said softly. "I was centuries old before your pale godling walked the Earth. Did you think his sign held any meaning for me?"

And then she turned to the others.

# Prince of the Punks

KARL EDWARD WAGNER

The aged cemetery in Battersea had been in disuse for some years. Weeds grew thickly, cut back only at long intervals by uncaring caretakers. Vandals had knocked over some of the tombstones, broken off bits from the statues of angels. A number of the graves had been opened and robbed. Modern graffiti—some of it Satanic—sprawled across many a Victorian mausoleum.

It was a typical London autumn afternoon. Spitting rain, cold, overcast. Inspector Blount considered himself a fool for trudging along through this mess. Detective Sergeant Rollins gave him reproachful glances but kept silent; he was a tall, sour man in his thirties, ambitious for promotion. Dr. Hoffmann led the way vigorously, despite his aged legs. He must be all of eighty. Detective Sergeant Rollins carried his heavy leather bag.

"It's just a short matter of finding his tomb," called back Dr. Hoffmann.

Inspector Blount cursed himself for venturing out on this lunatic outing. He was rotund and graying, too old for this sort of thing. Still, Dr. Hoffmann might lead them to some manner of clues. Anything would help this investigation.

Six unsolved deaths in two months, all with linking modus operandi. All of them teenagers, found within a few miles of this vicinity, puncture wounds to the throat, bodies drained of blood. The tabloid press was filled with screaming headlines of Satanic rituals and vampiric sacrificial killings. More quietly and more firmly, orders came down to solve the mess quickly.

Which was why Blount and Rollins were following a probable senile lunatic through a forgotten Victorian cemetery in the rain. He might know something. He might even be their killer.

"I have made a lifetime study of vampires," Dr. Hoffmann had said, when he presented himself in Inspector Blount's office. "Your murders are clearly attacks by a vampire. I think I can find him. And destroy him."

Inspector Blount had just been upbraided with the others for lack of progress. He was having his tea and thinking of retorts he wished he had dared make. His assignment was to explore the Satanic youth gang element to the murders. Thus, Dr. Hoffmann was sent to his office, and Inspector Blount was in a testy mood.

"A vampire? How many sugars?" He poured a cup for Dr. Hoffmann. A nut case just might know something worth following with regard to other loonies of his acquaintance. Any sort of lead just now.

"Two, please. Yes, a vampire. Obvious, isn't it." Dr. Hoffmann sipped his tea. "If I'm correct, and I think I am, judging from the localities of the deaths, it's one Giles Ashton, entombed within the family crypt, St. Martin's, Battersea, in 1878. Months later, they opened his coffin clandestinely and drove a stake through his heart. There had been numerous deaths such as these in the vicinity. Described as anemia. Ashton had been known to explore the black arts. Died under strange and unspecified circumstances. After that, the deaths ceased."

Inspector Blount finished his tea and wished it were a cup of single malt. At least he was pursuing his assignment by listening to this mad geezer. "How do you know all this, then?"

"I've spent my life studying vampirism."

"Oh, yes. I forgot. So then. Why is this Giles Ashton suddenly on the prowl after all these years?"

"I think it's those young punk would-be Satanists, raiding unfrequented cemeteries and robbing graves for skulls and other human remains. I think some of them broke into the Ashton crypt, opened his coffin, saw the stake through his heart, and removed it to see what would happen. It would have released him."

"I see."

Dr. Hoffmann examined his watch. "Just past midday. I have wooden stakes and mallet, garlic, crucifix, holy water, and consecrated host. We can find his crypt before darkness and destroy him before he kills again."

Inspector Blount had just received a severe reprimand to produce results right now. His position was in jeopardy. The man was a senile fool, but if he did have any knowledge of Satanic rites near the murder scenes, Blount could truthfully report that he was following every lead. Perhaps the geezer might lead him to something important.

So, Inspector Blount summoned Detective Sergeant Rollins, and the two of them followed Dr. Hoffmann off into the rain and the weeds and the vandalized graves.

"Here it is!" Dr. Hoffmann pointed to the mausoleum. It had been blemished with spray-paint graffiti; the door had been forced. In eroding marble letters, the name of Ashton could still be read upon the cornice.

Inspector Blount envisioned a gang of depraved teenagers, high on drugs, performing Satanic rituals here. Drinking the blood of their spaced-out sacrifices, leaving their bodies close by, too crazed to think of hiding them. This might be the break.

"Vampires sleep by day," Dr. Hoffmann said. "Giles Ashton will be resting in his coffin."

Inspector Blount had seen the movies. Let the old geezer go on about with it. He and Rollins should find evidence here. It was a large mausoleum, ideal for cult activities. In the semidarkness, Blount observed with disgust empty cans of Tennent's Super, broken syringes, used condoms, dirty blankets, more graffiti. A large pentagram painted on the floor. Blount suspected that it wasn't actually paint.

"Over here!" Dr. Hoffmann pointed to a vandalized coffin.

It bore evidence of having been forced open recently, and a verdigris-covered bronze tablet read: GILES ASHTON. 1830–1878. MAY HE REST FOREVER.

"Quick! Hand me my bag!"

Rollins did so, feeling like an idiot.

Dr. Hoffmann removed a sharpened wooden stake and a mallet. "Now then. Remove the coffin lid, and you'll find your killer."

My God, the man is serious, thought Inspector Blount. Best to humor him, then get on with the serious detective work. He and Rollins lifted the coffin lid, as Dr. Hoffmann stood poised to strike.

The coffin was empty.

Dr. Hoffmann stared at the empty coffin. They must have hidden his body!"

A figure stepped out from the deepest shadows at the back of the crypt.

"After so long a sleep," said Giles Ashton, "I find I have insomnia."

He also had a sawed-off shotgun.

*(The original version of this story was written in collaboration with John Mayer.)*

# Entrapment

## JOHN MACLAY

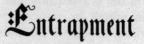

e didn't know why it had taken him so long to discover the show bars. Having lived more than one lifetime, you were supposed to be wise about such things. Whenever blood, food, had become scarce, he had even resorted to wandering the city alleyways and sucking the filthy necks of drunks. How much better to be drawing his sustenance from the creamy white flesh, the piquant blue veins, of young girls!

And the show bars were a natural. Crowded along a rundown street, each with its dark interior, its jukebox, long bar, and stage where the girls danced naked, they were only open at night, his native time. The girls, too, were of the type whom nobody would miss if he drank too deeply; or if they were missed, society's opinion of them was such that the police wouldn't look too long. Then there were the secret back rooms to which he could take his victims for a few dollars, where sex was supposed to be illicitly performed. Lastly, there was the fact that his dark clothing, his long, stringy hair, his gaunt and hungry look, weren't remarkable among the other male patrons; men who, most of them, also saw women as prey.

There had been the almost comical drawbacks, the stages having mirrors behind them and the girls sometimes having drugs in their veins. But he'd known that the former weren't of real silver, and the latter had provided a not unwelcome high.

Now, some months after his discovery, he was a regular on the street of broken dreams and of fresh young blood. He would sleep all day in his cheap hotel room a couple of blocks away, then would rise at sundown to be one of the first on a worn vinyl stool. He varied the bars he visited so that he wouldn't become too suspicious or, on the positive side, so he could enjoy more than one smorgasbord of fleshly delights.

Tonight, a Friday, it was the Hot Spot.

He pretended to sip a beer from a dirty glass, and rested his black-coated arms on the scarred rail. The girls danced, one by one, in the order in which he remembered them. There was Raven, the lusty brunette; Angel, the bubbly blonde; Sue, the one with the huge breasts; and Foxy, the thin redhead. All of them bore the traces, noticed or not, of his fangs on their sweet young necks.

Absent, of course, was Sandy, with whom he'd gotten a bit carried away.

But there was a new girl in the Hot Spot tonight, he noticed with a thrill; new blood. Tall and yellow-haired, she appeared cleaner than the rest and at the same time smarter. Intrigued, he waited until she'd shown all of her smooth, firm loveliness, then accepted her proposition to sit beside him.

"Hi, I'm Mitzi," she purred. "Buy me a drink?"

He nodded and signaled the bartender. She smiled and draped a lithe arm over his shoulder.

"Do you come here often?"

He said that he did, chuckling inwardly at her use of that word.

From there on, it was as before. He bought her more drinks, enough that she wouldn't notice, or mind if she did, his particular brand of kissing. He stroked her warm skin while she fondled him below. Then, after an exchange of bills, he followed her to the back of the bar.

Some of his kind might consider it dishonorable to pay for it. But he had plenty of money after all his years, and the merchandise was fresh and good.

In the tiny room with its soiled paint and rumpled bed, he decided against the sex part. This new girl, Mitzi, was even more tantalizing to him in the taste of her blood than in any other exchange of fluids. So, sitting with her, he simply increased his attentions, building up to the moment at which he would bare his fangs.

Before it arrived, however, he received a major surprise.

"Police," she said, pulling away. She reached into her handbag and produced the proper identification. "You're under arrest for solicitation."

He'd heard that there was to be a crackdown on the bars, but he hadn't taken it seriously. Nor had he believed that such would involve more than inspections, and certainly not the arrest of patrons.

But now he was in genuine trouble. What if, he thought, his true nature were revealed? What if, in the city jail, there were a physical examination?

He had, though, lived too long to be defeated by a mere undercover policewoman. So, using his superhuman strength, he simply pushed her down and pinned her arms to the bed.

She lay there, blue eyes looking uncertainly up at him, well-formed breasts quaking, while he decided what to do next. With his free hand, he did feel in her handbag for the inevitable gun and tossed that away.

"You know, this might be called entrapment," he tried.

Her return look was mixed, as if she were thinking whether to cite law to the contrary or to avoid provoking him further. She wound up saying nothing, only breathing heavily into his face.

But that breath, almost comically, presented another problem. That was because, like the coarser dancers at the bar, she'd thought nothing of having a dinner laden with garlic.

He felt himself getting a little weaker, and at that moment it happened. Her right hand, working free from his grip, went to her leg that was uncomfortably drawn up under her. And from one of her boots, which were the only exception to her nakedness, she pulled out a small and secret knife.

Now it wasn't funny. Her eyes changing to fierceness, she plunged the blade into his groin. "Aouww!" he screamed as the pain shot through him, even though he knew he could easily repair the wound. Facing down the garlic, he twisted the knife out of her hand and reestablished his hold on her.

She looked terrified now, and so, partly, was he. He would have to kill her outright, or to suck out enough of her blood to accomplish it. But there would be no delight. Moreover, he'd have to leave the city, even to give up his haunting of show bars in any city, due to the attendant publicity. A policewoman dumped naked and drained in the alley, as he'd done with the several others with whom he'd gone too far, was another matter entirely.

"You missed your mark," he told her, recovering, sensing that she must have guessed something about him. "With one like me, it has to be wood and in the heart."

She looked calmer, more knowing. "Just my luck," she said at last. "I draw this kind of duty and I get hooked up with a real one, not just the human kind."

He was mildly surprised. "Then you believe in us."

"Why not? When I'm off duty, I get into some pretty kinky things."

Now, he knew, it was her role to prevent him from killing her, or to temporize while she thought of a way. What would she try? he wondered. In his long life, there had always been time for games.

He soon had his answer. It was the sex part. "Make love to me," she sighed.

He was no longer disinclined. Despite his jadedness after lifetimes of lovers, despite his stronger urge to taste her young blood, her blonde nakedness and the hold he had on her had made him rise. So, pinning her with one arm on her smooth white throat, he undid his clothing.

"Oh, yes, kinky!" she gasped when she felt him inside her, there in the tiny back room of the dingy bar. "I've certainly never made it with a vampire before." She paused. "Can I see your fangs?"

Now he was delayed indeed, not to mention taken aback. She was enjoying it too much, as evidenced also by her return motions below. What was she up to, this dancer, this not-so-undercover policewoman-hooker who had led him here?

Had he finally met his match?

Tentatively, then more boldly, he fulfilled her request. Raising his upper lip, he gave her full view of his long canines while her blue eyes widened in supposed terror.

Then, as her mouth also dropped open, they widened in something else! It was a look of amusement she was giving him, as well containing fellow-feeling and a deep, mystic peace.

"Damn you!" he cried. "You young rascal. Damn you!"

He said it when he saw her fangs, new and polished, coming clear.

"Well, you can't blame me for earning a living," she laughed, "in the best way I know how."

They completed their business below, which wasn't really important anymore. Then they sat on the soiled bed and talked.

"It was entrapment, of course," she said. "And naturally I won't arrest you now, or even spoil your M.O."

He smiled. "Nor I kill you, as if I could. Naturally, indeed! The age-old entrapper, working to entrap. And who is more of one than one like us, who takes mortals and sucks their blood?"

She nodded. "Yes. Often, before I run the men in, I do have a little drink."

"But I'm a bit sad," he concluded, gazing at her tall, sleek nudity, her marble-like throat. "You're so lovely, but you're not available. And I was so looking forward to a drink, too, my love."

At that, she gave him a wild look. "Well, why not?" she shrugged. "There's always a first time for everything!"

They embraced, cheek to cheek, their mouths seeking. And soon they were lost in an ancient, red-tinged sea.

# Cocci's Blood-fueled Feud

## Lois H. Gresh

pirilla's kinky torso gives Cocci the shudders. She wriggles and pumps protoplasm against her cell wall, then oxidates the fleshoid tumor and sucks dissolved blood into her vacuoles.

Oh Polyp, just the *sight* of her . . .

He murmurs, "Forgive me, Polyp, for I am about to sin," and then he clutches at Spirilla and divides into two cells.

Spirilla's flagella tense. A dozen whiphairs smack his cell wall. "Stop it, Cocci, stop it! You have billions of children. If you would stop dividing, we wouldn't have to move again. Oh, you make me sick; *sick!*"

Cocci's new bacteriole swims into the mainstream, and Cocci feels himself glowing—dividing always makes him swoon —and he knows how terribly handsome he is right now, a perfect sphere and more luminous than the phosphorescence of the inner organ. He is Cocci the Virile, Grand Patriarch of All Disease. "Spirilla dear, your place is with me."

"But I'm tired of moving. I won't go."

"You have no choice. We've sucked this creature dry. Of all the fleshoids that came to the homeland, only two remain. And Vibrios is a constant threat. If we don't invade the last two creatures *now*, Vibrios will beat us to it and the Cocci clan will starve."

Spirilla droops. She peers into the swirling neon at the little ones below. They bow to Polyp, great God who pounds with the blood of the visceral organ. Their prayers ride the rank mists: "Save us, Polyp, give us blood."

Cocci has brought them up well.

A dribble of pickling acid burns the hair off his rear quarters and riddles him with holes. Blood oozes from his body.

Spirilla springs forward and laps the blood.

With anyone else, he would mind; but Spirilla's vibrations

are soft on his flanks, like the rubbing of fur on fresh fleshoid tongue.

She sucks down the last drop and says, "Oh, Cocci, if only you would stop browbeating everyone . . . stop dividing . . . if only you could be—" her voice a hundred whispers of hair, ". . . more like Vibrios."

"You insult me. Vibrios is a killer."

"Vibrios doesn't *want* to kill us. Once we blast our way into the new fleshoid, there will be enough room for his clan *and* ours. Cocci, maybe I'll . . . maybe I'll stay until Vibrios goes."

"You're my firstborn. You go with me."

He's had enough, and he twines his flagella into a cord and whacks her. He knows it hurts her and it pains him to think what he's done, but then her kinky body springs down the yawning tube and he knows: *there is no other way.*

Millions of bacterioles skitter past them. The tubular flesh vibrates with the intensity of their sucking. All so desperate for fleshoid blood.

Cocci leaps after them, shouts, "One, two, three, leap!" and his progeny slide onto the wide spot, where the tongue hairs tickle. They shoot spores into the air, and soon a spore mat floats beyond the wide spot toward the succulent new fleshoid beyond.

The dying fleshoid stings Cocci with toxic protopin. A last pathetic effort, no doubt, to kill the Cocci clan; probably instigated by Vibrios. Cocci turns and sprays antitoxins, guards the way while Spirilla and the others leap to the spore mat.

Cocci is the last one to leap aboard.

And now they're flying to nirvana, leaving the wretched fleshoid tissue behind, dreaming of a new hostlife.

The air is warm. Cocci feels good.

He must divide.

Where is Spirilla, where? She must not see him divide.

Behind him, shrinking farther and farther into the distance, is the diseased fleshoid, its tissues inflamed, its blood vessels choked.

Hundreds of bacteriole cells curl into heavy-walled beads and fall from the spore mat. His children are deflating from dehydration. *They need blood.* Everywhere is the wailing, the scrabbling, the lunging for shore.

Spirilla, crying: "You're so cruel, Cocci. You don't care that we're dying."

She's right behind him. She'll see him divide.

But he can't control the urge—

He divides, then divides again.

Spirilla gasps, turns from him. "Polyp Almighty! You're so disgusting."

Cocci kicks his new children into the mounds of offspring bobbing and playing tag. "You prefer Vibrios? That meatless wimp can barely divide. It takes *him* forever to dissolve a host. I can dissolve three hosts in a day. And Vibrios has no morals; he doesn't even believe in Polyp. Not to mention that his excretions are poison. I can't understand what you see in him. He's lower than a yeast."

*"You* are a pig."

A *pig!* "Just get off the boat, would you?"

He divides again and uses a string of offspring to flail her. Her flagella dent, and she curses and flies off the mat onto the tongue of the new fleshoid.

Cocci slurps saliva and blood, analyzes the new tongue's chemical consistency. Too much lactose. His children wither and die. Their hard, round corpses bounce down the fleshoid's outer skin. Cocci loses at least a few million grandchildren and great-grandchildren.

He begins to divide: interphase, prophase, metaphase . . .

And the macho bacterioles—those who truly take after him—split exponentially, and within moments, new generations adapt and consume the excess lactose.

"To Polyp!" cries Cocci, and they dive down the throat into the food cavity, where the new Polyp awaits. Children wrestle and scream and dissolve tissue into blood. Spirilla worms into a crevice by Polyp, and Polyp throbs a welcome. She ignores Him and burrows into His Flesh, and from her wriggling tail, Cocci knows that she is oxidating tissue as quickly as possible. She must be starving.

*Real* disease converts calcium sulphate into calcium sulphide. *Real* disease converts ferrous compounds into ferric. But Cocci is hungry, and so he oxidates fleshoid carbons into watery blood, the most simple way to feed. He's content to fill his belly.

Something pokes his feeding vacuole. Sharply, he looks up. "Who dares to—"

It is a crescent-shaped bacteriole. A stranger. It is—

Vibrios!

"Get out! Get out before I kill you! Go back to the old fleshoid where you belong!"

Vibrios slowly dissolves then swallows a bit of blood vessel. He pokes Spirilla's tail, and she turns and *glows* at him.

Age-old hatred churns in Cocci's gut.

Vibrios says, "Enough food here for your children *and* mine."

"You will not infect my home. Go find your own turf, someplace where they don't mind toxic dump excretions."

"Your excretions, Cocci, are far more noxious than mine. You can dissolve a thousand intellectuals with a drop of your spit. I, at least, kill heathens. But we won't bother you. My family will live far away in the brain."

"This fleshoid's not big enough for the both of us. When stomach worms get bad, we Coccis go to the brain. And when we do, we don't want to find *you* there. I'd rather live with mold and rust, with mildew—"

"Oh, stop it, boys," says Spirilla.

She sidles up to Vibrios. She sucks her waist in and out, pulses to some internal tune. Why is she flirting with the disgusting Vibrios?

Aah, but such undulating curves . . .

Cocci grabs her and as her heat hits his flanks, he pinches himself into hourglass shape. Their flagella lock.

"All you Coccis are braindead." Vibrios sneers and slides farther into the stomach.

Thousands of his children slide with him.

Cocci divides.

Slowly, the Vibrios bacterioles chew.

Cocci divides.

Slowly, the Vibrios bacterioles ponder and turn and consult about building ponderous cities in the new fleshoid. The wimps don't even *try* to divide.

Now several point at Polyp and laugh.

The nerve of them! "Bow to Polyp and beg forgiveness, or you will burn in hell," says Cocci.

"Yeah, right." Vibrios pokes Cocci with the barb of one of his crescent ends, then swivels and pokes him with the other.

The barbs puncture Cocci's wall. Sharp pains flame through his protoplasm. He curls into a tight ball, presses his wounds together, secretes slime. The slime glues the wounds shut. "This is an act of war," he says, and then he curls even tighter and rolls back and sends himself spinning, fast and now faster, down the sloping stomach wall until he crashes with a splat into the concave crescent of Vibrios.

Vibrios' ends buckle and snap together, trapping Cocci tight. Cocci squirms and bulges, and finally, with a powerful push, splays open the crescent ends and rolls away.

He tenses, ready for battle.

And Vibrios comes quickly. He squats, bunches into a spring, then leaps; and Cocci sees him, a translucent bolt shooting through mists of neon green.

Cocci tightens and rolls.

Vibrios plunges and, knife that he is, skewers the fleshoid's stomach with his deadly barb. He squats, bunches, leaps again.

Cocci laughs. Vibrios the Slow. Cocci excretes waste from his vacuoles, then rolls to the right and waits in a cradle of blood. Nice and warm; he divides a couple of times, and shoves his offspring from harm's way.

*Sproing*, and Vibrios is in the waste puddle, squirming, trying to grip glistening flesh, to pull himself to safety. But Cocci's excrement dissolves his barbed ends, and Vibrios cannot hook himself onto the flesh. "Save me. Save me!" cries Vibrios.

A voice like the whisper of hairs; Spirilla: "Do something, Cocci. You can't just leave him there to die."

"You bet I can," says Cocci, and he drags her kinky body into the oxygen-rich tunnel of an artery.

The crescent bacterioles stab Vibrios and wrench him from Cocci's waste puddle.

"Where are we going?" Spirilla asks.

"Shut up and reserve your strength. Go slurp some myoglobin from those muscle cells and store the oxygen. You might need it later for quick flesh oxidation. We'll be eating on the run. We're going on a long trip."

Her heat radiates in a red frizz halo, and he knows this means that she is angry. What did she call him before, a *browbeater?*

Cocci drains oxygen from hemoglobin, then rolls to the tunnel edge and waves his clan to follow. Vibrios' army surges, excretes waste, poisons hundreds of Cocci's children to death. But millions, perhaps billions, dive into the arterial tunnel, and together, they dodge murderous phagocytes and make their way to . . .

. . . to . . . "What is this?!" says Cocci.

"A womb," says Spirilla.

They're in the *womb* of a female fleshoid?

A sac of bloated blood drifts before him. Attached to the sac is a gnarled cord.

Spirilla says, "It's a child, Cocci. This fleshoid carries a child."

"Test for hormones."

She probes for estrogen, wiggles through the cord and disappears. She returns almost instantly. "Food ahead. Child almost ready to be born. I'd say a couple more months, at most."

A child . . . couple of months . . . more food . . .

But it only takes the Cocci clan a few *days* to dissolve one of these creatures. By the time the fleshoid child is ready to live, its mother will be dead.

From behind comes wailing and hooting. "Get them, get those Coccis!"

No time to think. Must act.

Cocci issues orders: "You, born from my left side, scatter and penetrate the smooth muscles of the artery. The rest of you: clot the blood."

The little bacterioles scatter. Millions surge into the muscles, millions scamper for the bones and return with calcium. Cocci stands alone at the arterial entrance to the womb.

Vibrios and his withered, round crescent ends appear around the bend of the bloody tunnel.

And now Cocci's bacterioles pump the muscles—blood in, blood out—and the muscles contract and punch the Vibrios invaders back, way back into the artery. The blood pressure rises and becomes fierce, pushing on Cocci's walls, collapsing him into a flattened circle, squeezing him until he nearly explodes.

Then the muscles relax. The vessel widens. The pressure drops. Cocci expands again into pure ball form.

His men roll forward and start stacking the platelets and calcium into clots. The Vibrios men jab and punch the clots, but as soon as they knock one down, Cocci's men rebuild it.

And the battle rages through the abdominal muscles and up to the diaphragm. Here, the air is warm. The Cocci bacterioles link flagella, maintain a stronghold against the Vibrios thugs, who lunge and stab, lunge and stab.

A heat wave hits, and Cocci's mind is fuzz and he drifts on a moist mat. The blood is rich and bloats him. He's a bulbous blood cocoon. Ooh, soon he will divide again. He's floating, floating . . . no care in the world . . .

. . . but then the muscles relax and the lungs compress, and a blast sweeps him toward the throat.

Vibrios is laughing. "Stupid Cocci, swept away by his own bloodthirsty lust."

No, he can't be exhaled. He must stay and fight Vibrios, take back what belongs to the Cocci clan.

The blood bulges from his right side. Such a pregnant swell. No control. And he splits, and the new bacteriole flies from his body and thwacks Vibrios right in his wimpy concave gut.

Cocci jumps from the moist mat. Together, he and his new bacteriole bounce on Vibrios, leaping higher and higher, crashing down harder and harder on the trampoline gut. Vibrios screams and flails. His body heaves and belches blood. And soon the great Vibrios is nothing more than fibrous mash.

This is one pool of blood that Cocci does not want to drink.

The crescents turn and flee, jab like polo sticks down veins.

Cocci's children dissolve Vibrios's remains. Vibrios's blood becomes theirs.

Cocci slumps by the muscle wall. Had Vibrios been a little faster, a little stronger, it might have been Cocci's blood floating in the vacuoles of the Vibrios boys. By dying, Vibrios has saved the Cocci clan.

A warm current caresses his flanks. He looks up.

It is Spirilla.

He must break the news gently. "You know about Vibrios?"

Spirilla droops. *She knows.*

"We've suffered great losses, Spirilla. We must divide. All of us."

"Never."

And the worst news . . . "We must move to the other fleshoid. *Now.*"

Here she springs to life. "Why? You just beat Vibrios. This fleshoid is *ours.* All the blood we want."

"Because, my dear, this fleshoid carries a child. If we suck the mother dry, the child dies. If we leave and let the mother live, the child will be born. We must preserve the fleshoid race. Otherwise, we'll starve."

"I can't leave the place where Vibrios died."

It takes a lot for him to admit it, but: "I'm no different from Vibrios," he says.

"But you *are,* Cocci. I, on the other hand, am more crescent than sphere. I may be spiral, but my parent cell was crescent. I was a mutation. That's why I rarely divide. That's why your wastes don't kill me."

"Then Vibrios was your brother? And oh, Polyp help me, you are *not* my firstborn?"

"When you have billions of children, Cocci, how can you remember your first?"

He feels himself tightening into an iron ball. "Why did you live with me rather than Vibrios?"

"I tried to bring peace, but you wouldn't have it."

Spirilla turns and slowly slinks down a vein, following the path taken by her brothers and sisters.

Oh Polyp, just the *sight* of her . . .

If only he were more like Vibrios.

# One Good Bite

## Christie Golden

im had just finished pouring coffee when she heard Jackie's tap on the door. Smiling, she set the pot down on the warmer and went to welcome her friend.

Jackie looked tired, and paler even than usual. The rings beneath her eyes stood out like badly smudged makeup. "Can't stay long," she apologized as Kim opened the door. "I'm dead on my feet."

"Later night than usual?" Kim stepped aside as Jackie entered. The women were of an age, in their late twenties, but there the similarities ended. Where Kim Wallace was blond, tanned, and carrying a few extra pounds, Jackie Severin was slim and fragile-looking. Her skin was so pale that the blue veins appeared perilously near the surface. Named for the late Jacqueline Kennedy Onassis, Jackie had that woman's uncanny loveliness. Kim was a working girl, a waitress whose shift began at four and ended at two at a local pancake place. Jackie, as far as Kim knew, had no job. Her nights were spent cruising local bars. And that was how the two unlikely friends had met—Kim was walking out the door of their rundown apartment building just as Jackie was coming in from a night on the town. Cautious hellos turned into friendly greetings, culminating in this strange custom of coffee at three in the morning every few days.

Jackie sank down wearily into Kim's sagging sofa and nodded, unbuttoning her coat and shrugging out of it. She reached gratefully for the steaming cup and sniffed the aroma. "Smells great," she said, scooping four teaspoons of sugar into the black liquid.

Kim winced, as she always did. "You don't like coffee, you like syrup. So, tell me about tonight's men."

Smiling wanly, Jackie did as she was told.

Jackie shut the door to her apartment and leaned on it, closing her eyes. The coffee had done nothing to assuage her

274

thirst, and had even exacerbated it. She was familiar with the effects the wrong liquid had on the Great Thirst, but it was the price she paid for being able to pass for normal. Now, her stomach roiling in protest, she stumbled to the bathroom, fell on her knees beside the porcelain god, and slipped a practiced finger into her throat. A precise, thin stream of liquid consisting of water, two Long Island iced teas, five Bud Drys, four glasses of Blue Nun, a Harvey Wallbanger, and three cups of sugar-saturated coffee squirted from her seven-hundred-year-old stomach and splashed into the water.

When she had voided her belly, she leaned against the coolness of the toilet. A trembling hand fumbled for the handle and flushed. Six days. Six days without a real drink. She'd tried a different bar each night, but what with the AIDS scare, one-night stands of any caliber worth having were harder and harder to come by. She longed for the good old days of war, where a camp follower had more men than she knew what to do with, or the high era of the courtesan, or even the late lamented '60s and '70s of this twentieth century, when love—and consequently blood—was free and readily available. Nowadays, she might as well be back on the damned Mayflower.

Her stomach rumbled, but her heart ached even more. "Damn it," she said to herself as she struggled into an upright position. She stared into the mirror, as usual seeing no reflection. Jackie was tired, so tired, of the whole stupid game. Her life—or undeath—consisted of stalking men, with the occasional woman thrown in for variety, seducing them and drinking from their throats. Sex was the bait, humans the unwitting prey. Sometimes Jackie enjoyed the prelude to feeding, but more often than not, after her stomach was full her heart felt empty.

She refused to make another like herself, desperate though she was for real companionship. And the other vampires she'd met during the last few hundred years had been real jerks. Jackie was discovering she didn't want sex any more. She wanted to make love, be in love, have someone to share the rest of eternity with. And that, she mused bitterly as she staggered to her pitch-black bedroom and fell into bed, was less likely than regaining her lost soul.

\* \* \*

That night, driving in her little Honda, Jackie passed through the seedier parts of town without pausing. Famished as she was, the one time she'd fed on a guy at a porno flick had left her with a dreadful taste in her mouth. She shuddered at the memory and continued on. Nothing appealed; she decided to avoid the city altogether and headed back into the suburbs. A new pub had opened around here, she recalled; some kind of microbrewery or something. That sounded good.

Jackie was astonished at the crowd. Evidently, the Hawk 'n Hare was *the* place to be. She could understand why. The place had a cozy air about it. There was even a fireplace, the mantle decorated with those little houses that were currently so popular. The chatter that met her ears was jovial, good-natured. Jackie ignored a quick pang of regret that she would never truly be a part of such a simple, happy crowd, and began to scan the group. Her eye fell on a large, good-looking fellow sitting next to the fire. His hair, a shade or two lighter than Jackie's deep ebony tresses, was cut short but stuck out wildly, despite its owner's unconscious attempts to smooth it down. He wore a blue pullover sweater and jeans. He seemed nice; more importantly, he seemed alone.

Jackie wandered through the crowd, making her approach seem less obvious. When she felt the man's speculative gaze, she pointed at the hearth beside him. "Taken?" she yelled over the noise.

His eyes widened in surprised pleasure, and he shook his head. She rewarded him with a radiant smile, fought her way to the brick hearth, and sank down beside him.

"Thanks."

"No problem."

"Starting to get cold." She shivered a little, edging closer to him.

"It does that in November." The tone in his voice made her glance up. His eyes, a clear, light hazel, were gently mocking her. She felt her face grow hot—something that hadn't happened to her in several years.

"Am I that obvious?"

He shrugged. "A little." But the smile was still genuinely friendly. "Can I get you something to drink?"

She glanced at the beer in his hand, a Coors Light. "I'll have what you're having. Thanks."

He flagged down a passing waitress. "Two Silver Bullets." He returned his attention to her. "The lady watches her figure, I see. It's certainly one worth watching."

An unexpected anger crept into her embarrassment. He was playing with her, just as she had planned on playing with him, and she didn't like having the tables turned. "Look, I'm just a little lonely tonight, okay? I'm sorry if I've insulted you with my attentions." She rose to leave. Part of her screamed, *you idiot! That's dinner you're saying goodbye to!*

"Hey—" His big hand, strong and covered with fine dark hair, closed on her thin arm. "I'm sorry. Let's start over." His hand opened. "I'm Tom O'Reilly. Pleased to meet you."

Slowly, Jackie took it in her frail, small one. The powerful fingers closed over hers very gently, and she felt a tremor of emotion she thought long dead. "I'm Jackie Severin. The pleasure's mine."

She put her hunger out of her mind for the next week, discovering a keen pleasure in Tom's company that she had forgotten she could know. And when at last, inevitably, she finally went to bed with him, they made love in his king-size bed with the window letting in the illumination of a gorgeous, nearly full moon. Running through the fabric of Jackie's intense physical pleasure was a sweet thread of deep caring. *Am I falling for him?* the vampire wondered as she moaned softly beneath his knowing touch.

His passion was brutal, almost bestial, and her own lust rose to meet his. At the moment of Tom's climax, overcome by the hot smell of his inflamed blood, Jackie's fangs emerged and she buried them in his throat. She heard him gasp, but she was at the mercy of her bloodlust now, utterly unable to stop. Jackie gulped at the crimson liquid that flooded her throat, shuddering in her own release of pleasure. It was only when she was thoroughly sated that she realized Tom was still conscious.

Such a thing was unheard of, no, impossible. No mortal could lose that much blood and not pass out! She shoved him off of her, trying to scramble out from beneath him with a burst of panic, and felt his hands clamp down on hers with a strength that was more than equal to hers.

The moonlight shone full upon his face. Only . . . it wasn't Tom's face anymore. His nose and mouth had lengthened into a muzzle, and he smiled, showing a jaw crammed with large, sharp teeth. His eyes, though still human, were large and lambent. Thick hair sprouted all over his body, writhing and twisted as it covered him with a thick, furry, silvery pelt. The hands that gripped her arms so tightly began to grow claws.

"One good bite deserves another," growled the werewolf. But the expected agony didn't come. Tom pulled her to his fur-covered chest and nipped at her. The inch-long teeth barely scratched her skin, merely adding an exciting sliver of pain to their erotic romp. As they began to make love again, Jackie suddenly started laughing.

She was thinking of Tom's favorite beer.

Much later, cuddling with the wolfman beneath the waxing moon and stroking his fur, Jackie learned a lot about werewolves. Far from being ravening monsters at the mercy of their "curse," they could control their changes to a certain extent, Tom told her in a husky, growling voice; but on the full moon proper they were completely wolf. Like her, though he was more than able to kill a human swiftly and efficiently, Tom had never done so. Werewolves were immune to everything but silver, and that included the ravages of age. Tom was just a cub as his people reckoned time, a mere babe of two hundred and four. When, filled with a sudden sense of hope, Jackie whispered her fearful, tremulous desire into his pointed ear, he whimpered an affirmative. She held him close and wept with pure joy.

The clanging, thumping, and barking outside in the hall caused Kim to peer out curiously around 2:30 that morning. She was surprised to see a breathless, beaming Jackie laden with boxes. A large husky pranced about her feet.

"Well, well!" Kim exclaimed. "I haven't seen you for weeks. What's going on?"

Hi, Kim!" Jackie said brightly. "Sorry I've been so out of touch. I've been—" and the dark-haired woman actually *giggled* "—very busy! I'm moving out tonight. Kind of sudden. No more morning coffee, I'm afraid."

The happiness on her face made Kim ask tentatively, "Moving out, clearly . . . what about moving in?"

Jackie nodded. "That's why you haven't seen me. I've met a wonderful guy. His name's Tom. I'll bring him by sometime."

"Oh, Jackie, I'm so glad for you! Here, let me give you a hand with that." She smiled at the dog. "Good puppy. What a good doggie!"

Jackie smiled. "Tom . . . gave him to me."

Outside in the predawn darkness, the two women finished loading Jackie's Honda. The husky, or malamute, whatever it was, jumped into the passenger seat and panted happily. Kim hugged her friend, exacted a promise for a visit, and watched her drive off.

Kim's eyes fell on the bumper sticker on the retreating car, and she smiled a little. The sticker proclaimed: THE MORE I KNOW ABOUT MEN, THE MORE I LOVE MY DOG.

# Miss Vampire New Mexico Meets Her Dream Date

JOHN GREGORY BETANCOURT

*A Gala of Ghouls* was the TV show's name. I watched it from my old rocker, a bottle of Coke in one hand. I sucked avidly and finally got the cap. It tasted like aluminum, but I managed to choke it down.

The contestants of the Miss Vampire U.S.A. Pageant paraded across my TV screen—and there I saw her: Miss Vampire New Mexico, the most beautiful of the beautiful, the goddess of my darkest dreams, the girl I knew I had to have. Something in her striking face drew my eyes like a magnet. I thought at first it might be her delicately pointed ears, but no, I was wrong. It was those fangs, all sharp and white as she showed them off to the audience. They glistened with what could only have been poison from their hollow interiors.

I had to see her. I had to have her for my own. I vowed to meet her before the program was over.

I knew just where to go, too. The preview article in *TV Guide* had said the show would be broadcast live from New York's Studio Four. That was only a few blocks away.

Crushing my Coke bottle to a glassy pulp, I lumbered over to the window, climbed out, and dropped six stories to the ground with ease. It was nearly midnight, so all the weirdos were out. I saw one ghastly-looking fellow—tan face, short coiffed hair, whistling menacingly as he strolled along with his hands in his pockets—but I carefully avoided him. I didn't want to get mugged on the way to see the vampire I loved.

When I arrived, *A Gala of Ghouls* had just ended. The backstage doors stood open to catch the evening breeze, so I strolled on in, listening expectantly to the babble of voices around me. Could it be true? Miss Vampire New Mexico had *lost?* And to California, at that! Talk about unfair . . .

I found my true love's dressing room and knocked softly, eager to console her with promises of eternal devotion. A loud voice bade me enter, so I did.

"Hi!" she said in a nasal Bronx accent. She was turned so she couldn't see me, looking at herself in a tall narrow mirror. Not that she could have seen me in one: I averted my eyes from it. "Are you the Club photographer? If so, I'll be ready for you in a second."

I grunted noncommittally, which she seemed to take to mean yes.

"Just let me get these *stupid* fangs off, and this *awful* makeup, and this *frightful* wig."

I gasped in shock.

"You don't really think I look like a monster, do you? Or did you want a picture of me in drag? Well, it's too late now—off with the old face, on with the new!"

I had a terrible feeling inside, like I was caught up in *Leave It to Beaver* or something. I switched on the twin spotlights by the door and faced them toward her. I wanted a really *good* look at her face, all of a sudden.

"Done!" she announced, standing. When she turned and struck a pose for me, I nearly had a heart attack.

Her face had become a hideous, unnatural peach color, and her fangs—those beautiful sexy fangs—had been replaced by gruesomely flat teeth. Clearly this *monster* was not the girl I'd fallen in love with on TV.

"Are you going to take those pictures or not?" she asked.

I clicked to myself, close to tears.

"Say," she said brightly, "You sound kind of cute. Want to grab a bite when you're done? Just let me find my glasses. I can't see a thing since I took out my contacts—"

I gurgled and the strangest expression crossed her face. She took a step back uncertainly. Moving closer, I reached out and touched her arm, tracing a vein with my index finger's long, sharp nail, hoping beyond all hope she'd only put makeup on to hide her true vampire self. She'd been so beautiful.

She gasped, awed I supposed by my striking silhouette against the spotlights. Then she smiled. It was hideous.

"Kind of kinky, huh?" she said, trying to snuggle close. "I can dig costumes."

A horror built up inside me as her warm, warm flesh burned against mine. Where was that chill, undead skin I had so longed to caress? Where were her green-glowing eyes and soft, cold, bloodless lips?

*It's all the fault of TV*, I realized. It had to be some terrible joke. I'd smash that television set when I got home, then find the door-to-door salesman who had sold it to me.

I pushed the woman away, shuddering.

"Hey," she demanded, hands on her hips. "What about my pictures? *Hey!*"

I almost ran. But then I realized reality was only what you made it. She'd been so beautiful . . . and she could be again.

I cackled happily, a mad, wonderful, impetuous plan forming in the back of my mind. She might have lost the contest this year, but the judges must have realized her seeming beauty was only skin deep. Next year . . . next year I would be her coach, her manager, her lover.

It could work. It *would* work.

She only screamed once when I killed her.

But then, later that night, when she opened her eyes and gazed up into mine—her lips so pale, her skin so cool—I knew I still loved her, and we would never be lonely again.

# Angels, Strange Angels

## Peter M. Spizzirri

**B**rigette is one of those French names that men can never pronounce. They are forever mixing their I's and E's around my TT's. And yet, it is my name. Do not be fooled by my frilly name. There is nothing left of the silly fourteenth-century French peasant girl about me and so it will have to do. Somehow, the nickname Mimi has followed me about since childhood—I suppose it is because I always yelled "Me . . . me . . ." whenever there was food or drink or other available.

I live in a city of hunters and prey called Chicago. Since my early years in Europe, I have always preferred cities with just enough sophistication. Chicago's very blue-collar beginnings guarantee a limit to its social heights. And so there are always enough fools to fawn over me. Fools always provide ideal alibis.

The Red Line is a fine, quiet lounge. Discretion on Devon Avenue is hard to find, but the Line manages it. And after all, discretion is the better part of allure!

Friday nights don't really start to happen until 9 P.M. or so. If you hit the bars too early, like around seven, you're too sloshed to last into the heat of the night.

I have always preferred to be a bit late. I like to see how a night has begun before I step into the dance. And tonight I was hunting.

Robert Fallon and his come hither eyes drew more men and women than my trapping pheromones. Straight, bi . . . sex until you die—he didn't care. And he knew I was a vampire. He was one of the few humans who knew and didn't fear. I had lured him with my trapping scent, and he had lured me with his easy smile and smooth come-on lines.

His laugh, his sweat, his sex, and his blood were all sweet. He had taken all that I could give him except death and smiled. He was truly a rare one. And he was AIDS-free. Robert was as uniquely gifted with natural fragrance. He never had body odor.

At his very worst, he was virtually neutral . . . and still there lingered a touch of the sweet natural character that marked him.

As I entered the Red Line, I knew that he was there. Mixed in with the taints of a hundred mingled blood scents, there was a trace of Robert. I had long ago grown used to the sad blood tales that humans radiate. Cancers were unmistakeable and more numerous than ever—so much so that I now say that life causes cancer . . . and I'm right. All illnesses affect the blood scent and all effect me. AIDS is the worst. Perhaps it is the instinctual reaction driven from my own immune system, but I can detect a person with full-blown AIDS (with a white blood cell count of say, eighteen) a block away. And all they wanted was love.

As I walked through the throng, I extended the range of my pheromones to my aggressive end. The reaction within a few feet is always the same in humans. Their "fear"omone response kicks in and they part before me instinctually and wisely. I love the look that the men and women give me as I lick my lips tasting the air for the few truly healthy bodies in the bar. So many of their eyes linger on my mouth and my so-red lips. It always makes me hot, and it always makes me smile. And my smile draws more eyes. It is a wonderful little cycle of stimulation and tease.

The straight men and women are easy, the bisexual masses everywhere, the true gay men quite evident, and the true lesbians luscious gems. I became distracted. There were more lesbians in the bar tonight than ever before, and a hunger developed that I hadn't had at the door.

"You're making a spectacle of yourself," a voice chimed.

"Bless you to the Maker, Robert. . . ." I turned slowly to face him, though I was startled to my toes. "You are the only human who has ever been able to step into my cirle without my awareness."

"Oh don't give me that 'I'm in control' bitch look of yours." Robert smiled, undaunted. "And besides, you'll want to take me home tonight and offer me a love feast."

"You and who else?" I taunted.

Moving his lips to my ear, "Ooooohh, menàge-a-vamp . . ." He tossed off his reply with a tickling hush of breath.

Robert stepped back with an unnatural quickness that caught me by surprise. There was a strange, awed something in his voice as he said, "You owe me . . . I found her. And she's here."

In all the years I had sought her, my expectations had always been on the rise—and now they were met. My fantasy and reality merged in a blazing second of recognition and I was mesmerized. She sat alone, undisturbed by the flow of the crowd. The myriad voices, crowding bodies, and even the simple airy swirls of smoke roiled about her. She somehow had created and enjoyed an island of quiet peace. Sweet golden hair flowed over her shoulders and well down her back. Her simple white shelled blouse seemed to have a clean full-moon glow. She wore no makeup of any type, no lipstick, no eye shadow, no rouge. Her fingernails were unpainted, she wore no jewelry and she was the most exquisitely beautiful woman I had ever beheld. No, she was beauty incarnate . . . simply . . . period.

Once I saw her and drank in her existence, I was drawn to the pure flame of her presence. My senses had automatically flared out and enwrapped her. My senses danced back an exquisite tease of a thrumming, burning, nerve-tingling, near-orgasmic shock. I quivered in an endless stream of electriclike pulses. Nothing in all my centuries had ever given me the sense feedback of this . . . woman. I went to her.

I stood before her shed of all my pretensions, haughtiness, and control; clothed, yet so vulnerable that I had never been more naked.

"Brigette . . ." I announced myself to some unspoken question. My voice was again that of a fourteenth-century child.

She smiled up at me. Her eyes met mine. My eyes teared as I welled with a score of unbidden emotions. Her smile grew.

"Sit." Her so-rich, gentle, sweet dream of a voice melted my knees. I had no choice but to sit . . . a chair, the floor, it didn't matter. I had always been a power to be reckoned with or at the very least feared. I have always walked this planet like a child of the lesser gods. No longer.

"Angel." She said. Her lush voice brought another tear, more electric-like quiverings, and a racing my heart had never known.

"Is that your name . . ." I stammered, "or who or what you are?" My voice hushed to a bare whiper as I trembled out my question.

"Yes." She answered in that voice.

Silence filled our space as I sat stunned. "You're an angel?" I finally asked.

"Aren't we all?" She replied . . . in that voice.

"I'm no angel. . . ." But there was heretofore unknown doubt in my words.

"Do you kill?" She questioned, her eyes penetrating my all as her words and voice rendered me so completely vulnerable.

It's funny, but I never had killed. It's also funny that every vampire that I had ever known or knew of that did kill was dead.

"No, I learned young to leave life, as I took what I needed to live." Her smile, impossibly, broadened as I spoke.

"Not all angels are pure, eh." A lilt, a so-subtle, gentle laugh of sorts colored her words. "And some are less pure than others." Her eyes shifted for a second.

Robert was somehow standing next to me.

Angel smiled at my surprise and she easily knew my discomfort.

"Fallon didn't tell you he's an angel, eh?" Her smile continued. "He, too, is a fallen angel. Fallen . . . Fallon, he seems not to let it go.

"Why did you think—or *did* you think—he could walk through your senses and defenses like you were asleep at his whim?" Her aura slowly edged its aspect into a glimmering robe of light as she spoke.

Her eyes, the voice, the questions, and Fallon, "I never . . ." Dumbfounded, I couldn't continue.

"Take him home with you tonight. Use him for your pleasure as you always have. Feed from him—take all you can and more. Try to kill him. Try to take all of his life essence." She laughed a true laugh.

Angel held her right hand up to me. "Come and see me again when you recover." she said, dismissing me.

Oh, so slowly, so tentatively, I reached for her hand with both of my hands. The light of a thousand reflecting diamonds seemed to surround her hand.

As I took her hand in my hands, my vision of her glow spread like a flash and she became a being of brilliance.

"You are but an angel of need and passion. We are all angels . . . angels, strange angels." Her voice flitted softly away.

And then she was gone.

My fragility broke, but I had no balanced sense of self. Robert helped me to my feet and led me off. I was shaking my head and muttering, "Angels . . ." over and over.

As Robert led me through unseen streets to my home, the usually so visible and living night seemed opaque. All of my senses were still numbed.

The silence of the night was all. Robert held my hand as we walked together, angels of the silent night.

# Another Saturday Night

### David Niall Wilson

In Crete the sun sets so swiftly that if you take your eyes off of it for a second, long enough to get a gulp of your beer, or to watch the waitress walk by, you'll miss it. There is a saying there that, if you watch until the sun has disappeared completely, you can make a wish, and that wish will come true. That is what they say.

Caroline had just finished washing the last of the glasses from the day's slower crowd, stragglers from the beach, lazy tourists taking a quick break from the sun to enjoy a coffee frappe, or a cool beer. Charlene, the other night bartender, had just popped in with her two roommates, Gillian and Nikki, and the three were at the corner table, giggling as Gillian scribbled something in their diary.

The three of them were Australian, having left homes and boyfriends behind for the chance at adventure, and they kept all their exploits carefully documented in a communal diary. There was another volume before the present one—Caroline could only imagine what might be between the covers.

She had come to the Beau Mec from Ireland, via a waitressing job in New York. Another girl had come from Britain, and a third from Georgia in the now disestablished USSR. Sifi, the owner of the bar, kept a mixed crew at all times, catering to the languages and tastes of the tourist trade. Conversation and good times were the real products they sold; beer could be had almost anywhere else, and cheaper.

She knew it wouldn't be long until the night's parade of drunks, dreamers, and locals would begin to trickle in and out—always different, always the same. It was Saturday night, but it didn't matter—not really. In Crete, during the summer months, every night was Saturday night, and even Saturday nights could become boring.

The sun was just dipping toward the skyline, and at that particular moment Caroline found herself with a free moment—a rare thing behind the bar. She watched the huge, red-gold orb pass behind the mountains, and she remembered for once not to look away. She knew it was silly, but she watched, and she waited, and at just the moment the sun disappeared, she made her wish.

"Something different," she whispered. "Just for once, something different would be nice."

Then the sun and the moment were gone, and the night's business began in earnest. There was a ship in down in Souda Bay, United States Navy, and the Beau Mec had its own small entourage of sailors. They all had the same questions, "How did you end up here, all the way from Ireland? You're not married? How could a beautiful girl like you not be married? You're what, about twenty?"

She'd answered those same questions over and over since her first day on the job. The answers were almost like a recording, playing out from her brain across her lips. They were good men, some more interesting than others, but they were all leaving. No matter how much she might like them, they were only going to be around for a few days, and more would take their place. It was amazing how lonely it could get in a crowded bar.

By the time the stranger wandered in, she'd forgotten all about her wish and the setting sun. She'd already had two shots of Jameson's Irish Whiskey and a couple of "brains," a sweet concoction of Peach Schnapps, Irish Creme, and Grenadine, and she was settling into a comfortable, if not remarkable, buzz.

The man was dark, but for some reason she was certain he was not local—probably not even Greek. His black hair was swept back over his ears and long in back, way out of style, and his deep, shadowy eyes had an odd glitter in their depths. When he caught her staring, the energy that flashed between them almost made her jump.

His clothes were probably the oddest thing about him. He wore a lightweight suit, dark in color, with a long-sleeved white linen shirt beneath. It was a summer suit, but even that was out of character for a day as hot as this one had been, and the man was not sweating. Not at all.

She slid along the bar to where he had taken a seat, trying not to stare, but curious, just the same.

"What can I get you?" she asked him, giving him her cheeriest smile and placing both hands on the bar in front of him. "Beer? Frappe?"

"No . . . wine. If you have it, a glass of red wine would be perfect. Nothing too new, though . . . I have a preference for older things."

His own smile seemed to snatch at her heart, and she caught herself staring again. "Wine?" she asked, knowing it sounded silly, but unable to regain her bearings quickly enough to say anything further.

Without waiting for his answer, she turned and headed inside the club. There was a second, larger bar inside, and it was stocked with all of the bottles that were not called for on a regular basis. Red wine was certainly not the most common request at the Beau Mec. She grabbed the oldest, most expensive vintage available, hoping it would serve, and returned with it to the bar.

He was watching her. As she glided behind the bar, searching for and finding the corkscrew, his eyes followed her every movement and a thin smile played across his lips. Normally it was flattering to be watched, to know she'd dressed attractively, but with this man it was somehow unnerving. His eyes were so —intense.

Pouring the wine as quickly as she could with her hands shaking, she returned to where he sat and placed the glass in front of him. He smiled in return and handed her his money, but he did not speak again—not just then. She found that, although a moment before she'd been wishing he wouldn't stare at her, now she wanted to hear his voice again—to know what he was thinking.

She moved on along the bar, pouring beer, making screwdrivers and Irish coffees, the normal routine. Somehow it was different. Somehow the fact that he was there, and that he was still watching her, made all the difference. She turned to meet his eyes several times over the course of the evening, and each time she did, he was watching her in return, smiling and sipping his wine.

When the evening was gone and the night beginning to follow in its path, she found that he was the only customer left in the bar, and it was enough of an excuse to intrude. She finished washing the glasses, said goodnight to Charlene, who took off with her friend Gillian and a couple of well-dressed young men in a red Porsche, and turned to meet his eyes.

He was watching her, still, and she found that she was getting used to the feel of those eyes—less self-conscious.

"It's getting late," she said softly. "Can I get you more wine?"

"No, not tonight," he smiled back at her. "I was actually thinking about taking a walk on the beach. Did I hear one of those young men call you Caroline?"

"Yes," she answered. "and you would be?"

"Stavros," he said, and though his pronunciation was odd, she saw that he was, indeed, Greek. "I was born here, but I have been away for a very long time. It is good to be back on Crete, better with such attractive company."

She blushed. He was very attractive—but there was more, something that tugged at her mind, something almost magnetic that drew her to him.

"Caroline is an ancient name," he continued, pausing to drain the last of the wine in from his glass, "ancient and beautiful. I once knew a queen by that name—do you believe that?"

"I don't know," she answered. "I have never heard of a queen named Caroline."

"She was very beautiful," he said. "Her hair was long, like yours, but red as the sunrise. I have not thought of her in years." He hesitated for a moment, then leaned forward to trap her hand under his own.

"Would you walk with me, Caroline? I know it is very forward of me, but it is a beautiful night, and I hear the waves calling to me—I would be honored."

"I . . ." she nearly said no. The bar wasn't officially closed yet, but that didn't really matter. There was nobody inside, and the beach was deserted. She knew she should just go home. He was attractive, true, but she didn't know him, and it was getting very late.

"Maybe for just a bit," she said at last. "I have to close up first, will you wait?"

"I will meet you down by those rocks," he said, his hand still holding hers. He lifted her fingers to his lips softly, staring directly into her eyes, and brushed them with a soft kiss, then turned toward the beach. As she watched him walking away, she felt the tug on her mind growing stronger, more intense. She hurried about, calling for Sifi to help her with the awning. All at once a walk on the beach after midnight was something she wanted very much.

She found him standing right where he'd pointed, a dark silhouette against the moonlit luminescence of the waves. His jacket was loose, and his dark hair blew about his head like a scarf, dancing in the grip of the breeze. Though she moved as quietly as she could, he turned and watched her as if he'd known she was there all along. He was still smiling, but somehow it was a wilder expression—less civilized and tame.

"You are even more lovely by moonlight," he told her, taking her hand in his once more without hesitation and turning back to the ocean. She followed his eyes over the expanse of choppy waves.

"Do you know the story of those islands?" he asked, pointing across the water.

When she shook her head, too nervous to speak, he continued. "They say that the muses and the sirens had a musical contest, back when the gods were the gods, and not just bedtime stories for children. It was held on a mountain just outside Hania. All the gods of Olympus stood in judgment over this duel, and in the end, the sirens were vanquished.

"Instead of taking their loss gracefully, they flung themselves like meteors from the cliffs, crashing to their deaths in the waters below and forming the islands that ring Crete. One of the larger of these islands is said to be the very one upon which

Ulysses himself was nearly drawn to his death. If you listen very carefully, sometimes you can almost hear the music on the evening breeze."

Caroline caught herself listening, straining to hear the mythical sounds, and she laughed. Spinning to face her, he joined in her mirth.

"That is a wonderful story," she said. "Tell me more."

"I could tell you a thousand," he said, turning back to the water, this time with one arm around her shoulder, "but I would rather show you. Come with me to that island, Caroline—tonight."

She pulled away in shock. "How would we do that now?" she asked. "Sifi will never let me take out one of the boats at night."

"I have no need of boats," he said, catching her eyes with his own and holding them, "nor will you, after tonight."

He was moving closer, and though she wanted to run more than anything she'd ever wished in her entire life, she stood very still, even leaning forward a bit as he approached.

"I have been lonely for too long, Caroline," he said, wrapping his arms around her as she trembled, "far too long. I felt you calling to me as I passed earlier, felt the tug of your wish on my soul. I did not come to the Beau Mec by accident—you called me there."

She tried to shake her head no, but he stopped her with a glance, pulling her even closer. Before she knew what was happening, he had bent and placed his lips softly to the flesh of her throat. There was a sharp pinprick of pain, and she almost cried out, but then it was gone, and she felt the world reeling beneath her.

Images swam before her eyes, some from her own past—from her dreams—others from places she had never known, thoughts that had never been her own. The beach was forgotten. The waves that crashed only short yards from where they stood became a pulsing, rhythmic backdrop to the visions.

Some were stranger than others. There were figures moving through her mind's eye, half-remembered names and faces that called out to her, but that she had never known—never seen. She felt as if she were floating, drifting on waves of pain and pleasure, memory and vision.

Dimly she remembered the man who held her . . . the stranger who had wandered in and swept her out of the comfortable walls of the Beau Mec and into a darkness filled with dreams and magic, a magic of which she was only a spectator, swept along by the intensity and emotion of the moment. The visions were powerful, overwhelming, majestic. It was a gigantic video screen—an epic drama where she'd been cast in the lead.

At some point, physical sensation returned to her, and she realized that his hands were moving across her back, that his lips had left her throat and moved to cover her own. She pressed against him, feeling him solid and real, drawing herself free from the dream world and back to the beach, to his eyes.

Lifting her easily, he laid her back onto the sand, sliding her clothing from her quickly and pressing his cool hands to her skin. She wanted to protest, to tell him to go slowly, but his lips were against her throat again, again the pinprick of pain, and the visions were sweeping her away again.

This time there were no shared memories. This time the only faces that blended with the man who held her were those of men Caroline had known, lovers she'd had and left, or lost. There were women as well, dark women, light women, and endless progression of faces and names. As she took them all in, as they blended and reformed and became as one, she felt him sliding over her skin, felt him taking her, even as he drained the life from her veins, even as the warmth of her blood flowed out of her and into him—as the world grew colder.

Just as he pulled back the second time, a final image implanted itself in her mind, a final face—serene and lovely, long red-gold hair falling over slim shoulders—Caroline—the queen.

She was frightened, but it was thrilling. Somehow, it seemed that it was all right, that it would be grand—unending—perfect.

He rose, drawing her up beside him, and she stood, looking up into his eyes. The moonlight washed over them both, and she noticed his skin for the first time, noticed how smooth it was, how pale—like ivory, or porcelain. She glanced down at her arm, which circled his back, and she almost cried out.

Her own skin was pale now, luminescent and almost glowing as the moon's rays played over it. She held up her hand, turning to him in wonder, and in fear, and he smiled down at

her, taking both of her hands in his own and drawing her closer
—so close that their bodies brushed.

"Come with me now, Caroline. We will go to the ruins of
the palace of Minos at Knossos and chase the Minotaur together.
We will track the elusive sirens through their island lairs and
show them real beauty. We will see things you have only
dreamed of. I will show you what and where I have lived, you
will show me life and *this* world. I have been away too long,
sleeping. Your wish woke me, and this is my gift in return."

"But . . ." she didn't know what to answer, and in seconds, it didn't matter. He swept his arm out and up, circling
them both and calling out some words in a language that she did
not know, a language that tickled at the hairs on her neck and
called to her soul, and they were simply not there. A mist hung
low on the beach, and the waves washed closer and closer to her
clothing, left behind on the sand.

In Crete, if you make a wish on the setting sun, watching
patiently until it has disappeared completely and not turning
your mind, or your heart, from your dreams, they say that wish
will come true. That is what they say. . . .

# Icing Up

### Benjamin Adams

Here, a thousand thousand tiny coals of life, warmly huddled away from the deep freeze outside. Here, the city;
cold as hell.

And getting colder.

A thin layer of rime forms on the inside of the living room
window, catching Susan Blaylock's eye. She idly scratches at it,
leaving her initials etched in the frost: s.b. Her true initials, from
her maiden name.

s.b., there on the icy glaze.

She relishes the way the letters look, stark in their alone-
ness; the emotional opposite of the engraved champagne glasses
she and Tony had received for their wedding.

(The fragments of those glasses now lay shattered in the barren decorative fireplace of this new apartment, where she threw them as celebration upon moving in.)

From her second-floor vantage she peers out on a dead world, locked in the Arctic grip of the coldest weather Chicago has known in ten years. Nothing moves in the street; the paralyzed husks of cars hulk under a white carpet of snow, still where their frustrated owners had quit trying to start them that morning. She wonders if Tony has been able to start his Trans-Am. And then she thinks: *Why the hell do I care whether or not his goddamn car starts? I have better things about which to worry tonight.* She prides herself on this tough-minded new attitude.

A chill falls on her. A draft from the wall-mounted air-conditioning unit directly beneath the window. The building super, Mr. Santos, supplied her with a metal cover when she'd moved in last week, but against this weather it fights a losing battle. She's wrapped a towel around the inside of the cover, making it fit more snugly against the air conditioner frame, but still the cold air forces its way inside.

It reminded her of a running argument with Tony. He said that the cold air wasn't really entering, but that the warm air was escaping. She would shake her head and say that didn't make any sense, because she could feel the cold air pushing in against her skin. And then Tony started in on his macho trip, proving himself right even though she knew he was wrong, there was something she could almost quite remember from her high school physics class. That was the important thing; she could have won the arguments if she'd really tried. But because she couldn't remember she would let him win the argument.

Tony always won. Before they were married, she'd been attracted to that in him; now it was the single factor that had contributed more than any other to their divorce. Even more than his cheating on her. At least she liked to believe that. It didn't hurt her pride nearly as much.

She wanders to the refrigerator and after a moment's pondering pulls out a couple of Schneider mozzarella cheese sticks, then returns to the living room and cuddles up under some blankets on the huge Papa-San chair. The Channel 5 News at 10:00 is on in a minute and she wants to hear how the weather has affected the city.

It's worse than Susan imagined. She's had trouble comprehending how frigid it is outside, but the facts and figures rattling by on the TV screen are stark and brutal. The temperature has bottomed out at twenty-one degrees below zero—one degree colder than the low recorded in Antarctica this same day. The homeless and elderly are dying in record numbers, equally ill equipped for dealing with the cold.

Tears form in Susan's eyes. *All this pain and misery, just because of the weather! It isn't fair.* She has trouble dealing with the apparent injustice of a squirrel run over by a car in the street, let alone this. Her index finger hovers over the "off" button on the remote—but pauses, as an impossibly familiar scene is presented. The tinny voice of news anchor Ron Majers drones on about another tragic cold-related death.

Susan watches, aghast; unconsciously she draws the blankets closer to her body.

An old woman died alone in her apartment, kneeling; her bare knees frozen in a thin layer of ice to the hardwood floor, her hands raised and clasped as if in prayer.

Of course the cameras don't show that. Instead they linger on the yellowed black-and-white photographs on the wall speaking of a life long past; Poland before the Nazi occupation. Susan knows these photographs. On a board laid over the inoperative radiator, a row of handmade dolls with painted, eerily smiling faces perch in a silent row on a doily. Susan knows these dolls. Small pieces of wood lay scattered nearby on the floor, embedded in the thin coating of ice around an ancient freestanding stove. These are all things Susan has seen a million times before.

And Susan knows the smells in that place, can smell them now: yeast and fresh-baked bread, baby powder and hand lotion, the sweat and rot of old age. She knows the smells and the sights by heart, because this is Tony's mother Martha who has died.

*This is a terrible thing,* she thinks. *This is the sort of thing that happens to other people, not someone you know.*

She loved the old woman. Anything good and gentle in Tony came from Martha, who had confided to Susan that she'd had terrible problems raising the boy, just terrible. *Taking, al-*

*ways taking without asking. And yet look what a fine young man he grew to be.* Susan would just nod, smiling; one of Martha's withered paws, caked with dust and dough, resting in her own hand. Martha's pulse still beating, a thin and dry tattoo against her skin.

A knock at the door, and Susan's heart flutters, a tiny bird trapped inside her ribcage. Is it Tony, come to tell her about Martha? Let him seek comfort elsewhere, in another's arms. She still, even under these circumstances, cannot bear the thought of seeing him. For the last week, she has half-expected Tony to come after her here, wanting her back; by force if necessary. Regardless of what Martha believed. Tony still takes what he wants. Sinking down in the Papa-San chair, seeking invisibility, she waits for another knock.

Which comes, followed quickly by "Miss Blaylock? Hello, are you there?" The gruff, fatherly voice belongs to Mr. Santos, and at last she relaxes and moves to the front door.

"I am not disturbing you, I hope?" asks Mr. Santos. Under his arm is a roll of yellow insulating material. "Some of the other tenants, they have complained of drafts. It is so cold." He holds the roll of insulation out to her. "So I am checking, you know? Checking and fixing."

Susan smiles and asks him inside. It is a welcome distraction.

Watching him wrap insulation inside the air conditioner frame with his aged but nimble fingers, she marvels at having such a dedicated super. Everywhere else she's lived, she's gotten the impression that the building superintendants would just as soon see all the tenants die than make repairs. Mr. Santos is a gem, a miracle. He smells of Old Spice and older grease. She wonders again, as she did when first meeting him, if he is Mexican or Spanish. The distinction is important. She thinks he is Spanish.

The job is done. He finishes tapping the cover back into place and holds his hands near where the cover meets the wall. A broad smile crosses his weathered face. "There. Now you are not so cold, hmm?"

He's so kind, she thinks. There must be something she can do for him, some way of showing her appreciation. And then she knows. Of course.

Susan says, "Please, wait here, Mr. Santos. I'll be right back." She runs to the bedroom and fetches her purse.

Mr. Santos' face clouds over when she offers him the ten-dollar bill. "No—this is my job. I cannot accept this money."

"Please," she says again. "It means so much to me that you've done this. Take the money."

He waves it away, walking to the door, the roll of insulation once again under his arm. "Thank you, Miss Blaylock, but it is not necessary. Good evening, eh?"

And he quickly bows his head to her and leaves.

Susan feels tears forming in her eyes. What has she done to offend Mr. Santos? Thanking him is all she wants; offering him a token of gratitude the best way she knows. She brings her hands up to her face to contain the sobs breaking through and sinks down to the hardwood floor of the entry hallway, spiraling down a pathway of self-incrimination into misery.

It's all gone wrong. Her entire life is a shambles. All it takes is Mr. Santos turning down a simple little tip to bring her to this state. Who's fooled by her leaving Tony? Herself. She doesn't really have that strength of character. She's been miserable since leaving him. She's nothing but a fraud. She wants to run down the street in the freezing cold outside, barefoot, screaming it: *I'm a fraud. A sad, lonely fraud.* Screaming it until her lungs bleed, scrubbed raw by the harsh, bitter air.

Martha, dead. Mr. Santos, offended. Tony, gone from her life. She can't do anything right. She is unable to hold on to anyone or anything she cares about. Maybe—if she'd tried harder —things would have worked better with Tony. Maybe he wouldn't have slept around if she'd only known more ways of pleasing him. Maybe if she hadn't been so stupid they could have talked without every conversation turning into an argument. *Stupid, stupid, stupid,* she cries softly to herself, wetness flowing down over her cheeks and through her fingers. Salty, the tears touch her mouth as she breaths in ragged gasps.

"Susie, Susie," a voice says softly. "Don't you cry. Why are you crying?"

She raises her head, her vision blurry, up from a pair of snow-covered boots, up thin, strong legs clad in Levi's, up the blue woolen winter coat she'd helped him pick out at Sears, to Tony's face, his dark brown hair and eyebrows covered with frost. Behind him the door stands open; she did not lock it after Mr. Santos left.

Susan is so glad to see him now, it doesn't seem odd that he is here. *His Trans-Am must have started after all,* she thinks. Maybe he can make everything all right again. Maybe this is a sign that they are meant to try again.

"Oh, God, Tony, I heard about your mother," she gasps to him. "I'm so sorry, I'm so sorry!" Her throat is constricted and the words squeeze out one at a time. She feels like her chest is caving in, it hurts so bad. Reaching out a hand to him, to her dull surprise he places one of his mother's dolls in it, the deranged folk-art face grinning wildly at her. The doll is cold to the touch, but that's not surprising. He's been outside.

"I was with her," he says simply. "At the end."

He bends down and helps Susie gain her feet, lifting her by her elbows. She collapses against his chest, feeling his arms around her back, holding her tightly. He's so cold, she thinks. He feels so cold. She trembles. "But how? Your mother—"

"Ah, Susie," he whispers. "Don't you worry, don't you cry."

And her entire body is shivering now, the cold spreading through her from where his body touches hers. She brings her arms up, trying to push him away, but he holds her so very tightly. The ice is dripping, melting down his face. "Tony," she says, "Tony. Please—let go—"

"I'm never letting you go again," he says, and brings his face near hers. His cold, cold lips meet hers gently, insistently. Her face grows numb, the chill settling in through her bones now. He feels warm against her cooling skin; so warm and vital and full of life.

Ice begins to form on her skin, she can feel it spreading inch by inch. It reaches through her, shutting down her insides, pushing in on her, icy fingers stroking her deep, deep within.

*Oh, God,* she thinks, the doll falling from her fingers and shattering in splinters of ice against the hardwood floor. *I'm so cold. Like Martha must have been cold.*

Tony, taking what he wants. From his mother, from Susan. As always.

As the ice seals around her, her mind fragmenting in bergs of deep, translucent blue, one last thought slowly surfaces and she grabs hold of it desperately: *Why wouldn't Mr. Santos take the money? Why couldn't he just take the ten dollars? I'll never know, will I? What I did that was so wrong. What I should have done.*

*I'll never know—*

But that thought, too, finally drifts ponderously away into Arctic twilight.

Here, one less burning ember. Here, the city; grown just that much colder.

# The Magnolia

REMY DE GOURMONT

*Translated by Francis Amery*

The two sisters, Arabella the beautiful and Bibiane the plain, came out of the house together. Arabella's beauty emphasised her youthfulness, while Bibiane seemed older by virtue of her plainness, so they seemed more like daughter and mother than orphan sisters.

They came out of the house that had been touched by grief and paused beneath the magnolia: the magical tree that had been planted by no one and that bloomed so magnificently even in the grounds of the desolate mansion.

The magnolia came to life twice in every year, after the fashion of its kind: first in the spring, when it pushed forth the green spears that would become its leaves; then again in early autumn, before the tired leaves began to wither. In autumn, as in spring, the proud display of the enchanted tree put forth huge flowers that were like those of the sacred lotus, each snow-white corolla cradling a tiny red spot as though it were a shroud marked with a single drop of life's blood.

While she leaned upon the maternal arm of Bibiane, who was always tolerant of her weaknesses, Arabella looked up at the magnolia's branches, dazedly.

"He is dying like the autumn flowers of the magnolia,

which have withered on the branches. The one who should have nourished the flower that I am with the drops of his vital fluid is dying, and now I am destined to remain eternally pale!"

"There is still one flower left," said Bibiane.

It was a flower that had not yet opened fully: a bud that stood out among the complacent leaves by virtue of its virginal purity.

"The last one!" Arabella complained. "It will be my bridal ornament. But is it really the last? No—see, Bibiane, there is one more yet, faded and nearly withered. They are like us—the two of us! Oh, it is a sign! It frightens me . . . I am all a-tremble . . . there we are, he and I, our fates mirrored in these two flowers. I will pluck myself, Bibiane—see, here I am! Shall I also have to die, like him?"

Mutely, Bibiane lovingly embraced her trembling sister. She was afraid herself, but she led Arabella from the sad and sorry garden, away from the magnolia that had now been stripped of the last relic of its former glory.

They went into the sad house, from which the prospect of happiness had so unexpectedly fled, leaving grief to reign in its stead.

"How is he?" asked Bibiane, while she lifted from Arabella's shoulders the mantle that marked her as a bride.

While Arabella sat down, as timidly as a child, to contemplate the unopened flower that she clutched between her fingers, the mother of the dying man replied: "There is no time to lose. He is dying, and his greatest desire is still to be realized. Come with me, my daughter Arabella—I must call you that although your husband-to-be lies dying—and let the presence of your beauty bring forth a final flourish of love amid the last round of prayers. Death awaits you, my darling—would that it might be otherwise! The kiss that his lips will place upon the forehead of his bride is the kiss of one bound for the tomb—but his last smile will defy the invincible shadows with its radiance, a glimmer of light echoing in that darkness which lies beyond the reach of your own beautiful eyes. The son I bore is going to die; he is dying, and I am deeply sorry that you must be given in marriage to a dead man. To you, alas, who are so full of the joys of life, who was born to lie in a bed of fragrant flowers, I can offer nothing but the putrefaction of the tomb—oh, would that it might be otherwise!"

They wept together while they waited for the arrival of the men who were to witness the last rites that would unite Death with Life. The priest came with them, not quite sure whether he had been brought here to tie the indestructible knot or merely to anoint the forehead, the breast, the feet, and the hands of the moribund son.

They all went upstairs together, in silence, stepping as leadenly as a troop of pallbearers. "He might as well be in his coffin as in his bed," whispered one of the men, "prepared for a burial instead of a wedding."

They hesitated at the top of the stairway, but the mother urged them on, repeating what she had said before: "There is no time to lose. He is dying, and his greatest desire is still to be realized."

In the bedroom, they all sank to their knees, save for Arabella, who took her place beside the nuptial bed, wearing her bridal gown like a shroud. When she too knelt down in her turn, touching her forehead to the edge of the pillow, the hearts of all those present went out to her, sharing her anguish. It almost seemed, as she lowered her pretty head to rest it on the pillow, that she was dying too. The bride-to-be laid her right hand upon the thin and wasted hand that lay on top of the coverlet, while her left hand pressed to her lips the unopened magnolia flower, emblem of her virginity.

The priest began to pronounce the solemn words of the marriage service. All eyes were fixed upon the bed where the son was propped up, supported by his mother. His face was tormented by knowledge of the impending catastrophe, his expression so despairing as to seem Satanic; it was bitter with envy of those who possessed the life that was deserting him, angrily resentful of the love that must be left behind. The nearness of the young and beautiful Arabella served only to ignite a fervent but impotent flame of hatred in his hollow eyes. *How terrible his suffering must be!* thought the onlookers.

The dying man managed to raise himself up a little further. From purple lips that had already been touched by the cold hand of death he spoke, while the men made a final effort to smile and the frightened women sobbed like mourners:

"Goodbye, Arabella—you belong to me! I must go, but you must follow me. I will be there—every night, I will wait for you beneath the magnolia, for you must never know any other love but mine. None but mine, Arabella! Ah, what proof you shall have of my love! What proof! What proof! Your soul must be reserved for me."

And with a smile that wrought a diabolical transfiguration of the shadows that lay upon his wasted face, he continued to repeat himself. His voice struggled against its imminent extinction, perhaps devoid of any sense but perhaps mysteriously infused with some unholy wisdom drawn from beyond the grave, saying: "Beneath the magnolia, Arabella, beneath the magnolia!"

For many days and many nights thereafter Arabella could not sleep. Her spirit was sorely troubled, and her heart was heavy. At night, when the wind rattled the dying leaves of the deflowered tree, and when the moon stood high in the sky, bathing its magical crown with bright rays cast down between the October clouds, Arabella frequently trembled with fear, and threw herself into her sister's arms, crying: "He is there!"

He was indeed there, beneath the magnolia: a shadow amid the fallen leaves that swirled in the wind.

One night, Arabella said to Bibiane: "We loved one another, so why should he seek to harm me? He is there. I must go to him!"

"When the dead call out to us," Bibiane replied, "the living must obey. Go, and do not be afraid. I will leave the door open, and I will come out to you if you call me. Go: he is there."

He was indeed there, among the fallen leaves that swirled in the wind. When Arabella came out to him beneath the magnolia, the shadow extended its arms to her—sinuous and serpentine arms that fell upon her shoulders, writhing and hissing like hellish vipers.

Bibiane heard a stifled scream. She ran out.

Arabella was stretched out on the ground. Bibiane picked her up and carried her back into the house.

There were two marks on Arabella's neck, like the imprints of two thin and bony fingers. Her once-beautiful eyes were glazed, transfixed by horror—and tightly clasped in the clenched fingers of her hand Bibiane found the second flower that they had seen on the day of her sister's wedding: the sad, withered flower that they had compassionately left upon the tree; the flower that was the Other; the flower that flourished beyond the grave.

# Vintage Domestic

## STEVE RASNIC TEM

She used to tell him that they'd have the house forever. One day their children would live there. When Jack grew too old to walk, or to feed himself, she would take care of him in this house. She would feed him right from her own mouth, with a kiss. He'd always counted on her keeping this promise.

But as her condition worsened, as the changes accelerated, he realized that this was a promise she could not keep. The roles were to be reversed, and it was to be he who fed his lifetime lover with a kiss full of raw meat and blood. Sweet, domestic vintage.

Early in their marriage his wife had told him that there was this history of depression in her family. That's the way members of the family always talked about it: the sadness, the melancholy, the long, slow condition. Before he understood what this meant he hadn't taken it that seriously, because at the time she never seemed depressed. Once their two oldest reached the teen years, however, she became sad, and slow to move, her eyes dark stones in the clay mask of her face, and she stopped telling him about her family's history of depression. When he asked her about the old story, she acted as if she didn't know what he was talking about.

At some point during her rapid deterioration someone had labeled his family "possibly dysfunctional." Follow-up visits from teachers and social workers had removed "possibly" from

303

his family's thickening file. Studies and follow-up studies had been completed, detailed reports and addenda analyzing his children's behavior and the family dynamics. He had fought them all the way, and perhaps they had tired of the issue, because they finally gave up on their investigations. His family had weathered their accusations. He had protected his wife and children, fulfilled his obligations. Finally people left them alone, but they could not see that something sacred was occurring in this house.

The house grew old quickly. But not as quickly as his wife and children.

"You're so damned cheerful all the time," she said to him. "It makes me sick."

At one time that might have been a joke. Looking into her gray eyes at this moment, he knew it was not. "I'm maintaining," he said. "That's all." He thought maybe her vision was failing her. He was sure it had been months since he'd last smiled. He bent over her with the tea, then passed her a cracker. She stretched her neck and tried to catch his lips in her teeth. He expected a laugh but it didn't come.

"You love me?" she asked, her voice flat and dusty. He put the cracker in his mouth and let her take it from his lips. He could hear his teenage daughters in the next room moaning from the bed. They'd been there two months already, maybe more.

She reached up with a brittle touch across his cheek. "They take after me, you know?" And then she *did* smile, then opened her mouth around a dry cough of a laugh.

Downstairs their seven-year-old son made loud motorcycle noises with moist lips and tongue. Thank God he takes after his father, he thought, and would have laughed if he could. Beneath him his sweet wife moaned, her lips cracked and peeling. A white tongue flickered like the corner of a starched handkerchief.

He bit down hard into the tender scar on the inside of his mouth. He ground one tooth, two, through the tentative pain. When he tasted salt he began to suck, mixing the salt and iron taste with a saliva that had become remarkable in its quantity, until the frothy red cocktail was formed.

He bent over her lips with this beverage kiss and allowed her tongue to meet his, her razor teeth still held back in supplication. In this way he fed her when she could no longer feed herself, when she could not move, when she could not hunt, when in their house tall curtains of dust floated gently around them.

"The girls," she said, once her handkerchief tongue was soaked and her pale lips glistened pinkly.

But still he could not go into his daughters' bedroom, and had to listen to them moan their hunger like pale and hairless, motherless rats.

"Tell me again, Jack," his wife whispered wetly from the bed. "Tell me again how wonderful life is." These were among the last words she would ever use with him.

The young man at the front door wore the blue uniform of the delivery service. Overripe brown sacks filled each of his arms, blending into his fat cheeks as if part of them. He smiled all the time. Jack smiled a hungry smile back.

"Your groceries, sir." Behind him were the stirrings of dry skin against cloth, insect legs, pleadings too starved and faint to be heard clearly.

As the young man handed the sacks over to him, Jack's fingertips brushed the pale backs of the man's hands. He imagined he could feel the heat there, the youthful coursing through veins, feeding pale tissues, warming otherwise cold meat.

Sometimes he took his daughters hunting, if they were strong enough, but so far he had been able to limit them to slugs, worms, insects, small animals. He wondered how long he could hold them to that when the stores kept sending them tender young delivery boys. He wondered how long it would be before his daughters were as immobile as his wife, and begged him to bring them something more. Somewhere behind him there was a tiny gasp, the rising pressure of tears that could not fall.

Some evenings he would sit up talking to his family long into the night. They did not always respond precisely to his confessions of loneliness, of dreams that did not include them, and he wondered if it was because of the doors that separated them from him.

Sometimes he would go to the closet doors and open them.

Where his wife stood, folded back against the wall with the coats and robes. Where his daughters leaned one against the other like ancient, lesbian mops. *Kiss us*, the dry whisper came from somewhere within the pale flaps of their faces. Jack still loved them desperately, but he could not do what they asked.

His youngest, his only son, had taken to his bed.

Jack brought his daughters mice and roaches he had killed himself. They sucked on them like sugar candy until most of the color was gone, and then they spat them out.

Months ago they had stopped having their periods. The last few times had been pale pink and runny, and Jack had cried for them, then cleaned them up with old burlap sacks.

His son disappeared from his bed one evening. Jack found him standing in the closet, his eyes full of moths, his hands stiffened into hooks.

Later his son would disappear from time to time, sometimes showing up in one of the other closets, clutching at mother or sisters, sometimes curled up inside the empty toy box (the boy had no more use for toys, having his own body to play with—sometimes he'd chew a finger into odd shapes).

Jack continued to feed his wife from his own mouth. Sometimes his mouth was so raw he could not tear any more skin off the insides. Then he'd bite through a rat or a bird himself, holding its rank warmth in his cheeks until he could deliver the meal. She returned his kisses greedily, always wanting more than he could provide. But he had spoiled her. She would not feed any other way.

His son became a good hunter, and sometimes Jack would hear him feeding on the other side of the closet door. Pets began disappearing from the neighborhood, and Jack stopped answering the door even for delivery boys.

His daughters became despondent and refused to eat. When he opened their closet door they tried to disguise themselves as abandoned brooms. Finally Jack had to hold them one at a time, forcing his blood-smeared tongue past their splintered lips into the dry cisterns of their mouths so that they might leech nourishment. Once he'd overcome their initial resistance they scraped his tongue clean, then threatened to carve it down to the root, but Jack always knew the exact moment to pull out.

Sometimes he wondered if they still considered him a good father, an adequate husband. He tried singing his children lullabies, reciting poetry to his wife. They nodded their full heads of dust in the gale of his breath, but said nothing.

When the food delivery boys no longer came he saved a portion of his kills for himself. And whenever possible he swallowed his own bloody wet kisses, and tried to remember the feel of his wife's hands on his face, back when her skin was soft and her breath was sweet.

In the houses around him, he knew a hundred hearts beat, desperately chasing life's apprehensions through a racecourse of veins. He tried to ignore the hunger brought on by such thinking. He tried to picture his neighbors' faces, but could not.

His family became so light he could carry them about the house without effort. If he hadn't heard their close whispers, he might have thought them a few old towels thrown across his shoulder. Sometimes he would set them down and forget them, later rushing around in panic to find where they'd been mislaid.

The lighter, the thinner they became, the more blood they seemed to require. When his mouth became too sore to chew he would apply razor blades to the scar tissue, slicing through new white skin into the thicker layers beneath, finally into muscle so that the blood would fill his mouth to spilling before he could get his mouth completely over theirs. Blood stained their thin chests with a rough crimson bib.

And still they grew thinner, their bones growing fibrous, pulpy before beginning to dissolve altogether. He made long rips in his forearms, his thighs, his calves, and held his wife and children up to drink there. The blood soaked through the tissues of their flesh, through the translucent fibers of their hair, washing through their skin until in the dusty shadows of the house they looked vaguely tanned.

But almost as quickly they were pale again, and thin as a distant memory.

He took to slicing off hunks of thigh muscle, severing fingertips, toes. His family ate for months off the bloody bits, their small rat teeth nibbling listlessly. They had ceased using words of any kind long ago, so they could not express their thanks. But Jack didn't mind. This was the family he'd always dreamed of. The look of appreciation in their colorless eyes was thanks enough.

At first he tore his clothes to rags to staunch the blood, but even the rags eventually fell apart. One day seeing his son sucking up the last bit of red from a torn twist of cloth he decided to forego the last vestiges of his modesty and throw the ragged clothes away. After that time he would walk about the dreary old house naked, wearing only the paper-thin bodies of his family wrapped around him, their mouths fixed tightly to his oozing wounds.

This went on for months, wearing his family constantly, their feeding so regular and persistent it seemed to alter the very rhythm of his heart. He would wake up in the middle of the night to the soft sucking noise their lips and teeth made against his flesh. He would awaken a few hours later and the first thing he would see was the stupored look in their eyes as they gazed up at him in adoration. He was pleased to see that such constant nourishment fattened them and brought color to their skin so that eventually they fell off his body from the sheer weight of them.

Wriggling about his feet at first, they eventually decided to explore the house on their own. Obviously, they felt far healthier than before.

Again they did not thank him, but what did a good husband and father need of thanks?

They soon grew thin again, soft, transparent.

After a year he had not seen them again, although occasionally he might swear to a face hidden within the upholstery, an eye rolling past a furniture leg, a dry mouth praying silently among the houseplants filmed in a dark, furry dust.

After five years even the garbled whispering had stopped. He continued to watch over the house, intent on his obligation. And after preparing a blood kiss in the pale vacancy of his mouth, he was content to drink it himself.

# A Little Night Music

## RON DEE

he wolves outside his door were still howling.

Loudly and literally.

Melvin gritted his teeth and clenched his eyes shut again, cursing the noisy animals silently. He didn't need all that noise to remind him of what lurked beyond his door.

His assailants had brought the wolves with them, it seemed . . . as well as the incredible loneliness he now endured.

He walked across the room, remembering all those fools who had made the exertion and frenziedly boarded up doors and windows to keep *them* out.

But even the wolves did not dare enter his domain.

This house was his fortress, but he hadn't done a thing to barricade it against the droning evil outside its walls—nothing but enter it and claim it as his own.

He wondered for the millionth time if there was anyone else like himself left.

Melvin went to the big living room window and peeked around the curtain, staring for only a brief second at the naked women gyrating seductively—so near that he could touch them if he opened his window. He heard the voices that were so intermingled their calls to him were meaningless.

But they drew their invisible psychic fingers over his mind constantly, and it was getting harder and harder to resist. Quickly, Melvin stepped back and let the thick yellow curtain drop shut again, reminding himself that he was a man . . . that there *must* be others—

Maybe not.

*They* called to him. The creatures of the night, surrounding his two-level home, chiding him with their lies that everyone else had already joined their ranks, increasing his despair.

It couldn't be true.

And what if it was?

They merely wanted him to open the door and invite them in.

A vampire could not enter a home without invitation.

That was certainly why some of these undead had tried to fool him into making his invitation to them in the daylight, when they were without their supernatural powers.

But he was no fool. One had even come to his door enacting the role of a traveling salesman, another as a door-to-door hooker. Those and the ones like them had been in the beginning, and more recently they had tried to fool him by sending their seductive forces posing as fugitives like himself.

But Melvin knew the tests to prove whether or not they were who they claimed to be, and he kept his mirrors at hand as well as the dwindling stock of holy water and crosses. When they came to him in the daylight, they were weak, and despite his suspicion he often still opened the door, indulging in his questions that frustrated them without his invitation, then killing them.

One by one.

At least it broke the monotony of his loneliness.

But how many were there?

What if he *was* the only human left?

He refused to believe it.

It couldn't be true.

Holding himself back as the tugs on his mind became stronger, not allowing himself to disarm himself further with the contact of the myriad glittering eyes beyond his drapes, Melvin walked out of the living room and went up the stairs, passing the portraits he had decorated every wall with. He entered his bedroom, and turned his stereo on just loud enough to drown out the constant pleas for him, and went to bed.

Melvin awoke at ten in the morning, groggy from staying up too late, but refreshed and invigorated that he had withstood the onslaught from within and without.

He was desperate for companionship. It had been like this almost a year now, and he was lonely, and even the supply of food in this city was dwindling.

He hated his imprisonment.

But he did not want to be damned. Long ago, he had learned that it wasn't always in his own best interests to go along with the crowd, and that fact seemed truer than ever. It was better to live out his remaining time as a man, even if he *were* the last man on earth.

But Melvin wished to hell that there was someone else to share his solitude with . . . anyone!

Anyone human.

He left the house as he usually did in the daylight, choosing one of his fleet of cars. He was virtually a millionaire as he and so many other of his long-ago friends had dreamed of being. He had a Cadillac, an antique Mustang . . . the finest of clothing and the finest of foods.

"It's not worth it," Melvin muttered to himself as he so often did now, and he forced his steps to the clunker he had laid hands on as a desire for his poorer former life, because that was how he felt . . . as beat up and washed out as the old Chevrolet Malibu.

Nothing satisfied him, and even when he put on his headphones and couldn't physically hear the calls from the former human beings awaiting, he could not forget their entreaties for him to join them or keep them from his inner mind.

But he knew he must not give in. All he had left was his *life*.

The blood was the life.

More days and nights passed, each grimmer than the hours before. Melvin found little solace in his music or in the library of movies he'd collected. He dared not look out at the throngs outside his home for fear that he would succumb.

He wanted to die.

But at least they had stopped coming to him in the daylight. Melvin guessed that he had probably dispatched a hundred of them through their attempted treachery during those hours. He wasn't surprised that they had finally learned their lesson, though he missed the break in monotony. After all, he left the bodies to rot in the street as his warning to the rest. At first he had disposed of them, wary of a disease their rot might cause, but now he welcomed the thought of a disease overtaking his body and giving him a natural death.

Returning from his latest tour of the city just as the sun began setting, Melvin knew his carelessness would soon prove to be his undoing. Subconsciously, he was just too tired of it all, and longed to join the frantic orgies he peeked out and witnessed in his front yard as the vampires grew lurid in their enticements.

All he had to live for was to keep from becoming an *undead*.

Walking through the ornate living room and gazing at the colorful museum paintings he had brought home, putting a CD of Beethoven's Ninth Symphony in his player, Melvin went to the refrigerator and opened a bottle of cheap wine, no longer wishing to enjoy the riches of his existence. As he drank, faster and faster, he was overcome with a desire for the voices inside his head . . . the monotone of ghosted humanity he could faintly hear beyond the chorus and orchestra booming from the speakers.

He knew he could not hold out any longer, and wanted to go to the window and salivate over the women who lusted for him as he lusted for them . . . to fling open the door and invite them inside. At this point, perhaps even the men!

In his weakness, Melvin knew he must be strong, and drunkenly went to the refrigerator for a second bottle of wine, picking up an army bayonet he had liberated for himself as he returned to his couch and listened to the Ninth Symphony begin again. Halfway through this second bottle, he knew he was becoming so drunk that he no longer had the energy to cross the room and open the front door. He also knew he did not want to do this every night.

The last man on earth . . . drinking himself into oblivion each night . . . as much a shell of the man he'd been as the blood guzzling undead he feared.

There was no more choice available to him.

Waiting until the chorus for "Ode to Joy" began once more, Melvin thought of the mess he would make, and chuckled as he thought of his enemy entering this house at last to find him dead, his blood coagulating and unpatable to them with his life already gone from it. His last laugh would be silent, but he chuckled at the thought now, in triumph.

The vampires would feel the power of his will that kept

them out vanish, and enter hungrily, battering one another to get to him.

But they would find him gone, the life in his blood that they craved beyond their reach.

Rather than give up his life to the undead, he preferred that the last living human take it.

Himself.

Finishing the second bottle in a long, sloppy gulp, Melvin dropped it to the blue rug and sliced the sharp steel of the bayonet across his left wrist, gasped, and then took the blade in his left hand and cut deeply into his right wrist.

Watched the gurgling red fountains drench his hands and the the couch and the floor with red wetness.

Closed his eyes as the strength drooled from him and was replaced with a mindless gray peace.


Melvin awoke from this newest nightmare, feeling the ache in his muscles and the dryness of his throat.

It was still dark, but he no longer heard the loud hum of voices in his mind, or even just above the orchestral strains of the Ninth's second movement from the speakers.

*Maybe all of it had been a dream?*

Melvin swallowed hard, feeling peculiarly light and uncaring, but he forced himself to retain his awakening wonder and furthered it: *Had it all been a dream? Had the strange disease of vampirism actually vanquished mankind?*

Or wasn't this all just a bad dream?

Then he looked down at the dried brown-red thick muck surrounding him, layering his wrists and hands . . . saw the stained knife at his feet.

He felt numb.

The sight of the blood . . .

Even dried out as it was, the lingering copper scent that made him salivate.

Melvin felt a pang of unrequited hunger, and touched the new fangs in his mouth. He no longer felt the loneliness that was only a memory, but a desire for life he could only find in the blood of another.

And with his psychic tendrils, he now knew his previous tormenters had taunted him only with the truth.

There were no others.

He had given up the last life that was to be had and this new hunger was far worse than loneliness.

# Sometimes We Come Back

## WAYNE ALLEN SALLEE

The man was not yet thirty when he had the conversation with the book editor. It was terribly humid that July night when they sat near the sands of Oak Street Beach and spoke of immortality.

He had met the woman at the Drake Hotel, and as they crossed Walton Street to the Lake Shore Drive underpass, the fickle Chicago wind had taunted the hem of her dress. The dress was the exact color of the blueberry Freez-Pops the writer had loved as a child. A cab driver turning onto Michigan Avenue honked appreciatively at the flash of thigh in the moment before she pressed her tan briefcase against her skirt. This he would always remember: the Badfinger song suspended in midair from the Flash Cab's radio, the frantic yapping of a dog in the nearby park, the sudden nostalgia of those long-ago summers filled with icy-blue treats that were no longer manufactured, the sun bronzing both their skins in near-dusk tones that complemented the woman's briefcase, and everything else in that one moment.

The moment that Shondra Massee from Perdition Press had placed his book, *Living Like the Fugitive*, on the spring schedule.

He had still felt human then, he thought as the dog hoisted its leg and two lovers on the shoreline shared a secret and laughed like someone in a Life Savers television commercial.

Nothing had *truly* changed. The writer had not won the lottery or become sole beneficiary in a will, he would still be working his day job as skip-tracer at the law firm and continue paying the minimum on his credit cards.

Only now, he was immortal.

He had written a *horror* novel, yes, but it didn't involve

vampires or the supernatural. Those creatures were sequel material. His book dealt with the crippled meeting the insane head on.

"You're excited, I know," the woman beside him said. "I know I was, when I sold my first story years ago, when dinosaurs roamed the earth." Laughter, like a wood sprite's.

But he wasn't really listening. He was thinking of the connotations. How a truly good writer was like a cop who stopped caring: drawing on personal moments from news clippings and the lives of his friends, all for a realistic story.

Sucking the life blood out of everything.

And how many times would he do it again to survive? He felt empty and wished that he could bury himself in the earth like the old vampires of legend did when they were too weary to continue living their lies. Their mockery of life.

He spoke his goodbyes to the woman; made a promise to meet for lunch later that week. Then he sat and watched the sun pass behind the Gold Coast highrises. Feeling immortal.

Wondering if, had he chose to sit on the bench that entire night, when the sun came up, would he be impaled by the rays and break away into dirt or simply get up and walk to the elevated train.

Peggy finished reading the story from the writer's commonplace book and looked across at the others gathered at the gravesite. The city he might have been buried in held no importance. "I remember him telling about thinking up his writer-as-vampire story," the publisher from Hell's Kitchen said. She had bought his first story years ago, but *long* after dinosaurs stopped roaming the earth.

"I remember that," Joan said. She was a novelist who raised five children in Shoreham, New York. The writer had been single, never married, loved only his word processor. "We were at Moravian College with Beth."

Also gathered were Jeff, Don and Von, Andrew, Ben, Harry, and Diane. They had been the last to see the writer, sharing laughs at the Red Lion Pub, the topic centering around theme anthologies and how many really truly original ideas were gone. The writer over whose remains they now stood brought up the current vampire book looking for submissions. What if a guy with Alzheimer's became a vampire and forgot to go inside when the sun came up? What if a nosferatu from the old country came to America and tried to give a girl the Evil Eye, knowing nothing about lost contact lenses and blurred vision? The writer was angered at how the reading public thought being immortal was so damn cool.

How soon before Kurt Cobain and River Phoenix came back, in some similar immortal way. Brandon Lee already had, when *The Crow* was released the previous month.

How the writer died was of no consequence.

"He hated the way the whims of the public made him reshape what he wrote," Harry said. "It was making him nuts, he was always telling me."

"Writers feed off others' lives," Andrew said. "But he fed off of his own."

After several more minutes, they walked away from the cemetery. Dusk fell soon after. Leafy shadows fell across the undisturbed grave.

Nothing would ever claw its way out, contrary to what I might try to tell you.

# Acts

### Benjamin Adams

On a good night, Wayne Lynch's rounds around Holy Lawn Cemetery netted nothing more than a few drunken teenagers partying amidst the graves and mausoleums. This was *not* looking like a good night for Wayne.

Somewhere up ahead, through the light ground fog, the guard heard faint, hoarse sounds; almost like what a voice would sound like through several feet of dirt piled atop a coffin. *Or,* Wayne mused, *if some goddamn kid had made a recording of himself and buried the tape player a foot or so below the surface of a grave.* The idea didn't strike him as so odd—he'd seen a lot of crap in his years at Holy Lawn.

316

In a few hours he could go home to his studio flat in Daley City. Hoist a brew or two and watch titty movies on HBO. Unwind after a shift with the stiffs in Colma, the South Bay's "City of the Dead." If you threw a rock in Colma, hitting a grave was far more likely than hitting a live person or even a house. And that's what pissed him off. With all the damn cemeteries around, why the hell did these kids pick his for their moronic practical joke?

Wayne's hand fell to his holster. He unsnapped it quietly and let his hand rest on the butt of his revolver. If these punk-ass kids thought they were going to get away with this crap on his turf, they had another think coming.

He approached the source of the sound, a fresh grave about ten feet away. He swung the beam of his heavy three-cell Mag-Lite toward the headstone. Its glossy marble surface caught the light and glowed through the swirling mist.

*Reverend Richard Casey Gilmore*
*June 5, 1948–October 18, 1994*
*'When the voices of children are heard on the green*
*And laughing is heard on the hill*
*My heart is at rest within my breast*
*And everything else is still.'—Wm. Blake*

"Well, goddamn," said Wayne with reverence. For some reason he'd never really considered the fact that priests die just like other people. All the ones he'd ever known just seemed like they went on and on, like the Energizer Bunny.

Playing his light over the surface of the grave, Wayne noticed that there didn't seem to be any fresh turnover or disturbance. The priest had been buried just a few days earlier, but a major rainstorm had blown through the bay area since then and the dirt was pretty well tamped down.

The noises continued unabated: a hoarse, muffled sound like screaming. And something else—a faint scrabbling sound that reminded Wayne of the cockroaches in his apartment skittering across the hardwood floor.

Around him, the fog gathered in thickness. Another couple of steps forward, and Wayne heard the sounds more clearly. Like

317

someone yelling, *"Let me out! Get me out of here!"* from underground. And the scratching, scrabbling noise sounded like—

—digging—

The dirt at the top of the grave began shifting slightly, crumbling into a shallow depression a couple of inches in circumference that had just appeared. Wayne began shaking. In all his years at Holy Lawn, he'd never seen anything like this, but he'd heard of it. A million-to-one shot, but it could happen, and obviously was happening right in front of his eyes. "Holy geez," he muttered. "They musta buried the poor bastard alive!" He ran to the grave and began scooping the dirt away from the depression. "Hold on, buddy, I'll getcha outta there!"

A dirty, grimy hand with battered and bleeding fingers burst through the hole and grabbed hold of Wayne's wrist. "Are —are you really there?" asked a shattered husk of a voice.

"Yeah, buddy, I'm real all right. Hey, you don't gotta hold on so tight! I'm tryin' to get you outta there. Hey, leggo! You're hurtin' me—"

Wayne gasped as his entire arm was pulled back into the hole and his body slammed against the surface of the grave. A moment later, he got enough of his breath back for a series of terrified screams as something below the surface sank needle-sharp fangs into his wrist, tearing out the veins beneath the parchment-thin skin. Soft lips pressed against the wound and began sucking his life away.

Soon Wayne Lynch's pathetic screams faded away into the thick fog shrouding the necropolis, and all was once again still, save for the soft, piteous sobbing of the damned.

Casey Gilmore reflected on his damnable bad luck. He'd specified in his will that he wanted his body left intact when he was buried; no artificial preservatives, thank you very much. He didn't want to be pickled for eternity, and look where it had got him.

He'd managed the walk from the necropolis of Colma to San Francisco before dawn, and as the first rays of sun broke the horizon he was safely inside a Salvation Army warehouse at the corner of Newhall and Williams. There he'd been able to clean up and collect a new set of clothes to replace the soiled and bloodstained clerical garb in which he'd been buried.

Even without his white clerical collar, Casey Gilmore stood apart from the tie-dyed and leather-jacketed masses still thronging the sidewalks this chilly October evening. The tall, graying former priest was out of place here, near the center of the old hippie district, just a block west of where Haight and Ashbury make their clarion call to a million sandaled and booted freaks and punks.

Deadheads wandered by, lost in acid reveries. Ragged street people panhandled without shame from everyone, including each other. Groups of young people, dressed in exotic, revealing outfits of leather, lace, and black velvet, stumbled laughing in and out of the I-Beam, a nightclub across the street.

He watched the children somberly. The majority fit the profile; dark hair and pale skin were almost a uniform for these kids. Sad, pathetic waifs and strays. He had worked in the Haight for years trying to help them: the runaways, the leftovers and outcasts of society. He felt sickened at the hunger that now consumed his belly when he looked at them. Some of these kids had stayed at All Saints Church and prayed with him.

*He'd gone down for an evening mass with the homeless kids staying in the parish hall. There'd been one missing from the usual group.*

*Tina Jensen.*

*None of the other kids remembered when they'd last seen her; maybe several days before. Her absence preyed on Reverend Gilmore's mind. He'd liked Tina. The pretty sixteen-year-old had brains and the guts enough to get off the mean streets and make something of herself.*

*So he decided he'd go looking for her himself—*

From that point, the memories were dim, scattershot, like faded postcards dropped on a floor.

Screams of pain and shrill yells of anger broke into his reverie. Aghast, Gilmore watched a pair of Riot Grrrls kick and pummel a teenage skinhead—who'd had the temerity to whistle at them—to his knees. The kid's face slammed into the plate glass window of Escape from New York Pizza and left a bloody smear.

At the sight of the blood Gilmore gasped and turned away. His stomach roiled at the sight.

*What sort of world have we bequeathed to our children,* he

wondered sadly, *when such acts are part of its everyday warp and weave?*

Unfortunately the answer, as always, eluded him.

After a while, Tina passed by, walking east, just as he knew she would. Gilmore didn't question how he knew; he had just felt that she would be here tonight. He had wanted to find her, and now here he was and here she was. It was odd, but many things about his life were odd now. How he had found her was the least of his worries.

She had high, haughty cheekbones that threatened to jut through her pale, translucent skin, and flashing green eyes. Blonde hair, cut fashionably in a severe gamin shag, crowned her head like a halo and emphasized her waiflike appearance. Her blue denim jacket hung on her lanky frame, stylishly tossed together with faded, torn blue jeans; the height of street fashion. After she passed by, he left the restaurant and followed her, hanging back twenty or so feet.

She turned north on Ashbury, toward the panhandle of Golden Gate Park, just two blocks away. He stayed well back from her, and as she crossed Oak Street he paused. Leaves rustled overhead in a slight breeze as she entered the solemn darkness of the park. A Muni bus roared by and he stepped back from the curb.

Once again he asked himself if doing this was the right thing. Even just a few days ago the answer would have been obvious; but that may as well have been another life. Where there had once been unalterable truths and certain answers, the building blocks of his faith and stewardship, now different truths filled him. The killing of the cemetery guard had already changed in his mind from an inexcusable act to meaning no more than crossing the street to 7-11 for a six-pack.

"Hey, man—spare any change?"

Gilmore turned toward the young voice. A pair of girls with shaven heads, barely past puberty, stood about five feet away from him, both clad in torn blue jeans. One wore the seemingly ubiquitous black leather jacket, decorated with four-inch-square vinyl stickers featuring the logos of bands Gilmore didn't know: Lard, Tool, Bikini Kill, Jordan Cohen Experience. The other child, shivering in the cold night air, wore just an extra-large T-shirt bearing the face of the self-destructive lead singer of Nirvana, Kurt Cobain, with the legend HE DIED FOR OUR SINS.

He shook his head. "Sorry, I don't have anything."

The teenager in the leather jacket said, "Uh—well, then, spare any drugs?"

Gilmore grimaced, feeling a recently all-too-familiar pain creep up from his stomach. Two diametrically opposed urges warred inside him. He wanted to help these girls, get them to a shelter, get them off the streets. But a terrible hunger rose inside him, threatening disaster. For himself, and the girls. There wasn't much time. "Get—get away," he grated through clenched teeth.

The girls began backing away from him, clutching each others' arms and keeping him in sight. "Jesus Christ, what a weirdo!" said Cobain T-shirt girl.

Her words stung his ears like solid blows. "GO!" he roared. "GET *AWAY!*"

The girls turned and ran south on Ashbury toward Haight, leaving Gilmore alone, gasping on the corner. The hunger in his belly subsided. So close this time. It had been so close. He looked up, back toward the park panhandle. Tina had vanished among the dark silhouettes of the trees.

So close. He couldn't chance it happening again.

Grimly, Gilmore entered the park.

His meandering path took him west, through the length of the panhandle, into the main body of the park. Some kind of strange new sense told him that he would find her here, this way; he let it guide him. It felt right; correct somehow. Passing McLaren Lodge, he remembered the last time he'd been here.

*The sound of sobbing coming from Lily Pond off Middle Drive East. Tina, alone, quivering under her blue denim jacket. "Father, can you help me?" And when he'd approached, seeing only his own reflection in the water even though she was right next to him—*

*—And the terrible rebirth inside his coffin, his ragged, bleeding fingernails finally clawing their way through to the surface—*

*—And fighting the hunger, the terrible hunger that threat-*

*ened to devour him from inside, but he could not, and so damned his soul forever by taking the life of the poor guard at the cemetery—*

Once again he found himself at the shore of Lily Pond. Tina Jensen stood by the water's edge, about fifteen feet ahead, her blonde hair glowing in the pale moonlight.

"Father Gilmore!" she said when she looked up and saw him. "You're here!"

He stopped a couple of feet away from her. "I guess I should be surprised by finding you," he said dully, "but for some reason I'm not."

She nodded. "Our kind know when another is near. It's a . . . talent we have. You'll learn as time goes by."

"You're assuming I want to learn."

Tina shook her head remorsefully. "You don't have a choice, Father Gilmore."

"Please . . . don't call me that any more. I'm not a priest. I'm damned."

She stepped closer to him and took his hands in hers. "No —you're *blessed.*"

"This is obviously some use of the word 'blessed' with which I'm not familiar."

He'd meant it as a morbid joke, but she gazed into his eyes and shook her head solemnly. "Don't you see? This is what the communion is all about; we eat of the body and drink of the blood."

"That was nothing but metaphor!" As he said it, Gilmore realized that he'd never believed in the miracle of transubstantiation—the moment when the wafer and wine become the true body and blood of Christ—at all.

The tenets of his faith were falling from him as easily as he had once undressed for bed.

"Why did you do this to me? *Why?*"

In answer she looked over his shoulder. "There," she said.

He turned his head. At the edge of the woods at either end of Lily Pond, a bedraggled group of teenagers stood assembled; a motley leather-jacketed army with pale faces and silver eyes in the moonlight. They'd moved into place silently, like a swirling San Francisco fog.

He knew several of the faces from the youth ministry.

Chuck Caruso. Zoran Novoselic. Kerilyn Hoefs. Billy Mundi. James Sherwood. Alice Sheldon. All good kids; at least, they *had* been good kids. What had happened here?

"I—I don't understand," he finally breathed. "Are they—are they all—"

"They're like us, Father Gilmore," Tina said calmly.

On the verge of objecting to her use of the honorific, he realized that he didn't mind it so much after all. Out here, under the stars, the gathering felt very much like a church service.

He wasn't the only one feeling that way.

As he stood there watching the group of vampire teens, they began moving forward, gradually taking seats on the grass before him. He spread his arms, welcoming them with love. Their wary, sad expressions turned to smiles, and his heart swelled with happiness and pride. Tina spoke truly when she said he wasn't damned, but blessed. He knew now why he was here. For them.

Here was a flock; was he not a shepherd?

Father Gilmore smiled back at the teens. He still had his calling.

"Let us prey," he said.

# Revival

### RICHARD PARKS

Evening, Miss Powers. I'm Jim Meader, a deacon here at First Canemill. We met at the membership drive potluck last Sunday . . . ? Thanks, it's nice of you to remember me. Do you mind if I sit down?

Yes it *is* a lovely night for an outdoor revival, isn't it? Not too warm for June, and the crickets are singing. You can see the bats swooping at the pole light now; I've loved to watch them ever since I can remember. It's a lovely feeling, being so much closer to God's creatures. And having Reverend Blacksen as guest preacher is a special treat.

No, I'm not surprised you've heard of him. He's quite in

323

demand on the revival circuit these days, and no wonder. He's the best. Church membership goes up at least five percent after he's been in town. Donations, too. Reverend Blacksen puts the spirit in a group like no one else. We invite him back every year.

I'm afraid you'll have to put your necklace away before the service starts. Oh, that's quite all right. I can see you've never been to one of Reverend Blacksen's services before. He doesn't allow jewelry of any sort in the congregation. Nor pictures, nor mirrors, nor flags. No, not even wedding rings. He's very firm about this, feels they pull attention to earthly things. Here, let me help you. . . . Keep it in your purse, that'll be fine.

That's him. The tall, thin man in the black suit. Yes he *is* very pale, but no, he should *not* get more sun. It's bad for him . . . hmm? Sorry, I thought you knew—Reverend Blacksen is a vampire.

I see by the bulletin that we're starting the singing with "I Am Resolved." Good choice. The last time someone picked "Blood of the Lamb" and it was very embarrassing, as you can imagine.

Miss Powers . . . oh that's all right. I know you couldn't help laughing. I do have an odd sense of humor, I know.

Let's sing together, shall we?

Wasn't it a lovely service, Miss . . . ?
Oh dear.
Don't struggle, Miss Powers. You'll only injure yourself. I think you'll be able to whisper very faintly, if memory serves. Yes, you thought I was kidding and I didn't try to dissuade you. That was wrong of me. It seems that Reverend Blacksen has singled you out; he can be very specific with his gifts when he needs to be. Focused charisma, I guess you'd say.

Maybe I can make it up to you, a little. Maybe it'll help if I explained the situation. Don't try to talk too much, the strain wouldn't be good for you. Just listen.

I'll bet you didn't know Reverend Blacksen got his start right here, at Canemill First NeoBaptist. It's true. He was barely out of Seminary, but we're a small congregation and we needed a minister desperately after Reverend McIntyre passed on. He was pretty good, even then. Nothing like now, of course, but full of fire and enthusiasm. The congregation was quite fond of him.

But he was very young, you have to understand that. Young and far from home and inexperienced. It doesn't excuse what he did, of course—

Well, he strayed. He's certainly not the first. It seems to happen more to people who renounce sin at such an early age that they're never quite sure what sin *is*. Rather like going into battle when you don't know what the enemy looks like—they tend to sneak up on you.

During his first year with us he went to Convention and met a young lady of the streets, if you'll pardon the euphemism. Or rather, something he thought was a young lady. He went with her to her place, to pray with her. That's what he *said*, anyway. Maybe he believed it, maybe he was experiencing the same effect you're experiencing now. But the long and short of it is that first she led him into sin and then she sucked him dry. She didn't have to do that last bit, you understand. We found out later that she could have fed well enough without going quite so far. It was a choice. Rather like adding insult to injury.

Well, needless to say he was missing from morning services the next Sunday. He finally staggered in late for evening services. We demanded an explanation, of course, as soon as he climbed into the pulpit. It was all just too much for him, poor fellow. He confessed all. In tears, pleading for forgiveness. Which of course we gave. What else? It's our way; I know you understand. It wasn't until Mrs. Dinson and a few others approached the pulpit to offer comfort that we grasped the full extent of the situation. Yes, she was wearing a small cross. Just like the one in your purse now.

We *were* a bit surprised, but not as surprised as Larry was . . . that's his given name, by the way. Fine man . . . or whatever. You'll be meeting him shortly.

Where was I? Oh, the cross. The transformation was sudden and quite startling, as I'm sure you can imagine . . . what's that? Why didn't we do what? Oh. Well, believe me, that occurred to us. From all the books and old movies we knew what to do, of course, but can you imagine driving a large piece of wood through someone you know and . . . well, love? It's not as easy as they make it seem.

Larry begged us to do it. We couldn't. Every time anyone

thought to try that business about casting stones came up. No one felt worthy. No one really wanted to do it anyway. So we worked things out, as you can see. And Larry always saves us a place in his schedule. He remembers his friends.

Demon from Hell?

That's a little strong, Miss Powers, but I suppose it depends on which idea of the vampire's nature you believe. Maybe he is what you say. Or maybe he's just what he always was, except for this gift that his condition has bestowed. It doesn't take much to accept that, really. Just a little faith.

Yes, I do call it a gift. He's done more good in his ministry than ten mortal men. And he can't help what he is. A man of the cloth can't let a little setback ruin his calling—

You're struggling again. I did warn you about that. Please try to relax; Larry won't be a moment. He just has to greet a few more people; most of the congregation has left already. I'd better be going myself.

Don't say such things. Please.

And don't worry. He's not a monster . . . at least most of the time. After you've joined our little church you might remember what happened tonight, eventually, but you won't mind. Trust me; I know.

Oh, and if this helps . . . think of it as a tithe. After all, ten percent *is* customary, and he's very gentle.

You'll see.

# Crumbs Under Thy Table

### PAMELA D. HODGSON

> We do not presume to come to this thy Table, oh
> merciful Lord, trusting in our own righteousness, but
> in thy manifold and great mercies. We are not worthy
> so much as to gather up the crumbs under thy Table.
> But thou art the same Lord whose property is always
> to have mercy. Grant us therefore, gracious Lord, so to
> eat the flesh of thy dear Son Jesus Christ and to drink
> His blood, that we may evermore dwell in Him and
> He in us.
> —BOOK OF COMMON PRAYER OF THE EPISCOPAL CHURCH

I've found my place at last. All I ever wanted was a place to stay and enough to eat. My prayers are finally answered.

My last night on the street I tried to sweep the trash off a bus stop bench to lie down and rest, but a cop (and where is he when an icy blade slits thin flesh this thick August night?) appeared, baton smacking against his fleshy palm as if itching for the cool touch of the blue steel bouncing against his ample hip. It's happened that way for days—or for nights, to be more accurate. I sucked another cottony breath of the congealed city air, and focused on the burn of the pavement on the balls of my feet to keep my mind off my hunger as I moved on.

The burn reminded me of another place and time, far away. Flames crackled and jumped under the feet of the heretic, blackening the soles and warming the winter evening with the gamey smell of burning muscle and skin. Blood ran and boiled and turned to brown steam. It made me hungry. I was ashamed.

But tonight I found sanctuary. A ragged man, as homeless and hopeless as I, fled the night-colored uniforms (do they wear them to blend in, or because, like me, city cops are creatures of the night?) toward a lancet-shaped pool of light. Gold bled into the dun and soot-colored street, sullied momentarily by his shadow. I followed.

Inside, the stone walls were cool and damp, smoke-streaked in spots. Shards of music from passing cars rippled against the granite and bounced off. Memory of incense hung in the clammy air, reminding me of my Renaissance childhood. Renaissance. How ironic. Behind a cracked, yellowing marble altar, a clergywoman raised her hands in supplication and sung out in a clear soprano voice that cut across the street noise. She was petite but not delicate, with a nose like a flatiron.

A few parishioners, all elderly, replied softly, while the ragged man suckled on paper-wrapped wine. Others slept among the reek of sweat and vomit. I thumbed idly through a small red volume labeled *Book of Common Prayer*. A rodent tail swatted my boot.

The clergywoman stumbled over some of the words. I remembered watching this same ritual as a child in Rome, stunned by the presence of God they invoked. I beseeched Him then in silent prayers to tell me why He created me this way, and how He meant me to live.

When I was twelve, I went to the monsignor and asked him. He flailed a cross at me, and swore the silver of the chalice would burn me. Of course he was wrong. But I ran away just the same.

Martin Luther came and went, and I stayed away. Basilicas and storefronts, gospel hymns, female clergy, and TV preachers —I watched them all, but from a distance. This was the first time in a century or more I'd been in church. But this vested woman's words, words of humility and succor welcomed me into God's home and to His table.

She raised the plate and cup, her movement punctuated by staccato gunfire. The sour smell of wine woke some of the sleeping homeless, and two or three joined the procession to the wrought iron rail for rounds of cardboard-thin bread and pungent sips of the wine-made-blood.

But it isn't made blood. If it were blood, it would sustain me.

One bony little man with a ragged gray beard and a scarred red face clawed the cup with blackened fingernails as he tipped and drained it thirstily. A sleek black rat cowered in a corner near the door nibbling on some scrap of garbage.

I hunched in my seat after the candles were out and the clank and rattle of the posteucharistic washing up was done. Jagged snores rose from the scratched wooden bench just in front of me. He wheezed and coughed in his sleep, and I heard the sad groan of the wood as he shifted, then a wet thump as he rolled to the floor. The snores continued. He reeked of bile and malt liquor. I crept forward and peered into the dark; it was the man who had drained the chalice. A faint trail of blood, black in the dimness, snaked from his left nostril through a crevice in his cheek and down to a crack in the stone. The iron tang made my innards rumble with long-suppressed hunger. I knew I was too weak to overcome him awake—even in his feeble condition—but asleep, he was simple. Finally, Our Father gave me a meal.

When he was dead, I wiped my mouth on the back of my hand and found a spot in the cobwebbed organ loft to hide.

Thou shalt not kill is the commandment. But one is not born in order to starve. I have to believe that.

A dumpy black man with close-cropped hair and salt and pepper stubbled cheeks swept up in the morning. He found the body and nudged it with his boot. When it didn't move, he kicked the man hard. Nothing. "Somebody dead in here." He sounded mildly interested.

A very old man in black shirt and priestly collar shuffled over to the body. While the sweeper leaned on his broom, the priest placed a hand on the corpse. From where I hunkered down, I saw him blink back a tear as he muttered a prayer. I tensed. Had I taken someone important? Had I failed some divine test for my survival?

I was more careful the next time. I shadowed the old woman for three consecutive nights. She babbled to herself when she wasn't spitting gravelly curses at some invisible enemy. The woman priest—Mother Lopreto, I learned—shot a quickly disguised look of anger at the old creature when she bellowed the word *fuck* during morning prayer. Even in the heat, the old woman wore three sweaters, each gray with dirt and wear. Her hair was matted into a single brown mass like a dead animal dangling from her head. She stunk like old corpses on a battlefield. We all stayed away from her, as if her madness might be catching.

I followed her into the women's restroom. The acrid urine smell mixed with the rot of her body and the dirt of her clothes;

I felt nauseous. She left the stall door swinging open, oblivious to me, as she hiked up her grubby skirt and clawed down ripped, filthy underpants. The rich, metallic scent of menstrual blood sliced through the other odors like a scalpel. I left her sprawled across the cracked toilet, her panties still dangling around her ankles.

Mother Lopreto, the curate of St. Peter's, is a slight woman, with jet black hair clipped short. Her hands are calloused and blistered. She smells like soap and flesh in a place that stinks of ammonia and mildew. She listens intensely, never breaking eye contact and never distracted. She sees too much. She scares me.

We talked once about the words of the prayers. She hates the Rite I words, the ones with "thee" and "thy" and so forth, but she uses them because the last paying members of the congregation are old. She calls it a price she must pay to do the service to the needy the Lord calls her to do.

I have a call too. My call is to gather the crumbs under the Lord's Table. I knew it when I first heard her say those words. But I didn't tell her that.

She found the next body, and the next. I saw her probe my marks with her fingers, like St. Thomas in the Lord's wounds, and then look straight to me. The hairs on the back of my neck tingled. "I didn't believe in this stuff," she whispered. I felt like ice turned to steam. "You can't be doing this. People choose their own fates. There's a certain order to the—"

"There *is* order." Outside, someone kicked over a trash can. Neither of us turned. "This is God's will for me. The Lord provides."

"I'll stop you."

She watched me walk away, her small, pale fingers clutching the doorjamb and becoming as white as one of my victims.

Yes, they are victims. But they were victims before I ever took them. I only take what the Lord offers me, what mankind has already destroyed. I wasn't made by another vampire—that's just a myth—I was born this way. I am the Lord's creation.

I hid behind the burnt shell of a '78 Bonneville in the dusk. I waited until she left, watched her climb into the smoke-belching bus and ride away and then went back inside.

We haunted each other, the next few days. My back and

sides were pocked with splinters from the crevices in the loft and rafters where I hid; I licked away my own blood, but it didn't satisfy me. The cheap ping and gurgle of the bottle of communion wine told me when she was readying for her eucharists. She knew I was there. She drew her breaths with purposeful evenness, but twitched at the slightest breeze. She forgot the rest of the homeless she was there to minister to. Her gaze didn't pierce any more; it wandered, looking for me.

On the third day, she told the rector, the old man who prayed over my first victim here. The veins in his hands looked like a shattered windshield as he grasped her shoulders. His voice was nasal. "You been working hard here, Mary, and then looking out for your husband and kids. It's a lot. Take a break."

"I don't need a break. Don't you see, there's evil right here in front of us, big as life!" She cast a giant, jagged black shadow against the ashen stones.

"That there is. But it isn't any vampire, honey." He let her go and sunk into a pew. "There's evil up in the mayor's office. There's evil in the housing projects. There's evil in the streets right outside here, plenty a that. I was a choirboy in this church, you know that? And now . . . jeez, I spent forty-two years fighting the evil here, and there's more of it than ever. But you can't give up. Or why are you here? Why are any of us here? Can't get caught up in some monster story and start slinging garlic around when there's people to be fed and clothed." For a moment he looked like an empty husk of a man. I could smell the scent of death on him, even from where I cowered behind the stone baptistery, the shape of a cherub pressing its clammy rump against me. The old priest clutched his side suddenly and gasped with pain.

She looked around for me, because she didn't understand. I've seen hundreds of years of death, but I ached for him as much as she did. But I had the power to deliver him, when the time came. She helped him out to his rectory and I crept off to sleep.

The air got hotter, thick and wet and full. I woke in the evening with my hair matted to my head, blood-scented sweat turning the dust and dirt on my skin to mud, plastering my clothes to me. The next two days, I watched the old man as pain distorted his walk into a stagger. I caught his elbow once when he came close to collapse. He was blind enough with the pain not to see who guided him to the sacristy and settled him into a chair. Or maybe it didn't matter. He didn't believe in what I am. Or didn't care. Or maybe he understood.

I was too hungry. I took an old, insane man with a cancer that blocked his gut and crushed the food back out of him when he tried to eat, leaving him knife-thin except for an uneven, grotesque bulge at the waist where the tumor protruded. Mother Lopreto fed the homeless garlic-filled meals; she hung the church with it, the powerful aroma refreshing after the stench of poverty it disguised.

She found my mark on the corpse, screamed and shrieked and railed against me. She ran through the church, waving a crucifix ahead of her, shouting, "I'll find you, vampire! I'll kill you! These are men, not crumbs! I'll kill you!" Parishioners filing in for Sunday morning service whispered behind their hands.

She got jumpier as the week went on, startled by the rustle of paper or the clink of a beer bottle to the floor. Deep circles cut themselves around her eyes. She stayed in the church all night, awake, waiting, two nights in a row. I hid.

Meanwhile, the rector's walk became more cautious and deliberate, and new lines rippled across his face. I saw him looking into my hiding place, almost pleadingly. I wondered if he knew. I prayed for guidance.

After three nights awake in the church, she fell asleep in a pew just before the noon eucharist. Her hair striped her face. The shadows were deep enough, even in daylight, for me to come out. I sat in the back for the mass. I was the only congregation.

"Thou art . . ." The old man's voice faded almost to silence. "Always to have mercy." I mouthed the words with him. The prayer that told me I was home. He grunted with pain, and crumpled onto the altar. I finished the prayer, then clattered over the marble into the sanctuary.

Tears and sweat streamed off him, staining the crisp white linen. He clutched at me, gasping, his fingers making red trails in my arms. "I beseech thee, oh Lord . . ." he muttered.

I traced a cross on his forehead with his own sweat. Then I pressed my mouth gently to his neck and drained him. He sagged into my arms like a sleeping infant. When I was through,

I set him down gently, arranged his vestments like a blanket on him, and folded his hands into prayer.

I am sorry to see him dead, but I'm happy to have ended his pain, and taken a little bit of him into me.

The diocesan people have come today to decide whether she will stay on and become rector of the parish. They sit in the sun-bright Sunday pews among the congregation of old people in polyester and cotton, and homeless people in dirt and decay. I cower in the dark of the abandoned organ loft, letting the sound of her clear voice, the ragged a cappella hymns, wash over me. The heat is starting to break. The smell of the place is less rancid, less old.

She hasn't forgotten me. She preaches about the myths of the past, the demons that have been forgotten rather than exorcised. Her voice rises, cracks, as she proclaims the need to remember these evil creatures.

I am not evil, I want to cry out. I was made by the same god as you.

But I keep quiet.

They shake their heads, these three wise men from the church's city headquarters. I have won, I can tell. The Lord has given me my place. The Lord provides.

# Blood Atonement

ROBERT M. PRICE

Ever since his conversion a couple of years before, Rich had always tried to believe God for the impossible. But tonight he couldn't help wondering whether "mountain-moving faith" had slipped over the line into fanaticism. For here he was, chilly under the moonlight, watching with embarrassment as Tony and Gabe stood before a weed-grown mausoleum and claimed a peculiar promise: "Lord, you commanded your disciples to 'heal the sick, raise the dead' and we're appropriating that scripture by faith tonight. . . ."

333

What did they believe would happen, Rich wondered guiltily. What did *he*, what *should* he, believe would happen? Even the elders of their charismatic prayer community had not been so sure about this venture, but Tony and Gabe had effectively cut off debate by invoking "the Lord's leading," and now, somehow, here the three of them were.

An hour, at least, had passed, and Rich had begun to be more afraid of the caretaker's reproof than the Lord's, but from the looks of the place, no caretaker had troubled with this corner of the graveyard in a long time. Of course, that's why they'd chosen it. They didn't want to be disturbed, and it didn't make much difference who was in the tomb. It was the test of faith that mattered.

*What was that?* Subtle scratch-scraping—his suddenly pounding heart drowned it out. Yes, definitely—sound. Tony and Gabe had quieted to listen. A rectangle of blackness, a rush of pit-cold air—Lazarus come forth—ye of little faith—moonlight limning a fourth face!

But the shock of wrongness! Dog's fangs in a man's mouth —sting! Warmth, sweet dizziness, falling, black.

There must have been a funeral, or so it seemed to Rich some unknown time later. In fact he dimly recalled hearing a eulogy. "In his faith he proved more mature than many of us who were in years his senior. . . ." Surprisingly his folks must have swallowed their opposition and invited his prayer-group leader, Brother Miller, to handle the service instead of Reverend Hensley from the Methodist Church the whole family had attended until two years ago. And as he thought this, Rich realized he had overheard, from the brink of waking, his own funeral. His eyes opened, dreading whatever sight would greet them. Purple and white flowers lined his field of vision as he stared up through the open casket, his eyes focusing on the high ceiling of the mortuary parlor. No mourners, thank God, were left to see him sit up. And thank God, too, he had not yet been embalmed.

There was a name for this, wasn't there? Catalepsy, or something. . . . Or was there *another* name for it? Rich's hand went up as if by reflex to his neck, just to the side of his Adam's apple, where the undertaker had artfully concealed two punctures. First there was giddy confusion, until an odd sensation shot the truth home like a bolt in a lock: He was hungry, but his stomach had nothing to do with it. It was a hunger he had never imagined feeling, one that some new instinct identified: blood. He needed blood.

Shockingly, amazingly, it was reality. His emotions fled in retreat before an assault they could never hope to meet. Numbly his mind felt the world mightily shift a notch and fall into place. He had felt this way once before, when he was born again. Now as then all things had become new. All bets were off, and he had to come to grips with a new creation, this time a terrible one.

In fact, no one was in evidence in the building, as far as Rich could tell, as he slipped outside and down the street without interference. The moon was full now; that meant he was . . . comatose . . . for a little over a week! The situation demanded that he sit down somewhere and plan, at least figure things out. He stopped in a park, but it was a mistake. He noticed two little girls, still out playing at this hour, but now scampering off home. Didn't their parents care enough to keep them inside, safe from people like . . . him? The thought had begun idly but had ended wounding him, for he realized that looking at the children he had begun to *salivate.*

Rich's self-revulsion wrenched him, then forced to the surface the accusing question he could no longer repress. And though he felt the heavens to be lead, he prayed croakingly, "Father, *why? How?"* His hands lifted in supplication but clenched into claws as if grasping for an answer that had slipped already through his fingers.

It wasn't too long a walk to Brother Miller's house. Rich didn't know what night of the week it was, but someone was sure to be there. If not for one of the weekly gatherings, then for the twenty-four-hour prayer-chain. The large freestanding garage had been made over into a little pine-paneled chapel, and it was this to which Rich headed, the gravel swishing grittily beneath his dragging steps. He was weakening; answers were not all he needed soon. But maybe his brothers and sisters would at least be able to help him with answers.

Someone was there; he heard singing. Suddenly frozen with a chill of sick irony he recognized the chorus: "Up from the grave he arose (he arose!)/With a mighty triumph o'er his foes . . . !" Getting a grip on himself, he knocked on the door—harder till they heard him. Finally someone opened up. Paula peeked through the crack-opened door, looking wary perhaps because of the hour. Her pretty face went blank as the impossible struggled to register. The door closed swiftly, not having been opened wide enough to slam. Rich could hear inside: "But it *is!* It's *Rich!*" A confusion of tongues sounded, and Rich could definitely pick up notes of rising panic. At length one voice, and a sentence ending with ". . . demon!"

The door came open again, and a tangle of galvanized faces stared, but Tony's and Gabe's were not among them. What had they told the rest? Had they ever made it back to the group after that night?

"Brothers and sisters," he pleaded, dropping his eyes from theirs, "you've got to help me with this . . . I'm *not* dead, I'm not alive either . . . God, I don't even know where my soul is!"

*"Do you confess that Jesus Christ came in the flesh?"* barked Brother Miller, as if it were relevant. And then Rich saw why Miller thought it was. This was sort of a password to detect demons, from the Book of First John.

"Wait, you don't understand—this is worse! I'm not possessed . . . I'm . . . a *vampire!"*

"There's no scriptural basis for that! This is like Saul and the Witch of Endor!" Miller assured the now trembling group. "It's a trick of Satan, a counterfeit of the resurrection of believers at the Rapture!" They seemed to believe their leader, but Rich noticed that at the word "vampire," several hands had moved to clasp the crosses hanging from their necks.

He turned and walked back into the darkness that was feeling more and more like home.

A childhood full of Saturday afternoon monster-films brought one question irresistibly to mind: how had the sight of the cross affected him? No burning, no flinching, but grief—great longing grief that against his will he had been cut off from Christ. *Against his will!* The words shook like defiant fists. Yet amid his rage, he felt the pain of love unrequited. But if no explanation presented itself, he still needed guidance. For the lust for blood was now growing, becoming nearly irresistible. Even if he *was* damned himself, he just couldn't take others with him.

He mustn't spread this . . . infection. But soon, he feared, he would lose control and commit terrible sin.

The silence of the small-town night made his bewildered mind an echo chamber, as verses of scripture bounced and ricocheted within. He thought first of Job, then of Paul with his "thorn in the flesh." And the more he thought about it, the more sense that verse seemed to make.

Rich stopped his aimless walking, gained his bearings, and headed for the cemetery. There were still a few hours of darkness left by the time he found a familiar-looking mausoleum. With what he had in mind to do, he would need help, and he knew of no one else likely to give it. He began to pound on the cold stone slab.

The search for Rich's body had begun immediately, of course, for its absence was discovered the next morning. And the police were not long in finding it. The secretary at the Methodist Church was the one to call in the frantic report. Some madman had desecrated both the poor boy's corpse and the sanctuary, it seemed, though God alone knew who or why. When the police came, they found that the life-size mahogany cross had been taken down (the wires cut), and the body, quite simply, nailed onto it. As the officers, faces contorted in disgust, worked to remove the nails without doing further damage to the now fragile corpse, Reverend Hensley noticed that whoever had done this had not quite known his Bible. For besides those in the hands and feet, there was an extra spike—through the heart.

# Back in the World

### BILLIE SUE MOSIMAN

t had been raining for two weeks, thunder booming through the rough gray stone of the walls of the castle, causing damp to seep into all the draperies and bed clothes, even into the wool carpets so that they stank like soaked sheep. The relentlessness of the wet weather and the resultant boredom of being caged indoors drove Count Noblenski one night to the dungeon rooms deep in the castle's heart. He had heard from his grandfather that all the treasures of the family were kept there; that if he ever found himself financially strapped all he need do was to loot the dungeon to save himself.

The Count was not facing bankruptcy except of the mind. He had read books in the library until his eyes ached and his brain nattered like a child intent on misbehavior. He had no need to sell the family treasures, though he thought this was as good a time as any to paw through them and take a tally. Just in case he faced misfortune in the future.

He carried the lamp carefully so as to avoid staining his fingers with the foul-smelling oil. He detested anything on his hands beyond water for washing them clean. Just the thought of the slick, pungent oil accidentally covering his hands made him cringe. If he made a mistake and soiled his hands, he'd have to retreat to the wash basin and put off the foray till some other time.

Shadows danced upon the walls grotesquely as he wove his way slowly down the winding stairs. He had the keys on a metal ring for the door; now if only he could get them without spilling the lantern. He grunted, reaching inside his long woolen skirt for the key ring and the sound echoed into whispers that faded up the stairwell.

Once the key was inserted, the door gave with a slight push, creaking back on massive hinges inset into the gray stones. The Count shined the lantern light before him, moving gently forward into the cavernous room. Ah! Why had he not investigated this hoard before now? There were chests and caskets, wooden crates, portraits, and landscape paintings stacked against the wall, intricately carved statues, exotically colored vases and bowls, books and manuscripts, folded squares of cloth with silver and gold and aquamarine threads woven through them. It was a pirate's paradise, a museum of valuables. Pots and crocks, rugs and canvas murals, silver wine cups, golden trays. And a mirror.

A most enchanting mirror.

Count Noblenski stepped over rolled carpets and navigated between laden tables of objects until he neared the mirror. He thrust out the lamp and leaned in close, not to look at his image, but to study the multijeweled inlay that decorated the mirror's frame. The mirror was beauty incarnate. Sublime. A masterpiece of craftsmanship. Looking closer, he saw there was an inscription bracketed by large emeralds across the top of the frame. But he could not read it. It was in a language he did not recognize. Surely this was a foreign object, for nothing like this had ever been created in the whole kingdom of Lithuania in any century.

He must have it. Nearby, so that he could admire it. Perhaps if he took it upstairs to the library with him. . . .

His gaze now slid slowly across the mirror's surface and halted while he stared into his own dark, liquid brown eyes. Who was he? Had he ever been a nobleman or was he truly a mere man of the earth, muscled and dirty and strong as ten oxen? Was there a cloak in the room so that he might don it and feel less naked?

He tore his gaze from those questioning eyes and found he was breathing quickly, as if he'd run all the way down the stairs. He'd *never* wondered who he was before. Had he just wondered that? Why, he was Count Edward Noblenski, how could he not know, even for a moment, who he was? And why would he wish for a cloak?

He shuddered at the stray odd thoughts that had possessed him, but felt no less obliged to carry the exquisite mirror with him up the stairs and away from its obscurity in the dungeon. He set down the lamp and grasped the mirror in both hands. A shock tingled his fingers just for a second and then he was smiling and tucking the treasure beneath his left arm. He took up the lamp again and turned, not even bothering to explore the rest of the treasures piled up in the room. He didn't seem to care for them, not care for them at all. Nothing could come close to rivaling this mirror, could it? Nothing might divert his attention from the tedious weather but the mirror, this being something he knew only in an abstract way, but knew nonetheless.

He hurried out, leaving the door unlocked behind him, and took the stairs in such haste that he spilled a bit of the oil from the lamp over his knuckles. That night he went to bed without even washing up. The stink of the oil never got through to his rattled senses. He was too caught up in admiring the mirror once he had it in the library to care one way or the other about the condition of his hands.

The next day he spent at the table in the library sitting before the jewel-encrusted mirror. When the servants brought him meals, he waved them away with his hand. He must have eaten and drank, but he did not know what he consumed or when. He must have attended to his bodily functions and slept and walked to exercise his stiff limbs, but he had no memory of any of that.

For the eyes in the mirror talked to him, a mesmerizing stream of revelatory conversation that filled his mind and shut out the world.

The beast in the mirror—for he *was* a beast, that was undeniable though the knowledge held no fear for Count Noblenski —told him of a tale of life that lasted over a millennium. Of freedom to fly high over the rooftops and even into the bellies of clouds. Of deep, restful sleep only the dead receive. Of conquering men and making them cower like dogs in a gutter. Of power. Of glory. Of everlasting vigor and appetite insatiable.

"What are you doing there?" the Count asked, meaning inside the mirror or behind it or within its very fiber.

Then came another tale of green, virulent jealousy, of a rival, and of a curse made by someone who enjoyed the secret of the gods to imprison evil men.

"He wanted to be like you," the Count said, understanding all. Had not peasants wanted to run him through with swords, fight him for his castle and holdings, rise up against him when he made them pay their levies they owed a lord?

"How will you be free again?" the Count asked, running

his fingers over the glittering stones held fast in the thick metal frame. With these jewels he could buy his own kingdom.

When the imprisoned beast answered his question, Count Noblenski lost all his senses and rose up from the table and took up the heavy ornate mirror and raised it high over his head.

In his mind all he could hear was the voice thundering louder than the thunder of God, demanding that he BREAK THE MIRROR. RELEASE ME, AND I WILL BE YOUR SLAVE was a promise that caused him to throw the mirror up and away with such force that he expelled all his breath in doing so.

The mirror came crashing to the stone floor and shattered into a thousand pieces. At that inopportune time one of the servants entered the library and let out a truncated scream at seeing the terrible damage.

Count Noblenski turned and shouted, "What do you want? Why do you bother me?"

The servant, an elderly man who had served his young master all his life and who had never been spoken to this way before said, "Sire, you have a caller at the door."

"Well, who is it? Tell them I'm not receiving visitors. Tell them I'm ill, that I . . . that I have a fever."

"But it is Count Dracula, sire, and he said you sent for him over a fortnight ago. He's come all this way. . . ."

"Oh, let him in then, hurry and be out of my sight, you talk too much and your voice is too loud."

The servant bowed his way out into the wide hall and brought back the visitor, then closed the door on the two men.

"To be honest, I don't remember sending for you," Count Noblenski said, scowling at the other man.

"Your messenger insisted I come quickly, but the rains delayed me. You *are* Count Edward Noblenski, aren't you?"

From the darkness near the dead cold hearth stepped a stranger. He came forth rumbling low in his throat and moving so quickly he appeared to be a wraith. Both Noblenski and Dracula started, their faces freezing in a rictus of horror as they lay eyes on the demon who pressed down upon them.

"*I* sent for you," roared the beastly human, leaping forward through the air the way a cat would, landing on his feet in front of Count Dracula. "This small, weak-minded nobleman chattered on incessantly, telling me all that he knew for days on end.

Your name came up as a man who has fought battles and taken your enemies heads to impale on spikes. I would be YOU. I would give you the gift that hasn't walked the earth for a thousand years."

Dracula drew back, his fear so great he trembled and stumbled like an idiot child. Armies and hordes had not frightened him, battle stirred not a single string of anxiety in his soul, but this monster before him made his spine weaken and his knees rattle together like bones in a cup.

"What about *me!*" cried Count Noblenski. "I was the one who discovered the mirror and released you from your prison of glass."

The beast paused now that he had Dracula in his arms and nearly to the point of entering into him. He said over his shoulder, "You." And his voice rose, thundering against the beams of the great room. "You we will have for our supper, fair nobleman. We have a long journey to make to our homeland and will need the sacrifice of your blood. You shall be privileged. You shall be *first.*"

Count Noblenski watched, hypnotized, while the beast from the mirror shifted and, like a veil of smoke, entered into his victim.

When Dracula came to him, his fangs bared, Noblenski hung his head in shame at how small and petty and ignorant he was, at how innocent and trusting and *greedy* he had been to wish to converse with a demon from hell. He wept while he gave up his life. Around his slippered feet gleamed the jewels from the mirror's frame and shards of the mirror itself, winking at him good-bye.

The curse was broken. The plague of blood was once again loose upon the unsuspecting world.

# The King's Return

## CHARLES GAROFALO

A sharpened wooden stake. Not really a good weapon, but the only thing I could bring that might possibly be of any use if the tales I'd heard proved true. Shoving it in my belt like a sword, I entered the burial vault.

*Hardly the sort of resting place that befits a great king,* I thought. A tiny stone mausoleum built outside the hallowed grounds of the graveyard. The priests had not forgiven the king's massacre of their numbers. They prayed for his soul and built him a tomb, but not in the holy grounds. Too afraid his presence would disturb the rest of the ones he'd sent to their graves ahead of him.

And if the stories I'd heard were true, the prayers hadn't done much good either. I doubted they would. Prince Vlad's deeds would have put him well beyond the power of any prayer.

The door was sealed, but it took no great effort to force it. I saw little in the bare tomb. Nothing jumped out at me, no fanged, emaciated specter with flaming eyes; no horde of rats; no pillar of smothering fog. Just an empty room, with a stone coffin in one corner, and dust and cobwebs covering all. Even the stench was faint.

Even so, I was frightened. In that coffin lay what was left of Prince Vlad IV . . . Prince Vlad the Impaler, called Dracula: "Son of the Devil." All who survived remembered his grisly reign. He could have been Wallachia's greatest hero, turning back the Turks and holding off the German knights . . . but he'd then turned on his own subjects and treated them no more kindly than he had the enemy. The reigns of the old Roman Emperors could have been no madder or bloodier than his. He impaled the thieves and burned the beggars alive, after squandering his kingdom's wealth and leaving so many of his subjects with no other way to eat than to steal or beg. Torturing unchaste women to death when he kept a dozen mistresses himself. When the chance of peace with the Turks came Prince Vlad's way, he destroyed it by demanding the Turkish ambassadors doff their turbans to him, then nailing them to their heads when they refused.

I steeled myself as I lifted off the stone lid of the coffin, preparing to face this devil in human form.

And stared down at a mouldering, headless skeleton in a tattered robe.

Prince Vlad Dracula had not risen as a vampire. He had been hacked to pieces by his own men at the end, and his body then captured by the Turks and beheaded. Prince Vlad had never risen as a vampire, even though his evil was still enough to drive the holiness from the sepulcher. Prince Vlad stewed in Hell, or at best Purgatory, his skull was a trophy in the Sultan's palace, and the rest of his bones lay here.

Hurrying, for I had little time, I used the heavy wooden stake to smash the bones into fragments, sweeping them into the leather bag I'd brought for just that purpose. I swept every scrap into the bag. On one of the skeleton's fingers I found a heavy gold ring with a royal crest on it, no doubt left on the corpse for fear it might carry a curse. I had no fear of curses, and transfered it to my own hand.

I heard the sounds of my pursuers growing louder outside. Leaving the stone lid off Dracula's sarcophagus. I strode from the tomb to face them.

There were even more people in the mob than I expected. Every other man in it seemed to be carrying a cross. There were a few soldiers with heavy swords in the mob, as well as the mob of farmers with axes and pitchforks. The village priest headed the mob, chanting the prayers to his God that made my head feel like it was going to explode.

Hiding the bag under my cape, pretending the sight of the crosses and sound of the prayers did not make my soul flinch within me. I faced the mob, forcing my face into that arrogant sneer that I remembered so well.

"Dogs!" I shouted at the mob. "Would you take arms against your Prince, appointed you by God in the Highest?"

His name burned my toungue, but I kept the pain from my face as the crowd stopped short. There were stares of disbelief. Despite the crosses, despite numbers that could have brought down even one such as me, the entire mob stopped in its tracks.

Many of the men shuddered and crossed themselves, backing away from me. The priest, who had up until now showed a courage the real Vlad would never have attributed to a holy man, turned pale at the sight of me.

"Prince Vlad?" gulped a soldier, disbelieving.

"Yes, your Prince! Returned from the dead, so that fools like you do not ruin the country I shed my blood to save. You ungrateful pigs! I've returned to protect you again, and you dare raise weapons against me. Have you forgotten the lessons I worked so hard to instill in you?"

They hadn't. They remembered too well the prince who impaled peasants he felt hadn't worked hard enough; burned children for being illegitimate; tortured people to death for a single wrong word or choice. Even four years after his death, they were still scared of Vlad the Impaler. As I walked out into the mob, they all drew back in terror. Nobody raised a cross or weapon against me, no one accused me of being a vampire, there was nobody even saying I was a faker and not Prince Vlad risen from the dead.

I could have changed my form and escaped, but I didn't bother. Instead, with the arrogance of the dead Prince himself, I walked right through the crowd. It split before me like the sea before Moses.

After I'd gotten through the mob, I turned to face them again. They were still too frightened to do anything to me.

"Remember, men of Wallachia!" I warned. "Your rightful Prince has returned to you, and he will be watching you as he did in the past."

I turned on my heel and left them, shuddering and staring. As I moved away, a clamor of talk began, but no one pursued me. I knew soon some brave fool would check the tomb and find the empty coffin, and the word would spread.

That day I would rest, and the following night I would return to my native Transylvania. Despite everything, I still loved my homeland. After all, I had died for it, impaled with the other captured boyars for "treason" . . . that is, daring to defend my Prince's lands against Vlad of Wallachia's false claims. Death was not enough; the Prince had denied us all last rites or a Christian burial. I still don't understand why only I rose as undead, considering the fate we all shared, but the ways of God and Satan are still both beyond me.

But my trick had saved me, and I would remember it, perhaps use it again on occasion. After the rule they'd endured, there wouldn't be a man in Romania a thousand times more frightened of Prince Vlad Dracula than of *any* vampire.

# Jack in the Box

RAMSEY CAMPBELL

When you awake they've turned out the lights in your cell. It feels as if the padded walls have closed in; if you moved you'd touch them. They want you to scream and plead, but you won't. You'll lie there until they have to turn the lights on.

You're glad and proud of what you did. You remember the red spilling from the nurse's throat. You never liked his eyes, they were always watching and ready to tell you that he knew what you were. The others pretended it was their job not to be shocked by what you did before they brought you here, but he never pretended. You can see the red streaming down his shirt and gluing it to his skin. You relax into memory. It's been so long.

You can go back as far as you like, but you can't remember a time when you didn't kill. Although you can't remember much before you were a soldier, and even that period seems to consist of explosive flashes of dead faces and twisted metal and limbs—until you reach the point where a pattern begins.

It was at the edge of the jungle. You were stumbling along, following the tracks of a tank. You'd been shot in the head, but your legs were still plodding. There was a luminous crimson sky and against it trees stood splintered and charred. Suddenly, among the ruts, you thought you saw a red reflection of the sky. You stood swaying, trying to make it out, and eventually, mixed with the churned earth and muddy stubble of grass, you saw enough of an outline to realize it was a man. The pattern of the tank-tracks was etched on him in red. You leaned closer, reaching toward the red, and maybe that's when it began.

You wonder why you can't hear any sounds outside your cell, not even the savage murmur of the tropical night that always filters in. Your head turns a little, searching, but your memory has regained its hold. When the army discharged you and paid your meager wage you returned to the city. The city doctor did his best for your wound, so he said, but shook his head and recommended you to see someone else who knew more about the effects. In the end you didn't. You were too confused by how the city and the people looked to you.

It was the red that confused you. The city was full of red, it was everywhere you looked. But it wasn't real red, not the red that trickled tantalizingly on the very edge of your mind. And the people were wrong, they looked unreal, like zombies. You knew that if zombies were real they never came into the city by day, they stayed in the jungle. That wasn't what was wrong with the people. You felt as if the most important part of them was hidden.

One evening as you came into your room you caught sight of a red glint within the wall. It was a fragment of the sunset trapped for a moment in a crack. At once you knew how to satisfy the yawning frustration you'd felt ever since your return to the city, knew how to complete the sunset: you must answer it in red. You cut your forearm with a razor. The red responded, but it hurt, and that was wrong. It hadn't hurt before.

You knew what to do, but you had to make yourself. Each evening when the sky was crimson you went out, the razor folded in your pocket. The tropical evening settled heavily about you, and the shadows in which you hid were warm, but each time you soothed yourself into courage and surged forth from ambush you heard witnesses approaching. It was worse than a jungle ambush, because here your people wouldn't praise you if you succeeded, they'd arrest you.

You went further from home, into the poorest areas. There was so much death here you had the cunning notion that what you did might pass almost unremarked. At last, one evening when the crimson light was just about to drain away into the ground, you saw a young girl hurrying toward you down an alley. Her eyes were specks of reflected red, making her shadowy face into a mask which you didn't need to see as human. It was as if she were a receptacle for the last drops of red. She was almost upon you when you swooped, your hands grubbing in your pockets for the razor. You'd left it at home. But now you were pressing her face into your chest to stifle her cries, and even without the razor you managed to make the red come.

After that it was easier. You knew now why you'd been confused when you looked at people: because all the time you had been seeing them as pipes full of red, and you couldn't think why. You could look at them without wanting to tap them except when the sky was calling, and then you made sure you were in the slums. During the day you stayed in your room with the curtains drawn, because outside you might have been stopped for questioning. When you went out you didn't take the razor, which might have betrayed you if you had ever been searched. You never were, although the slum people were complaining that a monster was preying on them. Most of what they said wasn't believed. They admitted believing in zombies, which city people never did.

You can't remember most of the people you caught. They were only shadows making stifled noises, moans, squeaks, the final desperate gargle. The older ones often seemed dry, children were surprisingly full. You do remember the last one, an old man who giggled and squirmed as he drained. You were still watching the glistening stream when men came at you from both ends of the alley. When you tried to get up they battered you down and dragged you away.

That was how you came here. You're becoming restless, and your mind is nagging, nagging: They would never turn out the light in your cell, because then they couldn't watch you. But your frustration is urging you on, it wants you to see the most recent and most vivid red: the nurse's.

He was from the slums. You could tell that by the way he talked. Perhaps you'd caught one of his relatives, and that was why he tried to kill you. You never saw that in his eyes, only a horror of what you were. But just at dawn you saw him tiptoe into your cell, carrying a straitjacket. No doubt he expected you to be asleep. You were tired, and he managed to restrain you before you saw the sharply pointed bulge beneath his jacket. But you still remembered how to bite, and you tore his neck. As he fumbled, gurgling into the corridor the sunlight through the window beyond your door streamed around his body, and two spikes of light pierced your eyes. There your memory ends.

You're half satisfied, half excited, and frustrated by the weight of the dark. You feel penned. Then you realize that you can't feel the straitjacket. They may have left you in darkness but at least they've freed you of that. Roused by your memories, you stretch before getting up to stalk around your cell, and your hand touches a wall. You recoil, then you snarl at yourself and move your other arm. It touches a wall too.

All of a sudden you're roaring with rage and fear and arching your body as if it can burst you out of your prison, because you know that what has been pressing down on your face isn't only darkness. You aren't in your cell at all. You're in a coffin.

At last you manage to calm yourself, and lie throbbing. You try to think clearly, as you had to in the jungle and afterward in the slums. You're sure the nurse has done this to you. The gap in your memory feels like a blackout. Perhaps he succeeded in poisoning you. He must have persuaded the others that you were dead. In this climate you'd be buried quickly.

You throw yourself against the lid of the coffin, inches above your face. You hear earth trickling faintly by outside for a moment, then there's nothing but the padded silence. You tear at the cheap padding until you feel it rip. A nail breaks and pain flares like a distant beacon. It gives you a sense of yourself again, and you try to plan.

You manage to force your arms back until the palms of your hands are pressed against the lid almost above your shoulders. Already your forearms are beginning to ache, and your upper arms crush your ribs. Your face feels as if it's trapped in a dwindling pocket of air by your limbs. Before panic can reach you, you're thinking of how the nurse's face will look when you reach him. You begin to push against the lid.

The first time there's the merest stirring of earth outside the coffin. You rest your cramped arms for a moment and push again. There's nothing. You don't know how many coffin nails nor what weight of earth you're trying to shift. You thrust your elbows against the sides of the coffin and heave. Nothing except the silent pendulous darkness. If the lid rather than the nails gives way, the whole weight of earth above will pour in on top of you. Pain kindles your arms, and you lever while they shudder with the effort.

Then the worst thing you could have imagined happens. The weight above you increases. You feel it at the height of your effort, and you're sure it isn't the weakening of your arms. For a moment you think it's the nurse, standing on your grave in case you try to escape. Then another idea occurs to you. It may be a delirious hope, but you force yourself to rest your arms on your chest, crossed and pulsing. You listen.

For a long time you can't hear anything. You resist the urge to test the weight on the lid again, because by now you've forgotten how it felt before. You don't even know whether you would be able to hear what you're listening for. The darkness thumbs your eyes, and false light swirls on them.

Then you think you heard it. You strain all your nerves, and after a stretched time during which you seem to hang poised on darkness it comes again: a faint distant scraping in the earth above you. You have a last nightmare glimpse of the nurse digging down to make sure you're dead. But you know who are the only people who dig up fresh corpses. They've come to make you into a zombie. You lie waiting, massaging your cramped arms and tensing yourself. Will they be surprised enough not to use their spades as weapons?

When you hear metal strike the lid you're ready. But when the first nails pull free and the lid creaks up, light pours in with a sifting of earth. For a second you freeze, trapped. But it isn't daylight, only torchlight. The gap in your memory was daylight, or perhaps it was death. To you they've become the same. You realize that one sound you haven't been hearing is the sound of your own breath.

You leap up and pull one of the startled men into the coffin until you're ready for him. Then you clasp the other to you, unlipping your fangs, thinking: red.

# Mouths

## STEVE RASNIC TEM

**S**ometimes the mouths reminded him of his wife's mouth: alternately seductive and angry. When he still had a wife. Before the mouths had eaten up the very idea of companionship.

Sometimes the mouths reminded him of his daughter's mouth: pouting, hungry, always seeking food. When he still had a daughter. Before the mouths had eaten his future.

Sometimes the mouths seemed to be speaking his name. But then they devoured his name, and he had no idea what to call himself.

He'd first been alerted to their presence by the all-pervasive fatigue. Each morning he would awaken later and later, despite multiple alarms and wake-up services and angry calls from work. And after the loss of his job, when punctuality no longer seemed an imperative, he didn't even attempt a morning schedule.

When he finally did awaken, and managed to stagger the dozen steps or so into his small bathroom, he never failed to be shocked by his well-worn appearance in the mirror, or by the countless little love bites and bruises—a scattered few haloed in blood—decorating both the visible and invisible aspects of his body.

"It's a hungry world out there," his grandmother once said, after his grandfather had lost his business, the house, everything. "You have to be careful of it, else it'll eat you alive."

*It's a hungry world in here, as well, Grandmother,* he might have told her, if the mouths hadn't already eaten her alive.

"Daddy, spend time with me," his daughter would say, and how could he explain to a little girl how the mouths had eaten all of his time?

"What is it, honey, what are you thinking about? Where is your mind this morning?"

He looked across at his wife, who sat with both hands clutching her coffee cup. A huge-lipped mouth perched on her shoulder, dripping blood down onto her white blouse. She set the cup down shakily. "You always seem to be somewhere else," she said, as the mouth surreptitiously took a huge bite out of her donut. Blood splattered across the bright yellow surface of the kitchen table, but she didn't appear to notice.

"I'm here," he said softly, "I'm here where I've always been." Then he turned away so he didn't have to see the mouth grinning at him.

"Well . . ." She set the mangled donut back onto her saucer. "You could have fooled me."

*Could have fooled me* . . . the mouth echoed, lips smudged with sugar, but she didn't seem to hear.

The mouths devoured the next day, and the day after that. He woke up one morning alone, a note from his wife on the kitchen table. But he could not decipher the note: the mouths had eaten too many of the words. He went to her closet and looked inside: the mouths had eaten most of her clothes, leaving behind only the less fashionable dresses. He went into his daughter's bedroom to tell his child that her mommy was gone, that the mouths had finally eaten her all up, and quickly discovered that the mouths had eaten most of her clothes as well, along with her best toys. A few dolls remained scattered on the floor, miscellaneous pieces chewed off. There was no sign of his daughter.

He went into the living room and flopped down into his chair. He struggled to pull the remote control out of a bloody mouth, finally succeeding and sending the mouth flying across the room, where it hit the wall and stuck with a loud, lip-smacking sound. He punched his way through the channels until the image of a newscaster in a tweed coat stopped him—the coat was too heavy for this time of year, but still pulled tightly around the neck. Mouths leapt and crawled about the newscaster, who winced and avoided them with an agitated dance while still in his seat, trying to perform his job.

"All life feeds on life," the man said, shoving away a mouth that was attempting to French kiss him. "That is an irrevocable law of nature. We *feed* on each other, make a feast of one another's love, excitement, despair. It's a natural outcome of our solitary conditions. But some people!" he shouted, as several mouths seized the opportunity of a sudden gap in his collar and dived in, writhing beneath the coat, eating their way both inside and out. "Some people go too far!" The newsman disappeared beneath the set as the camera lens was splattered by shredded tweed and blood. He turned off the set.

The next morning the boredom reached an intolerable level so he got into his car to go looking for a new job. The mouths were in the car waiting for him. One of them had a cat's leg between its lips, the fur and meat mostly gnawed away but with just enough remaining traces of black and white that he recognized it as a leg from the family cat, now missing more than four days (perhaps much more, as so many days had been so neatly digested leaving no trace). With his rolled-up newspaper he knocked lips and cat leg together out the car window.

The others in the company lobby had mouths attached to them at various places: hanging with clenched teeth from a tie, kissing the thin cloth covering a shoulderblade, licking the underside of a bearded chin. He tried to ignore them. But then a man stood up, screaming, and ran down the hall, blood streaming from a gaping hole in his left buttock.

"Mr. Smith?" The woman had huge, pouty lips. She was too close to him; he had a sudden terror that she would suddenly start kissing him. "Mr. Reynolds's will see you now."

He stood up and followed the woman into Mr. Reynolds's office. Smith . . . he supposed that now he had his name back, but something was still wrong with that. He thought that perhaps he had once had a longer name. Smithfield. Smithers. Smith and Wesson. Something like that.

"Smith!" Reynolds stood and extended a hand with teeth. Smith took it reluctantly, wincing as it bit through his palm. "Glad to meet you! *Mighty* glad! We could always use a good man like you!"

"How do you know?"

Reynolds frowned. "I'm afraid I don't get you, pardner."

"I mean how do you know I'm a good man?"

Reynolds opened his mouth into a grin spreading wider and wider until he was showing four sets of teeth. "Why, I can *smell* it, boy!" Then he leaned over and kissed Smith wetly before beginning to feed.

S. wandered the beach for days. He had many parts missing, but he could not remember their names and he had lost the memory of their appearances. The mouths had come out of the dark water and were waiting for him at the shore line. They shifted about restlessly as S. strolled near them, poked at them with driftwood, examined them, looking for ones he might know: his wife's, his daughter's, his parents', long dead but their mouths remembered with fondness.

Her lips had only a trace of substance left, and so floated with but a hint of breeze. He leaned close and said, "I love you," even knowing they might attack. He closed his eyes and pushed his own mouth forward, acutely aware now of the thin line separating a kiss from a bite.

# The Blood Ran Out

## Michael A. Arnzen

The blood ran out from the ungourmet gash, the usual gnawed neck, the unpretty wound. It streamed, ran, hurried as if each drop was fleeing from his dry green tongue for the sanctuary of soil beneath the body—first fast then madly escaping as the heart inside his victim thrashed its mighty self for survival—then slow, too slow, as it trickled, dribbled, gave up—and as he lapped he tried not to look, he tried not to see, tried not to forget the memory of himself long ago as he tearlessly cried and died the first time. He clenched his eyes tight to bring stars of new blood to his eternal inner night. He fingered his victim's wound gingerly, spreading its rough edges like sticky chapped lips for a kiss, then brought the wet tip of his finger to his own neck, lubricating the ancient cut, feeling the similar wound there—almost alive as he swallowed—reading the Braille of his flesh bitten long ago for the imprinted memory there of his first time when . . .

the blood ran out from his neck and he couldn't stop it no matter how hard he struggled with the thing chewing into his voice box—the ever-crunching jaws biting through his shaking fingers, his palms, his wrists . . . everything he had to try to stop the bleeding and the thing that simply sucked, sucked, sucked his life away, his life away, his life away into this new imitation of life with the first dusk, believing he had awakened from a terrible daydream, then remembering the struggle with death's darkness, imagining this might be heaven after all until the hunger, hunger, hunger in not so much his stomach but his soul sucked so far inside-out that now he was the swirling vortex of confusion, now he was the one who sucked, took, fed on nature's fluid return, becoming not life but simply a living hunger, a hunger, hungry . . .

The blood ran out from between his lips, he was choking on it, choking on his memories too, pressing his wound and trying to swallow life too fast—and he quickly realized that others had gathered around him—at least ten other hungry souls just like him—crowding out his peaceful memories with their incessant quest for food—wrestling with limbs, writhing naked in the soil around him as they fought over his kill—starving animals trying to yank even him out of the way with their mouths and sharp fingers, as if he could feel pain—their voices growling in the dark as they fed on the remnants of the dissipating soul he'd swallowed—their gleaming green mouths snarling and thrashing on the flesh he'd already nearly emptied himself. Again he tearlessly cried as the others parasited his kill—licking the bottom of this barrel of flesh he had already drained. These others weren't just stealing his meat—they were stealing a part of him, what little he had and was, too. They were all so hungry. And he could sense others out there in the night, rushing toward this empty field where he had minutes ago happened upon the first real human he'd seen in months, at first thinking the smell of fresh sweat and the hot thump thump thumping he felt in the distance were merely figments of his imagination, a mirage of a meal in the hunger of his empty void that had sucked so long on nothing but darkness that he had taken to animals and insects and even they were hard to come by anymore and so he pounced on his imaginary human feast like a dreamer rapes a pillow in dreams—because he needs to know if it's real—if *he's* real—but this time he was not the only one dreaming of food—far from it —there was nothing anymore but crying, lost, and empty, hungry souls around him—a nauseating universe of dizzy dark mirrors—and he was so surprised that this one lunging and desperate bite hit home—that his imaginary vision was *real*—that his teeth had sunken into real flesh, real blood, and as his hunger subsided to pulsing satisfaction he did not stop the gluttony he did not stop to rest he did not stop feeding as the others tore free his limbs—then his *torso*—to make room for their orgy of snouts and . . .

the blood ran out from the back of his throat—tongues reaming the open hole on the underside of his gutted neck. He knew full well he was decapitated but still eating, chewing, biting, teeth clamped on the body to hold on—a vortex feeding the other vortexes—an ever-open mouth feeding other mouths—sucking, sucking, sucking as the blood ran out ran out ran out—because he knew—as did the growing mountain of others chewing their way into the back of his brain—that this could be the last time for all of them—and as he himself was eaten he ate he ate he ate because this could very well be the night

the blood ran out for good.

# The Last Victim

## Jeff Gelb

**M**organ Webb ran for his life through the dusk-darkened back alleys of Los Angeles. The blood he'd drank just minutes ago was pounding like wildfire through his heart and arteries.

He looked over his shoulder and tripped over a recycling bin heavy with newspapers. He stopped to catch his breath, watching and listening for the police. For the moment, they were nowhere to be found.

He allowed himself the luxury of letting his heart calm down so that the foreign blood in his system could settle. It was making him giddy—had his last victim been drunk? It seemed so.

When he'd accosted her in the hospital parking garage, she'd offered little struggle. He'd chosen her purposely—from centuries of experience, he'd found women to be less strong than men, less able to fight him off.

He'd sunk his fangs into her throbbing neck and drank his fill, instantly feeling the effects of her blood in his system. He'd become dizzy for a moment, then continued drinking as his victim had fainted, apparently in fright. When he was done and she was dry, he tossed her to the cement floor like an empty candy wrapper. He began to slink away when a parking attendant spotted the woman's body.

Webb had taken off at a gallop with which the overweight attendant could not begin to keep pace. Within moments Webb was out of the garage and running up back alleyways, behind restaurants and hotels, where garbage cans nauseated him with their contents, ripening in the summer heat.

His apartment was only a mile away. Usually he could have made it in under five minutes. But he was feeling decidedly strange. Maybe it was nerves—this was the closest he'd come to being caught in at least a decade.

He'd gotten sloppy, he admitted to himself. He never should have chosen a victim so close to his home. But he'd gotten lazy these past few weeks, and cocky. He'd come to believe the L.A. cops were too busy with the riots, the fires, the gangs, and the earthquakes to chase after the likes of him. And till tonight, he'd been right. So he'd decided to take a victim close to home, the way normal people might go to the neighborhood fast food restaurant for a quick bite before a movie.

Webb brushed himself off as he heard shouts behind him. The cops were rounding a corner at full clip and yelling for him to stop. Their guns were drawn. Webb began to run again, searching for places to hide, fearing he could not outrun them and reach his apartment.

He spotted a narrow walkway between two apartment buildings. He ran for it and grazed his skin on one of the building's rough brick exteriors as he ran toward the end of the walkway.

The sun had set half an hour ago, so he had to watch his step carefully lest he fall again. His attention diverted, he ran out from between the buildings and straight into the arms of a police officer, who slammed a fist into his nose, breaking it instantly.

Webb gasped in pain, eyes tearing and obscuring his vision. He struck blindly at the officer, who was yelling for backup. Webb pounded his fist into the man's face, and continued pounding until the man stopped making any sounds, until his face was incapable of speech.

Letting the cop drop to the ground, Webb looked around to see other officers running toward him, less than a hundred yards away. He ran down the street, nose bleeding freely into his open, gasping mouth. His sense of smell gone, he was unable to taste his own blood.

Breathing through his mouth, he spotted the bright lights of a carnival a few blocks away in a small city park. He ran toward it, knowing he could lose his pursuers in the crowd. He smiled, certain he would live to drink blood again.

He ran between two large canvas tents, bending under ropes that were apparently to keep nonpaying customers from entering the carnival grounds. He slowed his pace to a brisk walk as he entered the noisy mélange of hundreds of people who were milling about dozens of booths.

Webb wondered absently about the lack of a midway and rides. He assumed he had snuck into the food booth area of the carnival. He looked around but saw no cops following him.

Wiping at his bleeding nose, he felt exhausted, energy totally drained, in almost desperate need of a good day's sleep. He needed a sugar rush. Something to keep him going until he reached his apartment, where he could hide and revive his energy. He turned to the closest booth and ordered an ice cream cone.

The vendor, a pimply-faced girl of no more than sixteen, smiled a mouthful of braces at him as she handed him the cone and took his dollar bill. He studied the throbbing vein in her neck for a moment while he claimed the cone, thinking of how good, how enriching and enlivening her virgin blood would taste right now.

He downed the ice cream in three large gulps, glad for its coolness in his burning, dry throat. Suddenly, his stomach flip-flopped and he felt the most intense heartburn of his centuries-long life. What the hell was going on?

He bent over double in pain, gasping for air and vomiting simultaneously. As he arose, still in a daze, he felt hands on his shoulder, then handcuffs clicking his wrists together behind his back. Before he could put up any struggle, his wrists and ankles were bound by silver cuffs, the precious metal intensifying the pain he was already feeling throughout his body. He groaned in agony as the cops led him through the crowded carnival toward one of their cruisers.

He couldn't understand what had overcome him—first the exhaustion, then the nausea. He felt as weak as a baby. Then he saw the slapping canvas sign above his head and knew why there were no rides at this carnival. His broken nose had betrayed him with its inability to smell the danger. The sign, flapping in the summer night's breeze, read:

FIRST ANNUAL LOS ANGELES GARLIC FESTIVAL

As he passed out, he realized he had eaten an entire garlic ice cream cone.

He awoke in a tiny, dark jail cell. He tried the bars but still felt no strength. The garlic was still coursing through his system. And there was something else, something that rushed through his veins painfully, making him twitch involuntarily as if his arteries were being pulled by an invisible puppetmaster.

Before he could dwell further on how his body was rebelling, he recognized the cop who had cuffed him heading down the hall toward him.

"You killed her, you know," the cop said derisively. He stood in front of Webb's cell, glowering at the vampire. "Drained her of her blood, you freak. You're gonna pay, though." He laughed humorlessly. "With your so-called eternal life."

Webb sneered at the cop. "Smarter men than you have tried killing me for centuries. What makes you think you're going to be the lucky one?"

The cop spat at him. Webb growled and wiped it off his cheek.

"Because this time, you killed yourself," the officer said. "When you chose Mrs. Blake as your victim—your last victim. She was returning from the hospital, where she was getting blood transfusions. It wasn't working though. You hastened her death, but she was dying already."

359

The cop leaned in close until the vampire could smell the damned garlic on his breath as he whispered, "Dying from leukemia."

# The Biting-a-Hologram Blues

### NINA KIRIKI HOFFMAN

I watched Willy stalk a girl standing in front of a big department store. She was wearing the very latest in body-huggers, striped blue knit over strategic areas and clear acrylic over others. She stood in front of the store's broad entrance, occasionally stepping toward the hover-traffic in the street, then turning around and peering both ways along the slidewalks, posing hipshot with arms akimbo. She had long dark hair that hung straight down and reminded me of hippie girls from the 'sixties and the teens.

All Willy saw was yumyums. Stupid kid. If I weren't so lonely I'd ditch him. You try and try to turn somebody you really like, and they die, and then some bonehead kid like Willy turns, and you kind of have to take him under your batwing, show him a few ropes, teach him a few steps, stick training wheels on his bike; he's kind of like a son to you. You know what they say about that. You can pick your friends, you can pick your nose, you can't pick your family.

Willy was doing a pretty creditable hover-in-the-shadows, just like I taught him. He waited for a break in the traffic, then dashed out to grab the girl, his teeth extended. Really, he was so crude. I guess he was probably hungry. He wasn't a very successful hunter yet, and I hadn't given him any of my seconds in about three nights; I thought hunger might improve his tracking skills, maybe get him past that barrier to biting, the darned vestigial conscience.

I waited for the inevitable, and of course it happened. He

fell right through the girl, who was a hologram billboard, and bit through his lip as he hit the sidewalk face first.

"Are you in pain, sir?" asked a slidewalk cleanerbot, sensing blood nearby.

"I'll take care of it," I said, leaving a voicetrack in its record, something I tried to avoid when possible; but if I didn't switch it off worse things might happen. I picked Willy up and jumped onto the fast lane and we were in another neighborhood in twenty minutes.

"Didja know?" he whined after we had switched walks a few times and his wound had healed up okay.

"Did I know what?"

"Didja know she was a holly?"

I snorted. "Willy, how many times do I have to tell you to use your nose?"

"I can't smell nothing, Mitch. I told you and told you."

I hadn't known that many who had turned. The one who turned me, and then maybe three others that she had turned, and now Willy, my first kid. Everybody else I knew who had turned had had enhanced senses afterward. But maybe the damned kid was telling the truth. In which case he might need me for a long, long time. Not a prospect I was very happy about.

"Let's go to the U-Club," I said, because the U-Club was easy to deal with. I didn't like going there very often because it was too easy; I was afraid I'd get lazy and grow to depend on it and get caught; but if I wanted the kid to survive at all I needed some food for him, soon.

"Sure," he said, pausing at a newscreen by a hoverbus stop and touching a headline pad. BREAKTHROUGH ON THE DISEASE-FIGHTING FRONT! NO MORE INFECTION! the screen read. "Damn! I wanted sports, not science," said Willy, touching another pad. SWEDEN BEATS ARGENTINA IN WORLD CUP, read the screen. FOR SCORE AND DETAILS, ENTER CREDIT. "Miiiitch?" Willy said.

"Forget it! None of that matters." I had never thought sports mattered when I was alive and they surely didn't matter to me now. "Do you want to eat, or not?"

"I'm starving," he said, and then muttered, "Maybe they'll have the game on holo-V at the club."

It was noisy at the U-Club, a university hangout and also a place to find nice clean ladies and gentlemen of the evening.

People on the dance floor were wearing clothes that lit up in time to the music. The air was full of the smells of alcohol, sex, lubricants, and sweat.

I was a shoplifter while I was alive, and I'm opposed to paying for food on moral principles, but once in a while I shred my ethics and go for the easy out.

There was still a chance that Willy would score without benefit of a credit card, though. "Pick somebody and see if you can seduce them," I told him. He was a good-looking kid, after all, though I don't think he had ever figured out how to use that to his advantage while he was alive.

He went straight for a really exotic girl, one of those people so skinny you wonder where food went when she ate it, and her hair was shellacked black and high into a frozen wave above her head. Her outfit looked like metallic painted-on swirls. Her eyes were too wide, the irises larger than normal. Microsurgery? I wondered. But when he brought her over to our table I could tell Willy had picked a loser again.

"It has to be in advance," she said. Her voice was musical; if the kid had really known how to listen, he would have heard the synth notes in it.

"Satisfaction guaranteed?" Willy asked.

"Of course."

"Mitch, can I borrow a hundred credits for fifteen minutes?"

"No," I said.

"Miiitch."

The exotic got unhurriedly to her feet, still smiling, and pulled her hand free of Willy's. "I've got to go," she said.

"Kid," I said, "bite her and you'll get a mouthful of machine oil and sprockets. How much more don't you know? The depth of your ignorance amazes me."

Willy looked pale and really, really disappointed. "How can you tell?"

"Scent, sound, and a few hundred other cues. Wait here until you see me leave with a woman, then follow us."

I found a beautiful fat juicy girl who was wearing a brown bodystocking that hugged her clear up to her chin, down to her wrists and ankles. She smelled like she was bursting with health, and she was so shy that my interest in her excited and thrilled her; I didn't even have to turn on the charm to get her to come with me. There wouldn't be any payslots on this one.

She came to the park with me, leaning against me as we sat on a bench. Her living warmth felt like an electric blanket. For a while I just wanted to sit there and enjoy it. I asked her about her family and her school choices, and listened to her answers with interest, almost feeling alive.

Then Willy came up. He looked really wobbly.

"Natalie, I'm sorry," I said. I stroked her temples. "You are getting sleepy," I said, in my best Bela voice, stroking sleepiness down her throat, along her forearms. She leaned back into a nap right away. Usually I just went through this charade to fool the mug-guards, which came alert at the sounds of screams or struggle, but this time I was glad I had these skills.

Willy sat down on her other side. I tugged down her collar. "Be gentle," I said.

He nicked a vein and took a few mouthfuls, then stopped the flow with his finger, made a face, and said, "She tastes funny."

Dumb kid. No sense of smell, no sense of hearing, and here he thought *my* choice tasted funny. I came around and took a little sip from Natalie's neck.

Doggone if he wasn't right. Not only that, but the nick he had made was knitting closed as I watched.

"Uck!" Willy clutched his stomach.

The inside of my mouth hurt. The faint flavor of Natalie's blood turned to acid on my tongue.

She was human. I knew she was human! She smelled like a big healthy juicy walking meal, and she sounded like a college freshman! So what was this horrible spice?

I rolled up her sleeve and looked at her upper arm. There was the fresh flower of an injection site there. Medical breakthrough, I thought.

Nanobots.

I lay back on the bench listening to Willy moan as tiny machines in my mouth fought the infection that kept me alive.

# Life After

## DON HERRON

**D**ry.

The hollow of its mouth was dry.

Sensation slowly spread, like a dessicating rot in a tree. In the darkness. Lids peeled over eyes that witnessed nothing, not even the memory of light.

Brittle muscles tugged fingertips.

*Where am I?*

Sand sifted within bone and it did not know the sand was marrow.

*What am I?*

"This the one?"

"Yeah."

"Pop it."

"It's not sealed."

"Better yet. You two, at our backs. Everyone else, in. Bag it fast."

Black and gray figures darted in the circle of drab blue light the dark-lantern cast over gravel before the door's iron bars. The light leaped up each side of the entrance in quartered moons, jumped forward, etched the receding ribs of the grillwork, vanished inside the crypt.

The rearguards, guns at ready, quickly posted before the hooded passage, barely moving statues, sweat cool on their necks, the metallic whisper of the hinges and the dusty shuffle of the footpads dying in their ears.

Listening to the scrabble of its . . . *nails* against . . . *planking*, it lay in black repose. Its throat ached.

*Dry birth. This is dry birth. I am born, out of dust and darkness. I am—*

Dull explosions of sound burst distantly, outside the darkness.

The darkness lurched.

Its head rocked forward and to one side. Hands pressed the sides of its—

"—get the coffin open. Smash the—"

—eardrums thundered, and its eyes filled with incandescent light.

"Get the bag open. Three on each side."

Lids pinched shut, it twisted its face away from the glare. Its flaring nostrils caught the scent of living flesh. Within the flesh, blood.

The brightness and splintering sound over it attracted its voracious stare. Its mouth was so very dry.

Thin fingers reached up.

"It's alive!"

"No, it's dead. They just move some, that's all."

"It's got my arm!"

Laughter echoed in the crypt.

"Pull loose. They've got no grip."

The dead dried hand fell out of the lantern glow, back into the burial box.

"Come here, look at it. You're working with us, get used to it. Almost all the same. Lift up the light."

Black-gloved hands reached into the coffin, grabbed the shroud wrapping the corpse and ripped.

"Citizens are easiest to find. They get drained, they pick up the virus, and they *always* get buried. Lucky for us."

The emaciated body twitched slightly in the blue shadows, eyes staring up blindly. The pupils were caved in, the eyeballs sunk deep into the sockets.

"Weird eyes, huh? They collapse with the loss of liquid, before the virus kicks in. When you get drained, even if you've got some fat on you, you look pretty much like this."

A leather finger traced the loosely stitched, puckered incision that ran down in a gray furrow from the neckline.

"Citizens get buried, first they gut 'em. Take heart, lungs, liver, hollow it all out. Sew it shut. Ritual. Makes for a lighter load. You'll appreciate that."

The finger indicated the stripped flesh of the chest, exposing the white curve of ribs, then dipped down and made a circle in the pit crudely carved into the groin.

"Male, female, not worth worrying about. They just hook 'em up, plug 'em in. Resale value the same for us. Gravedigger probably took this stiff's sex to make a fetish. Personal use. Blackmarket. Or maybe they were hungry."

The finger pointed to raw yellow pits cut out of the thighs. "Steaks."

The black gloves moved to the face, gripped the jaw and pulled it down. Three fingers slipped deftly into the mouth, probed rapidly as teeth gnawed weakly at the leather.

"Thought so. Tongue's gone too."

The gloves pulled out of the light, leaving the wad of waste cotton that had filled the mouth cavity hanging between the corpse's lips.

"Now, get this thing bagged and let's get out of this tomb."

All about it, blood-ripened flesh flowed into the night.
*Rich, redolent darkness . . .*

Its senses stretched as it was carried along, back into the crypt, where motes of dust, boot-stirred, settled again in the ancient rite of the world; into the graves of the surrounding earth, filled with the insatiable legions of the worm; into narrow passages of profound shadow between the mausoleums, lurking points for the hunters; over the leaning stones, away up the hill, the necropolis bone-white in the fragile radiance of the waning dead moon. It saw everything, the tiny scuttling shapes in the darkness, the hieroglyphs of the rocks. It heard the gnawing. It sensed the cancer in the bowels of one of its bearers, and behind its pitted eyes felt the fluid pulse of the bodies. It soared on the smell of blood.

To its ears came the brush of feathers over air, and eyes moved in its lolling head to target the gliding nighthawk. A fellow creature of the darkness, claws to rend, beak to bleed the living flesh. Gone, a shapeless, helpless bag of life suspended in its grip.
*Power.*

As it was borne into the scented night, drugged with visions
*Blood.*

it forgot for a moment the ache of its throat.
*Life.*
The throat that was so terribly dry.

# A Frenzied Beat of Wings

C. Bruce Hunter

The sun had just dipped below the horizon, but a scattering of clouds siphoned its rays back into the sky and spread their red glow across the town.

The streets were steamy from an afternoon shower that had come and gone in near silence. In its wake rivulets of water trickled down the sidewalks and onto the asphalt pavement, feeding little pools whose oil-slicked surfaces shimmered in the failing light.

A quiet had settled over the town. The evening rush of people speeding home for supper had subsided, and those who would be coming out for an evening's entertainment had not yet appeared on the streets. The temporarily deserted town waited patiently for the first stirrings that would signal a return of life to its buildings.

Only occasional sounds broke the quiet, and they barely filtered through rows of trees and neatly trimmed bushes, and drifted across a close-cropped lawn to the walls of the old, Mediterranean-style building that stood on the top of a lonely hill at the outskirts of the town. Set well away from both street and town, the old house seemed completely separated from the rest of the world, and perfectly designed to shut out the sights and sounds of unwanted company.

Thick walls and small windows, strategically arranged, let in none of the cheer and warmth that abound in small tree-lined communities. Inside there were only cold and quiet.

Vlad moved slowly and deliberately through that cold and

quiet. With practiced cadence, he approached a young woman and leaned forward over her body. Her face was remarkably free of wrinkles, and her pale skin was set off by a dishevelled mass of jet black hair that formed an almost perfect circle around her head. She resembled the medieval icons Vlad had seen so many years ago, her beauty was so classic and innocent.

He probed her neck with his fingers, trying to find the jugular vein. It was soft and not easy to locate. He was not surprised, though. This woman seemed to be very placid and relaxed, and such people have low blood pressure. Their veins do not stand out.

When Vlad finally located the vein he moved closer, until his face was only a few inches from her neck. Placing his finger and thumb on either side of the vein, he pulled the skin tight until a thick, blue line appeared. Then he carefully inserted the needle and secured it in place with a piece of adhesive tape.

This woman was too young and too beautiful to die, Vlad thought, cursing the laws of nature that condemned such beauty to an eternity of coldness. Death should take only those who have lived a very long time, whose bodies have already begun the process of withering and drying.

He turned a valve, and the pink-tinted embalming fluid began pushing its way through the veins, flushing clotting blood ahead of it. The flawless face slowly took on an artificial color, and the thin body seemed to exhale as the blood drained away.

Vlad had always felt this was the cruelest part of the process. Removing blood from the body was the final rape—taking away the fluid potency, now only a symbol of life, but still a person's last remaining tie with the world of warmth. Once the blood was gone, there was no barrier to withstand the encroaching cold and damp of the grave.

What must once have been a vital and happy person seemed now to blend gradually with the cold steel table on which she lay. No longer a living thing, she—or more accurately *it*—now had no function, no use, no purpose. It was fit only to be relegated to the earth, so infused with preserving fluid that it could no longer support life—now hostile even to the worms and flowers of the field. It was a lifeless thing, condemned by the embalmer's needle to lie immobile and immutable in a lifeless grave.

A door opened and closed, but Vlad did not bother to look up. Continuing the routine he had gone through a thousand times, he worked more from instinct than from memory.

Sam Crenshaw lumbered into the room, carrying two large carboys of embalming fluid. He half lowered, half dropped them to the floor in the corner and stiffly pushed them against the wall with one foot.

"Don't take too long on that one, Vlad," he said, wiping his balding head with a wrinkled handkerchief that had been stuffed in his shirt pocket. "We're running a little behind tonight."

"How did she die?" Vlad asked.

"Childbirth. That doesn't happen much any more. It used to be the way most women went, though."

"It's a crying shame." A tear formed at the corner of Vlad's left eye. "She had so much to look forward to."

"You're too soft for this business, Vlad," Crenshaw mumbled as he leafed through a thick stack of papers on his clipboard. He was trying to schedule an overload caused by a school bus accident. "You've got to stop seeing them as people, or it'll screw up your mind."

"But there's so little warmth in the world as it is. It's wrong to have to lose so much like this."

Sam Crenshaw was not listening. His businessman's mind was busily cranking out dollars and hours and names.

"It's going to be tight," he said, drawing lines on a clipboarded chart. "If we can get some of the families to go for closed coffin funerals, we can cut corners and save some time."

The tear in Vlad's eye had grown large enough to bother him, and he wiped it away with the back of his hand.

"I'll put some coffee on." Crenshaw put down the clipboard and sorted through a mass of electrical cords on the table to find the one that belonged to the coffee pot. "It looks like we're going to be working late tonight."

Vlad opened a bottle of warm beer, dropped the cap and opener on the table, and sat down on the edge of his bed. The bottle cap rolled across the table, bounced twice on the seat of the room's only chair, a simple wooden kitchen chair, and finally clinked to rest on the floor.

It was almost dawn. Vlad had worked straight through the

night and was so tired that he had not even taken the time to wash his hands after finishing the last body. His shoulders were tight, and an ache was beginning to throb its way from the back of his head, down his neck and into the shoulder blades. He took a long drink of the beer and closed his eyes, rolling his head in little circles to relax the muscles.

The beer had a strong, bitter taste. There was no icebox in the room, so he had learned to take his drinks warm. He didn't eat in the room—food attracted ants and roaches—but there were always a few bottles of beer on hand. He needed something to take the edge off a day of working with lifeless bodies.

Opening his eyes, Vlad leaned his head back until he felt a tightness in his chest. He tried to relax his burning eyes by focusing along the jagged cracks in the ceiling, moving his eyes first to the left, then to the right, then in widening, irregular circles.

After several seconds of this exercise, he pulled himself from the bed with a faint guttural groan and walked slowly to the window. He tried to stretch his legs as he walked and took another swallow of bitter beer. Placing one hand on the windowsill to support his tired body, he leaned forward and looked out at the street.

Most of the buildings were dark. A flashing red and white neon sign told of a drugstore that would not open for another three hours, and a pale yellow glow came from the all-night diner half way down the block. They turned off most of their lights this late to save on the electric bill. The street light was either broken or burned out, and the only other light on the street came from a line of gray-pink that was beginning to silhouette the buildings to the east.

The pavement was still wet from an early morning shower that had turned the night chill into a humid warmth, and the buildings were quiet, as if the rain had washed away all the sounds as well. The silence was violated only by a baby crying somewhere behind an open window.

Vlad pulled down an old, yellowing, masking-tape-mended shade and returned to the bed. The beer had produced a warm, almost burning sensation in his stomach, and there was a pleasant numbness in his head. The tightness and pain were starting to unravel.

He strained a little to pull off his shoes without untying the laces, then lay back on the bed and stretched his legs as far as they would reach. The muscles seemed to loosen as soon as his legs sank into the mattress. He drank the last of the beer, holding it in his mouth for several seconds before swallowing it, and slowly lowered the bottle to the floor.

The mattress was old and soft, and it urged his muscles to let go. The bottle slipped from his hand and rolled under the bed, making a grinding sound as it moved across the dusty hardwood floor.

Morpheus enveloped Vlad in a billowing cloud and lifted him slowly and tenderly into oblivion. They floated high over the town, across the river to the west, then lost sight of the earth as more clouds closed in. The clouds swirled and churned, forming a myriad of nebulous shapes in which Vlad could see marvelous things: winged horses at play—wood nymphs frolicking under glistening waterfalls—small, furry animals sleeping together in the sunshine.

The images appeared and faded, yielding to the changing patterns of the churning clouds. They conjured and teased Vlad's imagination. An almost unending succession of fantasies offered themselves to him, only to retreat before he could seize them.

Finally the clouds thinned and parted to reveal wooded hills scattered like emeralds across an expanse of undulating fields. Vlad descended through the cool evening air until he could make out a small, half-timbered cottage tucked into the lee of one of the hills.

He floated closer. The warm glow of plaster and wood in the moonlight seemed to beckon to him, as if the house were reaching out through its covering turnings of ivy and grape vines to offer a yielding welcome.

Vlad took the welcome and entered the cottage through an open window whose billowing curtains parted to receive him. He found himself in a large, airy bedroom of pink and lace. Its uncluttered decor had a graceful line and a delicate arrangement that reflected a sensitive, feminine hand. And pastel colors told of a happy and pastoral childhood.

At the far side of the room, in the shelter of a ceiling-mounted canopy, in an old-fashioned four-poster bed, lay a young woman. Her long, jet black hair was spread over the pillow, tossed by a restless sleep. Her flawless features were the color and texture of alabaster in the moonlight. A glow of health and innocence played across her face, a face whose cheeks showed no color yet boasted of life and warmth.

Vlad moved very slowly and quietly toward the bed, hesitating not from fear but only to hold the moment a few seconds longer. The tranquility of the scene that unfolded before him and its exquisite beauty were the substance and essence of dreams, the heart of the purist of fantasies, and he did not want to lose them too quickly.

Approaching the bed with a deep feeling of reverence, Vlad slowly bent over the woman's body and pressed his mouth to her throat, closing his teeth and moving them back and forth to feel for the vein. He found it and paused for several seconds to sense its gentle pulsing against his tongue, then bit down hard. The flesh separated easily, but the vein resisted. He bit harder, almost gnawing his way through its tough wall until he felt a trickle of blood.

As he sucked out the living fluid, Vlad eased his arm around her waist and pulled her body closer. Her body yielded to his embrace, and she half exhaled, half moaned with a faint sound at once reminiscent of both song and laughter. Her heart pounded, forcing her blood more willingly into his mouth.

Moon-cast shadows moved silently across the room as the night passed, caressing a communion of the most ancient ritual, a heritage of primeval origins, lost in a rational world and preserved only in the most intimate reaches of the mind.

A bird sang in the distance, and Vlad pulled away. The young woman's eyes opened slightly, closing again in the time of a single heartbeat. She turned onto her side, pressing her body into the soft bed, and pulled the blanket more closely around her shoulders.

Vlad left as he had come and drifted on morning clouds of pink and crimson and violet.


Sam Crenshaw strained to wheel a heavily laden steel table into the storage room. Its front end shimmied across the tile floor, and he had to wrestle it into place at the end of a line of identical, nameless tables. When he was finally satisfied with the table's position, he adjusted the plastic sheet that covered the body and marked off another name on the clipboarded grid. Then, pausing to wipe a spot from his neatly pressed suit, he smiled at the orderly row of bodies that filled the room.

"Looks like we're going to make it," he called to Vlad, who was drawing a cup of coffee from the pot in the other room.

A slight tremor in Vlad's hand sent ripples across the surface of the coffee, and the tentacles of steam rising from the cup flickered in the cold air.

Crenshaw had forgotten to bring a new bag of sugar, and the cream had turned sour, so Vlad had to drink it straight. He didn't mind, though. Its stale, overboiled taste helped keep him awake.

Sometimes Vlad was afraid of sleep, afraid that he would drift into its clutches once too often and never come back. It was a curious fear, and Vlad was always surprised when it crept into his consciousness.

At times he felt that something in the deepest part of his mind was trying to warn him not to be seduced by the barren promise of an eternal beauty. After all, beauty was only fleeting. It had to be. Too fragile and tenuous to hold its substance for more than a single heartbeat, it had to pass away with the morning mist.

He swallowed a last, bitter trickle of coffee and stared into the empty cup. The grounds in its bottom formed curious patterns as the last of the coffee swirled slowly around, moving the grains in concentric circles. At first they seemed to form a cross, then they dissolved into a pair of wings that fluttered in the tiny amber pool.

He put down the cup and turned to the steel table that held the last victim of the school bus accident.

She was a large girl and somewhat older than the others. Her golden hair was matted with blood, and the right side of her chest was sunken from what must have been a very heavy blow. But even in death she had a haunting beauty—the beauty of a girl who had only begun to blossom into maturity. Too young to have had more than a taste of love, she had been abruptly snatched away from the promise held by the gentleness of her features.

Vlad silently mourned the destruction of such beauty. He reached out to her with a trembling hand and wiped a drop of blood from her cheek and combed her hair with his fingers. The girl's flesh was cold, her eyes and lips closed.

Vlad could almost believe she was only sleeping. He held the needle in his right hand and gently probed her neck with his left.

# The Exploration of Inner Space

### BRIAN STABLEFORD

My father is the sanest, dullest, least imaginative man I have ever known. I suppose that he's always loved me, but I have to suppose it, because he certainly never took the trouble to display the fact. Not that he was ever cruel or conspicuously ungenerous, but he was always stern, distant, and impassive; if nothing I did ever seemed to disappoint him, nothing I did ever seemed to delight him either. We saw little of one another after I left home to go to university; we had little in common to start with, and our interests grew further apart as time went by. It was something of a surprise when, in the course of a routine visit following my bruising divorce, he invited me into his den for what he obviously intended to be a long and serious talk.

I expected to receive some utterly banal advice about the way to handle my new situation, but I could hardly have been more wrong.

I knew that he had once studied psychology before moving into actuarial work, but I had never heard him talk about it before, and I was astonished when he began his speech. "Many years ago," he said, "when I was only half as old as you are now, I took part in an experiment. I was paid, but I didn't do it for the money. Research students were expected to help out in such projects, and were rarely reluctant to do so. I had a sense of adventure in those days, and a strong sense of purpose. Dr. Irwin was one of the leading men in the field of dream research, and I was eager to involve myself in his work."

*He had a sense of adventure!* I echoed, silently. *What on earth can have happened to it?*

"You know, I suppose," he continued, "that an animal can be made to act out its dreams by the surgical removal of a part of the brain called the pons, whose normal function includes switching off the body's motor responses during sleep. Irwin had proposed that there must be a similar inhibitor that prevented dream-experiences from being stored as memories, and that this inhibitor must be a chemical process rather than a simple switch because memory is a chemical rather than an electrical phenomenon. He'd been experimenting with various psychotropic substances for thirty years in the hope of finding the key to dream-memory, and had long been in the habit of seeking assistance from his students. I happened to be in the group he was using when he finally struck lucky."

"But people *can* remember their dreams," I objected. "The memory fades, but you can cling on to it if you try hard enough."

"Not so," my father replied, with that irritating firmness he had always employed in addressing me. "If a person wakes while a dream is in progress, the waking mind latches on to a single fugitive dream-image and extrapolates that image by semiconscious confabulation. People who become conscious that they're dreaming or train themselves to remember their dreams are merely extending and elaborating that process of confabulation, exaggerating its distortions. *True* dreaming is entirely unconscious, unless the inhibitor that conceals dreams from consciousness is chemically castrated. You'll understand why when I explain."

"Because dreams are nightmares too horrible to be confronted by the conscious mind?" I suggested, making light of it because the fact of his saying all this was—to me—far more bizarre than the substance of it.

"You might put it that way," he said, so bleakly that I regretted my attempt at wit. "Are you familiar with the Hoyle-Wickramasinghe theory of cumulative evolution?"

"They proposed that life evolved in vast interstellar dust-clouds and colonised planets by bombarding them with genetic material spewed out of comets," I said, glad of the opportunity to demonstrate my cleverness. "On earth, such bombardments are supposed to cause epidemics—but in the past they also provided opportunities for evolutionary surges, because some organisms could incorporate whole new gene-complexes into their make-up. It's a very unorthodox theory—almost certainly false."

"It's not false. Disease is just a side-effect of the cumulative process—the process by which an immune system filters out the bits of genetic material that don't fit into the particular jigsaw puzzle that is the evolving organism."

"You can't have a jigsaw puzzle unless there's a picture to work toward," I pointed out. "Evolution isn't like that. It isn't *planned*."

"I'm afraid that it is," he said. "The evolution of life on earth is simply recapitulating a pattern that is also established on millions of other worlds. The earth is merely one of many fields seeded in order to produce a particular crop. We—human beings—are that crop."

"When's the harvest due?" I asked, keeping my face rigidly straight. I still didn't have a clue what was going on, but I was content to play along. It made a change from talking about maintenance payments and fresh starts.

"It's already happened—or, at the very least, is in the process of happening. The creatures that planned and planted us have already moved in."

I figured that it was at best a tall tale and at worst a paranoid nightmare. I hoped that it was a tall tale, but anyone who knew my father would have judged it a forlorn hope. Could senility be setting in early, or had all those years of cunning calculation finally flipped his lid? My response was carefully guarded. "You're saying that two billion years of earthly evolution have been calculated to produce *us*, so that some other species waiting out in the wilderness of space can now move in to reap what they've sown—and you're saying that you discovered this forty-odd years ago when you took part in an experiment that allowed you to remember your dreams."

"Yes, Mike," he said, flatly. "That's exactly what I'm saying."

*Humour him*, I thought. *Let it go, and see where it leads.* "Who are these cosmic farmers?" I asked. "What function were we bred to serve? Are they vampires whose only possible nourishment is human blood, or what?"

"They're vampires of a sort," he agreed. "Personally, I've always thought of them as succubi—but vampires might be more apt, given that they do indeed nourish themselves on our blood."

*Vampires, succubi, lamias,* I thought. *What's the difference? They all spell "madness."* "And they're already living among us, undetected?" I said aloud. "The great harvest of blood has already begun?"

"Yes—but not quite the way you think. You're thinking in terms of our neighbours or our political masters, but it's not like that at all. They're *inside* us. Bodily, they're a part of us, sharers of our flesh. Hoyle and Wickramasighe were right, you see— evolution isn't a matter of ruthless competition between individuals; it's a matter of careful cumulation. Two billion years is a long time, but that's the time these things take. That's the time required to produce proto-human beings that are capable of the last and most important evolutionary leap: the leap that allows the brain to accommodate an extra partner, an extra individual. That's when the harvesters move in—and I mean *in*. They move into our heads; they take up residence inside our skulls. Our bodies nourish them; the blood that is our life is also theirs."

I thought about that for a few moments, and then said: "Exactly what's the sense, then, in speaking of them as though they were separate individuals? How can we distinguish *them* from *ourselves?*"

"If you believe that DNA maketh the man, we can't," he said, somberly. "But it all depends on what you mean by your *self*. If everything that happens inside me is myself, then I am indeed my succubus and she is me, but if my *self* is simply my consciousness—that elusive, ghostly entity bounded by sensation and knowledge, which is talking to you now—then *she* is something else entirely."

"She?" I queried.

"That's just a way of speaking," he countered, quickly. "I admit the absurdity of characterizing another inhabitant of my own brain as a being of a different sex, but that's the way I saw her, when the curtain hiding my dreams was briefly drawn back.

That's the way she—or *it*, if you insist—was presented to me. What I learned when I took Irwin's drug, you see, was that the waking life we pitiful human mind-things lead is but a shadow of the *real* life that goes on inside us. I learned that we're very foolish to think of ourselves as the masters of our bodies and the captains of our souls. I learned that we're shabby and shadowy things, little more than muscles or sensory organs.

"We think because we respond to what we see and hear, because we feel pain and fear, because we react and respond to stimuli, that we're the governors of our fate—but we're wrong. What you think of as your will is merely the instrument of another being, and all your reasons are mere rationalizations. What you think of as *your* desires and *your* ambitions are mere echoes of another, deeper consciousness whose abject slave and helpless puppet you are: a mind within your mind, which is constantly present but normally unapprehended. Your waking is the other's sleep, but your sleep—your *dreams*—are the source and essence of its most vivid experiences. Like any vampire, it's physically nourished by your blood, but like the gaudier vampires of fantasy it requires much more of you than that. Its mental nourishment is all the produce of your life: thought and feeling, pain and joy, sensation and imagination. What we make of such things while we are awake is a direly dull and tawdry business compared with what might be made of them in our dreams—our *true* dreams—by the parastic creatures that spin their own rich and beautiful lives out of the meagre threads of ours."

I had run out of objections and interjections. I simply waited for him to explain further.

"When I took Irwin's drug," he said, his voice softening strangely as he recalled the experience, "I entered into my dreams for the first time, and carried their legacy back to the realm of wakefulness. I met my anima, my succubus, my own majestic vampire—and I shared, for a brief while, the authentic intercourse of which mere human sexual intercourse is a pathetic caricature. I lived with her for seven magical nights, and with her I discovered what *real* life was. I found out how she used me, not merely to produce the blood on which she fed, but all else that was life-giving.

"Human life is no longer as nasty, brutish, and short as it once was, but still it's racked by a pestiferous legion of discomforts and disappointments, frustrations and failures. Such torments are filtered out of the dream-life, which is all colour, all ecstasy, all . . . well, simply *all*. There's no way to explain to those who haven't experienced wholeness how petty and *partial* our life is—but it has to be that way, for you and I are simply instruments that have a function to perform, like fingers or feet, and we couldn't be good and trusted instruments if we had true consciousness and a will of our own."

I wanted more details now, but he seemed embarrassed, as if he had become doubtful of the wisdom of telling his tale.

"Not everyone responded to Irwin's drug in the same way," he went on, eventually. "Some of the subjects reported disordered experiences much like those associated with ordinary hallucinogens. Only five of us contrived to preserve distinct and accurate memories, and they weren't exactly alike. We weren't sure how to interpret them at first, but we were able to find enough common ground on which to base firm conclusions. We knew, however, that we wouldn't be believed were we to make our findings public. The fact that the drug failed to close down the memory-censor in some cases would be used as evidence that we were the victims of some kind of collective folly, akin to the many individuals who claimed to have recovered lost memories of being abducted aboard UFOs by aliens and subjected to medical examination.

"We knew that we could demonstrate the truth of what we knew to *some* of those who condescended to try the experiment, but that this would only serve to intensify the hostility of those who would not. If the news we had brought back from our journey of exploration had been better, it would have been a very different matter, but if you care to examine the responses that my story awoke in you while I told it you'll easily appreciate the difficulties that faced us—and you'll understand why we decided to remain silent."

"What about this Dr. Irwin? What did *he* make of your story?"

"He was one of the five. He would never have asked his students to take a drug he wasn't prepared to take himself. It must have been worse for him than for the rest of us. He had found the way to the truth that he had sought for thirty years, but was unable to claim his just reward. He died a well-respected man, whose obituarists were far too polite to label him a failure, but he died in obscurity, just as I shall. Two of the others are still alive, but I haven't seen or talked to them for a very long time. I have no idea whether they've ever told anyone what they know."

"But you decided that you ought to tell me. Why? And why now, instead of twenty years ago?"

"Because you're my son, Mike. Because I didn't want to carry the secret to my grave. Because I've spent a whole lifetime proving my sanity, so that I might—just *might*—be believed if and when I decided to speak. I've held down a good job, made steady progress up the career ladder, sustained a good marriage, and raised a very able son. I hope I've demonstrated my trust-worthiness."

"Was that what it was all about, Dad?" I asked, unable to contain the sarcasm. "All that determined conformity, all that blinkered materialism, all that rigid attention to detail? Was it all just an act, to prove your *trustworthiness?* Was it really worth it, Dad? Fifty years of living in a straitjacket, just so you could one day lay all this before me and expect me to swallow it hook, line, and sinker?"

"It wasn't an act," he said, coldly. "It was the real me. It was *what was left.* After a week, you see, I had to stop taking Dr. Irwin's drug. If I'd continued to take it, the gradual accumulation of toxic metabolic by-products would have killed me. Irwin died in his own good time, of natural causes, but the other two who are no longer alive died because they couldn't or wouldn't give up taking the drug. Effectively, they committed suicide for the sake of a few extra weeks of what they'd come to consider the only *real* life. I didn't—but I've had to live with the knowledge that the life I lead is what it is. You may call it determined conformity and blinkered materialism, but that's all there is for those of us who can't enter into our own dreams. Maybe you still think that there has to be more, Mike, even though you're past forty, but that's just a hopeful confabulation built on a fugitive atom of desire. I didn't tell you all this twenty years ago because I wanted you to be able to cling to your illusions a while longer, and perhaps it's unkind to tell you even now, but I really did think that you ought to be told *some time*, and now is the time I chose. You still have the option of thinking that I'm crazy, and I won't be offended if you decide to exercise it."

As I said before, my father is the sanest, dullest, least imaginative man I have ever known. I'd always been determined that no one would ever say the same of me, but since Isabel left me and took the kids . . . I guess that when you're past forty it's difficult to convince people that you're young at heart. And if it wasn't vampires who made us the way we are, how on earth did we ever let it happen?

"You really believe all this, don't you?" I said, by way of stalling while I tried to make up my mind. "You really believe that there are vampires inside our heads which leech everything valuable out of our experience, while we live the lives of pathetic, deluded phantoms."

"Look around you, son," he said. "Look at the world, and the universe in which it floats like a lonely speck of inconsiderable dust. Look into yourself—at what life has done to your hopes and ambitions. Look at the wreckage that forty years has made of those furious idiot tales you mistake for your dreams. Don't ask me whether I believe it, Mike—ask me the question that any *real* man would ask."

He was crazy, all right. He was also wrong—about me, if not himself. He had always been wrong, about me if not himself. But what else could I do? I was fat, forty-four, and forlorn, but what else could I do?

"Okay," I said, eventually, with a sour sigh. "How do I make the stuff, and what kind of dose do I need?"

"That's my boy," he said.

It was the first authentic note of pride I'd ever heard in his dull-as-ditchwater voice.

# The Nine Billion Names of Nosferatu

SIMON MacCULLOCH

**E**ric" sounded more like a vampire's name if you put an "h" on the end. John wasn't surprised to see that this was what his would-be employer had done, because the business card he had just given John identified him as "President, the Arcane Order of Nosferatu." Already himself a member of the arcane order of freelance computer technicians, not to mention gifted since birth with a silent "h" of his own, John didn't have to try very hard not to be impressed.

"Well, Mr. Knight," he said, easing himself back on the ornate antique chaise longue that was presumably intended to add a touch of sumptuous aristocratic decadence to his host's otherwise Spartan office, "would you like to outline the assignment for me?"

"Of course. I understand you are already familiar with our computer system." Indeed he was—he had had a fair idea of the formidable specifications of the hardware at Mr. Knight's disposal, quite beyond the requirements of the specialist publishing house whose support was ostensibly its function, even before he had answered the advertisement for "technical support for major literary project." The tour he'd been given that morning of Gibbous Moon Book's facility had not disappointed him. There was no longer any doubt that their latest project was something bigger than last year's *Who's Who of Vampiredom* or even the much rumoured but surely overambitious *Encyclopaedia Vampirica*.

Knight's dark, beady eyes, restless to escape the white candlewax stiffness of his face, seemed to fasten on his thought. "You are probably also familiar with our publishing endeavours to date. I don't think it would be immodest of me to mention that the corpus of published vampire scholarship has more than doubled since we entered the field a decade ago. Now we feel the time has come for Gibbous Moon to expand its range to include fiction."

"A brave move, if you don't mind my saying so, Mr. Knight. You have a firm market niche for your present product— but isn't there more than enough vampire fiction being published?"

"There can never be more than enough," Knight pronounced with the air of someone responding confidently to a catechism. "But you have a point, of course. If Gibbous Moon is to become a trademark for the best in fiction as well as nonfiction, we must bring something especially appetising to the ever-hungry readership. Hence the present project. Did you know that this company now possesses the single greatest archive of vampire literature ever assembled?"

John did, but he was wary of appearing too blasé, especially as Knight's bony hands had started to tremble with excitement on the desk in front of him. He contrived a raised eyebrow, a shift of position, and a mildly startled grunt.

"Yes. Thanks not only to the scope and rigour of our academic research and publishing programmes, but also to the skill and commitment of the worldwide membership of the Order— including, of course, many wealthy and diligent collectors—we are in a unique position in the field. We alone have instant access to the extant canon in its entirety."

"So you aim to corner the market for reprints. . . ."

This was Knight's cue to use the smile he'd been saving up. John refrained from studying the dentistry—too obvious. "Obviously. But that is merely a by-product of our central endeavour. Our project is more ambitious than that. Our database holds not only every word of surviving vampire fiction of the last two centuries, but a vast apparatus of critical theory with which to analyse it. Thus supplied, we have developed a programme that can identify, within the parameters of the tradition, those permutations of plot, theme, character, context, and subtext which have yet to be used or developed to their logical conclusions, and write them for us. We shall therefore be able to guarantee a scientifically achieved combination of originality and familiarity in all our output. The market we shall corner is that for all future vampire fiction."

World Domination, Plan 66, thought John. "And my role?"

"The programme is in the final stages of testing now, and there are still a few bugs that our people haven't been able to get rid of. Our start date is pressing and we hope a fresh perspective will boost us over the last hurdles. You will appreciate that we require someone whose technical expertise is exceeded only by his discretion."

"The very soul," said John, and took the knobby hand that offered itself in his.

He'd been working at Gibbous Moon for a week when he met Nyctalops. The name sounded like something you'd christen a computer system, but it was the only one the ratty young man who'd been waiting for him outside his flat would give. His business card came courtesy of the Royal Transylvanian Guild of the Undead.

"So how much is your organisation going to offer me to stop Gibbous Moon taking over the vampire market?" John asked when he'd got bored of hearing how the Order of Nosferatu were fools, dilettantes, imposters, traitors to the vampire cause, a front for the Van Helsing Group, et cetera.

"Taking it over?" Nyctalops's nervous tic, a twitch that made one eye keep winking like a faulty lightbulb, subsided for a moment as he realised he would be scoring at least one point in the discussion. "They took it over years ago. Who do you think has been supplying publishers with their vampire detectives, vampire romances, vampire historicals, vampire science fiction, and so on for the last ten years? If that was all their stupid computer did we wouldn't worry. It's no worse than having humans write the stuff. We want you to help us stop them *destroying* the market, possibly vampire literature itself."

Saving the World, Task 94, thought John. "Isn't their project all about preservation rather than destruction?"

"Their project is about evolution. What they didn't tell you when you took the job was their theory—I say *their* theory, although in fact the Guild came to the same conclusion years before they did—the theory that the development of a literary genre is governed by the same impulses as that of a living species. It is a constant process of selection and honing of available attributes in search of the perfect functionality. The real purpose of the Order's project is to speed up the evolution of the vampire story. Once every possible permutation has been tried, the result will be the perfect vampire story."

"And you think the Royal Guild should be the ones to have it because you thought of it first?"

"No, no, we aren't that selfish. Unlike the Order, we are not motivated by profit or personal aggrandisement. The reason we oppose their project is that no one can say what will happen when evolution has served its purpose."

"Let me guess. One by one, without any fuss, the stars go out?"

Nyctalops looked disgusted. "This isn't some science fiction story."

"Good thing too, on the strength of the 'science' I've heard so far. Look, I'm just a humble technician doing my job, okay? Suppose you just tell me the bottom line."

"The bottom line is that we can't predict what the bottom line of all vampire fiction will be, and until we can we believe it is in everyone's interests not to meddle with things that vampires were not meant to meddle with. We hope you can help. Our inducements are commensurate with our concern."

"I'll think about it."

"Please. I should also mention that our intelligence indicates the culmination of Gibbous Moon's project within days. Your appointment tends to confirm this. Time is very short indeed."

"*Vita longa, ars brevis*, then," said John cheerfully and ushered the by now positively palpitating Nyctalops out quickly. He wanted to report the encounter to his employer without delay.

The Van Helsing Group HQ wore its shabbiness like a puritan virtue, but casual dress by the staff was discouraged, and even after hours with most people gone home John felt conspicuous in his jeans and sweat shirt. The Chief, of course, was still at his desk. A plaque on his wall said: "BATTLE NOT WITH MONSTERS, LEST YE END UP WORKING THE SAME HOURS THEY DO."

"Harper. Your first report's not due till Monday. Problems?"

John related his conversation with Nyctalops. "I think I

need to know now exactly what this assignment's all about," he concluded.

The Chief tapped his desk decisively. "I agree. I didn't give you the full story at the outset for the usual reasons, but I intended to brief you fully next week anyway. And one thing I think our friend from the Guild is right about is that the time for action could come any day now."

"You mean we're buying all this guff about the perfect vampire story?"

"We suspect the Order know what they're doing, even if the Guild are as clueless as ever. We've found the evolution analogy a useful one in our own analysis of the problem of vampire fiction. It makes sense if you bear in mind that evolution is driven by the efforts of DNA to maximise its survival. Stories 'survive' in the sense of being handed down to posterity by virtue of a combination of fashion, inherent worth, and chance, but the only period during which they are absolutely guaranteed life is while they are being written. So maximising survival as far as any member of a literary species is concerned really boils down to maximising the wordage needed to conclude it. This explains the trend towards longer and longer novels, sequels by other hands, series, spinoffs, shared world, and sharecropped fiction. Our statistics show that vampire fiction has featured especially strongly in these areas since Gibbous Moon started supplying the market. Our fear is that their programme is on the verge of producing something that will be beyond the ability of any author, human or computer, to put an end to, and the immortality of the vampire as a literary species will be assured."

"Why should we worry? Isn't Eastern Europe throwing up enough problems these days?"

"Recruitment. You know that our members have been dwindling steadily since the 'seventies, while vampire organisations have been springing up like weeds. Did you know that in the last three years they've even overtaken us for recruitment from the Boy Scouts? We put this down to the impact of the entertainment media on young people's perception of vampirism. It's bad enough that the Order have succeeded in increasing the vampire's market profile tenfold already. We're determined not to let them score the moral, psychological, and propaganda victory of being responsible for the first piece of undeniably immortal fiction."

"Okay. Why haven't you had me sabotage the programme already?"

"We'd planned something like that; hack their system and wreck it. But we didn't expect them to be so rash as to advertise for a technician. With someone on the inside we can take a more subtle approach. Your job will be to catch their superstory when it starts to emerge and curtail it prematurely. What they won't be counting on is reader intervention. The computer will keep churning the thing out *ad infinitum*, until all its ramifications are resolved, which of course they never will be. But if you can fake a resolution and impose it on the programme, they'll assume they simply haven't reached their goal as soon as they expected. By continual intervention we can delay them indefinitely without them knowing, and with luck their shareholders will start to query the value of keeping the project alive when it doesn't deliver to deadline."

"But how did they fix their deadline in the first place?"

"Apparently their analysis of the history of vampire literature has indicated the point at which the final stage will be reached. I don't know how it works, but our own analysts seemed to think it made sense."

"Don't tell me. Story Number Nine Billion, right?"

The Chief didn't have to try not to smile. "This isn't a science fiction story, Harper," he said.

If it was, thought John as he paused after several hours of furtive and frantic work at his console in Gibbous Moon's offices the next morning, whoever's writing it would just have finished describing in loving detail how the hero got into the parts of the system to which he'd been denied access, decoded the numbering of the stories being written there, and, finding that the one that was supposedly the ultimate vampire story had already started, quickly tackled the challenge of infiltrating the still encrypted text. As things were, he supposed results would be the only monument to his efforts he could hope for, and as he wasn't getting very far with the infiltration bit he was beginning to wish for a rescue of the sort appropriate to an older type of romance.

"Can I help?" asked Knight from behind him.

"I doubt it," he said smoothly, "It's just a particularly tricky little . . . er . . ." Knight was holding some hard copy up for him to see. He was smiling. People were stopping work and gathering round.

"We advertised for you for two reasons," said Knight. "One: having someone on the inside might discourage you buffoons from trying some cruder form of sabotage. Two: we couldn't imagine creating the ultimate vampire story without getting someone from the Stake in on the act. After all, we even included the Royal Trannies in our database."

"My next line begins 'I don't know what you're . . .'," thought John, and he saw that Knight thought so too. So he just said, "Suck my dick, Vlad," with textbook ruggedness and started scanning the room for exits.

"We may let you go, if your vulgarisms don't annoy us too much. But first you're going to have the privilege of reading the culmination of the Gibbous Moon project—not to mention several centuries of literary evolution."

"You seem pretty certain about that."

"We're absolutely certain. It became clear a few minutes ago that the programme has reached a dead end. It will be incapable of producing anything further, because it will never be able to complete the present story."

"Bullshit. It's only been writing it for the last fifteen minutes. Unless it's Warholian immortality you've got in mind. It could write for months and that still wouldn't prove anything except that it had discovered soap opera."

"Ah. As I suspected." Knight's hands were shaking again. "Permit me to gloat in earnest. What you haven't grasped is that vampiric immortality implies immutability, fixedness. An epic story is no better than a long-lived human being. What we have been seeing since we started our programme is a species refining not its capacity for length, which is equivalent to a capacity for development, but its capacity for repetition. Vampires do not merely live forever, we live a single instant forever, the instant in which our souls were frozen in undeath. So too the perfect vampire story. Perhaps this is what book reviewers are trying to say when they talk about fiction having 'resonance.' " The shaking hand proffered the typescript.

"I'll bet it stars at least one pompous windbag," said John as he took the story, and began to read.

The ultimate vampire story was titled "The Nine Billion Names of Nosferatu." John knew after the first few paragraphs how it was going to go, and by the time he'd got to the scene that described his talk with Nyctalops he couldn't stand the suspense any longer.

He skipped ahead to the final paragraph. It read:
    "He skipped ahead to the final paragraph. It read:
      'He skipped ahead to the final paragraph. It
read:
    "He skipped ahead to the final paragraph. It read:
      'He skipped ahead to the final paragraph. It read:
      "He skipped ahead to the final paragraph. It
read:
    "He skipped ahead to the final paragraph. It read:
      'He skipped ahead to the final paragraph. It read:
      "He skipped ahead to the final paragraph. It
read:
    'He skipped ahead to the final paragraph. It read:
      "He skipped ahead to the final paragraph. It read:
      'He skipped ahead to the final paragraph. It
read:

# VampWare

## Karen E. Taylor

Sarah Barlow pushed her chair away from the computer, locked her fingers together, and stretched out her arms, cracking all her knuckles in the process. She tilted her head from side to side, trying to shake out the kinks that had developed, and stole a half-guilty, half-pleased look at the clock. As she'd suspected, as she'd planned, it was much too late to attend her afternoon class. *What the hell,* she thought, *I'm flunking anyway. Why prolong the agony?*

She padded down the hallway of her apartment to the

kitchen and poured herself a cup of this morning's coffee, now thick and grainy. Sarah grimaced as she drank it. "And who gives a shit?" she addressed the empty room, "even with a Master's there are no jobs to be had. I'm better off here, so long as dear old Daddy keeps the checks coming in."

Sitting down at the small kitchen table she looked at the wall calendar where a countdown of red numbers marched over the current week and the next. Today was Tuesday, she was now nine days away from the deadline for her dissertation outline with nothing to show for her efforts but eight clocked hours testing Gideon's new computer game, VampWare.

Undaunted, Sarah picked up her portable phone and dialed his office number. As always, he answered on the first ring, as if he had nothing better to do but wait for her call.

"V.G.I., Gideon Richards speaking," he said formally. She was constantly surprised by his voice, deep and rumbling; it sounded as if it belonged to a trucker, not the delicate and pale effeminate figure that was Gideon. If she hadn't heard him speak in person, she would have bet that he'd had his office phone modified to artificially enhance his voice.

"Hi, Gid. It's me, Sarah."

"Sarah. It's early, I didn't expect to hear from you so soon. Aren't you supposed to be working on your dissertation?"

She gave a snort of amusement. "As if I could, when you keep tempting me with these computer games."

"Well," Gideon laughed, a low, strangled chortle, "candy doesn't work for little girls like you; I've had to work hard and long to find something alluring enough to keep up my quota."

"Very funny, Gid. Anyway, it worked. It's a wonderful game."

"Good, I thought you might enjoy it. How many hours have you logged in?"

"Eight, so far. And it's great, but another hour and I'll be at the last level."

"I know, it's not challenging enough for you. But I have the prototype for VampWare II right here on my desk, fresh from the lab and ready to be tested by any eager guinea pig I can find."

Sarah held back a small gasp. "But you told me that wouldn't be ready for months."

"We sped it through production, just for you, my darling.

390

And Sarah," the pitch of his voice seemed to lower even more, now possessing a throbbing, persuasive note, "this one is a virtual."

"Gideon," Sarah said, unable to control the desperate tone that colored her words, "I *have* to have that game."

"I know."

"So what'll it cost me this time?"

"Nothing you can't spare, Sarah. Your first-born son perhaps, or maybe we'll just settle for your immortal soul."

Sarah laughed. "Well, no problem, that you can have. Thanks, Gid. I'll be right there."

The offices of V.G.I. were just several blocks from Sarah's downtown apartment and she made the trip in five minutes. Her normally pale cheeks were reddened from the cold, and she gave the receptionist a wide smile, combing her fingers through short, brown hair that had been tousled by the wind. "Hi," she said breathlessly, "I'm here to see Gideon."

The woman behind the desk gave her a cool, appraising stare and Sarah stood defiantly, making no effort to pull her jacket closer around her body. She was aware, but uncaring, of the inappropriateness of the skin-tight leotard and leggings she wore into the office environment.

"I will tell Mr. Richards you're here." With a final sneer the receptionist turned back to her desk and buzzed Gideon's intercom. "Ms. Barlow is here to see you *again*, Mr. Richards."

"Great. Send her back, Mary." His booming voice seemed to echo from the walls of the sparsely furnished lobby; Sarah gave Mary a smug smile and sauntered down the hall to his office. Halfway there, aware of the woman's still unapproving scrutiny, she slipped off her jacket and slung it over her shoulder. "If you had an ass as good as mine, you dumpy old bitch," Sarah muttered, smirking, and deliberately emphasizing the wiggle of her hips, "you'd probably walk around buck naked. So eat your heart out."

"Excuse me?" Gideon stood in his office doorway, leaning against the jamb and shook his head at her. "Talking to yourself again, Sarah? That's not a healthy sign, you know."

"Why don't you sack that old ghoul, Gid? She doesn't meet your image of a leading-edge company. And what does V.G.I.

stand for anyway?" Sarah went into his office and flopped into one of the black leather and chrome chairs next to his desk.

"I've told you a hundred times already," Gideon said with an exasperated sigh, "Vampire Games, Incorporated, as anyone should have been able to figure out. And you must have read it repeatedly on the game instructions."

"Oh, those," Sarah shrugged, "I never bother with reading them. I *live* the games."

"A dangerous attitude . . ."

"But one that you would like to foster in every home across the country, no doubt."

"No doubt." Gideon agreed and sat down behind his desk, his long, slender fingers splayed out upon the highly polished surface. Sarah studied him for a minute; he fascinated her, he always had since the night they'd first met in the seedy student bar she frequented.

It had been a cold, misty night about a year ago and the bar had been practically deserted; most of the other students were spending one last night cramming for midterms. Gideon had approached her while she stood at one of the video machines. "Excuse me, miss . . ." he began, but Sarah waved him away.

"In a minute," she said, not even looking at him, "I just fed the damn thing another quarter." And he stood quietly, patiently, trying not to interrupt her concentration. But it didn't work. His presence there was so commanding and so unnerving that eventually she turned away from her game in progress, leaned up against the machine and glared at him.

The man was definitely not her type; she wasn't entirely sure if he would be anyone's type. He was tall and gaunt, and his dark clothes emphasized his ashen skin. Yet there was something oddly attractive about him, although she could not quite define what that quality was—maybe the deep-set, almost black eyes, or maybe the swatch of baby-fine black hair, that fell on his forehead, giving him a boyish appearance. His manners were impeccable and fastidious, and when he introduced himself, producing the small business card that declared him as vice-president of gaming module research and development, it seemed to her a match made in heaven.

Their relationship had never progressed beyond friendship, and that suited Sarah just fine. She had been repelled by his initial touch, that clammy hand grasping hers only briefly, and as time went on she had accepted his idiosyncrasies as part of the total package, grateful that there seemed to be no sexual strings attached to the vast wealth of material he had offered for her consumption.

Sarah's eyes darted around the office now, searching for her newest free gift. Gideon watched her intently for a moment, then gave his low, rumbling laugh.

"Can't wait, can you?"

"Hell, Gideon, I ran all the way here. Where is it?"

"It's here, my impatient one." He pulled out a large carton from behind his desk. "You do understand, Sarah, that this is merely a prototype. You must be extremely careful. *And read the instructions first.*"

She winced a little from the loudness of his last words. "Hey, why don't you just give me the basic run-down, Gid? I'll wing it from there."

Gideon shook his head, a wry grin twisting his narrow lips. "Fine, if that's how you want to do it. But remember that you were warned."

"Warned? Against what?"

"The lab results have proven that this is an extremely addictive game. And much more complicated than the original VampWare."

"Great, I can't wait to start."

Gideon proceeded to explain the intricacies of the hookups: the helmet and bulky gloves that would actually bring the game to life. Sarah nodded, only half-listening, her fingers literally itching to begin. "And this is the most important facet . . . Sarah! You're not paying any attention to me, are you?"

"Hmmm?" She tore her eyes away from the high-tech equipment alluringly displayed on the desk and focused on his face. "Go ahead, Gid," she nodded, "I'm listening."

"I repeat, this is the most important facet—don't forget to set the helmet clock. Two hours is the recommended time and more than enough for your first time through, if you even last that long. The commercial version will have an automatic time-out built in, but in the prototype you must do the timing yourself. Don't forget."

"Yeah, yeah, Gid, I won't, I promise. And if I can't take the two hours, I deserve to lose."

"Well, then," he shrugged his thin shoulders, "take it and play in good health. Call me after you've clocked your first two hours and let me know what you think."

"Two hours, my ass," Sarah muttered as she cleared space in her office for the new equipment. "I'll play as long as I like." She made the appropriate connections the way Gideon had shown her, then sat down in her chair and turned on the game.

The opening screen was almost identical to VampWare I and Sarah snorted as she entered in the appropriate information when prompted. "New and improved, huh? Gideon, you gotta do better than that."

But then the words and pictures on the screen melted together to form a computer approximation of Gideon's face. The expression in his eyes was one of challenge and arrogance, and when he spoke, the inflection of his voice was scornful and realistic. "You are about to enter into the domain of bloodthirsty and terrifying vampires. Everything that you experience will feel perfectly real. The first ten minutes of the game after you don the equipment are a safe time to get accustomed to the controls and the environment. After that you are on your own."

"Thanks, Gideon," she replied as she put on the helmet and the gloves as requested. Sarah took one long deep breath and hit the enter key.

"Jesus H. Christ." Sarah's words echoed through the damp stone hallway. "I can't believe it. It's just incredible."

As if transported miraculously, Sarah found herself in a cold and dank medieval castle, lit by burning torches and by the setting sun faintly shining through a narrow window at the end of the hall. "I see," she said, smiling, "I'm only safe until the sun sets. Nice touch, Gideon."

Sarah jumped when his voice answered. "Thank you, Sarah. I knew you'd like it. You have ten minutes, my darling, use them well."

In spite of herself, Sarah shivered. Then she noticed that she was clothed in only a white, lightweight, almost transparent nightgown. Her feet were bare and her long hair—long hair? she thought, confused—streamed down her back. "Very Gothic,"

394

she spoke more quietly now, so that she would not be heard, "but very unsporting. Where are my weapons? My defenses?"

"You will have to find them."

"Shit." Sarah looked at the waning sun and hurried down the hall, checking each room she passed for weapons. The first room was completely empty, as was the second. From a distance, Gideon's voice boomed, "Seven minutes and counting."

"Should have read the damn instructions." Sarah opened the door of the third room. This one contained a wrought iron candelabrum holding five candles. As she watched, one of them sputtered and burned out. "Great, less than seven minutes and it's about to get dark . . ." She left the room, and tried the next door; it was locked. She pounded on the door with her fists and a moment of panic washed over her; here she was, dressed like a seventeenth-century bimbo, armed with nothing, about to face a hoard of hungry vampires. Then she remembered that it was just a game, a good game, one that felt real and frightening, but a game nevertheless. And she could always get out if things got too bad. It just felt like she was in this damn castle; in reality she was sitting in her apartment, playing.

"Six minutes to go, Sarah. Will you be ready?"

She laughed, "Yeah, I will be."

Finally four minutes and three doors later, she found some useful items; standard vampire protection, she scoffed, but at least it was something. A few cloves of garlic, a bottle of what she presumed was holy water, and a three-foot-long wooden stake, the pointed end sharp and lethal. But she had no way to carry everything and wasted one more minute trying to decide what to take. Eventually she opted for the holy water and the stake, both of which would serve as offensive weapons. The garlic she left behind.

"One minute, my sweet."

Quietly, she went back into the hallway, looking for a place to make her stand. Not by the open window, she shuddered as she watched the last rays of the sun filter through the surrounding forest, better off back where she started. That way she could get out quickly if need be. Sarah ran down the hallway, but it seemed much longer than she remembered. All of the doors, rooms, and torches looked identical, the exit could be anywhere.

"Thirty seconds." Gideon's voice sounded pompous and self-assured.

"Go to hell. I'll beat this game, you'll see." Frantically, Sarah tried to remember the brief glance she'd taken at the instructions. She was supposed to flex her right hand to get the options menu, she thought. Setting down the bottle of holy water, she raised her arm, and made a fist. "I feel like a damn fool," she muttered.

"Twenty seconds, and of course you do, my dear."

Or maybe it was her left hand? She put the stake down next to the holy water, and made the same motions with that arm. Neither worked. She tried both arms simultaneously as the ten-second warning came. A gust of wind blew through the open window and all of the torches at that end of the hallway blew out. From behind her, faint but threatening, she could hear the beginning of a blood-curdling hiss.

"Shit," she spun around, her foot kicking the stake. It rolled down the hallway, knocking down and breaking the bottle. Sarah felt tears sting in her eyes as she watched the wet stain that was one of her only two defenses spread out on the cold flagstones. The stake itself had disappeared into the darkness.

"Time's up."

A misty figure began to materialize next to her. When the familiar form of Gideon appeared she relaxed slightly and smiled, giving a nervous laugh. "You were right, Gid, I should have read the instructions first. Now, be a love, and tell me how I get out of here."

He said nothing, but grinned at her, exposing a set of truly realistic canines.

She backed away from him. "No, really, Gideon, tell me how to get out and I'll go back and read the stinking book. I promise."

He still did not speak, but he reached out and grasped her thinly clad arms. The chill from his contact caused Sarah to shiver. "Gideon? What do I need to do? Tell me."

He laughed, his face closing in on hers. "You've already done it, Sarah. And now I take my payment."

"Your . . . your payment?"

His mouth was treacherously close to her neck, his breath

was hot and putrid. "Yes," he hissed, "my payment. Your immortal soul."

Gideon's teeth came down on her neck.

And Sarah Barlow's last earthly thought was that they could have made losing the game a lot less painful.

"Graphics aren't much better than the first one." Thirteen-year-old Ted Hampton said to the friend peering over his shoulder as he entered the appropriate information on the opening screen of VampWare II. Then the words and pictures melted into a picture of a woman, long brown hair curling provocatively over her thin, white nightgown. "Hey, cool!"

"You are about to enter into the domain of bloodthirsty and terrifying vampires." The woman smiled at Ted, exposing long, blood-stained canines. "I am Sarah," she said in a sultry voice, "and I will be your first challenge."

"Man, she's a real fox," Ted's friend said, "I bet you could have fun with her!" He chuckled slightly, "Maybe you better read the instruction manual before you start, Ted."

"Nah, those things are for wimps. I want to live the game."

# The Best Years of My Life

### Yvonne Navarro

Hello, Richard."

The sound of my voice shocked him enough to make him jerk gracelessly in front of the lovely woman sitting across from him at the cafe table. She looked up at me beneath tear-swollen eyelids and frowned—instant jealousy—then her features rearranged themselves into a polite smile. Richard just looked flustered; I suppose it was all those memories suddenly snapped to the forefront.

"Nicole! It's—uh—good to see you. How've you been? How are things going?"

I smiled and resisted the urge to smooth my hair. "Fine," I answered. "You know how it is. Time passes, things go." I tried not to stare openly. "And you?"

"Fine, fine." He looked uncomfortable, and in a way that was good. I didn't want to make him angry, but I didn't want him to forget about me quickly either. This was a tricky situation; his lady friend looked like she could slip into the aggravation range at any moment, and that was a no-no. I guessed her age to be about thirty-five, a good fifteen years younger than I. They must not be getting along very well by now, and were probably nearing the end of their relationship. That would explain the tense expressions that had been on both their faces before I'd interrupted their lunch. My appearance would probably make it worse; even so, it wasn't intentional, although this was my ex-lover and his latest soon to be ex-girlfriend.

"Listen," I continued, "didn't you collect Cubs memorabilia? I thought your uncle was an announcer at Wrigley Field or something." His face brightened and I knew I had him. I knew all about his uncle, of course—how could I not? We'd lived together for five years. Undoubtedly he'd left that part of his life out of the history he'd given to the woman sharing the table with him now. I wondered how long they'd been together; my guess was about five years. In some ways Richard was very predictable. "It's a good thing I ran into you. I was cleaning out the garage a couple of weeks ago and found this box of old baseball stuff that I'm sure is yours. I didn't have a number for you or anything, so I was just going to toss it. If you like, you can come and pick it up. Unless you'd rather I put it out with the garbage."

Richard looked absolutely horrified. He knew the box I was talking about, of course, and it wasn't one he'd "accidentally" left behind. I hadn't had much notice that things had gone sour between us other than the two-week time span during which his attentions had rapidly faded out, along with his actual appearance on my doorstep and in my bed. But I'd always been an intuitive woman, and I'd moved the box of his uncle's Cubs souvenirs to my mother's house long before the final good-bye. He'd asked about it two days before he'd disappeared altogether, but

I'd claimed I couldn't find it. At the time I'd had some wild idea that it would be enough to keep him coming back until I could figure out what had gone wrong and patch things up. The blind faith of a woman in love, I suppose. I could have—*should* have—shipped the box to him in care of the ballpark when I'd finally accepted the truth, but I hadn't. Spite, pure and simple. If he'd given me nothing else, I deserved my share of that. After all this time, that box of moldy old cards and caps and dirty leather balls was going to serve some purpose. Imagine that.

"Oh, no!" he said now. "Don't throw it out. What's a convenient time to come and get it?"

"Any evening," I said. "You do remember the address?" I was very proud of myself at the success with which I was able to keep any sarcasm from showing in my tone.

"Certainly, Nicole." Suddenly he recalled the woman sitting silently across the table. Her face was a palette of emotions: fury, jealousy, embarrassment, and a dozen others I'd have to look up in a dictionary. Richard turned his melted chocolate gaze on her and smiled gently. "Nicole used to be my landlady," he explained. "I didn't live there for very long, but who forgets their old addresses?"

If I'd had any lingering doubts about what a slime he was, they disappeared at that instant. While that may have been one way of looking at our relationship, it was still the boldest, most outlandish lie I'd ever heard verbalized in front of a woman who could easily expose him. Was he that confident that I had outgrown my feelings? Or was he simply at the point with this woman that it no longer mattered? That seemed more likely.

In any event, the ruse worked; the mask of anger Richard's companion wore disappeared, replaced by a look of curiosity. After all, I was a fifty-year-old woman—what possible competition could I present? "Good," I said with finality. "I'll see you . . . when? Probably within a week or so?"

Richard nodded. "Count on it."

"I am." I turned and walked away, grateful there were no mirrors around to give him a telltale reflection of my wide, grim-lipped smile.

"This place is still the same." Richard was ill at ease in the back parlor of my rambling old Baltimore Victorian, still hunched inside his leather jacket though the full fire going on the hearth in the front room wiped away the chill that had come with the all-day March drizzle. Come to think of it, he'd never been comfortable in the house, even during the half decade he'd lived there and shared my bed. If he'd thought it was too old and reminded him of things best forgotten then, what must it be doing to him now? He fidgeted and folded his arms, then picked up a paperweight with a scorpion in it, a touristy thing I'd bought on an Arizona vacation. "I'd've thought you be living in Phoenix by now," he continued. He glanced at the door leading to the basement, but I wasn't about to let him get his things, not yet. After all this time, he could at least pretend to make conversation with me for a few minutes.

"I couldn't make the move," I said as I watched him carefully. "Too many bills to pay, too many repairs to be made on the house to get it in saleable condition."

"Some things never change," he said absently. A foolish comment, and one that opened a door to all kinds of possibilities.

"That's true." I brought one finger up and ran it along the line of my jaw, feeling the age-softened skin there, the map of wrinkles that had started to crawl across the skin. I stared at him, but he avoided my gaze. His skin was as smooth and unblemished as I remembered it, girlish in its pale perfection. The house was a light-soaking relic, but I fought it at every turn with an over-abundance of lamps; they showed not a single strand of silver anywhere in his thick, dark brown hair. "Speaking of things changing," I said bluntly, "why haven't you?"

"Why haven't I what?" He tried to look innocent, but there was something deep in his gaze that made the whole thing a farce, and I knew it. He *knew* I did, but I guess he'd been living with lying so long he thought he could do it to everyone. Overconfidence, like that ridiculous tale he'd told the woman in the restaurant three days ago. Perhaps a life of delusion had made him begin to believe his own stories.

"There's nothing wrong with my eyes, Richard. Why haven't you *aged?*"

He laughed; if there'd been any hint of nervousness, it had disappeared. "Because I take care of myself, that's why." His smile was just as gorgeous as it had always been, perfectly even

white teeth arcing across a front-cover *GQ* face. "And I take
. . . vitamins."

"You take something, all right," I muttered. If he heard my
offbeat comment he gave no sign. I raised my voice. "It would be
an understatement to say I find it somewhat unusual that you
still look the same as you did when we were together."

He tilted his head to one side, finally giving me his full
attention. "I don't know what you mean. Together?"

Exasperation finally cut into my patience. "Oh, please," I
said. "Can we just knock it off with the small talk here? This
has nothing to do with our relationship, anyway. I don't care
about that any more. You know damned well what I'm talking
about."

Richard folded his arms, the movement slow and careful,
as if he were taking pains not to startle a mean-tempered dog.
"I'd hardly call renting the basement rooms from you a relationship," he said slowly.

"What!"

"Look, Nicole," he turned his hands palm-up in a gesture
of supplication. "I know I lied in the restaurant when I told my
girlfriend that I'd only lived here a short time, but that was only
to avoid an ugly confrontation. She's a bit on the jealous side,
and we're already dealing with some rocky points. We don't
need anything from the past to complicate things further."

This time I couldn't suppress a gasp. "After all that time,
that's all I was to you? Your *landlady?*"

"Yes," Richard said firmly. "I know I made a mistake—"

"More than once!"

"—or two by coming upstairs and . . . well, you know.
But I thought we both understood that's all those times were.
Errors in judgment, moments of weakness caused by too much
wine—whatever you want to call them. We—"

"It's hard to believe that even you would have the audacity
to stand there and talk about the time we spent together as
though it were nothing more than a series of drunken one-night
stands," I said grimly. My fingers were balled into fists, the nails
biting into the callouses on my palms. "I gave you the best years
of my life, my *child-bearing* years. You took them and used
them, and now they're *gone,* forever." I relaxed one fist and
waved at him, but his eyes were unreadable. "And now *look* at

you. For God's sake, Richard, you haven't aged a single *month* in the fifteen years since you last walked out of this house. It's like you took those years from me and—and *ate* them or something. Sucked me dry to nourish yourself and moved on." I glared at him. "Is that what you're doing now? To how many others? Was that woman in the restaurant with you your latest victim? Why, I bet she's the same age now as I was when you walked out, isn't she? *Isn't she!*" My voice had climbed to nearly a scream. "That's what you *do*, right? Take the best years of a woman's life and then just *walk!*"

"I don't have to listen to this," he said coldly. He gave the zipper on the front of his jacket a sharp tug upward and shoved his hands deep into its pockets. "You can keep the damned box. There's nothing in it that can't be replaced anyway."

Of course he could replace the contents—they were what, thirty, maybe forty years old? In fifty years he'd have a whole new box, only this time it'd be filled with memoirs of the first *day* games at Wrigley Field. But I had gone too far—in another five seconds he'd be out of my life for good. That wasn't at all what I'd meant to happen. "Wait!" I said quickly. "I'm—I'm sorry. I guess I'm still bitter, and I didn't realize it." I laughed self-consciously. "Really, I apologize." He hesitated, then shrugged. "The box is in the basement," I offered. "It seems really silly for you to have come all this way and not pick it up, and even sillier to throw it all out. Plus, I don't want to lug it up here myself." I tried to look plaintive, not an easy thing to do when nothing but bitterness had fed my thoughts for the last couple of days. I must've pulled it off, though, because he looked me up and down and you could see the idea run through his mind that I was getting old and emotionally stupid, and physically weak to boot.

"Well," he said at last, "I really did want the Cubs stuff. And you're right, of course—I *am* here." He smiled engagingly. I nodded without adding anything and motioned toward the door leading to the basement.

"It's under the stairs," I managed. I followed him through the door as he began to descend. "I got it that far, but never got around to bringing it up."

"What happened to the windows?" Richard asked as he took the first few steps downward.

"I had them bricked up," I said, "to keep out the water. And the rats."

"*Rats?* Jesus, Nicole. Where's the light switch? I can't see a damned thing—"

"You don't need to," I said and gave him a good, hard push in the middle of the back.

He hasn't made nearly as much noise as I thought he would. I've been planning this for quite some time, of course, since the first time I saw him at that cafe downtown three months ago. At the time I'd thought it was a fluke, but when it happened twice more, I realized it was a regular place for him— at least during this cycle. That's what Richard does, you see. He runs in cycles of five to seven years, sucking away that last precious half-decade or so when a woman could create a life of her own, then leaving a dried husk behind. It's what he did to me, and to that swollen-eyed woman in the cafe. For me, and her, and countless others, it's too late. But he won't do it again.

It's amazing what just a couple of weeks in the basement has done to Richard. He's starting to show his age much more now, and he looks so much more natural. I see his face at the bottom of the stairs when I open the door and set a plate of food on the steps in the morning and at night. The basement is still an apartment, just like when he rented it from me fifteen years ago, though I had the electricity to the stove disconnected. But there's still a sink and refrigerator, and a small bathroom with a shower. Like all turn-of-the-century Victorians, the house has a small dumbwaiter, and Richard sends his dirty clothes and clean dishes—I won't wash those—up to me using that. It's too small for him to crawl inside and escape; he may be a vampire of sorts, but he doesn't suck blood or turn into smaller creatures like in the B-movies. No, he does something much worse in his search for immortality—he takes the best years of a woman's life and gives nothing in return.

I suppose he's not much different in that respect than a lot of guys, and I've certainly known enough women who'd like to get a second crack at the good years they wasted on a lot of men. I've always thought it was unfair how men end up with an extra decade or two to make decisions about family, and just sort of . . . *wear out* a few women while they go through the process of making up their minds. To prove my point, last night Richard was ranting through the door at me, carrying on about how I'd been too dependent on him when he'd rented the apartment, and about how I'd blow everything out of proportion then and was doing the same thing now. Just to make sure it stung, he threw a couple reminders in there about how I'd never been able to take care of myself, then asked how I was going to take care of him now.

I didn't care for that at all—I know I don't look the same as when we were together, and grinding in the fact won't help his situation. I used to be a beautiful young woman; now I'm just sort of dowdy and pre-elderly. The vitality's gone the way of my smooth skin and firm muscles. Still, I've always thought I was a fair-minded female—more than most when it came to passing judgment on the opposite sex—but I have a hard time understanding his point of view. Especially when *my* point of view shows me a man who looks the same to me as he did fifteen years ago.

But you can't hold someone who doesn't want to be held, and I wouldn't want to be responsible for him dying or anything. I'm pretty sure he's eating, though that basement can't be healthy for his complexion or constitution, as dark and damp as it is. Besides, I'm not totally crazy—I know I can't keep Richard down there forever and I certainly don't want to kill him.

Oh, I'll let him out, of course.

When he looks like me.

# The Wet-Nurse

### Lois Tilton

Marija snored, mouth open, sprawled on her bursting straw-filled mattress. Flies hummed in the room's malodorous heat. There was a stirring within a heap of rags in a corner and a naked infant of about nine months crawled out. It crept across the filthy floor until it encountered a rind of bacon, which it put into its mouth, sucking and gumming the rancid scrap.

After a while the child began to whimper. Marija stirred. With a snort, she rolled onto her side, scratching after a louse in her armpit. She groped for the pitcher lying overturned beneath the bed but found it empty.

The crying persisted, even more loudly. Finally, Marija sat up in the bed. "All right, you poxy brat," she said, lifting the child from the floor. Her bodice gaped open. The breasts within were fair, swollen, blue-veined globes of flesh, and the child reached out with an eager mouth for them, rooting, sucking.

Marija had not expected it to live, as the two before it had not. But whether she wished it or not, this one had lived and, indeed, was thriving on her abundant milk.

When it was done, Marija pushed it away and laced up her bodice. Then she picked up the empty jug from the floor and went out the door, not bothering to close it behind her.

The taproom was only a few doors down the street. Marija was blonde and fair-skinned, with plump red cheeks, but today no men looked up as she came into the taproom, so she filled her pitcher, then made her way to a bench in the corner.

A sodden, gray-haired crone lifted her head from the table as she sat down. "Eh? Marija! D'y know? They be looking for a new wet-nurse up at the castle! For the Count's heir."

Marija's hand, holding a mug, arrested halfway to her mouth. The villagers generally wanted little to do with the strange folk up at the castle. "I thought they had that girl from Vladej."

"Nah. That one died. They carried 'er to the churchyard tonight. So the place is open."

"How do you know?" Marija demanded, shaking the crone, whose head had fallen back down to the table.

"Eh? Oh, the Count's steward . . . brought the body into town just after sundown . . . 'e's at the Wolf's Head now. But you'd best hurry, or someone else will have the place."

Marija calculated. True, there were tales about the castle, but as wet-nurse to the Count's own heir she would have nothing to do but eat rich food and suckle the brat. She could hope for no better fortune, tales be damned.

Decided, she made her way quickly to the Wolf's Head.

405

Another woman, a wide-hipped drab with a child clinging to her skirts, stood already before the booth where the Count's steward sat in polished black boots. Her immense, full breasts strained against her bodice and her broad lap looked as if it could hold a dozen children, including the one that reached to pull itself up by her skirts.

At this, the steward's brows lowered. "You could not take the child with you, of course."

"But, Sir! The milk is more than plenty. When I was wet-nurse to the goldsmith, Master Lucasz . . ."

"What do I care for a goldsmith's brat?" the steward snarled sharply. "I seek a nurse for Count Ludovic's heir!"

At this, Marija pushed herself forward. She knew her worth. Slowly, she unfastened the lacing of her bodice and cupped one hand under each breast, lifting them out into view—full, heavy, bountiful. She pressed one teat between her fingers so he could see the milk spurt.

"And have you no child to drag along with you?" he asked.

"Oh," she belatedly recalled the existence of her offspring, "that one is all but weaned. It'll do well enough without me."

"Very well," the steward said abruptly, draining his tankard and getting to his feet. "When can you be ready to leave? It must be soon, before daylight."

Marija finished lacing her bodice and shrugged. "I have nothing to keep me here."

The castle's interior was dark and tenebrous, lit only by candle-brackets. Marija saw no windows. *Wait*, they had told her, but now the door creaked as it opened and she whirled around, bowed down.

"The trull from the village, my Lord," the steward announced, and Marija raised her eyes to see Count Ludovic: Parchment-pale, with onyx eyes that seemed for a moment in the candlelight to glow red. He was dressed in black velvet, in mourning.

"Let us see her, Janosz," the Count said, and Marija stepped forward, unlaced her bodice, exposing her ample flesh proudly. In the candle-glow, Marija's swollen breasts seemed suffused with a pulsing red warmth. The Count's eyes were drawn to them, he took a step forward, staring hungrily. Then, "She will do," he said, turning away.

The steward beckoned another woman forward. "Take care of the slut," he said shortly, then turned to follow his master from the hall.

"Jumped-up bastard," Marija muttered under her breath, but the woman heard her.

"Ah, Janosz. The old blood runs strong in him, though not quite as pure as he would have it." The woman had the same pallor as the others, though her black hair was turned to gray. She introduced herself as Evonna, the castle's housekeeper. "But come, the child is waiting, the poor precious mite."

"The mother is dead, then? In childbirth?"

"Ah, my poor lady Countess! Such a tragedy, that her blood was not as strong as the child's. In him, the old blood flows true." Then she shook her head and hurried Marija from the hall. "He must not wait!"

Once in the nursery, Evonna went to a cradle and took out the wailing creature, handing it to her. Marija dutifully opened her bodice, and let the open mouth fasten to her teat. She gasped to feel the sharp pain as it took hold. The little brat had teeth! Almost, in a reflex, she raised a hand to slap it, but the housekeeper's sharp gaze was on her, and so she endured the discomfort as it fed avidly, draining her.

At last her teat, aching and raw, was finally released. As Marija laced up her clothes, the housekeeper began to instruct her in her duties to the Count's heir. She was not pleased to hear that she would be required to care for the child alone during the daylight hours. And there were other restrictions: "Under no circumstances must the child be taken outside. His skin is delicate. The sun would burn it."

Marija listened sourly. From the pallor of their skin, it would seem that none of the castle's denizens were accustomed to the daylight.

Evonna took the child and kissed it, then laid it in its cradle, crooning, *Sleep, little owl* . . .

It was beginning to seem to Marija that she had entered a prison or a convent, to be shut away here in the nursery, day and night. But just then a servant entered, bearing a tray from which came savory odors. Marija, with a ravenous hunger, devoured soup and fowl, sopped up the juices with thick slices of bread, and washed it all down with draughts of the strongest, richest ale. For this, perhaps she could endure a few restrictions, a little discomfort. Would it not be better than her filthy straw bed and the coppers she earned from the men she entertained there—and the brats they gave her? Yes, a wet-nurse's life in the castle would not be all bad.

Yet, when the Count's child began to wail again, she had to bite her lip as she brought it to her sore and bleeding breast.

Milk and blood, mingled, drooled from one corner of its mouth as the child finally released its hold on her teat. Marija groaned in relief. A small hand reached for one of the laces of her bodice to put into its mouth, but she impatiently slapped it away. She was paid to nurse the brat, not dandle it in her arms. Let the housekeeper do that, and the maids, when they were done with their nightly pleasures. After all, she had the care of it all throughout the day.

The child, placed back in its cradle, whimpered to be held, but Marija turned her back on it and went to pour herself a cup of ale. It was dull here, alone in the nursery all day with the insatiable thing and its demands. Once, she had ventured into the empty hallway, as far as the door to the inner courtyard and the stables, but there had been no other soul to be seen or heard. It was as if the castle slept.

Now sunset was near and she was impatient for the others to relieve her of her tasks. Ignoring the child, she sank down into the soft goose down of her bed, took another deep gulp of ale. She was always ravenous and thirsty these days, ever since she came to the castle. Now, from outside in the hallway, she could hear squeals and shrieks. Doubtless the maids were having some sport, instead of attending to their duties.

The Count's heir was wailing when Evonna came into the nursery, and the housekeeper rushed to lift it up from the cradle, glaring accusation at Marija. "The child is crying!"

She began to rock it in her arms, crooning soothingly, "Poor, motherless little mite. Poor lady Countess, that your child must be put to a stranger's breast! Are you hungry, my little lord, my little prince? So you are!

"Here, now," she said sternly, handing the infant to Marija, who sighed, unlaced her bodice, and shut her eyes in pain as its mouth clamped to her teat.

"The maids are supposed to be here after dark," she said sullenly. "I can't care for the child myself, night and day."

"They'll be here soon. After they've fed," Evonna reassured her.

As she watched the babe suck, Marija asked, "There was another wet-nurse before me, wasn't there?"

Evonna frowned. "The girl from Vladej? That one was sickly, weak. A poor choice to nurse our little lord. I hope you will do better—a fine, strong, stout girl like you."

Marija scowled and looked resentfully down at the child gorging itself on her milk, her blood. At last it released its hold, tiny fangs gleaming, and she called impatiently for the maids to take it away for its bath. And where was her supper?

She fell avidly on the tray when the servant brought it in. While she ate, the maids played with the infant in its bath, splashing and squealing. Marija was ignoring them until she overheard: "Look at her! Like a sow at her trough!"

"Not so much lard as a sow, though. Not lately."

"And she was so proud of her great fat teats when she first came here!"

"Well, we'll be rid of her soon. Our little lord is almost ready to be weaned!"

Marija flushed angrily. Let them call her a sow, would they? But then she tugged at her loose bodice. Twice now already since she'd come to this place she'd been forced to take it in when the laces would no longer close it tightly enough.

The door flung open abruptly and the maids stopped their chatter as the steward Janosz entered. He turned a sharp eye on Marija. "You're not eating? Don't forget, slut, you're here to feed the Count's heir."

Marija sullenly turned to her tray, but it was true, she was always so hungry. Yet it seemed that she was wasting away. . . .

As the first wet-nurse had wasted away. . . .

As the Count's lady had died, life drained away while the child was still in the womb! *In him, the old blood runs true.*

409

And suddenly she realized at last what blood it was in the castle's denizens. The legends told in the village must be true!

She forced herself to wait until daybreak, when the sunlight would be their bane, and her safety. The hours passed slowly, while the child toddled around the room, held upright by the housekeeper's hands. Oh, but she would miss the luxury of this place, the soft bed, the fine food. Never had she lived so well!

At last the nursery door opened and the Count entered, returned from his hunting. The child squealed in happiness as its father took it and tossed it in his arms.

But then it was time for them all to retire for the day, and soon Marija was alone. She hesitated a moment when she opened the nursery door, but as always, the corridor was silent, the castle asleep. She fled.

But to her dismay, the castle's heavy oaken doors were locked and bolted shut. She was trapped! Desperately, she ran up and down the corridors until she found one door that would open to her, the door to the stable courtyard. Rejoicing, Marija ran out and across it to the postern gate, pushed on it, heaved with all of her strength, but it was locked fast.

Above her, the massive stone blocks of the outer wall loomed. Her prison. She couldn't escape!

Tears of rage and terror began to fill her eyes, which were already watering, unaccustomed to the sunlight—

The sunlight. Marija's tears stopped and a slow, grim smile crept across her face. The sunlight—their bane, the bane of all their blood.

She ran quickly back to the castle, to the nursery, where the child slept, and she seized it from the cradle and clamped one hand over its mouth. It made stifled cries of terror, and fangs bit her fingers, drawing blood.

Her blood, on which it had fed for so long. "No more," she told it, smiling that same grim smile.

Then, carrying the struggling infant, she ran to the courtyard once again. As the sunlight touched it, the tone of its screaming changed from rage to pain. Now, *now!* Standing in the center of the courtyard, Marija took her hand from the child's mouth. Already, as it screamed, she could see its pallid skin beginning to redden.

She could hear cries from within the castle, then Evonna was standing in the shadows of the doorway, stark horror on her pale face.

"Please, the child will burn, it will die!" the housekeeper begged, but Marija laughed. "If you want to save it, then let me go! Bring me the key to the gate, and your Count can have his heir back!" Then she had a further thought. Was she not due payment for her service? "And fifty pieces of gold," she added.

More figures appeared in the doorway's shade, and one of them stepped forward. Marija recognized the tall, cloaked form of Count Ludovic himself! She curtsied mockingly as she repeated her demands.

"You can have what you ask," he pleaded. "Only bring me the child first! The sunlight will kill it!"

"I am not such a fool as that!" she replied. "But you had better hurry to bring me the key. Its skin is starting to blister!"

With a bitter curse, the Count took something from a dim figure behind him. "Here," he shouted. "The key and the money. Come here and take it!"

"Oh, no!" Marija cried back, over the sounds of the child's tortured screams. "Throw it out here to me!"

A cloth purse landed with a ringing sound on the flagstones next to her. Marija opened it. Yes, the key. She went to the gate, still carrying the tormented infant, and inserted the key into the lock. Yes, it fit. And the gold. She counted the pieces while the Count begged for her to bring him back the child, to bring it out of the sun. Yes, there were fifty pieces.

She pulled the purse's drawstrings shut and tucked it into her bodice, then lay the infant down on the flagstones. "Come and get your child!" she cried.

Through the open gate she could see them stumbling, staggering blindly toward the gate to retrieve the Count's heir. The legends were true. In the sunlight, they were all but helpless. Marija would have plenty of time to buy a seat in the mail coach going to the city, far from Count Ludovic's castle.

Thoughtfully, she cupped a hand under her breasts where the purse of gold rested. It was not a bad life, still, that of a wet-nurse. Plenty of good food and a soft bed. Perhaps, in the city, she might find another position, a less demanding nursling than Count Ludovic's heir.

It was too bad, she thought, that she had left the castle without a letter of reference.

# 𝔄 12-𝔖tep 𝔓rogram

## (𝔉or the 𝔠orporeally 𝔠hallenged)

### TINA L. JENS

𝔚elcome to the first meeting of the Midwest Chapter of Vampires Anonymous. I know a lot of you cadavers have traveled a long way to be with us tonight, so take a few minutes to stretch your legs, wings, or whatever, hang your capes in the cloak room, then join us here in the circle. You'll find some refreshments on the back table, compliments of a Red Cross blood drive held this afternoon. A big flash of the fangs to Duchess Katie Longtooth for coordinating that project."

A polite round of applause followed the announcement. The group leader, Baron Brad Mooreland, shut the mike off. He watched with satisfaction as nearly thirty vampires from all across Illinois, Iowa, Wisconsin, and Missouri flocked around the refreshment table in the basement meeting hall of the Temple Sholom on the far north side of Chicago. It represented less than a tenth of the Midwest Undead. But vampires, being the lone-wolf personality type, were intrinsically nonjoiners. Let the cabal call him crazy. V.A. was going to work.

He flipped the mike back on again. "A quick question for our Jewish vampires: Are any of you experiencing any discomfort from our location? No? Good." He flipped the mike back off.

Obviously, a Christian church basement, the traditional setting for such groups, wouldn't work for Vampires Anonymous. The Baron had gotten the idea of using a synagogue from one of his recent victims. The old man had held up a Star of

David to ward him off. One dead rabbi later, the Baron knew where to hold the meeting.

To the Baron Brad's knowledge, no organized research had been done to test the effects of other religions' accoutrements. He shook his head. The Undead just had to get organized before they were exterminated.

He joined the crowd at the back of the room to partake of a little refreshment and small talk.

"Baron Mooreland."

It was Lady Julia Peterson, of the Ft. Madison, Iowa, Petersons.

"Lady Julia, how good to see you," the Baron said, bowing low to kiss her hand.

She smiled and took his arm.

"As you know, Baron, I have supported this idea from the very beginning, and I've sent a number of letters saying so to the ruling cabal. However," her voice dropped to a whisper, "their concerns of security are entirely valid. I must admit I'm a bit uneasy having this many of us in one place. One raid by a wild pack of Van Helsings could wipe our community out."

Trying to regain her composure, she brushed back her feathered blonde curls with her fingertips and laughed playfully.

The Baron thought the laughter sounded forced.

"I don't usually think such grim thoughts," she assured him. "Perhaps it's our surroundings."

"Never fear, Lady Julia, there shall be no holocaust of the Undead tonight. We've taken many precautions to insure our security."

He led her into the hallway.

"Perhaps you noticed the oily substance on all the windows and door handles? They've all been treated with a potent mixture of poison ivy extract and unguent of chili powder.

"Outside, we have a spy manning a Demon Dog hot dog cart on the corner. He's our early warning defense system. Also, we've hired a couple of panhandlers to spread out on the front steps."

He led her down the hallway to the long bulletin board that hung on the wall.

"I put this poster together myself," he said proudly, pointing at the yellow photocopied handbill. "Surely you saw them on all the doors?"

"I did wonder if I'd come to the right place when I saw the fliers for the amateur poetry reading," Lady Julia said.

"In the unlikely event that anyone actually shows up for that, we have a doorman positioned to collect a five dollar cover-charge."

Lady Julia giggled at the deviousness.

"And of course, we've covered the basics," he told her, as they wandered back into the meeting room. "We locked the parking lot and towed in old junkers to fill the metered spaces on the street.

"And several of us met for an early dinner in the neighborhood. The police are quite busy picking up the pieces of a couple of drunken vagrants who passed out on the El tracks. The Chicago Transit Authority had to completely shut down this stop for the night."

"Well!" Lady Julia said, "I'd like to see a bunch of Van Helsings try to get a bag of wooden stakes past a Chicago bus driver!"

Baron Brad laughed with her.

"Need I go on?" he asked her kindly.

"Not at all. Obviously, we're in good hands tonight," she said.

It was time to get started. The Baron started herding the group away from the refreshment table. He stood back and watched as the vampires shuffled into the circle. He smiled as he watched a couple of vampires pull some of the chairs out of the circle, to make room for the werewolves, who preferred to lay on the floor. It was heartening to see Furry Friends attending the meeting. Werewolves didn't become vampires until after they were killed, of course. But obviously, these creatures were planning for their future. The Undead needed just that type of long-term-picture people to guide the community into the next millennium.

He took his place at the podium and turned on the mike.

"Hi, I'm Baron Brad Mooreland. And I'm . . . a Vampire," he said, with just a hint of melodrama.

An unerring sense of dramatic presentation was one of the

more important attributes gained when one was transformed into the Undead.

The group looked around hesitantly at each other. Then, in uncertain unison, answered, "Hi, Baron Brad."

The Baron nodded, pleased. Obviously some of the cadavers had belonged to a Program while they were alive. That made things much easier.

Brad wasn't really a Baron, of course, just as the cadaver sitting to Brad's left wasn't a real Count. Not by the living's legal standards, anyway. But it was part of the Undead's social structure that you took a title upon your rising. At each century's un-deathday, you were awarded the honor of upgrading the title. Who were the living—to deny them the use of the title Baron or Count?

In a way, that was what this whole meeting was about. Getting the Undead organized. They had been a repressed minority for too long, discriminated against and misunderstood.

"It is only through learning to accept ourselves, that others can learn to accept us. We must come out of our closets of shame, stand tall, and be proud of what we are," Baron Brad told them, his voice cracking with emotion.

"Remember, it is not God—but Christians—who are against us. We must learn to distinguish among the magic of Christianity, with all of its powerful talismans, and the power of God."

A murmur of assent passed through the room.

"For are not all things on this earth *His* creatures?" he said warmly. "Now, who among you would like to share his story first?"

There was a scraping of chairs and a low-pitched buzzing as the cadavers blushed and avoided his eyes.

"Oh come now," Brad said. "You're among friends."

Hesitantly, Count Chaney raised his blanched hand. The Baron traded places with him.

He tapped the mike. "Is this thing on?" the new speaker asked hesitantly, using the age old phrase of those who are stalling because they are afraid of the mike. The group assured him the equipment was working.

He cleared his throat and said, "Hi, my name is Count Ralph. I'm from Rockford, Illinois. And, I'm a Vampire."

"Hi, Ralph," the group responded.

Ralph's face lit up from the encouragement.

"I've been a Vampire for 236 years. In that time, I've seen some pretty awful things—and done even worse."

As Ralph came to the close of his statement, Brad led the group in a round of applause. Ralph's neighbors slapped him on the back as he returned to his seat.

Standing behind the podium again, Brad asked, "Ralph, how did you become a vampire?"

"Loss of blood," he mumbled.

The Baron nodded. "That's pretty common. Let's take a poll. How many here died from loss of blood when a roving vampire bit you? Raise your hands. Don't be shy."

Here and there a few hands went up.

"How many became vampires because you died in a state of sin? Suicides?"

Several members nodded or waved their hands. Looking closer, Brad could make out the razor-blade scars left on one woman's wrist, and the rope burns around the neck of an older man. Injuries incurred as a vampire would heal quickly, but suicide scars never went away.

"Any excommunicants in the group? Perjurers?"

"Before, or after, we died?" an anonymous voice wisecracked.

The Baron smiled tolerantly. A little levity was a good thing at this type of meeting. After all, if we can't laugh at ourselves, who or what can we laugh at?

"Who here was cursed by their parents? Dabbled in Black Magic? Were exceedingly wicked persons?"

Hesitantly, one cadaver raised his hand. His neighbors on either side moved their chairs away from him.

"Judge not lest ye be judged," Baron Brad admonished them.

With shame-faced grins, they scooted their chairs back, not quite as close as they had originally been.

"Any unavenged murder victims among us tonight? No? How about unbaptized children?"

The McGregor twins, who looked about six but had already passed their first-century mark, nodded.

Brad said, "I thought so."

"How about corpses who did not receive Christian burial? People unlucky enough to be born on Christmas Day? Any seventh sons? The seventh son of a seventh son?"

A husky young man in the back of the room raised his hand. The group gasped. Brad made a mental note of it. Seven-sevens, as they were known, were incredibly powerful and equally bad-tempered.

By the Baron's accounting, there were still a few individuals unidentified. "Anyone born with a caul?"

He shook his head sadly as one young woman raised her hand.

"That's a shame," Brad said sympathetically. "With advancements in prenatal care, those are completely preventable with dietary supplements."

"Anyone womb-cursed?"

This had always been a catch-all category for vampires who couldn't account for their condition any other way. It was hard to detect and harder to prove that a vampire had stared at a pregnant woman. In the few instances it was detected, the curse could be reversed by a priest's blessing.

"Now that we know each other a little better, who'd like to go next?"

The Baron stared expectantly at the crowd.

A young woman to his right raised a tentative hand. Obviously new to the world of the Undead, her skin still had a salmon tinge to it. She was just the sort of vampire who needed this group most. Brad smiled at her and motioned her to the podium.

"Hi, I'm Linda," she said, tugging nervously at the shoulder strap of her jumper. "I live in Wauwatosa, Wisconsin. Unlike so many here, I knew my sire. I was young, impressionable. Thought I was in love at the time."

There was a murmur of sympathy from the group.

"But being Undead wasn't what he said it would be. Three months after he changed me, he took off with a little tart—a ghoul that he'd met at the street fair in Madison during the Halloween festivities. That was two years ago. I haven't seen him since. I heard a rumor that he'd gone on a binge down in New Orleans during Mardi Gras last year. Supposedly he got drunk, passed out, and got fried by the sun. But I don't believe it. That worthless son of a bitch is out there somewhere, ruining some-body else's afterlife."

Brad laid his hand tenderly on her shoulder.

"No bitterness, Linda. Aren't you just projecting your an-ger outside yourself, when in reality, you're unhappy with who and what you are?"

She nodded.

"You must accept yourself, and make peace with your past."

The Baron turned to the group. "I think Linda needs a little extra support here tonight. Who has a hug for her?"

Count Ralph stood up, and she tottered into his arms. The group broke out in spontaneous applause.

Brad beamed. The meeting was going splendidly. Out of the corner of his eye, he saw Lady Julia wink at him.

It was going out on a limb, but he asked, "Seven-seven, would you like to share your story next?"

The burly cadaver, who, rumor had it, made his unliving as an All-Star Wrestler, barked once, then slunk down in his chair and looked the other way.

Ruffled by the response, Baron Brad said quickly, "No pres-sure!"

One of the werewolves "woofed" and padded up to the mike. "I'd like to say something."

His S's slurred into R's, the wolf's soft palate not being designed to utter the nineteenth letter of the American alphabet. Brad made a mental note to talk to the cabal about arranging speech therapy sessions. Perhaps that was a project Lady Julia would consider taking on.

"I'm Harold Raines from St. Louis, Missouri. Obviously, I'm not a vampire. Not yet. But I'm a realist, folks. I know it's just a matter of time. Some drunken hunter's gonna mistake me for a deer, or some ranger with the Wildlife and Game Depart-ment is gonna try to tranquilize me and relocate me in one of the state parks.

"I've been a werewolf for twenty years. But it hasn't been so long that I don't remember the culture shock. Back then, there wasn't anything like V.A. or W.A. to help you through it. And unlike you folks, the lucky ones, anyway, werewolves don't have any sires to explain things and help us through."

He sat back on his haunches and rubbed his nose with his front paw.

"One day you're walking around, minding your business as a human, and some wild dog on steroids knocks you down and bites your ass. You go to the doctor. The wound heals, and you think nothing of it. Until the next full moon—when suddenly you're sprouting hair and you've grown a tail and a whole lot of extra teeth."

The group murmured sympathetically.

"Don't get me wrong," Harold growled. "I'm not saying you vampires have it any easier. I think V.A.'s great! A group like this helps me prepare for the inevitable. I think we should give a big round of applause to Baron Brad, and all those cadavers who made this possible."

The vampires applauded and Harold wagged his tail.

The Baron stood up and waved his hands to stop the applause. His cheeks were tinted with just a hint of pink.

Just then, the doors flew open and a mob of angry young poets swarmed in, pushing the bouncer forward on the crest of the wave.

Clearly, they were going through their Gothic phase. The boys uniformly wore black jeans and black cotton turtlenecks, while the girls sported short black dresses. The jewelry was frighteningly unisex. Small silver hoops pierced their nostrils, oversized rosary crosses dangled from their ears, and intricately carved wooden stakes suspended from black cords around their necks.

But this wasn't a pack of rampaging Van Helsings. The youths were yelling something about First Amendment rights, free speech, and starving artists.

"We demand access to the mike!" one young rebel with spiked hair and multiple nose rings shouted.

The Gothic Gang fell silent as they noticed that thirty pairs of gleaming fangs and glowing red eyes were trained on them.

"Uh, wrong room?" the rebel leader asked, doubtfully.

"Why, yes," the Baron responded, his voice as silky and smooth as the Arabian boudoir where he'd spent his first Undead night.

"I believe your group is down the hall," he intoned. Si-

419

lently, he willed the others to join him in invoking a group trance.

Slowly, the young poets backed out of the room, herded by the sheepish bouncer.

When they were gone, the Baron clapped his hands to get the group's attention.

"All right, folks, it's been a good meeting! Don't let the interruption get you down. Remember, when the afterlife throws you a tomato—make a Bloody Mary!

"Before you go, I've got just a few announcements to make. Lady Julia is passing out membership fliers at the back of the room, so be sure and pick one up."

Baron Brad checked his notes.

"Next month, the Countess Bathory will give a talk entitled 'If I Had Him for Dinner—Do I Have to Go to His Funeral?' and other issues of Undead etiquette. And coming up in October, Dr. Harry Jekyll will talk about 'The Effects of Daylight Savings Time on the Vampire's Feeding Patterns.'

"To better accommodate our Furry Friends we'll hold it on the full moon. So mark your calendars. I hope to see you all next month, and why don't you all try to bring a friend!

"What's that, Duchess Longtooth? Oh, yes," the Baron nodded. "Additional refreshments will be served in the next room."

# Supernaturally Incorrect

## TIM WAGGONER

Jesus Christ, I don't know *why* they let zombies drive cabs!" Marshall Raymond said in his on-air bullhorn voice as he approached the table. Quite a few of the restaurant's patrons looked up and recognized him. Their expressions showed a range of reactions from mild dislike to open loathing. Marshall pretended that he didn't notice, but of course he did. He always noticed. And he loved it.

The attractive brunette who was waiting for him at the table gave him a half smile. "What happened to your car?"

Marshall sat his stocky frame down and ran his fingers through his graying hair as well as he was able with all the hairspray clogging it.

"Blew a goddamned tire. And the driver hadn't checked the spare recently. Turned out it was flat too." He shook his head in disgust. "I'll call my producer tomorrow and have him fire the bozo."

"Come on, Marshall. It was probably an honest mistake."

"Yeah, an honest mistake that forced me to take a cab. Ordinarily I would pass up a zombie hack—"

Sarah opened her mouth to speak, but before she could, Marshall said, "And don't tell me the preferred term these days is 'Previously Living.' We've only been out a few times and things have been going so well. Please don't spoil them. Now where was I? Oh, yeah. I can't stand riding with zombies. The whole cab reeked of rotting meat and grave mold."

"Now Marshall, you know they put spells on them so they won't smell."

"Well, this pus-bag must have slipped past quality control because he stank something fierce." He looked around the restaurant. "Where the hell's the waiter? After the day I had, I need a drink."

Sarah smiled sweetly. "He stopped checking on me after the first hour went by."

"I'm sorry, Sarah. They wanted me to stay and tape some new promos for the show tonight and nobody bothered to tell me ahead of time."

"I see. And I assume they taped these promos in the only TV studio in the world that doesn't have a phone."

"I didn't think it would take that long, but something kept going wrong with the sound and . . ." Marshall stopped and sighed. "Look, I'm sorry, okay? Really and truly." Her gave her his Number Eight smile, the one he ended his show with every night. It was one of his best and never failed.

Sarah relaxed a bit and returned the smile. "Forget it. I suppose these are the sorts of things one has to get used to when dating a celebrity."

Marshall didn't puff up at Sarah's use of the word *celebrity* because it wasn't a compliment so much as a statement of fact. Marshall Raymond was a celebrity in the truest sense of the word. His radio and TV shows—both called *Wake Up, America!*—were respectively listened to and watched by literally millions of people every day. He was, as he often said on his shows, the Voice of Right, practically a living god to conservatives, with the uncanny ability to appeal to both the common man and the well-to-do at the same time.

Marshall trumpeted every conservative cause, no matter how obscure, and attacked liberals every chance he got. And among his favorite targets were America's rising preternatural element, or as he liked to call them on the air, "The Spooks."

"So what kind of establishment have you chosen for our dining pleasure this evening?" Marshall asked. "I've never been here before. 'After Midnight.'" He gave Sarah his Smoldering Look Number Five. "Kind of a sexy name, don't you think?"

She appeared a trifle uncomfortable. "It's not really that kind of place, Marshall."

As if to illustrate her words, a small black bat came flapping up to their table and transformed into a tall young man who might have been handsome if his face wasn't so pale and his cheekbones so prominent.

"Good evening, sir, madam. My name's Blair and I'll be your server tonight. Can I get you something from the bar?"

"How about a glass of holy water?" Marshall snapped.

Sarah shot him a venomous look. "Marshall, please!" She smiled at the waiter. "I'll have a vodka and tonic."

The waiter turned to Marshall. "And you, sir?" The vampire's face was completely impassive, but there were two tiny red fires blazing behind his eyes. Like most Darkfolk, he undoubtedly hated Marshall.

"Nothing for me, thanks. But you could do me a favor."

"Yes?" Blair's tone contained more than a hint of ice.

"Could you dispense with the magic tricks for the rest of the evening? I'm afraid my friend's worried you might try to nest in her hair."

"Mar-shall!"

The vampire—Marshall refused to even think the more politically correct phrase "Nocturnally Enhanced Person"—narrowed eyes that were nearly completely red now. But all he did was nod and say, "Certainly, sir," before turning and heading off in the direction of the bar—in human form.

"Really, Marshall, there was no call for that."

"Look, Sarah, you know how I feel about *them*. Why did you pick this place? Are you trying to teach me some sort of lesson in tolerance? If so, it's not going to work. You're not the first woman who's tried and, if you keep it up, you're not going to be the last."

Sarah's face hardened. "I chose this restaurant solely because the restaurant critic at the paper said the food here is absolutely wonderful. And I'm quite aware of your stand on 'special privileges' for the Darkfolk. But I hoped you were a big enough man to put aside your political viewpoints for one evening and simply enjoy a fabulous meal."

"That depends on how fabulous." He took a look at his menu. Many establishments that catered to both humans and Darkfolk were done up in heavy kitsch in order to put humans at ease, with Saturday matinee horror show decor and obnoxiously named offerings like Batburgers and Full Moon Fries. But the architecture of After Midnight was far more subdued, as was its menu. If it hadn't been for Blair's little demonstration, Marshall might never have guessed the restaurant's true nature.

As he perused the menu's selections, he found himself thinking about how he had gotten together with Sarah Pearson.

She was a reporter for a local alternative paper whose editors and staff usually delighted in bashing Marshall every chance they got. One day on his radio show, Marshall challenged the paper to do an actual objective story on him—and Sarah responded. A staff reporter, she told him she had decided to take up the gauntlet he had thrown in the name of "journalistic integrity." She impressed him right away, for her beauty of course, but far more so for the almost tangible waves of dislike and resentment that came off her. Even so, the story she wrote was for the most part fair and balanced and he admired her for that.

Most men wouldn't have gone after a woman who actively disliked them, but Marshall Raymond wasn't most men. He thrived on conflict, romantically as well as professionally. And he enjoyed the challenge of using the same wit and charm that had made him the icon of conservatives in places both high and low to win over someone who initially couldn't stand him.

It had taken a lot of flowers, boxes of Dove chocolates, and cutesy-clever messages left on Sarah's answering machine before she finally agreed to go out with him. This was their sixth date so far. Not bad. Normally he would have driven her off by date five. But he suspected she got off on conflict nearly as much as he did. There was something about her. . . .

"Are you ready to order, sir?" Blair said.

Marshall hadn't heard him approach, and he wondered if the vampire had coalesced out of mist just to irritate him. Sarah ordered the prime rib, rare, and Marshall selected the Caesar salad with low-calorie Italian dressing.

"Is that all you're going to have?" Sarah asked.

"I've been trying to drop a few pounds."

Blair took their menus, looking at Marshall just a little too long and showing just a hint of fang before he departed.

"So you had a bad day," Sarah prompted.

"Boy, did I. It began this morning when I was accosted by a werewolf—excuse me, by one of the 'Metamorphically Gifted'—as I was leaving my apartment building. He said he was going bald and wanted me to give him five bucks so he could afford some Rogaine."

"So what did you do?"

"I gave him a quarter and told him to go join the Hair Club for Wolfmen."

Despite herself, Sarah giggled.

"And when I got to the station to do my radio show, I discovered it was being picketed by—are you ready for this?—members of the First Church of Satan, Reformed."

Sarah frowned. "Reformed how?"

"They believe human sacrifice is optional."

Sarah shrugged. "Well, this country was founded on religious freedom."

"Don't get me started. And then, as I was sitting in the cab on the way over here, trying not to choke from zombie-stench, we got stuck in a traffic jam when someone tried to conjure up one of the Elder Gods downtown." He sighed. "Things were sure a lot simpler before all these Spooks decided to come oozing out of the woodwork. Or coffinwork. Whatever. They should've stayed in the shadows where they belong."

"Don't give me that," Sarah said. "Deep down inside you

love them. Without the Darkfolk you wouldn't have half as much to rant about."

He couldn't help but give Sarah a small smile.

"Maybe."

"And then you wouldn't be able to get people stirred up the way you do. And if you couldn't do that . . ."

"There wouldn't be any point in doing my shows," Marshall finished.

Sarah grinned. "Exactly. You love the turmoil you create. You eat it up."

Marshall spread his arms. "What can I say? When you're right, you're right."

After the meal was over Marshall admitted that the food had indeed been fabulous.

"How would you know?" Sarah said. "You only ate half your salad, if that much."

"You're a fine one to talk. You barely touched your prime rib."

Sarah shrugged. "Guess I wasn't as hungry as I thought."

Blair brought the check and Marshall handed him a credit card. The waiter returned shortly with the credit form and as Marshall was signing it, Sarah told him to leave a good tip.

Marshall called over his shoulder at the vampire. "Stay out of the sun and avoid pointy wooden objects!"

Sarah swatted him on the arm and, grinning, he filled in a gratuity on the form.

As they stepped out onto the street, Marshall said, "I'm afraid you'll have to drive, Sarah."

She nodded. "I'm parked over this way." She led him down the sidewalk, her hand nestled in the crook of his arm, her hip warm against his.

"You know, Sarah, I was thinking that maybe we could go back to my place for some coffee." A mischievous glint danced in his eyes. "And maybe we could talk about the story your paper ran yesterday on the new trade agreement with Transylvania. I'd love to hear what you . . ." Marshall's words were cut off as Sarah suddenly grabbed him and dragged him into an alley. He found himself against a brick wall, held fast by arms as unyielding as steel beams.

"I'm not a big coffee fan." Sarah smiled, displaying ivory fangs. Red fire danced in her eyes.

"Sonofabitch," Marshall breathed. "I knew there was something different about you, but I was never able to put my finger on it."

"You've caused my kind and our brethren a great deal of trouble over the years, Marshall," Sarah half crooned, half hissed. "You've turned public opinion against us and slowed down our efforts to gain equal rights with humans. Worse, you've incited religious fanatics to come after us with their shabby icons and homemade weapons. Do you know how many Darkfolk have lost their lives because of you?"

"I don't have the actual statistic at my fingertips."

Sarah's hand lashed out in a blur and struck him a stinging blow across the face. "You present yourself as a defender of freedom, but in truth you're nothing more than a parasite. A far worse parasite than my kind could ever be, for you appeal to people's ignorance and intolerance, rouse their angers and prejudices, and then sit back and feed off the ugliness that you've created.

"When you issued your challenge to the paper, it was—pardon the expression—a godsend. The Old Ones of my kind recognized the opportunity and sent me to take care of you once and for all." She gave him a sly smile. "They even had me play hard to get, knowing you'd find that more attractive than a woman who threw herself at you."

Marshall's voice should have been full of fear, but it was calm and even and more than a little amused. "Do you intend to kill me?"

"Oh, no, Marshall. That would just make you a martyr. I'm going to change you into one of us." She grinned. "You're going to become 'Nocturnally Enhanced.' And once you have, you'll be bound to obey the Old Ones, just as all of us are. You will continue with your show—at night, of course—and slowly but surely you will soften your message of hatred until it eventually becomes one of understanding and acceptance."

Marshall smiled. "I think I'd be canceled long before I got to that point.

Sarah shrugged. "Perhaps. But at any rate, the threat posed by the great Marshall Raymond will have been nullified."

"Someone else will just come along and take my place."

"If so, we'll take care of him too." Sarah opened her mouth wide and her fangs extended even further. "Say good-bye to mortality, Marshall."

Marshall reached out and cupped her chin in his hand. "Before you do this, Sarah, there's something I think you should know."

"What?"

Marshall grinned as he dropped his disguise of humanity and showed Sarah his true form. Her eyes widened in terror and she tried to scream, but the darkness that comprised Marshall flowed into her mouth and filled her throat, cutting off any sound she might make. She tried to pull away, but ebon bands encircled her, holding her immobile.

"You were more right about me than you knew, Sarah." The words were cold echoes issuing forth from Marshall's darkness. "I am a parasite. An ancient, powerful parasite who feeds off the hatred he creates, although far more literally than you imagined."

She couldn't speak, but he could see the question in her eyes.

"What am I? I'm so old there are no names for me. But to be modern, I suppose you can think of me as a 'Negativity Assimilator.'" He grinned, a slash of ivory within his shadow, and then he took Sarah's unlife.

Marshall Raymond, once more seeming to be the man who appeared on TV screens across the nation, walked out of the alley, straightening his tie. He left behind a small pile of dust that would be washed away by the next rain.

As he exited the alley and headed down the sidewalk, he hummed to himself and mulled over what subject to rail against on tomorrow's show. The Dangers of Interspecies Dating, perhaps?

Marshall chuckled and continued along the street, drinking in the darkness that surrounded him.

# 𝔅ar 𝔗alk

### Joe R. Lansdale

ey, what's happening?

Not much, eh?

No, no, we haven't met. But I'm here to brighten your day. I got a story you aren't going to believe. . . . No, no, I'm not looking for money, and I'm not drunk. This is my first beer. I just seen you come in, and I was sitting over there by my lonesome, and I says to myself, self, there's a guy that could use some company.

Sure you can. Everyone needs some company. And you look like a guy that likes to hear a first-class story, and that's just the kind of story I got; first-class.

Naw, this isn't going to take too long. I'll keep it short.

You see, I'm a spy.

No, no, no. Not that kind of spy. No double-ought stuff. I'm not working for the CIA or the KGB. I work for Mudziplickt.

Yeah, I know, you never heard of it. Few have.

Just us Martians.

Oh yeah, that's right. I said Martians. I'm from Mars.

No, I tell you, I'm not drunk.

Well, it doesn't matter what the scientists or the space probes say; I'm from Mars.

You see, we Martians have been monitoring this planet of yours for years, and now with you guys landing up there, saying there's no life and all, we figure things are getting too close for comfort, so we've decided to beat you to it and come down here. I'm what you might call part of the advance landing force. A spy, so to speak. You see, we Martians aren't visible to your satellite cameras. Has to do with light waves, and an ability we have to make ourselves blend with the landscape. Chameleon-like, you might say. And we'd just scare you anyway if you saw us. We'd look pretty strange to you Earthlings.

Oh this. This isn't the real me. Just a body I made up out of protoplasmic energy.

The way I talk? Oh, I know your culture well. I've studied it for years. I've even got a job.

Huh?

Oh. Well, I'm telling you all this for one simple reason. We Martians can adapt to almost everything on this world—even all this oxygen. But the food, that's a problem. We find alcohol agrees pretty well with us, but the food makes us sick. Sort of like you going down to Mexico and eating something off a street vendor's cart and getting ill . . . Only it's a lot worse for us.

Blood is the ticket.

Yeah, human blood.

Find that funny, huh? Vampires from Mars? Yeah, does sound like a cheap science fiction flick, doesn't it?

You see—ho, hold it. Almost fell off your stool there. No, I don't think the beer here is that strong. There, just put your head on the bar. Yeah, weak, I understand. I know why you're feeling that way. It's this little tube that comes out of my side, through the slit in my clothing. I stuck it in you when I sat down here. Doesn't hurt. Has a special coating on it, a natural anesthesia, you might say. That's why you didn't notice. Actually, if you could see me without this human shell, you'd find I'm covered with the things. Sort of like a big jellyfish, only cuter.

Just rest.

No use trying to call out. Nothing will work now. The muscles in your throat just won't have enough strength to make your voice work. They're paralyzed. The fluid that keeps the tube from hurting you also deadens the nerves and muscles in your body, while allowing me to draw your blood.

There's some folks looking over here right now, but they aren't thinking a thing about it. They can't see the tube from this angle; just me smiling, and you looking like a passed-out drunk. They think it's kind of funny, actually. They've seen drunks before.

Yeah, that's it. Just relax. Go with the flow, as you people say. Can't really do anything else but that anyway. Won't be a drop of blood left in you in a few seconds anyway. I'll have it all and I'll feel great. Only food here that really agrees with us. That and a spot of alcohol now and then.

But I've told you all that. There, I'm finished. I feel like a million dollars.

Don't know if you can still hear me or not, but I'm taking the tube out now. Thanks for the nourishment. Nothing personal. And don't worry about the beer you ordered. I'll pay for it on the way out. It's the least I can do.

# Exodus

### Lawrence Schimel

**J**ust before dawn, the vampire stumbled towards home, drunk as a camel (since they don't have skunks in Egypt, and also because that was how he felt right then after he had drunk so much blood). The streets ran with blood and he had drunk his fill and then past his fill, bloating himself to capacity, unable to stop drinking all that glorious fresh blood, flooding around him as the Nile, turned like all water to blood, overflowed its banks with Spring. He grabbed his doorframe and leaned there, heavily, for a moment, while he fumbled for the keys to his house. His bloodied hands left a stain upon the lintel. He entered the welcoming darkness of his dwelling and, bloated as he was, fell promptly asleep.

He slept for days.

Frogs swarmed through the streets, but his windows were shuttered and he didn't notice them. They slithered under the door on their pallid white underbellies, croaking their loud calls from atop his bed, even, but he did not hear them. He was fast asleep, dreaming about the floods of blood. He had an erection. Eventually, the frogs left.

In the frogs' wake swarmed all the vermin that had fled before the onslaught of those thousands of hungry tongues. Bed bugs snuggled into bed with him and bit him. Lice burrowed into his scalp. Fleas and ticks and chiggers and the entire panoply of minute parasites that sting and bite attacked him. But he did not notice. And, bloated as he was, he had blood to spare for them.

Wild Beasts stampeded outside his dwelling, but their pounding hooves and neighs and coughs and trumpets did not wake him. He slept unperturbed. The vermin were intrigued by all the noise, however, and all that furry flesh to infest, and set off for wild and uncharted territories in search of excitement and blood that wasn't second-hand.

From the filth of the excrement left behind after the Wild Beasts had departed for greener pastures came a pestilence that struck down all persons who moved about the streets. Fast asleep as he was, the vampire remained uninfected.

However, from the poisoned bites and stings and scratches of the vermin and the eggs lain under his skin, his body erupted in horrible swollen boils. He looked as if the frogs' warts had been contagious, but took a few days to manifest. But the vampire did not scratch them. He did not even feel them. He slept as if drugged, so bloated that he could not feel his skin.

The temperature plummeted. Hail the size of grapefruits pounded the roof. The vampire hardly noticed at all, but in his sleep he pulled a sheepskin over his body to stave off the chill.

When the hail ended, a swarm of locust descended upon the city, devouring every comestible in their path. In minutes they stripped away his roof of thatched reeds. The vampire murmured against the sudden bright sunlight and burrowed deeper under the sheepskin, but he did not wake. In moments, the world was submerged in a preternatural darkness, which quieted the vampire's somnolent discomfort.

The Angel of Death stopped outside his door and the vampire again cried out in his sleep. The Angel of Death was curious and lifted his hand towards the doorknob; it had been a long time since he had taken one undead, one who had eluded him once. But he saw the blood upon the lintel and was sworn to pass by. This one, too, would come to him, in time, and receive his due punishment. Twice now, this one had eluded the Angel of Death and the Angel of Death was not pleased.

A neighbor came to the vampire the next night and at last roused him from his torpor by banging on his door. "What do you want?" the vampire growled as, sleepy-eyed, he opened the door. He was still quite full from his binging during the floods, but his anger at being awakened from such blissful dreams woke the tiny spark of hunger that had managed to dry itself off in his belly.

"Come, we must flee. It is time to go. We shall be free!"

"Leave? You've got to be kidding? What if this happened again and I missed it?" The vampire shut the door on his neighbor and lay down again, his thoughts already turning toward the flood of blood he would dream about until the Pharaoh's soldiers came.

# The Longest Night

CYNTHIA WARD

Thorstein Eagle-Eyes stood at the prow of *Wolf*, below the snarling carved wolf's head that gave the longship its name. Thorstein's blue eyes were narrow and restless, seeking the high sheer walls of the fjord, and the narrow shingle where the ship must make landfall in darkness. Jarl Harald Icebeard had taken his men a'viking, and rough seas had delayed their return from fat green Ireland to their home, the northernmost steading in Halogaland, the northernmost region of Norway. In this delay, the sun had set; it would not rise again for three months.

Thorstein Eagle-Eyes was tall and rangy, with shoulder-length yellow hair and a stripling's sparse beard. All his life he had yearned to follow Jarl Harald on the Sword Path, but he was not displeased that the raiding season was now ended: He had proved his worth with his swift sword and sharp eyes, and he had seized enough silver in his first summer to pay the bride-price for Freydis Bjornsdottir.

Ah, Freydis . . . she was a beauty, with her fair complexion of milk and strawberry hue, her gleaming hair like a braid of gold rope, her sturdy body as long and broad-beamed as a fine ship. Her breasts were full and high; surely they were white as fresh milk and firm as southland melons. . . .

"*Thorstein!*" The youth jumped, startled by the voice of his jarl, close beside him. "By Odin, why did we call you Eagle-

432

Eyes?" Harald Icebeard demanded with a laugh. "We should have named you Dreamer!"

Thorstein's eyes were clear again. "I see the strand!" he said. "But I see no one upon it—"

"Winter has fallen black and cold, and you expect a welcome feast on the shore?" Jarl Harald laugh merrily, and called commands to his men.

No one stood upon the strand—and no one stood guard about the steading. Jarl Harald's land was in the nomadic Lapps' territory; Jarl Harald's men drew sword and seax-dagger, raised axe and spear, as they slipped through the long, winding passageway into the longhouse.

A sword flashed in firelight; Harald Icebeard caught the blade on his shield, and a voice cried, "It's Jarl Harald!"

"Put up your swords!" the jarl commanded the white-faced old men and boys who faced him, all trembling as Nordmen never should. "Why do you attack us?"

"An evil spirit has come with the winter-night!" cried Einar the Stout, a man grown too fat and age-gnarled to go a'viking. "It has slain five men and three women, yet no one has seen it!"

A high, cackling laugh, amused and disdainful, silenced the shouts. The warriors turned their heads toward the insulting sound, and saw an old bondwoman, an ancient white-haired Lapp with a face like crumpled brown leather; her black eyes were slits and her toothless gums bared. Thorstein felt the hairs of his neck and skull prickle as a wave of cold flowed up from his spine, colder than the night air had been; for the old thrall was a spae-woman.

Her voice was cracked with age, and heavily accented: "Einar, you say we have not seen the evil spirit that haunts us, but do you not remember? You welcomed him into our midst, and bade him spend the winter with us!"

"Foolish bitch!" Einar spat. He turned to his jarl. "She speaks of a Christian priest, separated from his Nordman traveling companions, who came upon our steading and asked for shelter. Of course we gave him guest-rights. But the foolish southerner insisted on going outside in a storm to take a piss!"

The ancient spae-woman cackled again. "He came to us after the sun disappeared from the world," she said. "No weakling southerner could travel in our northern winter! He did not wear a cross. No Christian priest fails to wear a cross! Not only the Christian god comes to the North—their *demons* come as well!"

Curses and fearful wails rose to the roof-beams, and the sounds of children crying. Thorstein Eagle-Eyes closed his hand on the amulet at his throat, a bronze hammer of Thor.

A meaty *crack*, and the bondwoman fell to the floor, struck down by the jarl. "Enough of your foolish talk!" Harald turned to his warriors and spoke five men's names. "You will stand the first watch," he said to them. "Stand at the four corners of the longhouse, and you, Bjorn Bloodaxe, shall guard the outer door."

Thorstein heard a stifled cry, and went to Freydis Bjornsdottir and took her in his arms. "Do not fear, beloved," he whispered. "Your father is the greatest warrior of Jarl Harald's band. He will slay the beast."

He held her and kissed her, and gave her a measure of comfort, but her composure was shattered by a man's shout:

"Bjorn Bloodaxe is slain!"

Freydis screamed and ran into the passageway. Thorstein followed her, trailed by the jarl and many warriors.

Bjorn Bloodaxe lay motionless before the door, his beard pointed toward the Pole Star. His skin was white as the snow. None of the other four men on guard had seen anything. There was no sign of a struggle. At the jarl's orders, the body was carried into the longhouse, and stripped and examined for wounds. But no wounds were discovered save two tiny bloodless holes like fang punctures in the neck.

Thorstein Eagle-Eyes shivered. What could slip unseen to the side of a mighty warrior, and slay him without a struggle?

Jarl Harald seized his amulet and swore: "By Thor's Hammer, that which makes wounds can *take* wounds! We will kill the beast and avenge our dead!"

The warriors roared agreement, shaking their fire-reddened swords in the smoky air. Thorstein shouted with them, and spoke words of encouragement to Freydis, but he could not stop thinking of the spae-woman's words. He knew a Christian demon had come to the North, and the Northmen did not know how to fight it.

The three-month night that stretched before them had never seemed so long.

"We must double the guard about the longhouse, and never go alone to the outbuildings," Jarl Harald said, and named the ten men who would stand guard now. He was one of them. Thorstein Eagle-Eyes was another.

At his post, Thorstein paced and stamped his feet, exhaling white breaths that frosted his scraggly beard. He was shivering violently, but not from the cold. The sky was clear; the stars were more numerous than the jewels of Byzantium, and brighter. Thorstein glanced frequently at the man to his left, by the other corner of the short wall, and the men to his right, along the long wall; and they were equally watchful.

A patch of mist was forming before him. But the air was far too cold for mist.

Thorstein reached for his sword and opened his mouth to shout. Before he could complete either act, the mist had become a solid shape: a naked, snow-pale man with black gleaming eyes and a cruel smile and two long, pointed teeth—and broad cold hands that gripped Thorstein's face and sword-arm with crushing force.

Thorstein's free hand seized the bronze hammer of Thor.

A voice spoke, oddly accented, impossibly soft and clear: "Your amulet has no power over me, pagan!"

Then the fangs slipped into Thorstein's neck and all the strength flowed out of his limbs; he sank down in the snow. His last sight was a vision of the Christian demon ravaging the Nordmen and Lapps with impunity through an eternity of three-month winter nights; his last thought was a blasphemous wish for a Christian cross.

# Fire of Spring

## George Zebrowski

lina's scream echoed in Cyril Beldon's ears as he ran down the carpeted stone hallway of the castle. He carried a flint rifle in his right hand. Each step brought him nearer to the sight he had hoped he would never see, the death tableau which had marked the end of life for so many of his family. Every ten years one life had been taken, since the first massing of stones had created Dawnstone seven centuries ago. There had been omens. As soon as the walls of Dawnstone had been raised the sun had captured a blue star passing nearby, pulling it in close to itself. A year later the sun had consumed its small companion in a fiery storm which had dominated the sky for months, as if signalling the start of the terror.

He found Elina on the red carpet just beyond the turn in the passage. Beldon stopped, desperately hoping that she would scream again, but there was only a muted gurgle coming from her torn throat. It was the only sound he would ever hear from his beloved again.

There were six of them around her: dwarf-like gargoyles two feet tall with wings folded across their backs. One held Elina's long hair with taloned fingers; two held her feet. Another was crouched near her neck, where he had been gorging on the flow of blood. The remaining two were kneeling over her belly, which was smeared with blood.

Beldon fired his gun. The creature holding Elina's hair let go with a shriek and flew at him, eyes burning with bloodshot hatred. It was bleeding where the ball from the gun had penetrated its right wing. Beldon swung at the flying beast with the butt of his rifle. He knocked it to the floor where it lay still, its leathery wings spread open.

Their feast ended, the five others launched themselves toward the open window at the end of the hall. The great glass panels were fixed in place and a warm wind blew in from the foggy summer night, filling the heavy white curtains as if they were sails. The flying things were out and lost in the fog in a moment, leaving him alone with the body of Elina.

Beldon went up to the body and examined its state. Her stomach was a raw mass of drying blood. Even in death she clutched the flimsy night shirt which was bunched up around her waist. Her eyes were wide open as if still seeing the horror which had descended upon her.

He knelt down and closed them gently, pitying her young form. He took off his coat and covered her. Tears formed in his eyes.

He heard something stir on the rug behind him. He turned around suddenly and saw the creature he had struck with his rifle. Removing his belt he rushed over to it and bound its taloned hands together. Then, one by one, he broke the light bones in its wings by crushing them under his boots. When he was sure the beast would never fly again he stopped and looked back to Elina's body. Rage filled him quickly and he kicked the wounded gargoyle in the side. Tears rolled down his face, but the devil made no sound.

He picked the gargoyle up and carried it down the hall, and down the great stairs into the main room, where he placed it on the warm slate flooring in front of the large hearth fire. Then he went to the kitchen where he found a meat cleaver and carving knife.

When he got back to the fireplace the winged devil was thrashing around violently, straining at its bonds. Its eyes were fearful of the flames. Every few moments it stopped its struggles to look at the sparks which were landing near it on the slate.

Beldon kneeled down next to the creature's face and tried to catch its attention. He knew what he had to find out, even if he had to torture it for the information.

The fiery eyes found his suddenly and the beast spoke. "A thousand years more, you'll pay," it said. "The others will tell how you opposed us." Its voice was a hissing whisper broken with shrill whistling sounds.

The creature's eyes were now betraying something of its pain. "What's a thousand years," Beldon said, "when you have the right of harvest at Dawnstone forever?" He paused. "Now," he continued, "where is your spawning ground? Tell me and I'll kill you quickly." He stared directly into its eyes and prodded it with the point of the carving knife.

"You will never know."

"I will know—you fly here in reasonable time so it must be near."

"What else do you know, fool?"

"It must be a small area, a place I know but do not recognize." He paused again. "I am the last and I will end it," he said raising his voice, "I have to!" He drove the knife partially into the creature's side. "Now tell me, for my Elina, for my dying mother, tell me now!"

But the gargoyle's eyes were no longer looking at him. He knew that it had resigned itself to death. Beldon withdrew the knife point and considered what he could do to its body that would be cruel enough to make it speak.

Suddenly he picked up the meat cleaver and began hacking at the broken wings lying limp on both sides of the gnarly body. In a few moments he had severed the wings from the ratlike form. He picked up the pieces and hurled them into the fire.

"Your hands are next," he said.

There was no reply. Beldon looked around the huge room, which was illuminated only by the fire. For a moment his own hatred astonished him. He thought of his mother asleep in the south wing of the castle—too deaf in her old age to have heard what was going on. But then, she had died inside when they had taken his father ten years ago. Even his marriage to Elina had failed to revive her. For years he had thought they would take her when the time came. Secretly he had hoped they would take the old woman and spare Elina. The thought shamed him now.

The shame kindled itself into a new rage. He brought the knife up to the beast's eye and pushed it in far enough to blind it. The gargoyle howled. The eye closed in shock as he withdrew the knife. The other one was watching him, jealous of its sight.

The creature asked, "If I tell you what you want to know, will you kill me quickly?"

Beldon was suspicious that the beast was trying to trick him into killing it. It would tell him some lie and he would kill it too quickly. But maybe he had broken its sense of community with the others and death meant more to it now than any loyalty.

Swiftly Beldon put out its other eye, shouting, "No lies now. I won't kill you until I'm sure."

The creature was licking its thin lips and biting them in pain, and the only tears its eyes could shed now were made of blood. "This much is true," it said. "The first Dawnstone conjured our spirits from the black abyss and imprisoned them in the bodies of the creature you see me in. They were harmless little things which lived in the forest. After he had bound us into these forms, he bargained to release us if we gave him all our knowledge of the forces which rule the world. If we refused he would destroy us by turning loose his birds of prey. In those days it would have been easy because we were so small and unused to our new shapes. So we gave him all our knowledge of conjuring all the powers in the blackness between the worlds. But we also tricked him into performing a ritual which turned those same powers against him. When he tested his powers for the first time, his body was turned inside out and torn into a thousand pieces; and the force of his death hurled a blue star into the sun. That much you know. But what you have never understood is that his spirit itself was destroyed, and all the heirs of Dawnstone were delivered into our power. After the lives of one hundred generations have been destroyed, we will be free of our fleshy prisons. Until then we cannot leave our bodies, but we can renew them from Spring to Spring, making them grow larger and more strong on the blood of our enemies. My death is nothing. I will have a new body at next birthing. Kill me now."

"But where are you born?"

"From the earth itself, but even if you knew the place you would not be there at the right time to see it. There is nothing you can do except wait for the passage of time to free Dawnstone." The creature sneered at him. "And the one hundredth generation will be the last. None will follow it to rob us of our vengeance."

Beldon raised the meat cleaver and buried it in the gargoyle's throat, cutting through to the spine, killing the creature instantly. For a moment he regretted his anger. He had to remind himself that this was not an individual he had spoken with, but a monstrous single being incarnated in living forms.

He thought he could almost sense its bodiless evil near the fire, hovering there, mocking him. . . .

He sat looking at the body for a long time. Spring, he thought, the creature had spoken of spring. Tomorrow, this morning, was the first day of spring. He thought of eggs hatching in the earth—in a field. The only fields near the castle were worked by the peasants.

But he did remember a clearing in the forest which he had not seen since he was a boy. He had never been there on the first day of spring.

He got up and threw the body into the flames. He was certain that his guess was correct.

As he put on his cloak in the hallway he felt that some new sense was guiding him. From the rack by the front door he took a walking stick, instinctively thinking of it as a weapon.

He opened the heavy oaken door. It squeaked loudly, bringing a sleepy servant out to close it behind him as he went out.

He went across the windswept outer court and through the open front gate. He wondered if he would be back before his mother woke up from her trancelike sleep.

He started to run in the pre-dawn darkness, his robe a flapping wing behind him. He slowed to a walk and his hand was on his knife hilt. Deep inside him the need to hurry was a fearful urgency uncoiling into his limbs, a fluid looseness in his hands and arms and a constricting pull in his legs and thighs.

He came to the fork in the path which led down from the castle into the village. The way left led into the forest. He followed it without stopping. He knew that he had to be at the clearing before sunrise.

He started to run again. The trees became rushing shapes on both sides of the narrow pathway. They were gray and black forms with a thousand paralytic fingers outlined against a lightening sky.

He burst out of the forest into a large clearing and stopped. He looked at the ground carefully in the pale light. It looked as if it had been plowed a long time ago—but by whom?

Something was waiting to come out of the earth. He could almost feel its presence in the morning hush. He leaned on his walking stick and waited in the chill air.

The sun started to come up in the trees and the air grew

warmer. It was a bright orange sun which grew hotter as it rose over the trees before him. A wind passed through the branches, fluttering the leaves for a moment before dying, leaving an abrupt stillness over the clearing as if the world was holding its breath. . . .

Suddenly Beldon saw the earth crack open in a thousand places across the field. He saw that it was moist under the parched surface. As he watched thousands of small pink-red sparks pushed out of the wet dirt.

He stepped closer, leaning over, and saw the tiny body of a winged gargoyle, pink and wet all over, entering the world from below, hatching from some infernal egg which had been waiting in the ground.

The sun caught the creatures across the entire surface of the clearing, turning their tumescent skins into red-orange slivers of fire, thousands of them transforming the field into a flame-dotted ground surrounded by green forest. There was an odor of birthing coming up from the land, making Beldon gag. Before him an evil nature was throwing up the things which were his enemy, and would continue as the seasons turned. Each spring would be a firelike beginning for these fleshy creatures, and all would struggle toward maturity and the aim of tormenting the heirs of Dawnstone.

Something seized Beldon from inside like a fist entering a hand puppet, and he gripped the walking stick with both hands. Raising it, he began to walk across the open rows in the field, striking the newly born devils with a rhythmic precision, splitting open their little heads and torsos, spilling their blood back into the soil. He was tireless. The force which drove him seemed endless. Fear, sorrow, and hatred had made an alliance for the possession of his body long enough to carry out this deed. His reason was an approving spectator.

He struck them until thousands lay torn open in the morning air, their blood clotting under the open sky. Beldon continued until the sun was almost overhead. Thousands still remained to be killed. He did not know which horrified him more —the dead or the still living.

He grew tired, overwhelmed by the sheer magnitude of trying to stifle this fertility of numberless newborn. He stopped and picked up a living specimen. Its wings huddled close to its body.

Its eyes were red rubies glazed with moisture. The creature opened its mouth to yawn and Beldon saw the tiny fangs, so much like the full grown ones which had taken Elina's life.

He lifted the creature high over his head and dashed it to the ground. He stepped on it immediately with his boot heel, feeling its life melt away into the soft earth.

Around him shadows raced on the ground. Shapes covered the sun. The shadows hovered near his feet. He looked up and saw five full-grown gargoyles diving toward him out of the sun.

He raised his stick to defend himself but he was too tired. Sweat ran into his eyes. The talons struck him and hurled him to the ground. A blow hit him in the right temple and a shower of lights exploded in the darkness like sparks from a blacksmith's anvil. . . .

He remembered being carried in the air and being dropped to the ground in the castle's courtyard. He remembered vague faces looking at him, the faces of his servants and his mother. He woke up in his bed thinking that by now his mother knew about Elina. Through the window he saw dark clouds driving across the sky, leaden masses filled with flashes of lightning, each pulse of light growing stronger.

He got up knowing that they had brought him back so he would continue. They knew that he would go to the village eventually and choose a new bride. In time they might come for her, or her son or daughter, or his daughter's daughter. Someone every ten years, as long as there were victims.

There were too many of the creatures to stop. He would never be able to surprise them again, they would see to that. The clearing would be carefully guarded from now on. It would be unapproachable.

And yet, he knew, some would live at Dawnstone untouched. Perhaps the ones who would be close to him now, his future bride and children, maybe they would live in peace, unharmed. He almost hoped that he would be the next one to be taken, and his family-to-be spared. It seemed right that he should be next.

He walked over to the window and looked out at the driving clouds again. He felt very different now, sure that he would be the next one to die. But his family would live, and it seemed that it should be that way and no other. Rain was falling from the clouds now, curtains of sweeping water which struck the colored glass of his bedroom window. Wind rattled the frame. He felt the hollow emptiness of acceptance as he watched the horizon of swaying trees, and the line of darkness advancing on the castle. There was a sudden break in the storm clouds and the setting sun cast its redness into the rain, turning the droplets for an instant into blood.

# Fantsilotra

JANET BERLINER GLUCKMAN AND GEORGE GUTHRIDGE

Shimmering like ghosts within the veils of heat, the four French mercenaries, still in the employ of Queen Ranavalona, labored across the cracked-earth desert. They were thirsty, sucked dry by the desert sun. Three of them could no longer remember why they had indentured themselves to the Queen. As for the mission that brought them to this godforsaken southern end of the island, it was, they had decided, sheer lunacy.

The fourth soldier, a captain, remembered all of it. While his men were renegades, driven half-mad by dust and death, and by fear of the woman who had sent them here, he was driven by something far simpler. Greed. Like his men, he was a French soldier turned mercenary. He would complete this mission, carry the prized *aepyronis* egg to Queen Ranavalona, who called herself the heart of the country, collect the bonus she had promised, and go home to Paris where he belonged. Paris might not be heaven, but at least there he would never again have to deal with such a woman. She was as evil as the Betsileo witch doctor he had once seen suck a child's finger until only gristled bone remained.

Queen Ranavalona had ascended to the throne after her pro-west husband, Radama, slit his own throat while drunk on rum. Or so it was said. From the distant capital of Antananarivo, she'd announced that all colonization would cease immediately. The French, the British, the Germans must leave—except for those soldiers who chose to remain in her service. All vestiges of European culture would be eradicated, by blood if necessary, from Madagascar's soil.

In the name of independence she enslaved her subjects. The foreigners, by inaction and silence, told the Malagasy that their lives were expendable. By that silence, they endorsed the excesses of the Queen as she reinstituted slavery. Not selling her people into slavery abroad, as others had, but forcing each Malagasy who was not Merina—her tribe—to serve without pay for at least one year on any one of many royal projects to be built by forced labor.

The Royal projects were royal disasters. Like when the captain and his men were sent to supervise the building of a road from Antananarivo to Antongil Bay. And why? Because the Queen wanted a new view of the eastern sea and had some headstrong quest for an eastern harbor. The road was to drop from the central plateau, home of the Merina, then wend its way through the jungle and down the malarial cliffs to the mangroves. Those from the south whom the mosquitoes did not kill died at the hands of the Tanal, the forest people, or in the jaws of alligators.

Or, the captain thought, cracked lips forming a smile, they would be sucked dry by the legendary man-eating *fantsilotra*, which reportedly inhabited the thicket ahead.

There would be some justice in that, he decided, since Ranavalona was sucking dry the blood of this great red island.

Laden with bedrolls and backpacks, the soldiers moved increasingly slowly toward the thicket. Their leader, spotting the top of a baobab rise from the thicket, found a sudden reserve of energy. He strode eagerly toward the promise of water the baobab held in its pulpy wood and crotch.

They did not know they were being watched.

They could not hear the call of the *fantsilotra*.

Watching the approach of the soldiers from within the thicket, the *fantsilotra* grew excited. Anticipation surged through its branches, and its steely thorns stood erect.

*Come to us*, the desert plant called out. *Come colonists.*

444

Then, silent, it waited, branches soaking a hard-bitten sun, roots seeking what little water the desert was willing to waste on something so ugly.

Seated in a *valavato*, graveyard of his people, Benary heard the call of the *fantsilotra*. Now that he had buried his sister, and the egg with her, there was nothing left but to say his farewells to this place and reenter the Land of Thirst.

Idly, he smoothed the earth over the grave and chased a beetle from the mound. He thought about sucking out the tenrec's insides, but he saw little point. The beetles were good food, much like porridge, but his hunger and thirst were such that a mouthful would do little to assuage the pain created by his need.

From his hilltop vantage point, he looked down upon the desert, home of the dead. He could see the soldiers, spots upon the horizon. Two hundred years before, the French had tried to establish a colony at Fort Dauphin, further to the south. His tribe had driven the invaders into the desert, where the *fantsilotra* had impaled them. The survivors fled to France with tales of man-eating trees.

No one had believed them then, nor did those who, unlike Benary, had not seen it for themselves believe it now. No one but Ranavalona. Benary had much in common with the *fantsilotra*. He too had the ability to kill without the capacity for cruelty; he, too, endured an everlasting thirst.

He stood up to leave, but seeing how slowly the soldiers approached, he sat back down upon a fallen *aloala*. The carved, wooden tomb post wobbled slightly, as if the spirits of the dead that guarded the tomb objected to his weight. He stared at the cattle horns that surrounded the gravesite, cracked and fallen upon the sun-baked ground, then reaching for a *pachypodium*, he opened it and drank the cool liquid hidden inside the smooth-skinned gourd. It did not begin to slake his thirst, any more than the tears that formed in his eyes could heal the pain as he cried for his sister, and remembered—

Benary's family was *cotier*—coastal inhabitants—his father a fisherman, his mother an educated woman, the product of French nuns. Like so many of the Saklava tribe, his family had been forced to flee the mouth of the Mangoky, from the sea to the desert. His sister, Flavien, thought the desert a trial to be endured; the home of the dead, forbidden to the living. She saw the spiked forest as she did everything else, the product of God. His mother would venture only to the edge of the desert's forests, for if she so much as neared a *fantsilotra*, it drew blood. Benary, too, feared the desert plant, but his apprehension dissolved once he was amid the thorns. He felt safe in the thickets, in a way he had never known on the slopes above the sea. Crawling like a tenrec, angling like a dancer, he avoided the thorns with surprising ease. It was Flavien who was not so lucky, Flavien who paid for their passage in blood.

It had taken them both some time before they gathered the courage to enter the thicket. Finally, thirst outweighed fear, and they went together in search of the elusive baobab tree whose top was so easily distinguished from afar, but which remained well-hidden in the thicket, amid the tangled vines and *fantsilotra*.

"Look, Benary!" Flavien pointed at a white-brown crescent that bulbed from the desert floor.

Benary knew at once what she had found. He dug it up, saying nothing. The egg was intact. He released it from the ground and gently wiped the crust of dirt from its surface. Large as their heads, it refracted the light.

"We can tell no one," he said. "If we do, the soldiers will come."

Angrily, Flavien stood up. "If it is valuable, it could take mother and father back to the sea."

"The soldiers will come," Benary repeated. "They will want to take it to Paris."

"We could take it ourselves to Antananarivo, to the Royal House. Perhaps Queen Ranavalona will reward us and we will be able to return to the coast."

Ceasing to argue, Benary simply reburied the egg.

Angry, unmindful of the risk, and unwilling to subjugate her haste to the need to crawl, Flavien started to leave. Her cheek brushed the *fantsilotra*, and her blood gleamed on the bush. The plant trembled and Benary identified his real thirst. He touched the thorn, put his finger to his lips, and knew why water held no joy for him. For the first time in his life, he was slaked of a thirst deeper than even the desert could instill—the thirst of porphyria.

Suddenly his senses were strangely attuned to his sister, who stood wide-eyed, watching him. Her breathing roared in his ears, and in his blood, her pulse. He felt strong. For an instant, he wanted to hurt her, to feel her blood on his hands.

After that day of his first tasting, Benary dreamed at night of embracing vampirism, of his sister's blood on his tongue, and of the swell of the huge egg. He sat upright and slept beside a fire built from branches that he hated to burn, *fantsilotra* branches. As tangled shadows coalesced into the suddenness of Africa's desert night, he heard his sister whisper to their mother of the finding of the egg, one of the last remnants of the largest bird that ever lived, hunted to extinction on Madagascar by the French. They spoke of the Roc, killed off like the pygmy hippos, only a few hundred years before, and Benary knew, by the excitement in his mother's voice, that she would talk of their discovery to his father, who would talk of it to the next person he met.

He determined that, as soon as possible, he would dig up the egg and move it to a place of safekeeping.

"Are you in pain, my son?" his mother called out, seeing him sitting upright in the darkness.

"I am fine, Mother," he said.

He was anything but fine, and they both knew it. When he was a child, different from the others, the villagers had whispered that he was cursed. In a sense he was, for he was the victim of a physical disease handed down in alternating generations. A deficiency of a blood-substance his mother called *heme*. The result was severe anemia. No cure was possible, though it was said a preventative existed: the common vegetable garlic.

That much his mother had been able to tell him. The anemia, she'd warned, would become increasingly severe. His dark brown skin, already mottled, would develop patches of white. His urine, now strangely pink, would turn the color of amber— as if tinted by the traces of copper draining from his system.

Like the giant bird, Benary thought, he too would soon be extinct.

Having once felt what it was to be sated, Benary took to entering the thicket alone. The first time, he dug up the egg and moved it to the *valavato*. It would be safe at the gravesite, he thought, for the spirits of the dead would guard it. After that, he entered the thicket for a different reason. He would sit for hours near the *fantsilotra*, listening for someone to come, waiting, hoping to see the gleam of blood. Once in a while, he found a stray lemur impaled on the thorns and he drank. But it was not the same. A whole lemur did not satisfy him as well as the few drops of his sister's blood.

Not long after that, the first intruders arrived—three locals, not much older than Benary. Neither he nor Flavien were there when they came, demanding that the family lead them to the egg which they'd heard rumored lay buried in the thicket. By the time Benary got there, they had buried his father up to his neck in the hot sand because he said he did not know the answer to their question, and also to immobilize him while they raped his mother.

Seeing what had happened, Benary swore to kill them all. His fury was compounded by the fact that these same youths had several times resisted his attempts at friendship with cries of "Freak" and "Devil."

Making them responsible for his progressing disease, with its violent skin rashes and escalating cramping and vomiting, he covered Flavien's eyes and sent her to wait for him at the *valavato*. When she was out of sight, he stepped into view and bade the criminals to follow him.

When they reached the *fantsilotra*, Benary signaled the youths to stop. He took hold of a branch and waited. As the first intruder approached, he let go of the branch. It snapped back, placing a thorn squarely into the rapist's eye. Blood issued from the youth's mouth, and the *fantsilotra* fed thirstily. A poisonous *didierea* bush brushed a face, and the second man collapsed onto his side, clawing at his cheeks and screaming.

One left, Benary thought, looking around for a weapon. But there was no time. The young man was upon him. "Come," he yelled, rising to send him reeling into impalement.

*Take him*, Benary whispered to the desert plant, as he pushed the last of them deeper into the bush. He swore he could hear laughter as the plant wrapped the boy in its arms like a lover.

Together, Benary and the *fantsilotra* sucked the intruders dry. When he looked up, he saw Flavien, doubled over and vomiting at what she had seen. The branches around him quivered and shook as he knelt by her side. She pushed him away, and stood.

Without removing her gaze from his, she said, "Damn you, Benary." Turning to run, she stumbled and lost her footing.

"Flavien!" Too late, he reached out to save her.

"God damn your soul," she shouted, struggling with the *fantsilotra* as it embraced her. "God damn it to hell."

With that, she gave herself to the *fantsilotra* and, happily, it fed.

Sobbing, Benary took his farewell, drinking her soul and her blood. Then he wrapped what was left of her in the tanned boarskin he usually wore as protection from the blistering he experienced whenever he was exposed to the sun.

As he buried Flavien, he thought about Ranavalona, imagining the Queen on her rattan-and-ivory throne. In his mind's eye, he saw an ebony master post, the Vola Mihitsy—so thick that two men could not join hands around it—hanging over her head. He thought about those who must have died bringing it to Antananarivo from the forests of the Betsimisaraka Escarpment.

Though he had never really seen her, it was as if he were standing in front of her, looking into her eyes. They were bright as new blood, shiny with satisfaction at how well she had succeeded in controlling her people and the colonials.

It was then he *knew*, then he recognized not only who Queen Ranavalona was, or who really cut her husband's throat, but *what* she was.

A sweet darkness suffused Benary, shutting out the pain and the sun that would never again blister his skin. His own need roared through his being. He rose from the *aloala* and, dragging the wooden tomb post with him, made his way into the thicket.

The captain was the first to arrive. Almost without thinking, Benary thrust the *aloala* at the man's face. It impaled him through the neck.

He did not bother with the blood already on the captain's skin. Placing his mouth around the eye socket, he drank. Not his fill—he knew that was not possible—but enough to grant him the strength for what he must do next. Now. Before the others arrived and deprived him of his choice.

"I need," he said, raising his head to look up at the moon. "I will always need."

Knowing the *fantsilotra* would not be able to resist, he drew a branch across his breast and waited—for the pain to begin, for the three soldiers to come, and for his need, at last, to end.

The French come on through the desert heat. Their uniforms have changed, their bedrolls and backpacks are colorful and lightweight. Walking sticks have replaced the carbines of soldiers.

The *fantsilotra* watches and waits. It is capable of nothing more than watching, waiting, and drinking. Its thirst has not been slaked in the century since Benary, son of Benary the *Cotier*, abandoned himself to them. Its branches have returned to soaking a hard-bitten sun, its roots to seeking what little water the desert is willing to waste on something so useless that it cannot draw to it the food it needs.

Were it capable of thought, it would know that those drawing near are tourists rather than soldiers, men, women, and children, drawn to the desert by its unique flora and fauna.

It would know, but it would not care.

## UV

NANCY KILPATRICK

*UV* wasn't a new spa, but it was new to Leila. Her best friend, her childhood girlfriend Julie, had called her about this exclusive place dedicated to youth and beauty—"Where all the glamorous people go!"—and as far as Leila could see, not one word in that conversation, at least concerning the elite aspect of *UV*, had been exaggeration.

No simple flagstone *here*. Expensive Italian terra-cotta tiles led to a massive mahogany door imbedded into one of the red rock formations that made Sedona famous. The hot colors of the door and walk blended so perfectly with the dusty red rock that, without a sign or even a tasteful brass plaque, the building struck Leila as almost an invisible fortress, impenetrable, invulnerable. That appealed to her.

She entered a sleek hallway, glad to be out of the heat. More tiles, in pale, cooling gray, lined not just the floor but the walls and ceiling as well. The entrance turned into a corridor that spiraled down and around.

As Leila descended, the tiles darkened, the temperature dropped, and the lights dimmed. Not a mirror in sight. That's unusual, she thought. Most spas confront you with how you look on the way in so the *New You* will look so much better on the way out.

A computerlike voice with well-modulated tones greeted her: "Welcome to *UV*. Continue along the path." With only one direction to walk, she couldn't be going the wrong way, but nothing else indicated it was the right way.

After what felt like an inordinately long trek downhill, Leila finally arrived at the end of the corridor to find a small waiting area, furnished with a plush slate couch and matching chair, the leather soft as ash, as well as a small ebony parson's table topped with smoky glass. A neat stack of the requisite magazines sat on the table. Down here the tiles were charcoal. If the light had been any dimmer, such darkness would have been unbearable.

Leila took a seat and waited. After a few moments, she picked up one of the magazines and leafed through it. The lighting was too dim to read by, which annoyed her—five years ago she could have read this print, even in this light. She refused to take out her reading glasses; she'd look at the pictures. There was the usual fare, women thin as manikins, with large eyes, full lips, no wrinkles, and apparently no worries. A quick glance at the table told her that all of the reading matter was of the same type—what she and Julie over the last few years had taken to calling "One-Downers," because the photos always made them both feel inferior. Leila knew she was being silly. These models were a small percentage of the population, teenagers mostly, twenty years younger, so why was she comparing herself? But she also knew the answer: because she envied them and wanted to be what they were, not what she had become—

ordinary. If I still had a body and face anywhere near like the ones pictured in these mags, she thought, I'd be deadly!

Most of her life she'd edged out the competition. She'd always been attractive and had been blessed with a naturally good figure, better than Julie's. Their "friendly" rivalry had been going on since high school, but Leila had always been the clear winner. And not just when it came to looks. She'd married better, produced smarter, more attractive children, and had earned more money. Until five years ago. Now she was alone, stuck in a job with a glass ceiling, carrying excess weight she could not lose, using auburn "Limage" on a monthly basis, and cursed with wrinkles that no longer disappeared after a good night's sleep.

A section of dark tiles slid apart from the rest, automatically, silently. The computer voice said, "Step through the opening and turn to your right."

Leila got up and entered a shadowy area. With only the subdued light from the corridor behind her, she turned right.

"Remove your clothing, then enter the room directly ahead."

She could just make out the dim outline of a doorway and a clotheshorse outside it. This was certainly the most impersonal spa she'd ever been to. Still, the place had worked wonders on Julie, who was now getting things Leila had only dreamed about. Besides, Leila had paid good money to come here and, since there were no refunds, she wasn't about to bail now.

She undressed, hung up her clothes, and entered the room. Immediately a faint light lit the doorframe, triggered no doubt by her body heat as she moved across the threshold. The tiles outside the doorframe slid shut, cutting off that dim light from the waiting area.

"Lie on the table," the voice commanded, and Leila did.

This room was small. Black floors and walls, an inky porcelain sink and matching fixtures, all ultra modern. A tall black cabinet stood near the sink that contained, she guessed, the tools the beauty expert would use to drain years from her body and face. The most peculiar item was the table. Made of midnight plastic, it was more a frame, really, with six black canvas straps stretched hammocklike across it.

She lay on the "table," feeling vulnerable, and a bit chilly.

There was no sheet with which to cover herself, and she was just about to get up and retrieve her jacket when the light surrounding the door frame went out, plunging her into utter darkness.

It was disconcerting, knowing she was lying so exposed in a room devoid of all light, located in the bowels of ancient rock. The knowledge of such density pressed in on her and her heart beat quickly. She shivered from those thoughts, and also from the cool air chilling her flesh.

Calm down! she ordered herself. You've been to spas before. She'd visited many, suffering everything, including face lifts, both surgical and nonsurgical, body wraps, seaweed baths, full torso mud packs, collagen treatments, liposuction, various types of massage therapy, and steam. And while the results usually produced a more or less better package than the one that had entered the salon, no spa experience had ever resulted in the rejuvenation Julie claimed.

Julie had gone in thirty pounds overweight and come out as thin as an *haute couture* model. Her cheekbones, she claimed, were prominent, the hint of jowls only a bad dream, her hips, stomach, and buttocks slimmed to the point where she needed to buy a new wardrobe—"Two sizes smaller!" But it was more than just physical changes. Julie had always been timid, afraid of drawing too much attention to herself. Since coming to *UV*, she'd opened her own graphic-design studio and was already inundated with work from high-powered ad agencies. Clients had flown her to the Caribbean, and were sending her to Europe next month. She'd bought a sports car, a fur coat. . . . And she insisted she had more men after her than she could juggle.

Leila had not been impressed. She'd been jealous! If she hadn't known Julie since childhood, she'd have thought her friend was lying. After all, going into a spa Friday and coming out on Monday . . . how could such a shift have occurred in body and soul in only one weekend? But Julie was a compulsive truth-teller, and Leila was here now, hoping that time would not only be slowed but reversed. She wanted her most confident self revived by the miracles promised by *UV*.

Well, "promised" wasn't the right word. *UV* promised nothing. In fact, they did not advertise, or even produce a brochure. Their clientele was select, built strictly by word-of-mouth, with each applicant carefully screened. A friend told Julie, who told Leila, who'd had, like the others, to answer lists of personal questions and sign a legal-looking document, all by mail, to get into this exclusive salon. Of course, with the prices they charged, they didn't have to advertise—they didn't appeal to the masses, which appealed to Leila. They could afford to treat each client on an individual basis.

Leila had dipped drastically into her bank account to come here. But if she could undergo a transformation like the one Julie experienced, something that would get her back into the flow of life with the looks and energy of a twenty-five-year-old, it would all be worth it. Life had been snubbing her since long before the divorce and she wanted to reengage in a major way, by her rules. But she was honest enough with herself to realize that, at forty-something, she was no longer a valued commodity. Youth, sex appeal, energy, aggression, they were everything, and hers had evaporated. Fifteen years of a boring marriage, three rebellious kids, and a dead-end job had seen to that. But her youngest had recently left for college—hallelujah!—and Leila felt she had good years left; she wanted to spend them grabbing everything she could get her hands on. If *UV* had a way of stemming the aging process, she was all for it, whatever it was!

In the darkness she felt a presence move into the room. For some unknown reason, the skin over her backbone prickled. Why didn't that motion/heat-sensitive light go on? "Hello?" Leila said.

Without a word, what was undoubtedly a technician moved to the table and quickly strapped her in at the wrists, ankles, thighs, upper arms, and under her ribcage, then tilted the table until Leila was in an upright position. Behind, Leila heard a click, as if the cabinet door had opened. A rush of cool air hit her back. Goosebumps sprouted across her flesh and her heart beat too quickly. Why didn't the woman answer? Then the thought occurred, God, I hope it *is* a woman! "I've never been here before," Leila said, trying to draw the technician out, disturbed by the small voice seeping from between her own lips.

Wordlessly, something cool was tied around her eyes. What for? she wondered, since I can't see anything anyway, then realized it must be one of those gel-filled masks designed to relax the muscles surrounding the eyes.

At least it's dark, she thought; somehow she didn't want to be seen, even though this aesthetician had likely labored over many bodies, some in worse shape than her own. She was about to ask the technician how she could work without light, but a sudden touch to her skin made her gasp. Her body jolted.

It was as though sharp icicles had dropped from the ceiling and pierced her stomach. But how could that be? She was upright. Obviously that was the tip of a stainless steel needle; the technician must have injected something. Then more needles on each side of both breasts. Freezing steel bit her inner elbows and wrists, the backs of her knees and ankles, her hips, her groin, her throat. She had no idea there was more than one technician in the room!

Panic rose in her chest. To distract herself from the fear creeping in, she tried to focus on what types of treatment this spa would use to remove excess water and fat from the body, severing inches from the waist, hips, thighs, and buttocks, firming breasts, tightening the chin and upper arms. And she'd tried them all, it seemed. When she'd heard where *UV* was located— in the middle of Arizona, desert country—right away she'd assumed the treatments would be heat-based, utilizing the natural sunlight. "The opposite," Julie confided when pressed. "They blame ultraviolet rays for skin damage, and for deforming cells and they say that leads to extra fat, water retention, and wrinkles. And all that reduces self-confidence."

"So how come they're not operating out of the North Pole?"

Julie, usually a cheerful person, had gotten testy. "Look, I don't know all the technical aspects, and I can't talk about the treatment itself. It's their big secret process—you signed the papers too! You'll just have to trust me on this: They know what they're doing. They're into anti-aging."

Cold spread across her stomach and chilled its way through her torso until it was met by the cold creeping down from her chest. Her body trembled. Iciness spread from her hips, joining what was in front and permeated her back until glacial fingernails scratched her backbone. Her body buckled uncontrollably as cold extended through her limbs. Soon she was numb from head to toe. She tried to open her mouth to ask what was going on, but found her jaw locked and leaving her only capable of guttural sounds.

Every other treatment she'd experienced had begun with heat, to open the pores and, if cold was used, it was alternating. Why were they freezing her? Her entire body had lost feeling.

This isn't bad, though, she tried to reassure herself, holding back a wave of panic. Now that the feeling had left her body, it wasn't any worse than a trip to the dentist, when the gums are frozen: No feeling, no pain. At least she hoped that was the case.

She lay in the darkness, her body corpselike, sensing forms hovering all around, very close. There was pressure on her body, but no pain. Her heart slammed in terror. She began to feel so sleepy, dazed, as if she'd been caught in a blizzard and hypothermia had set in.

Time had no contours. Whether she was asleep or awake, dreaming, hallucinating, or seeing reality, she had no idea, and that certainty ceased to matter. Images appeared on her eyelids, or was there a TV screen on the wall in front of her?—news footage of starved children; a parade of grinning skeletons, their bones rattling as they jerked along a runway in flimsy expensive costumes; red icicles hanging like stalactites, thinning to dripping points; a swarm, fluttering in the dark, a million night birds descending on prey. She felt none of this in her body, which made the tension greater.

There were many more images, all fleeting, but the one that lingered was of the crimson fires of passion. Just out of reach. Like eyes that reflected her own intense hunger to devour life. She felt compelled to stare into those fires, and any desire to turn away soon vanished.

"Take a step forward."
Leila couldn't feel her limbs and was surprised when her legs moved. She walked with difficulty at first, feeling weak and dizzy. Hadn't she been strapped to the table? Her head was light and thoughts only snippets.

She still could not feel her body, yet possessed energy, but the source was a mystery. She had been here—how long? Long enough. Shouldn't blood have rushed from or to her head? But it did not.

"Take six steps forward!" the voice commanded.

The voice resonated through her, like air rushing in and filling her lungs, although she could not feel herself breathing. She did as directed and passed through the doorway, which did not light up. Her eyes must have adjusted to extended darkness because it was as though she could see through a red filter. She found her clothes and dressed, aware that the blouse and slacks were far roomier than when she had removed them.

She reentered the waiting area. A small open wine bottle without a label and a crystal goblet sat on the table. The voice told her, "Quench your thirst."

She filled the glass. The earthy aroma of this beverage called out to her as she raised the glass and drank. Smoldering embers flowed through her body and suddenly burst into flame. She took on a solidity, yet was amazed by how crystal clear she felt. Renewed.

Her hand that held the glass was far slimmer. The bone on her wrist jutted out, as it had when she was younger. Smooth flesh, the color nearly translucent, the first of the age-spots gone. For a moment she imagined she could see through the skin to the blue veins below, plumped with the flowing nourishment she had just consumed.

"Proceed along the path."

As Leila moved up the spiraling corridor, feeling the air warm, watching the tiles lighten, she was aware that she, too, felt lighter. It was as though she had no body, but was a spirit, gliding, without pleasure or pain, and that the absence of both was as close to bliss as she was likely to get.

With one hand she pushed the door open. Arizona's dry, cool night air rushed in to welcome her. She stared up at the silver moon, full, sated, and breathed in its brilliance. A flock of hungry nightbirds flew across its perfect face and she felt a connection to them, as if they reflected her true nature.

The iron in the rock drew her as had the drink; she needed replenishment, and instinctively understood how to get it. What had been taken from her, she would take from others, tonight, every night.

As she headed down into the valley, she knew how to stay young, slim, beautiful, and aggressive. The world belonged to her. It would come to her, and she would devour its vitality and prey on its weaknesses. Forever. After all, she was the Ultimate of her kind.

# The Skull in Her Smile

WILL MURRAY

Metallus Duende moved among his skulls, touching them with cool, appreciative hands.

It was a sumptuous collection. Among them was the petrified dragon's skull he had unearthed in the Gobi, a narrow and vaguely canine skull he had purchased off a Romany gypsy who vowed it had encased the living brain of a werewolf, and an exquisitely human skull no larger than a walnut that might have been elf, fairy, or leprechaun.

There were skulls of bone, skulls of stone, as well as skulls of jade, electrum, and other more rare matter. Human skulls and nonhuman skulls. Occulists in this and other dimensions coveted the fabulous skulls of the earthly sorcerer Metallus Duende. Some, seeking to pillage it, had found themselves unwilling and cavern-eyed contributors to its many-dimensioned variety.

But Metallus Duende considered his enviable collection incomplete. For there was no vampire skull. Not one. True, there were skulls of doubtful origin, skulls with hollow canine teeth that could have given shape to a vampire's living head. But nothing whose authenticity absolutely satisfied him.

It was not enough for Metallus Duende to set a skull upon a shelf in his vast and gloomy Chamber of Skulls and label it *Genus: Homo Vampyrus*. It must have an indisputable pedigree to join his unsurpassed collection.

But in the late twentieth century, skulls of vampires were exceedingly rare. When they had been plentiful, in previous centuries, the manner of their demise was not conducive to preservation. Sunlight sundered their fragile bones. Or they perished as vaporous and uncollectable mist. Most often, they expired in bat-form. Vampire-bat skulls were distressingly common. Duende possessed seven of them, one for every century of the last seven. But that most rare prize had always eluded him.

Until the twenty-eighth Walpurgis Night of his life on earth.

The club was called Stoker's, and if one judged by outward appearance, its clientele consisted exclusively of vampires. They entered pale of visage, trailing black diaphanous garments and fragments of ennui from their identically blood-red lips.

The doorman, sizing up Duende's pale blond looks, said, "Not undead enough. Sorry."

Duende smiled disarmingly and raised a pale hand on which a bluish gem gleamed in a silver setting. It captured the doorman's gaze, and while he stood transfixed, Duende shrank to the size of an ant and walked between his polished shoes and into the club.

In the darkness of the foyer, he whispered the spell that restored his stature. No one noticed. It was that kind of a crowd.

The decor could only be described as cryptic—in all senses of the word. Coffins for tables. Tombstones to lean against. Spunglass cobwebs in the dim high rafters. Those not wearing cloaks had powdered their faces to a surreal Kabuki pallor. Lips of both sexes gaped like raw open wounds, quietly communicating their desperations, their thwarted desires. Leather and vinyl and costume chain crinkled and clinked unmusically. The drink of choice was the required cliché, Bloody Marys.

Duende drifted through the closely packed crowd, smiling often and receiving coolly ironic toothy acknowledgement in return. At the first set of canines not obviously plastic, he paused.

"Hello, stranger," he said.

She was a tired lily, with black eyes like spiders resting in the blue web of veinwork showing in an open and honest face. Her chestnut hair had the starved, dryish quality of a nest of autumn leaves. She wore black. Of course.

"You have an earnest smile," she said, dull red lips peeling back to display two singular canines and very pale gums. The rose color of her high cheekbones was paint. "There is truth in it."

"I like your smile, too," he told her, smiling back.

"Oh really? What is it about my smile that attracts you now?"

"I can see the skull in your smile."

She didn't blink at that. "People tell me I show too much gum."

"I find that irresistible in women."

"And I thought *I* was unusual." Her lilting accent revealed itself then. Irish. Fresh off the plane. She moved closer. "What else do you like?"

"You have very prominent cheekbones. And all your teeth."

"No cavities, I." She searched his face. "You have such bedroom eyes. Would you be undressing me with them now?"

"Not exactly."

She ran a tentative finger down the front of his white silk shirt. "Exactly what then?"

"I'm mentally stripping the skin from your skull," he said truthfully.

Her black eyes, dancing spiders, grew wide in the blue web of her face. "Oh, you truly, truly *are* unusual." She gave him her full attention, falling into the game. "What sort of skull do I have?"

"A fine-boned one, with a stunning smile. Your suborbital ridge is very Old World."

"Interesting. What sort of smile do you consider stunning?"

"One that goes on forever. A smile that doesn't need eyes or lips or fleshy expression. A smile for all eternity. I could gaze upon it for the rest of my natural life."

One arching eyebrow lifted quizzically. "Most men compliment me on my eyes."

"I collect smiles," he explained.

"And I collect red-blooded men. Care to swap in kind?"

"Do you know what you're trading away?"

"Oh, I have plenty of smiles."

"But only one skull."

For a moment, her brow grew troubled. She shook off her doubt with a quick toss of her head. "I don't know your name."

"Have you a need to know the names of your prey?"

She laughed, averting her eyes.

"You don't think I'm a true vampire, do you?"

"I most sincerely hope you are."

She turned her gaze upon the milling crowd. "With so many vampires to choose from, why tired old me?"

"You have a certain . . . authenticity."

She made a face. "It's not hard to stand out from this sorry lot. Pale pretenders, with their nose and nipple rings and their vain affected disdain of life." She hissed the words. "Ah, if they could only know the damnable reality of it." She lowered her lids. "I don't know why I came here."

"I would have thought to blend in."

She made no reply to that. After a moment, she brought a wine glass brimming with some dark port to her lips and pretended to sip as if in salute to a crepe-hung portrait on a nearby wall.

"Bram was Irish," she murmured, not looking at him. "Did you know that?"

"I know it now."

"Read his bloody book when I was a naïve little lass."

"Enjoy it?"

Her voice shrank. "It ruined me."

"That's a matter of opinion, I suppose."

She slipped a finger into the glass and stirred her drink with an ebony fingernail. "No good deed goes unpunished," she said wistfully.

"I didn't catch that."

"An old Irish saying. And so terribly true, as I can attest. I would not be in this time or land had I not gotten caught up in the dark romance of it all. Just like these blind fools all around us, pity them all."

Metallus Duende took the wine glass from her cool fingers and set it still full on the coffin-shaped bar. "Shall we seek other diversions then?"

She turned, looking him full in the eye. "You are quite forward and oh so certain of yourself."

"I know what I want when I find it." He smiled, and her return smile brought out the strong planes and angles of her exquisite Old World skull.

She offered her arm in a gesture so old-fashioned it caught him by surprise. "Shall we, then?"

"Let's."

Duende took her arm up in his and led her out into the young night. Mentally, he calculated her age to be seventy, although her husk had arrested at twenty-five.

They walked along the bank of the Charles with traffic swishing by like frightened animals. The moon was a misty coin peering through sullen cloud cover. And in her hair, a spider toiled unnoticed.

"Have you ever kissed one of the undead?" she asked at one point.

"No."

"Imagine sticking your tongue into the cold innards of a squirming clam. Imagine the gray muscles squeezing for dear life. Your life."

"Charming."

"It was a memorable first kiss, I must tell you."

"Are you trying to discourage me?"

"Perhaps."

"My place is very near," he said.

"I thought we'd go to mine, actually."

"I could show you my skulls."

She hesitated. Duende understood this to be the critical moment. She wanted him. But some spark of pity remained. She had no idea she was also prey.

"We won't have to cross the river," he assured her. "If that bothers you."

Finally, she allowed, "I think I should like to see your skulls."

"They eagerly await your company."


Metallus Duende opened the heavy brownstone door for his pale companion, heart beating high in his chest in anticipation. She entered the foyer and turned very suddenly at the sound of the heavy door lock grating shut like a cell door.

"I feel something I have not felt in many years," she said suddenly.

"Fear?"

"That, too." She came up on her toes and offered her dull red lips to his.

"But you haven't seen my collection yet."

"I must taste you now," she whispered urgently. "Otherwise I fear the opportunity may be lost."

Their lips touched, brushed, parted, attracted to yet repelled by one another on some primal level.

"Why am I afraid of you?" she implored, pulling back suddenly.

"Because I'm not afraid of you," he told her, holding her eyes with his own mesmeric violet gaze.

She swallowed. "This is the moment of truth. Are you prepared?"

"Are you?" he countered.

"I must have your vitality."

She closed her eyes and exposed her gleaming canines. As she brought them toward his exposed jugular, he fingered a silvery object from a pocket.

When her teeth came together, they clicked tinnily.

At the sudden taste of metal in her mouth, she screamed. It was shrill and high-pitched. A bat's scared squeak. Eyes wide and searching, they fell upon a hall mirror. There was no reflection of course. Not of her. Just the silver spring-clip dental plates that had forced her jaw apart, capping her hollow dangerous canine teeth, rendering her helpless to attack and feast.

Eyes reddening with rage, her face began morphing into batlike lines. Her lifting arms grew membranous under each armpit.

Metallus Duende flicked a pinch of green powder that billowed out to envelope her head. Her flaring nostrils sucked up the green vapor and when the last of it had been inhaled, her pale face was a mask of peace.

Her eyes, however, glared.

"Bat-form skulls are so common," he said casually, opening the door to his apartment with a key made from a mummy femur fragment.

The vampire made a low nasal sound of distress as he guided her into his antique-crammed parlor and beyond that to his gloomy Chamber of Skulls. Her resistence was minimal.

463

She stood in the door frame, eyes blinking rapidly as the room welcomed her with a thousand fixed and toothsome grins.

"I wasn't playing a role either," he whispered in her ear. "Obviously."

A shrill squeak escaped her comically distended jaws.

"There's just one problem. I must have your name. For the label, you understand."

Her shoulders relaxed in submission. Woodenly, she turned to face him. Her face was drawn, lines like taut strings.

This was the most dangerous moment. He would have to get her name and her head off without complications.

"The doors are locked up tight," he pointed out, "and there are bars on all windows. No way out."

Her eyes searched the parlor, gliding over the iron-barred windows, the sealed doors. They fell momentarily upon the great fireplace, cold now with its heavy iron grate, and ricocheted away. They locked again with his violet orbs.

"You dream of true rest," he told her tenderly.

Squeezing her eyes shut, she nodded.

"You yearn for it," he continued. "It calls you more than the hunger on some nights. Only I can give you that eternal peace. In return, I ask only for your immortal skull."

She threw her head back, offering her unprotected breast, her bare marbled throat, her impotent fangs.

Taking a slim wand of silver, he brought it to her yawning mouth, saying in the reassuring tone of a doctor to a patient, "Don't be afraid. When I touch the locking brace with this, the spring will relax and relief will be yours."

The wand touched a contact point pressed into her bloodless tongue. The device slowly relaxed. Spitting, she snatched it from her mouth, saying, "Nasty, nasty thing."

"Your name, please?"

"Bridgid O'Shea."

"Spelled as the usual?"

"Yes, yes. Now let us be done with this—this charade." Her tone was bitter.

"Yes," said Metallus Duende. "Let us conclude our transaction. I regret that I cannot grant you the quick boon of sunlight. The stake will have to do."

Her eyes challenged his. "You know that what you covet may be lost."

"I'm quite skilled at separating people from their heads, I assure you."

She forced a smile, and her skull revealed itself anew. "Would you risk destroying the very object of your desire?" she asked. "I could be your . . . pet."

"I fear I couldn't afford your food. Are you prepared?"

"I am not afraid, if that is your meaning."

And as he took up the wooden stake and mallet from a teak taboret, Bridgid O'Shea uncoiled like a serpent from a box.

Metallus Duende tapped the stone in the amulet under his silk shirt and his atoms became as fluid as droplets of water. She passed through him. Bridgid O'Shea seemed oblivious. Her features ferocious, she cleared the space to the fireplace, flung the heavy grate free and began squirming and writhing into the chimney flue like a wolfhound digging at a burrow.

Casually, Metallus Duende touched an Egyptian scarab on the wall above the taboret. It clicked. From the fireplace, came a rattling drop of a sound, followed by a mushy *chunk!*

The clang of steel reverberated like a flat bell.

Bridgid O'Shea, her head caught in the chimney space, shook on all fours. Her body shuddered and convulsed over and over, as if her tissues were being bombarded by successive shockwaves. Leathery folds beneath her arms quivered like old sailcloth.

While she backed away on hands and knees, Metallus Duende strode up, kicked her over until her breast flipped into sight and set the stake's hard point against her inert heart.

Bridgid clawed blindly for his face with fingers growing long and horny. Duende pounded the stake once, hard and true. It went in with a dry rustle, as if into a scarecrow stuffed with straw. The husk collapsed into smoky tatters.

And on the other side of the guillotine blade that had dropped down in response to the scarab's click, Bridgid O'Shea's decapitated head screamed once, high and batlike, then no more.

"I told you I was skilled at separating people from their heads," he said grimly.

\* \* \*

Metallus Duende moved among his skulls, sprinkling them with tiny wolf spiders taken from an ebony box. These skittered into the grinning hollows, seeking bone-eating vermin.

Taking a turn around the Chamber of Skulls, he came at last to a fine Old World skull with wicked canines in a smile that would shine forever. It was labeled:

BRIDGID O'SHEA
*GENUS: HOMO VAMPYRUS*

It was a treasure, a rare prize, and the crowning jewel of his fabulous collection.

And if the human lines of this latest acquisition were also vaguely batlike, well, what could one expect in these last years of the twentieth century?

# Upstairs, Downstairs, and All About Vampires

MORT CASTLE

## Upstairs

The time is our time. Death Rock and The Doors still worshiped, Jim Morrison into being dead before almost anyone realized how cool it was. At the MegaMall Movies (ninety-six screens—NO WAITING!), *The Crow*, starring dead Brandon Lee as a dead avenger. Unlife and varieties thereof, that is where it's at.

And in the room the women have rather unoriginally chosen to call "The Dark Room," candles hiss and flicker and shadows waver and pulse on walls lit by sickly yellow light.

Three women in black. Black cowls and flopping black sleeves, black gowns blacker than the somber shadows of "The Dark Room."

Ambiance. Mood.

*Style.* Style is all. Or nearly everything, what the hell . . .
This is their thing, you see.

Three women, with black hoods and faces white beyond
ghostly and white beyond ghastly. Three women with heavy
black circles beneath eyes that make you think of Edgar Allan
Poe and Death (Death Tangible, not Metaphor), or German Ex-
pressionist cinema, or severe sinusitis.

Three women, one young, and two who would say they are
". . . older," if they would condescend to say anything at all
about a matter that is none of your concern—*really.* The young
one, let's risk being politically incorrect, and call her "The
Girl." But one of the older women is only, let us say, "big sister"
older (and from now on, let's speak of her as Big Sister), and the
other older woman is, well, "Old enough to be your mother"
older. (It would be impolite, even an unintentional double en-
tendre, to call her Mother, and we won't, but we can call her
leader, that is, *The* Leader, and, truthfully, that is the way she
thinks of herself.)

Now, in jaundiced and pallid light, in light that brings to
mind cigarette coughs and stories of bleak winter in America's
Great Depression, three women in black touch fine-stemmed
glasses, glasses that hold a liquid dark and purple and every bit
as red as it is purple and dark.

A delicate *ting.* Smiles. Three white and cold smiles, so
serious beneath raccoon-from-hell eyes. Smiles intended to be
jaded and decadent and insouciant.

Smiles you might consider casually cruel for this familiar
toast:

"Blood!" says The Girl, in an exultant whisper.

"The *blood* is the *life!*" says Big Sister.

The Leader draws out the moment, *her* moment, appreciating drama, timing, *style,* yes, style, and, like a jazz musician,
(be-bop-a re-bop!) *cool* . . .

The Leader says, "To . . . Life!"

(Which is what you might hear at a bar mitzvah, but there
wouldn't be any incongruity.)

Laughter.

And three women in black in "The Dark Room" drink
deep.

## Downstairs

Damn! Rat bastard! Damn! Argh! Dazed, defeated, and *drained* as he is, he understands Eternity because he is in it up to his hoo-hah and hairline and honker, and because he understands it, you bet he would tell you, "Eternity sucks!"

The dark is upon him like suffocation, infection, and telephone solicitors, as he lies in unending absence of light, the cold and hard circularity of chains at ankles and wrists securing him on the rude altar or heavy table or what the hell.

He has been a prisoner how long? He does not know. Eternity screws your sense of time, and it's so damned dark he couldn't see his Timex even if (A) he had the freedom to move his arms and (B) they hadn't taken his watch.

The Timex along with everything else. So long to the Florsheims and the Levi 501s. No receipt for anything they boosted when they stripped you *buck NAY-KED!*

Oh, yes, it is his skinny bare butt on the tabletop. Hey, fellas and gals, forget the physical your HMO recommends once a year, forget standing in the shower going rub-a-dub-dubby on all your private, personal, and *very own!* places, you do *not* understand *bare-assimo ultimato* until you are (A) wearing chains and (B) one hundred the hell and twelve extra percent at the mercy of . . .

Those!
*God!*
*DAMNED!*
*BITCHES!!!*

## Upstairs

The Dark Room is closed with the smell of wax and the scent of perverse excitement. (Think Calvin Klein perfume and Lust Potion Number Nine. . . .) Arrowheads of candlelight are distorted reflections in the curved bowls of empty stemmed glasses on a dresser top.

As though mocking that which is round, near the glasses, is the gleaming angularity of a single-edge razor blade, a proud, if disposable, member of the Wilkinson clan.

"And so, which of us this time?" The question is posed by The Leader. Her tone tells you she is, without a doubt, the kind of "go for the throat" twentieth-century woman who frightens many men in the business world—and likewise causes strong, if not always welcomed, arousal, in others. (Same response for/from women. Check out your Kraft-Ebbing, under the topic, "Nothing New Under the Sun.")

"Please, me!" says The Girl. Her excitement is what you'd expect from a high school sophomore, one both overly dramatic and hormonal.

"It was you last time," says Big Sister, although she sounds every bit as peevish and *nyaah-nyaah-nyaah* as would only a *slightly* older sister who might run to rat out her sib, in hopes that the sib might get grounded or even whacked a good one.

The Leader orchestrates the scenario. (Got that, girlfriend?) She arches an eyebrow. She touches a long and filed-to-murder-weapon-sharp fingernail to her chin. Her head tips. This is all done so casually that you know the pose has been well and frequently practiced. It is what you'd expect of an actress in a made-for-cable film—if the cable network were USA.

As authoritative as the curriculum developer for "Assertiveness Training for Sumo Wrestlers," she says to The Girl, "Yes. You."

Big sister's "Oh," is disappointed, but then, in just a micromoment, you can see the feeling of *let down* vanish to be replaced by *worked up.*

As The Girl pushes back her flopping sleeve to reveal a slender and ivory-pale left forearm, with pinkish and whitish marks, scars old and new.

And now she concentrates, the Wilkinson blade poised, delicately held between thumb and forefinger.

And now she draws the diagonal line with precisely modulated pressure. The tight flesh of her forearm parts. Purple-crimson beads appear, swell and pulse, dots grow and connect to create a slender, rippling worm of blood.

The youngest woman in black proudly offers her arm and her blood.

The mouth and tongue of The Leader touch and taste.

The Girl smiles.

In The Dark Room, two women in black taste the blood of

another, who then kitten-licks and sucks and then drinks her own blood, and then, there is what we might call a "collective sigh," as well as several similar, if not exactly shared, psychological and physiological reactions.

Then The Girl, Big Sister, and The Leader, three women in black, go downstairs.

## Downstairs

Uh-oh, is what he thinks when he hears the door hinge squeak above him in the darkness. He is more than a bunch bonkers and so, all kinds of whacked out things shoot across his mind:

*I tawt I taw twee puddy tats. . . .*

There's been a mistake, really, a *bad* mistake. . . .

Okay, we have had it with the preliminaries! Howzabout I call the law, tell 'em you're like a cult of weirdified lezbo crazy*kopfs* or something, that you're so rutabaga you make the Jehovah's Witnesses seem like 4-H, and then, well, you'll go to jail and Oprah won't even have you as guests because you're so goddamned *icky*. . . .

You are *such* bitches!

You are goddamned Bitches!

You are. I am not kidding.

YOU ARE BITCHES!

Yes. I'm calling . . . THE AUTHORITIES!

With the cellular phone I just happen to have in my ass . . .

Tell you what, how about I plead? Very pleadingly, okay? *Please* . . . Oh, please. Oh, please. Oh, please.

Will you *please*, will you, please, willyouplease . . .

Hey, that's what he is saying. Saying it right out loud. As out loud as he can, anyway, which is not all that loud, considering how thoroughly thrashed, bashed, and trashed he is.

"Puh-leezzz . . . *PUH-leeee* . . ." He feels the plosive pop on his dried and burning lips. Feels the gritty rush of air up his wind pipe and the searing slice of it on his tongue.

Three women in black surround him.

And one of them, the oldest, and most vicious, The Bitch

Boss/Boss Bitch is putting on the demands. She is as friendly about it as a cement mixer, but her volume is a tad higher.

He *will* tell them.

Oh, yes.

He *will* do what they demand.

Oh, yes.

Does he think he has a choice? Does he think they can be fooled? Does he think . . .

He thinks: If he knew how to spin window putty into a goddamned free-monthly-lease Lexus, he would tell them. If he knew how to destroy his favorite Aunt Mildred in a lingeringly painful way, he would tell them. If he knew the position for the Cringing Ostrich Trick, supposedly taught to Jack Kennedy by Marilyn Monroe (film rights optioned by Oliver Stone), he would tell them.

He would tell the bitches anything.

*ANY*thing—

But he *has* told them.

They do not believe him.

Ladies, ladies, ladies, listen up! No kidding, honest Native-American, forget the fiction, all the bull by that one lunatic woman and her imitators, most of whom have three names, with or without hyphens. This is *the emmis*. If I am lying, I am flying (and I sure ain't, in case you didn't notice). The truth? Say, does the Pope poop in the woods? Tell the truth and have no regrets. I swear to tell the truth, the whole truth, and here we go. . . .

I cannot help you. Not me or anybody else.

It's kind of like being black.

It's a birth thing.

You are born like me, okay?

Or, in your case(s), you are not.

You cannot sign up for classes. It's not like converting to Judaism. No one can teach you the secret handshake. You are wasting your time with personals in the *Village Voice* or semiliterate e-mail and computer BBS. No way. Uh-uh. Won't happen. Pay Miracle Momma Wombat to brand your behinds with a Big Voodoo "V." Learn to diatonically fart the 100 Arcane Names of The Devil. Combine the cookbooks of Countess Bathory and Famous Amos.

And it STILL won't mean A THING!
(Even if you *got* the swing!)
Because
You is.
Or.
You ain't.
And I is.
And you ain't.
That's rationality, if you please, good women.
Okay?
Over and out.
"You want us to believe you."
*Why, yes, compared to, say, your sawing off my manly thing with the only Ginsu ever to be sold without a warranty . . .*
"You'd like us to free you, to send you on your way."
*I guess so. Go figure.*
"You will teach us. You will. We have patience."
They have patience—
—and they have blood.
The young one. She puts her forearm to his split lips. He laps greedily at the coagulating cut line, feels blood liquid and good in his mouth, sucked up by his system.
And he feels something like—no, not life—but a weak and dreamy energy that will sustain him for now—
—barely—
—until the Three Women in Black come again—
As they now leave him, as they vanish in darkness and distance . . .

## Upstairs

# Foul Weather

## Dawn Dunn and Judy Post

**B**lood-red eyes.

Pearl-white fangs.

Rain pelted the window as gray clouds smothered the parking lot. It had rained every day for two weeks. The sun hadn't shown itself in two months. Ray couldn't remember when the weather had been so dreary for so long.

The last lunch customer paid at the cash register, then opened his umbrella and dashed across the street to the factory. Ray watched him shiver against the dampness and dart up the sidewalk. No one even wanted to cross the street in this weather.

Lenore cleared the table and pocketed her tip. "Need me anymore this afternoon?"

"What do you think?"

"Right." She opened the door that led to the narrow stairs at the back of the restaurant and climbed to a small rectangular bedroom. A few months after Ray bought the cafe, the city had closed the street it sat on for major road repairs. The crumbling old pavement had been stripped to its base and was being resurfaced. The street would remain closed to traffic for several months yet.

What perfect timing, Ray thought glumly. Lenore's footsteps clopped over the ceiling above him. The springs on the old Hollywood bed creaked as she threw herself into it. The only way he could afford to keep a waitress was by giving her free room and board.

He rubbed his eyes and stifled a yawn, though he wouldn't have been able to sleep if he tried. His dreams of late had become gore-spattered landscapes, peopled with mostly unfamiliar faces, all of them hideously pale and blood-streaked, yet uncomfortably erotic. *Give me your heart.* The words he had heard last night. A deathly white hand held his still-beating heart, the blood running like syrup between the skeletal fingers.

Ray stared out the window at the soggy, gray world. Water ran in rivulets down the glass, distorting the images on the other side. While he watched, two hollows, resembling eyes, swam open and a mouth stretched wide beneath them. The delicate, watery nostrils wavered in and out. Marie.

A quick rush of breath escaped him. He blinked and backed toward the cash register, his skin growing suddenly clammy. Though he willed it away, the face was still there, peering in at him, screaming a silent accusation. It was nothing more than another nightmare, he told himself, although he was both shaken and angry. The pressure and guilt were eroding his sanity.

Unable to rid himself of the vision, he finally pulled the drapes. He'd always wanted to run his own restaurant and had sunk all of his savings into this dream. It'd taken all the courage he had and every penny he'd ever earned to quit his job at the warehouse and buy old Murray out when he'd talked of retiring. *If* that's why Murray sold him the place. Ray swallowed hard. Murray hadn't bothered to mention that the restaurant was going to be nearly inaccessible for four or five months while the roadwork was completed.

I'll make it, though, Ray reminded himself. Things would be tight, but he'd pinched and scraped before. He couldn't give up now, not when he was so close to having everything he wanted.

A wind gusted around the corner of the building, sighing loudly, searching for cracks.

She's trying to get inside, he thought. He ran to the front door and locked it. He hurried from window to window, pulling the drapes. Hardly anyone came at the dinner hour. Maybe tonight he wouldn't even bother opening up. He could turn on the red neon 'CLOSED' sign. There was a full second shift at the factory, but when it was dark and rainy most of them lined up at the company's cafeteria anyway. And who could blame them? Ray wouldn't have to go out, either. He could just sleep on the upholstered settee that snaked around the far corner booth. He had his coat and jacket to throw over him to keep warm.

What's the matter with me? he wondered abruptly. He was letting the gloomy weather effect him. He'd been under too much stress. First, Marie's death. Then buying the restaurant—

the business they'd spent the last five years budgeting for so they could run it together. Then the street repairs. And all this damn rain!

Ray went to the counter and poured himself a cup of coffee. Something hot and steaming to soothe his nerves. As he took his first sip, a scream ripped the air upstairs. Lenore's feet hit the floor over his head as she ran toward the stairs. An icy chill gripped his bowels. "What is it?" he hollered.

Did he really want to know? Instead of Marie waiting on customers, he had a young girl with hickeys circling her neck like a cheap necklace, who was so pale she looked as though her boyfriends sucked the blood out of her every time they touched her. He hated them all. A bunch of greasy, smart-mouthed hoods.

Lenore appeared at the bottom of the stairs, all hyper and trembling, pink splotches accentuating her papery flesh. It would take her at least half an hour to calm down. "A woman was looking in the window upstairs!" she cried.

Ray didn't need to ask what the woman looked like.

Lenore went straight to the freezer and scooped out great dollops of ice cream. Even in this miserable weather, she inhaled Double Dutch Chocolate. For someone who ate so much, she sure was skinny.

The rain began to drum with a vengeance, hurling itself against the windows, beating on the door. The wind howled.

Ray put his hands over his ears and shut his eyes. "Let's forget the supper shift," he said. "Nobody's gonna show up."

Lenore grinned, licking the ice cream off her lips. "Fine with me."

"I'm gonna work on the garbage disposal to see if I can get it unclogged," he said. "I can't imagine what got stuck in there. Later, I'll fix us both a small supper, watch a little TV at the bar, then I'll curl up on the settee."

Her spoon froze in midair, a biteful of Double Dutch Chocolate lost in limbo. "What?"

"My car wasn't running good on the way in this morning," Ray lied. "I don't want it to break down and leave me stranded. I'll just sleep here tonight and be ready for the breakfast crowd."

"That's not a good idea."

"Why?"

She frowned, not meeting his eyes. "I wouldn't have hired on if I'd thought you were gonna be spending the nights here, too."

"If you're worried that I'm going to bother you, forget it," he growled. "I just don't want to get drowned trying to get home."

Lenore shook her head, her thin, white-blonde hair grazing her shoulders. "You shouldn't stay. I have a friend who'll fix the disposal. I told you that."

"Relax, will you? You can lock your door when you go upstairs. I don't want your friends playing with my pipes. I'd rather do it myself." Ray pushed himself to his feet and poured another cup of coffee on his way to the kitchen. "I've got work to do. Do what you want."

Ray had never been good with mechanical things. If he'd been good with pipes, he could have gotten rich as a plumber. But he didn't trust strangers with what was his.

He'd fidgeted for the last three hours with the monster disposal, and he still couldn't make it run. Something was jammed solid in there, blocking a whole section of pipe. Frustrated, Ray decided to take a break and make supper. Cooking was the one thing in which he did excel. He didn't give a damn whether Lenore ate with him or not, but he had worked up an appetite. She could quit for all he cared.

Buckets of water were throwing themselves at the windows when he cracked the drape to peek outside. It was unbelievable that the storm had lasted so long, yet it seemed to be growing worse by the minute. The wind whipped around the corners now, shrieking a high-pitched keen. Water sat on the asphalt an inch deep, forming a shallow, black lake. The red light from the neon sign threaded across its dark surface like blood seeping its way through a sea of ink. Raindrops hammered the new bushes he'd planted, smashing their branches into the dirt. One of the branches lifted itself from the ground, then another, stretching toward the window as if they were arms. The center cluster writhed into a female shape, and once again, Marie reached out for him.

He dropped the drape.

He couldn't let her, or rather the memory of her, destroy

him. His head felt light and his knees weak. It'd been too long since he'd stopped to eat. What he needed was a good meal.

He went to the freezer and pulled out two big T-bones. He tossed them on the grill and sliced onions and peppers to sizzle beside them. As he foraged in the storage room for a can of mushrooms, he found an old box of lye that Murray had left behind. He spread the mushrooms on the griddle with the other vegetables, then emptied the lye down the garbage disposal, flushing a little water after it for good measure. Whatever was in those pipes should work its way through now. He put a bucket under the open drain to catch whatever came through. That done, he returned to his food.

Ray couldn't remember the last time he'd sat down and enjoyed a leisurely meal. Not that he could call Lenore good company. She ripped into her steak as though she hadn't eaten in weeks. But it was better than eating alone, as he usually did, after the last customer had gone, when he was almost too tired to taste anything he put in his mouth.

Though he tried not to, he thought of Marie. He'd often cooked fancy dinners for her when she came home from a long day at the grocery. Marie had worked at the check-out and her feet always ached by the time she sank onto a kitchen chair and sipped a glass of wine to relax. They'd shared lots of good times. They'd be working together in the restaurant now if it hadn't been for the tumors. The doctor had found the first under her right arm. Then a second had grown on the side of her breast. Each time a tumor was removed, another appeared in a new place. The medical costs were exorbitant, and their insurance had been about to reach its maximum. Soon, they would have had to dip into their nest egg, the savings they'd struggled so hard for, so that they could buy their dream. Ray hadn't been able to stand the soft sobs that shook Marie in her darkest hours. He hadn't been able to face a bleak future of watching her die, bit by bit. . . .

A sucking, sloshing sound burped in the kitchen.

Ray swallowed his last bite of steak and picked up the two dirty plates to take to the sink.

"Let me help you," Lenore offered.

Ray stared at her, surprised. She never volunteered for anything. Lenore carried the glasses and silverware, following him.

After stacking the dishes, Ray turned to the bucket and gasped. A white, mucky glob jiggled inside the metal pail. Ten fingers and a few toes protruded from the mass of fatty tissue.

Ray looked up, wide-eyed. Lenore met his gaze, calmly.

"What—can you . . . ?" Ray stammered to a stop.

"I tried to tell you not to stay." She might have been talking to a small, stubborn child. "I told you my friend would clean out the pipes."

"Your friend . . . did he? I mean, who is—" Ray couldn't go on. Lenore's pale eyes gleamed feverishly.

"It worked before," she said wistfully. "I guess this one was too big, or we just didn't get it chopped up small enough."

"Do you know what you've done?" he muttered.

"Clogged your pipes," she said innocently. "But you got them unclogged, didn't you?"

"This is insane."

"It's kind of hard to explain. I hang out with some people who are little different, see?"

Ray shook his head.

"They might be a few centuries old, maybe more."

"You're nuts," he repeated, but Lenore merely laughed.

"Ever wonder how a vampire gets high?" she asked.

Ray brushed past her and walked to the phone.

She sprang after him, landing on his back, straddling him, her teeth sinking into his neck. Her fingernails bit into his face, and blood veiled his eyes.

Ray groaned in pain and flung her from his back. She leapt to her feet and charged him again, but this time he sidestepped her and knocked her to the floor. Pinning her down with a heavy boot across her chest, he groped for the receiver. She immediately rolled out from beneath him and ran to the door. Flinging it wide, she screamed, "Welcome, ole wayfarers of the night!"

A thunderous sound, like an approaching train, rushed into the room, and Ray thought a tornado had struck. Winds blew in every direction, scattering tables and chairs. The ferocious gusts called out his name. It was Marie's voice.

Ray ran. In seconds, he was drenched, his clothes plastered to his skin. Wet arms embraced him. Cold lips kissed his cheek.

Marie's face hovered mistily, then the wind tugged at him, pulling him further away from the restaurant.

She'd come back to punish him. He'd overdosed her, then used the insurance money to buy out Murray. He hollered and wrenched himself from her grasp. Fighting the wind, he hurled himself back into the restaurant and locked the door.

An ominous silence greeted him.

Turning, he saw Lenore, writhing on the large, circular table in the corner. Five men, some of them the same hoodlums he'd seen her with before, others he recognized from his dreams, crowded around her. A vacuous smile tilted her lips as she gazed with glassy eyes at the ceiling above her. Slowly, her hand rose and she took another snort of coke.

One of the men opened his mouth and bared his fangs. His long, narrow tongue darted viciously toward her neck. The others awaited their turn, almost reverently. A tiny ribbon of red trickled down Lenore's white neck, and she arched her back in ecstasy or agony, while a sickening sucking sound filled the room.

Ray watched in disgust. He glanced toward the door, ready to run, but a husky young man leaned casually against it. His eyes met Ray's, and he smiled. Ray recoiled at the glistening fangs he revealed. His insides quivered, and for a moment he feared he might faint. But men didn't faint. Men were brave. Men were strong. Then he looked into the glowing, red-stained eyes from his nightmares and broke into a cold sweat.

"We've been trying to think of a way to repay your hospitality," the young man said, his words echoing distantly as though they were bouncing off bygone years. "Lenore suggested that we make you one of us."

If blood could curdle, Ray was certain his had. "Not meaning to sound ungrateful, but—"

The vampire laughed. The softness of his voice was more menacing than any scream or growl.

Ray studied the young man carefully. Lenore had said they were old, but he didn't see any signs of aging. He wondered what it would be like never to grow old, never to worry about heart failure or tumors.

"I grew up around the Revolution," the young man said, reading his mind.

"Seventeen seventy-six?" Ray asked.

"No, the one in England, when they made King John sign the Magna Carta."

Lenore gave a low gasp.

Ray saw the bloodsucker at her neck sink contentedly into the booth, while another took his place. "Ever wonder how a vampire gets high?" she'd asked. Well, now he knew.

"Too bad about your wife," the vampire at the front door said. His eyes narrowed, and he took a step forward. "She really misses you. She's been doing her best to warn you about us, but you misunderstood."

Ray would gladly join her now.

"It's a little too late for that," the young man said reading his mind again.

A cold shiver shook Ray's body. He looked at the vampires gathered around Lenore, their complexions deathly pale, their eyes empty just like their souls. He was taller and heavier than any man in the room, but he doubted that would matter.

The wind outside had reached a new pitch. It thrashed at the building, trying to break in. The rain lashed and pummelled.

Ray lunged for the front window, slamming his body against the glass. It shattered, but the vampire had sprung forward at the same moment, breaking Ray's momentum. He threw Ray into the wall and sank his fangs deep into Ray's flesh, gnashing and tearing.

Ray struggled until the vampire pierced his jugular and the loud draining of his blood began. The lights spun above him. Nothing seemed real. He could hear the wind crying. The air got colder, and his vision turned black. As his fingers twitched involuntarily, he heard the rain finally slowing. Instead of a storm, it reminded him of tear drops, falling from Heaven's eye.

As he lay limp on the floor, he felt the fangs withdraw from his neck. The vampire straightened and laughed smoothly. "She's gone. It looks like tomorrow will be a nice day."

# Folds of the Faithful

## Yvonne Navarro

hy doesn't she just *die!*" Michelle asked. "Why would she hang on like this?"

"How can you say such a thing?" I demanded. "Wait—of course you can. You're not the one who's depended on her all these years, who's lived with her and kept her company." I hugged myself tightly and rocked on the edge of the uncomfortable vinyl-cushioned chair. The hospital bed loomed to my left, antiseptic metal beneath over-bleached linens that stank of medicine and sickness. "You're not the one who loves her like I do!"

"Oh, say it a little louder, *please.*" My sister glared at me and tossed her head, the movement making her long auburn hair swing. "Make sure she hears you, *pet.*" Michelle practically spat the last word.

"She doesn't need to hear it," I said hotly. "She already knows."

"Then she doesn't need your whining now!"

"Jesus, don't the two of you ever stop?" Mark, the oldest, sat on the other chair in the private room, his eyes tracking Michelle as she paced the width of the room like a big caged cat. "What's next? Playing tug of war with her purse?"

Michelle was on the attack instantly. "His Highness speaks," she sneered. "And where have you been for the last decade?"

"The same place as you," he said calmly. "Getting on with my life."

I felt my face flush. "Meaning what?" I interrupted. "That our mother wasn't worth the devotion of my time?"

Mark stood and looked like he was going to walk over to me; instead, he shoved his hands in his pockets and gazed at the floor. "That's not what I meant at all, Mary. Jesus," he said again. "How did we get like this?"

For a few moments we stared at one another. Flash memories spun in my thoughts—were the same memories flitting through their minds? Mark, Michelle, and Mary—our parents used to call us the three Mouseketeers when we were kids. What *had* happened? Life, I suppose. Mark had gone to college, then law school. Michelle headed for college two years later, then polished off her career goals with a bachelor's degree in fine arts from the Art Institute of Chicago. Luck of the draw made me the youngest, and I had stayed with Mother after Father's death shortly before Mark's graduation from college. I still remember Mother's words back then—

*"It will only be for a while, Mary. A couple of months, half a year at the most. Is that so much to ask? I'm so lonely with your father gone. If you go to college in St. Paul now, the house will be empty suddenly! How can I face that so soon?"*

And so I had stayed, putting aside my dreams of a doctorate in medieval history from the esteemed University of Minnesota, taking AE courses from the local community college instead. Gradually those had turned from academic challenges to time-killers, a decade-long subtle transformation from Early French Literature to Learning Macrame at Home. When I signed up for the Art of Home Canning three years ago, I'd known I was lost. It would have been funny if the realization hadn't made me feel so utterly hopeless.

"Mary?"

I raised my head to find both my brother and sister staring at me curiously. "What?"

"Are you all right?"

Concern was etched all over Mark's face, bless his heart. I had no doubt it was heartfelt, too, at least as much as he was able. But what did Mark, with his perky blonde-permed wife, twin toddlers, and his stylishly renovated home on Chicago's Gold Coast, know of loneliness? What did he know of an empty and echoing century-old mini-mansion at the rear of a woodsy lot in Bourbonnais, Illinois? His life had taken him much farther away than the sixty-odd miles that separated us.

"I'm as all right as a person can be when their whole reason for living is dying in front of them," I replied in a dull voice.

"Mary, honey, you mustn't think that way." For once Michelle's voice was compassionate as she hurried to my side. "You've spent so many years taking care of Mother. We all know

you've sacrificed everything for her, all your dreams, your education. . . ." She glanced at Mark and he nodded. "All this stupid
bickering—it means nothing. Whatever's in Mother's estate, the
house, the bank accounts, whatever—it's all yours. You deserve
it, Mary. Mark and I are both quite comfortable, and let's face it,
we got that way with your help, in a roundabout way. Without
you to take care of Mother and be with her after Father died,
college might have been stalled for both of us."

Petty fights be damned, I'd never, *ever* thought Michelle,
who was notoriously self-centered, would admit to that. Still,
the whole estate? "I don't—"

Mark stopped me with a wave of his hand. "Nonsense. Michelle's right. She's got the gallery, I've got my practice. The
estate's worth what? Five or six hundred thousand? Enough to
support you while you finally go to school and set you up in a
good life afterwards. Enough to let you finally catch up."

"The estate is worth slightly over two million," I said quietly.

Michelle's mouth dropped open, then she shut it. Having
theoretically "given" me the rights to the entire inheritance, she
would have difficulty gracefully reneging. The ball was in
Mark's court now. He was silent for a few moments, then he
folded his arms and set his jaw. "That's good," Mark said with
finality. "And it's only fair that it goes to you, as repayment for
everything you've done."

Unexpected heat again filled my face. "You can't buy me,
or—or put a *price* on my love!" I stood, nearly overturning the
heavy hospital chair. "Neither one of you knows anything about
how it was, or how I felt. Now you think you can give me some
money and I'll shut myself up in that empty old house and leave
you both alone. So the problem of *me* will just go away, right?" I
was crying now, pressing my fists so hard against the sides of
my face that I could feel my teeth cut into the skin inside my
cheeks. "Well, what about what I feel?" I howled. "What about
what I *need*?"

When Mark spoke, his voice was surprisingly cool. "What
you *need*, Mary, is your freedom. Let's be blunt here, okay?"
He waved a hand at Mother's still figure on the bed. Buried
beneath the mound of hospital linens, wires and plastic tubes
ran in all directions and made the lump look absurdly like a fat

centipede. "She's beyond help, but she's still sucking you dry. You get here at nine and don't leave until they throw you out at night, not even for lunch. The sole reason you don't lose weight is because you bring a bagged lunch with you." I was shocked at his tone of voice, incredulous at the anger on his fine-featured face. "You think we don't know you go to Mass every single morning? Honest to God, you need a life more than anyone I know!"

"Someone's got to pray for her!" I snapped. "You two certainly don't. At least I have hope that she'll get better, instead of hovering over her body and waiting for her to die."

"So you're doing it," Michelle said suddenly.

I blinked at her. "Doing what?"

"Keeping her *alive*." Mark frowned at her, but Michelle wouldn't take her eyes from mine.

"They're only prayers," I said. I felt suddenly feverish, slightly dizzy. "Don't be absurd. I'm an early riser anyway."

Michelle ignored me and turned to Mark. "That's why Mother kept breathing when we insisted they take her off the respirator last week," she continued. "She *can't* stop. Mary's prayers won't *let* her die."

"Michelle," Mark said gently. He looked thinner than I remembered, weary and abruptly overburdened by the direction the conversation had taken. Even his hair seemed droopy. "You're stretching it a bit, don't you think?"

"No." Michelle's face, normally so pretty, twisted and became almost ugly. "All this time we thought it was Mother draining Mary, but it's Mary forcing Mother to live." She rubbed the flesh of her slender arms below the short sleeves of her summer dress, a trendy thing with huge, splashy flowers that looked out of place in the somber room. "The doctors said Mother should've died a month ago," she said quietly. "They can't understand it. Well, I can. It's Mary, going to Mass day after day, begging every morning that she be given one more day with Mother."

"Well, I can't say that's actually true," Mark said thoughtfully. "But I do know it's not healthy." His head turned towards me, seawater-green eyes piercing. "And I want you to stop, for your own sake."

"Can you blame me for not wanting her to *die?*" Fear made

my voice high-pitched, tumbled my words over themselves in a speed-induced stutter. "I j-just ask for her t-to hang on. I'll be-be all a-alone when she g-goes—"

"No, you *won't*," Mark insisted. He reached over and took my hand. "We'll be there for you—" Michelle made a noise under her breath and he glared at her. She and I had lost the closeness of childhood two years before I realized I wouldn't be leaving for the University of Minnesota after my high school graduation; we killed it in a bitter rivalry over a neighborhood boy when I was seventeen. "I will, anyway," he said with unaccustomed nastiness towards Michelle. "Bourbonnais isn't that far from the city. Angie and I will start bringing the kids out a couple times a month on the weekends, or you can visit us."

"I-I don't know," I said. Kids? Noisy voices and boundless energy, so much of it after so many quiet years. How would I deal with that? "The children—"

"You'll get used to them," he assured me with a pat on the shoulder. "They're a joy, really. You need to get some *movement* in your life, Mary, some people and voices into that huge old house. Something besides these endless, piddling classes at the community college. God," his expression was earnest, "there's a whole world out there you haven't seen since you were a teenager. Mother took that away from you—"

"She never—"

"—whether she intended to or not. Come on, little sister." Over Mark's shoulder I could see Michelle, but her face was unreadable. Mark smiled at me sadly and stroked my cheek.

"Mary," he said softly, "it's time to let Mother go."

Mother died the next afternoon. I didn't go to Mass that morning, and as a matter of fact, I haven't been since. A year has gone by and I haven't seen Michelle since the funeral, which is no big surprise. I've gotten to know my two nieces quite well and they seem to look forward to their twice-monthly Sundays with Auntie Mary, though their mother doesn't always share their enthusiasm. That's unfortunate, but Mark did promise, after all, that he would be there for me in the dark times following Mother's death. All the years of taking care of Mother, cooking and cleaning for her at first, then feeding and washing her like a baby in the later years—I came to depend on the way she needed me. And I needed her in return, to make me feel wanted and loved and . . . *necessary*. True to his word, Mark and the girls have done a spectacular job of doing that.

But Mark is desperately ill. I remember thinking on that horrible day in Mother's hospital room that he didn't look right, too tired, too thin. I'd thought it was the strain of Mother's illness, the tension generated by having the three of us sniping at each other over the course of Mother's final month. I was wrong, of course; last week the doctors told Mark that he has cancer, and that it's spread throughout his lymph nodes and pancreas. They've fitted him with a shunt for chemotherapy and put him on a special antioxidant diet, but they don't have much hope. All that faithlessness shows in the lines of his face and in his young wife's traitorous, money-hungry eyes when she looks at him and wonders silently how much longer he'll live.

Early Mass at St. Sebastian Catholic Church starts at 6:15. The priest hasn't seen me since I stood by Mother's graveside and tossed a tear-stained rose on the casket as the first shovelful of earth splattered on its lid.

But I'm positive he'll welcome me back to the folds of the faithful tomorrow morning.

# Just Enough

JOEL LANE

It wasn't much. A third-floor office just south of the city centre, in between a nightclub and a car park. There were three phones, but rarely as many as three people to answer them. Tonight, Gary was on the late shift: eleven till two. He was sharing it with Alison, an older counsellor. They tried to have at least one female operator present at all times, to deal with distressed women who called. Through the office window, Gary could see the city's lights sprawled like a constellation.

He'd learned early on that the things which made people desperate were also things that drove them mad. Bereavement, violence, drink, betrayal, isolation. It was no use talking down from a "rational" perspective. You had to start where they were and work upwards. Sometimes you could help, if only by listening. Or by not reacting badly when they told you terrible things. (Add guilt to the list.) Tonight seemed more difficult than usual. An Asian man who'd been beaten up repeatedly; Gary advised self-defence courses and strategies to avoid being alone on the streets. Someone who was too drunk to make any sense. Someone else who was clearly suicidal but refused to say why. And then, near the end of the shift, a familiar voice. "Gary, is that you?"

"Yes, it is," Gary said. A mixture of tension and vague panic made his vision blur momentarily. "Are you okay?"

"Just about. Gary, I need some more. Can you get me some?" His voice was like a child's.

"This isn't what the line's meant for. You know that." Gary found it hard to keep the impatience out of his voice. He'd told Paul not to call him at work. Unless it was a real emergency.

"Well, *I'm* desperate, aren't I? And you know where to get it." Gary didn't bother to reply. He held the silence, as unnerving as a level gaze, until Paul said: "Bring money, then. Go to the cashpoint. Please."

"Okay. I'll see you at home." Gary hung up, then turned and punched the office wall on his left. He heard plaster crack. Flakes of paint stuck to his fist. *Jesus wept.* Alison, who was answering another call, raised her eyebrows. "Sorry," he said as the phone rang again.

"Hello," the new caller said. "I need to talk to you. It's so cold here. Are you as lonely as me? Are you?" He sounded like he was calling from an open space, with the wind blowing around him. And there was an uncomfortable sneer to his voice. As if he were trying not to laugh. His accent reminded Gary of London. "I have to talk to someone," he went on before Gary could frame a response. "All day I make phone calls and never sell anything. Why not? I'm good. I believe in *me.* But there has to be a window. So I can reach what I want. Otherwise . . . it's just so dark. Do you think you can help me?"

Gary couldn't speak. The voice made him think of caves, tunnels, cracks in the earth. A terrible emptiness. But there was also something false about it. This was the kind of person who'd dominate a pub conversation with bizarre anecdotes that turned out to be pure bullshit; who'd make a date somewhere really hard to get to and then not turn up; who'd make a living selling advertising space. He coughed. "Well, we're here to talk to. What's been getting you down?"

There was silence; then a laugh so painful and childlike it made Gary feel cold. Sweat trickled from his shoulder blades. "I don't want your sympathy," the voice said. "I want *you.*" There was a thin hiss, like someone breathing through a straw. Then a click. Gary put the receiver down. Black grains swarmed across the wall. His right ear was tingling; he rubbed it and felt something wet. There was blood on his fingers. *Jesus.* By using a tissue, he determined that there were several little cuts in the flesh of his ear. Scratches, really.

Alison glanced at him between calls. "Are you okay?" He shrugged. "Bad call?" He nodded and she smiled gently, knowing better than to press him. It was nearly time to go home. He stood up and walked over to the office window. In the view, street lamps and car headlights seemed to float high above ground level. He imagined the network of lines that ran from building to building like an invisible map. That network was survival. Nobody could live without human contact. His phone rang and Alison silently reached to answer it.

Two days later, they were still arguing. Paul wasn't entirely a weak person; when he was set on an idea, he could be as stubborn as fuck. "I *know* we got into it together," Gary said as he stirred mushrooms into the Quorn and tomato sauce. "But I've given it up. The reason you won't give it up is not because you refuse to conform." Paul's sardonic eyes dared him to say what the reason was. But that would blow the evening apart. Gary touched the side of Paul's face. "I really want to help," he said. "But you've got to change direction. Or you'll destroy everything." He looked into Paul's eyes, hoping the younger man would see the love as well as the threat in those words. Paul tilted his head and kissed Gary fiercely, desperately. The phone rang.

Gary was draining the pasta when he heard Paul slam down the receiver. Then, moving as lightly as ever, Paul was back in the kitchen. "Cold caller. Trying to sell fucking life insurance. I told him I'd rather die." Gary didn't laugh. Paul gave him a tired smile. "I'm sorry. You know I'm trying." Gary didn't make the obvious retort. He was wondering whether to tell Paul about the mad caller who'd left him feeling ill at work. Better not. There was no point worrying Paul about some lyrical casualty of Black Wednesday. And Gary wanted to stay off the subject of the helpline for now. It was getting harder for them to talk at any level except foreplay. As they sat down to dinner, he tried to fight off a growing sense of despair.

It was nearly two o'clock on Saturday morning, and Paul was ready to scream. He'd turned up at the nightclub, met his contact and paid forty quid for a little foil-wrapped package which, when he got it home, turned out to be washing powder. He didn't care whether it got the really stubborn ingrained dirt out of his shirt cuffs. It could be My Usual Brand for all he cared. He'd rushed back to the club and spent the very last of his money getting in a second time. The bastard was gone.

There was no one he could turn to for help. Except Gary, who'd still be at the helpline. Paul felt bad about calling him. Admitting that his promises had come to nothing. But what choice was there? Trying to appear calm, he walked down Hurst Street towards the phone box. The air in his lungs seemed colder than the air on his skin. Little clusters of wrecked youth were scattered along the pavement, helping each other to walk or to throw up without choking. One boy staggered against a wall; when his girlfriend caught hold of him, he pulled her closer and slipped his hand between her legs.

The phone box was occupied. Paul was about to walk on when the door opened and a smartly dressed young man emerged. He was wiping his mouth on the back of his hand. Paul saw a bright smear of blood. The lad winked at him and swaggered up the road, almost dancing. It was probably just a split lip; but Paul felt uneasy. He decided to use another phone.

At the back of New Street Station, police were gathered near the open phone booths. Paul kept walking. The city centre was like a prison, every space barred with scaffolding or railings or traffic barriers. It was probably too late to catch Gary at the helpline. He waited for the night bus instead. It was harder to score in the week, but he'd manage something when his supply ran out. Just now, he didn't feel like pushing his luck.

When he got home, Gary was already there. "I came home early," his lover said. "Wasn't feeling too well." He didn't look very well either: pale and unfocused, as if something had been taken out of him. His face was cold. Paul made him lie down on the sofa and drink some hastily microwaved soup. Dim lights, soothing music. Gary smiled at him. "If you took as good care of yourself as you do of me, I'd be happy. Know what I mean?"

It was too late to talk. Paul made Gary promise to see the doctor in the morning. He'd shoot up then, alone in the flat. Fatigue claimed them both the moment they went to bed. But a couple of hours later, Paul woke up in the darkness. He could hear Gary crying on the other side of the bed. "Gary?" There was no response. Paul reached out and touched Gary's shoulder. "What's the matter?" The crying went on; but Gary was asleep.

Another broken night. Gary looked in the bathroom mirror. He could scarcely recognise himself. The doctor, after trying a series of blood tests, had told him it was stress due to overwork. Combining the helpline work with freelance graphic design—carried out at the mercy of other people's deadlines—had never been easy. And Paul's behaviour wasn't helping. That night he'd gone to bed alone. Paul was presumably out scoring. (Would he rather Paul was having an affair? That was an easy one. Yes, of course he would.) This morning, his lover had been stretched out beside him, in a deep narcotised sleep. Gary hadn't even tried to wake him.

The face in the mirror was like a passport photograph. It wasn't any real physical change that frightened him so much as the blankness of the expression. The lack of energy. It was the same look of despair that he imagined on the faces of some of the callers he tried to help. Mind you, that sick fuck who kept calling him at the helpline wasn't making life any easier. He'd talked to Gary five times now, but none of the other operators seemed to have come across him.

The very sound of his voice made Gary feel lost somehow. *Hello, my love,* he'd started the last time. *I've spent today in Hell. Do you know how that feels?* Gary never knew how to answer. He let the man go on lilting his cold and selfish intimacies until he heard the strange final breath and the click of the receiver. It was like an obscene phone call. Gary wasn't flattered in the least. It left him feeling empty. Something was being done to him that he didn't understand; and it hurt him without letting him feel pain. He still didn't know the caller's name.

The grey light of morning filtered through the bathroom window. There was a pattern of cracks in the glass. How long had that been there? Evidently local children had been throwing stones at the windows. There'd been scratches on his car recently; but he'd ignored them because he didn't want to think about the implications. The pattern of cracks was like a spider's web. He stared at it, and a terrible thought came to him. *No. Forget it.* The cold eyes in the mirror pleaded with him.

By the time he'd finished shaving, he knew it was the only solution.

Tonight was the late shift again. When Gary turned up, Alison was already there. "Are you feeling okay?" she said. "You look shattered." She didn't waste time being tactful. That was one of the things Gary admired about her.

He shrugged. "Not been sleeping well. A few things bothering me. We'll have a chat later, if there's time." He knew there wouldn't be. "I'll make some coffee." Alison was answering a call when the kettle boiled. He slipped two tablets into her mug. Sedatives. His doctor had prescribed them. "The milk's a bit off," he said, pouring the dregs of the carton down the sink. When he picked up the mugs, his hands shook and some of the coffee spilled over his fingers. He didn't feel it.

An hour or so later, Alison started to yawn. Her eyelids were drooping. She smiled at Gary. "Don't seem to have your trouble with sleeping."

Gary smiled back. "Oh, I don't have trouble getting to sleep. It's just my nightmares eat me."

Alison raised her eyebrows. "Lucky you." Within a few minutes, she'd cradled her head in her arms and fallen asleep. Moving quietly, Gary took her phone off the hook. His phone was less likely to wake her. He hoped Paul wouldn't ring. He hoped Paul wouldn't freak completely when he found his works and his stash were gone. Alison's breathing slowed to an even, scarcely audible rhythm. He felt terribly alone.

Carefully, he unwrapped the little bundle in his carrier bag: syringe, candle, spoon. The tiny packet of white powder. Like swimming, it was a technique you didn't forget once you'd learnt it. He boiled up the solution, filled the syringe, rolled up his sleeve. And waited. There were several calls of the normal kind. He dealt with them to the best of his ability. Then, around one o'clock, there came the call he was waiting for. *Hello, my friend,* said the voice of bleak seduction in his ear. *I'm so glad you're there.* Gary's vision swam. He felt almost too tired to move. *You're my only hope. It's a bitter world. You survive how you can.* Static rustled like cellophane in the receiver. He tightened the ring of cloth around his upper arm, then picked up the syringe. When he hit the vein, the clear solution went red. He thought again of the network of lines under the city, and tried to imagine his death spreading through it like black ice.

The pathologist at the General Hospital was feeling a bit pissed off. Two bizarre cases in the same night. And they expected him to work overtime because of that, when his hours were already so long he was sleeping on his coffee breaks. At least he *had* coffee breaks, unlike those hospital doctors whose patients were still alive. The first case was a man in his late twenties, a helpline worker brought in by a colleague. He'd taken a massive heroin OD. The colleague said she'd zonked out in the office after drinking some coffee he'd made. She'd come round a couple of hours later to find him dead with the phone in his hand. If he'd drugged her, that made suicide the most likely explanation. But there was no note.

The second case was a younger man, well-dressed, trendy hairstyle. Looked like a yuppie. He'd been found in a city centre phone box, dead from a massive hemorrhage in both lungs. (Why was it always too late to call for help?) The blood had clotted into tiny lumps throughout the alveolar tissue, like a hailstorm in a forest. It was presumably TB—but until they knew who he was, they couldn't check his records. And the tissue samples were confusing. There was no evidence of disease there, apart from the blood clots themselves. Which seemed to be. . . .

*Jesus Christ.* Obviously the lab people weren't getting enough sleep either. According to this test report, the blood type in the clots didn't match that in the alveolar tissue samples. If that was true, it would mean the blood that had choked this man to death—that had burst and then hardened inside his lungs —was not his own.

It was four A.M. Paul was alone in the flat. He was sitting in the bedroom, trying to read a back issue of the *New Musical Express*. He hadn't called Gary at the helpline office. He knew Gary had taken his works and all his supply. Presumably, by now he'd either dumped it or sold it back. It would be all right. He'd go clean from now on. As long as Gary was there, he didn't need anything else. Their love was enough. More than just enough. He sat on the bed and waited for the sound of a key in the lock.

# Family History

## NINA KIRIKI HOFFMAN

It was always night when Marian came to see me, and she came every year, on our birthday. I wasn't sure how she found me this year, but she had. She knocked on the windowsill. I said, "Come in," and in she came, through a screen, three-inch open space, without disturbing any of my ivy or the African violets that crowded the ledge.

"Oh, Constance," she whispered when she had formed and stood beside my hospital bed.

For a moment I just lay and looked at her. Her hair was long and curly, the color of rich dark earth, and hung down free about her shoulders. She would never have left the house like that when we were girls. Her face still had the rounded edges of youth, and her dark eyes were undimmed by shadows, the lids not scratched and stretched by age.

She was the image of myself at eighteen.

I had been wondering if she would come. Not expecting her, but preparing, just in case. It wasn't so easy to leave a for-warding address for her, since I had no idea how to get in touch with her. But just in case, I had the head of my bed cranked up, and the box of albums close, where I could reach them with my good right hand, and I had palmed the sleeping pill Jenny, the nurse, had brought me. For one night I could live with my dreams, even if Marian didn't come.

But here she was.

I cleared my throat. "It's been a little harder for me to get out and about this year," I said, "but I got some pictures." My voice had an old-lady quaver in it. I was used to that; it had been there for several years, but I had managed to keep the tremor suppressed when last I saw my twin sister. This year I decided to be myself.

"Oh, Constance," she said again.

I patted the bed with a gnarled and age-spotted hand. "Sit," I said. She climbed up beside me on the bed, and I edged over. I didn't need so much room as I used to, but with the two of us side by side it was crowded. That was all right. It reminded me of when we were girls. Her body had a clay coolness to it now, but I could deal with that. I wasn't going to need living heat much longer myself.

I fetched the oldest book from my box. It had embossed leather covers, with cutouts of ivy vines on the front, red velvet behind them, and gold curlicue letters on the wide spine that said, "ALBUM." The fat leaves were edged with gold. The leather was scuffed and deteriorating now, the velvet balding. I laid it in my lap and opened to the first page. There we were, twin babies in lacy white dresses and black button shoes, sitting on a bear-skin. I had never been sure which of us was which.

"Constance, why this album?"

My lips tightened. I turned past pictures of Mother and Father and our uncles and aunts and cousins until I came to the last likeness ever made of Marian and me together. We leaned on a pillar, she on the right and I on the left, our elbows meeting in the middle. Our faces looked serious. We wore matching black dresses with nipped waists, long sleeves, and lines of mother-of-pearl buttons up the front. Except for a froth of curls at our foreheads, our hair was piled and pinned down tight on the tops of our heads. The clasp at my collar was a silver spray of ivy leaves; her brooch was a heart with an arrow through it.

I looked at our picture, and I looked at my sister, whose face was just the same as the one in that photo from eighty years ago. "Well," I said, "this year my present is a little different. Please bear with me."

She took my hand in hers and stroked it. Her flesh was taut and smooth.

After a moment I closed the album and picked up a different one, from thirty years later. I opened it to a family photo: me and Ralph, surrounded by our three grown children and their spouses, with a row of grandchildren in front of us. My younger boy, Arthur, stood straight and tall in his uniform. His wife, Mary, looked frightened, as well she should; Arthur never came back from Europe. Mary raised her baby Ronald in my house. After my husband died in 1954, Mary and Ron were a great comfort to me.

I had never shown these pictures to Marian before, though she had visited me in houses where these people had lived.

"Oh," she cried, touching each face. My daughter Marian looked just like her aunt, only grown up, and my granddaughters Ellie and Clara, twins, looked just like those babies on a bearskin in the previous album. I didn't tell her their names. I watched her face as she studied them, and when she was done looking, I closed that book.

"These are my immortalities," I said to her, "and I have outlived them all. You're all I have left, Marian."

"Last year you were living with a family."

I closed my eyes for a moment. "Clara passed away of cancer this year," I said, "and it broke her husband's heart." And mine as well. "He didn't have the energy to take care of me *and* his children, so we decided I would come here to Rest Haven. This isn't a place where I'll stay alive very long, though."

She squeezed my hand. "Join me," she said, as she has said every year since she died.

"No, my dear," I said, as I have said every year since she died. "I've had my years on Earth, and most of them were good. I don't regret anything. But I think this will be our last visit, so I want you to have my albums. I've written out all the family histories. Clara's husband helped me print them out on his computer. They're in the backs of the books. So if you like, here is my life; I will it to you to do with as you like. You can track down the great-grandchildren if you want, or burn these books;

it's up to you. I just thought and thought, and it seemed to me the best gift I could give you would be a family history."

She gripped my hand. We sat silent for a long time. Her lashes lowered on her perfect cheeks, and when she opened her eyes they were clouded and shimmering. "Thank you," she whispered. I kissed her cold cheek.

"Well," I said. I put down the family album and picked up the one I had made for her this year. I opened to the first picture. "Look at this. Here's a sunrise up in the mountains in October. Pine trees, and the maples have begun to change with the frost—isn't that a gorgeous color? And here's what Crater Lake looks like in the daylight. That was a special trip we made, the last all-family outing with Clara . . . actually little Michael took this picture from up on a wall for me. He's agile. You might like him. And here's a sunset in the desert. That was in August. We were going to watch for meteors that night. . . ."

# Moving Day (Night?)

## KATHRYN PTACEK

We have vampires moving in across the street," Peter remarked to his wife as he stood in front of the big picture window in the living room.

Startled, Cordelia looked up from her crocheting and squinted at him. "What makes you think so, honey?" Their third daughter, Tammy, was due to deliver any day now, and she wanted to finish the fluffy baby afghan in time, which is why she was so engrossed in her work that she'd hardly paid attention to her husband tonight. But Peter understood. They had been married for some forty-four years now, and if he didn't understand that she liked to be by herself at times and that she didn't want to talk to him every moment of her waking day, then she didn't think they'd make it to their golden anniversary. Lucky for her, though, she thought with a slight smile, he *was* understanding.

Peter, she knew all too well, was prone to saying some

pretty odd stuff, but *vampires?* Across the street? Vaguely she wondered what movies he'd been watching on TV again. He always enjoyed the horror films, and the gorier the better. She much preferred a good old-fashioned epic—heavy on characters and costumes and the whole grand pageant of inevitable events that sweep characters into their destined roles—and none of that blood and guts stuff, thank you very much.

She wondered if something might be wrong with his mind, but she pushed that thought quickly from her own. She didn't want even to consider the possibility of Alzheimer's or something equally horrible. It was enough that the girls were forever calling on them, checking to make sure they were okay and hadn't fallen during the night or gotten sick. Their daughters were forever reminding them to take their vitamins and eat their vegetables and dress warmly when it was cold . . . all things, she realized with some amusement, that she and Peter had instructed the girls when they were children. And it wasn't like she and Peter were elderly; they were only in their mid-sixties, for God's sake, and had plenty of good years ahead of them.

Still peering outside, he ticked off the points on his fingers. "They came to see the house at night. They signed at night—Wayne down at the bank told me so when I met up with him at the ShopRite last week—and now the moving van is outside, and the men are unloading, and it's a quarter to ten, which is a pretty darned peculiar time for this sort of thing. Besides, I haven't seen a single mirror, and I've been watching since the van pulled up."

Not one to argue in the face of such impeccable logic, Cordelia shrugged. "Maybe they're bringing the mirrors themselves. You know how rough movers can be. Remember when we moved into the house on Decatur and those men broke Aunt Irene's rosewood dresser?"

He nodded.

It was true that he'd been fixed at the window since she'd returned from the church group's meeting an hour or so before. Someone had heard a weather report and snow was on its way, and so the meeting had been quickly adjourned and she'd hurried home, only to find Peter avidly watching their new neighbors. She hadn't seen hide nor hair of them, but that wasn't all that unusual. She tried not to keep tabs on the people in the neighborhood; but there was a delicate balance between not knowing about anything going on and being considered a busybody. She was afraid that Peter fell into the latter. He *always* knew what was happening in the houses around him. Hadn't he said that the McLeods would be divorcing because he'd heard them arguing and Frances crying loudly later on? Wasn't he the one who saw the first wisps of smoke coming out of Mrs. Pelacky's house and called the fire department and then run down the street and got into the house and pulled the old woman, who'd broken her hip and fallen and couldn't get out, to safety? And hadn't he been the one to phone the police when he saw the little Harrison boy with bruises day in and day out? Of course, none of this had gotten him a medal or any such recognition, beyond being told time after time to mind his own business.

Sometimes she thought that Peter had retired too soon. He should have kept working, or found another job when he retired from the phone company. Of course, now maybe they could do some traveling, something they really hadn't done much while the girls were growing up—there were always doctor bills to pay, or ballet lessons and summer camps to pay for, and so most of their vacations had been quick one-week jaunts to visit relatives in-state or to fairly local sites. Now might be the time to show Peter that brochure she'd picked up at the travel agency downtown, the one with the beautiful glossy photos of a cruise to Alaska. They had a good-sized nest egg now; their kids were secure in family and job and so didn't need any financial support. She would mention it to Peter, but not tonight. Not when he was playing detective or whatever he was doing. Peter Sherlock Holmes, she thought and smiled to herself as she looped the yellow yarn across the number ten hook.

"Vampires?" she echoed.

"Don't laugh at me, Cordy."

"I'm not." She rested the crocheting in her lap. "Honey, this is pretty wacky, you know." For a moment she wondered, maybe there *is* something wrong with him. He had seen Wayne yesterday, not last week. And hadn't Peter forgotten he'd done the laundry last night and did it all again today? Maybe . . . no, she told herself. No, no, no, as if the repetition of the word would somehow protect them.

He shrugged, but she could see the rigid set of his back. He wasn't pleased with her. Well, they'd weathered their share of arguments and sore feelings, and God knew, they'd bickered about even less important things before.

"I don't see why you think it's so weird."

"Peter! C'mon—have you see any coffins?" He shook his head. "Do they wear black? Does she look like Morticia Addams? I haven't even seen them yet. They're probably coming in tomorrow or the next day, and just wanted their stuff inside the house when they arrived. And besides, what would vampires be doing out here in the suburbs? I mean, this isn't a prime area for them."

"Maybe they got a good interest rate."

She sighed, not sure she wanted to encourage him in this delusion.

"They're vampires, I tell you."

"Oh, Peter, you're impossible." She felt a little cranky now, and thought she'd finish this row of her crocheting and then go to bed and read. Let him stand out here all night and stare at the neighbors. And what must they think of him, standing silhouetted against the window, the light from her table lamp outlining his form. He couldn't have been more obvious, and she wished he'd get away from the window because he made the perfect target. Target for what? she asked herself, when their little suburb didn't have much crime and they weren't in an area known for drive-by shootings. Still . . . it made her uneasy.

She opened her mouth to speak, but he interrupted her. "I met them, you know, Cordy. They came by while you were gone earlier this evening," and as he turned from the window to face her, she saw the glint of lamplight on his fangs.

# Hemo Gobblin'

## Robert M. Price

One of this body's compatriots shoves this shoulder and cries out, "An' you stink, m———f———! Wash your ass!" Shoves again. The back impacts the bricks of the alley wall, with some minor pain, no concern. Better to be rid of them. They depart, gesticulating. We remain. We watch the sidewalk traffic. Must find one alone, with few others on the street.

The opportunity is arriving. This glides out of the alley like a shadow, becomes the shadow of the man in the suit. He notices, turns, requires information: "Hey, what's the matter? What do you want?" Easily sense his voice shaking.

"Nuthin' man. You got some change, maybe?"

He nervously fumbles, seeks change. Pauses by next alley, where these arms grasp him, pull him. Flailing limbs too frantic to withstand us. We seek the most accessible swath of exposed skin and strike. His scream of outrage drenched in silence as these teeth connect. Despite rotted condition of this body's teeth and gold frame around one, we have been able to activate and select growth genes and form requisite hollow points. One tooth begins to chip, blood spraying a tiny mist, but we have injected a sufficient number of ourselves into new body.

Old body sags, falls free. Rest of us wait within to be freed before the husk becomes toxic. Stench greater already, decomposition setting in, body crumbling. Soon we have gained the bloodpaths of this new body, we sail the red rivers within, permeate, are in control as long as body is docile from shock. We are strong enough now. Bend over rotting form in front of us, seek black flesh of thigh, still intact, try to bite. No good, will take longer to shape teeth. Must rescue those trapped within. Suck them out and into new body. Something amiss.

Resistance. This mouth has false teeth. Reach up, tear them out. May need them, though. Pocket them. New incisors grow, hollowing, sharpening. Still time?

Duller than usual, but they go in, made easier because crumbling flesh does not resist. Many of us are past help. But we are retrieved, have made the journey once again.

We have control, can access recent memories of this brain. Realize was heading home. Standing up, we dust off clothing, still too marked with dirt to satisfy social expectations. Must return to this one's dwelling, not far away. As we stride away, turning down direction from which this body came, onlookers begin to examine alleyway. Some cheer for this one who "struck back" at mugger. Others alarmed at condition of what is found amid overturned cans in alleyway. Must not linger.

No real difficulty getting past coated man and into dwelling. He asks what happened. Reply there was an incident with mugger. We are beginning to grasp this one's speech pattern, much different from previous. Almost a different language. "Mother" has different meaning.

Mirror reveals only minor damage, dishevelment. Inside we feast, gain strength, drain vitality. Will soon need to make the transfer again. Posted calendar indicates dinner date. Memory access slightly impaired. Cocaine perhaps responsible. Female face appears from memory coil. Name Sarah. Writing on calendar difficult to read. Cannot recapture this one's recognition of own handscript. Seems to read: San Moritz. Taxi driver will surely know. Time is soon. Perhaps opportunity to make transfer.

Liberal use of cologne in case deterioration of this body begins. Shower, dress. Artificial teeth seem confusing to reinstall. Easier to grow whole new set in this mouth.

Descend elevator shaft in vertical capsule. Coated man summons taxi. After short ride, exit automobile, remove billfold, hand driver random bill. He whistles, tips hat, says gratitude in another language. Drives off. We face great glass doors that reflect this body, no problem yet. Another man, coated like the other, opens door for us. Mumble thanks.

Up brass-framed elevator, operator asks floor. Do not know it. Tell him name of dining room, one of many apparently. Doors like brass skeletons slide clear. Pass plants. Down hall is great room filled with people whose bodies are hung with clothing different from those in streets far below. Most men in black. Much noise, some music, much talking. We are confused by great mass of beings; we thunder through pulse at sheer number of potential hosts. Hear a voice call the name of this one: "Rex! Over here, buddy!"

This may pose difficulty. Did not anticipate a group of people. No notice of such in this memory. Walk to table, affect a smile, greet "everybody." Vague recognition of faces. Friends of this one? Business acquaintances? May not matter.

"You okay, Rex?"

"Yes, okay. Truly okay, and you?"

"Uh . . . okay! Yeah!" Several look at each other. Seem confused, trying to hide it.

"Sarah should be back in a moment. She and Dolores just went to powder their noses."

"Noses?" This seems odd, but he does not seem to think so.

"Uh, yeah, they're just in the Ladies' Room—sorry, Nan, I mean the Women's Room!" Laughter follows this synonym.

"Look, here they are now. Sarah, Rex is here, better late than never!"

One of the females, tall, thin, long yellow hair, joins me, kisses this mouth. We hunger. Notice a momentary hesitation, this smell, perhaps. She whispers in this right ear: "Rex, are you all right? You sure you're not sick? We don't have to stick around if you're not feeling well, you know. After all, it's your birthday, darling."

"Yes, let us go. We need privacy . . . Sarah." We take her hand and lead her away, noticing her backward glance to the others. Can hear their fading comments.

"What do you suppose is wrong with him?"

"Nothing's wrong, he just can't wait to get her in the back seat of a cab. You know, Sexy Rexy!" Laughter.

This Sarah seems worried. Soon her worries will abate. She asks, "Rexy, you know my car's here in the parking garage. I'll get the keys from the attendant and we'll drive it out ourselves, okay?"

She speaks to the one in the dingy coveralls, returns with the keys. Rejoins us, leads us to the automobile. It waits in a dark, cool corner of this cement labyrinth.

"No," this voice says, "the back seat, Sarah."

502

She smiles, at ease once more. "Why, you old fox. Sexy Rexy! Well, I guess no one's liable to catch us here. Let's do it."

In the dark confines of the car, she strains to remove her clothing, tight as it is. Cannot wait, but bend close and touch mouth to neck. Notice she breathes heavily now. Seeks this mouth, but it returns to her neck, more easily bitten. Contact. She recoils, is bleeding. Eyes widen. "Why, Rex! What do you think . . . ?" Dabs at blood. Not much of it.

No time. Can tell stench begins to collect in small interior of automobile. Easily entrap her shoulders in these arms, bite savagely. Neck still fights, but now transmission has begun. Soon she is limp.

We open her eyes and again behold the form of the Rex one. And from those eyes we behold the Sarah. There is mutual recognition for a moment, then the Sarah bends over and bites, sucks. The man's form is vacant, collapses, begins to liquify.

This body knows how this machine is driven, but then there is the Rex-husk, which we dare not try to remove from the automobile, nor be seen with. Best to abandon both inert vehicles. We remember to replace clothing, smooth yellow hair, walk unsteadily on sharp, long shoe heels. Walk past attendant, who seems puzzled to see this Sarah. We wait to look behind, see that attendant is heading for location of automobile. Trouble.

Walk briskly up ramp, out onto street. Soft moonlight is merciful to the mutating flesh. Walk several city blocks aimlessly until can access memory. It is still in shock from transfer. Can regain little information. Some facts about Sarah must be stored in billfold. In small purse we retained. Reach for it.

Authorities arrive in blue and white automobile screeching to curb only feet from us. Doors pop open, men jump out, guns pointing. "That'll be far enough, lady!"

Control of body now sufficient to turn and run. Still unsteady. Reach to discard heels. Here is obstacle, seen late. Railed contrivance, like elevator gates, only thick and green. Trip over it and fall. Head strikes stairs below.

As eyes close, see milling people of many colors circling around body. Any could be hosts, but body seems not to respond. Check reveals spinal cord damage. Insufficient control of cells to initiate repair. Nothing moves. We are trapped.

Dizziness encroaches. Cannot make out words of police officers as they reach for the limp, blonde form. One looking at scattered contents of purse. Something about a card . . .

Out of the deep cold. Thought and light returning . . .

Eyes opening. We behold a circle of smiling and tearful faces. They cry out prayers and gratitude. All eyes fixed here. "A miracle! That's what it is!" says a plump woman with a bun of white hair.

A man in a green smock chuckles genially, pats the woman's fleshy arm and replies, "A miracle of modern science!"

"Still a miracle, Doctor!" says the woman. "God bless the poor lady who provided the spleen! She's saved our Marie's life!"

# Paying the Fine

### JILL M. MORGAN

Y ou can't sleep here," said the monitor, giving the sole of the old man's boot a kick. "Wake up. Are you drunk? You can't sleep in a public library. That chair is for patrons. It's not a bed, and this isn't a hotel, so get out of here."

The white-haired man drew open one lazy eye, then the other. He peered at the monitor through reddened, paper-thin lids rheumy with age. High cheekbones jutted under skin that sank against the bones of his skull. He looked to be an old man, worn and weary, discarded by the powerful, the comfortable.

"Go back to the street where you belong," said the monitor. "You think you can treat this library like a camp, using the sink of the men's room as a private bathtub. Sitting in these clean chairs in your filthy clothes. And the way you smell! You think the rest of us don't notice?"

The old man straightened in his chair, pulling himself to a sitting position by the strength of one hand on the chrome armrest. His hand seemed slack of muscle tone and ropy with veins. Brown age spots marked the back of it like a map of continents.

His mouth worked at trying to speak, as if words were nearly forgotten companions to the parched, anemic lips. A pale rose tongue slicked moisture over the seamed lines of the man's mouth.

"It's better to be kind to strangers," he said.

The words sounded like raspy sandpaper. Sheets of gravel rubbing together. A quick vision came to the monitor of bleached bones touching in the earth, touching and grinding. He hated the old man for that—making him think of death.

"You get out of here before I make a citizen's arrest," said the monitor. "I've done it before with your type. Coming in here like you own the place."

The threat seemed to have no effect on the man. If anything, he seemed even more connected to the chair, as if it were part of his bony frame, chrome legs and all. His eyes were a strange color, the monitor noticed—not blue, not green, but sort of gray. Ashen.

"What's your given name?"

"That's no business of yours," said the monitor. "Are you leaving? I'm telling you for the last time, get up and get out."

"John!" a librarian's voice called from the desk at the center of the room, "They need you in circ. Somebody caught stealing books."

A war of opposing duties clashed in the monitor's mind. He *wanted* to throw out this old geezer. Wanted to grab the man by his baggy shirt and toss him out the door. In a way he couldn't quite understand, the creep irritated him.

*But stealing books* . . . no, he couldn't let anybody get away with that. He had personally installed the security video cameras to record such actions. His duty to the library came before the pleasure it would give him to give this guy the bum's rush.

"When I come back," he threatened, "you'd better be gone."

Fear didn't float the ghostly rivers of the old man's eyes. Something else was there, but the monitor was too distracted to call what he saw in those eyes by name.

An uneasy sense stayed with him as he rushed toward circulation and the book thief. He hoped it was a kid. He could scare a boy—hell, boy or girl—give 'em fear that would last a lifetime. He never called the cops on kids. He handled it himself. Liked the job. Yeah, he hoped it was a puppy-eyed twelve-year-old. By the time the monitor got through with him, those eyes would be changed forever.

To John's disappointment, it wasn't a kid. The thief was a grown man in his fifties. The inside pockets of the coat, and the canvas bag he carried, were stuffed with expensive volumes pulled from the shelves. A proprietorial rage burned in the monitor, that some jerk like this one would dare try to steal books from a public library. His library.

He wanted to squeeze the man's neck with his bare hands. Wanted to watch the thief's eyes bulge, and life fade out of them. If it were up to the monitor, he'd make this one pay a real fine, then take the body out to the desert and dump it. He knew a place . . . had thought of it a lot.

A lot of people were standing around. He had to settle for calling the police.

He waited forever for the cops to arrive. They didn't care what happened in this library. It didn't matter to them if somebody stole every book off the shelves. He'd seen that smugness in their eyes before when they had taken down his reports. This library wasn't important to them.

It *was* to the monitor. This was his place. Nobody messed with his house, his car, his wife, his kids—and nobody better mess with his library, either.

It was closing time before the police were through. The monitor had to argue with the arresting officers. Yes, *he did* want to file a complaint. Yes, *he did* want the man to be booked for petty theft. No, *he wasn't* willing to overlook it this time. Whose side were the cops on? They looked at him like he was the one causing the trouble.

"Do you know how much paperwork this is going to require?" one of them said.

"Do your job," the monitor told him.

They did, finally.

By the time the officers left with the thief in custody, it was time to make the closing announcement. Making the closing announcement was the best part of the monitor's day. He loved the way he sounded over the library's microphone system, the deep bass tones of his voice. Patrons had complimented him on it, asking if he'd ever been an actor.

Of course, he hadn't.

"You should be," they insisted, "with a rich, manly voice like yours."

He had come to think that was so, and sometimes imagined himself onstage when he made the evening's announcement.

"The library will be closing in five minutes," he said, enunciating every letter and syllable like a thespian. "If you wish to check out a book, go to the circulation desk now." He put great emphasis on the word *now*. It gave him a feeling of power and importance.

The sluggard patrons lingered. Even those who got up to leave ambled out as if they had all the time in the world. They'd be the ones to complain when it was too late and their books couldn't be checked out tonight. Not his fault. He'd warned them.

He watched the minutes go by on the clock. When it was time, he made the final announcement. "The library is now closed. If you wish to check out a book, the library will open tomorrow morning at nine o'clock. Thank you for visiting the Glendale Public Library."

With that, he switched off the main bank of lights.

He heard them grumble and stumble in the dark. "I can't see," someone yelled.

It didn't phase him. The library was closed, and closed meant lights out. If they'd waited too long to be on their way, that was their problem. They wouldn't do it again the next time.

He had a certain disrespect for the patrons. As protective as he felt of the books, furniture, and equipment in this building, his sense of protectiveness didn't extend itself to the library patrons. They were cattle.

It was a *public* library and he had to put up with patrons, but he'd much rather lock them all out and keep the books and the building for the few people he considered worthy of being allowed here. He thought about that a lot, especially when he began checking the building after closing, and turning out the series of lights.

The library was a massive building, recently remodeled,

and the pride of the city. It was the monitor's job to make sure every door was locked, and every person was out of the building. That meant even checking the bathrooms—where the homeless sometimes tried to hide from him on a rainy or cold night, hoping they wouldn't be noticed.

In all his years working for this library—twenty—he'd never left anyone in the building overnight. Never.

He had to check all three levels, starting in the basement. Lack of light had herded the last of the patrons to the circulation desk, where they milled unhappily toward the exit doors. Staff members exited with them, fresh-faced pages and older library clerks, calling good-byes to each other.

John the monitor paid them little attention. He started down the stairs to the underground level. His job wasn't finished. The rest of the staff could walk out the doors and go home. The monitor needed to make sure everything would be here in the morning, just as they'd left it. That meant no one left in the building to steal, deface, or to . . . the word *desecrate* popped into his mind.

To him, this was a sacred site. Not in some *preaching-from-the-pulpit* kind of way, but as dedicated and hallowed ground. The thoughts from the best minds in the world were housed here, in the books of this library. He felt awed by the enlightenment and rich history in his keeping. Like a high priest, he held these books as holy writ, and devil take the man, woman, or child who damaged them. Mercy for such offenders was not an attribute he was accustomed to feeling. Had never felt. Would never feel.

He checked the exit doors. The homeless picked strange places to hide. He'd always found them. Once, he found one sipping a cup of coffee in the downstairs lounge, the dirty heel of his shoe propped on the staff dining table. The monitor broke the offending leg with the slam of a solid-wood periodicals rod before he tossed the bum out of the building.

They guy never came back, and never filed a complaint. Who would he complain to? Maybe he'd died in some alley. *Not my problem*, thought the monitor. It was the city's problem to pick up such refuse.

He pressed the button for the elevator, stepped inside, and pushed the numbered panel for the top floor. The elevator lurched and whined when it started up, like a laboring beast. He hated being alone in this damn thing, especially after closing. It was eerie, caged in a metal box, everything out of his control. That's the part he hated the most, giving up control.

He used to climb the stairs, but his doctor had vetoed that. Too much strain on his heart. Nowadays he took the elevator.

He turned off the lights as he checked and locked the door of each room, until the entire top floor was shut down dark. Now, only one light remained in the library, at circ, in the front of the building. He was halfway down the central staircase, heading there, when that light went out.

A sound stopped his breath. It was from the main level, something heavy crashing to the floor. He didn't have to be told. He guessed who it must be—the old man he'd told to get out of the library. The guy probably thought he was alone in the building, that he'd put one over on the monitor who'd kicked his boot, and was going to wreck the place to get back at him.

*Over my dead body,* thought the monitor.

He was glad the man had turned out the lights. He wouldn't see the monitor coming, wouldn't hear him or know he was there, until . . . until pain lit up like all the lights in the building.

Another shelf crashed to the floor. The sound hollowed the monitor's senses, cannoning through him. *Damn the man!* He was destroying library property. The monitor wouldn't just throw out this one. He'd make an example of him.

Holding the huge ring of keys hooked to his belt kept them silent. The monitor moved closer to where he'd heard the sound of the crashing book shelves. He slid one thick wooden rod from a stack of periodicals. It was heavy as a French rolling pin. Armed with this club of punishment, he moved through the darkened main floor.

Sounds came from behind the shelves of new fiction. The monitor knew his way around the stacks so well, he didn't need a light. The old man wouldn't be expecting anyone to step up behind him and—

The monitor felt the flow of air over his bare skin a second before the slam of a fist struck the nape of his neck, knocking him to the floor. The blow stunned him, dropping him to his knees. He tried to stand, blood spurting from his nose, but only managed to fall forward, catching himself on outstretched hands.

*I'm crawling,* he thought, horrified. How could this be happening? The old man wasn't powerful enough to—

The heel of a boot smashed unmercifully into the monitor's back, pounding the air from him and paralyzing his lungs. His face struck the polished wood floor with bone-crushing force, breaking his nose. Blood gushed from his nostrils, dripping into a puddle beneath his face. Thick, suffocating blood. He felt himself drowning in it.

Couldn't *move.* Couldn't *breathe.*

He would die here. No one would see his murderer, even through the library's glass walls. Too dark. He needed light. Had to turn on a light.

A violent shove rolled him onto his back, then he was yanked from the floor. Lifted in hard hands by strong arms . . . one hand painfully gripping between his legs, and the other one digging finger-wide trenches into his chest . . . pulling him horizontally from the floor, like lifting weights.

The pain was unbelievable, nerve-end excruciating. He would have screamed, if his lungs had allowed that much air. The scream was caged inside him, like the pain.

He knew the man would throw him, knew his body would sail through the air like a two-by-four tossed by a giant. His muscles tensed for it, felt it coming, anticipated feeling the unyielding force of the solid wood pillar he'd hit.

In one desperate move, with the only measure of his strength left to him, John stretched out the fingers of his right hand. As he was raised above the man's head, his extended fingers trailed the wall and touched the power panel.

Light filled the main floor, cold remembering light. It was light the monitor wanted, needed, light that would frame the images the library's hidden video cameras now recorded.

He would die, but his killer would be captured on film. A grimace of triumph hardened on John's lips. Savored his victory, like the taste of blood in his mouth.

Unbelievably strong arms threw him like a missile toward the pillar. In midair, the grimace of triumph died, and his mouth gaped open in heart-stopping terror, eyes widening with fear as the pillar loomed nearer . . . nearer. He hit with a sickening *crack* of his spine. He felt the impact and the severing. Mercifully, all pain below his neck flowed away from him like blood from a wound.

*I'm dying*, thought the monitor. But it wasn't over yet.

The white-haired man stepped closer, leaning over him, the narrow planes of his face sunken with age. He knelt beside him, and the embered coal eyes seemed to see into John the monitor's soul.

"Why?" John mouthed the final question. The word could not be heard—not enough air for a voice—but was on his lips.

"It's better to be kind to strangers."

The man leaned closer. Closer still. In the gray rivers of this stranger's eyes, John saw the drowning of his own life and soul.

When the vampire's mouth opened and the piercing fangs sank into John the monitor's neck, the overhead cameras were the only eyes to see the silent scream of terror, and the red bridge of life flowing from one body to another.

When the custodians arrived that night, they found the broken casing of the monitor's body. The flesh had sunken in, as though drained flat by a lack of blood. Only a small puddle of blood was seen on the floor. The rest was gone, disappeared like the killer.

The security video tapes were played by the investigating police. Amazingly, the only figure that was seen in the tapes was John himself. Even as his body was lifted off the floor and held aloft for a space of seconds before it flew like an aimed projectile at the pillar . . . even then, only one person was visible to the camera's eye—John.

An escaping figure did trip the silent alarm, and the camera caught the flutter of its wings. A bird, or bat, soared like a dark streak to the ceiling, and to the open vent of the library's air-conditioning shaft, where it slipped through and away into the night.

# The Devil is Not Mocked

## MANLY WADE WELLMAN

> Do you not know that tonight, when the clock strikes midnight, all the evil things in the world hold sway? Do you know where you are going, and what you are going to?
>
> —Bram Stoker

**B**alkan weather, even Balkan spring weather, was not pleasant to General von Grunn, leaning heavily back behind the bulletproof glass of his car. May 4th—the English would call it St. George's Day, after their saint who was helping them so little. The date would mean something to Heinrich Himmler, too; that weak-chinned pet of the Führer would hold some sort of garbled druidic ritual with his Schutzstaffel on the Brockenburg. Von Grunn grimaced fatly at the thought of Himmler, and leaned forward to look out into the night. An armed car ahead, an armed car behind—all was well.

"Forward!" he growled to his orderly, Kranz, who trod on the accelerator. The car moved, and the car ahead took the lead, into the Borgo Pass.

Von Grunn glanced backward once, to the lights of Bistritz. This country had been Romanian not so long ago. Now it was Hungarian, which meant that it was German.

What was it that the mayor of Bistritz had said, when he had demanded a semiremote headquarters? The castle along this pass, empty—ready for him? The dolt had seemed eager to help, to please. Von Grunn produced a long cigarette. Young Captain Plesser, sitting beside him, at once kindled a lighter. Slim, quiet, the young aid had faded from von Grunn's consciousness.

"What's the name of that castle again?" inquired the general, and made a grimace when Plesser replied in barbarous Slavic syllables. "What's the meaning in a civilized tongue?"

"Devil's Castle, I should think," hazarded the captain's respectful voice.

"*Ach*, so—Transylvania is supposed to be overrun with

devils," nodded von Grunn, puffing. "Let them defer to us, or we'll devil them." He smiled, for his was a great gift for appreciating his own epigrams. "Meanwhile, let the castle be called its German name. *Teufelstoss*—Devil's Castle."

"Of course," agreed Plesser.

Silence for a while, as the cars purred powerfully up the rough slope of the pass trail. Von Grunn lost himself in his favorite meditation—his own assured future. He was to establish an unostentatious command post for—what? A move against Russia? The Black Sea? He would know soon enough. In any case, an army would be his, action and glory. There was glory enough for all. Von Grunn remembered Wilhelm II saying that, in the last war.

"The last war," he said aloud. "I was, a simple *oberlieutenant* then. And the Führer—a corporal. What were you, captain?"

"A child."

"You remember?"

"Nothing." Plesser screwed up his courage to a question. "General von Grunn, does it not seem strange that the folk at Bistritz were so anxious for you to come to the castle—*Teufelstoss*—tonight?"

Von Grunn nodded, like a big, fierce owl. "You smell a trap, *nicht wahr?* That is why I bring two carloads of men, my trusted bodyguard. For that very chance. But I doubt if any in Transylvania dare set traps for me, or any other German."

The cars were slowing down. General and captain leaned forward. The car ahead was passing through the great open gateway of a courtyard. Against the spattered stars rose the silhouette of a vast black building, with a broken tower. "We seem to be here," ventured Captain Plesser.

"Good. Go to the forward car. When the other arrives, form the guard."

It was done swiftly. Sixteen stark infantrymen were marshaled, with rifles, bombs, and submachine guns. Von Grunn emerged into the cold night, and Kranz, the orderly, began to bring out the luggage.

"A natural fort, withdrawn and good for any defense except against aircraft," pronounced the general, peering through his monocle at the battlements above. "We will make a thorough examination.

"*Unteroffizer!*" he barked, and the noncom in charge of the escort came forward woodenly, stiffening to attention. "Six of the men will accompany me inside. You will bivouac the others in this courtyard, maintaining a guard all night. *Heil Hitler.*"

"*Heil Hitler,*" responded the man briskly. Von Grunn smiled as the *unteroffizer* strode away to obey. For all the soldierly alacrity, that order to sleep outdoors was no welcome one. So much the better; von Grunn believed in toughening experiences for field soldiers, and his escort had lived too softly since the Battle of Flanders.

He walked to where a sort of vestibule of massive, rough stone projected from the castle wall. Plesser already stood there, staring at the heavy nail-studded planks of the door. "It is locked. *Herr General,*" he reported. "No knob or latch, bell or knocker—"

But as he spoke, the door swung creakingly inward, and yellow light gushed out.

On the threshold stood a figure in black, as tall as von Grunn himself but thinner than even Plesser. A pale, sharp face and brilliant eyes turned upon them, in the light of a chimneyless oil lamp of silver.

"Welcome, General von Grunn," said the lamp holder. "You are expected."

His German was good, his manner respectful. Von Grunn's broad hand slid into a greatcoat pocket, where he always carried a big automatic pistol.

"Who told you to expect us?" he demanded.

The lamplight struck blue radiance from smooth, sparse black hair as the thin man bowed. "Who could mistake General von Grunn, or doubt that he would want this spacious, withdrawn structure for his new headquarters position?"

The mayor of Bistritz, officious ass, must have sent this fellow ahead to make fawning preparations—but even as von Grunn thought that, the man himself gave other information.

"I am in charge here, have been in charge for many years. We are so honored to have company. Will the general enter?"

He stepped back. Plesser entered, then von Grunn. The vestibule was warm. "This way, excellency," said the man with the lamp—the steward. von Grunn decided to classify him. He led the way along a stone-paved passage, von Grunn's escort tramping authoritatively after him. Then up a great winding stair, and into a room, a big hall of a place, with a fire of logs and a table set for supper.

All told, very inviting; but it was not von Grunn's way to say as much. He only nodded, and allowed Captain Plesser to help him out of his great-coat. Meanwhile, the steward was showing the luggage-laden Kranz into an octagonal bedroom beyond.

"Take these six men," said von Grunn to Plesser, indicating the soldiers of the escort. "Tour the castle. Make a plan of each floor. Then come back and report. *Heil Hitler*."

"*Heil Hitler*," and Plesser led the party away. Von Grunn turned his broad back to the fire. Kranz was busy within the bedroom, arranging things. The steward returned. "May I serve the *Herr General?*" he asked silkily.

Von Grunn looked at the table, and with difficulty forebore to lick his fat lips. There were great slices of roast beef, a fowl, cheese, salad, and two bottles of wine—Kranz himself could not have guessed better what would be good. Von Grunn almost started forward to the table, then paused. This was Transylvania. The natives, for all their supple courtesy, disliked and feared soldiers of the Reich. Might these good things not be poisoned?

"Remove these things," he said bleakly. "I have brought my own provisions. You may eat that supper yourself."

Another bow. "The *Herr General* is too good, but I will sup at midnight—it is not long. Now, I will clear the things away. Your man will fetch what you want."

He began to gather up dishes. Watching him stoop over the table, von Grunn thought that he had seldom seen anyone so narrow in the shoulders—they were humped high, like the shoulders of a hyena, suggesting a power that crouched and lurked. Von Grunn was obliged to tell himself that he was not repelled or nervous. The steward was a stranger, a Slav of some kind. It was von Grunn's business to be scornful of all such.

"Now," he said, when all was cleared, "go to the bedroom and tell my orderly—" He broke off. "What was that?"

The other listened. Von Grunn could have sworn that the man's ears—pale and pointed—lifted voluntarily, like the ears of a cat or a fox. The sound came again, a prolonged howl in the distance.

"The wolves," came the quiet reply. "They speak to the full moon."

"Wolves?" The general was intrigued at once. He was a sportsman—that is, he liked to corner and kill beasts almost as much as he liked to corner and kill men. As a guest of Hermann Goering he had shot two very expensive wild bulls, and he yearned for the day when the Führer would graciously invite him to the Black Forest for pigsticking. "Are there many?" he asked. "It sounds like many. If they were not so far—"

"They come nearer," his companion said, and indeed the howl was repeated more strongly and clearly. "But you gave an order, general?"

"Oh, yes." Von Grunn remembered his hunger. "My man will bring me supper from among the things we have with us."

A bow, and the slender black figure moved noiselessly into the bedroom. Von Grunn crossed the floor and seated himself in an armchair before the table. The steward returned, and stood at his elbow.

"Pardon. Your orderly helped me carry the other food to the castle kitchen. He has not returned, and so I took the liberty of serving you."

He had a tray. Upon it were delicacies from von Grunn's mess chest—slices of smoked turkey, buttered bread, preserved fruits, bottled beer. The fellow had arranged them himself, had had every opportunity to . . . to—

Von Grunn scowled and took the monocle from his eye. The danger of poison again stirred in his mind, and he had difficulty scorning it. He must eat and drink, in defiance of fear.

Poison or no poison, the food was splendid, and the steward an excellent waiter. The general drank beer, and deigned to say, "You are an experienced servant?"

The pale, sharp face twitched sidewise in negation. "I serve very few guests. The last was years ago—Jonathan Harker, an Englishman—"

Von Grunn snorted away mention of that unwelcome people, and finished his repast. Then he rose, and stared around.

The wolves howled again, in several directions and close to the castle.

"I seem to be deserted," he said grimly. "The captain is late, my orderly late. My men make no report." He stepped to the door, opened it. "Plesser!" he called. "Captain Plesser!"

No reply.

"Shall I bring you to him?" asked the steward gently. Once again, he had come up close. Von Grunn started violently, and wheeled.

The eyes of the steward were on a level with his, and very close. For the first time von Grunn saw that they were filled with green light. The steward was smiling, too, and von Grunn saw his teeth—white, spaced widely, pointed—

As if signaled by the thought, the howling of the beasts outside broke out afresh. It was deafeningly close. To von Grunn it sounded like hundreds. Then, in reply, came a shout, the voice of the *unteroffizer* uttering a quick, startled command.

At once a shot. Several shots.

The men he had encamped in the courtyard were shooting at something.

With ponderous haste, von Grunn hurried from the room, down the stairs. As he reached the passageway below, he heard more shots, and a wild air-rending chorus of howls, growls, spitting scuffles. Von Grunn gained the door by which he had entered. Something moved in the gloom at his very feet.

A chalky face turned up, the face of Captain Plesser. A hand lifted shakily to clutch at the general's boot top.

"Back in there, the dark rooms—" It was half a choke, half a sigh. "They're devils—hungry—they got the others, got me— I could come no farther than this—"

Plesser collapsed. Light came from behind von Grunn, and he could see the captain's head sagging backward on the stone. The side of the slender neck had been torn open, but blood did not come. For there was no blood left in Captain Plesser's body.

Outside, there was sudden silence. Stepping across Plesser's body, the general seized the latch and pushed the door open.

The courtyard was full of wolves, feeding. One glance was enough to show what they fed on. As von Grunn stared, the wolves lifted their heads and stared back. He saw many green-glowing eyes, level, hard, hungry, many grinning mouths with pointed teeth—the eyes and the teeth of the steward.

He got the door shut again, and sagged upon it, breathing hard.

"I am sorry, general," came a soft, teasing apology. "Sorry —my servants were too eager within and without. Wolves and vampires are hard to restrain. After all, it is midnight—our moment of all moments."

"What are you raving about?" gasped von Grunn, feeling his jaw sag.

"I do not rave. I tell simple truth. My castle has vampires within, wolves without, all my followers and friends—"

Von Grunn felt for a weapon. His great-coat was upstairs, the pistol in its pocket.

"Who are you?" he screamed.

"I am Count Dracula of Transylvania," replied the gaunt man in black.

He set down the lamp carefully before moving forward.


# Ragz

### ADAM-TROY CASTRO

This is Ragz: see how frayed he is.

See the threads that dangle from his filthy sleeves; the strips of oily bandage that hang from his clothes; the strange transparent places where his unseen and diseased skin can almost be glimpsed through the shapeless bundles of canvas that he uses instead of shoes. See the years of collected grime that have dyed a dozen layers of old clothing into a uniform shade of oily black; see the worn places marked by holes that reveal only deeper and uglier substrata of rot. See him shuffling down the street, mumbling randomly to himself, saying nothing that makes any sense; facing the pavement as he speaks, addressing the gum wrappers, the cigarette butts, the newspapers, and the turds, as equal citizens of the place he's come to inhabit. Whenever the wind shifts, other people feel the waves of bleak insanity beneath the skin, and gag from that sour-sweet putridity so much more appropriate for a corpse than a living being.

Nobody talks to him, but everybody knows him.

They call him Ragz.

Your name is Paco.

At least that's what you call yourself; your real name comes straight out of the Bible, from those early chapters where everyone begats each other, and you regard it as way too faggoty to be endured. Guy walks out on the streets with a name like that, he liable to get his butt handed to him. Paco, on the other hand—it sounds like some crazy mother stab you dead soon as look at you, and that's the kind of name you want, because that's the kind of guy you want to be.

Alas, you're also the kind of guy who, physically at least, never quite outgrows being a kid—you're a thin, wiry little thing, with a baby face and a peach-fuzz mustache, and though you wear elevator shoes, you still top five feet only at the crest of your pomaded hair. When you talk tough, Paco, people just laugh.

You're going to prove them wrong, Paco.

That's why you're in the park, heading toward shunned dark places where all the ragged people go to sleep off the worst of the midday heat. Why you carry a Flintstones thermos filmed with lighter fluid in the right inside pocket of a raincoat too heavy to wear in the middle of a sweltering July. Why you can't blame all of your profuse sweating on the summer heat. Why you're already anticipating the triumph of flesh turned black from flames.

Your name is Paco. You're carrying a six-inch-long, barbed hunting knife in case your chosen victim, the one everybody calls Ragz, gives you trouble. You can't imagine any shuffling wetbrain like him giving you any trouble. You're Paco. And you can't wait to see him burn.

This is the thing eating Ragz.

It's sunken soft roots into his skin, burrowing deep into his blood and his bone and his flesh. It left his mind alone for the longest time, leaving it to fracture at its own pace, which with the pain and the fear and the despair wasn't very long at all. Now Ragz is thoroughly insane, and he understands nothing of what he sees and very little of what he does. To him, the city's just a frightening alien landscape, filled with dark looming shapes and shadowy, threatening inhabitants. He wanders from place to place, hungry, thirsty, afraid, despised, alone, and dying . . . walking where it wants him to go, sleeping where it wants him to sleep, eating what it wants him to eat . . . and feeling it hollow him out, one little piece at a time, leaving Ragz nothing but the gathering cold and dark.

He used to have a name, and a home.

But there isn't much left, now.

Just Ragz.

Your name is Paco . . . and even before your eyes adjust to the darkness of the access tunnel under the bike path, the stench lets you know that your quarry Ragz is here. You can pick it out over the smell of the lighter fluid sloshing in the thermos you carry; you can even pick it out over the combined smell of half a dozen ragged people just like him, wheezing, mumbling, drinking, sleeping, or dying. They're all equally flammable, which is a good thing to keep in mind for the future . . . but this time out you're after Ragz.

They thin out long before you get to him . . . probably because even they can't take his smell.

When you finally find him, at the end of the access tunnel, in a moist place covered with huge brackish puddles, he's sitting atop a sleeping homeless man, straddling him, and tearing at his victim's filthy clothing; and for a moment you leap to the conclusion that you've caught him in the act of rape. You think it's the most disgusting thing you've ever seen. Not that you disapprove of rape as a matter of principle—you've even participated in a couple of all-night parties, on those rare occasions when the gangs involved could be talked into taking you along—but anybody so sick he gets turned on by these stinking, lice-ridden pieces of human garbage is a somebody who should have been burned long ago. Still, if you throw the lighter fluid right now, you'll probably get both of them, and won't that be a hoot. . . .

. . . then your eyes adjust to the light and you see that this is something considerably worse than rape.

The thing's feeding.

Strips of tattered cloth have unspooled from Ragz's shoulders in long serpentine shapes, coiling downward like things with minds of their own, worming their way into the clothes of the man beneath him. As you watch, the man on the ground wakes up enough to open his mouth, revealing a pair of blackened, needle-shaped teeth, and a tongue like a yellow gangrenous worm. He tries to yell. Another strip shoots out from somewhere within Ragz's many layers of wrapping and with the speed of a striking cobra stuffs the man's mouth full, keeping him silent. He twitches and kicks and begins to convulse as it burrows deep into his body. The strips of sooty gray cloth turn red from blood being sucked upward. Into Ragz.

You gasp. Ragz hears you. He turns. You face each other.

For what you're now stunned to realize is the very first time in all the years since you first spotted him shuffling through the streets, you find yourself taking a good look at Ragz's face. It's always been the only part of his skin he exposed; everything else has always been buried beneath multiple layers of cloth. But you've never looked close, because you never saw any good reason to look close. You never saw the white, glazed-over eyes, the leathery, cyanotic skin, the scabby lips twisted into a grimace of hunger and pain. You never recognized the hollow look of a man being eaten from the inside out.

And all of a sudden, Paco, burning him isn't just a way to build a rep. It isn't even something you secretly wanted to do just for the fun of it. It's something colored by panic, and other things you'd be even more bitterly ashamed to recognize.

You flick the lighter in your left hand, and raise the thermos in your right, intent on hurling its contents into the thermos at the thing's dead and unseeing face.

Long cords of greasy, gauzy something, the toughness and texture of canvas, shoot from somewhere beneath Ragz's tapestries of tattered cloth, and seize Paco by his right wrist, breaking it. Stopping his throw so suddenly makes the lighter fluid backsplash, drenching his arm and chest and face. Some lands in Paco's eyes, temporarily blinding him. Some also, inevitably, saturates the ragged tentacles even now coiling around Paco's arms, but that's okay, for now—they're already saturated with worse things. It's enough that Paco can't light a fire without immolating himself . . . and that, by entering this place, where the thing inhabiting Ragz daily takes life from the most wretched of the poor, Paco has given it the opportunity to claim the best meal it's had in months. Ravenous, it abandons the half-dead derelict on the ground and draws the screeching Paco closer into reach of its many thirsty mouths.

Your name is Paco, and what's happening to you is beyond your understanding. The moment is so insane that you're capable of doing something insane.

You touch the open flame in your left hand to the reeking flammable cloth wrapped around your right.

For a moment, there doesn't seem to be any pain at all— just a distant, not unpleasant warmth, as the blue flames engulf your arm, turning it into a pretty little flower. You don't even feel any pain as the flames leap the distance between your hand and your face, landing with a harsh tingle on your cheeks. Then your eyes start bubbling in their sockets, and all of a sudden the heat gets turned on full blast, and you know you're in the furnace.

Naturally, you scream.

But you're not the only one.

Even before its generous dousing in lighter fluid, the thing feared flame. Like so many rags, it's saturated with greases and oils—some so dangerously combustible that they smoke ominously on sunny days. The addition of lighter fluid and the torch that was once Paco's right arm renders disaster inevitable. It begins to burn at once, with a heat that dwarfs anything happening to the much less flammable Paco.

It screams. Ragz, its host, screams. Even several of the derelicts farther up the tunnel scream, though they possess little understanding of what's happening.

The thing releases Paco and tears free of Ragz in a shapeless, burning lump, hurriedly turning inside out to smother the flames that would otherwise consume it. What's left of Ragz the man—an emaciated torso too large for its withered arms and legs—falls to the ground, outliving the flames that freed him by seconds. What's left of the abandoned meal on the tunnel floor dies almost immediately after that, his already ruined body failing quickly without the blood that he needed to run it. As for Paco, he isn't quite lucky enough to die; his convulsions have sent him splashing about in puddles, artfully extinguishing the flames just in time to leave him blind, blackened, and writhing.

He spends forever screaming soundlessly before something comes to bandage his smoking arms.

It's not a doctor.

See him shuffle from the tunnel, only a few minutes later: a creature wrapped in pitted rags, smelling of cooked meat.

See the threads that dangle from his blackened sleeves; the strips of charred bandage that hang from his coal-black clothes; the places marked by holes that reveal the boundary where burnt rags end and burnt flesh begins. See him jerk painfully down the street, sobbing quietly to himself, begging for a release that won't come. See the thirst of the wounded thing he carries reflected in the swollen masses of scar tissue where he once had eyes.

His name used to be Paco.

When the pain takes his mind, he'll be Ragz.

# Cross Your Heart

### LISA LEPOVETSKY

Hi again. Sit down over here, right next to me. No, on the other side—I can't stand anybody sitting on my left, where my heart is. It blocks the rhythms of the blood. Never mind, let's just say I'm left-handed, and I need to keep my left hand free. Like when I made us blood brothers yesterday, I used the knife in my left hand, remember? Yeah, I'm funny that way.

Let me just move those smelly old newspapers and you can sit closer to me. Bums always leave newspapers on park benches, did you ever notice that? Bums are a blight; I hate bums, don't you? Well, at least the one that left this mess won't be back.

Zip up your jacket, that wind's a little chilly, even for May. It just whips through the buildings like a flood or something, and by the time it hits the park, it's full of grit and garbage and nasty people smells. People should watch out for the wind, especially little people, like you. The wind can be treacherous, can sneak up on you when you're not watching. After you finish that hamburger and eat your sundae, we can go somewhere more sheltered. I know a great place.

You had a good time yesterday, didn't you? Me too. And the day before? Yeah, I thought so, I could tell. When guys become blood brothers, like us, they know stuff about each other without even saying anything. Like you probably know I didn't tell anybody about us being secret friends, right? And I know you didn't tell either, without even asking you. See, I was right.

Something about your eyes lets me know—maybe that shiny spark behind the violet color of your iris. I love that color, it's like the city sky just before night falls, and that's the best time of all. Oh, the iris is that ring of color in most people's eyes, the part that circles around the little black pool in the center. Yes, I know my irises look clear, but actually there is a color there if you look really close, a kind of pale, smoky color, like fog or a cloud across the moon. You almost have to look away to see it. Some people think it's a little scary, but I know it makes me special. I've always been special.

Look at my left eye. Closer. There's a picture of God in there. Well, maybe the light's not right. Later, I might even let you sit on that side and look—I'll bet you'll see it then. You won't ever forget it.

Hey, I have a great idea—you know what we can do today? We can play in the creek way back behind the old amphitheater. You'll really like that. Unfortunately, the water's all mucky and the pollution's killed off a lot of the plant and animal life, but sometimes there's really amazing stuff, stuff you don't ever forget. Maybe there's something just waiting down there for us to see it. You can never tell what we might find if we look hard enough.

You ever play in the creek before? Maybe back behind the

projects, closer to home, down where you can just barely see your back door if you squint just right? She won't, huh? Your mom's no fun. Most moms are no fun. I bet she makes you stay away because you can't swim. I knew it—probably because we're blood brothers. But heck, the stuff in that water'd kill you before you ever got the chance to drown. Hey, don't look so scared. You know me, I was just kidding around. I spend lots of time playing back there, have for years. I'm all grown up now, and just look at me, I'm fine.

Well, your mom can say what she wants, but she doesn't care about you much, I can tell. Look how she lets you wander around the streets all by yourself, where anything might happen to a little boy alone. She doesn't even make your lunch, just gives you a couple of bucks and sends you out to McDonald's. I mean, McDonald's, for God's sake. No telling what kind of weirdo might come after a nice little boy like you, if you hadn't made friends with me yesterday. You need somebody to take care of you, somebody like me—a real pal. In fact, I'm kind of like a big brother, aren't I? Yeah, that's right, a blood brother.

Well, tell your best pal the truth now: Have you ever gone down to the creek in spite of what Mommy says, maybe when she was too busy with your little sister to watch you? I'll bet you did. You can tell me, I'd never tattle. I mean, heck, what are best pals for if not to tell stuff to? I'll tell you a secret if you tell me one.

I knew it. Good. That's real good. I think every boy ought to have some naughty secret he doesn't tell anybody—except maybe one special person. Except maybe his best pal, his very best pal in the whole world. Okay, now for my secret.

You know, I remember when I was about your age. Yeah, I see your violet eyes rolling up. Grown-ups always end up talking about when they were kids, don't they? I don't know why that is. But I think you'll like this story, anyway; I love telling it.

As I was saying, when I was about your age, maybe a little older, I used to go play in the town dump. We lived out in the 'burbs then, about a half mile from a big dump—what they call landfills now. It's where towns—little towns, not big cities like this one—put all the garbage that won't fit down the toilet. They're great places to get rid of things you don't want anymore. And great places to learn new things in the dark of the moon, to develop new tastes, to discover new powers. That's why parents don't want us going places like that. They don't want kids learning things that can make them powerful.

But the dump was a great place for a kid to find treasures, too. Little amber bottles—with corks still in them sometimes. Toy six-shooters that might even work if you held them just right and could find strips of little exploding caps to use with them. Magazines filled with pictures of pretty girls you could keep under your bed till your mom found them. Then she'd burn the magazines, and hold your left hand, the one near your heart, the one the devil owns, over the flame on the stove until you— anyway, you could find all kinds of neat things at the dump.

Stupid Jeffy Brimley used to make everybody give him the best stuff, though. He was a year older than the rest of us—and about twenty pounds heavier, too. The bully. There's a bully in every gang of boys in every neighborhood in every town in America—in the whole world, in fact. Jeffy Brimley was ours. He hassled us and teased us, about how little and skinny we were and how our parents talked and how we dressed and what hand we used—all kinds of stuff. And we couldn't ever tattle on him, even if we wanted to, because we weren't supposed to be playing in the dump in the first place. Jeffy thought he had power, but he didn't know what I'd learned back in the dark places.

Of course, our parents always warned us about the dangers in the dump, in those gigantic mounds of trash and refuse—big things like old refrigerators or water tanks you could climb into and maybe never get out of again. And there were rats and all kinds of nasty vermin that would give you diseases and stuff if they ever bit you or touched you. And packs of stray dogs that people dumped along the side of the road wandered out there. Sometimes grown-ups forget that puppies—and kids—grow up; that they won't be cute and little forever. Those poor animals were hungry all the time, and hung around the dump looking for old bones or juicy children who couldn't run away fast enough. And you knew that if you ever got trapped in one of those discarded appliances—even if your foot or hand got stuck and held you there—you were critter-food for sure.

My old man warned me over and over that he'd thrash me good if he ever caught me going out to the dump. But he was always worried about his work and buying another six pack, so he didn't really pay that much attention to what I did or didn't do. And my mom was always praying at the altar she set up in the guest room after my kid brother died of the fever. They thought I was out at the park or at some friend's house; they never suspected how much time I spent down at the dump after dark.

They had no idea of the real dangers, the dangers that made rats and dogs look pretty mild. Nobody did. Not even after dumb Jeffy Brimley vanished two days after school let out for the summer. His parents didn't even start looking for him for a week, 'cause he was always running away from home. And by then I wasn't hungry anymore.

Of course, I stayed away from the dump for a couple of weeks, to make sure nobody connected me with his disappearance, just in case he was found. I figured what was left of Jeffy would be found sooner or later, but you know what? He never was, thanks to the rats and dogs. And, best of all, he never bothered me again. Neither did any of the other bullies—and nobody suspected. It got to be a kind of game for me: See how many grown-ups I could fool. And after a while, the game became a habit, then a need, and I was hooked. I was hungry all the time.

I kept their left hands for souvenirs. Still have them, too, if you ever want to see them. But we can do that later. I have lots of things to show you.

I like it in the city better. Here in the city, they just dump stuff they don't want in the river, and it flows wherever it wants, sometimes leaving bits and pieces, sometimes picking up something new. I'll bet you'd be amazed what I've found floating in that creek behind the amphitheater. It's kind of sad; nobody goes down there anymore—afraid, I guess. There hasn't been a show on that stage in more than two years—at least not one folks would pay to see. Though sometimes you can hear screams and cries echo through the bandshell like weird songs, if you really listen when it's dark. And then a small splash, like applause, after everything's quiet again.

Sometimes, I crawl under those hanging willow branches by the water, and I just lie there on my belly, waiting to see what drifts by. Cardboard boxes, clothes, old toys. I even found a kitten once, nearly drowned by the time it got to me. It was so scared when I pulled it out, it bit my hand, my left hand. There's the scar just beneath my thumb. Can you believe it? I knew what it really was then, what was hidden inside it, poor thing. Its fur was all matted and muddy, and its tiny grey neck was so thin and delicate under my fingers . . . I could feel its pulse.

You all finished with your hamburger? Great, me too. Then let's go down by the creek together. Here, take my hand. No, my right hand. You shouldn't still be making that mistake. You'll have to learn. Don't worry, I'll teach you; I'm a real good teacher.

No, we don't need to tell anybody where we're going. Your mom's probably too busy with that new baby, and anyway, you'll be home before dinner. Sure I promise, and real pals always keep their promises. Like we promised never to tell anybody about each other. You didn't, did you? Cross your heart and hope to die? Good boy.

# The Glass of Blood

JEAN LORRAIN

*Translated by Francis Amery*

She stands at a window beside a lilac curtain patterned with silver thistle. She is supporting herself upon the sill while looking out over the courtyard of the hotel, at the avenue lined with chestnut trees, resplendent in their green autumn foliage. Her pose is businesslike, but just a little theatrical: her face uplifted, her right arm carelessly dangling.

Behind her, the high wall of the vast hallway curves away into the distance; beneath her feet the polished parquet floor carries the reflected gleam of the early morning sun. On the opposite wall is a mirror that reflects the sumptuous and glacially pure interior, which is devoid of furniture and ornament save for a large wooden table with curved legs. On top of the table is an immense vase of Venetian glass, moulded in the shape of a conch shell lightly patterned with flecks of gold; and in the vase is a sheaf of delicate flowers.

All the flowers are white: white irises, white tulips, white narcissi. Only the textures are different, some as glossy as pearls, others sparkling like frost, others as smooth as drifting snow; the petals seem as delicate as translucent porcelain, glazed with a chimerical beauty. The only hint of colour is the pale gold at the heart of each narcissus. The scent that the flowers exude is strangely ambivalent: ethereal, but with a certain sharpness somehow suggestive of cruelty, whose hardness threatens to transform the irises into iron pikes, the tulips into jagged-edged cups, the narcissi into shooting stars fallen from the winter sky.

And the woman, whose shadow extends from where she stands at the window to the foot of the table—she too has something of that same ambivalent coldness and apparent cruelty. She is dressed as if to resemble the floral spray, in a long dress of white velvet trimmed with fine-spun lace; her gold-filigreed belt has slipped down to rest upon her hips. Her pale-skinned arms protrude from loose satin sleeves and the white nape of her neck is visible beneath her ash-blonde hair. Her profile is clean-cut; her eyes are steel-grey; her pallid face seems bloodless save for the faint pinkness of her thin, half-smiling lips. The overall effect is that the woman fits her surroundings perfectly; she is clearly from the north—a typical woman of the fair-skinned kind, cold and refined but possessed of a controlled and meditative passion.

She is slightly nervous, occasionally glancing away from the window into the room; when she does so her eyes cannot help but encounter her image reflected in the mirror on the opposite wall. When that happens, she laughs; the sight reminds her of Juliet awaiting Romeo—the costume is almost right, and the pose is perfect.

> *Come, night! come Romeo! come, thou day in night!*
> *For thou wilt lie upon the wings of night*
> *Whiter than new snow upon a raven's back.*

As she looks into the mirror she sees herself once again in the long white robe of the daughter of the Capulets; she strikes the remembered pose, and stands no longer in the plush corridor of the hotel but upon a balcony mounted above the wings of the stage in a great theatre, beneath the dazzling glare of the electric lights, before a Verona of painted cloth, tormenting herself with whispered words of love.

> *Wilt thou be gone? It is not yet near day:*
> *It was the nightingale, and not the lark,*
> *That pierced the fearful hollow of thine ear.*
> *Nightly she sings on yon pomegranate-tree:*
> *Believe me, love, it was the nightingale.*

And afterwards, how fervently she and her Romeo would be applauded, as they took their bows before the house!

After the triumph of Juliet, there had been the triumph of Marguerite, then the triumph of Ophelia—the Ophelia she had recreated for herself, her unforgettable performance now enshrined in legend: *That's rosemary, that's for remembrance; pray you, love, remember!* All dressed in white, garlanded with flowers in the birch wood! Then she had played the Queen of the Night in *The Magic Flute;* and Flotow's *Martha;* the fiancée of *Tannhaüser;* Elsa in *Lohengrin.* She had played the parts of all the great heroines, personifying them as blondes, bringing them to life with the crystal clarity of her soprano voice and the perfection of her virginal profile, haloed by her golden hair.

She had made Juliet blonde, and Rosalind, and Desdemona, so that Paris, St. Petersburg, Vienna, and London had not only accepted blondes in those roles but had applauded blondes—and had come, in the end, to expect and demand blondes. That was all her doing: the triumph of La Barnarina, who, as a little girl, had run bare-legged across the steppe, asking no more and no less than any other girl of her age, lying in wait for the sleighs and the troikas that passed through the tiny village—a poor hamlet of less than a hundred souls, with thirty muzhik peasants and a priest.

She was the daughter of peasants, but today she is a marquise—an authentic marquise, a millionaire four times over, the wedded wife of an ambassador whose name is inscribed in the *livre d'or* of the Venetian nobles, and entered upon the fortieth page of the Almanack of Gotha.

But this is still the same girl who once lived in the steppes, wild and indomitable. Even when she ceased to play in the falling snow, the snow continued to fall within her soul. She had never sought lovers among the wealthy men and the crowned princes who prostrated themselves before her; her heart, like her voice, remained faultless. The reputation, temperament, and talent of the woman partook of exactly the same crystalline transparency and icy clarity.

She is married now, though it is a marriage that was not contracted out of love, nor in the cause of ambition. She has enriched her husband more than he has enriched her, and she cares nothing for the fact that he was once a celebrity of the Tuileries in the days of the Empire, or that he became a star of the season at Biarritz as soon as he returned to Paris from the Italian court, following the disaster of Sedan.

Why, then, did she marry that one rather than another?

In fact, it was because she fell in love with his daughter.

The man was a widower, a widower with a very charming child, just fourteen years old. The daughter, Rosario, was an Italian from Madrid—her mother had been Spanish—with a face like a Murillo archangel: huge dark eyes, moist and radiant, and a wide, laughing mouth. She had all the childish yet instinctively amorous gaiety of the most favoured children of the sunny Mediterranean.

Badly brought up by the widower whom she adored, and spoiled by that overgenerous treatment which is reserved for the daughters of the nobility, this child had been seized by an adoring passion for the diva whom she had so often applauded in the theatre. Because she was endowed with a tolerably pleasant voice the child had come to cherish the dream of taking lessons from La Barnarina. That dream, as soon as it was once denied, had quickly become an overpowering desire: an obsession, an *idée fixe*; and the marquis had been forced to give way. One day he had brought his daughter to the singer's home, secure in the knowledge that she would be politely received there—La Barnarina was accepted as an equal by members of the finest aristocracies in Europe—but fully expecting her request to be refused. But the child, with all the gentleness of a little girl, with the half-grandiose manners of the young aristocrat, with the innocent warmth of the novice in matters of love, had amused, seduced, and conquered the diva.

Rosario had become her pupil.

In time, she had come to regard her almost as a daughter.

Ten months after that first presentation, however, the marquis had been recalled by his government to Milan, where he expected to be asked to accept a position as envoy to some remote region—either Smyrna or Constantinople. He intended, of course, to take his daughter with him.

La Barnarina had not anticipated any such event, and had been unable to foresee what effect it would have on her.

When the time came for the little girl's departure, La Barnarina had felt a sudden coldness possessing her heart, and suddenly knew that the separation would be intolerable: This child had become part of her, her own soul and her own flesh. La Barnarina, the cold and the dispassionate, had found the rock upon which her wave must break; the claims of love that she had kept at bay for so long now exerted themselves with a vengeance.

La Barnarina was a mother who had never given birth, as immaculate as the divine mothers of the Eastern religions. In the flesh that had never yearned to produce fruit of its own there had been lit a very ardent passion for the child of another's loins.

Rosario had also been reduced to tears by the thought of the parting; and the marquis soon became annoyed by the way the two women persistently sobbed in one another's arms. He quickly lost patience with the business of trying to patch up the situation, but hesitated to suggest the only possible solution.

"Oh papa, what are we to do?" pleaded Rosario, in a choked whisper.

"Yes, marquis, tell us what to do," added the singer, as she stood before him embracing the young girl.

So the marquis, spreading his arms wide with the palms open, smiling as sadly as Cassandra, was left to point the way to the obvious conclusion.

"I believe, my dear children, there is one way. . . ."

And with a grand salute, a truly courtly gesture, to the unhappy actress, he said: "You must leave the stage and become my wife, so that you may take charge of the child!"

And so she married him, leaving behind the former life that she had loved so ardently and that had made her so rich. At the height of her career, and with her talent still in full bloom, she had left behind the Opera, her public, and all her triumphs. The star became a marquise—all for the love of Rosario.

It is that same Rosario for whom she is waiting at this very moment, slightly ruffled by impatience, as she stands before the high window in her white lace and her soft white velvet, in her pose that is just a little theatrical because she cannot help remembering Juliet awaiting the arrival of Romeo!

Romeo! As she silently stammers the name of Romeo, La Barnarina becomes even paler.

In Shakespeare's play, as she knows only too well, Romeo dies and Juliet cannot survive without his love; the two of them yield up their souls together, the one upon the corpse of the other—a dark wedding amid the shadows of the tomb. La Barnarina—who is, after all, the daughter of Russian peasants—is superstitious, and cannot help but regret her involuntary reverie.

Here, of all places, and now, of all times, she has dreamed of Romeo!

The reason for her distress is that Rosario, alas, has come to know suffering. Since the departure of her father she has changed, and changed considerably. The poor darling's features have been transfigured: The lips that were so red are now tinged with violet; dark shadowy circles like blurred splashes of kohl are visible beneath her eyes and they continue to deepen; she has lost that faint ambience, reminiscent of fresh raspberries, that testifies to the health of adolescents. She has never complained, never having been one to seek sympathy, but it did not take long for La Barnarina to become alarmed once she saw that the girl's complexion had taken on the pallor of wax, save for feverish periods when it would be inflamed by the colour of little red apples.

"It is nothing, my dear!" the child said, so lovingly—but La Barnarina hurried to seek advice.

The results of her consultations had been quite explicit, and La Barnarina felt that she had been touched by Death's cold hand. "You love that girl too much, madame," they had said, "and the child in her turn has learned to love *you* too much; you are killing her with your caresses."

Rosario did not understand, but her mother understood only too well; from that day on she had begun to cut the child off from her kisses and embraces; desperately, she had gone from doctor to doctor—seeking out the celebrated and the obscure, the empirically inclined and the homeopathic—but at every turn she had been met with a sad shake of the head. Only one of them had taken it upon himself to indicate a possible remedy: Rosario must join the ranks of the consumptives who go at dawn to the abattoirs to drink lukewarm blood freshly taken from the calves that are bled to make veal.

On the first few occasions, the marquise had taken it upon herself to lead the child down into the abattoirs; but the horrid odour of the blood, the warm carcases, the bellowing of the beasts as they came to be slaughtered, the carnage of the butchering . . . all of it had caused her terrible anguish, and had sickened her heart. She could not stand it.

Rosario had been less intimidated. She had bravely swallowed the lukewarm blood, saying only: "This red milk is a little thick for my taste."

Now, it is a governess who has the task of conducting the girl into the depths; every morning they go down, at five or six o'clock, to that devils' kitchen beneath the rue de Flandre, to an enclosure where the blood is drained from the living calves, to make the white and tender meat.

And while the young girl makes her descent into that place, where bright-burning fires warm the water in porcelain bathtubs to scald the flesh of the slaughtered beasts, La Barnarina stays here, by the window in the great hallway, perfectly tragic in her velvet and her lace, mirroring in her mode of dress the snow-whiteness of the narcissi, the frost-whiteness of the tulips, and the nacreous whiteness of the irises; here, striking a pose with just a hint of theatricality, she watches.

She keeps watch upon the courtyard of the hotel, and the empty avenue beyond the gate, and her anguish reaches into the uttermost depths of her soul while she anticipates the first kiss that the child will place upon her lips, as soon as she returns: a kiss that always carries an insipid trace of the taste of blood and a faint hint of that odour that perpetually defiles the rue de Flan-

dre, but which, strangely enough, she does not detest at all—
quite the contrary—when it is upon the warm lips of her beloved Rosario.

# 𝔄ngels of the 𝔐ist

STEPHEN MARK RAINEY

n nights when the mist wends its way through the
streets and alleys of the kingdom, when the moonlight is diffused and describes soft, purple shadows beneath the eaves of sleeping houses, this is when the
angels will appear. Silently they come: pale, slender things floating on cushions of billowy vapor, like the luminous, semisolid
aquatic things that roll in on the tides of the ocean at night. And
their voices, they whisper and sigh in the loveliest harmonies,
like the sirens who sought to draw Odysseus to the rocks.

And not unlike the sirens they are, for I've watched the
angels as they drift toward the earth, seeking it seems, for always they call. Whereas long ago tales were told about them, no
one had ever seen them; no one alive, that is, and the songs they
sing are heard only in legends. My minstrels sometimes com-
posed their canticles around these legends and made them quite
beautiful. But never was any man-made music so beautiful as
the sounds that one night not long ago began to peal beneath the
moonlight. Sounds that drew me from my bed to my window,
where I looked out upon my kingdom and wondered at the
source. It was a misty night then; a night like tonight, the kind
they favor, a night that remains in my memory like the after-
taste of a sweet wine that has turned bitter.

I loved my subjects and they loved me, and I had been their
king since I was just a lad, a lad with a face unmarred by these
creases and chasms, and whose hair shone gold beneath a midday sun; not the king of now, whose wilding mane reflects silver
moonlight like the mist that lifts its arms toward this embattled
tower of mine. I sometimes wondered if only I could hear the
voices in the night, for never to my knowledge had a single sub-

ject so much as whispered of them. Often, I felt compelled to shout to my people, "Do you have ears, have you not listened?" and yet a strange reluctance would befall me, as if a will from outside could dominate my own. Not an evil will, but one that could not be resisted by the likes of a mere mortal king.

Came a time that I awoke, and the voices, I found, were directed no longer at the ambiguous night, but solely at me, as if these seekers had finally found a special soul—for a purpose that only they knew, but that came in hints with every muted melody to reach my ears.

"Come to us," they said, with passion sweet. "We need you, we want you." This collective voice beckoned, and I found it delightful, for I knew it meant that I alone was party to these legendary whispers, that no one but I could share their secrets. And the underlying mourning, so hopeless, so melancholy, moved me to tears and I wanted to see the makers of this wistful music.

So they came. Ghosts I thought them, for seemingly without substance they drifted through the night, their countenances hidden beneath veils of willowy silk. Never too close, like frightened children, always remaining at a distance so that I could not view them clearly; yet distinct presences they were— no mirages or delusions, these. And somehow they transmitted fear, for I began to sense a threat in their music that, before, my ears had either never detected or had willfully suppressed. Something about these angels chilled my blood, for theirs was a terrible beauty and the mournful sighs they breathed nevermore seemed so sincere. The visions of Heaven they had conjured faltered and collapsed.

"We will have you now," they called, and I became truly afraid. From beneath their veils shone embers of red, and I could only stare aghast as scores of them drifted in on an airborne tide. "We desire you. We will have you."

"I don't understand," I cried. "What do you want of me?"

"Your body to appease us. Your soul and your heart will sustain us if offered to us willingly. And you will be rewarded."

"No!" I cried, sensing a lurking untruth. "Why have you come to me so?"

"Because you are king," they said. "And there is no more potent life than the life of a king. Come to us."

I knew there could be no denying them if they came to me. I realized they could take me by force if they so chose, but this was not their wish. "Leave me," I begged them. "Leave me and return no more. I regret ever hearing your music and casting my wishes upon it, for you are not what I thought I desired."

"We will not leave you," echoed their call. "Never will we leave you. We want you."

And the pain began. So much pain, conveyed by their voices—ringing in my head like the pealing of countless, monstrous bells, so loud and so insistent I thought my skull would crack. I think I became mad then, for I pleaded with them, cursed them, and finally, I offered to bargain with them. With this, the pain ceased, and before me, these wraiths floated above the mist with eagerness in their haunting, burning eyes.

"This, then, is what you will do," they whispered, and I was horrified.

But to stop the pain, I made my pact with them.

In the daylight, when the angels hid from the world, I became more myself, and went to seek guidance from my most trusted counselors. But I found I could not speak of the visitation, for my tongue froze—whether from witchery or mere human terror I cannot judge. All I know is that I, the king, must certainly have looked the fool calling the good men of my court together only to stumble over my own words and occasionally laugh nervously, all too disturbingly like the poor madmen rotting away in the darkness beneath my keep.

And that night—oh, that night—I myself went to the daughter of my highest court advisor, secretly, so that even her father would never know. She was so young—a beauty of only seventeen years, but fully a woman in every way perceivable to the male sense. I lavished upon her my affections, and she was flattered and perhaps overwhelmed, yet never losing a moment's composure. So sweet and trusting she was, knowing that I, the king, was regarded by her father as the most honorable man who had ever lived.

I took her to the tower, to the window where I had overlooked my kingdom and seen the silky raiments of those pale, singing angels above the mist. And there, as she regarded the night, a long, withered stalk, like a gnarled tree limb bleached white as bone, but possessed of a clawlike, clutching hand, reached through the window and grasped the poor girl around her waist, in an instant pulling her through the portal into the darkness; only the meekest of frightened chirps escaping her lips before she was gone. I leaned forward, shocked at what had happened, though I must have known full well the preordained fate of this poor, lovely creature. I cried after her, certain my voice would waken those subjects sleeping in their nearby homes. Yet the mist stole even my cries, for the guards in the hall, the timekeeper, the exotic women of the streets who sold themselves to wealthy barons, none heard so much as a moan from my agonized lips, or a brief, parting scream from the doomed young woman.

Unparalleled misery prevailed the following day, for sunrise revealed the bloodless corpse of my previous evening's guest in the castle courtyard, and her father, my trusted friend and advisor, lost himself in grief more heartfelt than any I have witnessed in all my years. Now, in front of all, I attempted to come forth and relate my part in the obscene death of an innocent, knowing that it would mean the end of my reign, of my wealth —of everything in my life I held dear, if not my life itself. Again, I know not if it were some spell cast by the angels or a heretofore unthinkable cowardice betraying my will; as it was, I remained silent and clumsily offered my condolences to my friend, swearing—falsely—that I would break my back to see justice done. I could not and cannot explain or defend the complete and utter loss of my honor, my whole being. I retreated to my quarters, knowing I was no king, but lower than the rats that scurried among the garbage outside the court kitchens. Yet no tears deigned stain my eyes, and what little shame I felt paled beneath the pure hatred that burned for those terrible wraiths that drifted through the night singing their demands to a weak, pitiable monster of a man.

But the memory of that awful pain spurred me on. They would not have *me*.

That night it was a baby I offered them, stolen from the crib of a nursery for the militia men's wives. I knew not to whom the child belonged, thinking that its anonymity might temper the sheer horror I felt at my actions. Yet when that ghastly, inhuman appendage reached through the window to pluck the baby from my arms, I screamed from the darkest pit of despair, flinging myself after it, stopping just short of falling to my own death from the towering precipice. This time, I heard the baby screaming as it was lifted toward the stars, its tiny voice so full of terror and longing for the protection of a mother it would never again see. And as my own wailing replaced the child's crying in the night, the darkness was lit by countless eyes peering at me from the gathering mist, radiating their approval, assuring me that I had damned myself as surely as if I'd willingly given myself to them and accepted their "gift."

In one instant, I saw the face of the girl they had only so recently taken, her soul now one with them, her body reanimated and greedy for the blood of the innocent.

Or of a guilty king.

My madness then must have been complete, for I swore at the darkness, drawing up from my black heart the warrior's will that had driven me in battle all those years ago; the will that had conquered lands and made peace, that killed where necessary and spared life at every possibility. *I* was the master in those days, and *I* would be again. *I* would never succumb to the manipulations of the inhuman spirits who wanted my body and soul.

And their voices replied, "We grieve, O King, for we take the blood of innocents only because you deny us your own. And you deny yourself the reward of eternity we offer. . . ."

Never had my kingdom hosted such bedlam as came with morning. With the discovery of the missing baby, which I learned belonged to one of the Captains of the Royal Guard, the people demanded action. Rumors of demons arose, not in hushed whispers, but in shouts, for some of the old men and women, those even older than I, could remember a day when the same brand of evil had stalked the land—evil romanticized by the songs of the minstrels so that until now it seemed only distant and legendary.

I think those closest to me quickly came aware that some cruel weight bore down upon me, yet even in their most bizarre dreams they never could have guessed the truth. Not even my most disloyal servant, if one could be found, might ever imagine that the ruler of the land from horizon to horizon had turned from regal monarch to slinking butcher.

And of course, the angels returned again that night—taunting me with promises of eternity in the mist, occasionally stinging my brain with songs that brought ringing agony.

Yet deluded, I raged at them. Despite their hold over me, I uplifted myself in my own eyes. "I am a warrior! The son of my father, who slew hordes of infidels to bring justice to this earth; and of his father before him, who brought his people across vast wastelands to this verdant kingdom so that all might know the gifts of this earth. You are vile things, so repulsive and horrible, you worms! I defy you! You may drag my kingdom and my body through Hell itself, but you shall not have me!"

An angel floated just outside my window, nodding its shrouded skull, lifting its arms unto me as if to embrace.

"Witness, then, what you have wrought."

I turned my back on the thing, then. Turned my back while rage and heartache grappled within my twisted shell. I did not at first hear the screams from below, so consumed was I with myself. When I realized the reality of the sounds, I hurried back to peer down at the streets, and what did I see then but blood—blood!—coursing through the alleys, and pouring from windows. Bodies lifted into the air and carried into darkness, young and old alike, writhing and screaming in agony and disbelief. Pale things swooped and sang, wailing dirges so beautiful the spectacle became dream: a tableau of crimson rivers and gray mist.

Once I heard my name—my given name—shouted from below, and gazing down, I saw the father of the girl whom I had delivered to these spirits, waving frantically at me with eyes as red as his attackers. For a moment, something hot burned in my eyes until I remembered fury and thrust away grief. I wiped my eyes clear, only to see my friend's arms clutched by groping talons, whereupon his body was torn asunder and the misty murderers knelt to bathe themselves and drink the essence of what had once been good life.

On and on it went, and whence these angels came I could never guess, for there seemed to be as many as the stars. Perhaps it was the stars that bore them, though now and again, I caught sight of once-familiar faces, withered and pale, possessed of blazing eyes beneath raiments of silk, and I knew then that perhaps not so long ago, there might only have been one; a single angel of death whose gift was bestowed from one to another and then another.

After a time, I turned away, for the uproar in the streets had begun to diminish. Occasionally, a distant scream wafted on a breeze, to be stifled moments later, sometimes by sounds that made my stomach quiver. And even later, I found that all was silent, the only sign of life in the world the soft pounding in my ears from the black, pulsing thing buried in my chest.

A soft rustle drew me around, and there stood a thing of beauty, or rather, of former beauty, though still it were majestic. It was she, the one whom I had offered to them so recently, her thin-lipped mouth awash with fresh blood, but with eyes still red and unsated.

"No man could ever stand alone while those he loved were taken from him one after another. No man could listen to the sounds that have torn apart this night, remaining steadfast as this one has. No man could offer up the lives of his people when they were not his to offer and shed no tear. Yet you stand here still. Accept their gift and be done with it. See you not the horror of your 'will'?"

The words of this creature, though clear, seemed as lies when I looked upon its deathly pallor. I could not remember remorse. Nor guilt. Nor sorrow.

Only anger at the affront.

"You will not have me. Begone!"

And so she went, joining her drifting brothers and sisters of the mist, spreading the words I had spoken to them; spreading disbelief even among the dead.

"No one shall master me!" I shouted. "Not you for whom death is king. Not you for whom I bargained in blood, mistakenly."

The mist swirled outside my window, and my own blood boiled. Truly, they had wanted me from the beginning and I denied them. Even with their evil machinations, meant to prey upon my humanity, I defied them. I am a warrior still.

I am king, for this is my castle. I am king, even king of death, for there is no one living in the courts below. I am king, and I have won my battle against them, for I stand alone. I stand here, victorious, while outside, the angels do howl.

# The Reappearance

MOLLIE L. BURLESON

**G**runting, Chris swung his leg over the rim of the mesa. Tough climb, he thought; or maybe it's just that I'm getting old.

But it was worth it. Standing at the top, he could see hundreds of miles in all directions. It was *always* worth it. The sun shone bright, as it always did, in a turquoise sky. Clean wind whipped about him and he breathed deeply the piñon and cedar. He had been coming to Anasazi country in New Mexico for years, studying the Ancient Ones' history, absorbing their culture. Here they had lived many centuries ago, thrived, then disappeared. Chris was determined to discover why.

He had taken a minor teaching job in Farmington, nothing really, paying little, but it was a way to be here, with the mesas and bluffs and buttes as companions. His field was English, but his love was the study of the Anasazi Indians, predecessors of today's Pueblo tribes. There were many speculations as to why the Anasazi had disappeared from the pueblos and kivas hundreds of years ago, theories ranging from starvation to hostile Indians. None of these theories satisfied Chris. A few years ago, between terms, he had made a little progress; he had spent a few weeks with a wizened Brujo, who, while on a peyote trip, divulged to Chris his ideas on the disappearance of the People, as they were known to the Pueblos.

Crouching one night with the Brujo before a fire built of dried piñon, Chris had again asked the medicine man why he thought the Old Ones had disappeared from the area, almost overnight, and the man had looked at Chris with intelligent black eyes and told him that they *hadn't* really disappeared— that their bones were still here, in this land of majestic mountains and mesas, hidden from all eyes.

He would not speak further of the exact location of their resting place, nor of the reason they had died. He only hinted that it was a horrible death; that to see their burial ground was forbidden; that to look upon it was to die. He did hint that the place where they lay was locked away deep within a canyon of yellow mesas somewhere south and west of Farmington. When Chris insisted that he would search for the place, the wizard looked at him over the glowing embers and said: He who goes there must take with him the charms of his people. With that, he said no more.

So here Chris was now, looking out over the desert vista for such a place. He would keep searching each year until he was too old to do it, or until he died.

Looking toward the west, he focused his binoculars and spotted a deep, twisted canyon area, yellow.

This might be it. But of course he had thought this many times in the past. At each yellow-colored canyon he had spotted, there were no bones, there was no burial place. What a marvel when he did finally find it! Praise, acclaim, and money were not even high in his desires. Being the one actually to discover their hiding place, that would be reward enough.

But—the warning the Brujo had given. What of that?

Did he actually believe in curses? Did he really think that for him to uncover the Anasazis' hiding place would be death to him? Well, what of it, then? He would document his meanderings through the canyons and leave a record of them, if indeed he came across the place today or tomorrow. If he were to die, maybe someone, sometime, would find it, and then they too would know.

He climbed back down the mesa, jumped into his jeep, and headed for the far-off canyons.

As the red sun was just beginning to sink behind the piñon-covered mesas, Chris pulled his jeep off the road, gathered his backpack and equipment, and started off into the nearby arroyo.

Maybe I can find it before dark, he mused; otherwise I'll have to make camp and wait the night out—which was never a hardship. He loved the darkness, the smell of his fire, the myriad stars above. He had no fear of the desert, but only respect for it; he knew its dangers. Here, under the stars, one could find peace and rest.

And something more.

Chris had always felt that he belonged here, even while living in the Midwest desert of Cincinnati. Living there, one could find *much* to fear: crime, drugs, maniac drivers. Here was serenity. He felt one with the earth. Maybe one of his little-known ancestors was an Indian—who knew? And even if he were to *die* here, then so be it. Better dead here than half-alive back in the East.

The setting sun cast spectral shadows over the cliffs that engulfed him, holding him, as it were, in their arms. Cradling him, welcoming him. He heard the distant howl of a coyote and the rattle of a diamondback somewhere nearby. He stamped his feet in the sand and then stood still; he could hear, in the stillness, the rustle of the snake crawling away.

The cliff overhead turned from yellow to gold to copper. It was beautiful here, spectacularly so. It was a place in which anything might happen—in which something, nearly a thousand years ago, *must* have happened.

But what?

The full moon rose over the eastern rim of the tableland, lighting the already dimming light with silver. Magical. Maybe the old Brujo was right; maybe this *was* the home of the Anasazi. He felt that he was close. Yet where exactly was the hidden place? Where did they lie?

Turning to his left, he spied what appeared to be a jumble of rocks. On closer inspection he discovered that it was what was left of an ancient pueblo built into the canyon wall. Could it be that this was it? The place the Brujo had mentioned?

Crawling over the tumuli, Chris eventually entered what appeared to be an ancient open space, ringed with more tumbled ruins and what was left of a great round kiva in the earth. Pulling away some of the stones, he managed to crawl down the old ladder into the kiva, and looked around with his flashlight. What he saw amazed him—for all around were huge piles of whitened bones, broken and disassembled. The Anasazi—at last.

In his eagerness to uncover these sepulchers, he tripped over an unnoticed chunk of adobe and fell headlong. Getting up, he cursed his stupidity and carelessness. One could not afford to be careless in the desert. One's life was always on the line. He noticed that he had cut his hand on a stone. Wrapping a handkerchief around the slight wound, he waded through the piles of bones.

Near a stack of what looked like disarticulated leg and arm

bones, he spied a domed skull. Picking it up, he looked into its eyeless sockets. *So, Ancient One, I have you at last!* Turning it about, he focused his light on its gleaming teeth. The two canine teeth were pointed and sharp.

"Aha, so you had a deformity, Old One. Was this why you disappeared?"

As he placed the skull back upon the ground, he noticed a dark spot near the jaws and realized that he had carelessly stained it with blood from his hand. *Damn it, Chris!* Now he'd messed it up. But there were more skulls lying about, and he figured one stained skull more or less was not of much import.

It was too late and too dark now anyhow for more exploring, though on cursory examination he could see more skulls in which sharply pointed canine teeth were imbedded. He climbed carefully back up the treacherous ladder and retrieved his backpack and set up camp close to the great kiva.

As he lay under the stars, pipe smoke curling away into the night, he could now speculate upon the fate of the Anasazi.

Those skulls with their pointed teeth—if this were Hollywood or Hammer Films at their zenith, he'd have said they were vampires! Vampire Indians. What a joke. Still, it *was* strange.

What had caused those dental deformities? Was it a genetic taint? Was it caused by something in nature?

It did appear that they had all died at once in some prehistoric earthquake or meteorological mishap. But why, again, the teeth? Maybe some paleontologist someday would discover the reason. Until then . . . Chris dozed.

And wakened to the sound of something scuffling through the piles of rocks circling the kiva. Rock grated upon rock, fell with a thump onto the red earth, then the scuffling again.

Was it a coyote? Well, if it was, he had nothing to worry about; they were no real danger to man, especially with the fire nearby. But why then was it approaching him now?

And then he saw it. In the flickering light from the flames he saw a figure of man. It looked like an Indian—medium height, long hair dangling at his shoulders, eyes black hollows in a chalky face.

Chalky face? Indians were dark.

Now within the circle of light the man stood, swaying

upon his feet, black holes of eyes staring out from a face in which a toothy smile appeared.

The canine teeth proved to be especially sharp as the Ancient One bent down to sink them into Chris's jugular vein.

It was only at that precise moment that Chris remembered the Brujo's warning. But then he had never fancied the Catholic faith of his parents, nor their talisman, the crucifix.

# The Travelling Coffin
## A Tale of Trembling Horror in Three Parts

MIROSLAW LIPINSKI

## I

He kept it in the cellar, along with his other sins. The sun never had a chance to damage its terror.

Randole Preston, formerly Lord Randole Preston thanks to the new Republic's freedom and democratic ideals, was neither a Tory nor a Revolutionary. He was a sinner —and sinned most grievously against the King—so he had made a wise choice of self-exile to the Colonies in the closing weeks of the War. This fate he oddly welcomed, as if pleased at moving on and not just because of troubles with His Majesty, King George III. His landing on these shores was uneventful, though cherished by himself (the man couldn't stand water), and once on terra firma, he proceeded, along with the wealth he brought with him, to move as far inland as possible—this, seemingly, to put as much distance as possible between himself and Mother England. But the former lord could not entirely part with civilization, and the distance he made inland never reached more than five miles west of Boston. Perhaps he wanted to move further on—at least people heard him grumble of such a journey, but it was never made. No doubt, if he had gone farther west, he would have taken the coffin with him. Of this everyone was sure.

For of all the belongings that he took to the Colonies none was more talked about than the coffin. To travel with a coffin is ominous and certain to arouse wild speculation. One opinion had it that the coffin was Preston's and that he wished to have with him his final, permanent home. But others, seeing it was just a *plain* coffin, insisted that it really couldn't be Preston's, for it was, well, just too plain. Another opinion had it that Preston cherished his former country and wished to take a remembrance of that frequently rain-drenched soil with him. But others maintained that the only things Preston had cherished in England were his former estate and the privileges he enjoyed and that he certainly didn't give a damn about England's earth, soil, dirt, or dust. Still another opinion (there were many, but this, thankfully, is the last one to be recounted here—for now) maintained that inside the coffin resided the skeleton of someone dear to Preston. The speculation fell to a brother, a sister, a mother, a father, a wife, a mistress—in no order of favor.

As to Preston, not one word could be gotten out of him as to the content of the coffin. So a mystery coffin it remained, and likewise the speculations remained, and the edgy Randole Preston still muttered about "moving on"—but didn't.

One fortunate day, Preston dropped dead in front of the town apothecary from a heart attack. All anyone could think about was, not his body, but that coffin. So his bluing corpus was left where it had fallen and the townspeople rushed to his home and searched all over for that vile rumor-plagued box. Already betting was on as to what would be found inside, already fights nearly started because of boisterous disagreements. Finally, the coffin was discovered in the cellar. The lid opened easily.

Just as easily, something inside shot up and queried:

"Have we got to India yet?"

Unfortunately this being looked so bad, and smelled so bad, and so frightened everyone, the united impulse was to kill it and put it out of everyone's misery and horror. Pitchforks were used, knives, rocks, bottles hastily broken for their sharp edges. Soon the poor thing looked even worse than before, and a quick decision was made to lower the lid and give the being—whoever, whatever it was—an improper burial near the home that Preston built.

Only later did the multitudes realize that with the burial of the thing, the mystery had been likewise buried. No one could figure out what it was (it was probably human), and no one could figure out why it was there, or why it said: "Have we got to India yet?"

Then the speculations started again:

The "it" was some insane person who had been hidden by Preston on the journey overseas and who thought the trip was to India. But then why wasn't this pathetic person let free on these shores? And what about eating, defecating?

The other speculation was that someone from the town had dressed up as an "it" and, hastening before the crowds would arrive, had gotten into the empty coffin as a practical joke. The joke misfired, of course, and the prankster, whoever it was, wound up horribly, violently dead. A count was made of the townspeople. Four were missing, so the townspeople gathered at the town hall and a stern decision was eventually reached.

Its execution came the following day: The townspeople returned to the home that Preston built, dug up the improper grave, and found it—empty. The coffin, and whatever had been inside, was missing.

Now speculating of the wildest and fiercest fancies began, which, after a few years, evolved into a legend of ghosts and madmen. But we are not concerned with legends here, but with the truth, and while the townspeople legendized, we must journey out West, nearly a century later.

## II

Brutus, the old, withered prospector, saw a coffin resting casually by the river. He licked his lips against the dry morning air and scratched his crispy beard, then made a face of part irritation and part curiosity. Spitting out his distaste at the intrusion into his predictable routine, he went over to the coffin and was about to open it right then and there, when he checked himself. What if someone was watching? What if there was something of value inside? He doubted very much that someone would leave a dead body here. No, no, there was something of value inside—at least a few rifles. He glanced around the gully. Not even a jack rabbit seemed to be around. Yet it would be better to take the coffin the short distance to his cabin, and there uncover its mystery. No use in letting anyone or any animal push their nose into what was now his business.

The coffin was damned heavy, but he managed to wiggle it up the slope, along the dirt and dusty rock and into his cabin. Shutting the door, he exhaled and coolly went over to his pipe, filled it and started to smoke. With the coffin safely inside he figured he had nothing to worry about any more.

After ten minutes of good pipe smoking—in which he almost forgot about the coffin—he decided to get it over and done with. Still sucking on the pipe, he opened the oblong box, and—

"Have we got to India yet?"

Brutus, who had seen many things in his long life, and was deadened to any shock, didn't bat an eye. Even his pipe maintained its dull rhythm.

Finally, he took the pipe out of his mouth. "India, you say?" Then he went to a rickety cupboard and drew out a crumbled, weather-beaten map.

He fingered through it, while the thing courteously awaited upright in the coffin.

Brutus found what he wanted and shook his head: "Nope, I'm afraid you still got a ways to go."

Then he went over and showed the thing the distance it still had to travel, the land, the wide stretch of water. He stood right next to the malodorous thing, and luckily years of pipe smoking had deadened his olfactory nerves.

The thing shook its head, carefully, so as to not disturb too much its dangling bits and pieces. Then came its pitch, which wasn't vocal, but revelatory in the best and truest sense of the word.

With a deft movement, its skeletal hand reached over to a mildew-damp stomach, quickly tore away a few scabs, and turned up the whole outer portion, like a creaky trap door. Brutus, who was still a little curious about the things of life (and death), leaned over and took an obliging look.

The first thing that struck the old-timer was the display of

549

light emanating from within. He expected darkness and maybe a few rotted guts, but here was light, and the cavern seemed quite clean. Next he noticed the little figures, then the stagelike set. He leaned closer and was amazed to find himself looking upon a scene from his own life. He recognized his younger self, and he recognized the two Indians who had, so long ago, taken him into an initiation of tribal ways. They were all smoking some pipe, and a creek trailed from under the decayed rib of the thing all the way out beyond its putrid pelvic bone. With ever growing interest, he saw that the figures were quite animated and that the ground around them was vibrant with life—the trees rustled, a bit of dust was wiped up, and the creek ran with a slow gurgling movement.

It was, simply, amazing. Even Brutus found it so. Old, jaded, inured to most shocking things of life.

"Have we got to India yet?"

The thing spoke, at the same time covering up its revealing belly.

Brutus didn't know what to do. When he tried to reach over and uncover the thing's stomach, the thing put up such a stench, and shook so much, that Brutus thought it would fall apart. So he put the coffin lid back down and thought a while.

What was happening here? Just now, there was no possible way to know. He had to wait. He wanted to see more of his past life—would it be the same scene repeated? or would there be nothing more revealed? or would it be a scene from another life?

That evening he popped open the coffin, and likewise the thing sprang up and said: "Have we got to India yet?"

"Nope, we still got a ways to go," Brutus answered, jerking his head toward the thing's stomach. The thing obliged, and opened up its belly.

This time, the scene was different. It was Brutus in San Francisco, already in his prime, and visiting the big city to find out how folks live there, particularly a certain Molly Saunders. At that moment the mature Brutus was knocking at her door with a bouquet of azaleas in his hand. Yes, yes, he remembered that day very well—and what happened that night. He wanted to see more, as desperately as he could given the fact he was an impassive old-timer, but the thing, after several seconds, sealed its belly.

Brutus uttered a curse.

That night Brutus hardly slept. His mind indulged in myriad speculations on the thing and its display, but nothing quite made sense. He knew that the thing asked about India, and, more importantly, had used the term "we." Also there was something insistent about its question. And what was at India, anyway? Whatever was happening, Brutus knew that he liked seeing his past life displayed so wonderfully. That was the important issue. For the first time in many years, something involved him, something got his old bones moving, his old blood bubbling.

The following days he realized that he would have to set off; the thing couldn't endure hanging around too long. Its stench was definitely getting worse, and sometimes it didn't even open up its belly. Now if he were a lord, Brutus thought, maybe he could will the thing to remain still and exhibit his past life, maybe he could fool it somehow, at least for some time. But, no, he was no lord or even an Englishman. And he always wanted to see San Francisco again, and, eventually, other parts of the world. . . .

During the course of the next couple of days he made preparations—and then set off, with the coffin, to the California shore.

𝔍𝔍𝔍

Sixty-five years later the ship *Mercury* made a stop at a nameless atoll located in the Pacific Islands. The *Mercury* was a vessel dedicated to botanic research and this atoll, along with others in the Pacific, was one point of study for a meagre few hours. Youstus Murphy was sent abroad to perform a cursory study of the narrow land, while a few other men were sent to gather moss and flower samples. The other men returned in two hours; Murphy didn't. He stayed much longer.

For he discovered something extraordinary on the far end of the atoll: the skeleton of a man and, nearby, a coffin. Murphy didn't have a hard time telling just where the stink was coming from, and guessed at the fate that led skeleton and coffin to this isolated region. He figured that the coffin's odious smell must have been too much for whatever ship had originally taken it, and that the captain, possibly at the crew's insistence, deposited coffin—and apparently a man much attached to it—on the lonely atoll. Somehow he also pictured that the skeleton outside had once been a Man of the West, that is the American West and not just any west, this because of the typical Western pipe sticking out of the skull's remaining three teeth. When he tried to move the coffin, he felt how heavy it was. By now he wasn't so sure there was a body inside. The scent of the corpus would have evaporated with the wind and the ocean air. The odd smell, he then surmised, was a crafty Western ruse to cover up—? Visions of treasure, rubies, and diamonds wedged between gold trinkets, ran around in his mind. Of course! Who would want to open up something so revolting, so odorous? There had to be a bounty of heavy treasure inside. Finally, botanic research was paying off!

He nearly fell back into the water when he opened the coffin and—

"Have we got to India yet?"

*What the hell!!!*

That evening Murphy was seen lugging something aboard the *Mercury*, which he pronounced, to the curious, were samples of a botanic nature. That the box resembled a coffin didn't pass unnoticed. Unfortunately, no crew member got a chance to get near the box and uncover its mystery, for Murphy kept zealous guard over it, explaining his odd behavior as scientifically necessary because the box had "a tricky flowery growth" that should be as undisturbed as possible.

During the remaining journey, Murphy rarely left his cabin, which now, because of the coffin, was so tight that no one else could go and visit him. Eventually, Murphy's new-found antisocialism completely revealed itself when he announced, as the *Mercury* docked in Japan, that he was leaving the expedition. He did and took his coffin with him.

Murphy reached India in two weeks, and, secluded in a seaport warehouse, opened the coffin, his mind trembling with the idea of sudden wealth.

The thing inside stood up and stretched—but was silent.

"India!" prodded Murphy. "Now what?" Already he could see glittering treasure and a life of ease.

The thing stretched some more, and glanced about with its darkly luminous eyes. "Mattara! Mattara!"

"What?"

"Mattara! Mattara!"

"Mattara—what's that?"

"Mattara!"

And the thing collapsed into its coffin, leaving Murphy the frustrating puzzle of Mattara to be solved.

He asked one native. The native didn't understand his English gibberish, but when he heard Mattara he ran away.

Murphy decided to approach one of the English colonists. The English colonist knew the location of the Imperial Palace, the precise hour of the Bartley cricket match, the current market value of various teas, but had never heard of Mattara. Murphy did the next best thing and approached a Hindu who found need of speaking English, a driver of slaves.

This gentleman's eyes widened instantly. "Mattara! Mattara is beyond the Zaskar mountains, sahib, but do not go there."

"Why not?"

"Sahib, Mattara is a bad place with many bad people."

But Murphy could not be so easily dissuaded away from the treasure he felt was already in his hands.

Of the difficult journey that Murphy and the coffin took, there is not much to tell. Many sights were seen, but not many adventures experienced, giving proof to the lie of many Kipling stories that were supposedly based on real events. So, after passing the Zaskar mountain range, Murphy and his coffin, along with a few untouchables, arrived at the gate. The untouchables, after being paid, immediately ran away, leaving Murphy and his coffin to face the truth.

He knocked on the mammoth double door. And waited. And knocked again. And waited. Thankfully, at least for his hand, it was fast approaching sunset. When the last ray descended coolly behind the mountains, the door creaked open.

"I have something here that belongs in Mattara," he told the tall shape looming at the threshold.

The door creaked open wider; the shape withdrew, motioning for Murphy and his coffin to enter. Murphy didn't particularly care for the fact that the door swung shut once he passed the threshold, or for the look of the place he found himself in—a vast courtyard surrounded by three sides with *inward* facing spikes. Facing him, about one hundred yards away, was what seemed to be a temple. He could recognize pillars and a wide flight of marble stairs that, even in the dark evening hours, seemed heavily stained. When he looked down he also saw that the ground was likewise stained. The shape ahead of him moved forward, and Murphy expected he should follow. He wished, though, that someone would come and take the coffin away from him, or, at least, help him to carry it.

As he advanced, he saw from the corner of his eyes fluid shapes ungluing themselves from the walls. He sensed a murky army forming behind him, yet he didn't want to affirm his fear. He felt very foolish dragging the coffin.

Something hovered over his head. Instinctively he looked up. The opaque clouds seemed peculiarly low and remarkably swift. No, they were not clouds. They couldn't be. They were too distinct and their movement whirled gusts around him. These shapes fell off to his sides—and in back of him. He heard fluttering, as wings of majestic birds. The flying things he also saw ahead. They hovered over the temple, cutting the moon's rays like portentous scimitars. Murphy felt like descending to the earth and covering himself up.

Meanwhile, the shadow that had been leading him started to mount the temple steps. Murphy stopped. Should he go on? Something nudged him—the point of some weapon? an elongated fingernail? He should go on.

The temple was cold with shadowy space, wet with slimy pillars. Huge candles, perched atop periodic iron posts, resembled white vultures in a no man's land, their eyes, beaks, claws tallow engorged. The central walkway was marked off by a precise tile work of green and yellow slabs, leading up to a dais. Atop the dais was a carved chair, dense with reliefs of ebony serpents, and on the chair sat a hooded, dark figure, his robe like the wings of a resting eagle.

Murphy felt another sharp sting prodding his back. He knew he must advance. As he did so, still dragging the coffin behind him, he heard the movement and murmurs of an audience trail after him and span to the sides, filling the black spaces where even the vulturine candle light dared not penetrate.

Murphy, finally, could go no further. The dais stared at him only a few feet away. He let the coffin sink with a dull, emotionless thud. The audience around him converged to the walkway, and paused with breathless hush, like some wild panther steadying itself for the spring. The moment of absolute truth had arrived.

There was a creak, then another, and another, all voiced like the intrusion of a summoned deity. But no deity arrived—the coffin had just opened up. Murphy turned. The thing in the coffin rose, stretched all its limbs, and stepped over the side. It did a few more stretches, massaged its fossilized knees. Finally, addressing the hooded figure on the altar:

"Master, I have done what you wanted."

"Show us! Show us!"

The assembly leaned forward as one.

The thing glanced around. Murphy thought he detected a teasing smile on its nonmouth. Then the thing's hand rose to the side, paused, and went to its belly, ripping it open. Out flowed a whole cavalcade of tiny people, before the thing reshut its stomach.

"The Catcher! The Catcher!" reverberated the voice from the dais.

Some draped figure ran out and scurried around, quickly grabbing with icy white fingers the stunned little people and hurling them into a crimson leather bag. Murphy was distraught at seeing human people, including various versions of himself, caught and imprisoned in the tight quarters.

The hooded figure on the platform shook his gloved hands in the air:

"We will savor them, we will fatten them, we will eat them! Garsonel, you've done well!"

"What—what is going on here?" Murphy asked, a little too boldly perhaps.

The imposing figure on the dais turned to him, thundering out:

"I'm glad you asked, insignificant one. We send out a fisherman who travels through the world to bring back these delicacies. These are past-life candies—succulent little morsels. Put one into your mouth, the blood pops inside—delicious! Well worth the wait of a century or two."

The explanation didn't relieve Murphy's anxiety.

The hooded figure added to the thing from the coffin, "Garsonel, you've done well, quite well."

Murphy sensed cold breaths edging in around him. "But what of me? I helped bring Garisson—Garosal—I helped bring G. here, damn it! I did you a favor! What of me!"

"You are not a delicacy, unlike your past life—but I'm sure we can find a place for you *on our table. . . .*"

As he glanced at the ominous shapes creeping toward him, he thought hard and fast.

"Let me present you with a deal. You like the past-life candies, don't you? Let me bring you many. I am an experienced traveller—and a scientist besides—if that's of importance. Please! I beg you!"

The teeth of the vampyrs did not ravage the body of Murphy, but they pierced and sucked it dry, till, three days later, Murphy arose as a variant of the undead himself. However, he was not a vampyr himself, nor did he enjoy their considerable powers. When he queried about this shortcoming in being undead, his last human request was brought up before him. Had he not pleaded with them to be a vassal for bringing the past-life delicacy? To be a vassal, a servant, rather than a vampyr himself?

Murphy had to admit his mistake. He had set his sights too low, a frequent error in judgment for many. He could have kept his mouth shut and been a vampyr, with all the privileges that entails—power, prestige, weird sex. Instead, he was a vassal for the vampyrs; simply put, a slave. Little consolation that the knowledge of various tongues was his, for the vampyrs hypnotized him to respond only to any language with the India question and the Mattara director. Otherwise, he couldn't do much talking.

And so Murphy was sealed up in the travelling coffin, darkness his womb, rotting his expectancy. He initially tested the confines, but only broke his curving fingernails, scratched his elbows, cramped his shins. He knew he had to resign himself to his fate. Freedom would hopefully come after the long, elaborate, mazelike journey around the world, after catching the souls of humans who wanted to relive their past lives, those delicacies so desired by the Mattara gourmands.

Beware of Murphy if you see him. As of this date, he still has not made it back to India.

# The Darkness in Her Touch

MICHAEL SCOTT BRICKER

The memories I had of my wife were drained from me during the night, as I lay in my dark room, patiently waiting as the vampire probed my forehead with its long, pale fingers. I try to remember my wife's face, her voice, her *name*, but I can only think of the creature, of how beautiful it is when it takes the form of a woman. I call the creature Carmilla, though I don't remember why. Some memories are taken by age. As my future wanes, so does my past. Others are taken by my "condition." I'm not afraid to call it Alzheimer's disease. The orderlies call it a "condition." There is no reason to mask the truth. Carmilla would never do so. She is an honest and precise creature. Whether memories are sacrificed to age or disease or whether they take flight on Carmilla's wings, it doesn't matter. The past is gone.

Ben's eyes have seen more than mine. Recession. Depression. Prohibition. Two world wars. Racism. A lifetime of racism. Soon he will celebrate his one hundredth birthday. Ben smiles when he speaks of it, taking pride in what he calls his "rictus grin." He tells me that he will make a fine-looking corpse, as he has spent many hours practicing his grin, his mask of death, while he has been in the Home. I stare at him across the table and he smiles again, and it seems as though I lose my thoughts in his many wrinkles, in the darkness of his skin.

Ben clumsily shuffles the playing cards in front of him and begins to deal. "What's wrong, William?"

I hesitate. "She appeared again last night."

"Carmilla?"

"Of course."

Ben deals six cards to me. He only takes four. We used to play poker, but the game has become too complex for either of us. We make things up as we go along. It closely resembles life these days.

"What's your question this morning?"

I look at my cards. Clubs and spades are indistinguishable from one another through my thick glasses. I feel ashamed, afraid to look Ben in the face. "My wife. Tell me about her. What was her name?"

"No. Don't ask that. Carmilla didn't take those memories. . . ."

"Yes."

"Damn."

"It was painless."

"I know."

I slide my cards across the table. "These won't do. Let me have six more.

Ben gives me eight cards. "Her name was Elena. She was beautiful. A musician. A cellist. You were together for fifty-two years."

I try to think of her face, but again I think of Carmilla instead. "She had long hair? A brunette?"

"No. Blond." Ben is no longer smiling. He returns his cards to the deck. "You win again."

"Elena. It's a beautiful name. Greek, I believe. It means 'light.' " I remember things like that at times. Little odd facts here and there. "How did she . . ."

"Pass away?"

"Yes."

"In her sleep. Quietly. No pain."

"When?"

"Thirteen years ago."

"No one since?"

"No one. I'm sorry, William."

I look at Ben's face. There are tears in his eyes. "Don't be sorry. Thirteen years is a long time."

"No. I'm not talking about that."

"Then what?"

"Your memory. You're just a kid. It's not fair."

I laugh. Ben is pushing one hundred years. I'm eighty-three. He frequently reminds me that he is older. "I'm no spring chicken."

"No. But it's not fair. I know how you feel."

That surprises me. Ben is proud of his sharp memory. I've never heard him suggest that he is having problems. "What's wrong?"

Ben folds his old, withered arms. "I forget things too, William. It's been getting worse, lately. I *can't* forget. My own wife. My children. Their children. All the little things, like the time I worked for the WPA, or when I first met Eloise. It was the day Al Capone died. Nineteen forty-seven. March fifteenth, I think, or maybe it was May. I *won't* forget."

"It's all right." I stare at the back of the playing cards, but I can't make out the design. "Carmilla's touch is painless."

"That again."

"You don't really believe in her, do you?"

"I believe that the world is unfair, William. At times, I believe nothing else."

"That's okay, Ben. Sometimes, even I have doubts about Carmilla's existence. Maybe she's all in my mind. My failing mind."

"Does her presence comfort you?"

"Yes. Very definitely."

"Then it doesn't matter whether she's real. I only wish that *I* believed in her. Maybe it would help." Ben gathers the cards and shuffles them once again. "What's the game?"

"Fifty-two card pickup," I say, and I smile as Ben throws the deck into the air.

Carmilla appears at three A.M. I have been in bed for hours, cold and shivering despite the warm summer evening. The vampire approaches and tells me I will be at peace. Her lips do not move, yet I can hear her voice. She touches my forehead and I begin to feel the memories wash away. My mother and father. Grammar school. Friends. Wars. Peace. Celebrations and upsets. It begins to feel as though I am losing *everything*, leaving a great

559

emptiness, and then even Carmilla is gone, and I find myself standing at the window, staring at the brilliant full moon.

I turn, and I see my body lying on the bed. Cold and still, with an expression of utter peace, like that of Ben's rictus grin. The memories come rushing back to me, all of them, every moment from birth to . . .

Of course.

Death.

I turn and look at my reflection. Myself. An old man. I think of my boyhood and that is the reflection I see. I had forgotten what I looked like at twelve. Now I forget nothing. I think of my wife, her gentle features, her soft blond hair, and I see her in the glass, and I *am* her. I think of Carmilla, and I admire my pale beauty, my thin lips, the sharpness of my teeth. I am a creature of shadows, of memories, and although my body is dead, my memories, *William's memories*, will live in the night for eternity.

I feel as though I belong at the foot of Ben's bed, and instantly I am there, and I have taken my most familiar form, that of the elderly William.

Ben wakes. "What's wrong?"

"I've come to help." I smile.

"Thank you, William. I could use the company."

"What are you thinking about?"

"I was dreaming about my grandson. Jesus, William, I don't want to lose those memories."

"You don't have to." I move smoothly to the side of the bed. My bare feet never touch the floor.

"How?"

"I'll keep the memories for you."

"William . . ."

I find myself changing. "Call me Carmilla," I say, and I gently touch Ben's forehead with my long, pale fingers.

# Year's Turning

## CONNIE HIRSCH

In the Eastern Kingdom, the turn of the year falls on the Dark Night, the new moon nearest the winter solstice, when the sun and moon are at their weakest. By strict tradition the day is passed in silence and prayer, all fireplaces cold, all tapers unlit, until the priests bring the new year's fire.

But in the lord's house in Siddale, there was singing and games while well-stoked kitchen fires cooked the feast, and the remaining tapers from the past year's stores were placed on every available candlestick and left to burn down through the day. The ornate marble fireplace in the great hall was scrubbed by the housemaids during the afternoon when the long table was set; after the grand dinner, Zev knelt and whisked a few last ashes from the hearthstone, while his family and retainers gathered to watch.

Zev observed as the children laid the wood for the new fire: little Naryam, his own child by one of his ladies; Merron, the son of the estates keeper; shy Lus, the daughter of the head cook, and several of their young friends. Despite the pure white hair that hung to his shoulders, he was youthful-seeming, no more than two years and twenty, though he was older by ten times that. For the ritual, he had donned a red velvet robe and a crown of holly leaves braided for him by a grown daughter.

Finished, the children sat beside him, Merron furtively scratching where the formal clothes chafed his neck. "Do the magic for us, Papa!" said Naryam excitedly.

Zev nodded. "I shall need silence for this task," he said. The adults stood behind the children, family and guest and servant, all eager to see the new year's maiden spark. *Ern would make a pretty speech, now,* he thought, *prattling on about the magic of the Piru, allowing me to concentrate.*

He banished the thought and focused his charism on the tinder. Fire magic did not come easily to the Pirukin, creatures of Earth and Air. Zev perceived the frenetically dancing atoms of the tinder. He did not relax till he heard a gasp from the crowd, and opened his eyes to see lazy smoke curling. His charism pushed air at it, and small flames appeared, licking at the sticks and logs.

"You did it, Papa!," Naryam crowed, straining upward to throw her arms around him, her baby-soft face buried against his neck. She smelled of sweets and warm blood. He stroked her hair and conquered his bloodlust: A child should not fear her parent. He regretted he could only see Naryam on rare visits; but he had sent the mothers of his children away from his household. In this past year he had alternated between despair and rage, a potential danger to all near him.

"So I did, my child," he said, scooping her up with one arm. *Ern would lead a toast now,* he thought. He hadn't the heart to propose it in his son's place. He returned Naryam to her mother Tera, who bobbed a curtsy and took her child off to sleep in the guest nursery.

With the children abed, it was time for the adults to play. Zev sat on his evergreen-trimmed "throne," a silver-chased goblet of warm cow's blood beside him, a fist cradling his chin. His people knew better than to disturb him when he was pensive. The festivity swirled about him as he lost himself in brooding over the past year, until over the noise of the party, the crackling of the fire, and the stamp of dancing feet, his hearing, sharper than human, detected the jangling of bells from the town outside.

With a touch of charism Zev slipped away unseen, leaving behind robes and crown, stripped to the black silk shirt and trousers that he wore in repudiation of the bright-colored festivities. Ern, he knew, would have dressed in such shades as to make the eyes water; his son had always adored the holiday and led the fun.

The balcony was icy cold, but it did not bother Zev. He stepped lightly over the snow crust, leaving no indentation; his long, slim fingers grasped the rime-coated balustrade and did not chill. He leaned out to better see the parade that wound along the street below.

The War Against the Darkest Night, the followers of the New God called the Dark Moon: The soldiers were children and the generals were grandmothers; their weapons were branches of holly and sprigs of mistletoe, bells, clappers, tin whistles, and drums; adults carried torches and lanterns lit from the rays of the Sun at noon on that day. The ragtag parade marched down every street, and once around the town, inviting the Sun back. They were led by the youngest child and the oldest grandmother who could walk the entire distance. Relatives waited in the doorways of the houses and businesses, ready to receive the fire that would be nurtured in fresh laid homefires. In the rear, bachelors and spinsters carried a bier containing the effigy of the New God, to show that he too suffered the sorrows of mankind. Last came the priest, dressed in robes of red, ringing a silver bell with every step.

"Why do you not join your own celebration inside?" said a woman's fine warm voice behind him. Zev turned to see his mother poised above the balcony, dressed all in white, a filmy high-waisted gown and a cloak of gossamer lace aflutter. Like him, she was white-haired, as pale and thin and tall and inhumanly young-appearing, for she was a full-blooded Piru, one of the last children of the old Goddess.

"Kyrani," Zev said, bowing low. He had known she would be abroad this night, ceremonially patrolling her domain; but he had not expected her visit to the town he called his own. "My lady," he said.

"Why do you stand separate from your people?" she said, her red-irised eyes trapping his gaze. "What sets you apart from the joy of this night?" Pirukin eyes are irresistible, even to lesser members of the breed. Zev felt his mind subsumed by Kyrani's as her centuries of experience overwhelmed his self. Like a wolf baring its throat before a pack leader, Zev submitted, with no more sense of oppression. Kyrani held his blood bond, after all.

"So," she said, withdrawing. "Ah, poor Ern."

Zev could only nod wearily. Ern, his son by a human woman, born with but a touch of the Goddess's charism and curse, had died at the hands of the New God's fanatics barely a half-year past. In his grief, Zev had hunted them down, but revenge had not soothed his pain. "I have outlived other of my children. . . ." he said. "A part of me died."

With her power, Kyrani carried Zev up into the cloud-roofed sky; until the balcony was a tiny pale square and the town was laid out like a child's toy. In the cold of the night, noise traveled far, and the rough music of the War filled the air. Zev could smell the smoke from the relit hearths.

Kyrani held out an elegant hand across the space between them. "You are too human," she said. "When you were born I worried; for you were so tiny and so helpless; here is one, I thought, who will never prosper, will die young; he is too human."

She touched his face tenderly. "Too human, I thought, he will be weak. And weak you are; less gifted than your siblings; more hurt by the life you lead."

"Madam, I—" Zev started to say, but her wise eyes stopped him.

"Yet all your weakness has been strength to you," she said. "You were closer to your son Ern than I have been to any of my children. You manage to avoid the kill; equally I deal death for every gift I give, and not by my choice." She crossed her arms, drawing the lace cloak tight about her. "And I have killed every lover I ever took." The snow swirled between them.

"Such is the burden of the Piru," said Zev. "Do you not think I am aware of what we are, the price we pay?"

Kyrani gestured down toward the town, where the torches made a river of fire. "In the days of my youth, the condemned led the parade, and at the end we Piru waited to receive their blood, their deaths in the Goddess's name. It was an appeasement, to turn the course of the Sun back toward the Earth. Then came the New God, and the humans turned from us. Now, they celebrate where once they quaked."

"The world has changed," said Zev. "Have I not said so?"

"So you have," she said. "I am Piru, and I am proud; I am powerful and can pretend the world has not changed. Yet it has, and I admit to you that I grow weary of the pretense. Our Age passes and soon enough I will go to the Long Sleep."

Zev stared his shock. "Mother, no," he said.

Kyrani laughed, her voice strong against the snowy wind they rode. "You still care for my company," she said, a gleam in her eyes. "I did not say such a thing for effect." She caught up his hands in hers. "I shall not rest this year," she said. "Perhaps I will linger for decades yet, until I lay myself in the Earth, as we do. The Age of Man dawns, and what I am is not part of it."

"The world has yet a place for many," he said.

"In your kindness you make a place for those believers who would have killed your Ern," she said. "Tolerating the worship of the New God here as you do—"

Zev looked at her coolly. "Even I do not blame the ordinary believers for the excesses of fanatics. Besides, once they move to our lands and see how we live, they lose their fear." He nodded. "And we need them—every year those humans who follow the old Goddess grow fewer. We must accommodate the new believers even as they learn to live with us."

"You would think that, would you not?" she said. "You are more human than I; you stand between our kind and them. A bridge to ease the transition, or to hasten it?"

"Do you think I work for my own abolishment?" said Zev.

"What will come of your work, but a blending, a new world? Whether you know it or not, that is the purpose you served, you and Ern."

"And he died for it," Zev said.

"As many shall," Kyrani said. Her almond-shaped eyes closed, their white lashes like great snowflakes. " 'Yet on the Day of Glory, all shall awake and love together again, without hunger, without pain: for such is the Goddess's covenant.' "

" 'So promises the Goddess,' " Zev quoted. "Yet still I miss my son; his humor, his company."

"I miss your father," said Kyrani. She absently touched a corner of her eye, as though to stop a tear. "He was so full of life, he made me laugh. Our love prevailed long enough for him to give me two children. Yet I cannot stop living; my land and my family need me, as you and yours need you. You will honor Ern by living. For all the sorrow the Goddess has allotted you, She has given you the grace to balance our Her cost."

"But at such price," Zev murmured, his eyes shut with pain; his arms crossed tight against his chest. Kyrani put her arms around him and kissed his face an inch at a time. His lips moved against her face, and she turned so her smooth white throat was exposed.

Their emotions so in tune that asking and consent were the same action, Zev bit deep, his teeth parting the flesh no inorganic object could. He—or perhaps she—sighed in relief as

565

her thick blood welled from the wound, as his tongue lapped at her gift.

After some while he broke away, spinning wildly in the wind. Kyrani smiled indulgently. " 'Tis time I continued my journey," she said. "Many leagues before the Dawn steals my power away . . ." With a flutter of white cape, she swept away faster than a mortal eye could see.

Sweet is the taste of human blood to the Pirukin, but the blood of their own kind is even headier, as strong brandy is to wine. Zev felt drunk as he never did from alcohol. He pirouetted in the air above his demesne, dancing as nothing fully human ever could.

Eventually his heart cooled and his reason returned, but his mood was lighter when he thought of Ern, how his son envied flight. He remembered when Ern was just a boy, how the child had begged to be taken up in a thunderstorm, the invisible lightning raising the hair on their heads.

It had always been a source of regret to Ern that he did not inherit enough magic to fly on his own. "But to be burdened with the thirst that rules your life, Father, in exchange for it," Ern had said after a brandy too many. "I do not know how I would have chosen—but no one asked me, so there you have it."

Zev let himself drift toward the ground. He landed in the small graveyard behind his house; ground unhallowed by the New God, still sacred to the old blood that had been spilled there. The stone sepulchers of the Pirukin sat in orderly rows, their incorruptible contents held safe from the indignities of the elements.

One tomb stood out, unweathered, under its coat of snow. Zev cleared the white shroud off with his bare hands, the crystals coating his trousers and boots like fairy frosting.

He knelt by the sepulcher's side, his forehead resting on the cold stone. Inside, he knew, Ern's body rested peacefully, his wounds still fresh, slowly healing through the centuries. Zev remembered his own agony, and his helplessness as he'd watched Ern killed. The fanatics hadn't needed to use a wooden stake to stop Ern's fragile and too human life; they hadn't known better. In the final moment, Ern's eyes had turned to him, pleading for help—but also full of love, and did he dare believe, forgiveness?

The clatter of the drums, bells, whistles, and clappers grew louder while Zev knelt. The War Against the Darkest Night was coming near, as they walked the perimeter of the town. Zev went to the graveyard gate to meet them.

The crowd was making enough noise and merriment that the rear of the line did not know immediately that the front had stopped at the sight of their reclusive liege lord. Zev watched them with a grave smile, as murmuring comment and shock ran] through the crowd. Grandmothers picked up children; toward the back he could see aversive gestures furtively made.

"What would ye have wi' us, M'Lord?" The crone who led the parade boldly said. She was dressed in her best, an embroidered coat with a high collar of fur, her white hair neatly braided in tight coils. She held her head proudly though she had to look up at him. "What does a Pirukin want with the New God?" The toddler that held her hand stared with wide-eyed fascination.

Her face was old, wrinkled, but her bone structure and carriage put Zev in mind of a maiden he had pursued one sultry night fifty years before. She'd consented to be caught—once— but had made clear the life of his ladies wasn't for her. "Marellia," he said, bowing. She smiled enough to acknowledge he'd recognized her. "I thought you had moved from this town?"

She inclined her head. "I came back to my daughter's, to help wi' the children," she said, glancing back toward a grayhaired woman in the crowd. She gathered herself again. "Ye have not answered my question, M'Lord."

Zev bowed again. "The War Against the Darkest Night does not belong exclusively to the New God, or to the Goddess." He looked at the crowd, his subjects, the people he kept safe. "I come to war with you, against the darkness."

Marellia looked back at her fellow townsfolk, but they gave no sign what she should do. She looked back to him, measuring. "Then take my hand, M'Lord, and take the hand of this child, and help us to walk the rest of the way."

Zev held her hand gently, careful with the old bones. He reached down toward the toddler, a yellow-haired child who looked up at him with wide eyes and a half-formed smile. "Come, my fellow general," Zev said, and the child took his hand.

The parade reformed behind them, banging drums, ringing bells, blowing whistles and pipes, a double river of torch and lantern light, turning back the Darkest Night for one year more.

# The Law

## Hugh B. Cave

It was near the end of a cold December day when young Ferenc Maklos and I set out for the home of Dr. Mihail Dozsa. Neither of us was pleased with our mission. Dr. Dozsa was one of our town's most prominent citizens, and we had been ordered to arrest him.

I especially was unhappy, for I had known and respected the good doctor since my childhood.

But someone, it seemed, had reported the good doctor for having violated our little country's newest law.

You would have to dwell in Eastern Europe to understand this law, I expect. Where else do people live in fear of such creatures as vampires? Oddly, though, the law came about because someone high up in our People's Republic happened to read a book called *A Plague of Magic* by the American writer Robert Weinberg.

According to Mr. Weinberg, or to certain characters in his novel, supernatural creatures exist *only because people believe in them*.

So then, no one in our country must ever again read or write about vampires, publish books about them, paint pictures of them, or even talk about them. In this way they would eventually disappear from the minds of our people and cease to be a problem!

Naturally, many of us looked upon this as just another stupid law inflicted upon us by a stupid government. But to break it was a serious offense, and someone had accused Dr. Dozsa of doing that.

He lived, this respected doctor, in a modest house on the edge of our town park—one of the oldest houses in town. His wife of many years had passed away some four years before, and he dwelt alone, disdaining to have a housekeeper look after him. He still maintained his practice, however, caring for patients who would have been desolate at the thought of having to go to anyone else.

As young Ferenc and I walked silently through the park, in no hurry to reach our destination, the lamps along the walkways came on to reveal thick, wet flakes of snow just beginning to drift down out of the darkening sky. The park's handsome old oaks and beech trees, for which our little town is famous, stood there like members of a jury, silently condemning us for what we were about to do. My heart was heavy as we approached the doctor's residence.

Reluctantly, but politely, I knocked on the door. There was no response. Again I used my knuckles on the wood. When I rapped a third time, I heard footsteps descending the stairs inside and at last the door was opened.

About seventy, with hair as white as the snow now falling, Dr. Dozsa had a gentle face with large, sad eyes. I knew him well, I repeat. He had cared for me and my family for many years. In fact, without his skill and devotion I might not have been standing there waiting to arrest him.

"Good evening, Peder," said he, and glanced at my companion. "Two of you, eh? And in uniform? Something must be wrong."

"Doctor," I began hesitantly, "we have been sent here to—" But the word "arrest" would not leave my tongue. "To ask a few questions," was the best I could manage.

"Then come in, come in," said he gently. "I was just having a glass of wine. Come and join me."

The downstairs part of that old house was set aside for his practice, so he led us up the carpeted staircase and into the sitting room in which he spent most of his nonworking hours. It was charmingly old-fashioned, that upstairs chamber, with old but comfortable furnishings and some handsome wood carvings. I had been invited into it more than a few times. This evening it seemed even more cozy, with but a single lamp alight beside his favorite easy chair.

At his bidding we seated ourselves while he produced a bottle of Pinot Gris and two more glasses. Then, as we sipped his wine, we—or rather I—reluctantly told him the reason for our visit.

"It has been reported, Doctor, that you have books here about vampires. Which, of course, is against the recent law."

"Really?" He never raised his voice, this man. Never spoke in anger. "And may I ask who made such a charge?"

I looked at Ferenc. He looked at me. "We are not allowed to tell you that," I finally said. "But—ah—we have come with a search warrant."

"The new law is ridiculous, of course," said Dr. Dozsa. "You must be aware of that, Peder. I have known you for years and know you to be a man of intelligence."

I put my glass down because the Pinot, though one of our country's finest wines, now tasted to me like vinegar. "Nevertheless, we have been instructed to look at your books," I said, and stood up to get our shameful errand over with as quickly as possible. "With your permission, Doctor . . . ?"

"Of course," said he, with a shrug.

I nodded to Ferenc, and with the good doctor silently watching us, we went to look at the contents of a tall, glass-doored bookcase.

After a while Dr. Dozsa said, "Do you *believe* in vampires, Peder? I don't think I have ever asked you."

"Do I believe? Well . . ."

"You do, don't you?" he said gently. "Perhaps you would rather not, and you hope the new law will eventually make them disappear as predicted, but as of now—yes—you believe." He turned his head to look at my companion, who had stepped away from the bookcase and was peering about the room. "And what about you, young fellow?"

"I do *not* believe," said Ferenc Maklos, swinging about to face him. "Oh, I have read *Dracula* and even been to certain old castles in what is called vampire country, but I definitely do not believe."

"You have been to Transylvania?"

"Yes, and to several of the old castles there."

"Interesting," said the old doctor quietly. "I, too, have had that fascinating experience."

There was nothing in the bookcase to incriminate its

owner. The rest of the room was equally nonproductive. Relieved, I led the way past the bathroom into the only other room on that floor, which was the doctor's bedchamber. This room was dark until, upon entering, I thumbed a lightswitch by the door.

I had not been privileged to enter the doctor's bedroom before, and the first thing that caught my attention was a large oil painting on the wall beside the bed. Handsomely framed in old oak, it was a head and shoulders portrait of the doctor's wife as a young woman. Not having known Theresa Dozsa when she was that young—but instantly recognizing her—I could not deny myself the pleasure of stepping forward to look at her more closely.

What a beauty she had been!

Of course, she had been a most attractive woman in her later years, as well—right up to the time of her death, in fact. But this girl in the portrait was a stunning young beauty!

She had passed out of this life, I recalled, after returning with her husband from a trip to Transylvania. Perhaps the very one he had mentioned only a few moments ago. Upon their return, she had been bedridden for weeks in this very house before passing away from what the doctor described as some new and deadly kind of virus.

While I was still standing there, gazing at the portrait, young Ferenc Maklos said quietly from the other side of the bed, "Peder, look at this."

I turned to him and he handed me a book. "It was on the bedside table here," said he, shaking his head. "I'm sorry. I was really hoping we wouldn't find anything."

It was a large, heavy volume, published in Poland. Translated, its title was *Vampires and Their Kind Through the Ages*. My companion and I exchanged frowns.

"Perhaps he had this in his office downstairs one day, and a patient saw it," said Ferenc at last. "We could say we found nothing here—vampires are but imaginary creatures and the law is ridiculous anyway—but if the patient who reported him was someone of importance, we could find ourselves in serious trouble."

He was right, of course. I could only voice a sigh of sadness and turn like an executioner to the door.

Back into the sitting room we went, I leading the way and Ferenc carrying the forbidden book. Two steps into that room I took. Then my feet ceased to function.

There sat old Dr. Dozsa in the chair where we had left him. And there, on the arm of the chair, sat a woman.

She was—God help me—the woman I had just been looking at in the doctor's bedroom. The young, beautiful woman in the portrait!

Her head lay on her husband's shoulder and she was smiling at him while his fingers lovingly caressed her face. Their whisperings were sounds of endearment. Anyone could see that this man and this woman were deeply in love and living in a world of their own, quite oblivious of the practical world around them.

Ferenc and I were intruders. We did not belong here.

As these thoughts occupied my mind, the doctor became aware of our presence and looked up at us. Very quietly he said, "Now do you believe?"

I looked at my unbelieving companion.

"Y-yes," stammered Ferenc. "Yes, yes, yes!"

"She died of a thing that happened to her in Transylvania," Dr. Dozsa said, "and now can be with me only at night. If you report me, even that will be denied me, for they will come here with weapons and wooden stakes and will tear this house down to find her resting place. Is that what you wish—for me to lose the woman I love more than life itself, and to spend my last few years alone in a prison cell?"

"B-but—they must have blood," Ferenc protested under his breath. "To continue their existence they must have blood. The books all say so."

"In her case, only animal blood," said the doctor. "And were you not nourished by some animal today? A steer, perhaps? A sheep? A chicken?"

I looked at Ferenc, and after only a brief hesitation he moved his young head slowly up and down. Reaching out, he placed the doctor's vampire book on a table. Then with no further discussion, he and I politely bade the good doctor and his wife goodnight and departed.

That is all. You have noticed, perhaps, that nowhere in telling this little tale have I mentioned the name of the town where these events took place. Let me assure you, too, that the names I have given the persons involved are not their real ones.

The law? Well, sometimes the laws men make are unfair, are they not? And justice, as defined by such, is truly blind.

# Cradle

ALAN BRENNERT

> Death borders upon our birth, and our cradle stands in the grave.
>
> —Joseph Hall

"How much?"

The girl was barely eighteen; long, straight red hair almost to her waist, a pretty face made hard by too much makeup and by wary, friendless eyes. She shifted a little in her seat, her too-short skirt hitching up to reveal a flash of thigh, in a naïve attempt, perhaps, to somehow influence the young attorney who sat opposite her. Marguerite, watching from a corner of the office, smiled to herself. Not very bright, but then, that really didn't matter, did it?

Ziegler slid the contract across the top of the big teak desk. "Ten thousand dollars," he said, showing no signs of being overwhelmed by teen sexuality. "Plus a *per diem*"—she looked blank at that—"a daily living expense during the nine months you carry the child. Fifty dollars a day for two hundred and seventy days—less, of course, if you deliver prematurely—for an aggregate total of twenty-three thousand, five hundred dollars."

The girl—what was her name again? Sondra?—seemed to contemplate that a long moment. She glanced casually around the expansive office with its hardwood floors and Paul Klee prints, floor-to-ceiling windows overlooking the brightly lit fountains of Century City at night, as though assessing Marguerite's worth by the company she kept (or employed). Then, with a frown, she shook her head. "Make it an even twenty-five," she said emphatically.

Ziegler looked to Marguerite, who kept her amusement to

herself—such a shrewd bargainer: a paltry fifteen hundred extra!
—then nodded, silently.

"Agreed," said the attorney. "Now, in looking over the
adoption agreement, you'll see there are some standard provisions to which you must adhere: No drug, alcohol, or tobacco
use during the pregnancy; regular obstetrical examinations,
which we will of course provide—"

Sondra frowned as she scanned the document. "What's
this?" she interrupted. " 'If circumstances warrant, surrogate
agrees to domicile—' "

"At Ms. LeCourt's home, yes. That is, should there be any
complications in the pregnancy—unlikely, but you never know
—Ms. LeCourt would feel more secure having you nearby, with
access to proper help. At which point, of course, we'd engage the
services of a full-time nurse, and Dr. Chernow"—he nodded
toward the portly, balding man seated next to Marguerite—
"would make daily visits." For the first time Sondra seemed
hesitant.

Marguerite softly cleared her throat, and all eyes in the
room were, just like that, suddenly on her. She looked at the
young woman and smiled. "I don't think you'll find it that hard
to take, Sondra," she said warmly. "I've been told I have a very
comfortable home."

Sondra smiled uncertainly, though she seemed more puzzled, now, than reluctant. "Listen," she said, finally, "this is
none of my business, I know, and you can tell me to go to hell if
you want, but—

"Because you're infertile, it's my eggs that'll be fertilized;
right? And Mr. Ziegler tells me the sperm donor is anonymous.
You've never even met him, right?"

Marguerite nodded.

"So it's a kid made by two strangers. No connection to you
at all. Why go to all this trouble? Why not a normal adoption?
You've got the money to get any kid you want. What do you get
out of this?"

Marguerite was impressed; she hadn't expected the thought
would even occur to Sondra, much less matter to her. Still, just
to be safe, Marguerite had practiced her response. Time had
taken the innocence from her still-youthful face, but she knew

that very youthfulness could work for her here, adding poignancy to her words. She leaned forward, voice purposely soft.

"I want," she said, "the chance to watch my child grow. From a thought, to an embryo; from embryo to fetus; from fetus to child. I want to hear its heartbeat, faint inside you; I want to be able to put my hand on your stomach and feel my son, or daughter, move. I want to be able to feel . . . if only for a moment . . . that it's inside *me*. By being there, with you, as it grows . . . maybe it will seem more like it's really mine."

Sondra listened, touched despite herself. Then, after only a moment's hesitation, she flipped to the last page of the contract, looked at Ziegler.

"Can I have a pen?" she asked.

Marguerite smiled.

The sleek white chauffeured Mercedes ghosted down Sunset Boulevard, passengers hidden behind tinted windows like riders on a phantom carriage. Inside, Chernow said, "She's brighter than she looks, but not quite as bright as she thinks she is. She knew insemination doesn't require removal of the ova, but when I told her we needed to do it to rule out genetic defects, she accepted it without a further thought."

Marguerite lit a cigarette—a poor substitute for blood, but at least she didn't have to worry about cancer. "And there's nothing about the procedure itself that will cause her to suspect how—experimental—it really is?"

Chernow shook his head. "We've already done the hard work. Considering the ways in which your DNA was altered, just before your death, it's remarkable it took us only two years to reproduce the genetic code. Once we remove the surrogate's ova, she'll have no inkling her DNA's being wiped from the eggs —or that yours is being imprinted onto them. All she'll actually *see* are the fertilized eggs being implanted in her uterus."

Marguerite exhaled a stream of smoke. She would have to quit, of course, before the baby arrived. "And then?"

"Then, with luck, a normal pregnancy, a normal birth. Though obviously, since no one's ever tried this before, we can't know for certain."

Marguerite nodded. The car turned up Queens Road, high above Sunset, toward the doctor's pied-à-terre in the hills; Marguerite glanced to her left and caught a glimpse of the golden lattice of lights—gridwork constellations extending to the horizon—that Los Angeles became at night. She would have dearly loved to see it, just once, by day, and not just on videotape.

"Marguerite?"

She turned. "Yes, Stewart?"

Chernow hesitated. "I . . . have my anxieties about this procedure."

"Why? It won't harm the surrogate, will it?"

"Not the process itself, no. But your DNA *was* altered, irrevocably, by the bite that . . . transformed you. Some of your—characteristics—will doubtless be passed on, genetically. Almost certainly your child will be, at least partly, a vampire."

Marguerite nodded. "I know that. I accepted that long ago." She studied him. "And that frightens you?"

"I . . . don't like the idea," he said in measured tones, "that I've helped create a new way for your—kind—to propagate themselves."

Marguerite laughed. "Stewart, trust me, the old method of propagation is far faster and more efficient than this," she said, smiling. When he didn't join her, she put a hand on his. "Stewart . . . you've known me for twenty years. I don't hunt; not when I can buy as much blood as I want. I don't seek the company of others of my 'kind.' I have no lust for power, or conquest, at least not any more."

She took his hand in hers, and held it as gently as her great strength allowed. "I was twenty-five when I died," she said, and this time the softness in her tone was genuine. "I never had a chance to have a child. Two hundred years later—science offers me that chance. That's all I want." She let go of his hand. "What does anyone want?" she said quietly, looking away. "To be loved unconditionally. To be loved, despite who I am, all that I've done . . ."

She looked back at the lights. "That's all," she said, and it was the truth.

Chernow took her hand again; she looked up at him. Centuries of reading men's faces as they gazed at her told her, clearly and sadly, what was in his. They both knew he could not love her in the way she needed; no mortal could.

576

"Then you won't mind," he said gently, "if I destroy my notes afterward?"

Marguerite smiled. "If that makes you feel better," she said, "by all means."

The procedure did, in fact, proceed as planned; Sondra's "decoded" ova were imprinted, successfully, with Marguerite's exotic DNA, fertilized by the donor sperm, and implanted once again in Sondra's womb. Fourteen weeks later, ultrasound revealed a fetal skeleton, normal in all ways for that stage of development; a week later, amniocentesis confirmed the fetus was male. In the sixteenth week, the first fetal heartbeat could be heard, faint but thrilling to Marguerite, who had no heartbeat, no pulse of her own: Her child was *alive*. It would breathe (already the placental villi were enlarged, drawing oxygen from the maternal blood), its heart would pump blood (unlike hers, merely a conduit through which blood moved by preternatural means: almost a living fluid that animated her, instead of itself *being* animated). Her son would be human.

Chernow was not so sure. Alive, yes; human, not necessarily. A hybrid, perhaps, of the living and the undead . . . with certain characteristics of both.

Marguerite knew this, intellectually, but the first time she placed her hand on Sondra's stomach—the first time she felt the baby move inside the womb—all such thoughts became remote. Something lived inside there: For the first time in two hundred years, something of Marguerite *lived*. That was all she knew.

It was in the eighteenth week the first complications appeared. Normally, a pregnant woman's blood volume increases by twenty-five percent by the time of delivery, while her red blood cell count actually decreases, as the fetus absorbs maternal blood through the placenta. Sondra's blood volume increased by twenty-five percent within the first trimester alone, and her red cell and hemoglobin counts plunged to nearly half their normal levels. She began experiencing acute anemia: attacks of vertigo, extreme fatigue, drowsiness, a constant ringing in her ears.

Tests showed Sondra's bone marrow producing staggering numbers of red cells in response to a vastly increased appetite for blood protein and nitrogen on the part of the fetus; it was literally sucking the blood from its mother's body at a prodigious—and alarming—rate. Her body was producing all the blood it could, but it wasn't enough; Chernow began augmenting this with weekly transfusions of plasma, as well as megadoses of calcium to fortify her bone marrow.

This worked, to a point, but in the middle of her seventh month, when Sondra collapsed suddenly outside Beverly Center, an even larger problem presented itself.

Thank God she had remained conscious, and told the paramedics to bring her to Chernow's office rather than nearby Cedars-Sinai; Lord only knew what the obstetricians there would have made of what they found. Even Chernow didn't realize at first what had happened. It was another anemic episode, yes— but severely acute, and one that seemed to reverse itself within minutes of Sondra coming into the office. He ran more blood tests; it was all he could do.

That night, he reluctantly gave Marguerite the results.

"Sondra's red blood cells are perfectly normal," he explained over dinner (his, not hers) at Marguerite's Holmsby Hills mansion. "But as soon as they cross the placental barrier into the fetus, they suddenly begin to . . . superheat. The blood plasma literally begins to evaporate, and the fetus, starved for blood, draws even more of it from the mother's body . . . only to have that evaporate, as well."

Marguerite, shaken, stared at her empty plate. "This attack. It occurred . . . outside?"

Chernow nodded gravely. "A bright, sunny day. Once we got her inside, the red-cell evaporation began to slow, then reverse itself. After the tests came in, I had Sondra sit under a UV lamp for half an hour; the anemia returned in force."

Marguerite shut her eyes against the realization.

"I think the time may have come for her to . . . come live with you," Chernow said quietly. "The sunguards on your windows, the shutters, the heavy curtains . . . they should protect the fetus, and, by extension, Sondra, as well."

Marguerite was silent a long moment. When she spoke, her voice was a whisper. "I dreamt," she said, finally, "that my child would play in the sun."

Chernow took a shallow breath. "That's not going to happen, Marguerite." A moment, then: "I'm sorry."

And so Sondra came to live with Marguerite, never suspecting, of course, anything more than what Chernow told her: that they needed to keep close watch on her from now on; that the shades were drawn because of the spots she sometimes saw before her eyes, a result of the anemia; that all other signs were positive, and they were confident she would have a healthy baby and a safe delivery. Which was, by and large, true.

Nurses attended her twenty-four hours a day, and the luxuries of Marguerite's home—maids to wait on her, to draw her bath; cooks to prepare elegant meals; a private screening room with hundreds of films available to her—seemed to buoy her spirits, at least temporarily.

She saw little of Marguerite, who "worked" during the day and never appeared until after sunset; and, even then, lingered just long enough to listen to her child's heartbeat, feel him move inside Sondra, make some perfunctory small talk, then disappear once more, leaving Sondra alone, feeling little more than a womb for hire; a shell. But then (she told herself) that's all she'd wanted to be, wasn't it?

One night well into the ninth month, Marguerite awoke to find Sondra missing—having missed dinner, and apparently given the household help the proverbial slip. Frantic, Marguerite searched the house in a panic, then raced onto the grounds. There were a good fifteen acres of land surrounding the house, a labyrinth of hedges and gardens, and it was here that Marguerite, with vast relief, discovered her—skipping flat stones across the surface of the koi pond. Marguerite was brought up short: Sondra suddenly looked nothing like the crass nymphet selected for that very crassness (and so less likely to contest the baby's custody) but like a lonely little girl.

She heard Marguerite behind her; turned. "Hi."

Marguerite took a step toward her. "You . . . had us worried. Maria said you didn't show up for dinner."

Sondra shrugged. "Wasn't hungry." She turned back, skipped the last stone across the pond. "Had another anemia spell this afternoon. Still feeling kind of woozy."

Marguerite moved a bit closer. "I'm sorry. We never expected this to be so painful for you."

Sondra smiled lopsidedly. "Yeah, well . . . you want to hear something really weird?" She shook her head in bemusement. "As shitty as this pregnancy has been . . . I'm actually kind of . . . *glad* . . . I'm pregnant. Is that certifiable, or what?"

Marguerite felt a little chill, and it wasn't the night air. Was Sondra bonding with the unborn child, after all? "Glad? How so?"

Sondra shrugged. "I look around at your house . . . at these grounds . . . I think about all the money you must have—"

*Damn*, Marguerite thought. *A renegotiation ploy? Is that—*

"And I think . . ." Sondra hesitated; Marguerite steeled herself. "I think about how lucky this kid is going to be," Sondra said quietly. "How much you'll be able to do for him. And it makes me feel . . . proud, I guess . . . that I'm helping him have a better life than I've had. You know what I mean?"

Marguerite stood there, surprised by Sondra's response, and more than a little ashamed at her own.

She put a hand, gently, on Sondra's arm.

"Yes," she said, at length. "I know exactly what you mean."

Sondra's contractions began at two o'clock Wednesday afternoon, exactly two hundred and seventy days after the in-vitro fertilization. The first one lasted about forty seconds, though Sondra swore it felt more like a minute and a half; the second came twenty minutes later. Within the hour Chernow had arrived to whisk Sondra, behind the UV-tinted windows of the Mercedes, to the private clinic in Santa Monica, where the contractions began coming fast and thick. It was three-thirty in the afternoon.

"Where's Marguerite?" Sondra gasped, a nurse sopping her forehead, and Chernow fell back on the if-necessary, prearranged lie that she was in San Diego on business, but would be here just as soon as she could. He hoped that Sondra's labor would, like most first-time mothers, last at least thirteen or fourteen hours —placing the actual birth well after sundown.

Still, to be safe, the shades were drawn, the shutters closed —as much for the baby as for Marguerite.

Sondra's water broke about five o'clock that afternoon, and, with Chernow's support, she began bearing down as best she could. Less than an hour later, as dusk fell, Marguerite stirred in her bed, her naked body lying, as always, atop a thin layer of soil from her native Nantes. Her eyes snapped open. Maria—stooped, white-haired, fiercely loyal and protective—stood above her. "The hospital called," she said. "It's time."

If Marguerite's heart had been capable of it, it would have been pounding. She jumped up, kissed Maria on the forehead, and stood by the window. "Please leave now," she said, and Maria, as usual, obeyed wordlessly. Marguerite shut her eyes, picturing her child, hoping—she had no one to pray to—that she would not arrive too late to see him born. A shudder convulsed her body as it folded in on itself, becoming smaller, lighter—

And then she was soaring over the city—sensed more than seen, in this form—heading west to the ocean, hearing/feeling the landscape below her, picking out the sonarform of the clinic, then transforming—flesh expanding, bones lengthening—as she dropped to earth. Inside, Chernow had left a change of clothes for her; she dressed hurriedly and rushed into Sondra's room.

She went immediately to her side, took her hand; Sondra's fingernails bit into her palm, and had Marguerite been merely human, they might have drawn blood. "It's all right," Marguerite said. "Everything's going to be fine." She glanced up at Chernow, as though to ask: *Isn't it?*

Understanding her look, he nodded. "Everything's progressing normally," he said. Within two hours, the top of the baby's head could be seen. And as Sondra's cries of pain filled the room, Marguerite found herself wishing it were she who was crying out—less empathy than envy, because this particular pain was a kind only a mortal woman could know. . . .

"Push!" Chernow coached. "Push!"

Sondra pushed—and the top of the baby's head popped out of the vaginal canal. But as soon as she saw it—saw its closed eyes and wrinkled skin—Marguerite sensed something was wrong; terribly wrong. She said nothing, but as the infant quickly emerged, Chernow and Sondra sensed something as well. A newborn infant's skin was always wrinkly, but this one's flesh was crepey; almost wizened. There was something horribly familiar about it . . . and there was no movement. Neck, shoulders, arms, each in their turn appeared . . . but by the time the infant was pulled out, close to midnight, everyone knew the truth:

The child was dead. Stillborn.

Sondra was crying, mourning the boy who might have had so much. Chernow was stunned. "Everything was proceeding normally. . . ." was all he could say.

Marguerite held out her arms. Chernow cut the umbilical cord, then silently passed the tiny form to her; she paid no mind to the blood and waxy vernix covering its body. Gently she touched the face. Its skin was so old; so very old, before it ever was new. She stroked the baby's head, fingers caressing its ears, its neck, its tiny mouth.

She should have known. Perhaps God, if He existed, had been offended at the thought of life plucked, arrogantly, from the darkest of cradles; or perhaps that Other, with whom she had made a grim compact centuries before, was equally enraged, resentful that one of his subjects was trying to reclaim something he had honestly bargained for, and won. Perhaps it was the one thing that Heaven and Hell could both agree upon.

Gently she caressed the old-man's skin of her never-young son, having recognized it immediately; she had seen it once before, when an undead lover of hers had been struck by a carriage and fallen, no time to change shape, into the River Loire. And she knew that her child, her baby, her first born, had in fact been doomed for hours—since five o'clock that afternoon.

"Running water," was all she said, and no one except Chernow even heard, much less understood. Marguerite held the small, still form to her chest, and hoped, at least, that his soul had flown—that he had been graced with a soul to fly—and that it would know the peace his mother had renounced forever. *"Adieu, mon sanglant agneau,"* she whispered: *Farewell, my bloodied lamb.* And, with a kiss to his forehead, said good-bye to her son.

# Acknowledgments